Secrets of Selparis

Sam Winters

SELPARIS BOOKS, SAN FRANCISCO

SECRETS OF SELPARIS

A Selparis Book

Visit our website at
www.selparis.com

PRINTING HISTORY
Selparis first edition / July 2008

Book Design by Selparis Books

For information address: Alight Publications
a division of Alight Natural Products Limited
P.O. Box 930, Union City, California 94587.
www.alightbooks.com

ISBN: 1-931833-52-4

SELPARIS
Selparis Books are published by Alight Publications
a division of Alight Natural Products Limited
P.O. Box 930, Union City, California 94587.

PRINTED IN THE UNITED STATES OF AMERICA

For my parents and sister,
who put up with me.

Contents

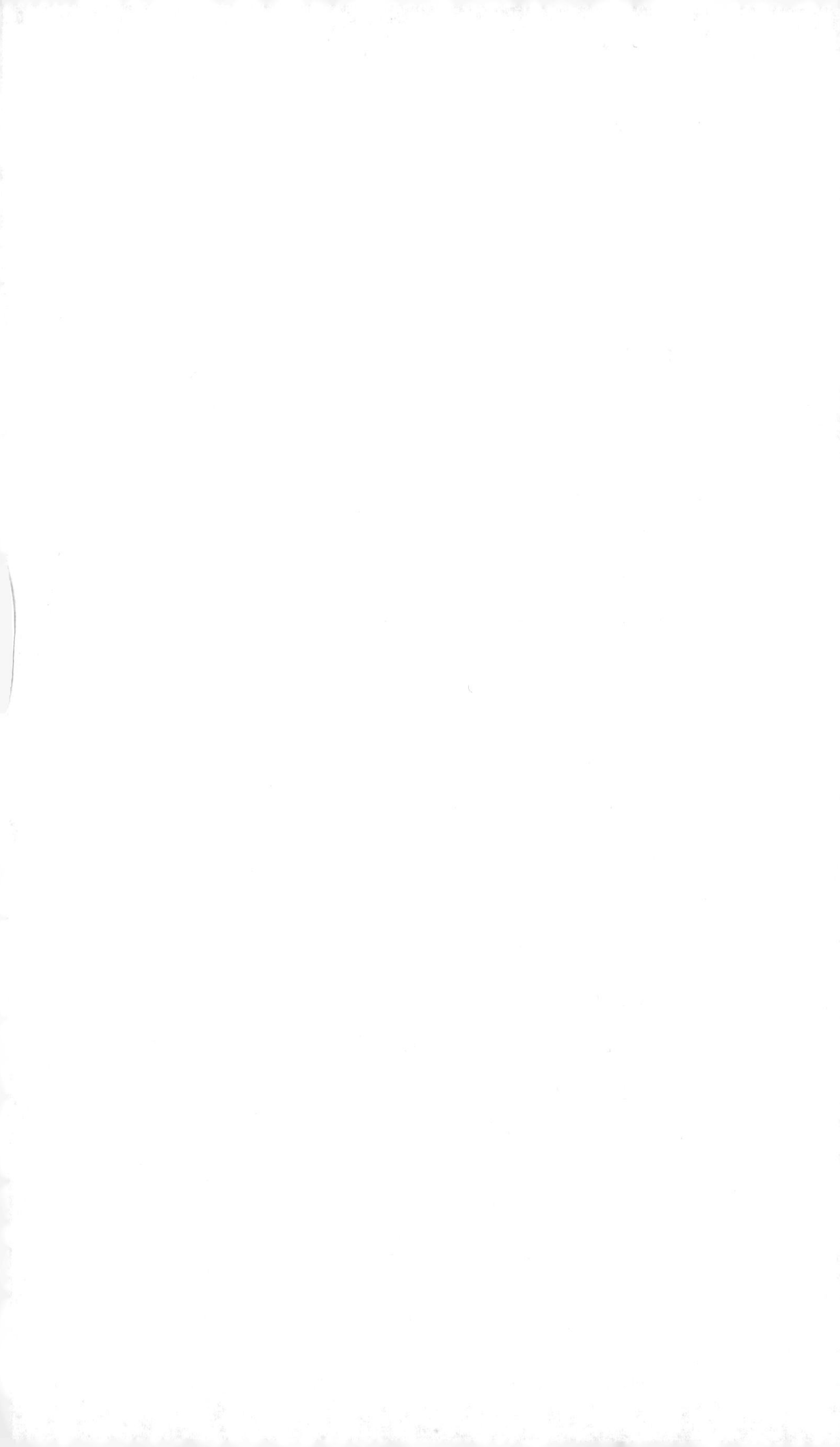

Prologue

As a city in space, Newport Station served many bizarre denizens of various shapes and sizes, but none of them was as fundamentally unusual, from Marcus Welder's point of view, as its commander, Tyler Raiz. Welder was an ambassador and diplomat, and in that capacity performed much the same role as Raiz, whose primary duty was to deal with interspecies issues in Earth's space. That similarity aside, the two of them could not have handled their duties more differently. Welder prided himself on his deductive logic and cool-headed ability to assess situations, while Raiz was charismatic, a tad flamboyant, and confident in his handling of anything that came his way. There was deep reasoning behind his madness, but he treated it as if it was an unwelcome necessity. Perhaps the age difference was the fundamental factor. Raiz was at least twenty years younger than Welder, and had thus avoided the tumultuous years when humans were first emerging as a spacefaring species.

What grated on Welder was Raiz's image as a genius; a prodigy with computers who somehow managed to make certain everything went his way. That reputation was even more annoying because it was well deserved. Called for a meeting with the station commander, the retiring ambassador anticipated some intricate plot, in which Raiz would use him indiscriminately for whatever purpose might improve Earth's standing in the Interstellar Community. There was no point trying to resist Raiz, since the commander had already accounted for all his possible reactions as part of the plan. It could be entertaining to try to make a move capable of surprising Raiz, but Welder was a utilitarian at heart, and did nothing frivolously. He would play it normally, trust that Raiz's goals really would benefit the human race, and hope that the maniac would not get him killed.

Newport Station was a collection of towers, each individually launched into space in sections, and linked together with enclosed roads exactly like their Earth counterparts except, from the exterior, they were cylindrical tubes. On approach to the station, it looked like a typical maze of metal, and gave no hint of its hidden charm. On board, only the lack of gravity and stunning view of the stars reminded visitors and residents that they were in a unique city. It had grown steadily over the past century, augmented regularly to match the demands for new services.

The commander's office stood at the very top of the station's tall central tower. Welder ignored the peculiarities of Raiz's décor choices as he entered, aiming straight for the man himself, who was dressed in a surprisingly conservative shirt with rolled up sleeves and khaki slacks. In the privacy of his office, Raiz typically looked as if he was at the beach, though he managed to be more presentable whenever television cameras and reporters were in proximity.

"Ambassador Welder, how are you?" the commander greeted with open arms, practically bouncing up to his guest, bubbling with energy. Tall and lanky, he strode forward with an imprecise rhythmless walk perfectly suited to him, magnetic soles on his shoes keeping him from floating. His black hair was predictably tossed about with reckless abandon. Considering his lofty position, his look and demeanor were disturbingly at ease. "I hope this meeting wasn't too inconvenient for you."

"No, no. I was on my way through the station to Eldrand, Raiz, as I'm sure you already knew," he answered in a gruff voice, his tone having both the natural gravel of years and a layer of casual irritation he reserved for people undeterred by it.

Raiz grinned. "I hope you don't mind holding off on your trip a little while. There's been some interesting activity on the hyperspace relays recently, and –"

"Unless this interesting activity has something to do with Eldrand, Commander, I'm not interested. This trip is sort of a farewell tour for me. I even have my wife along. I'm not looking to get into anything . . . difficult. Just going around to the worlds I've visited in my time to say goodbye to old friends and that sort of thing."

"It might have something to do with Eldrand, but I don't know for sure. Let's say that it did. Could you hold off on leaving for a week and a half, maybe two weeks?"

Welder stroked his chin, appreciating the cluster of white stubble developing there. "I was planning to anyway. My wife and assistants are still on Earth. They'll be coming on a shuttle in a few days. I still haven't made travel arrangements with one of our local captains. Business must be pretty good around here, because every one of them I've talked to already has commitments. Just recently, I seem to remember half the local boys just waiting here for something to turn up. I don't suppose you have something to do with this . . . shift, do you?"

"Well, you know me, Welder," Raiz said unabashedly. "I see my duty as –"

"– ensuring Earth an improved position in space. Yes, I understand that. You've only mentioned it as a talking point a hundred times. And I'm sure you do as much as you can to get our people trading runs. I mean have you deliberately –"

"No. I don't work that way, Marcus."

"Yes, you do."

"Not for one person," Raiz said, smiling broadly. "Now, do you want to hear what I know so far, or have you lost all sense of curiosity."

Welder sighed. The tone of the invitation made it all too obvious that, for sheer self-preservation, he should just walk out now. Fortunately, his survival instinct had never prevented him from prying into perilous affairs and seeking information he had no right to. He was too old to change his ways now. "Go on, then."

Not bothering to offer the veteran a seat, knowing that it would be refused anyway, Raiz plunged on, now with grave seriousness. "There is a planet we have been picking up a lot of buzz about. A mysterious and unnamed planet kept under a semi-official non-interference rule, like the one Earth was under for millennia. I have a contact on Ina Cur who says that there is evidence a group of Asparii mages has interest in it, and might try to . . . well, interfere. The location and name of the world isn't mentioned, but decades ago, Earth forces helped Asparii refugees reach a planet they said would be a safe haven, and this may be the same world. According to the people we helped, it has been populated by refugees from various worlds for ages, and it's one of the planets on the Interstellar Community's non-interference list, though we have no idea why it was put on the ISC list in the first place."

"So?"

"We've had word from that refugee world, Selparis, recently. Some of our people stayed with the refugees and have become part of the local culture, which doesn't get too surprised by newcomers, I guess. They say that there has been a discovery – an underground city containing ancient documents. Now, which ancient people was famous for its underground cities?"

Nodding to acknowledge that Raiz did, indeed, have an interesting piece of news there, Welder said, "And these Asparii magic users are after the information this . . . cache might contain?"

"It seems like it."

"You're playing a dangerous game, Raiz," Welder growled. "There could be anything down there, and the ISC will be up in arms if we break the non-interference rule, assuming your communication with the world hasn't done that already. You'll have to make certain these Asparii mages get there first, use them as an excuse to step in, and then try to get ahead of them. That's a mess in the making. Who are you going to send in? Wilson's got reliability on his side, and this is not the sort of thing you want to entrust to someone questionable. It's too bad Captain Pierce died recently, otherwise he could bring guts and inventiveness to the mission, and that might be just as important. Who got his ship, by the way?"

A concerned look on his face, Raiz answered, "I think you've hit it there. I thought about Wilson at first, but then it turned out my Inana friend had other plans. He hired Captain Pierce."

"What?"

"Captain Emily Pierce, the old captain's granddaughter. He had used his wealth to buy the ship in the first place, and he wanted to pass it on, and decided she was fit to inherit it."

Welder was aghast. "But she's . . . how old is she?"

"In her early twenties, I think. She just hired her new crew here a week ago, and she's heading to Ina Cur as we speak. The crew's a bit on the inexperienced side, but it's a solidly qualified crew."

"Led by an incompetent captain."

"I don't know about that," Raiz said offhandedly. "Anyway, the Inana has brought her into the equation, so she'll have to play her part. I will arrange for her to get a job that will bring her here. I would appreciate it if you delayed your departure until then, and perhaps we can get her to deliver you to Eldrand."

"What's the point?"

The commander put on an indulgent lopsided smile to indicate that his guest was being a bit denser than usual. "At the very least, I would like you to pretend that you know nothing about this, and to hear what she knows – what she might not be willing to tell me when I meet her. My Inana friend will definitely tell her more than he told me, and every nugget could be vital. I'm sure you'll be able to give her advice as well. You usually do that without any prompting."

"Pretend. I don't –"

"Yes, you do. This is just diplomacy, sir, and I'm sure you would have played the exact same game to get information even if I hadn't asked you to."

Now a tinge unnerved, the ambassador gave up. "I'll consider it. I don't like any of this, though."

Raiz shrugged. "We're behind of the other species in the space game. We have to take some risks if we want equal standing. Thank you for your time."

Welder nodded. After shaking the commander's hand, he left without another word.

Making his way to his rarely used oak desk, Raiz pressed the speaker button and said into the grill, "Olivia, go ahead and send that message to Jason Parell."

1
Ariki

"What do you mean the ship's orbit's deteriorating?" Emily shouted over the comm as the landing pod descended to the surface of Ina Cur. The pilot at her side glanced at her with a worried expression, but then turned back to the work of landing on the planet safely. Emily tried to keep the panic out of her voice, as much to imitate the attitude expected from a good captain as to avoid distracting the pod's pilot. On the bright side, the crew could not blame her this time. She was out doing the real work.

"Reason unknown," Liam, the ship's communications officer, relayed. "Kaz says that there're no errors in the orbit, and Brian followed the projection before he cut the main engines. It's not bad, though. Kaz says we'll be all right for a day."

After bearing snide remarks from Kaz, the navigator, on her bungling of their first job, Emily felt she had some license to bite back. "You mean you're using the maneuvering thrusters, and the orbit's still decaying?"

"Yeah, and at this rate we've got a day's worth of maneuvering fuel left. Then we'll have to light the main engines to regenerate our supply."

Emily saw the face of Kaz in her mind's eye, and it was sneering at her. Even though Kaz showed a full range of expressions, the sneer somehow fit him best. He had well-hidden venom in him, not far from the surface of his sallow face, but now it was her turn to be vicious. "And there's nothing obvious pulling on the ship except the planet's gravity?"

"No," Liam responded, seeing where the conversation was headed, and trying his best to slip out from between the two combatants. Kaz had just stood up, and was now striding across the bridge to the communication officer's station.

"Then do you think we've discovered some sort of new species that knocks space ships out of orbit? Or maybe Kaz made a mistake and doesn't want to admit it."

"A new species is entirely possible, Captain," this time it was Kaz's voice slithering coolly through the headset. Emily pictured him pushing Liam aside to take over the comm panel, even though Liam had almost certainly surrendered his post without prompting. "But the point is that you'll need to hurry and get the goods aboard ship, or we'll have to fire up the mains early. That'll be expensive fuel being spent to get us into a higher orbit."

There was a concealed barb in his words, and she felt it. The implication was that she had no idea where her priorities should be, and by extension lacked the acumen to captain a ship. As if she was unaware that fuel for the main engines was expensive. Her recent failure in their first trade run left her defensive and sensitive to even the mildest criticism. She was inexperienced, Kaz knew it, and wanted her to know he knew it, though he kept his points subtle. Since she looked and acted a few years short of her actual twenty-two, she surprised no one with her lack of expertise. Her parents had pointed out this likely pitfall, trying to convince her to sell the ship as soon as they had discovered the contents of her grandfather's will. Every reason why she should abandon his legacy had been articulated, even the possibility that he had not written his will in his right mind. The condescending and often insulting conversations had only hardened her thirst for independence, and the ship was her revolution. A part of her had to agree with her parents, though – someone who had done nothing since narrowly graduating high school had no place running a starship. Still, the chance to be her own boss, to answer to no one, and to make a fortune, thrilled every atom in her. It was hard to pass that up. Unfortunately, her grandfather's stories were her primary source for how to captain a starship, and none of them mentioned how to assert authority when a member of the crew was quietly undermining it. Either he had never dealt with such insubordination or she was being far too touchy.

"Should I take the fuel cost out of your cut, Kaz? Captain, out." Getting the last word was the best way to end the verbal sparring.

The landing pod was a small craft that took ten trips to fill the ship's cargo bay. It was actually a five-person escape pod converted for transport duty. A pilot and the ship's cultural specialist accompanied Emily to the surface. The latter was her friend Ethan, who had trouble articulating himself in English, much less any interstellar language, though he had a sharp mind, phenomenal memory, and was an excellent guitarist. While awkward with words in normal social situations, he could deliver the answer to complicated questions with bookish precision.

They landed roughly on a spot of developed land – a rare bit of paved ground on this planet of amphibious ocean dwellers. The Inanas were an odd race to be dealing with, but Emily was in no position to be picky. At least their planet had an Earth-like atmosphere that negated the need for breathing equipment. Once it was clear that the landing pod had settled, she headed for the hatchway, swapping the ship comm headset for a translator headset from the cabinet on the way out. Ethan pushed his glasses further up his nose and followed her, not entirely sure he would be contributing anything by doing so. The pilot remained in the pod, glad to be spared any criticism for the rough landing, leaving Emily to do the heavy lifting on Ina Cur.

Walking onto the parking apron alongside a mile-long runway, Emily mused that most Inana atmospheric craft must be like Earth aircraft – incapable of vertical landings. That was where the similarities between the two species and their worlds ended. The land itself was unfamiliar. The bare soil nearby was an oversaturated dark brown, and in some patches pitch black. The foliage in the distance was a wall of jungle – all of it a tangle and none of it in the distinct form of trees. Some unknown force held the wall in check. Even the paving of the runway was unusual, with a dark blue hue instead of a grey. Then there were the Inanas themselves.

Three scaly-skinned Inanas approached them, crawling on all fours. Their powerful forelegs and tails did most of the work, while they dragged their hind legs along. When they reached the trading captain and her associate, they perched themselves up to a standing position using their hind legs as pivots and their tails as counterbalance. Their forelegs – now arms – brought large backpacks forward, and all three simultaneously fished out translator modules, set the translators on their heads, and returned the packs to their backs. One stood well aside from the other two, and took out some kind of weapon. The whole maneuver was so comical that Emily almost burst out laughing. She smoothed the creases in her tee-shirt, glanced at her black cargo pants for spots, and checked her thigh pocket for her handheld computer as the two parties neared each other – her equivalent to a businessperson straightening out her necktie. Maybe her gestures looked as odd to the Inanas as their preparations did to her.

These Inanas were about six feet from head to tail, about half the length of the Great Inanas who never left the sea. Stretched full length, they had two or three inches advantage on Emily, but standing with their tails tensed for balance behind them, they were about four feet tall. They were olive green and sported a lizard-like surface. Their heads were frog-shaped, though a bit more streamlined. In the water, they no doubt swam like eels, since even while standing they had a slight side-to-side oscillating motion in their upper bodies. They looked weak to Emily, but it was difficult to tell. She instinctively sized them up in pragmatic terms, and decided she could fight two, maybe all three of them if necessary. Ethan might be able to handle the third, but he was a bit of an eel himself.

"You are . . . Captain Pierce?" a high-pitched whine was translated in the earpiece of her headset. Since she had not spoken yet, the output of the Inana's headset was uncalibrated, but after receiving the Inana language, her own device was now ready. Though slightly cumbersome, the translators were thoroughly programmed, and able to adjust grammar after a slight delay and even decode contractions as long as the source was in the standard form of one of the installed languages. Dialects and colorful phrases, especially those Emily preferred to use, tended to make the device buzz and choke, limiting her range of expression lest she risk misinterpretations.

Into her mic, Emily answered with forced formality, "Yes. I heard from a contact on Plani that you had a job for me."

"Welcome to Freeman's Canal, Captain. This is Ariki of Channel," the Inana said, gesturing to his companion. 'Ariki' was only the translator's approximation of the tinny name. "He will be your passenger. I am Aya . . . trade representative in Channel. It is important Ariki reach Plani safe. Land at Dael so our people can take him to Interstellar Community Headquarters. Does your ship have weapons?"

Ethan looked at Emily ominously, but the captain answered confidently, "One pulse cannon for defense." Whatever diplomatic mission Ariki had in ISC headquarters no doubt had its opponents.

"Turret?"

"No, fixed." Now that he asked, she wished it was a turret.

Aya and Ariki turned off their translators and murmured to each other, inaudible to Emily's own device. Ariki was clearly calming the negotiator and assuring him that a fixed pulse cannon would be enough. She wondered whether they were concerned about trouble from the Inanas or from the Plani. From her own bias, she assumed the Plani were the threat. Then again, she remembered how little she knew about Inana politics – or any politics. The contact had described Ariki as a religious leader, but provided no details. She had been quick to take the chance, and still shunned second thoughts now.

Ariki turned on his translator and addressed her for the first time. "My room . . . will have place for me to go in water? Cover in water?"

A bathtub. "Yes. It is this big." She outlined its dimensions with her hands.

"And your ship – a fast ship in normal space?"

Emily smiled. On that account, her ship was solid. "We can get from zero to a thousandth of the speed of light in an hour," she quoted from her grandfather's last letter to her, which had been a bit of an exaggeration, but not by much. Unfortunately, the word 'hour' failed to translate. The device beeped and repeated the word back to her to indicate this. The Inanas were left puzzled.

"Damn," she said. That also failed. "Ethan, you're the linguistics and culture person. Any help?" she asked in desperation.

"It is well," Ariki said, understanding the problem. "You are confident in its speed. That is enough. Aya, pay them first money and show them where cargo is. Captain, I will board your ship after you have taken up cargo. When I am on board, I expect we leave quickly."

"Okay."

Aya showed them the cargo – rare foods according to the job description. The boxes were piled on top of transport pads, which were nothing more than motorized carts of a standardized size. Without extra seating, the landing pod had enough space for one pad. Five were standing on the pavement, waiting for loading.

"Maximum temperature for goods is halfway point between freezing and boiling of water," Aya said, clearly having done his homework. "Of course, it should not be close to this. Also, it should not be frozen. We apologize for not giving temperature control boxes, but it would make cost too much. Cannot do business."

"No problem. Our cargo hold is set to –" she looked imploringly at Ethan, who whispered the conversion to her, "a quarter of the way between the freezing and boiling point of water. Should be perfect for the cargo."

Aya nodded. He brought his pack around again, and took out a handheld computer. Punching up the ISC banking system, he handed the computer to her. "Your account number, please."

It was displaying the transfer-to screen. She made it a point to check before typing her account number and pressing the confirmation button. The computer keypad used ISC standard digits, which Earth students now studied in school alongside the old Arabic numerals. It was odd that the ISC had standard numbers, but not standard time or temperature measures. Must have been politics. Giving Aya his computer back, she brought out her own from her right cargo pocket. It was all there – a million credits up front. The transaction remained incomplete until the information reached Plani through hyperspace, but the exchange was final as far as Aya and she were concerned. She could spend the million right now, and the signal would arrive at Plani after the first one, so there would be no financial complications. By the time she actually reached Plani with Ariki and the cargo, there would be another Inana ready to transfer another million into her account. That part went badly last time, though. Still, the Inana were not Plani, and the money they were offering for this simple mission would cover fuel and other costs while leaving a tidy sum for a few days' work.

She nodded to Aya, and he left – probably to attend to Ariki. Ethan turned to her and noted, "The planet doesn't smell that bad."

It was true. Before embarking on her space venture, she had recounted all her grandfather's spacefaring stories to Ethan, and they had always included vivid descriptions of the foul scents of each planet, and how visitors invariably got used to it after a few minutes. Plani was the exception, of course. It was sterile. Ina Cur, though, was not unpleasant smelling, just intensely salty. Maybe her grandfather had exaggerated.

Bringing out her communicator while still musing at the increased balance of her credit account, she commed the landing pod. "Pilot, we've got cargo coming on board. Make sure there isn't anything on the floor that could give the pads problems. We don't need them tipping over or anything."

They managed to get everything aboard ship before the day was up. When the main engines fired up, it was in preparation for their de-orbit and jump. Emily entered the corridor to the bridge with a deep breath, passing her hand through her short dyed-black hair. For someone who had never planned to be a space trader, she was getting along fairly well. The ship was still in one piece, after all.

She ran her hand along the panels at the side of the corridor, careful to avoid activating anything sensitive. The Eldrandii, the ancient species who held exclusive rights to hyperspace technology, had built the ship, but her grandfather had designed the interior. He had taken the money from his solar energy business, pouring it into this dream. The way the ship oozed his rebellious personality had made it impossible for her to sell it after he had willed it to her. She had thought about it, though. It would have fetched almost a billion dollars, but selling the ship would have been letting her grandfather down when he had shown her incredible confidence. As a result, even though she was unsuited to be the responsible captain-type, she was resolved to justify his trust in her.

Taking some comfort in the fact that a successful space trader had thought she would be a good captain for his ship, she stepped onto the bridge. There were no "Captain on deck" announcements or salutes. She had made it clear in her first speech to the crew that this was a merchant ship, not a military operation, and she was not an egomaniacal know-it-all who they had to obey blindly. Now, less secure in her ability to command, she regretted that particular speech, as a few signs to remind everybody that she was in charge would have helped.

The bridge crew was composed of herself at the center, Brian at the pilot controls up front, and Liam with Kaz on the consoles in the back. It was a spare bridge, and nothing like the glorified techno-mazes of some imaginings. Her chair, though, had more indicators and panels than she had names for. It was designed for a captain who liked to know exactly what was going on, and to take control in an emergency. Unfortunately, that described Kaz more than it did her. In only a week, Kaz had augmented his own panel, writing programs to aid him in his quest to act as a de facto captain for every second Emily was away from the bridge. She had disliked him from the start. She could get along with Brian, who was downright gorgeous and shot a charming smile at her every time he managed to do something right for the first time. Liam was too busy listening to communications to bother anybody, though he had a sharp wit and a good idea of what to say, and what not to say. Kaz was constantly serious, and always spoke his mind. There was no questioning that he knew his stuff, otherwise she would have given the job to someone with more . . . personality. He would make a decent captain eventually, though probably not a well-liked one like her grandfather had been. He had more experience on ships than the other three bridge crew members combined – though that wasn't hard since she had none, Brian had spent two years on a ship as the hyperspace backup pilot, and Liam had five years. Practically coming of age on spaceships, Kaz had a definite sense of entitlement that was stifled by Emily's deliberate reluctance to name a second-in-command. That was the crux of the cold war between them.

She flopped into the captain's seat and tapped open the general comm with her elbow. "Ethan, is Ariki fine in his room?"

It took a moment for Ethan to find a panel to comm back from. "Yeah, he says it's fine."

"Cargo Bay, is the cargo secure?"

"Yes," came the gruff answer. There might have been a tone of disrespect there, but it could also have been an attempt to sound weary. Always good to give the captain an impression of exertion.

"All right. Heat it up, engine room. You have control, Brian. Kaz, plot for the Sirius system."

"Anywhere in the Sirius system?" Kaz asked testily, still agitated from the way Emily had cut him off at the end of their last discussion. He projected the course he had plotted hours ago onto the main screen. "Maybe an orbit of Sirius A? I've always wanted to see how close we could get to a star that hot. Or did you mean a course for Plani?"

"Just Plani, Kaz," Emily answered, not biting. "You have it, Brian."

The pilot nodded. "Taking us out of orbit."

Briefly, Emily wondered what had been causing their deteriorating orbit, and whether it would cause complications as they left Ina Cur. Those worries faded as they accelerated out to the jump point, which was set safely away from the gravity of Epsilon Indi and its planets – a direct descent from the system's plane.

"Accelerating at minimum," Brian announced, "with jump point ETA at six hours."

"Go to maximum – the money from this job will be more than worth it."

"If we get a dime this time –" Kaz murmured so that only Liam could hear.

"Our ETA should be half, right?"

"Yeah," Kaz admitted grudgingly, "three hours."

Examining the waypoints on the screen, she said, "Making one and a half million miles in three hours sounds good to me." She leaped out of her seat. "I'll be in my room if you need me." She had to admit that, except for being held-up at gunpoint on the first job, captaining had been a breeze. The trick was delegation.

She had attempted to move all her belongings into the captain's quarters without luck, and left most of her accumulation on Earth. As far as she was concerned, what she had taken with her was essential, but she actually wore little of the wardrobe she had brought on board, and almost everything remained packed in boxes. Most of her posters featured bands out of favor, and her extensive music collection, condensed down to essentials, was on her handheld computer, so those boxes were still unopened. Part of a well-connected family, she had collected a horde of gifts and never felt right about throwing them away. They helped her remember all the people she cared about. All she really needed in her regular business were a few sets of jeans, some tee-shirts, her trenchcoat, the hair-dye that helped her realize the look she preferred, her computer, and the necessities of hygiene. The rest was home – as much a part of her environment as the walls – even if it was all hidden inside cardboard.

Home, though, was a place you occupied with people you knew. Her only friend on board was Ethan, and their conversations since the departure from Newport Station had been limited. In contrast, camaraderie between her grandfather and his crew filled his stories. She wished she knew how to create that same atmosphere, but as it was, she seemed to live in a different world than most of the crew. Maybe the obstacle was cultural. She was a nouveau punk rocker that had almost dropped out of high school, and they were a bunch of engineers or highly trained . . . whatevers. Nothing in common. She tried to start conversations, but only Brian and Ethan listened to the same music as far as she knew, or share the same generational touchpoints. Getting to parts of the crew was difficult, since they often kept to themselves when not on duty. All the cargo and engineering people ever talked about in the rec room was football, auto racing, and maybe basketball. She was athletic, but in an individual and unorganized way. Team sports were a foreign land filled with regimentation and structure that she found abhorrent. Therefore, since the inhabitants of the rest of the ship spoke an alien tongue, she tried to carve out this little home in her quarters.

"Captain," the comm blazed through just as she was settling down on her bed. The female voice was unknown to Emily, and the lack of recognition seemed a logical continuation of her uncomfortable thoughts. "We've got blips trying to follow us."

It was the signal officer, then. The signal officer worked in a quiet room directly behind the bridge, and usually sent anything important to Liam. Emily went to her desk console and opened the general comm so the entire ship could hear what was going on. "You've got blips – how many and can they catch up?"

"Can't tell – maybe two. They don't seem to be accelerating fast enough to get to us, but we have to keep the engines burning."

"So anything less than full acceleration would be a bad idea."

"That's right, Captain."

She pumped her fist. There was nothing better than making the right call. Too bad Kaz had stayed silent about wasting fuel when she had ordered full power – this would have been good payback. "Okay, keep me posted if anything changes. I'll stay in my quarters."

The blips rekindled her earlier questions, though. Who was this Ariki, and who wanted him this bad, to tail a ship in the openness of space? The pursuers had clearly been caught off guard, since the best intercept would have been while they were orbiting Ina Cur. Or was this just for show? Trying to intercept in open space was a hopeless cause. Of course, they could be trying to beat them to Plani. Maybe there were even ships already waiting at the other end, and these were only following to box them in.

"Damn," she said. Well, she could only beat out the ones definitely chasing them, and that meant jumping before they did. Opening the comm, she said, "Kaz, try to get us a closer jump point. I'm heading to the bridge. Oh . . . signals, make sure you tell me if you see any jumps anywhere. Not just the ships close by." She would really have to get the signals officer's name down sometime.

Back through the corridor, she passed the four-member exterior repair crew, who were off-duty and looking the part. They had picked up on the concern her orders had broadcast, but would get ready for work only when ordered to. She didn't blame them. Just the idea of a mid-space intercept was crazy. On top of that, the repair crew would be able to do little about an attack until it started. They handled the normal maintenance while the ship was in orbit.

If there was any planet that would allow piracy to happen in its orbit, it was Plani. The Plani had too many ships to deal with, and focused mainly on preventing ships from crashing into important parts of the planet's surface – any inch of the densely populated northern continent. Assuming their pursuers knew their business, they had a flock of ships waiting around Plani, covering as many trajectories as possible. Moreover, having so many ships meant that they either had government backing, or were a phenomenally successful bunch of bounty hunters.

Kaz was infuriated, and showed his alarm when she walked onto the bridge. "What do you mean 'get us a closer jump point?' Do you really think they could intercept us?"

She should have been upset at the shouting, but was instead comforted to see a natural reaction from Kaz. "I don't want to find out. They think they can. So, how soon can we jump?"

Kaz got to work. "Well, the whole distance from gravity thing is just regulation. The Inanas won't be happy with it, but I could plot us a jump point one minute ahead. But how do they think they can find us in Plani orbit? There're thousands of ships there. It's not like we're unique. We're an Eldrandii ship, just like the rest."

"Don't know. Just know they're chasing us. I don't think jumping close to Ina Cur will piss the Inanas off more than carrying our passenger already has." She finally reached the captain's seat, and tapped the code for a direct comm to the signal officer. "Signals, are there any blips chasing the ones chasing us?"

"No, Captain. Unless it's a close chase."

Emily looked at Kaz. "Can't be sure, but I get the feeling that this is official."

"You mean we've got an entire planet coming after us?" Kaz asked incredulously.

Shrugging, Emily had to admit to herself that she liked the idea. At least, a part of her did. The more practical part responded, "Maybe just one country."

This information distracted Kaz from his calculations. Trying to contribute, Liam piped in, "we can clear it up after we finish this job. I mean all we have to do is tell them the truth – we didn't know the passenger or cargo was not supposed to leave Ina Cur. I have our comm log to prove it."

"Even better – once we get to Plani, we'll complain to the Ina Cur embassy that we were chased, and put it on them," Emily decided. "Anyway, we have to get there first. Kaz, how's the plotting coming along?"

Kaz tapped a final key with a thump and the course showed up on the screen. "One minute to jump. Already sent the message to the engine room."

"Okay. Brian, looks like a tough turn to the jump point. You got it?" Actually, practically any turn would be difficult with their momentum as it was.

"Got it," the pilot responded, firing the maneuvering thrusters.

"Jumping in five," Brian announced, turning on the warning sign for the rest of the crew. Panels around the ship lit up. Emily gripped the corners of her armrests for no particular reason. They entered hyperspace without fanfare, but also without any idea how it happened. The mystery of hyperspace entry made the process consistently nerve-wracking despite a long history of safe transit. Folded space, as it was also called, was as bright as day, like a blue-greenish sky with a few dark patches not unlike clouds. Emily could not describe it any better, but instinctively balked at any comparison between it and the features of Earth. Hyperspace was a world all its own.

No course plot appeared on screen while they were in hyperspace, and Brian locked the controls. Changing course in hyperspace was the stuff of legends. The Eldrandii might be able to do it with predictable results, since they had created the jump systems and knew how it all worked. Maybe a bright physicist on Earth could manage it eventually, somehow. As far as Emily knew, no one had tried it. No reason to. Hoping Kaz had done the job right was harrowing enough without trying anything fancy.

"How long in hyperspace?" she asked.

"Fifteen hours. Time to get some sleep," Kaz suggested hopefully. He didn't look like he would be able to shut his eyes. Emily had been awake for far too long, though, and this was no party.

"All right," she said, and then addressed the ship. "Hyperspace crew to the deck. You'll take over for ten hours." It seemed like a long time, but you could rely on the alternate crew to sort out their shifts and breaks. They were only keeping the seats warm and standing ready to wake her up if anything went wrong, anyway.

Leaving the bridge with plenty of worries on her mind, she stepped by the signal room and peeked in.

"Hi. Good job spotting those blips. You should probably get some rest. Need you to be wide awake once we get to Plani."

"Yes, Captain," the signal officer said, rising from her seat – a cushion on the floor – amidst a hoard of detection hardware. It was an indecipherable mess from the look of it, but the signals officer managed to make it work for her, so Emily did not mind. Actually, she was thrilled. Her choice for signal officer had turned out to be a pro.

A bit embarrassed, but never showing it, Emily said, "what's your name, by the way? You've been so quiet –"

"Jessica Scott, Captain," the signal officer said, smiling. She was used to going unnoticed. "You can call me Jess, if you want. People always do."

"Thanks." Now that Jess was clear of the hardware, Emily saw that the signal officer was plump, but not unattractive. She had a patient look – the kind that bordered on dullness and made her easy to forget. Her workpants and collared shirt were both olive green, and her hair was tied back in a ponytail. Ready for action. Old enough to have some experience, too. Maybe more than Kaz had, in her own specialized way. Emily was no judge of aptitude in this area, but so far, so good.

Emily found it tough getting to sleep, and even more difficult staying asleep. Thanks to all her tossing and turning, her blanket had ended up on the floor. She didn't have the energy to rise and pick it up. Her mind was working overtime, taking the opportunity to use every ounce of energy while she was prone, stealing it from her muscles. The thoughts seemed to race by, but since they came mixed with dreams and bouts of real sleep, they might have taken hours to form. One involved her talking their way out of the situation if their pursuers actually caught up. Spacing the cargo and passenger was a last resort, but that troubling possibility floated across her mind as well. Ariki might even be noble enough to agree to give himself up. He was religious, so maybe he was prone to martyrdom. It was popular on Earth, after all. That last resort would cost her any chance at keeping up this space venture, though. It would be straight back to Earth with or without her consent.

Her dreams were increasingly more disastrous variations on what might happen in the Sirius system. Pretty vague and unrealistic, though – they were full of odd monstrosities and figures from her past popping up out of nowhere. She considered them illegitimate and less than satisfactory nightmares, since her mind could come up with far more convincing horror plots. One dream nevertheless managed to stick in her mind after she gave up trying to go back to sleep. In a brief gem of clairvoyance, she saw, from the point of view of a spacewalker, a huge lump tangled with wires fastened onto her ship. As the view moved backward, away from the device, she saw it spew out like a volcano in regular bursts. The view continued to move away, so that the ship became a nearby star. That star then went nova to end the dream. Emily leaped out of bed, recognizing the reality of the situation for the first time.

Not wanting to wake anyone up prematurely on this nocturnal hunch, she took the time to freshen up and to make sure she was thinking clearly. That meant consuming every sugary substance in the vicinity and following it up with some cold bottled coffee kept in the room for just this sort of occasion. Then she donned her battlegear – solid black jeans, tee-shirt, trenchcoat, and boots – and headed out with the kind of unfounded confidence she had shown to her peers while failing miserably in school. Whatever the scorecard said, she was in control of the game.

To her surprise, Kaz, Brian, and Liam were already on the bridge when she arrived. Brian had his seat turned toward the rest of the bridge, and he was clearly facing Kaz, waiting for some instructions. Working hard to keep to her established course, Emily opened the comm without sitting in the captain's seat. "External repair crew, to the bridge," she called into it. Then, to the bridge crew, she said, "I have an idea," and explained her dream and the reason for the course deviations.

Kaz tried to keep his eye on his work, but was forced to look at her in surprise. "I called the others to the bridge a few minutes ago, getting the idea that we had been sabotaged. I've asked the repair crews rig up a drone with a camera so we can take a look outside. Brian will control it from his console. Since the hyperspace crew was awake, we're having them check the interior. Liam's coordinating them. From your . . . dream . . . you're pretty certain the thing's on the outside. Makes sense."

"And you decided to do this . . . without telling me?" Emily struggled to say, ready to punch her presumptuous nav officer. Kaz's smug face was ripe for a shiner.

"You were asleep and there wasn't anything certain yet. It would have taken some time just to get the drone ready, and you wouldn't have been able to help with that, anyway. You needed your sleep, and it sounds like you were . . . productive," Kaz tried to explain. "On top of the engine section, you said? From your . . . dream, I mean." His face was expressionless, but he was aware that he was testing her line. He couldn't help doubting the usefulness of the captain's dreams while giving better estimation to his own efforts, but wasn't looking for an embarrassing confrontation. Being pummeled by a female would qualify as embarrassing.

Emily was visibly reddening, and her voice growled with threats underneath each word. "I give orders. I decide what to do. You wake me up." She was irritated both by the nav officer's steps to check for sabotage and his ridicule of her dreams. No matter how far-fetched they were, she relied on and trusted her intuition, and opposed anyone who berated her for that faith. It was her magic, and she would not have dared as much as she had without them.

"All right, Captain. What do you want us to do?" Kaz said, knowing that any command she could conceive of would only duplicate his own orders, at least until they had more information.

She shook her head stiffly, recognizing the ploy. "No, don't try that on me. You have an idea, you tell me. This is my crew. Clear?"

Kaz felt secure that he had won this round. The captain could not exactly go around to the crew and tell them not to take his orders – that sort of thing would only show them how insecure she was. Therefore, as far as they were concerned, he was still a legitimate authority. The captain simply failed to appreciate how much he did to keep the ship running smoothly. If she had to worry her ditsy head about it, she would not know where to start. It was only out of childish spite that she had resisted declaring him first officer, as if she could do without one. Anyway, he had tested the waters and found them just a bit too hot for now. "Clear, Captain."

"I'm warning you."

"Understood . . . sir."

She was still on the verge of a fit, and would have had trouble calming herself down, but the exterior repair crew arrived, and looked uniformly concerned. These four were the spacewalkers, the ones that took care of basic repairs and maintenance while the ship was in orbit. They looked fresh, but worried that they would be blamed for Kaz's proposed device. Emily had given that angle no thought, only calling them up because she needed someone to check out her theory. Fear of responsibility was written all over their faces. Judging from how they gave Kaz sheepish glances, he had already questioned them while preparing the bots. Only the cargo crew could claim to have more muscle and stature than these four, so it was odd seeing the ominous looks they gave the frail navigation officer.

"Okay," Emily said, taking a deep self-righteous breath, "Okay. So we might have some sort of device attached to us that knocks us off course . . . wait a minute," she looked at Kaz again, this time with panic, "doesn't that mean we're off course in hyperspace."

Kaz sighed. Case and point. "No, I set up a program for the maneuvering thrusters to fire regularly. I had noticed the deviations in our course even after we left orbit, and saw that it was all regular, so setting up a program to deal with it was no problem. Otherwise, I would have told you and jumping would have been out of the question."

"Why didn't you tell me before?"

"It's normal procedure for the navigator to deal with those problems," Kaz lied. "Besides, you didn't take it very well when I told you about the problem in the first place, while we were in orbit. I chose to save us both the trouble of another one of those . . . conversations."

She bit her lip. "So since it's normal for you to do that, this thing can't be just trying to knock us off course in hyperspace. What's it trying to do, then? Any ideas?"

Silence. She ended it quickly. Taking her seat in an attempt to reassure herself, she decided to talk to the crew, explaining the circumstances over the comm system. She made clear how little they knew for sure, and that she would appreciate suggestions. It took a few moments, but the first clue came in from the engineering room. Emily rarely got down to engineering to check things out, and Kaz had more interaction with them than she did. They seemed willing to take his orders, at least.

"Captain," the engineering officer said, "Whatever it is, we think it's knocking us off course because it vents regularly. If it's strong enough to do that, then closing the vents will make it overload and explode."

Emily was instinctively puzzled. "Why wouldn't they just use a normal bomb? Oh, wait –"

"They want us to know it's there," Kaz said, beating Emily to it. "Which means they think we can't remove it. They'll meet us around Plani, threaten us to get our passenger, and probably blow us up after we turn him over. Good news is, they want him alive. Then again, maybe they won't take much time to blow him up if we try to stall."

Having heard the captain's announcement, Ariki had made his way to the bridge and entered walking upright. Without waiting to be noticed, as if used to having himself heard wherever he went, he said, "Captain, we need to talk about situation." His translator buzzed the words, cutting through the collective thoughts of those in the room.

"Go ahead," she snapped back, with obvious irritation. Taking the opportunity, Kaz went up to Brian, and they started piloting the prepared drone out of its small vacuum chamber. The exterior repair crew waited uncertainly.

Ariki looked around at the many disheveled forms on the bridge, some having nothing better to do than to listen in. "Not in private, Captain?"

"No. Go ahead. We don't have much time before we exit jump into Plani space."

Ariki was standing as tall as his form would allow, and was rigid in his height. His words were going to be impossible for the crew to take seriously, but he did his best to back them with as much dignity as he could muster. "I am . . . prophet to major religious sect on Ina Cur. Opposition sect, you might say. In serious danger. Fleeing for sanctuary elsewhere – Plani first, no knowing where after. My pursuers will kill me if necessary, but do not want . . . martyrdom. Powerful ones would like to capture me and force public . . . recantation."

"But they won't wait to kill you, will they?"

"Perhaps for a moment. They will not risk me surviving free."

Emily sighed. "Kinda guessed that. Well, you know what we're dealing with. We know what's going to happen once we get out of hyperspace –" She paused as the drone's camera, filling the view screen with images of the ship's exterior, caught sight of an anomalous body in the distance, on top of the engine pod. As the drone proceeded, the complexity of the device became clear. It seemed to have a hundred wires attached to the ship's hull. It was exactly as she dreamed it, and the sight of her ship exploding popped into her mind. Emily briefly considered how she missed it on all her trips between the surface of Ina Cur and the ship, but her trajectory had been totally wrong. The device was at the top of the ship, and she had approached from below.

"Well, I can see why they weren't worried about us finding the thing," Kaz said, looking up to the view screen while standing next to Brian. "They definitely want us to know we've been screwed. Pretty effective, I'd say."

"Don't know about that," Ben, the head of the repair crew, piped in. "Not very sure, but it looks like a Plani device – something they stick onto ships carrying extremely sensitive material. They tell everyone about it. The idea is that if someone hijacks the ship, the captain will ditch in the escape pod, and then detonate the thing with the bad guys on board."

"Weird," Emily decided. "So, any idea about what to do with it?"

"Can't do anything in here. We'll have to wait until we're in normal space."

Walk softly, Emily reminded herself. "You can't go out and check right now? Just take a look and see if you can figure anything out about it?" She was asking them to violate one of the chief superstitions of space travel. There were no spacewalks in hyperspace. No leaving the ship whatsoever. It was silly – in theory, nothing could happen. However, people rarely held up their beliefs to the scrutiny of logic.

One look at Ben and his comrades made it clear that they would not yield to her – nor any captain – and they were offended that she would even ask them. "In normal space," Ben repeated.

"Okay . . . so what other ideas do we have?"

Kaz knew he would be the only one to propose the obvious. "Will our Inana friend be willing to turn himself in to save us? What are the chances that the guys following us will leave us alone if they get him?"

Ariki bowed his head, looking at the floor. "I would be willing, and if it is clear to them that you did not know of my status, they would disable the device. They are bounty hunters, not criminals. My followers, though, would hunt you to death. Lack many ships, though. Main peril for you would be on planets. I will send message to my people on Plani, so they know situation."

"You're basically saying that if we turn you over, we'll be all right," Emily said incredulously.

"Yes," Ariki admitted reluctantly. He had come to the bridge to say exactly that, but the word still exited his lips with difficulty.

Emily and Kaz glanced at each other. There was the definite sense between them that average space traders got into far less trouble than they seemed to. Word that the ship was cursed could easily spread like wildfire throughout the crew if they turned Ariki over to bounty hunters, and fanatical Inanas would be hunting them on every planet. They both saw that.

"Kaz, how long till we leave hyperspace?" Emily asked, indicating that she intended to stay silent about Ariki's words.

"Three hours and a few minutes."

A member of the exterior repair crew shifted a bit. Emily caught the uncertain movement and looked at the young man questioningly. Clearing his throat, and trying to avoid the looks of his companions, he said, "Captain, I wouldn't mind going out to look at the thing."

Responding before the captain because he had guessed what the young man was about to say, Ben hissed, "You don't know anything about it. What are you trying to do?"

"Trying to help," the volunteer said, accusingly.

Emily wanted to ask his name, but chose not to. "Are you sure?"

He nodded.

"Kaz, could you show him where the thing is?"

To Emily's surprise, Kaz shook his head. Usually as levelheaded and calculating as people came, the nav officer now defended the repair crew against this breach of their customs. "Captain, you can't let him do this." Emily had no words, so he continued, "there are ways of doing things, and a captain has to make sure that no one disobeys the unwritten rules."

That was it. She had to confront Kaz. He was only willing to let her play Captain as long as he agreed with her decisions, but otherwise, he felt perfectly comfortable with telling her off as if he was directing her how to act the part. Through grinding teeth, she said, "I'll talk to you in my ready room. Now." Turning to the volunteer, she said, "Get ready to head out."

"But Captain," Kaz again started to object.

"Do it," she said, menacingly. She left the bridge, heading for her tiny ready room on the right side of the corridor, immediately outside. It had a bare desk and two chairs, and this was the first time she had used it, so the machined air was stale. Kaz followed, his own temper rising. Resolved to get the first word in, though, she beat him to it. "Who's captain on this ship?"

"Captain," he said with emphasis to avoid directly answering, and then continued in a reasoning tone, "it is unlikely that the repair crew can do anything about that device. Asking one of them to do this will cause divisions within the repair crew, and make the rest of the crew dissatisfied with your command. Will you be asking them to go against their beliefs?"

"This is life and death."

"Not for the crew," Kaz said coldly, "we can just turn over our passenger –"

"Oh come on. You've seen the movies. They always take the guy then kill everyone else anyway."

"I don't think these Inanas have seen that movie. Ariki thinks they'll let us go. The repair crew knows it, so the rest of the crew will soon. You haven't done anything to show them you're a good captain, but now you've shown them that you don't respect them. I'm not religious, and I don't think there's any reason to worry about spacewalking in hyperspace. I'd go myself, but I have no clue what I'm looking at, just seeing the images the bot sends back."

"Well, maybe the guy going out isn't superstitious, either. Did you think of that?"

Kaz's stared at her, saturated with scorn. "He's part of a team," he said slowly, in case she needed the extra time to understand the information, "and you don't even know his name, do you? The only person on the repair crew I know is Ben Wetzler. He spoke for them, and that means he's their leader. His decision was theirs. The kid you're sending out won't be part of the team anymore. You can figure out what that means on your own. I was just trying to save you the trouble. If you need me, I'll be on the bridge."

He turned to leave and Emily thought about stopping him. If she just stood in front of the door, he would not be able to get past – she was easily quicker and stronger. But Kaz had been right, and as much as she hated to admit it, her decision was going to cause problems. She would have to deal with it later. For now, there were more pressing issues. Kaz could use his cold logic and throw Ariki overboard, but that would destroy the crew's confidence in her more than any superstition would. Just as she was about to leave the ready room, heading back to the hostile bridge, Ariki himself appeared in the doorway, and waited for permission to come in.

"Well?"

"Captain," the semi-biped addressed, still at full height, "tampering with device will cause disaster. I will surrender myself. You will be safe. I will inform my followers once we exit hyperspace. If pursuers overlook cargo, please deliver as planned. My followers will show gratitude, and pay you."

"It's more complicated than that," she said, a bit too sharply. "I've already botched one job. I don't want a losing streak."

"Losing streak?" Ariki repeated in English, clearly not understanding the meaning of the words.

That was a bit ironic, she suddenly realized. "You're religious. Do you understand superstition?"

"Baseless belief. Coincidence assumed to be pattern. That is not religion," he responded with what might have been a testy tone.

"How about . . . a bad omen?"

"Yes. And you are saying that failing to transport me to Plani will be a bad omen?"

"Yeah. 'Specially after I messed up last time."

"And that you will have trouble controlling crew after omen?"

She flopped into the chair on her side of the desk, propped her boots on the desk theatrically, and said, "I barely control them now. Kaz controls them, I think. But I think you've got the idea."

Ariki's physiology prevented him from sitting in the other seat, but he climbed onto it, and perched his forelegs on the desk while leaving his hind legs and tail in the seat. Emily put her own feet down instinctively, feeling that having her boots in his face would only be venting her anger at the wrong target. Her moment of hesitation allowed him to get settled and ready to speak.

"You are not an experienced leader, I see."

"Yeah. Don't have followers, that's for sure," she snapped back.

"As one who does, let me tell you what I discovered."

"I don't want followers, Inana. Don't need followers."

Ariki ignored her and continued. "You are worried your people will not follow you. Do not be concerned about this. Be a leader, and others will follow. Be strong and confident, and others will trust your judgment. If you fear, your crew will fear. If you are irrational, so will your crew be."

"So you think I should just magically stop being afraid or worried?"

Ariki thought about this, and then said, "There is rational fear, and irrational fear. After this passes, do not continue fearing. If you are afraid of your crew's . . . discontent, they will be discontented. If you see this as losing streak, so will they.'

Emily calmed down a bit. She had all too little experience dealing with other species, but Ariki had caught at least two words in her language, even if he voiced them in an eerie high pitched voice. "What should I see it as, then?"

"Unavoidable. How could you have avoided this? You could not. Where is fault? Nowhere unless with me. It is right for me to take responsibility and for you to get reward for the risk taken."

She still had a pit in her stomach at that thought. "Well, we'll see what we can do about that device first. I'm not going to call him back in."

The Inana seemed to slink back a bit. "Hyperspace is a magical place. Many superstitions about it. No good will come from challenging them. Eons of space travel have not shaken them. Ideas have . . . inertia. Be careful of ideas in future. This time should not cause too much trouble."

"My navigator thinks different."

"He does not have my experience," Ariki said pointedly.

There was a blank silence. Sensing that their conference was at an end, Emily rose and sighed, "back to work." Ariki remained in the room as she exited and stepped onto the bridge.

"Okay, what's up?"

To her surprise, it was Kaz who answered. The repair crew was still on the bridge, but they kept silent. "He's still looking. We can see what he sees on the viewscreen."

An exasperated voice crackled over the comm. "Captain," the spacewalker called in, his helmet cam aimed at a solid panel with a keypad devoid of symbols, "this is no good."

"No good as in no chance?"

"No good as in messing with this thing is more of a chance than I'd like to take. I'm pretty sure that the key wires are behind this panel, and it looks like even getting to them in the wrong way'll set this thing to explode. Could try . . . but –"

Emily felt like slamming something and cursing, and barely contained herself. A glance at the repair crew made her want to punch Ben. They were murmuring to each other, clearly considering this whole hyperspace excursion a transgression without reason. A pointless mistake. She could have sworn they were supposed to find the fix for this. Flushing from her mind the obvious conclusion that their trip was cursed, she cleared her throat and tried not to sound too disappointed. "All right. Come on back. Doesn't look like that'll work."

"It was a long shot anyway, Captain."

Kaz looked at her, trying to indicate something too subtle for her to catch. Seeing that she was only puzzled, he decided to move in a different direction. "It is looking like we might have to negotiate, Captain."

"Looks like," she said with reservations.

"You up to it?"

Once again, it was a cockiness check from Kaz. She had to admire how he was handling all of this. "If I'm not, I guess you'd like to take over from here, wouldn't you?"

"And be responsible for getting us blown up? It's all yours, Captain. I'll be heading for the lander as soon as we hit Plani space."

That was a bit more of a serious note, and the captain decided to take it as one. It was a good way to shame Ben and his bunch, anyway. Addressing the crew, she said, "Once we reach Plani space, I want everyone ready to bail out. Escape pods by stations – four per pod. If things start to go wacky, I'll turn on the red alert, and everyone except for the bridge crew should head for the pods. Don't go before the red alert, or the enemy will destroy your pod assuming that you are our passenger trying to escape," she remembered that tidbit from one of her grandfather's stories. It had been one of the more exciting adventures. "Kaz, program the trajectories into the pods now."

"I always do that prior to jump, Captain," Kaz said, with full exasperation. "Regulations."

"Right. Shouldn't come to that, but if things go nasty. On red alert, we'll maneuver the ship to cover the escape." She turned off the comm. and mouthed, voiceless, at Kaz, "can we actually do that?"

Kaz shrugged and said, "Depends. I'll try. The closer we are to Plani, the better. We'll be exiting into normal space in half an hour."

Emily decided to stay on the bridge. She dismissed the repair crew, but worried what they might do to the young volunteer when he got back in. By all rights, he should be considered a hero. Others had probably walked in hyperspace before, but he was definitely the first human. The real issue at hand quickly replaced that concern in her mind. Emily occasionally glanced at the door out to the main corridor, wondering if Ariki was going to come back in to say something useful, but he did not. Ethan popped onto the bridge, though, wondering if he could be of some help, and by the very offer making it clear that he felt powerless in the face of events that threatened his life. Emily sent him to the conference room to talk things over with Ariki – to get all the details. Whatever actually happened, Ethan would get some valuable experience and information. However long he had left to put it to use, she thought unwillingly.

She breathed out heavily. Of course, that was wrong. She was already getting used to the idea that they would be turning Ariki over, and that the Inana hunters would let them go in exchange. They wouldn't want to start an interstellar scandal, after all. As Ariki had said, she would be able to just sail away. With some profit for her troubles, like he had said. It was . . . wrong.

After an eternity of these thoughts chasing after each other in her mind, Brian finally broadcast the hyperspace exit warning. Kaz would have beaten him to it, but the navigator was completely occupied, tapping away like a master organist in a spiritual trance. Emily had no idea what he was doing, and wondered whether he did it all just for show. It was impressive, anyway.

As the ship left hyperspace, Emily instinctively ordered, "Engines full, maintain acceleration until we hit the Plani speed limits."

“Already plotted, Captain.”

“Signals,” she commed, “do you have anything for me, Jessica?”

“Not yet, Captain. Plani space is a mess, you know. Thousands of ships in and out. It’ll take me a minute to see if anything’s moving out of its way to get us.”

In an unpleasant turn, Emily realized that she wanted there to be something chasing them at this point. Otherwise, the signal to detonate the device could be light-minutes away without them knowing it. If the bad guys don’t feel like chasing, they could just push the big red button. To have any chance, she needed to be able to talk to them, if only to surrender.

Trouble was that she was far from a negotiator. She was used to getting her way. The first to admit that she was spoiled as a child, she still got frustrated easily when things went against her. Same with Kaz, when she thought about it. Anyway, she wasn’t eloquent or diplomatic. She was a girl of action. Maybe the language barrier would help mask her inadequacies – especially the way people always thought she was lying when she was trying her best to talk carefully. Maybe physical differences would keep them from reading her face, and seeing if she was bluffing. Reading her face –

“Ethan, to the bridge,” she yelled through the comm.

Ethan ran out of the ready room and onto the bridge. “What?”

“Ask Ariki about Inana facial expressions. How do they tell if someone is lying, or angry, or sure of himself. You know, we’ve got shifty eyes, folded arms, and stuff like that. Anything.”

“Got it,” he said. “And you . . . don’t want them to see Ariki on the bridge, just in case.”

“Right. And maybe they’ll also think they can bluff us. Not like there’s any reason for them to, but they might anyway. I want them to lie to us about something. It’ll give me something to try.”

Ethan nodded and went back into the conference room. Emily briefly congratulated herself on her ingenuity, and for being a horrible yet frequent poker player, but it was half-hearted. For all she knew, the Inanas could be stone-faced when they wanted to be.

“Captain,” Jessica called up, “I’ve got them. Three blips not trying to hide themselves. They’re coming right after us, already at high speed. They’ll catch us up in half an hour. Their acceleration can't match ours, though. We'll be able to break away from them eventually."

"They won't let us do that. We'll wait for them to comm us, but if they don't do it in fifteen minutes, Liam, I want you to open a channel. I want some time to talk it over with these guys."

"Yes, Captain."

After fourteen minutes, Ethan returned to the bridge and Liam announced that the pursuing ships were requesting a comm link.

"Let's get a good look at them, then," Emily said, standing firm and gripping the top of the captain's seat to help with the tension. Ethan stood beside her, hoping to find some point to deliver his information.

"Bridge comm or ship comm, Captain?" Liam asked.

"Ship. Want to make sure the crew knows what's happening," she said, eyeing the red alert button.

Two Inanas then appeared on the main screen, obscuring the external view but placed behind the flight path projection so that there was a blue line across the face of the one in the center. Evidently, the Inanas were using a more private screen to transmit the message, so only a minimal amount of their ship's interior was visible. There was some advantage in this for Emily, though, since she could give her opponents any number of false impressions about the state of her ship and crew.

"Captain, by now you know explosive device is on your ship. If not, notice constant course deviations. We want Inana known as Ariki, wanted criminal of our government. If he not delivered, your ship destroyed. If delivered, no hostile action." Emily could not tell one Inana apart from another, but this one's speech translated more roughly than Ariki's.

Just for form, she said, "we don't know any Ariki –"

"You lie." There was no indication of doubt. "You insult us. You die."

She quickly held up her hands in what she hoped was a gesture of submission. "Okay, okay, we have Ariki. Geez."

Ethan whispered to her quickly. "They're bounty hunters. They're not government officials or anything, but they're hired and given a warrant."

Emily doubted that the knowledge changed anything. Maybe she could take a different attitude with them, but they seemed a bit trigger-happy.

At the Inana end, they understood her next words to be, "we did not know of this. We transport passenger peacefully. We do not respond to threats. Company policy. Sabotage of ship leads to legal actions and interstellar crisis. Perhaps we can negotiate, but cargo cannot be transferred under threat." It was the best ploy she could come up with.

"You have no choice. We mean our threat. You will die."

Ethan whispered to her, "he's nervous and not sure about things. The gills are opening wider than usual, and Inanas take in more air when they're nervous."

Well, there could be a whole lot of reasons why this Inana could be nervous, but at least this was a start. "We do not understand. We want to cooperate, but cannot under these circumstances. There are regulations." Hopefully, the Inanas had no clue about the human propensity for violating regulations. She wanted them to think that humans, or at least the captain negotiating with them, blindly followed orders.

Their response gave her hope. "If you wish to show cooperation, decelerate to match our acceleration. Match us as long as we speak."

Without hesitation, she nodded to Kaz to adjust their thrust. While sending the calculations down to engineering and the new plot to Brian, he also took the liberty to prepare an emergency deceleration. A drop-back maneuver was within the realm of possibility, if necessary. With any luck, it would put their single pulse cannon in position to fire on the enemy ship. Since the Inana would detonate the device in response, he planned to execute the program right before the escape pods launched.

"We're decelerating," she said. "Now please tell us, is our passenger dangerous? Is that why you're chasing him like this? Our regulations make exceptions in special cases, to avoid violence."

The Inanas talked it over at the other end, turning off the audio as they conferred.

Taking the ideal opportunity to pipe in, Ethan said, "The other one – the first officer, I guess – is looking excited. A bunch of signs, especially the hand gestures. I think he just wants to blow us up."

"Their captain knows better," Kaz advised. "He wants some real proof to show the government. Blowing us up means they have no proof they killed Ariki, except our word for it."

"Good point. Definitely shouldn't invite Ariki onto the bridge, then."

The Inanas opened the comm again. "Your passenger is a religious zealot. It is . . . odd he would accept your help. He blames all things on off-worlders. We believe he seeks to disrupt meeting of Interstellar Community council. May plan terrorist act. He is real threat. Must be captured."

Out of curiosity, Emily looked at Ethan. He shrugged, indicating that there were no signs. But she knew that the Inana captain was lying. She had talked with Ariki enough to know that. The bluff was good, though, because she could not simply contradict him. She had to work around the lie. The mention of the ISC – the Interstellar Community – had given her an idea.

"Please, give me some time to check the . . . regulations on this. There should be . . . transfer guidelines." She tapped her side panel, pretending that the ship data LCD was an electronic rulebook. She took the time to think out a plausible counter. Something that would be in the law. The passenger was a criminal or a suspected criminal. Why would someone refuse to turn him over? After a moment's thought, she had the answer. "Our regulations state that criminals will be handed over to ISC personnel only. We cannot know that you are not accomplices of his. Maybe we are already handing him over to authorities, and you want to rescue him."

"Nonsense. You will –"

She shouted back, taking charge of the situation. "You have sabotaged my ship. You have threatened my crew even though we are not criminals. You seem to be terrorists to me. I have to be suspicious of you. Anyway, we are in open space. ISC has clear . . . jurisdiction. What do you have to say?"

As she finished, she realized that the push had been too far. The Inana first officer was now openly challenging the authority of the captain. The bounty hunters obviously preferred the more direct approach in place of negotiations. So, the Inana captain returned to more familiar ground. "Give us Ariki, or you will die."

Her success in the negotiation suddenly turned into a pyrrhic victory. The opposition had a clear upper hand thanks to the obvious and unconcealed device on her ship's hull. Stalling was clearly not going to save them. At least Ariki got a chance to send his message. Just in case, she threw her final stalling tactic at them, knowing that their patience was wearing thin. "Captain," she said in as affronted a tone as she had ever whined in, "I can't trust you if you keep making threats like this. I am trying to work with you. Maybe you have a warrant for Ariki's arrest?"

Another silent conference ensued on the other side, and it ended with the Inana captain ordering his first officer off the bridge. In the meantime, Emily sent Ethan to Ariki. Probably, her passenger had already heard how things were going, but she wanted to be sure that he was ready for the worst, including the bit about sending his message. He returned with confirmation that Ariki's message was sent, but there was no guarantee that it was received. On the bright side, the bounty hunters remained unaware.

"Transmitting order for arrest of Ariki issued by Empire of Most Fair. Will also transmit communications with Empire of Fair to show we represent emperor's will."

"Getting the transmission now," Liam said, "I'll have it displayed in a minute."

Ethan drew closer to Emily and murmured, "the Empire of the Fair's the largest country on Ina Cur, and the one with the largest military." He was reciting from memory.

"Ariki told you about their politics?"

"No," he said, a bit embarrassed, "I just watched a whole lot of Alien Species episodes when I was a kid. My qualifications, remember?"

Never surprised by her friend's memorization of television documentaries, Emily's view was suddenly full of documents tiled on the forward screen. They were all scanned plastic sheets imprinted with Inana writing. Liam pushed the button for a translation overlay, but its results were choppy. Nevertheless, the document on the upper left had all the seals that a person would expect from something official, with Ariki's name rendered in Latin script.

"Cut out audio," she ordered Liam. Once he nodded in her

direction, she continued, "what're the chances they're bluffing and we can call them out on it."

"Won't do you any good," Kaz noted, "and they're past impatient."

"It might. We could try to contact ISC authorities."

"By the time the signal got through the bureaucracy, we'd be dead. The bounty hunters might get fined."

"They're bounty hunters," Ethan repeated, "maybe we can pay them better than the Empire of the Fair's giving them. Maybe Ariki can pay us back."

Emily sighed. She knew better than that, but Kaz saved her the trouble of telling Ethan. The bounty hunters would have to be paid enough not only to make up for this job, but for all future jobs as well. If any hint got out that they let their target go for money, they could be criminals as well. Anyway, bounty hunting took in a whole lot more money than honest trading. Their price was too high for her. "Open our comm connection." Emily cleared her throat. This was going to be hard.

Then it got harder. Ariki stepped onto the bridge. "Captain," he started, "I will surrender myself. There is no choice."

"Will you get back to the –"

"I am about to fire, Captain," the translated voice came from the other ship. Then, realizing what he was seeing, the opposing captain said, "seeing my prey . . . makes me impatient."

"Your guarantee that the device will be disabled," she said quickly.

"We are locked onto you. We can destroy your ship with a shot. We disable the device now as a sign to you. Do not alter vector or accelerate, or we fire immediately. Device will be released. At a safe distance from you, we will explode it."

Emily and her crew waited uncertainly. The captain contemplated the red alert button, wondering if the sight of Ariki had driven the Inana captain to explode the device. After all, he now had his proof. She held her finger from the button, though, and when the explosion came, it only rocked the ship slightly. Once Kaz compensated for this, he said, "I'm taking the course correction program off. If the device is really off, we won't be off course at the interval. I'll be able to say for sure in a minute."

The Inana captain had been true to his word, so there was only one course. Some large cannon was no doubt now locked on to them and ready to fire. "All right, we'll bring Ariki to you using a pod. Please send us a course to your docking bay. Ethan, escort Ariki to the cargo bay's exit chamber."

"Course received," Liam said, "sending it over to Kaz."

"Got it. Programming landing pod one."

Emily ordered, "Pilot one, please get your pod ready. Course has already been sent."

After a few minutes, Emily informed the Inana captain that their pod was ready to head over. Receiving a warning that the Inana would convert the pod into energy if it deviated from the course provided, she assured the opposing captain of her good will through gritted teeth.

For all the confrontation that had occurred before, the finale concluded smoothly. As the landing pod was on its return journey, Ariki appeared on the bridge of the Inana ship, and met with its captain. Satisfied, the Inana captain declared their business at an end and shut the comm link. His ship and its two escorts decelerated, breaking away for the jump back to Ina Cur.

The bridge crew waited silently for the return of the landing pod. Ethan rejoined them, and did not bother to keep his words to Emily when he said in a choked voice, "Ariki wanted me to remind you that the bounty hunters didn't ask for the cargo. He . . . the last thing he said was that he wanted the cargo delivered as planned. He was real serious about it. I don't think it's just rare food."

"No kidding," Emily said, irritated at herself, but willing to take on convenient targets as well. "We're definitely finishing this job off. Not like we have anything to do with the cargo if we don't."

Brian turned around from his panel. "You don't think the cargo's weapons or bombs or something. I mean, what do we really know about Ariki?"

Emily was about to reply sharply, but checked herself. Heck, the Inana was a major religious leader – he could probably dupe people into believing he was a good guy without even trying. She suddenly felt the burden of her continuing naïveté – the fact that she had only ever posed as a rebel. Ariki was the real thing. What could she say about the lengths he would go to for his beliefs? He had already shown a willingness – maybe even eagerness – to sacrifice himself. She had no clue what she had in the cargo bay.

"Yeah, but what difference does that make?" said Emily. "We don't want his followers chasing us across the galaxy. And what if we break the locks and find out it's something totally harmless? The best way to get out of this is to deliver the goods without messing with them. That's what we would have done anyway."

Thankfully, Kaz had no objections, but Brian persisted, "Captain, what if we end up responsible for a huge disaster? On Plani, that could mean millions of people dying."

Kaz intervened. "Once we get down there we'll ask to see what the cargo was. If they refuse, we'll notify the authorities. That's the best we can do. If these are bombs, we can't go around with the crates in our bay. If we turn to weapons dealing, we'll really be in trouble. We're in the business of hauling cargo, not law enforcement. No one expects us to inspect the cargo."

Emily nodded, and added nothing. With the pod docked in the bay, she was eager to get this all behind her so she could work on her relationship with the crew. She already had a couple of things in mind, and had no doubt others would have proposals of their own. She desperately needed to learn some names, for starters.

"Plotting a course for Plani landing, Captain. We will need clearance to dock with the Dael city drop ship."

"Liam?"

"I'm on it," the comm. officer confirmed.

"It's too bad we can't just leave the cargo in the station for this job. Using the dropship and lifter will cost us," Kaz noted.

"They paid us enough to make up for it. How long will we have to wait for the drop?"

She waited for the response from Liam. "We're lucky. Next drop's in five hours Earth time, they say, and we'll be on board in three. It could have been three or four days."

Emily had never experienced a dropship landing on a planet before, but she had every reason to expect that it would be relaxing, or at least more relaxing than bringing the ship to a landing themselves. Her ship could manage an atmospheric landing and takeoff, but it would be more dangerous and more expensive in fuel.

As it turned out, the rendezvous with the dropship and the journey down was a breeze. The lander carried down all of the trading station's deliveries and at least a dozen other ships. Like with all things, the Plani packed it efficiently, and to the brim. That was impressive, since it was almost a quarter of a mile in each dimension. On its way up, it could serve as a lifter for entire stations, if necessary. It was just a vertical descent pod aimed at a clearing in the city of Dael. Its rockets were primarily directed to slow its approach to the surface, and small maneuvering units maintained its aim. Emily couldn't imagine the thing lifting off – the energy used must be impressive. Nevertheless, the Plani operators made the trip at least fifty times every Plani year. The lifter system was necessary, considering the massive trading volume that the planet handled.

Plani seemed like a mass of metal as they descended. They were treated to a full-on view of the northern continent. Its southern counterpart was mostly a dense rainforest preserved to provide a breathable atmosphere, inhabited by extremely hostile animals and criminals serving life sentences. In the sardine-can cities of the north, the air was painfully thin, and even species for which the nitrogen-oxygen atmosphere was nominally suitable found a portable air supply necessary.

In the key cities, though, clearly marked drop zones, landing strips, and the bullet rail path interrupted the grayness. Around the supersonic rail line, a broad greenway flourished – a forest of sorts. At the side of the slower lines, there were slim stretches of a grass-like plant. The supersonic line crossed the entire northern continent, and was as distinguishable from space as the world's coastlines. Ethan briefly mentioned to Emily that the parks around the rail lines were important to the Plani because they served as spots for social gatherings – especially for the lower classes who felt the world of the gray ignored their interests.

Emily's only experience with the Plani was when one of them took all the profits from her first job at gunpoint, after just having paid her. To rub it in, the bastard had used an Earth handgun – presumably because the station anti-weapons sensors had yet to be programmed to detect them. She had been forced to access her account, transfer the payment back to his, and then to face her crew with empty hands. She could have put off the explanation to the crew until it came time to split the profits, but that would have caused even more problems. As it was, her failure sparked Kaz's intense disaffection with her command. After she had openly wondered why the Plani had bothered to transfer the money in the first place, and then only asked for the same amount back, Kaz informed her of what everyone supposedly already knew. The Plani had some sort of honor-among-thieves thing, so that the way the Plani swindled her counted as fair. Ethan had pointed out that if she had pulled out a weapon after the Plani had, he would have left without any malice or standoff. If only someone had mentioned all of this to her earlier –

Anyway, this time they were delivering to Inanas living on Plani who, with any luck, were ignorant of Plani trading culture. There were enough complications to deal with as it was. What about Inana culture and the peculiar beliefs of Ariki's cult? Images of chaotic religious rituals and fiery sacrifices flashed through her imagination's eye, and she shuddered, only now realizing the bizarre possibilities that could be awaiting her.

The lander smashed safely onto the surface of the planet. Suddenly they were in the midst of a bustling port with a slot for everything that could come out of the ship. All cargo pods had trains waiting to take them to their final destinations, and all ships had a berth where they could conduct business. Standard transport pads were zipping through the place in every destination, sometimes under remote control. More impressive was when chains of them were rigged together, looking much like the trains that were waiting to haul them out.

The Inanas were already waiting for them at the berth by the time the tow truck released the ship and went out to take care of other business. Their quick arrival was no surprise, since the dropships provided a complete inventory to the port before leaving the orbiting space dock. Screens all over the place displayed ship arrival times for the benefit of those awaiting a passenger transport. The worrying part of the Inana presence was the look on their faces. It was easy to tell that they were angry. Rage flowed right out of the Inana gathering and filled the hangar-like berth. As a more astute student of Inana behavior, Ethan noted the erratic oscillations in their body, and the tension in their forelegs. They were all standing.

Emily wondered if there were any signs of grieving as the amphibians met Ethan and her at the edge of the open cargo hatch. She would have preferred to see grief. Remaining as close to the ship as they could get without being on it, she and Ethan engaged the Inanas without weapons. If the Inanas had guns hidden in their packs, there would be just enough time to get back into the ship and close the hatch.

"Human captain," the Inana at the center of the front row of seven called out, "where is Ariki, who paid to be brought here?"

Emily was about to ask whether they had received Ariki's message, but quickly deduced that all they expected her to do was make the bad news official. They had been expecting the worst even before she had stepped out. Heck, the fate of Ariki had probably been foretold or something. She steeled herself, and got ready to deliver the news in as dignified a way as possible, definitely wanting to make it clear that she respected Ariki.

"The danger was not made clear to me," she started, all apologies, "and my ship was sabotaged in orbit around Ina Cur. We tried to remove the sabotage device in hyperspace, but failed. After hyperspace exit, we were intercepted by bounty hunters. We tried to negotiate and failed. Ariki chose to surrender himself to save us. He told us to deliver the cargo to you despite the disaster. We obeyed." She thought the "obeyed" part was a nice touch. Hopefully, the translators caught all of that. She had kept it as simple and clear as she could.

The Inana leader was a bit ambivalent in his silence. The others were clearly looking to him for direction, so the reception was entirely in his hands.

"Have heard of this. Ariki died honorable, then?" the leader finally said, his words translating poorly compared to Ariki's because he spoke in a more peculiar dialect. "Saving your lives?"

Emily chose to avoid the fact that Ariki was still alive, and only captured, understanding that the difference was, in this case, irrelevant. "Yes, very honorably. My whole crew knows he sacrificed himself to save our lives."

"Very well. Certainly understand human captain could not have known what would come. Of cargo, Ariki followers will take possession now."

The transition had been so quick that Emily had no idea how to broach the subject. She had to try, though. "Umm . . . could we ask what it is? Cargo, I mean." She tried a different tact. "Was it important to Ariki? Will it help his cause?"

The Inanas were clearly suspicious, but their leader had planned to explain the cargo anyway. He said, "Bring cargo out, and all will be shown. By entering unlock code for crates, Ariki followers show . . . are rightful recipients, then pay rest of fee."

"You don't have to pay –"

"Will pay," the Inana insisted. "Now, cargo."

Emily signaled the cargo crew, who brought the pallets out. The cargo crew had spared the crates even the slightest damage, but the Inanas conducted a quick check anyway. Satisfied that the exteriors showed no sights of wear, the leader stepped up to a seemingly random crate and entered his code. There was a snap, after which he lifted the lid slowly. Swaying with obvious relief, he set the lid aside, and pulled an object from the crate. Emily had no guess about what it was at first, seeing only a light-greenish box, but then the leader opened it, turning one leaf after another. On the leaves were Inana writing, though in a more elaborate form than on the bounty hunter warrant. The object was obviously a book written on pages formed from an Inana plant. It was a marked contrast from the plastic sheets now practically universal throughout the ISC.

Ethan ventured a guess. "These are . . . Ariki's writings?"

"Yes. Only copy. Very important. Ariki did not wish copies made until his death. Now, Ariki's followers will publish."

Emily was stunned. "All of this? He wrote . . . all of this?"

Agitated at the disrespect implied, the Inana responded with quick words, "This is fraction of Ariki's wisdom. Time was too short for him to finish. Universal wisdom cannot be kept in crates, no matter how many. Ariki is thanked by all followers for doing his best."

The other Inanas then intoned something, clearly reciting a formulated thanks to their prophet.

"What's this all about, anyway?" she said as soon as they finished the chant, hoping she was not interrupting a more elaborate ceremony. "I mean, you put my ship and crew at risk without telling us why. I know things didn't turn out well, but I'd still like to know what's going on."

The Inanas were predictably flustered, but Emily felt it was time to sound stern – now that it was clear they intended to spare her life. Their leader composed his people, and adjusted to her change in tone. "Apologies for not informing Captain, but would make no difference. A chance Captain was not honorable, not worth such risk. Space travel is difficult to arrange. Ariki followers are persecuted on Ina Cur, against Interstellar Community's freedom of belief, and are here to petition community. Ariki ordered by Empire of Fair not to come here, but he wished to explain our position."

"So, why would the Empire care so much about what you believe?"

The Inana stood proudly. His oscillations were more rigid, as if he was standing at attention. "Because Ariki followers are anarchist, speaking against Empire on Ina Cur. Empire takes over other nations, expands breeding grounds forcefully. In ancient times, Empire coexisted peacefully with others. Outside influence, different from Inana nature and beliefs, influences Empire. Inana are simple species with small populations and low technology. Easy target for outsiders who use Empire to gain control over Ina Cur."

Conspiracy theories. Theirs was a reasonable one, at least, but still vague and virtually impossible to prove. Anarchists, though . . . it took some mental adjustment for her to think of these Inanas as anarchists, but she had no doubt they meant it. Anyway, religious heresy and anarchy went together just as well as religious orthodoxy and autocracy. Emily had the ideas, but lacked the words for them. The religion was clearly a secondary problem for this bunch, but they had to use it to bring their case to the ISC, and Ariki's bible would help prove to the ISC that there was a legitimate religion involved. Suddenly, a great deal was becoming clear.

"All right. But who do you think is causing this outside influence?"

The Inana hesitated, and tried not to tip his hand too much. If his enemies knew the extent of what he knew, there could be consequences. Caution was key here, but so were allies. In a confidential tone – a low pitched whine in contrast to the high pitch with which he made his more lofty declarations – he said, "Could speak privately?"

"Yeah . . . Yes, follow me." The Inana leader made his way up the ramp, and Emily led the way to the ship's conference room. Ethan looked uncertain about which way to go, but decided to stay out with the Inana horde. At least the cargo crew was still nearby, and this way there was minimal suspicion.

In the conference room, with its long table and eight chairs, Emily and the Inana faced each other standing, instead of taking seats. The Inana, almost breathless with eagerness to voice his thought, said, "Surely Captain knows of destruction of Asparis, and of refugee crisis tens of Plani years ago. Earth people were involved, yes?"

Emily nodded. "Yes." She knew where this was going, but didn't like the idea that humans were somehow involved in the political plight of the Inanas. Asparis had been a phenomenally powerful aggressor planet, feared and quarantined by the ISC. It had attacked Earth with the living weapons that ruled Asparis – the mancers. Earth had barely survived, but within decades mounted a spectacular retaliation, supported by the rest of the ISC. The cost of Earth's revenge had been hefty, and had to be additional justified by a desire to free the oppressed majority of Asparis, the mundanes, from the hammer of mancer rule. Asparis was subsequently left barren for reasons too complicated for Emily to understand. All she knew was that it had frozen over, and Earth's weapons alone had not been the cause of its climatic change. However, in the flood of Asparii mundanes fleeing to other systems, some of the mancers were unaccounted for. Captured mancers had been rocketed to the Andromeda Galaxy on a ship without controls, built to particular specifications preventing the metal manipulators among the captives from applying their abilities to it. Despite this extreme removal of the mancer menace, there were almost certainly still mancers lying low, waiting for an opportune time to regain power. It was a good thing they were instinctively distrustful of each other; otherwise, they could easily unite and become a powerful force again. Still, individual mancers could easily threaten a government into submission, and they would want revenge against Earth, if they could get it –

Emily was immediately skeptical as the Inana described the suspected Asparian interference in Inana affairs. Sure, it was possible, but it was also too convenient. The Inana had picked the one enemy that a human would be eager to ally against. Then again, it would explain why the Inana wanted her as an ally. It might even explain why they had hired her in the first place, as opposed to a spacious Karisi ship, for instance.

After going over the outline of his theory, the Inana moved on to the point – what he was hoping she would do about all this. It wasn't what she expected. "A planet exists, Captain, outside of ISC control. Few know about it, because only refugees settle there, and for hundreds of Plani years, refugees have kept quiet so former leaders would not chase them. Planet is legendary. Those in fear for lives try to go, not always knowing where to go. Planet has no space travel. Older . . . settlements do not believe space travel possible. Know this because branch of family went to escape famine on Ina Cur. Maintained communication all these years."

"So –"

"Planet is covered with small settlements, developing slowly. ISC maps label system as hostile, but family says planet is safe. Empire of Asparii refugees, a good empire with good Asparii, has peacefully built, ready to begin interstellar trade. No ships, though. Empire may be target for mancers, for takeover. Earth can provide . . . technological option, and can give defense against mancers. Bring planet into ISC, and planet will have protection. Asparian empire will welcome you. As a human, say Earth defeated mancers. Many Asparii mundanes are still afraid of mancers, and will be interested in hearing of human conquest of Asparis. Excellent trade opportunity, and will close possible haven for our enemies."

At this point, Emily wished she knew more about Earth's conquest of Asparis. All she knew was that Earth didn't really win – Asparis somehow self-destructed. She was therefore hesitant to pose as a vanquisher of mancers. Of course, this looked like the kind of break that would make her a famous trader. To be the first one to establish a trade run with a planet was the holy grail. Quickly, she saw things from the Inana's angle and was shocked at how clear his purpose suddenly was. Ariki's followers were outcasts, after all. This planet of exiles might soon be their destination if things continued to go badly on Ina Cur, but only if the mancers weren't secretly taking it over already.

They needed to ensure that it was every bit the sanctuary they hoped it would be. Well, at least things were making sense now, though it gave her a headache trying to think about it all at once.

"And no one else knows about this?"

"Some may know exiles there, but will not have reason or chance to pass information to starship captain. How long until another does? No one may say. Information is on standard data disc."

"No conditions? Just because I take the disc does not mean I will go there to trade, understand?"

"As Captain says. And Ariki followers have copies to give other captains, if given a chance."

"How long will you give me before you hand the discs to other captains?"

"Doubt will meet another trustworthy captain in a quarter of a Plani year. And another human captain . . . rare. Asparii will trust humans more than any other species. Earth people look like Asparii. Earth was an Asparian colony, yes? Was Atlantis, yes?"

Emily had always found it troublesome to believe the official ISC account of the origin of humans on Earth. The population of Earth itself was divided on the subject, confused because the idea that humans were descended from an alien species used to be the realm of crackpots, and legends about Atlantis the realm of fantasy. The science of the ISC account was difficult to follow, too, so no help there. She instinctively distrusted the theory, but whatever her own ideas, there was no denying the species resemblance. At the very least, she would not stand out among Asparii the way she did alongside Inanas or Plani.

"All right," she said, trying to avoid feeling pressured either way, "give it to me."

The Inana brought his backpack around, and grabbed the disk from one of its smaller pockets. He also took out his computer. Handing her the disk, he said, "your account number, please?"

Emily handed him a prepared slip with the number written on it, and he finalized the transfer. She checked the credits at her end.

"Thank you, Captain Pierce. Ariki group is straightforward in dealings when possible. Hope this experience does not prevent Captain from taking cargo in future." He said it solemnly. The way Emily read his words and the high-pitched tone of his actual voice, it seemed to her that all this had been planned ahead of time, even these words. Ariki had prepared for his capture. They had planned for her to feel guilty about it, and all this would lead her to feel obligated to go to the planet of exiles, or to take other jobs from them. Ariki's capture had been inevitable – they had all but admitted it – but this way it would help them in their case in front of the ISC. They had probably recorded her speech about his capture when she was apologizing outside the ship. For the moment, she stood awed by their foresight. It was plans within plans, all over the place. They were as bad as the Plani.

"I'll have to think about that. I'll have to think about a lot of things."

2
Downtime

She needed to get more organized. The time spent refueling at Dael gave her the chance to make some changes. When she had first put the trading mission together, she had more or less expected the crew to take care of their own business, and they proved to be entirely capable of doing so. They weren't children who required extensive management. The problem was . . . after two jobs she still didn't know most of their names. There was more to the problem, but the name issue was a salient symptom. She felt insecure with them, and the only way to change that was to take the independent professionals she had hired, and turn them into a crew.

If asked, she would have considered herself dynamic and flexible, and ready to adapt. In the final frame, though, the crew beat her to it and started suggesting changes as soon as the ship touched the Plani surface. Ben, from the external repair crew, came to her first, asking for permission to acquire external cameras and good repair drones. Clearly, they wanted to avoid any more requests for hyperspace walks. She gave them the okay, but put a price limit on it. Ben gave her the hint that there was strife within his team's ranks, and that he wanted to know whether she would recognize his leadership or not. Since he had been circumspect about it, she chose to ignore the issue, putting it off until later. Then there was Brian, who wanted the ship named. Since it was his first piloting job, he had quickly developed an attachment to the ship, and it was awkward to have no name for it. Her grandfather had called it the Intrepid, but that name had no special meaning to him, and she thought it sounded goofy, not to mention too military.

Naming the ship would be a step in the right direction, giving the place a unified character. She had left Brian in agreement, but without a proposed name.

After those two discussions, she settled in her ready room with a beer, mulling things over. Before she could prop her boots on the desk, though, Kaz came in. This meeting came a bit sooner than she had planned, so she thought quickly how to deal with it. Kaz seemed to be in the mood for calm discussion, and a bit too tired to arm it with fangs. His jet black hair, normally in perfect order, was in a slight but meaningful disarray as he ran his right hand through it. Emily noticed the sign, meant to indicate that Kaz had come unprepared for this talk, and was frustrated by the problem of bringing up the subject. Of course, she knew very well that he had been carefully considering it for hours, contrary to what he wanted her to think. Being so concerned about what he thought of her, she had developed a knack for reading him, not that he tried especially hard to conceal anything. Kaz only started something important with a clear idea of what he was getting into, and how to get around likely barriers.

"Captain, I know we've had our differences –"

There was really no need to go through the conversation, not if she really wanted to avoid strife with Kaz. What he wanted was a minor deal, anyway, since he already acted like a first officer. If things didn't work out, she could just take the job away from him, so no harm done, and maybe some good. Preempting him in the hope that he would be surprised, and forced out of his planned gambit, she said, "I'm thinking of making you my first officer." His stunned silence was definitely satisfying. "It's about time I had one. I need some advice on changes I want to make. We need to get the crew working together. You've been on other ships, any ideas?"

At this point, Kaz found it difficult to stay standing at attention, and took a seat. She could imagine the thoughts snaking their way through his mind. Kazuhiro Kamiki was officially first officer of a starship. He had taken on the job knowing that his comparative experience would give him an advantage over the young crew. Seeking to be first officer from the start, he had acted like one, and resented being denied the title he knew he deserved. Still, he had to be the youngest starship second-in-command ever. Whatever else happened, unless the ship was destroyed, this would look good on his résumé.

He had a few recommendations, now that she asked. "First, we need to establish who reports to who," he voiced his last words with an unusually thin pitch, so he cleared his throat. "There should be three or four departments, and the head reports to you. That way, you always know who to talk to, and you give people the kind of responsibility they're used to."

"Sounds like you've thought about this."

"I have."

Emily was skeptical, but sidestepped the sarcasm that initially came to her mind. "It doesn't sound like that'll bring the crew together. They're already in teams, and the teams've chosen leaders. Not a real change –"

Kaz held up a finger, indicating that he was about to offer a point. "Once we've got definite teams, we can have competitions. Friendly games. Not just between the four departments, but also between teams like rookies versus crew chiefs. That way, people on opposite teams one week might be on the same team other times. That's just one idea, though."

"Sounds interesting so far. Other ships have games like this? Didn't really hear much about this part."

Kaz nodded hesitantly. "All the ships I've been on so far did. Usually some sports, so I wasn't really thrilled about it. Maybe we could try something different, but sports usually work best."

"All right. What else do you have?"

"Basic rations are a bit harsh for morale. We probably have some decent cooks on board, so maybe we can give them some extra duty. On one ship, we also had the losing teams make dinner for the winners."

"We'll be needing some time when everyone's available. I like my sleep, so I don't want to organize stuff while we're in hyperspace –"

"On the other ships I've been on, we had some arranged downtime. It wasn't just job after job after job. After all, if you finish all the jobs waiting, you're going to end up with a lot of time all at once."

"Could lose jobs, though. And this is about the money, right?"

Kaz shrugged. "An officer on another ship told me it all evens out at the end. I've never done the accounts, so I don't know the business-end. That's your department, I think."

Emily scratched her head. It was time to make a list. Prone to disorganization, she was at least bright enough to recognize when her mind was flooded, and threatening to lose some ideas overboard. The ready room desk was fully stocked, so she just pulled out a notepad and a black pen from a drawer, and began to jot everything down, starting with Ben's recommendations. Finally, she got down to what Kaz had just said. "Okay. These three or four . . . I guess we'll call 'em teams . . . they'll have to have close to the same number of people each, right? Otherwise the whole game thing won't work. How were you thinking of putting them together? I suppose you've already thought all this through, right?"

Kaz cleared his throat to cloak a confirmation of her guess. "Well, engineering already reports to me, and Brian basically flies to my plot, so I'd be in charge of them. That's navigation. Signals sends its information to communications, so Liam will be in charge of his own post, Ms. Scott, and your friend Ethan –"

"Pretty small team –"

"– which is why we put the hyperspace crew with them, too. The technical and external repair crews will be put together, and the tech repair chief will lead them. I think his name's Harpaul."

"Don't know if Ben and the external crew will like being put under the computer geeks."

Kaz shrugged. "They should get to know each other. That leaves cargo and supplies. The transport pilots should be under them instead of navigation. Makes more sense."

Since it all sounded reasonable, and she was feeling more open-minded than she had the past few days, Emily just took it all down. She would probably end up taking more notes here than in four years of high school. "Looks like we've got enough stuff for a whole crew meeting."

Taking an upside-down look at the list, Kaz said, "just naming the ship could take some time, depending on how we do it. So yes, we should probably get the whole crew together for this."

The ship's crew was about double the size that could fit in the conference room or the recreation room, so the only place where everyone could congregate was in the cargo bay, which had some benches stacked in a corner for just such an occasion. The bay already had a rough basketball court set up, so that would be convenient. The makeshift court was close to the hatchway and pressurization chamber, so it was easy for the cargo crew to keep it clear – placing the transport pods as deep into the hold as possible. The whole place was empty now, though, and looked like quite an arena. They still set the benches close to the tail, opening the two sets of hatches to increase ventilation. The cargo bay had air, but even the thin air of Plani was preferable to the processed air of the ship's atmospheric system.

This was the first assembly of the crew since they held a meeting on Newport station, from which the ship had departed Earth's orbit. That time, she had just spoken to the crew briefly, trying her best to hide her public speaking inexperience. She had failed. The rolling eyes had actually been audible. It was time to make a new impression. With any luck, her deftness in dealing with the Ariki situation had given her an extra ace to work with. Unfortunately, the prevailing attitude was that, while it was her ship and she was free to run it, the best way to run it was for her to leave the people who knew about engines to the engines, who knew about repairs to the repairs, and to stay out of their way by sticking to the bridge where a captain belongs.

No one said this as they congregated in the cargo bay, but they were thinking about it hard enough so that it was plain on their faces. Seeing them all there, Emily was acutely aware that she had prepared little of what she was about to say. That was all right. She'd let her natural bravado take over in place of rehearsal.

"Okay, first thing," she started, benches of crewmates on three sides of her, "I want us to get to know some names and a little bit about each other." That met with immediate groans. Everyone recognized the pattern, and many were irate at being treated like a class of children. They had escaped that nonsense, and resented any implication that they were incapable of handling themselves and socializing like adults. She knew the feeling, but knew of no other way to handle this step. Taking a few words to explain her reasoning to them, and receiving a few scowls back, she continued. "We'll just do this the easy way. Introduce yourself to the people sitting next to you. Tell them your name and what you like to do in your spare time. Then I'll introduce Kaz here, and we'll go around, each person telling us about the person on their left. Okay? Go ahead and introduce yourselves."

They were slow to get started, but there was no point in disobeying. Emily went over to Kaz and said, "Kazuhiro Kamiki, right?"

He looked at her sardonically, still waiting for the official announcement of his new position. "Yeah. You won't have a clue about my favorite pastime, though, even after I tell you."

Not at all surprised, she asked, "why? What is it?"

Kaz sighed. "A board game called Go. It's . . . like chess, but that's probably the worst way to describe it. It's famous, but you haven't heard of it."

She hadn't.

"Tough to explain without showing you how to play it."

Emily shrugged. "Is it complicated?"

"Not the rules, but the way it's played gets to be."

Leaving it at that, Emily started off the introductions with herself – she liked to listen to music and play poker in her spare time. Moving onto Kaz, she said, "Kazuhiro Kamiki has been our nav officer, and I've picked him to be my second-in command. He likes to play a board game named Go." She allowed a bit of time for the news to settle in, and for Kaz to stand and bow. There was only scattered applause, but Kaz was unperturbed. He was now official. Emily then gestured to Kaz to continue the introductions, and they went around the room. As she had expected, there was no way to catch everything, but there were a few memorable names and activities. A lot of sports. Kaz had come up with another, less obtrusive way to learn names. As soon as the first phase finished, he fetched a roll from under his seat, unfurled it, and displayed it to the crowd. The poster was actually composed of taped-together printout sheets. It displayed the name of the captain at the top, and the four branches extending from her – Navigation, Communications, Repairs, and Cargo. Then it had the sub-branches, and empty boxes for the names of the crewmembers.

"Kaz and I have talked, and we decided to get the crew a bit more organized. Kaz got this chart ready," Emily said, looking admiringly at the poster. "We need you to get your names on here, then meet with your team to pick a leader. Then, each team gives us a list of suggestions to improve the ship."

The crew entered the process with more good will than she had expected. Still, "no more meetings" was a popular recommendation. The repair team picked Ben as their leader instead of Harpaul, but Emily had expected that. Activities were recommended, and basketball quickly took the lead there, followed by soccer and poker. Basketball seemed to satisfy the crew, but Emily vowed to find some alternatives. She had never been opposed to physical exertion – she had been athletic in the walking-on-handrails and jumping-from-extreme-heights styles. She just hated team sports. Maybe it was the chauvinism that men – even semi-intelligent ones – felt it necessary to display while playing, watching, and talking about them. Sounded like a lame excuse, though.

"Now for naming the ship," she said, finally hitting the last point on the list as the crew was getting impatient and uncomfortable on the benches. "My grandfather called it Intrepid, but that's not my kind of name." There were a few nods at this. In hiring the members of her crew, she had avoided any military types, or wannabe military types, so at least they were unlikely to name the ship after some admiral or war hero. "But I've got no idea what to call it. Any ideas?"

At first, it seemed like she would get a brain-drizzle instead of any sort of storm. After the first suggestion, a flood came. She used the back of the organization poster to jot them all down. Kaz was once again holding it up, but was having trouble keeping his arms up. Emily grinned at him, and he scowled back.

"All right. I think we've got enough. Let me just cross out the goofy sounding ones –" Earth Pride was off the list immediately, as were all animal names, anything involving a country or world, anything with a double entendre, and anything with a single entendre having to do with sex. She kept Freedom, and thought it was the best of the lot. It was how she thought of the ship, after all. None of the names was particularly striking or inspiring.

Ultimately, they decided on *Azar*. It had a decent ring, a spacey tone, and was unique. Emily conceded that it avoided the stereotypical ship names, and practiced saying a few times to get the feel for it. That settled, she was free to take care of practical business, and arranged a meeting to net them another job.

3
Sleepless Hyperspace

Like all Plani cities, Dael packed its residents tightly with minimal allowances for living space. This was easily the city's most memorable trait, since constant discomfort is hard to forget. Jostled and thrown off-balance so many times on the train to Dael's outskirts, Emily's recollection of the experience was a solid blur of agitation. Tossed around once, twice, or half a dozen times, she would remember each incident clearly, and might retaliate by shoving back, but the sheer frequency of it on the commuter train prevented her from doing anything except bear with it. As in a few Earth cities, the stations had heavyset Plani – about as strong as the average human – hired to pack people onto the trains, making sure the mass-transit company used every bit of train-space efficiently and quickly. The Plani were the most competitive species in the galaxy, and they expected that privately owned railroads would milk every credit they could manage from their operations. At least they also had the decency to be highly organized – every person in this train car was exiting at the same station.

Being surrounded by Plani made the journey even more uncomfortable. The grey stick figures could be described as elfish, if not for their sickly bureaucratic pallor. If you took newborn elves and raised them in cubicles, giving them desk jobs as soon as they could talk, you might end up with Plani. Maybe they were the extreme result of the evolutionary track Kaz was so ardently following. Their faces certainly had the sneer and cynical look down. She wondered what the Plani considered fun, and suspected it had something to do with ripping a fellow Plani off for his or her last dime. Maybe comparing them to vampires would be more accurate.

Long before her first direct experience with one of them, her grandfather's stories had soured Emily's attitude towards the Plani, but even after hearing those tales, she was willing to believe he had exaggerated their malice. Then one of them held her up at the end of her first job. Granted, he had only taken the payment back when he could have left her with nothing, but it was no less humiliating. Only later did she find out that this sort of thing was common in Plani business, and that it was nothing personal. They had rules so alien to what she was used to, she had to watch her step.

Thankfully, she was meeting with a human-run business this time. Earth corporations had only started building outposts on Plani recently, despite how pivotal the planet was to ISC trade. Every major interstellar company felt it necessary to have a branch on the planet, to have their influence, if for no other reason. Earth simply lacked anything to offer the other worlds yet, and any influence to extend. There was finally some spark of initiative, though. Earth had to develop ties to the rest of the galaxy, and that process was bound to cost a bit at first.

Land close to the Dael city center and its massive spaceport was so expensive that there was no way to locate a comfortable workspace within close proximity to it. Most non-Plani firms located their premises a fair distance away, and made use of the extensive Plani rail system. Businesses often sent goods to other cities, since ISC headquarters used Dael's ports heavily and the added demand drove up costs. With Emily in the neighborhood, though, one company felt that it could get a good price from her – human-to-human. She actually considered taking less from them to build up some good will. It was a facet of business that she had reluctantly picked up from her father's conversations during dinner parties that had doubled as ways to develop valuable contacts.

A short walk took her from the train station to the company's offices. Given the bland name of "Space Pier Imports," it was the Plani branch of a more respectably named Earth conglomerate. On the exterior, Plani buildings were similar to Earth structures; they were boxes of steel and plexiglass. Inside, the difference in looks seemed acute, but Emily guessed that the souls of Earth and Plani business buildings – the corporate sterility – were as similar as the cold exteriors. While she was here, though, she enjoyed the legroom.

Through the metal detector, guard, and elevator, she found herself in the office of a man who looked every bit a used car salesman – toupee, sleazy moustache, bow tie, and cheap suit. He was embarrassing to look at. The best she could say for Space Pier Imports was that someone else was in charge, and this lamentable individual just negotiated for transportation. However, the fact that the Earth conglomerate had sent him here instead of, say, Siberia, showed a degree of contempt for off-world business.

"It's Captain Pierce, right?" the slimy intrusion from the past addressed her, hand outstretched to shake hers. He said her name as if pointing out that he could pronounce it properly, unlike all the aliens doing business with her, whose translators would always have trouble with proper names. She looked at the hand for a moment before shaking it, at once not used to business etiquette and put off by the person attached to it.

The Space Pier Imports representative gestured to a seat on the visitor side of his desk. Like her ready room, the office was only furnished with the essentials – his seat, the desk, the visitor seat, and a few items of stationery. The representative had either just moved in, or was using the office temporarily. Emily tried to avoid jumping to conclusions, but after her first two jobs, she had a license to be suspicious. It was too easy to wonder about this guy, though. It would fit the humor of the universe if, with so much about him indicating the contrary, he was an honest man. She took the seat roughly and sat in a heap, resolved to play the part of the haughty space captain. In her mind, this meant a slouched and spread-legged posture like the insolent one she used in classrooms. While perfecting the position, she noticed the nameplate on the desk – Jason Parell. With her typical inability to remember names, she had asked her way up to the right office.

Focused on delivering his regular pitch, Parell failed to notice the way Emily looked at him. "Thank you for coming. I hope you found the place without trouble. We are a new firm, and we specialize in bringing both unique artifacts and visitors to Earth. All entry hassles will be taken care of by us – the clearances and biological checks and that sort of thing – so you will be able to enjoy your time on Newport

Station. If there's any trouble, we have a representative aboard you can contact –"

Since it seemed that Parell was going to be slow to get to the point, Emily interrupted. "I don't supposed you're going to tell me what I'm handling and how much you'll pay me."

Parell held his hand up to beg for patience, and continued his practiced litany. "We believe in creating a comfortable system in which space traders can flourish in safety and without hassle. We appreciate that the attraction of spacefaring mainly centers on the freedom and exploration it allows, and we work with traders to make certain they enjoy all the benefits they have come to expect from their ventures. We hope that your experience with us in this, your first assignment with our firm will encourage you to take future assignments from us." He took a breath. "That said, let's discuss this assignment."

Emily rolled her eyes. Giving Parell the benefit of the doubt, she assumed that this was some sort of lawyer-mandated greeting designed to avoid any interstellar misunderstandings. Even if that was the case, though, Space Pier Imports had shown incredible incompetence. Despite her limited experience, Emily realized that other species were quick to brush aside their misunderstandings and move on, and would sidestep a major incident unless they saw a definite advantage to making an issue of it – like putting an inexperienced negotiator off his game. There was no point doing that with Parell, who had an air of insecurity around him already.

She reminded herself that her end of this depended on the price Parell was willing to pay, and had nothing to do with his personality. On that, at least, Parell's company seemed to have the right sense. He plunged into price negotiations right away. It was a simple Plani to Earth run, after all, so there was a clear idea of what the price should be. She ended up settling for a price just a bit under her optimum. This left Parell looking like he had won, while giving her a healthy sum to boast to her crew about.

"We would like to keep the nature of the cargo confidential," Parell continued, "but you can be sure that it is not perishable, illegal, or weaponry. Mostly, just data and artifacts acquired from other worlds."

Emily nodded. That was normal. Heck, the Inanas had outright lied about their cargo. Some honesty was a bonus at this point. "Is that it?" she asked, sensing somehow that it couldn't be. If that had been all, Parell would have no reason to be cagey. His awkwardness had been leading to something specific.

"Well . . . ," Parell started with intentional discomfort, "we have a few passengers if you can accommodate them. They're strictly tourists. On your ship, they'll have to follow your rules. They're cleared at Earth end already . . . and they're human-size, so no Gols or Karisi or anything that'll need special accommodations in the cargo hold."

Emily sighed. "Human-sized . . . what species? What's wrong with them? No shapechangers, right?"

"No, no," he made a sequence of gestures with his hands to show how ludicrous and unacceptable that would be. "The first is a Plani –"

"A Plani tourist? No such thing."

Parell shrugged. "Scouting out the business opportunities, I suppose. Then there's a Dunorii Eldrandii. Knows what to expect as far as accommodations, and says it has no problem keeping the wings furled for a few days."

This didn't seem to be a passenger that would warrant hesitation, but it was still a bit odd. "Always happy to carry an Eldrandii, I'm sure. Sort of surprised it couldn't arrange for one of its own ships for transportation, but I guess there aren't any heading for Earth. The Plani had better keep any comments to himself. I don't want to hear how inefficient I am, or how the Plani will eventually takeover all Earth businesses because we won't be able to compete. But I'll carry them, sure." She hoped to draw the line there, before Parell mentioned the real trouble.

Clearing his throat, Parell said, "there's also an Asparii couple. Thing is . . . the thing is that the husband's a mage."

"No."

"Please, they're all checked out. He has papers from the ISC certifying that he is not a mancer. Same for his wife. They're not immigrating or anything. They're just curious about Earth. The husband's set up an extremely successful mage school on Anor, and just started a branch here on Plani. He's often acted as an ISC consultant, so Newport Station didn't take much time clearing him – his record's that good. Think of how good it would be for Earth, if he decided to set up a school there. Earth has a huge market for Asparian magic. Getting it homegrown'll make a big difference."

"No. I've seen how the Eldrandii and Plani talk about Asparii. There's thousands of years of blood there. I'll take the first two, and that's it."

"The Eldrandii and Plani have been informed and they assure us that they will have no –"

"Yeah, but they have to say that. The Plani might not do it since he'll have that code of honor and opportunity thing holding him back. All the talk about how nice and wise the Eldrandii are has fooled you, though. This trip will give him the perfect chance for revenge."

"Her, actually. Most Eldrandii blame the mancers directly, and wouldn't target a mundane Asparii. Anyway, the Dunorii are strict pacifists –"

"So are all Eldrandii," she noted. It was one of the few details of interstellar culture she was clear about. "But, somehow they still get into wars. Why not send them separately? Just get two ships."

"Because we only have one ship's cargo, Captain. We need to keep costs down, and attracting another ship will basically mean doubling the cost. With the sale of this cargo, we'll be able to expand our business, but we're in a tough place right now. We need your help on this."

Emily could appreciate Parell's frustration. Earth attracted very few interstellar tourists, so keeping these four waiting was bad policy all around.

"Amazing that you could get them clear for Earth. We have our fill of Asparii refugees already, and we've never really trusted the magic types."

Parell, sensing that things were starting to go his way again, relaxed and nodded. "There's definitely tension, and the refugee thing is a definite political issue. But all of the passengers are beyond question. As I understand it, the World Council will provide government tour guides to these folks, and the guides will make sure there's no . . . unpleasantness. The only issue right now is finding a transport willing to take them to Earth."

Emily shook her head, but said, "How much?"

The *Azar* exited the dropship and fled into open space, finally out of the Plani sardine can. Emily took special pleasure ordering Kaz to plot a course for Earth. As usual, it was a waste of breath, and Kaz had the course up on the viewscreen before she had finished the sentence. He tried not to look accusingly at her, but it was a struggle against his reflexes.

Some star systems had strange features that a pilot and navigator would have to work around, but Sol system was straightforward. They would approach Earth from underneath the system's plane. While there was something to be said for sightseeing planets on the way in, that would require a messy zigzag and cost fuel. There was plenty of chance for sightseeing later. From what she had heard, crews scheduled that sort of thing every eighth trip or so. Each crewmember would give up a part of their cut in exchange for a vote on where they would go. Even then, the system around Earth's sun was so plain that it probably wouldn't rate a nomination.

To Emily's surprise, the passengers had boarded without incident and resolutely stayed in their quarters. Dressed provocatively by human standards, the Eldrandii attracted some comments from the cargo crew when she boarded. Clearly, her crew was in desperate need of some leave time at Newport Station if other species were looking attractive. Aside from that, the passengers had been out of sight and, intentionally or not, they avoided each other. Emily was a bit nervous about what they might be doing in their rooms, but pushed away any thoughts of installing hidden cameras. She had a visceral reaction to that sort of thing – one that overrode her need to know what was going on in her ship.

For a welcome and anticipated distraction, the crew played their first basketball games on the trip into the jump point. Cargo beat both navigation and repairs, taking advantage of practice and physical presence. Each team managed to find a star and a non-participant. Brian netted most of the points for Nav, while Kaz failed to make a shot. Tembi on the repair crew made some incredible dunks, but the three-point shooting of Adrian Marquez, the cargo chief, won the game. Along the way, Emily learned a few more names and felt that the crew was gelling together, finally. The games had also given her a rare chance to relax in their company.

She went to sleep after the basketball games without any worries, or any intention of waking up before they exited hyperspace. As always, her dreams were dark and vivid. Somehow, her mind naturally arranged random flashes into epics filled with gothic imagery. It definitely had a talent for a midnight way of thinking. This time, though, as she stood in the shadow of a building with twin spires that touched the stars, the world was suddenly washed away and replaced with an insane whiteness. A corner of the white fabric came forward to form a figure. As the figure separated itself from the fabric, it also took on color and distinguishing features. It was the Asparii mage. He was wearing a robe instead of the conservative trousers and shirt he had boarded with. Like all Asparii, he could have passed for human if judged only by his body's form. This was not her dream.

Her temper boiled to the surface in a flash. "What the fuck do you think you're doing?" she shouted, dashing toward the figure and pushing him to the ground. To her surprise, he actually fell. She had expected him to vanish and appear behind her. His impact against the ground had produced a ringing thud, but the mage was uninjured, and got up immediately. The sensations in this . . . was it really a dream? . . . were far more acute than she had ever experienced in the recesses of her mind. Much more like real life.

"Please, Captain," the Asparii said with urgency in thickly accented English, sounding vaguely like Dracula. "I did not mean to do this . . . it should not have been possible. Please come to my room immediately. I had meant to contact you, to discuss an urgent matter concerning two members of your crew. Not like this. This was an accident. Please excuse me."

The Asparii disappeared. Emily bolted awake as if from a nightmare, and was out of bed a second later. She threw on her clothes and immediately made her way to the guest quarters in the other fuselage of the ship. The good thing about habitually wearing jeans and tee-shirt, and keeping short hair, was that it took no time at all to get out the door. She also chose sneakers over her normal boots, and dashed the distance in a fury.

The Asparii was waiting for her at his door, face full of distress.

She barely held herself back as every muscle in her body prepared to punch him, just as she had done in the dream. "What the hell do you think you're doing? Get the fuck out of my head!"

"I am out, Captain," he said in a compelling voice. "Please, come into the room. I had only been meditating when my mind wandered to the need to contact you and tell you the news I had when I found myself in your mind. I had no control over it. My news is serious, and we cannot discuss it in this corridor." The words came in the same English as in her dream – as what Emily supposed to be a Transylvanian accent. The mage was a bit taller than her, probably stronger, and only starting to develop the creases that marked old age. It was a rugged form made magical only by the flowing robes. She had no idea whether the robes were necessary for the magic, or if he changed into them to be more comfortable. They made an impression, though, and reminded her who she was dealing with.

She reluctantly stepped inside his quarters, walking a bit stiffly to keep her impulses in check. Though she made no conscious note of it, her mind maintained a strict duality. Instinctively, she defended her core ferociously, creating an exterior image that only allowed hints of it to show. Now, breaching her defenses, this magician just strolled into her ultimate sanctuary. He was clearly telling the truth about not meaning to do it, but the shock and confusion she felt remained.

The Asparii chose not to offer a seat to the captain, and instead started talking immediately. "My name is Verinus Tylan. I was going to contact you because you should be told that two of your crewmembers are criminals wanted by the ISC. They are not considered dangerous, and the ISC will not pursue them. The ISC sometimes asks me to help investigate certain incidents. I recognized the faces while walking in the corridors, and checked my computer for the names. Am I right in saying that Ben Wetzler and Jason Davison are on your crew?"

Well, this was a twist. "You actually remember them? Their faces? What're you trying to pull?"

Tylan looked confused. "I am sorry. I have a strong understanding of English, but do not know this . . . idiom."

"What?" she shouted, then thought it over. "I meant, are you trying to trick me? You seem to have something planned here. Don't tell me that you remembered their faces out of nowhere."

That seemed to puzzle the mage even more. "Of course I can remember. If I had any plot against you, I would not need subterfuge. I mean no offense, Captain, but you are simply not important enough to warrant my interest."

Emily literally growled. "What's all this about then? You expect me to turn them in? What did they do?"

Tylan extended his arms in an odd gesture of supplication. "No, I do not expect anything. I simply feel that informing you is my duty. These two men were accused of being accomplices to an act of piracy. A fairly grand act. Their roles were minor, and the major players have been brought to justice. They simply supplied some mechanisms. It is entirely possible that Wetzler and Davison were simply engaged in black market activities and did not know what use the devices would be put to. This was all . . . very complicated. However, you can see that this might be relevant for your ship's safety – and for that of your passengers."

Possibilities flowed through her mind, but she was in a suspicious mood. Tylan could have put this idea into her mind to deflect suspicion from himself. He could be plotting some sort of revenge for the Earth-Asparis War, which had left his home planet devastated. Then again, that was unreasonable. If he could put thoughts in her mind, surely he could prevent her from doubting him. And the whole idea of revenge was unlikely. Only the mancers, orders of magnitude more powerful than the man standing before her, had really been free and at home on Asparis. Even a mage would have been thankful for the chance to leave the planet for less oppressive soil, and the ISC had done an impressive job evacuating and finding places for refugees.

Emily's mind suddenly took a right turn at the thought of refugees. "I don't know about your warning," she said after confronting him in silence for a minute, "but I've got something else to ask you while I'm here."

"Yes?" he said with a natural uncertainty. He had faced too many unpleasant situations in life to approaching anything with instant confidence.

She was unsure why she should bring it up now, but went ahead anyway. "I've . . . been told that mancers might be playing their games on other worlds now, but keeping it secret. I think it's all sort of a conspiracy theory. What do you know?"

Looking as if this had turned out to be a familiar question, Tylan said, "I will tell you what I know, but it is not a great deal. Certainly, it is possible, but also unlikely for a simple reason. Mancers are so accustomed to complete domination that they cannot suddenly switch to covert control. They are not subtle thinkers. Any mancer still in the ISC would quickly find a way to announce himself. Undoing thousands of years of conditioning at a stroke is not possible. Look at how Asparii act on your world. They still act as if under the heel. Still, it is theoretically possible. I have not encountered a mancer since the war. Of that, I am sure."

"How would you know? Thought you would need to check their genes or something?"

Tylan sighed. "First of all, they would try to kill me on sight. Even if they did not, magic is . . . obvious when you have learned to see it. Anyone who uses it can see it all around. It is a sort of glow, I suppose you could say. The mancers are blinding. The gene test is a joke, really. They will never catch a mancer that way. Before they got close, they would be in so many pieces even I couldn't get solid evidence from their remains."

Losing interest in these details, Emily turned back to her original course. "I want to be real clear about this. What exactly can you do inside our heads? If you can mess with what we're thinking, I don't see why I shouldn't shove you into space."

"I cannot touch your thoughts. I cannot even enter the minds of others unless they are open to it, and most people keep theirs closed. While you were sleeping, yours was not only open, but it drew me in. I am still shocked."

"Not as much as me."

"If I had been able to see your body while you were sleeping, I would not have been surprised to see more magic around you than you have right now. I have not seen Earthlings while they are asleep, and have not been close to your people before. It is possible that having receptive minds while asleep is normal for you. I will have to arrange an experiment with your government to see if it is the case."

"You'd better think twice about pulling this kind of stuff on Earth."

Shoulders slumped and arms limp in an Asparian pose of exasperation, Tylan said, "I did not pull anything off. This was an accident, a coincidence. I promise you it will not happen again to you or your crew. Now that I know it is possible, I can be careful."

"So it was all me," she said.

"Perhaps. It is difficult to say for certain."

They stood in silence for a moment, and it was clear that the conversation was over. Emily was still bitter, but Tylan's demeanor had completely calmed her down. It was good to see someone powerful apologizing to her. She took her leave of the mage with a flock of doubts following her out, and increasing trust in his warning. Despite keeping the details of her recent trouble with the Inanas from Tylan, she nevertheless connected the dots and had very specific worries about Wetzler and Davison. Could they have been responsible for the *Azar*'s recent sabotage? She somehow doubted it, but it was unusually convenient that they knew all about the Plani device involved – one altered from its original function as a self-destruct mechanism and turned into a tool for sabotage. It was just the kind of item that would be altered in a sleazy Plani shop willing to hire humans, and sold through the black market to Inana bounty hunters.

She saw no easy way to deal with the subject. Turning Wetzler and Davison in was out of the question. Unless they were considered dangerous, or being pursued, then handing them over to the authorities would deny them a chance to change, and they might have joined her crew for precisely that opportunity. Guaranteeing that privilege was far from her primary consideration, but failing to do so would be a source of bad blood within the crew. Asking Wetzler and Davison about it was also out of the question, at least until she established a better rapport with them. Odd that humans had gotten into the interstellar black market so quickly – must be natural aptitude. It could be beneficial to have some crewmembers experienced in that sort of thing . . . but impossible to put it to use until she put some matters to rest. The mage had certainly caused her trouble, one way or another.

Returning to her bed, her mind was racing too fast for sleep. More than Tylan's warning, the question of the refugee planet plagued her. Why had she even mentioned it? The idea of it was lodged in her mind inconspicuously, lying low until an opportunity to further itself came.

In the meantime, it grabbed hold of her imagination, tapping into her childhood idea of what space adventures were all about.

Brought out of the mire by a comm signal from her desk, she slumped off her bed and walked with weary reluctance to the panel, opening the connection with a weak tap. "Yeah, what is it?"

"Captain, sorry to disturb you," the hyperspace comm officer said, presumably from the bridge, "but the Eldrandii passenger has been hammering the comm in his room and insists he should speak with you. I told him you were sleeping, but he just kept at it. He said he saw you leaving the Asparii's room. His accent doesn't get through the translator well, so I didn't get what he thought about that. As far as I can tell, it's a religious issue he wants to talk to you about."

She rolled her eyes. Suddenly, her quiet passengers wanted to annoy her. Couldn't they have done it before hyperspace? Well, she wasn't getting any sleep anyway. "All right. I'll head down there. It's a she, by the way."

"Sorry to disturb you," the officer repeated.

Off she went – sluggishly, this time. Averse to superstitious nonsense at all times, and on this taxing night in particular, she still had enough sense to humor her rich passengers in the hope for repeat business. If this Eldrandii was planning on talking her ear off, though, Emily was in the mood to speak bluntly and let the pious Eldrandii taste the bile.

The Dunorii were a minority among the avian Eldrandii. Like others of their species, they had slim, winged forms with weak arms and legs suited only to keep the body standing. They could walk short distances, but avoided it whenever possible. It was odd that an Eldrandii would choose to take a ship with a human-suited interior, since the shipbuilders were excellent at accommodating their own species' need to fly. Their ships were caverns in space, with maximum flying space and minimum privacy. This Dunorii had managed to walk her way through the ship without looking too awkward, so maybe she was use to more confining spaces. That contradicted what Emily knew abo the Dunorii, though. Known as naturalists leading simple lives in t wilderness, they were identifiable at a glance by their white-gr camouflage-shaded plumage, which stood in contrast to the strikir bold colors sported by other Eldrandii. Dunorii clothing was minim as well, as noticed by the cargo crew when the passenger had entered. Others of their species preferred to cover everything except their head and wings to protect against the harsh weather of their planet.

The passenger had been quite imposing when Emily first saw her. She had walked with slow grace, stood tall, and her plumage had been smooth and fine – even shiny. Looking at the crew, she had been imperious, with the same condescending gaze that Emily's mother employed on unpleasant acquaintances and disobedient family members. Thankful that she had so far been saved from dealing with that superior attitude, Emily had second thoughts about interrupting her already troubled sleep to confront it.

Before approaching the guest quarters, Emily checked the passenger's name using one of the corridor computers. It was A'anfu En. It probably meant something, but Emily had no idea what, and ignored it. She tried to compose herself as much as possible, and reminded her stormy side that the Eldrandii were the most important species in the ISC, and good relations with them was vital. This one was wealthy enough to travel to a practically meaningless junior partner like Earth, so reacting badly to her would be, at the very least, foolish. Politeness, combined with the way she tuned out when parents and teachers were talking, would be key. As isolated as the Dunorii preferred to live, they nevertheless shared the Eldrandii penchant for approaching the ISC with complaints and suggestions. The community tolerated this because, simple life aside, the Dunorii still sold other species unique technologies. They had earned their license to be parental. Having A'anfu En as a friend could mean access to breakthroughs before the competition even heard about them.

The passenger did not meet Emily at the door to her quarters, but captain chose not to use her access card to get in. She pressed the r at the side of the sliding door and waited. The door slid open any words exchanged. Usually, Emily would have expected ker under the buzzer button to crackle with the voice of the hecking who was there, but reminded herself that that was vay. Shrugging to herself, she stepped into the dimly lit the Eldrandii sat on the bed with wings outstretched, The thirteen-foot wingspan was an impressive and nd the effect was, of course, deliberate. Even though she saw through the affectation, the captain had to think twice before entering the room further. The stutter-step made A'anfu En smile. At least, it looked like a smile. As if she had just been stretching, she moved her shoulders back, rotated them slowly so that the tips of her wings cut circles in the air, and then folded the wings halfway.

"Have you never seen an Eldrandii in full glory, Captain? It is too bad this room is not tall enough for me to stand with wings open. Amazing how much other Eldrandii conceal under their cloaks, is it not?" A'anfu En said through her translator device. Emily, in her irritation, had forgotten to bring her own, but all the quarters were supplied with them. "But it is unhealthy to keep the wings folded too long."

"All right," Emily said, not knowing what A'anfu expected of her, but quickly getting irritated again. She hated when people thought she was easily manipulated, and that was precisely what this display was about. The sight was impressive, though. The subtle transitions from white to green in the midst of the fine feathers, and the fractal-like pattern of camouflage on the wings, were outright artistic.

A'anfu only saw the surface reaction, and proceeded based on the assumption that the captain was in awe. "I asked you to come here because I have some issue with the décor in this ship, and the food you eat. I am sure you know that your ship's atmospheric wings are of Dunorii make, as well as . . . key components of your hyperspace drive."

The Eldrandii's words came out in a flurry, and the translator gave them an airy, detached tone. Given a gap in which to respond, the captain started, "No, I –"

"Well, I suppose you are unaware that we Eldrandii feel quite attached to the well-being of our work. We provide free servicing and repairs to those who can bring their ships back to Eldrand. In return, we like to see our work put to good use. I go to your planet to advise your government about the possibility of adapting our engine technology to energy production, but I see I will have to inform them of proper conduct aboard Eldrandii-built ships. This is unacceptable."

"Really –" In Emily's eyes, all this talk marked A'anfu En as a particular kind of demon – the clueless valley-girl of the Eldrandii. Earth schools were filled with air-headed girls conditioned by the attention lavished on them to be entirely self-centered. Based on the way A'anfu En was acting, no one had ever told her to shut up.

"And," continued the Eldrandii, slowly furling her wings into a tight bundle behind her as the point of the discussion neared, "I am distressed to see the lack of plant life on board. The place is almost barren. It looks like something the Plani would have designed. This is unacceptable. I assure you that adding plants and animals to the ship will create a living atmosphere in which your crew will operate more efficiently. They are being subtly depressed, just as the Plani have been for millennia by their grey world. Like the Plani, your crew will soon be at each other's throats."

"Okay –" Emily said, her mind providing a violent tune to occupy her while she waited diplomatically. It was a shame that, when the ISC programmed languages into the standard translators, Eldrandaiz received priority, followed by Plani and Asparian, so an Eldrandii never had to pause to wonder whether the words were coming out as intended. They could speak with confidence that others understood. Emily could have pretended to speak an Earth language not yet added to the translator system – most of them – but even this Eldrandii wasn't so clueless that she would believe it.

"– the cuisine is as dry and depressing as Plani military rations –"

"They are Plani military rations. How'd you guess?" Emily said with sarcasm that went completely unnoticed.

"– and this is only harming your crew. As we learned in the frigid northern wastes of our world, spicy food can mean the differences between having the will to survive, and dying from lack of effort. It is very cold in space, Captain."

"We're . . . working on that," Emily yawned. Suddenly, she was facing a complete brain meltdown, which still put her a billion brain cells ahead of the alien in front of her.

"Speaking of the Plani, did you know that your Plani passenger is a vampire?"

At first, her mind refused to register the comment, but Emily's ears were persistent, and they forced her into alertness. The mental conflict that ensued was severe. A'anfu could be trying to get some predictable response from her. Maybe the translator had finally goofed. Maybe the Eldrandii idea of a vampire was a bit different from the human one.

Maybe A'anfu was using the word figuratively, like calling a person a leech if she lived off of someone else. Of course, there would be no reason to bring it up, then. While the rest of her psyche was trying to make sense of A'anfu's words, Emily's core laughed maniacally, seeing this as another confirmation of the fundamental chaos and bloody-mindedness of the universe.

"What do you mean?" she asked with Tylan-like caution.

A'anfu had an aloof manner as she said, "we Dunorii are one with nature, and have very sharp senses. I saw the signs of vampirism on him. It is a rare genetic defect among the Plani, you know. It shows how depraved the entire species are, really. Vampires are persecuted on Plani. It might be the only thing you can get persecuted for on that planet."

Missing most of this, the captain asked, "What . . . signs?"

The Eldrandii cocked her head in a gesture unfamiliar to Emily. "He smiled once, and I caught blood on the teeth and blood-stained lips."

"Could have got in a fight, or just needs a dentist," Emily murmured, knowing better.

"Plani do not fight with their fists, and their dentistry is as brutally efficient and sterilizing as everything else they do. He is a vampire, definitely. It is not a problem, I am sure. I just made a note of it as a curiosity. We rarely see vampires out of their safe places and communities, and then they only travel in packs and at night. Otherwise, a lot of Plani would not think twice about taking out their frustrations on them. It is a very frustrated planet."

"They . . . they can walk in daylight?"

That puzzled A'anfu. "Of course. Now, it is true that at night, the Plani are usually calmer and more reserved, so they are less likely to persecute the vampires. In daytime, it is the cutthroat world you are used to seeing, no doubt, and killing a vampire is not a crime."

"We . . . we are talking about the same thing, right? Vampires are blood-suckers?"

"Yes. Very much so. I understand they find more sanitary ways to satisfy their need for blood, but it has to be ingested. If they try to absorb blood intravenously, their immune system will attack the cells. The vampires are the only interesting thing about the Plani, since they fit the bloodless Plani character so completely and obviously that it is almost as if the universe created them as a sign to us all."

It occurred to Emily that, had A'anfu been human, she would have been the type of person who would constantly demean other races and cultures without hesitation. You had to appreciate the logic of the Eldrandii – they had sent this horribly flawed specimen of their species as far away as they could without wasting one of their own ships. There was also no chance that she would do any serious damage to the Eldrandii reputation on Earth, a backwater that was still awestruck by the older spacefaring races. The inevitable conclusion was that A'anfu was not as important as she pretended, and that being pleasant to the creature was unlikely to get Emily sympathetic contacts on Eldrand.

Feeling that speaking to A'anfu would be a complete waste of time, Emily bowed briefly and bolted out of the door before the Dunorii could object. The Plani was only two doors down. Exhaling heavily before pressing the buzzer, she reflected that things were suddenly getting way too interesting. Hesitating as her finger neared the button, she wondered what would happen if there really was a vampire on the other side, and he was in the mood for a meal. She could, before pressing the buzzer, head across to the bridge, grab a weapon, and then come back. Then again, that might panic the Plani and provoke a violent confrontation, which could end with her shooting a passenger. The Plani had done nothing unusual on board so far, but maybe he was waiting until the ship docked at Newport Station before feeding on a convenient victim. Maybe he was holding himself in check, and saw Earth as a massive feeding ground.

In a way, it wasn't her problem. Earth immigration was responsible for clearing interstellar travelers. But did they even know about these vampires? Would they believe it if they were told? The way A'anfu had said it, there was no problem or threat, so maybe she was overreacting based on Earth ideas about vampires. Still, she had to know.

She pressed the buzzer and Plani speech came through the speaker, completely incomprehensible to her. She shouted, "this is Captain Pierce" in response. There was a pause at the other end, some fumbling – probably for the translator – and then the voice said, "apologies, Captain. Could you delay your entry for a few moments?"

"No. No, I think I want to come in right now."

She was about to take out her access card when the door slid open. She walked through with trepidation. As far-fetched as the whole vampire thing was, and as fundamentally absurd as A'anfu En was, she had to take it seriously. The Plani looked as he did when he boarded, but there were details around the room that made Emily's stomach turn. Most obvious was a white cloth stained red and thrown into a corner, but the open suitcase on the bed, covered quickly with the blanket, was the clincher. The right side of its contents remained uncovered by the blanket, and Emily could see containers filled with a red liquid occupied every inch of it. Clearly, the Plani had just been feeding, and used the cloth to clean his mouth off before opening the door. It was uncharacteristic for a Plani, especially one that had to hide his identity to avoid persecution, to be so careless with evidence. The obviousness of it dismayed Emily. It was too easy.

Realizing that his feeble attempt to hide the traces of his abnormality had failed, the Plani desperately tried to talk his way through the awkward situation. "Captain, allow me to explain. I am not harmful. I am . . . a vampire. As you can see, I have enough blood for my whole journey. I am in control of my weakness, and will harm no one. It is synthetic blood, in case you were concerned."

"I was. Sorta hard not to be." She paused for a moment. Oddly enough, the Plani had more color to him than the average Plani, and was a bit less skeletal. His manner was tentative and uncertain – the complete opposite of the cold confidence practically every Plani had shown her. If he was typical for a vampire, then she could see why Plani society rejected them. Sensing that things were going fairly well – her jugular was still intact – she went on with an even tone. "Okay, so why should I trust you? Why are you going to Earth anyway? Trying to take advantage of a place where people can't spot what you are?"

"I . . . ," he started, and then paused to check his emotions. "People like me are hunted on our planet. We have to live in secret, relying on each other for our survival. I heard that, on your planet, there might be sympathetic people. I have seen . . . works of fiction . . . that show vampires . . . that show vampires in a positive way. I was visiting to see if there might be a place in your world where I could live without fear. I . . . have a family –"

Emily snorted. "I haven't heard much about Plani caring about their family. Heard the opposite, I think."

"We are not normal Plani," he said heatedly. "Please try to understand. I ask you – are there people that might accept my family and me? Will it be safe for me to walk in daylight? If not, this has been a great waste."

Emily sighed. Even at this late hour in hyperspace, she had a soft spot in her heart for the demon who just wanted to find a safe place to be demonic without some preachy exorcist coming around. "Maybe. Some people might try to hunt you, but not more than the usual crazies. There'll be people to hate you, but there's that for everybody on Earth. You've got a bit more muscle on you than other Plani. With some hair color and the right clothes, you could probably pass for a thin, pale human, and there're plenty of those. You've got to learn the language, though. There's definitely a vampire-style culture on Earth, in some places, but I'm not sure how they'd react to the real thing, and they won't be like anything you're expecting. How're you going to get the blood, though?"

The Plani seemed to brighten. "I will move my laboratory with my family. I am a specialist in blood synthesis. That is how I made the money for this journey. My knowledge of biochemistry will be as valuable on your planet as it has been on Plani. More valuable, maybe, since your people has little knowledge of the chemistry of otherworld species. I have great hope that my family will live a better life on Earth than we have on our homeworld."

Emily arched her eyebrows. She had a clear vision of human religious fanatics taking the vampirism thing badly. On the other hand, for every human actively trying to get rid of the vampire, there would be two ready to defend his rights. Heck, who was she to stand in the way of oppressed minorities trying to free themselves? Earth had cleared him. If he broke the law by attacking someone and drinking their blood, he would get the same punishment as anyone else on Earth. As long as he didn't do it on her ship, it wasn't her problem. If he did, he would be out of the airlock in a second, no questions asked.

"Well, I hope Earth's everything you think it is. Just don't do anything with the crew, okay?"

Abashed in a way Emily had never seen a Plani, the vampire

shook his head vehemently in imitation of human actors he had clearly studied, "not even with their consent. My status will be kept . . . confidential, then?"

She shrugged. "None of my business."

He bowed. "Thank you, Captain. I realize this is a very complicated situation."

No kidding – it was too complicated to be considered on so little sleep. With a yawn, she wondered how well the devices translated Earth television shows and movies. Odd that this guy, so interested in Earth culture, had never learned Earth's lingua franca, while the Asparii spoke fluently. Magic, she supposed.

Emily took her leave of the vampire, considering her unblemished neck a good sign for the rest of the journey. So, there were vampires. At least, there were blood drinkers – she was unsure how else they were similar to the Earth legend of vampires – probably not close at all. She could readily believe that all imaginable creatures existed somewhere in the universe. Carefully avoiding this train of thought, she focused resolutely on the prospect of sleep.

She might have been in bed for hours, but when the bleep of the comm panel woke her up, she still felt drained. Thankful that she was still dressed, since she lacked energy to get herself sorted, she opened the comm to hear who had woken her.

It was Liam. Before he could say anything, she mumbled, "How long till we're in regular space?" Her subsequent yawn forced Liam to pause before delivering his answer.

"About two hours. That wasn't why I called you."

She sighed. "Didn't think it was. What's up?"

"The Asparii says you talked to him earlier. He says he remembered something that might be important, to do with people pulling strings secretly."

"All right. I guess I might as well hear it. Are you the only regular on the bridge?"

"Kaz is here, too."

"Okay. I'll be up there after I talk to the Asparii and get some coffee."

"You sound tired."

"Feel tired. So that works out. See you on the bridge."

She tried to wipe out the most noticeable wrinkles in her tee shirt and jeans with no success. A cursory look in the mirror perched on a box near the door revealed her short hair standing on end, thanks to all the static she generated while tossing in her sleep, with the black dye wearing out in places to show her natural brown. She resolved to dye it red next, since black was working out so badly. Having no patience to look for her comb, she patted the hair down, ran her hand through it, and patted it down again. It looked positively horrible, but at least it was accurate.

Tylan was once again waiting at his door. Emily's memory of their previous conversation was a haze, blended together in the most bizarre ways with the other two discussions. She tried her best to remember that Tylan was not the airhead, and not the vampire.

"Captain, sorry to disturb you again."

Too impatient for pleasantries, she said, "what information do you have for me?"

"Please come in. I will explain."

Mrs. Tylan was in the room this time. She had a sheepish, submissive look about her, as if willing to consent to anything her husband said. Emily's distaste and basic anger at this were tempered by her inability to keep her eyes open. She just nodded to acknowledge the wife's presence.

"My wife spoke to me after our encounter. I will allow her to tell you what she told me," Tylan said, indicating to his wife that she should proceed. Emily mustered a scowl at "allow," but that was gentler than her normal response to gendered culture shock would have been.

Tylan's wife cleared her throat and adjusted the translator, feeling the presence of the device a bit uncomfortable. "I . . . ," she started with almost practiced hesitation, "do not know how to begin. In my village, before war, there was word from cities nearby that a . . . fanatical group controlled those cities. That group had to work secretly because mancers would kill them otherwise. That they captured some ships Lord Heinly, Asparii mancer lord that attacked your planet, built to use against you. Most in group were mages."

As the lady paused for breath – acting exerted after saying so many words – Emily said, "Good beginning. What were they fanatical about?"

"They looked for some secrets. Secrets to give them power – maybe power over mancers. They manipulated people with magic –"

" . . . exactly the kind of magic you feared I was using, Captain," Tylan said.

"And they left Asparis before you came for revenge. They took everything they could from cities before they fled. They left it in decay and ruin. Our village had nothing they wanted, so they left us alone."

"They are still looking for ways to gain power, Captain," Tylan clarified. "Of that, I am sure. I had heard of this group as well, but had forgotten about them. I have seen Asparii mages on many worlds and any one of them could have been part of these – the best way to translate their name would be 'Shadow Workers.' If anyone suspects that Asparian magic is controlling governments, then this is the group responsible. I should have been watching for them all this time, but they are good at hiding, and none of the crimes I have investigated showed signs of any mages being involved. I will also inform the ISC of this potential threat through contacts that will keep the information and source strictly confidential. Your source will have no reason to fear."

On it goes. Somehow, this revelation came as no shock to Emily. Maybe she was just too tired for it to sink in. If she had been more alert, she might have been suspicious of the Asparii mage, but it was best to put all judgments off until later. Seeing nothing else to say, the captain thanked the two Asparii and made her way out. She was supposed to be a trader, but the universe was intent on having her investigate this mystery. There was a part of her that was eager to cooperate, seeing this as exactly the sort of thing she had dreamt of when thinking of space travel as a child – exploring new worlds and evading dangerous enemies. Her essential rebelliousness overrode that tiny part, and pretended to defy the universe and its expectations.

What could she do, anyway? Never one to back down from a fight, she nevertheless had to admit that her crew was no match for a bunch of Asparii mages. These Shadow Dancers could steal a spaceship from under the noses of the mancers, meaning that they had a combination of cunning plans, raw guts, and sheer power. There was no chance of them spontaneously surrendering at her request. Anyway, she had enough to deal with as it was. Let the ISC take care of this menace.

Making her way to the recreation room to grab a cup of coffee, she spotted A'anfu exiting it. She tried to avoid eye contact with the Eldrandii, but the winged one addressed her without sympathy.

"Captain," A'anfu said, translator already in place, "you look horrendous. Clearly lacking in energy. It is the feel of the place, you know. A proper diet would help."

Emily shook her head in wonder. Sure, the feel of the place was doing it, not the total lack of sleep. At least it wasn't the vampire talking about a proper diet. "Right, right. Look, I really got to go. Ship to run, and all that."

"Surely you would not in this state. You should at least eat some stimulants. In this state, you could get us all killed."

Murder in her eyes, Emily said, "No, I won't," and stormed off before a small part of the Eldrandii's prophesy came true. Striding into the recreation room and pouring the coffee with desperate fingers, she downed it as if it was her first drink after days wandering the desert – careful not to drink too quickly, but getting the replenishing liquid deep into her body as soon as possible. She evened herself out before reaching the bridge, wanting to avoid directing her irritation at Kaz.

"Okay, what's up?" she said once the bridge crew was in earshot. Brian was still absent from the pilot's seat, but the other two were there.

Assuming that, as second-in-command, it was his duty to update the captain, Kaz said, "Still about half an hour before we're in Sol system. Nothing wrong –"

"Don't jinx it," she interrupted, then yawned.

"Right. If you'd like to catch up on some sleep, Captain, I'd be glad to handle the entry into Newport station."

She knew this would be coming, and held the reflex sarcastic comment in check. "No, no. Thanks, though. There won't be enough time for me to make up the sleep. I have to be awake for the Newport station bit since we've got passengers, and they seem to really like my company."

"I could take it in slow – we could spend eight hours or more on the way into the station."

"Umm –" As far as Emily was concerned, Kaz should have known that this was pushing it. On the other hand, his new title had not entailed new responsibilities so far. She would have to give him more of a part to play before he decided to carve out some new territory for himself. "Listen, I just want to get this over with. It'll be our first totally . . . successful job, right? And trust me, talking to the passengers, there's plenty that could still go wrong. So, first we finish this, then I'll find the time to sleep. Just drank coffee anyway," she decided. Kaz decided not to press the issue any further. Yet.

Existing hyperspace into Sol system was a relief. The universe was chaotic and confusing. So was Earth, of course, but at least it was a human mess. She knew how to deal with it. The amenities were also human. Newport station had been gradually built over the course of a century, serving many different purposes in that time. It was now an Ellis Island-like entry point for alien species, and a necessary regular stop for human ships. Everything was a bit cramped and there was weightlessness because of the constant freefall orbit, but it was still a city in space. Emily's mouth watered at the thought of the restaurants on board, and those were just the start of the comforts her crew would be longing for.

The station had its own denizens – permanent residents who staffed its services. The usual officers, repair types, and cargo people were there, of course. So were some less fortunate members of the World Council bureaucracy. Then there were those prepared to pander to the whims of the trickle of alien visitors, including merchants and cultural officers. However, alien visitors were few, and human visitors were far more common. Since those humans would inevitably be in the midst of three to six month tours in space before returning to the comforts of their surface homes, and very often single, the station's commander had allowed the presence of the place's most controversial denizens – the prostitutes.

Some objected to their presence on Newport station, on the basis that the money spent on this space welcome mat should be used to present the best of Earth, and therefore conduct on board should meet the highest standard. The charismatic commander of the station had countered that any prostitutes allowed up would be the best Earth had to offer, tested to ensure pristine medical standards. In reality, he was even better than his word. Extremely organized, the loose ladies and gentlemen of Newport required their clients to be screened for a full range of diseases beforehand, and were impeccable in the style they maintained. Station security also had a well-publicized protective attitude toward them.

Her crew was already anticipating a good time, and looking to spend the better part of a week in dock. She would have to advance them some credits. For her part, Emily had only been to Newport station once – when preparing her ship for departure. She had appreciated the food, but noticed a certain lack of . . . professional males. This was probably due to the lack of spacefaring females, which was in turn the legacy of longstanding human biases that few species except for the Asparii shared. There could have been a few, she had to admit, but it was so hard to tell whether they were doing it professionally, or whether they were hitting on every woman sitting alone. She was nervous about the entire prospect of looking for quick sex, but knew she had to get comfortable with it eventually. She was casting longing looks at certain crewmembers more frequently with every day that passed. When selecting the crew, she had counted appearance as a factor. Even Kaz was . . . if his attitude wasn't so damn annoying. Brian definitely got her attention, especially in this caffeine-fueled haze. As he stepped onto the bridge a few minutes before the exit into normal space, he noticed that her eyes were lingering on him more than usual. His reaction gave every indication that he was used to that sort of attention, and had previously used it to his advantage. He was only a mediocre pilot – Kaz did most of the work – but at least he looked good up front. No, she definitely needed someone soon. Hopefully, Newport station would offer some possibilities.

"Acceleration into the traffic pattern, Captain?" Kaz asked, bringing her drifting mind back to the simple command she had to issue. His tone suggested that, if she insisted on keeping command for a few hours, she should at least do the job right.

"Minimal acceleration," she decided without knowing why. Then, feeling all the discussions of the night in hyperspace crashing down on her, she suddenly needed someone to talk to. She had never been the quiet type – a person who kept everything to herself. She was a complainer – not a loud mouth speaking without reason or thought, but used to voicing her opinions. With no other choice, she said, "Kaz, could I talk to you in my ready room? Got a lot on my mind."

Surprised, Kaz raised no objection and followed the captain out.

"Yes? What is it?" he asked once they were in the tiny office. Thinking quickly, he added, "I didn't mean to –"

"No, no. I had some talks with our . . . passengers last night. They were a bit . . . stupid."

"Yes?"

"No, that's not what I wanted to say. The Eldrandii was just ditsy. The Asparii and the Plani were the interesting ones. Easy one first. The Plani's a vampire." She paused for effect, hoping that she really was the only human who knew vampires were real.

"What?" Kaz kept his tone level, suspicious that the captain was exercising her misguided sense of humor.

It felt silly saying it, but she was satisfied with Kaz's confused response. She tried to see how much more she could get out of him. "Drinks blood. The Eldrandii told me. It's one of those things everybody knows, so nobody bothers to tell us. Some Plani are . . . vampires. Cool, huh?"

"But –"

She held up her hand. "He doesn't want to drink anyone's blood. He's got a suitcase full for the trip. Wants to see if Earth will persecute him less than Plani does. Turns out the Plani don't like having vampires around them. Imagine that."

"And he thinks Earth'll be better?" Kaz asked at first, and then decided he had a more important question. "And you believed him?"

Kaz was a bit panicky, and Emily could appreciate that. Luckily, her chosen subculture on Earth considered vampires cool; otherwise, she would have definitely overreacted to the sight of the Plani and his blood. "I told him that as long as he didn't attack anyone on board, I don't care."

"But what will he do on Earth? He could just start killing people and we'd be responsible."

She held up an index finger to indicate a point was about to be made. "The clearance people will be responsible. Maybe Space Pier Imports'll get the blame. Anyway, if he tries anything, the police'll deal with him just like they do with any criminal. Our vampire friend has to know that. He watches our T.V. shows."

Kaz gave Emily a sidelong glance. "He didn't . . . charm you, did he? You didn't . . . do anything with him, did you?"

Emily rolled her eyes. "Would I be bothering to tell you if I was in that deep? No. I can't believe you said that."

Not sure why he had, either, Kaz changed the subject. "Why did you tell me?"

She picked the answer most likely to satisfy him. "Well, you're first officer, right? Thought you should know. We might come across other vampires, 'specially if this one thinks Earth's a nice place, so you need to know about them. This one was nice enough, but maybe they aren't all that way. Now, for the more interesting thing."

Something clicked in Kaz's mind. "The vampire thing . . . was the easy one."

The captain was now grinning maniacally. It was good to share the weirdness. Seeing the expression on Kaz's face was positively therapeutic. "Did I tell you about what the Inana leader at Dael told me in the conference room?"

"Not much. Something about trading with a planet outside the ISC. Sounded interesting. What was it really about?" Kaz had clearly caught on.

She told him everything, from the possible Asparian conspiracy to the chance that they could intervene on this planet of exiles, helping them resist takeover. He expressed the expected skepticism, to which she replied with the revelations shared by Tylan's wife. Along the way, she suddenly realized that, while the ISC might root out Shadow Workers on Ina Cur, it would leave the refugee planet to its own devices. She pushed that aside for now, and instead tried to explain her understanding of Shadow Workers, since Kaz was still confused about them. "It sounded like sort of a mafia to me. It sounded like a secret bunch that frightens people – with magic instead of guns and bombs – and really controls things. They rule the streets behind the scenes. And Tylan said that they are definitely still out there, and trying to get power. So, maybe the Inanas weren't paranoid."

Kaz was silent, clearly unsure of how to take the information. Emily had tried to imply that she was indifferent about taking the Inana tip, and had no firm intention of getting involved, but he had detected her leanings. Trying to avoid the topic until she had more time to think about it, she went ahead and told him about the final and most vital item of news – the criminal record of Wetzler and Davison.

He kept the cautious look on his face and avoided bursting out with the likely implications. "Sounds like something that will have to be taken care of delicately. I suppose the two of us will just have to keep our eyes out. If there're people looking for a job at Newport station, we could take them on just in case."

Massaging some stiffness in her neck, Emily leaned forward and said, "we'll need to talk to them first. And before that, I'll check their records on Newport station, just to make sure we're not stressing for nothing."

"You didn't check their criminal records before hiring them?"

Emily tousled her hair. "I didn't exactly know what I was doing when I started all this. My . . . guide sorta left the background check thing out."

"Funny, I would have thought that checking if the interviewee was a criminal would be an obvious step in the process."

"I was a bit new to the whole interviewing thing, okay? No surprises, right?"

Kaz backed off. "Okay, okay. So, it was a vampire, a planet that we need to protect from a magical mafia, and half of the repair crew being involved in sabotage. Anything else?"

Breathing in and out deeply, Emily said, "Listen. I told you this stuff 'cause you've got a right to know, not because you need to do anything about it. Just get us to Newport station safe, and I'll be happy. I need a break, all right?"

Kaz nodded. For the first time, he seemed to appreciate that she had some real thinking to do. Her brief stints in command on the bridge had been poor showcases of her mental prowess. Five minutes of "full acceleration" and "plot a course for Plani" were inadequate to qualify as work in his eyes. He could handle all of it without her. Having a superior officer who could deal with vampires, conspiracies, and criminal crewmembers, though, was something else entirely. He had enough trouble keeping the ship running as it was.

Emily yawned. "Man, I give up. You take command. Get us to the station in one piece. I'll be sleeping. Wake me if the vampire goes on a rampage or the Asparii mage decides he doesn't like humans, after all. No matter what, I want to be awake to see them off."

Kaz positively glowed at this, taking his leave before she could change her mind.

4
Newport Station, Earth

Newport station was a motley assortment of tubes, platforms, and solar panels. The service tubes were the oldest bits, being the original modules sent into space. Cramped and uncomfortable, only the station's engineers and technical staff occupied them. The platforms and road tubes created a huge continuous surface, dwarfing the maze of ducts underlying them, and were pocked with buildings that made the place look like a legitimate city in space. Cylindrical airtight shields sealed the streets so that visitors could move from building to building without spacesuits. Weightlessness was tricky, though. Spacefarers were used to the artificial gravity on Eldrandii-built ships and the stations of more advanced species. All visitors had some training concerning freefall environments before being allowed in space, and magnetic boots were a must. Stomp too hard in the boots, though, and you would find yourself free of the weak magnetic hold and destined to smash into a wall or ceiling. To avoid potential embarrassment, many visitors relied on the station's helpful guides or the taxis that supplemented the station's insufficient income.

The station was an ever-controversial monument to human ingenuity and community spirit. No other sentient species had a station quite like it – artificial gravity aside. Huge stations encircled other planets, but none was as pleasant to live in. They were miles long, but barely habitable. Depending on where you lived on Earth, Newport station could actually be an improvement. The cost, though, was a flashpoint. So was the man chosen to fill the post of commander.

Most of the station's funding came thanks to its information gathering abilities, which law enforcement agencies around the world were able to tap into. Its core computer could intercept and gather data from practically any transmitted source. The stored database was massive, and a serious privacy concern that conjured up visions of Orwellian government control. In practice, though, the amount of information was unwieldy unless the investigator already knew what he or she was looking for. Fortunately, the only person to have ever hacked into the station computer was now its commander, though that choice frequently drew unfavorable scrutiny.

Emily knew what everyone knew about the station, but didn't really care about the politics. She liked the hacker's story, and he had turned out to be a real gift to the station – his organization skills were impeccable. Even better, he was a media darling. Whether he was defending the cost, the database, the prostitution policy, or himself, he always looked good. She had seen him on the news, and had always impressed. She couldn't remember his name, though, or exactly what he looked like.

The *Azar* docked without hassle, and Emily woke to see the passengers off, finally feeling refreshed after the long night. Kaz looked smug as they met in the corridor, heading for the docking port. The passengers were already waiting, and all of them seemed satisfied with the journey. The Asparii mage and the Plani gave her knowing looks, as if trying to see what effect their imparted secrets had on her. The mage's wife still looked sheepish. A'anfu En, however, continued to insist that Emily should make changes in the ship, phrasing her words as friendly suggestions while using a chastising tone. It was the parental voice. Emily's contact with A'anfu had exceeded her time spent with all other Eldrandii combined, so the passenger had, unfairly, become her picture of the entire species.

With the passengers safely disembarked, the captain got her money from Space Pier Imports, and congratulated herself on her first successful job. The odd time in hyperspace aside, it had finally been a smooth ride. Of course, if her only straightforward jobs were going to come from human companies, the ship was going to be in dock for a very long time. As it was, defense ships and official vessels occupied most of Newport Station's berths. Next to these, there were a few with non-human crews, but these were just stopping by to enjoy the station's excellent accommodations. Even though the station's prices were unreasonable by Earth standards, the rest of the ISC found the costs cheap. The Plani, in particular, arranged business meetings on the station whenever possible, arriving in their own ships rather than employing Earth transports. They openly broadcast the fact that they saw Earth as a third-tier world that they would milk of resources with reckless abandon.

As captain, Emily was the last to exit the ship, and she sealed it with her code. In shifts, there would always be four members of the crew guarding the ship. Since the communications team had lost so badly in their first basketball game, the rest of the crew agreed that standing in the games would determine who got the first shift. As a result, Emily exited her ship while bearing the dirty looks of Liam and Ethan, who might have had one guard's muscle if combined.

Everything in the station was bright. Solar panels were the start of the place's power, but its nuclear reactor did most of the work. Day or night, the space city was a beacon in Earth's sky, and easily its third brightest light. For Emily's part, she preferred things dark, and had trouble thinking in bright light – always a problem in classrooms, which were always overelectrified. Here, she would spend her way through, and skip the thinking. It would be safer that way, if not cheaper.

Emily quickly found herself walking next to Kaz as they exited the portside, curious about how he planned to spend his time and money. After she blatantly tailed him through a few corridors, he turned to her and said, "I'm going to check the news, if you're curious."

"That's all?"

Kaz looked surprised at her insistence. "No. I was thinking maybe of a trip to the restroom. After I've booked my room, of course. Why do you care?"

"Come on. Are you going to find people who play that game –"

"Go," he said, intending the double meaning of the word. "I don't think I'll find anyone who plays. Maybe poker, if you really need to know."

"Are you good at poker?" Emily continued to prod. She enjoyed annoying him in a friendly way.

"If I wasn't, I wouldn't play it," he answered, quickening his pace.

Emily gave up, and was now off in search of more mischief. Unfortunately, her continuing worries dashed any attempts to come up with fun ideas. She decided to try and do a criminal check using the station's database to clear one of those concerns up. It was supposed to be unbelievably intrusive, right? If she had some suspicious types on board, there shouldn't be any need to go to Plani to find out. She hated herself for worrying. Just a few weeks ago, she would have flaunted her independent spirit on Newport station by doing everything. Simply enjoy everything. Don't think about it. Now, with the perfect opportunity to indulge her impulses, she was hogtied by responsibilities. She had never paid much attention to them before, but now she had something to lose. In the game of space, she was an underdog, but she had the one vital tool an adventurer needed – a ship. She did not like the idea of anyone sabotaging it.

How to get started, though? Unlike her ship, Newport station lacked convenient panels – not that they would have freely provided confidential information anyway. Moving awkwardly in the magnetic boots, she emerged from the docking level onto a sidewalk on the station's surface. There were handrails along the sidewalks, but crossing the streets was a bit more adventurous. Some people relied on station guides to help them across the asphalt, but she didn't even consider it. Instead, she asked a guide how she could find the records she was looking for. He simply led her to a tourist map, pointed to the center of it, and said, "Maybe someone at the command center can help you. They're not usually very helpful, but if there's any place the central computer can be accessed, it's there. Besides, you'll probably need to get someone to put in a password or something."

They had better be helpful, she thought, I'm bringing them business and docking fees.

Frustrated by her slow progress from the docking periphery to the heart of the city, she decided to take a taxi. She was here on business, so she might as well act like it. Time is money, right? And if she wasn't going to have fun, she might as well do it in style. Inside the plush interior of the taxi, she wondered how much one of the vehicles would cost, and whether it was possible to get a license to drive it on the station. Paying over two hundred credits for a five minute drive was off the wall. The *Azar* burned about five hundred credits every five minutes, but got a lot farther on that money.

The tower of the command center overlooked the entire city. As with all the city's buildings, it was designed to bear some gravity, but not Earth's full surface gravity. Most of the tower's floors were still unoccupied. All businesses with space aspirations had offices there, as did some intrepid billionaires, but both categories were small and the tower was huge. Emily's grandfather had considered buying premises in the city, but saw no benefit to it. The tower was stationary, while his business was on the move. The ship had a conference room that was perfect for doing business, if a more neutral location was elusive or inconvenient.

Nevertheless, the place had to have a tower – it was just a matter of style. The view from the glass elevator on the way up was breathtaking, though probably hell for anyone afraid of heights. From the top of the tower, the tails of ships docked at the edge of the city were visible, as were the solar panels that had facilitated the station's initial construction before the reactor was installed.

The highest floor accessible by the public was the lobby of the command levels, and five floors from the top deck. The floor below it was one of the high-class restaurants always found close to the top in skyscrapers. Help and information desks filled the lobby, and she approached the first one manned by someone who looked helpful. He was young, and had a smile on his face. That was all she needed to know.

"Hi, what can I do for you today?" he asked pleasantly, though a bit mechanically.

"Hi. I need to do a background check on my crew. I'm a registered captain."

"Ah, we don't handle that," he said, even more cheerfully. She quickly reassessed him. "If you want to access the database, you need some high level permission."

"What do you mean?" She tried to find the right argument to make. "I'm a registered employer. I'm the highest level in my company. I have a right to –"

"I mean high level here, not in your company. Maybe on Earth, maybe with the authorities down there, you could pry into your employees' lives at will, but things don't work like that here. People down there are real picky about who sees the information we gather up here, so there are data levels, and everything pertaining to individuals is strictly controlled. No one up here had any choice. Sorry."

For the first time in a while, one of her father's sayings popped into her head – persistence is the only way to beat a bureaucracy. "Okay, but the commander of the station has access, right? Let me talk to him."

The info desk clerk tapped up the commander's appointment book. She could see the screen obliquely, and noticed that he scrolled ahead a bunch of pages without even looking through them for an opening. "How's December Fourteenth?"

It sounded like a long time to wait. "What date is it today?"

He rolled his eyes. "November the Fourth."

Her jaw dropped. "More than a month. Kidding me, right? I saw some of the pages you went past. There were open slots. Don't lie."

"No good. I'm not senior enough to schedule an appointment that soon. If you want something sooner, talk to Commander Raiz's secretary."

"Okay, and how do I get to his secretary?"

"You'll have to call the front desk," he said, knowing that there was a long chain of phone operators employed specifically to prevent individuals form reaching the commander's secretary.

Emily knew it instinctively, and was ready to start shouting when a startled look took over the clerk's face. He was staring over her shoulder, so she turned around. Behind her was a lanky man in a red tank top, blue swimming trunks, and sandals. If you thought of space as an ocean, then maybe he was appropriately treating the station as a beach. For those who thought of space as a cold void, however, he was completely out of place. His hair was all over the place, and his face bore no lines of worry or concern, so it was hard to pin down his age. Emily could understand why the clerk had been surprised to see such an apparition, even when the oddest aliens didn't get a second glance around here. There had been a sense of recognition in the clerk's glance, though, and Emily had a suspicion that she had seen the face somewhere before.

"Captain Pierce," the figure greeted, extending his hand, "nice to finally meet you."

She shook his hand, then stumbled through the words, "how did you . . . are you . . . you're –"

"Sorry. Commander Tyler Raiz, at your service."

"And how –"

"I know everything that happens on this station, Captain. It's my job. 'Course, there aren't that many human ships to begin with, so it's not hard to remember their captains. Anyway, your grandfather was a frequent visitor. I never actually met him, though. He was a busy man, and never needed any help from me. I was sorry to hear about his death, but I'm glad he left the ship to you. You seem interesting already," Raiz said in spitfire fashion. Even when speaking on television, he had a definite air of hyperactivity. Here, in his domain, he was completely unrestrained, and made no effort to slow down for clarity.

Having met a mage, an Eldrandii airhead, and a vampire, she brushed off his unusual behavior with a blink. "I need to check criminal records for my crew. Should be pretty simple, shouldn't it?"

"I was wondering when you would get down to that. You did your hiring on board the station, but you never tried to do basic background checks before leaving. You might have had someone do them for you on Earth, but I had a feeling you weren't the type to think about it."

"You . . . keep this all in your head?"

He shrugged. "Have to. That's why they gave me the job. Come on, I'll get the files for you if you'll just follow me."

He led her to an elevator that took them to the top level of the tower, where Commander Raiz had his office. On the way, he flew through the security checks and entered his pass code on the elevator panel. His office was less spacious than offices preferred by those who conducted business over a golf game. Panels and screens, all labeled with the specific area of the database they handled, filled one wall of it. There was actually one called "background checks." Instead of bending down or grabbing a chair, Raiz kneeled to tap on the keyboard below that screen. He got the program to the screen where names had to be entered, and then slid over to the "known ships" database, bringing up the listing of her ship. He exported her crew listing, sending it to the "background checks" screen. In a few more moments, the printers whirred up and started churning out the sheets. When they were done, he proudly handed her a stack of details on her own crew, including her own file.

"There you go. These are the short records, but they should do. Any criminal activity is highlighted. Glad to help. I see my job as helping Earth get into space, so anything I do for you is just working toward that goal." He meant every word, too. It wasn't just a Parell-like meaningless pitch. "Anything else I can do for you?"

"Umm –" All she could think about was the exile planet. She hesitated, but couldn't help asking. "I've heard about this planet. I have coordinates in my ship computer, but it's supposed to be outside of the ISC, but have exiles from all sorts of worlds. Someone told me about it as sort of a . . . trade opportunity. I've also been hearing about an Asparian group that calls itself something like 'Shadow Workers.'"

"I don't know about any Shadow Workers, but exiles . . . I think I remember. When all the Asparii refugees flooded into Earth, some wanted to be taken to another planet about thirty light years away. That about right?"

"Yeah."

Raiz nodded solemnly. He led her to two beanbags placed on the same side of a coffee table covered with paperwork. He completely ignored the desk and its more formal seats, though he used it for paperwork as well. The black leather chairs didn't suit Raiz, anyway. To the desk's right was a suit hanging form a wall peg and a door that led to the commander's personal restroom. Clearly, even Raiz recognized that a tank top and shorts were inappropriate for press conferences.

The beanbags were a bit worn, but relaxing. Emily felt genuinely at ease – not something she would have expected in the office of a top commander. Raiz got straight to his explanation.

"When Asparis was destroyed, a lot of the refugees we were handling wanted to go to a planet they called Selparis. Occasionally, the mundanes of Asparis managed to build spaceships in secret to escape the mancers. And I mean about one every hundred years. Well, Selparis was the place they aimed for. When I asked them why the mancers never attacked Selparis, they said it was because all the

ISC species had exiles and refugees there. Every government quietly knows about it, and there's an unspoken agreement that its neutral ground. We sent about a thousand families there with some of our own people who volunteered to go. That was about forty years ago. We brought the ship back so none of the other species would think we were trying to interfere with the planet. That's all I know."

"So . . . I'm guessing I can't trade with the place," she said, almost hopefully.

"Sure you could. There shouldn't be any problem with trade, as long as you don't try and take over the planet. The only reason people haven't been trading with it is 'cause they don't think it has much to offer. It's still close enough to the ISC that, if it had anything valuable, it would have been colonized in a second. But maybe it's developed enough now. You can expect the technology there to be about where Earth was a hundred or two hundred years ago – electricity in cities and wealthy places, and old time villages everywhere else. If you're lucky, you'll get some plumbing. The exiles and refugees had to remake everything from scratch, which is difficult when you're talking about technology. So, they're back to being primitive. Watch out where you land – not all of them'll react well to a spaceship landing."

"Thanks for the info," was all she could manage to say. She was still trying hard to believe someone like Raiz existed. Wrapping her head around the details he had offered proved impossible. Again, a part of her wanted to be suspicious. How could Raiz have possibly known all this off the top of his head? Then again, how did he hack into the most secure computer in the world, and still become commander of this station? Trying to fathom him, his abilities, and his motives would inevitably prove futile.

Filling in the silence, Raiz said, "Happy to refresh my memory about that planet, especially if you're going to get involved there. It's pretty unique, with all the species there. Too bad I didn't know anything about the Shadow Workers. I'll have to look into that. But you can't just be going to Selparis for the money."

"I can't?"

"No. Why were you told about it? It can't just be that someone wanted you to trade with the planet, and it's a pretty secretive place, as far as hiding a planet goes. Does it have something to do with these

Shadow Workers?"

Emily wondered whether the Inana who had started her on this track would have wanted his private words told to public officials. Then again, Raiz had proven himself a mine of information, and answering his questions might be part of the deal – trading information could be even more valuable than trading goods. And she had already tipped Tylan off. Maybe she could get to it without saying too much. "The . . . person who told me was paranoid – a conspiracy nut. He knew someone on Selparis who said that the world was too weak to stop a secret group of mancers from taking over. I brought two Asparii here, and they said that mancers didn't do things in secret, but a group of mages called Shadow Workers was sort of famous for it, so maybe they're the ones threatening the planet. Anyway, that's why I was told about it. I haven't decided to go there yet, so I don't know why I'll be going."

Tyler Raiz stroked his bare chin and said, "Never heard about any of that." Leaning far back in the beanbag, he added, "it's possible, but there's not much way to check for evidence. Can't help you there." He seemed genuinely disappointed.

"Okay . . . well . . . ," she said, starting to rise out of the beanbag.

"Hold on," Raiz said quickly, got up, and went to the desk to retrieve something. It was a cell phone. Emily was mildly surprised – the usefulness of a cell phone to a star captain was minimal. "I give one of these to each Earth captain, for when they're in the vicinity. It's programmed with lots of useful numbers, including my own, some people to do business with, and some people who can get you out of trouble. I want to make sure things are as smooth as possible for our people up here in space –"

" . . . Because that's your job," she repeated his frequent refrain.

He brightened with a blinding smile. "Because I want to see us establish ourselves. Because space is open to us and we aren't taking advantage of it. People still look up at the stars and see them as unreachable. This is my job because I'm a dreamer."

"You got this job because you hacked into the station's system computer and you know it better than the people who built it."

Raiz pretended to be taken aback, but the smile never fully faded from his face. With a bit more edge to his voice, hinting at the vast intellect he camouflaged behind a jovial exterior, he said, "no. That'd be a good reason to put me into prison. I got here because I knew what to do with the station and its computer. I knew why it was all here. Everyone knows I broke into the system, but no one ever asks why. No one except the previous commander. You might not know your ship better than the Eldrandii that built it, Captain Pierce, but you know what to do with it. The day you stop knowing what to do with it, your ship won't have a crew or a captain."

Emily nodded. It was a good point. She liked that kind of thinking. Deeming this a good note to end their meeting on, they parted ways with quick thank-yous. Emily soon found herself at the station's ground level again, and waited for a taxi at the edge of the sidewalk. During the short wait, she felt uneasy, as if someone unfriendly was watching her with malice. She looked around and saw no one, though the far left corner of the tower made her inexplicably suspicious. Before she even considered investigating, a taxi was in sight. She hailed it, making her destination the station's main hotel, having decided that she desperately needed to cool down or risk her imagination running away.

After getting a room, she found herself sitting on the bed, looking at the files Raiz had given her, and hating herself for it. This was far from her idea of relaxation, but with the pages in front of her, curiosity took over. At least she had resisted during the taxi ride. It took little time to filter out the two criminals – Ben Wetzler and Jason Davison. They were the only ones, and everything was exactly as Tylan had said. The two were wanted for black market trading of illegal devices. That . . . sucked. Now she actually had to do something about it.

Dumping the reports on the floor, she grabbed some of the blanket, and napped with the lights on. Her mind was once again too busy to sleep. Without knowing how long she was lying there, she finally decided to float around the station for a while. By her own clock, it was afternoonish, and she wanted to do something fun before midnight. With any luck, that something would lead to satisfaction before dawn. Too much to hope for, though. She had always led her social life while carefree, and she was anything but that now. Chances were that she would be sitting alone, brooding over a drink.

She almost bumped into Kaz striding speedily along the corridor outside her room. He was dressed in an upscale blue suit, and looked like the consummate professional with his black hair immaculately parted.

"You look like you're ready to lie to somebody," Emily observed, "You playing poker, or picking up a date?"

The captain's wit so surprised Kaz that he almost failed to throw a sarcastic comment back. "We're on the same floor. Incredible. Another example of the divine sense of humor at work. I'll be playing poker, Captain. It's officers only, so the stakes are high, and they expect people to dress –"

"Like mafia hitmen. Got that part. Sounds fun, mind if I tag along?"

Emily could guess the quick calculations Kaz was making. He saw her as someone he could beat easily since she wore her emotions on her sleeves, so she was welcome in any of his poker games for the economic value. On the other hand, she could easily embarrass him in front of the other officers and captains. Balancing these out, he decided that he could get over the embarrassment if his bank account received some extra padding. He nodded and led the way, confidently walking with a quick pace and showing his microgravity experience.

Kaz's preferred gambling venue was close to the hotel, so they didn't call a taxi. Showing a deplorable lack of imagination, it was named "Officer's Club." It was an all-purpose recreation club with stage acts, a casino, and a restaurant. Emily knew immediately that it was not her kind of place, but she was already committed to annoying Kaz, and refused to back down. Besides, it would be interesting to see Kaz in the company of his peers.

The gaming hall, set aside from the other two areas of the club, had an atmosphere of solid sound making it difficult to focus on anything until the mind adjusted. There was a lot to see, and excited people of all shapes and sizes. There were as many Plani as humans in the hall, but they were more restrained, and matched the stereotype of their species exactly. They maintained a calculating, business-like look, seeing the place as a profit opportunity instead of a recreation spot. At least, that was what they looked like they were thinking – they might have only been living up to expectations.

After spending less than a minute observing a pool game in the far right corner – the first thing she saw of interest in the huge, ill-lit and elaborately decorated gaming hall – Emily was impressed but bored. They could have been the best players in space, but that only meant that she would look foolish trying to play against them. On the bright side, few people in the hall were as well-dressed as Kaz, and many were dressed in simple polos and slacks. The sloppier dressers were clearly the more competent players. She was the only one wearing a tee-shirt, but clearly broke the trend. Emily made a mental note to limit her bets. This bunch could easily bait her, getting her carried away so they could take every last credit in her account.

Kaz, out of some strange sense of responsibility, had kept with her while she looked around, but now he led her to one of the private poker rooms. The tables had six chairs, and five were occupied. A dim chandelier hanging three feet above the table's center lit the room. Every indication suggested that this table was invitation only, but no explicit sign declared it. In contrast to the casino outside, a tense silence filled this room. The five men were taking their game very seriously.

Despite their concentration, though, they willingly broke it to greet Kaz, who was instantly ushered to the last seat. Kaz introduced Emily in a stiff voice, leaving off her rank for reasons that Emily would inquire about later, and then went around the table with introductions. She caught two names – Captain Jack Wilson, who looked like Kaz's model for style, but had a muscled, broad-shouldered bearing, and Emilio Rabella, a tired, wrinkled man whose name was only memorable because of its resemblance to Emily's own. The table greeted her with raised eyebrows and nods. Only her position as captain rated her this much recognition. The table had an economy of conversation. The player with the fewest chips in front of him, a military officer still in his uniform, smiled at her, stood up from the table, and thanked the others for the game. After exchanging his chips for credits with the player acting as banker, he exited silently. The others, including Kaz, looked at her expectantly. Realizing that she was being invited in, she took the vacated seat. Already, though, she was out of her element.

They broke the silence to tell her that the table minimum was five credits, and the maximum was two thousand. She transferred two thousand credits to the bank, getting the same in chips. Kaz did the same. By the looks of it, two of the other players had about three thousand in play, while both Wilson and Rabella had over five thousand. The game was seven-card stud, which had been growing popular in recent years, replacing a resurgence of five-card draw. An hour in, she was a thousand down, despite having some decent hands. Competitive though she was, Emily knew her limits, and anticipated her losses. Blowing a daringly constructed straight to a magically conjured flush in the hands of Wilson was infuriating, but otherwise she kept her expectations realistic. Hopefully, that was helping her keep her expression flat and her lack of skill hidden. She managed to take a few small pots, so maybe she wasn't making a total fool of herself. Or maybe they had just felt sorry for her.

Kaz was less lucky. The best hand he had put together was a three-of-a-kind, and that only once. Probability was kicking him hard, and the frustration was starting to show. When a newcomer came in looking for a seat, Kaz vacated, folding with a thump. Emily decided to leave as well. Normally, poker involved a lot of shouting where she came from. She had gotten no sense of the other players, and it was difficult to play for fun with total strangers. Interacting was the best part of the game. At least she had come out better than Kaz.

"So –" she said to Kaz, considering whether to leave him to his woes. She could try her luck at the pool tables while she was here, having saved a thousand credits from the poker bunch. The place was still alien to her, though, and she was really only here because of Kaz. The high-class attitude could quickly get on her nerve without having something else to focus on – namely, the humor of seeing Kaz acting with that attitude. Sure, he acted that way all the time, but her presence was definitely throwing him off, as much as the club's atmosphere was throwing her.

Before she could say anything more to him, Captain Wilson, who must have left the game only one hand after they did, approached Kaz. The man was clearly a captain – he wore some self-adulating insignia on his suit, reminding her of airline pilots. He was clean-shaven, crew cut, and looked ready to run for President. His smile was designed to charm and it nearly made Emily puke. She was allergic to politico-business affectation, and he reeked with it. He was a master. Space Pier Imports would have been thrilled to have him, kicking Parell out the door in a second. After shaking Kaz's hand in greeting, he immediately introduced himself to Emily, saying, "Captain Jack Wilson, and you're Emily Pierce. So pleased to meet you." He put special emphasis on the title "captain," as if it set him apart from mere mortals. He made his introduction with enthusiasm that the even-keeled Kaz could not match in his most ecstatic moment. Kaz's face, though, lit up with delight, as if he had been worried that Wilson had forgotten him, and was thrilled at being recognized. Wilson was clearly Kaz's image of a good captain. Emily felt a pang of disappointment in her first officer, who she had at least considered intelligent until now.

When Wilson followed up by asking, "And what is it you do, Ms. Pierce?" with a naturally patronizing voice, she resigned herself to the need to strike back. If Kaz got embarrassed in the process, it was his fault for not introducing her as "Captain Pierce" in the first place. Clearly, Wilson had classified her as a commoner – a peon – and expected the same kind of fawning that Kaz was ready to give him. He was the spitting image of a politician shaking hands and smiling at the peasants, who look up to him admiringly and swear to vote for him on Election Day.

"Oh, just hyperspace communications. I'm new to the whole space thing, trying to take after my grandfather and all that," she said quickly, just as Kaz was opening his mouth to tell Wilson the truth. "Kaz wanted to show me around the station. I've only been here once, when we set out." It was always good to mix up truth in with the lies. That way, even if you don't get away with it, you can at least confuse people.

Wilson looked puzzled. "Kaz . . . asked you?"

"Yeah. Sort of a date, you know." She looked at Kaz, and was pleased to see him shocked and speechless. It was subtle, though, and it didn't tip Wilson off.

The other captain furrowed his brows but kept the smile on his face. The expression showed as much cluelessness as Raiz's cautious smile showed sharp intelligence. "Well . . . opposites attract, I guess."

"Oh, yeah," Emily said, nodding. "Didn't take long at all. He likes strong women, I think. I catch him staring at the only woman on our cargo crew. She's got these muscles," Emily indicated the size of them by hovering her right hand two inches over her left arm, "but

I think she was a bit too intimidating for him, so he settled for me. Anyway, he's a lot looser in bed."

Kaz nearly choked, his face red. He got his breath back in desperation and immediately interfered with Emily's ruse. "Captain Wilson, this is Captain Pierce, who likes her jokes. She decided to join me here for the poker game, but that's all. I wouldn't want to leave you with a false impression."

The expression on Wilson's face faltered as he tried to decide how to take this. After a few seconds, he chose indignation. "Well, I hope the laugh was worth it, Captain Pierce," he said, turning 'captain' into an accusation. Directing his next words to Kaz, he said, "You had the makings of a good navigator. If you would like to be part of a serious crew, I could recommend you to some of the other captains. They know I train the best, and sharp nav officers are in high demand. Old Captain Pierce would have seen your talent right away – might even have made you first officer. It's too bad his ship's been left in immature hands. I'm sure you're doing more than your part to keep the ship together."

The words wiped Emily's smile off her face. Wilson was ignoring her, as if she was a nonentity. He had known exactly how to strike back – ruthless despite the charming veneer. In a different time, she would have socked the pretentious asshole without a second thought, but even in her anger, she now kept herself in check. She would hate herself for it later, but she let her temper swell in her mind and face instead of in her fists.

Without really seeing how angry Emily was getting, Kaz automatically corrected Wilson. "Actually, Captain Pierce has made me first officer, sir. She might have more of the old Captain Pierce in her than you give her credit for." Then, looking at Emily and seeing her calmed down by his unexpected vote of confidence, he added on second thought, "she does have some immature impulses, though." He said the last words with a scowl at her ill-treatment of his old captain. Behind the scowl, he was still surprised and unsure what to think of her. While he had absolute respect and reverence for Captain Wilson's abilities, Kaz had never been comfortable with the artificial charm. It was fascinating to see how quickly Emily had pushed Wilson out of it.

"If you say so, Kazuhiro," Wilson said, turning to leave. "The offer stands." He gave Emily a curt nod, and moved to the restaurant side of the club.

Once Wilson was clear, Kaz turned to his captain and asked, "Did you have to do that? You embarrassed all of us."

"He was an idiot."

Kaz straightened tensely. "He's one of the best captains Earth has. Maybe the best."

"He acts like an idiot."

"He acts respectable."

"Fake respectable. He's faking it. I can't respect that. Plus he was so damn arrogant; someone should bring him down a few pegs. Should've punched him to wipe that smug look on his face."

Kaz sighed. "You have a point, but sometimes contacts like Wilson could be useful, Captain."

"To get you another job, maybe. For me, he's the competition."

"We have enough competition from the other species," Kaz said, her attitude making him sour. "Humans have to work together to build our place in the stars. That's Captain Wilson's attitude, anyway."

"'Cause it suits him if everyone else believes it. He can get the better of them while looking like he's some kind of prince."

"A dozen other captains – half of Earth's private space fleet – see how useful it is to know him."

'He just hasn't figured out how to stab them in the back, yet."

"Captain . . . ," Kaz said through grinding teeth. A bright ringing coming from Emily interrupted him. She fished out the cell phone Raiz had given her, and took the call.

Raiz's voice came excitedly through the earpiece, and she heard the rumbling of many conversations behind him. "Sorry to disturb you, Captain, but I have a job opportunity that might interest you – one that will definitely make you more visible. The customer will not want to leave for a few days, so your crew can have their leave. He just wanted to line up his travel arrangements. I'll give you details in person if you can meet me at the Café Diplomatic. If you'll tell me where you are, I'll send a driver to pick you up."

As usual, Raiz packed so much information in so little time that Emily had to take a few seconds to register it. She then looked at Kaz, and then said to Raiz, "I'm at the Officer's Club."

"Really?" Raiz said. "Not your kind of place. Did you tag along with someone snotty, or maybe you didn't know about the other entertainment establishments on our station? Hope you're not bored out of your mind – they can do that to you. But I'm sure you're finding some way to amuse yourself. Our female adventurers usually head straight for The Spot when they pass through. Anyway, the cab'll be right over. See you in a bit." And that was that.

"Who was that?" Kaz asked immediately, staring at the phone as she put it away.

"A real valuable contact. Wanna come and meet him?"

Brows furrowed in suspicion for a moment, curiosity eventually got the best of Kaz, and he nodded.

They left the club and, during the cab ride over, Emily murmured to Kaz, "We really should think about that mystery planet. I don't like the idea of Wilson beating me to it, and he's just the type that would sleaze the information out of someone. And the Inana had hinted that he would eventually tell other people if I didn't go."

"Risky. I know you want to show everyone that there's a new Captain Pierce in town," Kaz said with surprising perceptiveness, "but that world's labeled hostile on the star charts for a reason, and we're not trained for exploration missions. We could get into trouble as soon as our landing pod touches down."

"We might have to land the ship, just for the manpower to back us up."

Looking at her appraisingly, he said, "even riskier." They left the topic there, spotting their destination through the cab's windows. Exiting the cab, she felt uneasy, and scanned the surroundings as she had in front of the command tower. There was nothing suspect in sight, but she still shivered as a chill ran up her spine. Awkward moment over, she refocused on the business at hand, leading Kaz to the doors of the café.

If anything, the Café Diplomatic was more upscale than the Officer's Club was, but also louder. Spirited discussions, mostly on politics, peppered the place, and the atmosphere was relaxed even if the décor and dress code was not. This was a haven for ambassadors, dignitaries, and political pundits. Newport Station provided a unique neutral ground for them to discuss matters of state, and this café seemed to be the public location where they would start the conversations that would be finished in private conference rooms. Emily was the only one there not in a suit. Well, except for Commander Raiz, now in a loose-fitting shirt and slacks. Still, he had increased the formality of his attire a few notches above the Bermuda look he had been sporting earlier.

Kaz was wide-eyed as they made their way to Raiz. Careful not to tip off their destination, Emily was eager to see again the surprise on his face. She was satisfied and delighted that he was, at least in this respect, entirely predictable.

Seeing them approach, Raiz rose to greet them and introduced the three white-haired and balding male bureaucrats seated at the table with him. The names were meaningless to Emily, but they impressed Kaz. Her first instinct was to dismiss them as the same class of people she had always despised, but then noticed that they looked enthusiastic, or at least bemused, instead of awkward in Raiz's eccentric presence. That was telling, since he was the ideal antidote for someone with a stick up their ass. She knew that no one so stuck up would be at ease in his company. On the other hand, they might just be enamored by Raiz's influence. She decided to reserve judgment.

Raiz had been speaking to the diplomat at the center in particular. The station commander emphasized that man's name, but mentioned no reason why he should merit special attention. Raiz had clearly expected her to recognize the name, but quickly readjusted after seeing her lack of response, adding for her benefit, "Mr. Welder was the Secretary of Interstellar Affairs for the United States. He's spent twenty years traveling throughout the ISC, establishing ties with other species for both the World Council and the United States. He's retired now, but still gets around."

"Oh," Emily said, choosing the minimal reaction to satisfy the situation. She might have heard of Welder at some point, but knew nothing about him. The way Raiz was introducing him, though, it was clear that the former ambassador was her intended passenger.

The table had five seats around it, which would have been the right number if not for Kaz. Her first officer moved to excuse himself, but Raiz offered him the last seat, choosing to remain standing instead.

The café was full of standing figures, wildly gesticulating as they regaled their seated audiences with elaborate political positions, so taken by their own ideas that they could no longer stay seated while explaining them. Caffeine-induced oratory filled the place, so Raiz fit in completely while he stood and explained the situation – though being outlandishly conspicuous would have made him perfectly happy as well.

"So, Captain Pierce," Raiz started, "who've you got with you? Wait . . . let me see if I remember . . . Kazuhiro Kamiki, right?"

Kaz nodded, but couldn't speak. Emily said, "Yeah. He's my second in command."

"Well, Kazuhiro Kamiki, my name is Tyler Raiz. I'm the commander of Newport Station. I'm sure you already know that we are meeting on some business, but from the look on your face, Captain Pierce didn't tell you who you were meeting with. She likes seeing the surprised look on your face, I think. Anyway, Mr. Welder wants passage to Eldrand, and I suggested you might be available."

Welder took the initiative now. As old as his wrinkled face and balding head looked, his eyes were ancient. There was a shade of hawk about him, softened by a sincere smile. His voice had a focused gravity that was ideally suited to make important points. Behind his eyes was the experience that had earned him that voice. "While I was working for the government, I used official ships for everything – more than just official matters, I don't mind saying. Now that I'm retired, I still have unofficial visits to make throughout the ISC, and I'm looking for a flexible captain who can accommodate me about once every three months. I am an old man, and I don't have the time to wait around for a ship to become available, so when I send a message to you through hyperspace it means I want to get to another planet as soon as possible. Would you be willing?"

Emily knew how this had to work. "That depends on what you're paying."

"A million credits a trip. I'll be bringing my two aides and my wife, but no cargo. Will that be enough to make it worth your while?"

It was enough to make her a bit suspicious. "Seems like a lot if you're just making social calls. You planning to make a lot of money from these trips?"

Welder accepted the question with good grace. "Captain, I can make half a million at a single speaking engagement on any planet in the ISC. I think I'll manage."

Emily decided not to quibble any further, since it was a patently solid offer. "All right."

The old ambassador stared at Emily penetratingly. She made no sign of discomfort, but definitely felt awkward. He seemed to be trying to decide how to approach a problem or to lay some groundwork with her. Finally, Welder asked Raiz, "Why did you recommend Captain Pierce, Raiz? I know you have your reasons. You always do."

Raiz pretended to be taken aback by the implied accusation. "I've told you already. She's new to the business and we need to give our captains as much of a head start as possible. The other captains are better established and connected. Ms. Pierce's grandfather had that, but I know he didn't have the time to introduce her to all of it. You know I always help the underdog."

Welder's probing gaze fixed on Raiz, as if trying to pry information from the commander's expression. "Yes, but I also know you can base your decisions on all the information in the world. Something superficial like support for the underdog is a good excuse, but it can't be your real reason."

"Ah, my dear Welder," Raiz said, mimicking some vague conglomeration of characters, "if I haven't already told you –"

It took a moment for Welder to realize that Raiz expected him to finish the sentence. Clearing his throat, he said, "You don't plan to. But I suppose it will be worthwhile for me to find out."

"Of course. Of course. No fun otherwise. But it won't kill you if you don't find out," Raiz grinned.

"I'm too old for adventures, Raiz," Welder grumbled. "Ask these two. They have been assisting me every step of the way. We spend most of our time complaining about our pains these days. They know I'm not up to anything that might fascinate you. You get interested in the damnedest things."

Raiz gave him a sidelong glance. "Maybe one last adventure. No? Well, it's your choice." Turning to Emily, he said slyly, "don't tell the old man anything unless he comes to you. You might get him to pay a fair bit for it. He's filthy rich, so don't hold back out of pity for an old man, and his one weakness is his curiosity. You won't believe the trouble it's gotten him into." Thoroughly enjoying himself, Raiz said "old man" with sarcastic emphasis.

Emily blinked. For the length of the conversation so far, she had been completely lost. Suddenly, Raiz was speaking to her as if she knew his secret, and she struggled to cross-reference the exchange between him and Welder with the thin body of knowledge he and she shared. The word "adventure" stuck in her mind, since she hadn't associated it with space travel in weeks. She used to think of it in those terms all the time, especially before she became a teenager and set aside childish dreams for hard reality. Only one thing she might be doing could possibly have the word "adventure" applied to it, but there was no way she was sharing that discovery with this aged diplomat. Comprehension dawning, she looked at Raiz incredulously. If Welder was as famous as everyone seemed to think he was, he would get all the credit for establishing a trade agreement with Selparis. She wanted that glory for herself. And how could an old man complaining about his pains help anyway?

Reading her thoughts, Raiz said, "You never know. He knows as much about exploring planets and negotiating agreements as any human. That's knowledge that a merchant captain might find useful, Ms. Pierce. But, still, the decision is yours. I never force anyone to do anything, just in case someone suddenly decides to impose on me."

Welder shook his head. "I'm not interested in spending any time teaching a trader how to make deals, Raiz. I have enough on my hands –"

"And I'm not interested in hearing about it," Emily said, defiantly. Her instincts had been favorable to Raiz until now, but his dark side was quickly becoming apparent.

"Well, sounds like you two are a perfect match then," Raiz said with an incongruous glee. "You don't want to say it and she doesn't want to hear it. Perfect. Do as you like, and I'll sit back and watch." Standing without even a piece of wall nearby to lean on, much less a chair, the station commander didn't look like he could possibly live up to his words. He had the stance of someone not only involved, but at the center of the action, so it was difficult to take his pretended aloofness seriously.

Welder and Emily looked at each other across the gulf of generations, silently agreeing that they were in the presence of an ingenious madman. Worth listening to, certainly, but still bizarre. Bypassing Raiz, Welder asked Emily, "So, do we have a deal?"

Emily nodded. "Yeah. When do you want to leave? My crew'll mutiny if we don't spend at least four more days here."

"A week. I have business to take care of first, and my wife won't be arriving until Friday. After that, our destination will be Eldrand."

"All right. We'll say a week from right now. I guess that's . . . ," she looked for a clock and found one near the center of the café's back wall, "around eleven o'clock station time. My ship's at berth twelve."

Welder nodded. "We'll be there."

That settled, Emily thanked Raiz and Welder, and left the café with Kaz tailing her."

"You . . . Welder," Kaz said as they floated out to the sidewalk. Emily tried to hail a cab, once again looking around to see if someone was watching her. That feeling . . . would she ever step out of doors on Newport station without feeling uneasy? Maybe it was the way the place was, barring the atmospheric shield, open to the vast expanses of Earth and space. The captain shook her head, decided that must be it, then registered that her first officer had just spoken.

"Hmm?"

"What was all that about, anyway? I knew Raiz was eccentric, but that was something else."

Emily sighed. "I think he wants me to tell Welder about the planet. He thinks Welder might be able to help somehow. That's what I'm guessing."

Eyebrows raised in concern, Kaz said tersely, "you told Commander Raiz about the planet?"

She answered defensively, "yeah. I was checking the records of our two criminal crewmembers, and I decided he might have some info about it. He did."

"He could pass what you told him onto other captains –"

"Not if he wants to helps the underdog."

"And you believed him about that?" he asked sharply. "Welder said it was a lame excuse."

"We wouldn't even have met Welder if Raiz was going to tell everybody he met about the planet," she shot back, "so yeah, I think he'll keep it quiet. And he's got no reason to tell anyone else. Not as much reason as you do, anyway. He's got everything he could possible want, but you could tell your favorite captain over at the Officer's Club, and he could give you a nice place with a captain he likes. Maybe he'd even pay you a few million on top of that. It's worth –"

"Stop," Kaz snapped.

"I don't –"

"Stop. You're right. Raiz probably had useful information, and nobody could pay him off if he didn't want to pass it on to him, so you trust him. Fine. Just don't insult me." The last words were feeble, but had a bitterness that Emily could taste before her tongue could move a hair's breadth.

She remembered his mixed defense of her at the Officer's Club, and the bad taste in her mouth intensified. She said, "Sorry," and left it at that.

"I'll see you back on the ship," Kaz said, drifting away from her just as a taxi pulled up. Her eyes were on his back for a few seconds before she shook her head, and pulled her magnetic boots off the sidewalk and onto the cab.

"The Spot," she said, hoping the place Raiz had suggested would let her finally forget all the business she was caught up in, wash her mind of the complications so many people loved to wallow in, and wipe away any lingering paranoia.

Newport Station was devoid of sleazy dives. Emily was beginning to appreciate that now, seeing half the city flash by. Well, no one would have consciously recreated a lower-middle class neighborhood in space. Getting out of the taxi at The Spot, though, she quickly saw that it was the closest thing she would be able to find to what she was looking for. At least, no one walking was wearing anything formal. The signs outside the door were all in gaudy neon instead of the sedate colors preferred by the Officer's Club. That was a start.

Inside, the place was exactly what Emily had expected, though lacking the haze of cigarette smoke because of the station's stringent clean air rules. Bar, tables, and a stage were all a place needed, and all The Spot featured. The gender ratio was firmly at the female end, which was technically favorable for the men. However, many of the women had an off-duty air that indicated they weren't interested, and were either trying to get over a long day with friends, busy enough in bed as it was. As a result, the bar hosted a few lonely men glancing admiringly at the flocks of female friends grouped at the tables. Other men had already acted, and were dancing in front of the stage with their newfound partners to some heavy electronica. The band used the latest array of synthesized instruments to play everything from classic techno to the latest stuff. The pulse of the music was intoxicating, but not so overwhelming that it denied weary patrons their right to sit still and gossip with friends.

To Emily's surprise, Ethan was one of the lonely men sitting at the bar. He wasn't gawking at the women in the place like some of the others were doing, but he did attempt the occasional covert glance, especially at a tall, leggy brunette who was dancing with anyone on the dance floor willing to join her. Emily could have laughed. Ethan could never get into a one-night relationship, particularly with a woman who seemed to have a five-minute attention span. He had sort of a clingy nature partly a result of his lack of self-confidence. He had clung to her all the way into space without there being a hint of a relationship between them, just because she was his best friend. If only he could let go like everyone else, he would have had no problem striking a chord with the girl of his choice. There was a geeky charm to him mixed with a well-hidden nihilistic side – the same combination found in so many other heartthrob musicians. As it was, the only hope the bar offered Ethan was alcohol, and he had never been a drinker. On her many nights out with friends, he was a consistent designated driver. Always whined about having to drive, but eventually did it anyway.

Not seeing her, he seized up when she sat down on the barstool next to him.

"Oh. Hello," he eventually greeted with complete lack of enthusiasm. He knew that she knew how his mind worked, and how thoroughly pitiful his current motives were. She was truly the last person he wanted to see here as he wallowed in self-loathing.

Understanding all of this, she said, "thought you'd find something better to do while we're here. Finding something out about different species, maybe. You know, your specialty."

"Too . . . lazy," he said, slumped. "I just wanted to do what everyone else was doing. Couldn't."

"Yeah, I know." Emily felt that she should at least try to console him. "It's not like I've found anyone or had any fun. It's been all business so far."

"Why don't you just find a prostitute like everyone else. There's one over there," he pointed, "and another one over there," he gestured again.

She looked at them, and felt that the first one seemed attractive from a distance. She couldn't make out the fine features, though. "How can you tell?"

Ethan slumped further. At first, he kept his mouth shut tight. Her eyes eventually forced him to mumble, "They asked me whether I was interested."

If she had been drinking, a spray of alcohol would have left her lips. "But even I could see how you were ogling that girl over there."

"You could?" he asked, horrified and blushing. Throat suddenly parched, he took a gulp out of the full mug in front of him. After he shook off the effects of the beer and made a face at the aftertaste, he said, "They asked before she came in. I guess . . . I wasn't being so obvious then."

Emily arched her eyebrows. "How long've you been in here?"

"Hours. I don't know. Just don't have anywhere else to go."

"You're hopeless."

"I know."

"Haven't you gotten a room, yet?"

Ethan sighed. "I . . . should do that, yeah."

"How much have you drunk?"

Feebly, he answered, "This is the second. I hate the taste, but I couldn't just . . . sit here."

Emily rolled her eyes. She hailed the bartender and ordered a Red Eld, just to make a point. This disappointed Ethan further, as he had hoped that she would leave him alone. The drink was a signal that she intended to irritate him further.

"I could order you to get something done."

Seeing no alternative, he rose from the stool. "Don't bother. I'll . . . go find a room." He stalked out, making her feel like a bully. This had been his normal defensive mechanism for years. He thrived on this sort of exchange, which usually resulted in a spurt of effort that would imbed information in his mind useful for years to come, and remembered longer. That information would come from television documentaries, more often than not. Good thing the hotels on Newport Station received every channel available. The effort would soon fade, so while he was off his usual sluggishness, it was important that he had the resources to make a go of it.

Turning her thoughts away from her wayward friend, Emily appraised the two men Ethan had pointed out. The second was totally out of the question – he was too short and had a silly grin on his face. It also looked like he had recently been indulging himself a bit more than was advisable for someone in his profession. The first one still looked smooth. His expression had a Bond-like suave, and his tight-fitting vinyl clothing made eloquent advertisements all over his body. He was tall and trim – not too much muscle, but with enough meat to show he had put some effort in.

She decided to take a closer look. After all, these were high-class consorts – only a license from the church could make the pleasure more guiltless.

That night had been dreamless. She noticed this only because of a vivid dream that haunted her every subsequent night for the rest of her stay on Newport Station – both waking and asleep. Awake, she felt eyes around every corner and enemies in every square inch of darkness. In her dream, she saw them there, watching her. Black cloaked figures were in every shadow, keeping a close tab on her every move, and they were there, no matter where she went. On the first night, she tried to sneak around, but no matter where on the station she went, they followed, even onto her ship and into space. She ran on the second night, but to no better effect, waking up panting and sweating. Next time, she went straight for her ship, undocked it, landed on Earth, and headed home. They were there.

In the day, there was always the feeling that they were lurking, but try as she might, she could never catch sight of them. It ruined the rest of her days on the station, and she mostly kept to herself for the remainder of the week. She detested being fearful, but saw no way to diminish her sense of alarm. Somehow, telling herself that it was all in her head didn't help. After days of pondering how this was affecting her, she finally hit on a possible solution on the last night before she would be departing the station. Unable to see them in real life, but she could in her dreams, so even though she had no chance to catch them in real life, maybe in her dream –

Before she slept that night, she focused on the idea of catching one of the Shadow Workers, if that was who these stalkers were. She had no control over what might happen while she was dreaming, but did her best, before closing her eyes, to influence what she would see. At first, she was running through her dream again, but she felt no fear. Then, just as she would have turned into the tunnel that would have taken her to the *Azar*, she ran to the nearest corner and snatched the figure she had always seen there. The grab worked, and she yanked the body out of the shadows by the collar of the cloak.

In the instant it was out in the open, the world of the dream changed into the same white space she had been in when Tylan had accidentally walked into her nocturnal wanderings. Like that time, everything had a great deal more reality to it, and her senses were as sharp as they were in real life. And like that time, she was furious.

"You! You're in my dream! What the fuck are you doing to me? You've really been chasing me around, haven't you?"

The figure, face still concealed by the hood, turned its robe red hot so she was forced to let go, and then said in a hoarse whisper, "You interfere in our affairs. We can destroy you, along with this entire station, if we choose to –"

Aha, she thought, so I've really got an enemy. That made it all so much more interesting. "Oh, yeah. Then why're you hiding, huh? You can do all that? Go ahead. Why don't you?"

There was a vicious smile somewhere deep in the hood. It oozed out in the figure's next words. "You are not worth the trouble, human."

"Seems like a lot of trouble, you getting into my dreams."

"Fool, you are one of our concerns. You dream about us and your fear brings us here."

So, this is like the accident between her and Tylan. His magic . . . and maybe some of hers . . . had forced them into the same dream world. That meant this creature was as rattled by this as she was. It was certainly acting like it – unable to stay still as if it was unsure of itself. "A concern, eh? Yeah, well I should concern you bastards. You think threatening me will throw me off? You've just got yourself an enemy, buddy."

"There are forces in this universe you cannot possibly understand. Stand in our way, and all that you love will be crushed."

Emily rolled her eyes. Even the supposed-to-be-scary voice struck as being too movie-like to be believed. "Oh, come on. You're putting me on, aren't you?"

"I have said all I have to say." The figure disappeared, and Emily woke up with teeth and fists clenched. She wouldn't have thought of doing it before, as uncertain and, to be honest, frightened as she had been all week, but it was time to find out about any Asparii on board, and especially about any ships carrying Asparii. They would need a ship to follow her when she left the station. She had confronted the shadow in her dreams and now it was a known enemy. Maybe something had been lost in translation, or there was a cultural disconnect, but the shadow's threats had seemed very weak and desperate. Then again, it had been caught by surprise, thinking that it had been walking a one-way street only to find someone hurtling at it in the opposite direction. Was it enough to throw her pursuers off their balance and make them rethink their strategy? Not for long. And maybe after this, they'd just decide to kill her off.

Dressed, and on her way to Raiz, she wondered why they didn't kill her. She couldn't think of a good reason, unless they felt her position as captain meant that her demise would bring too much attention, and may reveal their once quiet manipulations. Maybe the opportunity hadn't presented itself, yet, and they were just waiting for the right time. That was a happy thought.

Offering deceptive comfort, the streets were free of any hint of watchers. If the stalkers were there, she couldn't feel them anymore. She reached the tower with no less paranoia, but was told on her arrival to the information desks that Raiz was on Earth, at a political conference in New York. Bad timing. Suddenly remembering the cell phone, she checked her pants pocket to see if it was still there from last night. It was, but she decided not to use it, even though it certainly would have been able to reach Raiz. Instead, she asked for a listing of ships at dock from the information desk, with the names of all passengers. If she had been a normal visitor to the station, the request would have been out of the question. As a cell phone-armed captain, she still had to use every bit of leverage she could, including the threat of calling the commander during his meeting, before the stalwart defenders of the station's information capitulated.

One Asparian ship in dock, and it had no name. Well, that fit the picture she had formed of her newfound enemy. Some of the other ships in dock had a couple of Asparii passengers, but her guess was that Shadow Workers didn't mix well with other species. Asparii-controlled ships had been fairly rare since the fall of Asparis, since most of them had been sold by the refugees to fund their new lives. She wasted no time, and headed for that ship's berth. No idea about what she would do when she got there came to mind, and her instincts were neutral on the matter, neither driving her forward nor holding her back. Her anger carried her forward, but she had already released a lot of it when demanding the ship listings, and it was bound to run out soon if no new target presented itself. Considering its mistake in challenging her in the dream world, the enemy was showing an unusual understanding of human psychology by staying away from her now. If she had still felt them around every corner, fueling the flame burning behind her eyes would have been no problem.

The ship was there, sitting calmly in the berth, cold, silent, and solid. Emily had envisioned something painted completely in black, but it was bare metal all the way, with the berth's lights gleaming off of it. No one guarded it, and after checking the many walkway arms from the observation concourse to the ship, she knew why. There was no visible way from the exterior to open any hatches. She supposed that the only way to get in would be to send a signal, and have someone open it from the inside. A hassle requiring the ship to be continuously manned, but secure.

Emily sighed, drained. Having done all she could from the concourse, scrutinizing every inch of the enemy ship for markings and waiting for someone to emerge from it, she was eventually forced to give up. Her own ship was heading for Eldrand tomorrow, and she'd just have to see whether this thing followed. On the bright side, the enemy ship's exterior showed no signs of weaponry, but maybe it was concealing its teeth. Her guess was that this Asparian ship would avoid entering Eldrand's space, since the Eldrandii would be suspicious of any Asparian ship. That, and the *Azar*'s substantial acceleration, provided some breathing room. Getting away for the short term would be easy. Dealing with these bastards for good was going to be a trick. If she could just find a way to get one step ahead of them, and stay there, that might be enough. For a while.

5
Murder on Eldrand

Despite a week of near neglect, the *Azar* was perched pristinely in its berth. For a fresh visitor to Newport station, it would have been an awe-inspiring sight, with the space city on the sunlit side of the world, and the Eldrandii metal skin gleaming with an unearthly brilliance. Shuttles from the surface sported paler reflections that humans were more accustomed to, and were put to shame by the true spaceships, though the Asparian ship's surface had been less luminescent. The shine on the *Azar* had character, dancing across the ship like an ethereal sprite. It was difficult to tell what the ship's original color was, especially when its surface caught images of Earth, and skewed the globe along its own gentle curves. To the veteran space traveler, of course, this was all old-hat.

Welder certainly didn't gawp, or seem taken by the view from the concourse. Nor did his assistants. His wife, though, was agog, staring at the ship with the eyes of a green venturer. As elderly as her husband, it was refreshing to see she could still manage such childlike wonder. On the other hand, when she turned to look at her husband, her eyes were filled with decades of wisdom and experience, but no weariness, disappointment, or regret. Her white, thinning hair seemed perked up in the presence of the starship, and some of her wrinkles were shallower as the ship's brightness was reflected in her face. Nearing the tunnel to the ship's portal, Welder turned to his wife, saw her still trying to catch a final glance of the ship's exterior before they entered. He felt a pang of envy in his tired heart, knowing that he could never see anything in the universe in that way again.

His travels had taken him far outside the tiny area of the galaxy carved out by ISC-controlled territory – to lands so alien that English lacked the words to describe them. Being forced to take it all in while dealing with intricate negotiations, he was conditioned to minimize reactions to new stimuli, no matter how spectacular, just so he could keep his focus on the business at hand. His lack of fascination didn't mean that he missed details, he just reacted differently to them the way others might. It was going to be nice, having his wife with him this time. Now that he was technically retired, it would be nice to enjoy the universe for once.

The former interstellar ambassador was feeling the finale approaching. His last journey would come, and soon. He couldn't stop – too many people around the galaxy called on him now, asking for his opinions and respecting his decisions. Dozens of species recognized him as Earth's greatest asset, and there was tremendous pressure on him to continue even though he was now acting as a private citizen. He would have continued anyway, and only the weakening of his once-ironclad health gave him second thoughts. If his last days would come away from Earth, at least his wife should be with him. She had spent almost half of their marriage without him, and that with minimal complaints. Her own career had occupied her almost as much as his did him, but every time the hyperspace relay from him, assuring her that he was all right, had ended, she would have given it all up to join him. The feeling passed quickly, and no lingering regret remained. Even now, space was a field over which humans traveled with difficulty and caution, and unknown dangers were hidden in the darkness between the stars. Welder had faced death many times, and had been imprisoned on five worlds, possibly setting a record. He had never mentioned this to his wife, keeping only the best of the galaxy for her ears, but she could read between the lines, and guessed what he had been through.

On this trip, the worlds would all be friendly. No more of the unknown. With nothing more to prove, he was visiting only on invitation, trying to spend his time constructively. He couldn't risk feeling useless, since that would be inviting the end to come.

The party of four boarded the ship as dignitaries, with most of the crew lining the passage way and the central corridor of the ship, waiting to greet the famous Marcus Welder. He was a legend in space traveling circles – a culture which Emily had yet to gain full admittance. She might have been the only one who didn't know about him, and to her annoyance, Ethan was excitedly telling her all about the ambassador. She had never seen him excited by anything in his life, and would have preferred it if things stayed that way. She couldn't care less about Welder, with all the fear, confusion, and frustration of the past week.

Kaz was no help, raising more questions instead of helping her answer the ones she already had. She refrained from talking about her dreams, but flat out told him that she had been followed the whole time she had been aboard Newport Station, and that she was sure the Asparian ship held the group of mages they had been warned about. His response was purely practical, poking holes in the bizarre affair without filling them in with solid sense.

"Look, if they're mages, why don't they just kill you? Why all the secrecy?" he reasoned, meeting her in the captain's ready room just before they departed from Newport Station.

Of course, she had thought about that herself, arriving at no good answer. "They don't want to blow their cover. This way, they stay secret until they're ready."

"They can hire assassins, Captain."

"On Newport Station?"

"Okay . . . maybe not here. Let's assume that they really are tailing you, and it has to do with this planet. Why don't we just stay away from the planet, then? That seems like the obvious solution."

She tapped the table, irritated. Of course it was the obvious solution. And she couldn't tell Kaz that she felt directly challenged by the Shadow Workers, and that an unofficial war had been declared as far as she was concerned. The crew would be unsatisfied by that explanation, too, if she was really going to drag the ship to Selparis. She needed something more compelling – some definite compensation – to justify the money and time the venture would take. Much as she hated to remind herself of it, this was a business, and the members of the crew were employees with a stake in the company's success. They had flat wages, but because she was a captain without a reputation, she also had to promise them percentages of the profit. It was common practice – though usually companies were publicly traded and simply gave their employees stock – but it limited her, unless she wanted to risk the displeasure of people keeping this ship running.

Before Emily managed to come up with a good answer to Kaz's question, he had already voiced an even more compelling argument. "What if they want us to go there? That would explain why they're goading you but not attacking you. We would do the hard work, then they would swoop in and take over. Did you think of that?"

No, she hadn't, but she wasn't going to admit it. That was a cunning plan, but why would these Asparii mages need to follow her? Surely they knew the location of the planet, if it was home to enough Asparii refugees to build an empire . . . but maybe not. After all, the only Asparii to go there in the last hundred years went on human ships, and Asparis was a world large enough to ensure that the secrets of one group of people might not have reached the ears of a manipulative bunch of mages. Kaz was better at thinking through these things than she was, so she put the question to him. "If Selparis is important enough for them to play around with me to find it, don't you think they would've just tailed the refugees when we took them there? Would've been much easier."

Kaz leaned back, thought about it, and said, "that means it's only become important recently. They only just realized there was something worth going there for." After a brief silence, he said, "you know, if it's something we can trade for, like a rare resource, you might be right, it might be worth going. But I don't think mages are really interested in that sort of thing, unless they're the type that would stoop to buying influence when their magic can't get it for them."

"They might be," was all she could find to say. "I'll . . . have to think about this."

Pondering this discussion as she welcomed the guests on board, she saw two men who were causing her an entirely different set of worries standing in the corridor outside the ship, getting a last breath of station air. Emily had found no exterior repair specialists available to replace Wetzler and Davison, and had lacked the time to arrange to meet anyone on Earth. While there was some flexibility in crew numbers – the *Azar*'s total complement was currently twenty-six out of a possible thirty-five – the external repair crew had to have at least four members. Usually, three or all four went out to handle the orbital checkup for a ship of *Azar*'s size.

Her ship had two criminals in its crew. For now, there was no avoiding it. There was a chance that they had already sabotaged her ship once, and that the other two had also been in on it. At least they had installed better cameras while they had been on the surface of Dael, recording activities every second so there wouldn't be anything fishy happening now. Come to think of it, Ben Wetzler had been the one to propose the cameras. She didn't know whether to be relieved or suspicious. Anyway she looked at it, she was caught in a quandary. Considering the inadequate result, she would have eagerly given up all the worrying and thinking of the past week for a good, old-fashioned spark of inspiration. If only her dreams brought her solutions instead of new problems.

Her dreams . . . they were another puzzlement, but easily ignored. As far as she could tell, her mind was still her province, but she was no longer confident that she understood it like she once did. There was a mystery in her mind that she would eventually have to solve.

Giving Wetzler and Davison a last, ominous look, she led the passengers to their quarters herself, and made sure they were comfortable. The adulation of Welder made extra care seem necessary. In no time at all, though, she was back on the bridge, and to her delight, it really felt like being back home. Worries aside, she was finally settling in.

The captain's chair still had an uncomfortable feel to it, and she spent as little time in it as possible. It wasn't her type of chair – more purpose-driven than comfortable – so maybe something with fewer panels and switches, and more velvet, would be more suitable for her tastes. If her first year in space ended in success, she would see a new chair installed. For now, with nothing preventing her from doing so, she paced around the bridge, occasionally standing in place to stare out of the main viewscreen into space. Kaz gave her a few glances, all of them complicated, filled with conflicting thoughts. He was as worried as she was about Wetzler and Davison, but though his first instinct was to stay at the station until replacements could be found, he also recognized that displeasing Marcus Welder would be a bad idea. He took the lack of solutions as a personal affront. When he displayed the plot that would take them to Epsilon Eridani, around which the planet of Eldrand revolved, it was without a word. His silence was in sharp contrast to the constant flow of words coming from Liam, who was inundated by the station babble. Newport Station lacked the practiced and expedited flow of other space destinations – the control tower had volumes of procedures and regulations that made arrival and departure something of an achievement. Liam referred to a checklist of his own to avoid forgetting anything that would delay clearance.

Free from the station half an hour later, and angling away from the system's plane, the ship accelerated smoothly to the jump point. Liam let out a breath of relief and set down his headset. "Someone's got to tell these guys how this is supposed to go. It doesn't have to be this bad."

A thought struck Emily, allowing her a brief smile. "I'll pass that on to Commander Raiz. He says making things easier on us space travelers is his job, so he should take care of it."

For the first time since their meeting in her ready room, Kaz spoke up. "Well, he needs something to do. He has too much time on his hands."

Caught off guard, Emily could only say, "What?"

"He cooks up this whole Welder thing for us, and from the way he was talking to Welder, it's part of some sort of plan of his. Too much time on his hands."

"Umm . . . okay," Emily said, stunned by Kaz's directness. Usually the master of subtle hints, stating things coarsely and clumsily was out of his character, unless there was something buried in the statement that she could not see. In any case, Kaz quickly returned to monitoring his station, aware of how odd his words sounded to the others. For the sake of Liam and Brian, who sensed some unseen tension and didn't know how to take it, Emily shook her head, looked up at the ceiling, and sighed. Hopefully, this trio of signs would indicate that she dismissed Kaz's comments as fruitless. It worked, and the other two turned back to their own business.

Awaiting the jump to Eldrand, she went to her ready room, to its full stock of pens and legal pads, with a compulsion to doodle. Her artistic talent was completely unrefined, but it was there if she ever felt an urge to put it to use. For now, sketching random cartoonish figures was a form of stress release, though she had never thought of it that way. She had spent hundreds of long hours in classrooms doing nothing else. Should have kept all those scraps of paper – if she became famous, she could sell them for some serious spare cash.

She wouldn't get famous if she kept herself adrift, without a direction of her own choosing. She had to take charge of where she was going, which was a hard chore when the universe was doing such a good job of choosing her way for her. It was depressing. The image of starship command shining through her grandfather's stories had been fast-paced and full of action. Not this. This was worse than school, because she had no one else to blame for either her boredom or gloomy thoughts. She was free, and on a road trip that most twenty-somethings – most humans, even – could only dream of. If only her grandfather had left her a small ship, something with a super-smart computer that she could fly on her own, that would have been real freedom. Except . . . she would have to find someway to buy fuel, and the ship would lack the cargo space to take normal trading jobs. Problems, problems –

"Jump point approaching," Brian called from the bridge. Rising from the desk, she glanced at the blank notepad sheet for a moment, and then went out. Somehow, she had spent hours pondering aimlessly, and after spending a few minutes of her time to see the transition into hyperspace, a formality more than a necessity, she anticipated a few more hours of blankness. As she stepped out of her ready room, Jessica Scott poked her head out of the signal room and said, "Captain, an Asparian ship has been following us out from Newport Station. It looks like it's breaking off, now that it can tell our hyperspace vector is aimed at Epsilon Eridani. Just thought you should know."

"Thanks, Jessica. Good work," Emily said, with hollowness to her voice. No surprises.

The entrance into hyperspace happened with its usual deceptive casualness. Emily was about to call the hyperspace crew to the bridge when Liam interrupted her. "Captain, Mr. Welder's asking to speak to you. He wanted to catch you before you went to sleep."

"Nice of him," she said, her three previous passengers coming to mind. "All right, tell him to meet me in the rec room." Then she looked at Kaz. "You might want to come along."

Kaz nodded, stone-faced. Time seemed to crawl as they marched to the recreation room at the front of the ship's right fuselage, and Emily let out a breath when they finally reached the sliding door of their destination.

The rec room was directly across from the bridge, which was at the front of the left fuselage, separated from it by space, and connected to it by the cross-corridor that ran between the ship's forward and reverse engines. All the essentials of running the ship, including the crew quarters, were in the bridge's body. Behind the rec room was the moneymaking area of the ship, including the visitor's quarters and the cargo hold. It was an odd design by Earth's standards, but very Eldrandii, with their sharp distinctions between different areas of life. One of them would have identified the left body as 'active' and the right as 'passive', but Emily rarely felt active in either one, but at least the logic was straightforward and easy to understand. Not everything about the Eldrandii was.

The view of space from the rec room was complementary to that of the bridge, so that combining the two gave a full forward field of view. The room was the ship's restaurant and general mess, though the crewmembers usually just picked up their food and ate elsewhere, so that the arrangement of the place was more suited to enjoyment than a quick meal. A nominal cook prepared food for the crew when it suited him, but his meals were no more than reheated rations. If he didn't double as a janitor for the place, operating under the auspices of the interior repair crew, his contributions to the crew would have been questionable. His qualifications mainly rested with his ability to pick out from the rations foods palatable by nonhuman passengers, a skill no one else on board had. With teams losing basketball games, though, the crew occasionally treated itself to something different. Unfortunately, even the best talents could do little with the limited resources on board.

The crew added means of recreation to the room haph*azar*dly. Its only fixture was the pool table, cloaked in an aura of steady dignity in a corner lit only by a dim chandelier. The crew sprinkled dartboards, chess sets, and poker sets around the room. And that was it – the rec room in all its glory. The main attraction was the panoramic view of space, anyway. Anyone easily bored by that view was unsuited for space travel.

Welder was already seated at a table with a board game on it – one that Emily didn't recognize. He was alone, and was examining a position he had laid out on the board. Kaz started for a moment, and then looked on interestedly. It didn't take Emily many brain cells to guess that this was Kaz's board, and that he spent some of his time pondering over it just like Welder was doing. If the great ambassador wasn't careful, he might become Kaz's all-time hero. A dubious distinction.

The two newcomers sat at the table, and Welder tore his eyes away from his board analysis. He fixed Emily with learned eyes and growled without prologue, "All right. What's it all about? What's Raiz's game?" Insatiable curiosity had once again won against an otherwise reasonable mind. Emily supposed that a famous space traveler like Welder must have a formidable inquisitiveness unimaginable by those who lived their working lives behind desks in cubicle offices.

For Emily's part, she doubted she wanted to tell Welder everything, or anything. She trusted Raiz, as bad an idea as that might be, but Welder could do little except take credit for the discovery, whether he wanted to or not. Agreeing to see him, she had known exactly why he had asked to meet her, and would try to satisfy his curiosity. She just had to be careful about what she chose to divulge.

"I'll tell you – but only if we're clear that you're not involved unless I say you're involved. This is my break, and you're just a passenger we're taking to Eldrand. If I tell you anything, it's just 'cause you asked nicely and I didn't see any problem with it. Okay?"

Welder smiled grimly. "You don't want some money out of me, then? Raiz told you to get something from me before telling me anything, didn't he?"

"He didn't tell me, he suggested, and I don't have to take his suggestions. I can't say you weren't any part of this if you pay me to hear about it. Get it?"

"Yes, Captain, I understand. I just happened to be a passenger on your ship. Go on."

Emily breathed out, gave a quick glance to Kaz, who looked noncommittal, then plunged ahead. She told Welder everything from her conversation with Raiz – no more and no less. As the details poured out, Welder's jaw became set in grim satisfaction, providing half a smile while the rest of his face refused to follow suit. His tired eyes looked right past her, visualizing what she was saying, only glancing directly at her to gauge what she was thinking. He wanted to know whether she would be acting on the information or not, but since she was indecisive about that, there was no way he could read her plans from her face. That bitter smile, though, suggested that he did have an idea about her future that she had yet to decipher. She bristled at this, but finished her explanation without commenting, keeping her apprehension in check until it had something solid to chew on. Once she was done with her story, she turned the tables on him. "So, why do you think Raiz wanted me to tell you? I guess you'll have some advice or something."

Welder scratched his head and said, "I could tell you plenty, but it would all depend on the situation. I have always preferred a minimalist approach, no matter what. Don't try to land your ship – that will cause too much of a stir. Take a landing pod down to somewhere out of the way. Make sure it's an Asparian area, and not occupied by any of the other species, because you'll have a better chance of blending in. Your skin will be paler than the normal Asparian yellow, but at least you'll be the right shape. Take weapons, but don't hesitate to give them up when you meet with the authorities. Oh, and expect to spend some time in some sort of prison."

"Prison?" Kaz repeated, suddenly deciding that, as first officer, he should stay with the ship in case things went badly. There was no firm regulation or standard to that effect, since most ships got into far less trouble than they seemed to, but this was as good a time as any to introduce one.

"A normal reaction if they think you're a spy from somewhere, or a criminal escaping the authorities in a foreign nation, which happens more often than you think. Don't walk in if you're not ready for the worst."

"Is that it?" Emily said. She could have come up with the same advice without too much thought, and at least two of her recent dreams had been worst case scenario planet landings, complete with quicksand, fierce jungle creatures, imprisonment, torture, and people speaking in painfully stereotypical German or Russian accents. Too many old movies. "I can imagine worse than prison," she said with absolute conviction, "and you should hear some of the stuff we've been through already. If people think we're spies, that's at least something you could figure out might happen. We're more used to the kind of thing no one expects."

Welder nodded knowingly, with somewhat more satisfaction. He respected confidence and experience because he had both qualities in volume. "There might be someone on Eldrand I could direct you to. Someone who will want to come with you, I'm sure, but I'll leave that up to you. She's a doctor who specializes in disease development on isolated worlds. She's been to many worlds lacking hyperspace technology, so she'll have dealt with everything. I'm more of a big central government type – she's better with the fragmented, decentralized societies." Sensing that he might lose the captain if he continued in this vein, he stopped short.

Emily shrugged noncommittally. "I'll meet her and we'll see. Is she famous?"

"Only in medical circles."

On firmer ground now, Kaz said, "it might be a good idea to bring her along, then. Diseases jump easily from Asparii to humans, and this planet's bound to have things we're not inoculated against. We've got one medical technician on board the *Azar*, and she'll need to stay with the ship. Not to mention, she's more suited to first aid and paramedical care than disease research."

"I'm not going to say anything until I meet your doctor, Welder," Emily said firmly. "We've had our fill of crazy people already. I'm not ready to add a mad doctor to the list."

Hyperspace was blessedly uneventful, and since the Asparian ship had broken off before they jumped, not as tense as it could have been. As far as Emily knew, being tailed in space was supposed to be unusual, if not unheard of, but her ship had a recent history of attracting unwanted attention. This was the second time in four tries that a ship, however briefly, had been following them. It was unnerving to be so popular, especially since space didn't allow you to take a sharp turn around a corner to throw off the stalkers.

Even without the tension, it was another rough night in hyperspace for Emily. This time, she was plagued by dreams instead of people constantly waking her up. Her midnight visions were becoming almost as taxing as life itself. They were clearly more than the dreams everyone else got, but that didn't mean they were useful. As with all prophetic visions, their meaning would remain ciphered until it was probably too late to do anything.

A precious few images seemed to be from Eldrand – a planet she had so far only heard about. Cone-shaped houses dotted the icy landscape like pimples as her landing pod passed over. Five Eldrandii were perched high above the floor, where she and Welder stood, and their gaze was menacing. A hawk-eyed Eldrandii with vibrantly colored blue plumage and unusually loose clothes of iridescent neons, was lecturing her on the underestimated value of diversifying plant life. An Eldrandii lay on the floor of a room, but there were no marks on it, so that it was impossible to tell if it was dead or just knocked out. The body faded into the floor like a chameleon.

Plenty of unrecognizable images filled her mind, as well. Maybe they were just random dreams, so she generally ignored them, even though she could remember each one clearly. She had seen two men shaking hands on a stage who were suddenly startled by a scream from the crowd watching them. An elevator with glass walls plunged down a tube through a deep darkness which almost made the transparent cylinder pointless. She flipped through the pages of a book with unrecognizable writing when she suddenly encountered a vivid image of a whole city exploding. It had been amazing for a book plate – providing delicate details to the architecture underneath the fire and debris being thrown up.

Emily felt no more rested when the hyperspace wake-up call chimed than when she had first set her head down. Briefly, she considered letting Kaz take the ship down to Eldrand, but nothing about the night so far gave her hope for the hours to follow if she chose to sleep some more. Left with no recourse, she dressed and zombied up to the bridge. The hyperspace crew was still there, playing cards on the deck floor. Monitoring data filled the main viewscreen, allowing the crew to keep tabs on their business without actually being at their stations. She felt comfortable with the atmosphere maintained by the hyperspace crew, but knew she was intruding on it. They immediately paused the card game on her approach, and she could almost have cursed at them for the looks they gave her.

Not wanting to break it up completely, she said, "just stopping by to see how things were going." After they assured her that everything was running normal, she walked straight out and made her way to the rec room.

She must have set her wake-up call too early, because a third of the crew was still enjoying breakfast in the rec room. She usually ate at odd times, and had never seen the place so occupied. A group of five around the table at the center of the room were closing up some practical ship-talk, and moving on to news they had heard during their week on Newport Station. A few others were scattered around the room on their own. No one paid much attention to her arrival, so she tried to avoid the large cluster in the fear that she would throw ice onto the proceedings. Kaz was easy to spot, alone at his gaming table and tucked safely away from the vibrant, noisy tables. She grabbed some coffee and joined him.

"You look like hell," he said, placing a black piece on the board.

"Feel like hell," she admitted as she took the opposite seat, "but at least I'm not playing a game by myself. It's supposed to be between two people, right?"

"That's why there are black and white pieces, yes," he said caustically. "But it's not a game you can stay good at without practice, and there isn't anyone on board who plays. I've checked."

"Except Welder."

As usual, Kaz took the opportunity to change the subject to more important matters. "What do you think about all of this. We're being tailed again. I've been on ships for years, and haven't heard of it happening once. Didn't even know the signals officer existed, really."

"Maybe you didn't have one, then. I know it isn't normal, you don't need to tell me, but it happened to my grandfather a few times, if I remember his stories right, so maybe we're in the middle of something to tell our grandchildren about."

"I'd pass on that. We're signed on as traders, not adventurers or explorers. This is looking like more than we can handle."

"So, if I decide we should go to this Selparis, you'll bail on me?"

That made Kaz uncomfortable, as Emily had intended. He stayed silent too long for a vehement "of course, not," so Emily continued. "What if I got solid money for it? What if someone like Welder hired us to do it?"

"Well, put that way, I guess I'd go along with it, no argument," Kaz said, thankful for an honorable way out.

There it was – Emily's challenge to the powers that be. She had been pushed on this road for a while, and it was time for her to start making her own conditions. Money up front. Let's see if the universe'll pay up.

"Still, Captain," Kaz went on, "we're already a step behind. I know we're not up against mancers – if we were, I'd be off this ship in a second – but magic is magic."

"If they're tailing us, maybe they're afraid of us."

Kaz didn't even have to respond this time. His stare was enough.

"All right. I still want to hear what Welder's Eldrandii has to say before I decide anything."

"There's absolutely nothing an Eldrandii researcher can do to help us. Don't kid yourself, Captain."

In a deliberately quiet voice, she said, "You'll do it if we're paid, right?"

"Yes, yes, but –" Kaz said, taken aback and deciding to hold his tongue. She was right, of course. He had said no argument, and only seconds later was stating objections, going back on his word. Flashing a weak smile, he said, "all right, fine. But Captain, it hasn't exactly been boring around here, you know. We don't really need more excitement."

She returned the smile. "Yeah, but this is the sort of thing I imagined doing when I got this ship. Wasn't it what you pictured doing when you became a captain? Don't tell me you've worked this hard just to do a bunch of trade runs, then retire."

Kaz nodded. "You're right. Been a while since I've remembered those old dreams, but they're still there. And there's a part of me that wants to do it even though I'd like better odds. But not everyone in the crew thinks like that – most of them really are in it for the money. They're mercenaries, Captain, and they signed up to get rich."

"I'm not expecting them to do anything. It'll be just me, Ethan, and a couple of others down on the planet, and they'll be the type that have dreams. We're just taking a look around, finding the authorities, and trying to see what they'd like to trade for. I'm not fighting any mages or getting tangled in any weird conspiracies, even if I decide we're going." Her brain was suddenly kicking into gear, probably fueled by the coffee. "We'll plan everything out before we go there, if we go there. I'll give you my contact list, and maybe you can find some jobs while I'm down there. You could talk to Raiz. I'll call you when we're ready to get back on board."

"You'd . . . let me take on jobs without you?"

It did sound amazing when put like that, but Emily had to concede that Kaz was reliable. Stinging comments aside, he had been trustworthy. "Sure. You'll be acting captain and everything. You'd get a bonus, of course, 'cause we wouldn't want to give you the extra work without paying you for it."

Kaz waved the whole question of pay away. "I couldn't. I wouldn't feel right about going off while you're down there."

"You'd have to, just to fuel up."

"But that's different. Taking on work without the captain would send the wrong message to the crew," Kaz said, hopelessly.

"I don't think so. My grandfather did it all the time, and his first officer used to come over for dinner to talk about old times. He ended up with his own ship," Emily said pointedly, leaving out that the first officer only became a captain in his own right a few months before her grandfather died.

"Yes, I know," Kaz said testily, annoyed at being given such an obvious counterexample. "Captain Ramiano's been a friend of Wilson's for as long as I've been in space. Listen, does this mean you intend to go whether we get paid for it or not? That my doing jobs while you're on Selparis will make up the difference?"

"No," Emily said, in a firm tone that was directed more at the universe than at Kaz. She wanted to make sure her conditions were clear. "We don't go unless we get money up front. The jobs you do will be extra."

Kaz calmed himself and nodded, checking his watch. "We're almost out of hyperspace. Time to get back to the bridge." Indeed, the rec room was almost empty now, as the crew went back to their stations to keep eyes on the instrumentation as they returned to normal space.

"Let's get this bit over with, then. Might have time for another basketball game on the way in. What do you think?"

The quick grimace on Kaz's face was filled with the discomfort he had felt while being watched during the last match. Emily reflected with amusement at Kaz's predictability. "Only if you're playing."

Emily leaned back and smiled broadly. "Maybe I will. Can't do worse than you, can I?"

The surface of Eldrand was exactly as she had dreamt it. As the landing pod skimmed over the pokey white surface, she could see the cone-shaped homes occasionally broken up by larger pyramid-like structures. A few instances of architectural creativity could be spotted, but on the whole it looked like an entire city composed of Native American teepees.

As much as Plani was known for its grey, Eldrand was blanketed in white. Ethan had taken the opportunity to warn Emily about the murderous winter of Eldrand, especially in the far south where they would be landing, so she was bundled up with layers of thermals, tee shirts, a hoodie, and a trenchcoat. Stepping out of the pod's hatchway after the landing, her face was brutally assaulted by the wind chill. Her gloved hands were all right, but the attack on her face was painful. She turned her back to the wind and looked on as her passengers wrapped scarves around everything but their eyes, covering mouthpiece of their translators while adjusting the speaker/receiver so that it remained out in the frosty air. Welder was actually putting some sort of eye drops to protect his eyes as well, and passed the tiny bottle to his wife so she could do the same.

The Eldrandii hated the weather of their home planet, and they made it known to other species that they once had a different, more temperate home, and that a disaster on their planet of origin had necessitated their mass departure. Spiritually tied to their sun, named Epsilon Eridani on human star maps, they had chosen to settle again within the same system, on the planet closest to their original world's temperature. This was far from a perfect match, and the new home world had remained sparsely populated for thousands of years while the species colonized more enticing worlds, only visiting their home as a form of pilgrimage.

As a planet of ritual significance, though, Eldrand had always been kept sacrosanct and dearly protected. In a clear bid to discourage intrusive visitors, the port of entry to the planet was located in its southern-most city, called Vananora locally, a place even less hospitable than the equatorial and tropical regions of the world. In the winter season, the port was practically empty. A few guards were walking slowly with their wings furled tightly around their bodies, bulky under the tight cloaks covering every inch of their surface. Their hoods and masks gave them a vaguely ninja-like look, but with their weak legs, they walked awkwardly, breaking the resemblance. They would have liked to fly instead, and to give their wings a bit of a stretch, but that would have only given the winter more opportunity to gnaw at them. Since they were guarding this port, they were undoubtedly among the best guards on this world, which just went to show that being exceptional was rarely rewarded as expected. Still, they weren't the types to sit in a comfortable room in front of monitors, and took their duties seriously as they went around the complex on patrol.

Emily was no longer sure whether she wanted to stick around on this planet to meet Welder's friend. The weather conditions aside, her dreams had been right about the planet so far, and that meant Welder and her would soon be facing a bunch of mean, hawk-like Eldrandii, and somewhere along the way, there would be an unconscious or dead Eldrandii lying on the floor. Maybe it was time to take some hints from her dreams. Then again, maybe the blue-plumed Eldrandii she had seen was Welder's friend, so at least the meeting would happen. That assumed her dreams were visions of what was really going to happen, instead of what could happen.

She couldn't pass this opportunity up, though. The Eldrandii had no love for the Asparii, and would be more likely than any other party to investigate rumors of rogue Asparii mages. Humans reconciled themselves with the dispersed people of Asparis after the war, but it had been easier for Earth to curtail ill feelings because it had escaped the relentless threat that the dread planet had posed to the rest of the ISC. At least, it had not faced the eons of hostility that could condition a species to viscerally oppose the existence of another. On this occasion, it might be good to have the more critical point of view along for the ride.

As far as she could tell, humans couldn't appreciate the fear every other species had for the Asparii. The similarity in physical appearance must have been a part of that, as did the long history of atrocities humans had perpetrated on each other. More importantly, though, humans had gotten involved at the very end of a long struggle, facing only one defeat before being a part of the ultimate victory. Earth came out of the Asparis confrontation stronger, finally joining the ranks of interstellar species, so it had been a good fight. The Asparii were a defeated people, and nothing to worry about. Sure, the mancers and their godlike magic were spooky, but they were all gone now, and only the underclass mundanes that they once oppressed remained, refugees scattered around the ISC and the nearby galaxy. It was tough to take them seriously after that.

"Welcome to Vananortaris," Marcus Welder said in a voice muffled by his scarf, using the official ISC name for the city. His tone came through, and he was obviously irritated by the lack of a reception, or at least someone to welcome them. "We can take the automated train to where we're going. At least it will be warm."

They wasted no time getting out of the cold. The guards didn't hassle them – they had been properly cleared. Considering the weather, it came as no surprise to Emily that no one wanted to brave the chill to greet them, but Welder was important, and had absolutely expected someone to be there. After all, if he had to be out in the cold, his hosts should be willing to do the same. Anyone who wanted to meet them would have had plenty of warning, just by checking the port's arrival schedule, so no excuse there. Bizarre.

Vananora's accommodations were designed to suit the variety of species that could be expected to pass through Eldrand's only entry port. Everything was roomy, to avoid cramping the larger species. The automated train had enormous cars – twenty feet tall, just as wide, and each car was at least a hundred feet long. There were no seats, but for the Eldrandii residents, perches were placed about eight feet up the car's walls – high enough that most species would not bump into them. Being careful, an Eldrandii could fly through the car without trouble.

Not so warm that they would feel hot under their bundles of clothing, the train kept them safe from the wind chill, and they shifted their scarves down to their necks as soon as they entered. With business still being conducted throughout the city despite the season, they were in good company in the massive vehicle. There were four Eldrandii perched in the heights, but about two dozen members of other species in all shapes and sizes. Most were Plani. Emily's eyes were drawn to the Gol. It was gigantic, easily sixteen feet tall, and made full use of the extra headroom. In an almost comical way, the Gol was trying to be inconspicuous, standing in one of the car's corners flush against the wall, looking at the front wall of the car, which was right next to him. Emily couldn't be sure, but she thought it looked embarrassed. It did sort of stand out, didn't it?

The Gols were accustomed to a different atmosphere on their home planet, and this one was wearing a face mask connected to a tank on its back, much more cumbersome than the smaller systems she would have to use on some planets. Humans were lucky, sharing a similar home atmosphere with the ISC's most powerful species – the Eldrandii, Plani, and Asparii. Ina Cur also had an Earth-like atmosphere, but other systems had wildly variant air compositions. The Gol's size and atmospheric problems aside, it had a typical bipedal form, and two arms. With gray, rugged skin, and painfully slow movements, there was something rock-like about the being. Ethan had mentioned them to her after learning about them, long before she had contemplated space travel. The Gol were supposed to be excellent technicians, construction workers, and philosophers. A lot of them had adopted Eldrandii spiritual practices, and they were generally reverential to the Eldrandii. That was probably why this one was here. They were otherwise rarely seen off their homeworld of Delaur.

Emily knew less about the other species represented by the train's passengers, and gave them little thought, anyway. You saw them all in the Plani spaceports, as well. They were the normal sights of the universal zoo, and expected background presences wherever you happened to go. Though it did remind her vaguely of an elephant, Emily had trouble relegating the Gol to the background of the picture, and even more difficulty imagining a world full of them, slowly lumbering around. The buildings they built must be enormous. She wondered how much they ate in a meal, and decided there couldn't be many Gols on Delaur, simply because food production would be limiting. Or maybe everything on Delaur was supersized. She had never been there – maybe it was a big planet overall. That wasn't right, though, since a big planet would have too much gravity to allow the Gol to move at all. You couldn't just increase the size of everything, and expect it to work the same.

Her curiosity about the Gol held her until they reached their destination. Back in the bitter cold, they walked a short way and found themselves in front of a cylindrical building. Its structure already announced it as a haven for off-worlders, and the scrolling multilingual sign over the doorway confirmed it. Unfortunately, none of the forms of writing was English, so Emily had no idea what she was walking into. Welder was in no mood to explain anything, so she just followed silently. Welder's wife and two assistants seemed worried as well, so it was a thoroughly guarded party that entered the building.

The massive doors of the building slid open as they approached and shut as soon as they were in, as if defying the winter to sneak in. The atrium was as colorful as the outside world was white, reminding Emily of a peacock's plumage. Everything had symmetry built into it – from the twin staircases in front leading up to the lobby, to the tiling of the floor, you almost expected your own twin to be standing next to you. A mirror down the middle would have betrayed no difference. It was striking because the decorators hadn't used solid colors, and instead employed intricate mosaics dizzying to look at. As Welder took off his scarf again, Emily could see the scowl on his face. She felt exactly that way about the décor, but guessed that Welder was once again reacting to the lack of people, or anything living, around to meet them. The atrium, and from the sound of it, the lobby as well, was empty except for themselves.

"This is not good," he said bluntly, "We're supposed to have a meeting in the conference room a few floors up. The person I wanted you to meet would have been there, Captain."

"So . . . shouldn't we go to the conference room . . . ," she tried.

"There should be people here, at least security. Something has happened. It might be best if you return to your ship, Captain."

Emily looked at her four companions, all in the twilight of their lives, and said, "I think I'll stick around until I'm sure you're all right. Want to make sure I get all those other jobs you promised me."

Welder's wife was trying to choose between worry and annoyance. "Marcus, don't turn this into one of your mysteries. Maybe it was rescheduled. Maybe they got the date wrong."

"Eldrandii don't reschedule unless a disaster's taken place, and they couldn't get the date wrong if they tried. Marvelous sense of time, but really bad at reacting to trouble. They always overreact. Always."

They stood in the atrium for a hew moments as Welder thought things over. Occasionally, he would glance at Emily, trying to indicate that she had a separate decision to make, but as far as she was concerned, she had a reason to be here and wouldn't turn back until she saw it through. She had made her choice.

"Empty," Welder repeated through gritted teeth, then led the way up the left stairway to the lobby. This heart of the building's business was a bit more conservatively decorated. Halfway up the stairways, the colors became dominated by the reds, and that was the color of choice in the lobby. The specificity of the selection still allowed for intricate patterns – Emily had never realized how many shades of red there were. The general impression was stately, and maybe a little regal as the shades neared the purple end. The lobby was an open space stretching for the entire breadth of the building, and the cylindrical walls were obvious. A pair of stairs, built for human-sized beings, curved up the wall from the huge space. For the larger patrons, elevators were concealed by the pattern on the walls, but could still be spotted by their outlines. The front desk, opposite the stairs they had just ascended, was unoccupied. In sheer size, the lobby was built for the same purpose as the trains – to accommodate all species – but this made its emptiness only the starker. Emily had heard of ghost towns only once, during Halloween, and the memory was forcibly brought back from the bowels of her mind by this sight.

Welder's wife was shaken. "What could have happened, Mark? Why is it like this?"

Before Welder could answer with another ominous comment, Emily heard the softest echo of talking – so soft she couldn't make out words and her translator wasn't picking it up. She held up her hand to indicate that no one should talk. None of the others seemed to have heard it, so it was up to her to locate it. Slowly walking about, she decided it must be coming from the left wall of the lobby, where she could barely make out a pair of twenty foot tall doors camouflaged by the pattern of the wall.

"There." She pointed. "Someone's talking behind there."

Welder wasted no time, and marched toward the indicated door. "That's the way to the conference room. Looks like we'll get some answers after all." As he strode, the harsh etches in his face softened, and he composed himself in preparation for some diplomacy. When he looked back to his wife, it was with a comforting smile. She smiled back, though weakly. Through the door, a massive stairway curved up and back over the lobby. In the concealed stairway, they could clearly hear someone shouting, loudest at the top where a single set of doors matching those from the lobby stood.

"Remember," Welder whispered to them, "the Eldrandii overreact to problems. They don't know how to handle them. Don't draw any attention to yourself. I'll do all the talking." Then he opened the door.

They didn't get very far into the room when they entered. It looked packed, but the real obstacles were the guards at the door who barred their way. An Eldrandii on the dais was lecturing the throng with a harsh, high pitched voice, the voice heard through the door. The anger and impatience in it was unmistakable, and very similar to the caw of a kicked crow, Emily knew from experience. She made the barest sense of what the translator was giving her – snippets about cooperating with the authorities and unholy actions. Most of the beings gathered – well over a hundred – were here against their will. Her first thought was that she had walked into a hostage situation, and was now trapped in it. The continuing flow of words from the Eldrandii in charge didn't support that, though, and neither was the way members of the crowd occasionally shouted back at him, as if they were hassled more than they were afraid. And the Eldrandii on the dais responded to them with words like "we have the situation under control." Maybe the translator wasn't getting these words right, but on reflection she couldn't really imagine a bunch of Eldrandii going nuts and taking hostages.

The guards didn't let them move, but also didn't disturb their leader's announcement. They were suited up in tight, form-fitted, slightly padded uniforms. Their wings were folded behind them, but out in the open, free to spread if necessary. Long faces professionally neutral, only their gaudy skin color defied expectations. Eldrandii spirituality held that an individual's work was the essence of his or her life, so that the species took its work very seriously and did everything pedantically, with the Dunorii sect, to which A'anfu En belonged, being the exception. These guards were orthodox Eldrandii.

Eventually, their leader's eyes moved to the gathering near the door, and his words came through the translator loud and clear. "Who in the worlds are you?"

Having had a minute to survey the situation, Welder proceeded confidently. "I am Marcus Welder, known by your government as the troubleshooter. I was scheduled to meet with the Universal Compendium editorial council in this room today. I have just arrived with my wife, two aids, and the captain of the ship which brought me."

"We will not be needing your help in this matter, Troubleshooter. We have this situation under control."

"Forgive me, but what is the situation? It looks like everyone in the hotel is in this room, my fellow council members included. Please tell me what has happened."

"You have just arrived," the Eldrandii on the stage started to say, but then changed direction in mid-sentence. "But that could be the best excuse. You and your companions will have to be questioned as well. Let them in."

Out of the crowd, an Eldrandii voice shouted, "there has been a murder, Welder. First in two years."

"Silence!" came the warning cry from the stage. "I have introduced myself to the others, Troubleshooter, so I will do the courtesy to your party. I am Ja'ani Orenis, captain of security in this city. I expect everyone's full cooperation."

Welder's exasperated glance back at Emily said it all. The galaxy's worst adaptability record was at work again. Earthlings, though civilized for a fraction of the time, had social structures designed to weather massive disasters. Those same structures on Eldrand somehow managed to make the disasters worse, employing the social equivalent of amputation to solve even the most minor disease or difficulty. Of course, it was this same propensity for lashing out unexpectedly that had allowed them to survive in their longtime rivalry with Asparis. Unpredictability was an asset in war. In a murder case, though, they would likely arrest everyone who had the remotest chance of being involved. There was no death penalty on Eldrand, and no prisons. The punishment of choice was exile to a planet with even worse weather.

This conference room was filled with all sorts of creatures, though, and rough treatment of them would get the sort of unwelcome diplomatic attention that even Eldrand couldn't manage. If Welder was the Earth representative, some of these people had to be important on their own worlds. There weren't any striking figures – no Gol or Karisi – but everyone was richly adorned in accordance with their particular cultures, signifying an expectation of respect. Even deporting this bunch could touch a nerve. Orenis' eyes were mostly on the Eldrandii VIPs, who made up a quarter of the room's population, and could take a more direct role in making his life uncomfortable, if he chose to inconvenience them. They had stood silent but conspicuous in robes that matched their plumage colors. None of them had shouted at the stage. The Eldrandii who had shouted at Welder was in blue. Emily couldn't tell for certain from a distance, but she would have bet that it was the same Eldrandii as the one from her dream – the one she was supposed to meet, and who would tell her about diversifying plants.

Orenis, whose orange and red plumage clashed horribly with a sickly green uniform, clearly lacked a firm grip on things, reinforcing his own inadequacy every time he professed to have everything under control. His instincts were to go blitzkrieg on the place, and haul in all the occupants. Then he would question them, and arrest anyone they named in the interrogation. With any luck, someone would be the killer. He was chosen as captain for this city's security because he showed greater restraint than his colleagues. Some days, though, it got tough. Whatever respect the people in this hall deserved, he had a good, honest policeman's distrust of power and the powerful, and he really didn't like the way this bunch thought they were entitled to shout their complaints to him. He would have taken delight in frustrating their smug sense of superiority, at least for a little while, if he wasn't so worried about having no clue about the murder.

He was a natural conspiracy theorist. A dignitary had been murdered, and it didn't take any stretch of the imagination to see an assassination and accompanying plot. Plani businesses had been known to arrange such assassinations as part of a competitive strategy. Could the victim have had dealings with the Plani? Could other species, Eldrandii included, have started to adopt Plani strategies? What about these younger species. He knew little about the Earthlings, except for the fierce in-fighting they continually engaged in. They didn't look physically strong, so maybe they were prone to underhanded tactics. He tilted his head to dismiss the thought. He didn't even know the deceased's background, awaiting records from the office that were still on the way. Cause of death still had to be determined, and the psychic on the job wasn't offering even a hint. He had nothing to go on.

Welder made his way through the crowd, which could only stand in wait for Orenis' next pronouncement. The wily veteran negotiator knew a stumped peace officer when he saw one, and knew how to offer help without transgressing cultural conventions. Emily tailed him, hoping desperately that her near future was free of legal trouble. She was in Welder's hands, now.

On the way to the front, Welder approached the blue-plumed Eldrandii and exchanged silent greetings. In halting English, the Eldrandii whispered, "I am glad that you are here. This . . . could be a mess." At that simple comment, Emily's respect for Welder's friend grew exponentially, and she was suddenly much more interested in their formal meeting. Too bad that would have to wait until the crisis at hand was straightened out.

Welder nodded, then continued forward. By now, Orenis had spotted him approaching and didn't look happy about it. "You are a suspect, Troubleshooter. I do not require any advice from you. Stay where you are."

The elderly ambassador stopped in his tracks, close enough so he could speak to, instead of shout at, Orenis. "Captain, there is a reason your people gave me my title. It is my calling to deal with the most difficult matters, just as it is yours to protect the people and investigate when the public peace is disrupted. Please be reasonable, and allow me to do what I am meant to do."

"In this case, you are directly involved, and must therefore recuse yourself."

"Captain, I –"

"Silence!"

Before Welder could try a new tact, a new Eldrandii guard entered the room, saluted, and said, "The investigative panel has been brought here at your request. They have been set up in the –" The last word didn't translate – some room that had no human equivalent.

"Good. Escort these humans there first. They entered after the incident," Orenis said, hesitatingly, stifling his more acute instincts, "so they are least likely to be involved in the murder."

"But it could be a conspiracy, sir," another guard pointed out.

"I know that," he snapped back, "and the panel will as well. Let the troubleshooter say what he has to say to them."

If he had been alone, and much younger, Welder would have objected and pressed the issue. This time, he went without a fuss, following the guard with the other humans in the room behind him.

They didn't have to go far. The panel was convened in a huge basement room that was either an Eldrandii-only conference room, or a gymnasium. It was almost as big as the hotel's lobby, and had more than enough space to allow and Eldrandii to fly laps around it. All around the room, there were perches set about seven feet above the ground, with every five placed in its own box, as if the place doubled as an opera theatre. The boxes were ornate, but in slight disrepair. The ground had a marble look, and also showed signs of use without maintenance – regular nicks and holes. Equipment was scattered around the room and along the walls, but for the life of her, Emily couldn't figure out what they were for. If this was a gymnasium, then they were exercise equipment, and the boxes were where the Eldrandii landed to cool down, rest a while, and socialize. If this was an interrogation room –

In one of the boxes, the five investigators were perched high above them, exactly as they had been in Emily's dream. The guard led the humans to a position close to the front of the box, so that they needed to look up at an extreme angle to see the five panelists, then took a few steps back, indicating that they should stay in their place.

"What are these?" the center panelist roared. A titanic sinking feeling swept over Emily.

The guard started to say, "Earthlings, sir, who . . . ," but Welder stepped back and interrupted him. "You know who I am. I have faced you before."

Exchanging looks of surprise, the five had not recognized him at first sight, but his voice was unmistakable to them. "You have changed, Troubleshooter. Are you . . . involved in this?"

"I was scheduled to meet with the Universal Compendium council here, your grace. By the time I arrived, though, Captain Orenis had already gathered everyone into the conference room. He sent us here first because we were least likely to have been involved."

"Please answer the question, Troubleshooter. You know our ways."

"Your grace, we are only involved by coincidence of being in this place at this time."

"Which could be considered enough reason to be suspicious."

"If that was the case, then Captain Orenis himself would be a suspect. He was here before us, after all. I am sorry, your grace, I do not mean to quibble, but you know how it is."

The chief investigator nodded. "Captain Orenis is well-restrained. I am surprised he did not want your help, though."

"He said that since I was involved –"

"Nonsense. Troubleshooter, you have helped us with our previous investigations to great effect. Forgive the captain for his rudeness. He is . . . new. I trust that after the fifteen years since we last saw you, your skills have not blunted. I know humans have short life spans, and that near the end of your life –"

"Still as sharp as ever, your grace."

"Very good. Guard, take the troubleshooter to the crime scene, then inform the captain that every consideration is to be given to him. Is there anything you will be needing, Marcus Welder?"

"I promised the captain here that I would introduce her to a friend of mine. If my friend could be released from custody, I would vouch for her."

The panel conversed quickly. Emily's translator picked out some of the babble, but nothing interesting. After a while, the chief investigator asked Welder, "Who is this friend? Of what species?"

"Eldrandii. Her name is Arisin Oris."

Another discussion ensued. "She is known to us. She will be freed," the verdict came. "However, this is on your honor, Troubleshooter."

"I understand."

The guard led them out, and up the elevator to one of the higher floors, one with a standard height ceiling, finally. Since the corridor allowed little room for wings to be spread, this level was probably not meant for Eldrandii. The door to the room was keycard-activated, and slid open when the guard used his security pass. At either side of the door, two guards waited to challenge anyone who wanted to enter, but clearly they were outranked by the newcomer, because they didn't say a word or make a move to challenge him. Inside, another Eldrandii was staring around the room, at a loss. This one was wearing a gauzy dress, revealing the curves and skin patterns of an Eldrandii female. She must have set her outdoor robes aside somewhere, because it was inconceivable that she could survive long in the cold wearing that dress. Emily didn't even realize Eldrandii were capable of it, but this one was visibly sweating. At their intrusion, she first looked panicked, as if not ready to confront a superior, then relaxed into anger.

"What are you doing here? Can't you see I am trying to divine what has occurred here? Your presence disturbs the memory of the room. Your own thoughts and memories will leak out."

"Any luck?" their escort asked in all seriousness.

"I need more time. My meditations are troubled by the scene. This is my first murder investigation. It is . . . unnerving. Now, please, let me be."

"By order of the investigative panel, this troubleshooter is to be allowed full access."

The crime scene investigator seemed to see the humans for the first time. "What are they? Look like Asparii to me. Should arrest them right away just for that. Aren't they suspects?"

"They are Earthlings," the escort said, exasperated, "not Asparii. Surely you remember the Earthlings – they destroyed Asparis. Listen, the panel said –"

"All right, all right," the investigator conceded, partially opening her wings in a stretch. "I need to refocus anyway. If you have any questions, Troubleshooter, now is the time to ask."

The escort, seeing that things were settled, left them to report to

Orenis.

"Well, I do have a few questions. Where's the body?"

The Eldrandii cringed. "In the bedroom. It is . . . messy . . . in there. And it is a bedroom, not a perch, since this room was designed for Plani . . . or you, I suppose. Please do not disturb anything, it will make this place depart further from the way it was, and divining the past will be harder."

"How long ago did the murder happen?"

"It happened right before sunrise."

"It's about noon right now. All right, let's see . . . has anything been removed from the scene?"

This time, the investigator looked shocked. Her plumage was standing tall. "Do you know nothing of our customs?"

"I know, I know. Unclean, right? That means no Eldrandii has come in contact with anything in there. What about others?"

"You are the first off-worlders in here since the murder. The body was found by an Eldrandii of the hotel's cleaning service. He is still trying to calm himself after the ordeal. He is, of course, the prime suspect."

"I'll have to question him. All right, let's look at the body."

They crossed the living room with the eyes of the investigator on them. The place was spotless, with nothing out of order, and had the bare amenities that a Plani would expect. Emily was unsure how prepared she was to look at a dead body, even though she technically already had seen it in her mind's eye. Everything to do with the parallels between her dreams and the unfolding reality was disturbing, and she had no idea how to take it. In a way, it was cool. Maybe she had a bit of magic in her, which was an enticing thought. But what if these weren't her own dreams, and instead the planted machinations of a true mage? After all she had been through, she doubted they were, but had to consider the possibility. She relieved her disquiet as they approached the bedroom by talking about something else.

"Umm . . . what's that Eldrandii doing anyway?"

"Meditating on the murder. That's how Eldrandii solve crimes. It's similar to the way some police agencies hire psychics except that here it's the regular way to investigate, and they're legitimate." Welder's voice held no disdain or judgment, making it clear that different species did things in different ways, and you just had to accept it. "The good thing is that they leave the scene untouched – even for theft and other crimes. The bad thing is, I'm not much of a forensic scientist. I know the basics, but I'm a politician. I solve problems by talking to people."

He made his best effort, though. The bedroom itself was no surprise to Emily, and the body on the floor looked as pristine as she had imagined. It still made her feel a bit sick in the stomach. Gesturing for them to stay near the doorway, Welder looked carefully at the floor before moving into the room. A real professional would have been more methodical, with all sorts of gadgets at hand, but the old ambassador always projected the concrete sense that he knew what he was doing. There were no obvious stains that Emily could see, so a blunt or bladed weapon was probably out of the question unless the perpetrator had some thorough cleaning method. Energy weapons could leave blood spatter, but not always, so that was still possible. Welder crouched down, examining the tiled floor with minute care. If there was even a hair – or maybe a fiber from a feather – he would spot it.

"Oh, Marcus," his wife suddenly said, her face a shade paler and draining fast. "The body . . . I've never seen –" Emily knew that the sight could have been much, much worse, but she could sympathize with Mrs. Welder. Lack of a mess aside, it was a sad scene.

"Hey, wait," Emily said, something finally clicking, "that psychic said the place was messy. What did she mean?"

"She was seeing it in her way," Welder answered. "I'm trying to figure out what she saw. David," he said to one of his assistants, "could you take my wife outside? She doesn't need to see this."

"No," his wife said abruptly, "I'll stay. If I want to leave, I don't need any help, Mark."

Emily had another thought. "Why would an Eldrandii be in a room designed for Plani, or a species like us?"

"I don't know what to make of it, but it's definitely something to look into," he affirmed, approaching the body with his measured crouch. Before looking at the corpse, he took another puzzled glance at the floor behind him. He found nothing, but there should have been some spot, or some debris, simply because the place was lived in. In this case, the lack of a clue was, itself, a clue. "I think I see what's so messy about this – at least in the mind of our meditating friend out there. Let's see what the dead has to say."

He released the clasps of the Eldrandii's robes, revealing its upper chest and wings. Though the signs were well-concealed and almost cosmetically covered, the body was not as pristine as the face and lack of blood suggested. Some fine feathers were missing from the wings. Hidden bruises pocked the chest under the soft layer of downy chest hairs.

"This had all been cleaned up, and that must have been done with magic. The murderer took time to beat up the victim before killing him, and there are still signs of penetrating wounds, so the main attacker did not use magic, but committed the murder with ordinary weapons. That gives us something to work from, but not much. The authorities can bring a mage in to check the conference room for other mages who might have done the clean-up, since they will be able to see the magic, and they will likely check the rest of the city while they are at it, but chances are that the actual murderer's long gone. Explains why the investigator said it was messy, though. She's trying to see what it was originally like, and trying to slip past whatever magical interference the accomplices set up. The murderer knew that there would be a psychic investigation, and his accomplices set up magical blocks to keep our friend out there from getting to the bottom of this. The clean up is something else, though. The low level magic used to clean up the place was just a curtain that a trained Eldrandii investigator will just move aside without thinking."

"Then why bother? Just for us?"

"Hmm," Welder stroked his chin, "Maybe. Or someone else who would actually take a look around, come in and try to figure things out." He didn't voice his final thought for the sake of his wife, but what if the murderer had known that Welder, the troubleshooter, was on his way to Vananora, and had to clean the place up, lest a more specific clue was left behind?

They left the room and found the investigator still standing, practically waiting for them to leave so she could really get back to contemplating the past.

"Do you mind answering a few more questions?" Welder asked

her, tone oozing with, and encouraging, patience.

"Yes, but if it will speed your leaving, ask them."

"Could you describe the room as you have seen it?"

The Eldrandii was poised to say something sarcastic, then realized why Welder asked the question. "Magic. It was a mage. I have been so stupid, so blind, I did not even notice. These are magical blocks, then? I have never faced them before. I cannot tell you how many illusions I have had to pierce through. It is hopeless."

"Not necessarily. Is there anything about the room, even the slightest detail, that you can be sure is real? Can you take a look at the room right now, see what it is like, and tell us what is missing?"

"That would only set me back. I am trying to go into the past. I do not care what it looks like now."

"Please. I know your goal is to see the murderer's face, but maybe in expending magic to conceal that detail, the mage failed to conceal other details from you, knowing what you would be focusing your efforts on."

The investigator was the picture of reluctance, but Welder was persuasive. Standing in the doorway, but staying carefully out of the room, she took some time. Letting the illusion of the present cloud her vision was a struggle. Finally, she said, "unbelievable. It really is all gone. That . . . you must understand that this place had blood everywhere. The body had open wounds –"

"What kind? What might the wounds have been caused by?"

"Slits. Like from a small knife. One anyone could get anywhere on this planet for ritual purposes."

"Anything else different?"

The investigator took a while, traveling back at the room as she had seen it, looking around this time instead of focusing on the killer. "Yes. Sheets on the floor. There was part of a star chart, a folded map, and what looked to be a printed report."

Emily and Welder looked at each other, sharing the same thought. Suddenly the ambassador was wide-eyed in surprise, but he didn't miss a beat. "And what did these look like? Do you know what coordinates were marked on the star chart?"

"Yes. Let me draw them out for you." She took a white opaque plastic sheet and a marker from a nearby table. "I did not study astronomy, so I do not know what it means. Do you think it is important?" She was definitely excited now. After hours of staring at mask after mask, this human had given her something else to look at.

"I think it was either information being traded between the murderer and victim, or some secret that the murderer didn't want the victim to spread. Either way, it's important, yes. Would any normal investigator be able to look at the chart in this detail? Since you're on this case, I assume your talents are . . . exceptional."

"No one else would be able to, no. Not that they would give it a look. I am the best, but today it has felt like a curse. Today has been a punishment for my presumption and arrogance. Still, there is no point adopting false modesty." She finished the chart and handed it to Welder. "I cannot be sure I caught the important details. Can you see where it was indicating?"

Welder handed it to Emily, translating some of the star names from Eldrandaiz to Earth nomenclature so she could orient it. She only had the vaguest idea of where stars were in relation to each other, but had stared at the information given to her by the Inana for quite some time. "That's it. That's the planet I was told about."

Not letting the puzzled psychic think too much about the comment, Welder asked, "could you reproduce the map? We might not know who did it, but we can find out what this murder was about, what the motive was, if we go to this planet."

"Only the visible portion, and even that is difficult because of the details. I can get the large features and lettering, but nothing is marked out or encircled on this side of the map, so the important side is likely facing the ground. Is it necessary?"

"Every little bit would be helpful."

Taking Welder's word for it, the investigator did her best on a new plastic sheet. Emily guessed that she was used to having to draw details for superiors – especially the faces of the criminals. The humans waited patiently for the result, but the map handed to Welder was clearly only a small portion of the planet.

Emily looked over his shoulder, unable to read the writing. Pointing out one territory's name, Welder translated, "Empire Atparis, which is Asparian for Empire of the New World. I think that's where you need to be headed, Captain." Then, to the investigator, he said, "I will tell

Captain Orenis what we suspect and he'll have a mage brought here to check everyone for magic. Make copies of both of these for him. Keep trying to see more of the murder. We'll leave you now, but I will return after I have taken care of business down below."

Wasting no time in leaving the scene of the crime, Emily's mind was racing. Her picture of events had the poor victim receiving some information about the mystery planet, then getting killed by an Asparian mage for it. By that reasoning, Emily herself was just as much of a target, and no match for a mage. Her geriatric companions were no comfort, and she wanted to leave this planet as soon as possible.

The way the body had been beaten up before the killing suggested that there had been something personal, though. Picturing the dead Eldrandii as an ally of the Asparian mage made no sense. Asparii didn't have a monopoly on magic, so the culprit could easily have been another Eldrandii, or one of a half dozen other known species. On the other had, strange planets made strange allies.

"It's . . . not worth it. I'm all for adventures, but these people have us beat," she finally said to Welder, hating herself for every word.

"I don't see that you have any other choice, Captain. But hold off on your decision until you've met Arisin Oris."

Emily sighed, and looked again at the map. What kind of place would this empire be? It didn't sound like a haven of freedom-loving peace. Of course, that didn't matter to her, if all she was doing was establishing trading ties with it. The empire was far from the lone territory on the map, which looked as populated with nations as a typical Earth continent. Directly below the empire, she saw a collection of nations dwarfed by the bulk of their northerly neighbor.

"What are these?" she asked as they approached the conference room.

Welder looked at the map and said, "they all have their own names, but there's a collective name for all of them. It translates to 'Independent Cities.'"

"Hmm." That sounded better. If that name meant that these cities had managed to stay separate from the empire, then those were the kind of people who would resist a plot to take them over.

Back in the crowded conference room, Orenis listened respectfully as Welder relayed everything he had noted in the victim's room, then released them as the panel had instructed. Arisin Oris ended a conversation with two other Eldrandii as soon as Welder caught her eye, and joined the troubleshooter and his team as they left the hall. Like most of her species, her face was unworn, so it was hard to tell her age. Her smile was a friendly greeting, but also hinted at some mischief. It was an unusual attitude for her to show when so many of her nearby brethren were serious and obsessive, especially given recent events. Oris had clearly benefited from her extensive contact with other species, because she saw some of the absurdities her own people exhibited. Freed from the potentially irrational clutches of the local peace officers, she was giddy and optimistic about how the rest of her day might go.

The warmth Oris projected gave Emily every reason to believe that they would get along fine, which was good, considering how much trouble she had borne through to make this meeting happen. They sat at a table on the side of the cavernous lobby. Like everything else at this level of the hotel, the tables and chairs came in various shapes and sizes to accommodate the spectrum of species that passed through. The humans grabbed what they considered normal seats, while Oris brought a stool to the table, which better accommodated her wings.

Saving Emily the trouble, Welder told Oris about the planet Selparis, and included their suspicions about the murder. The Eldrandii disease researcher took it all in placidly, as if she had come to expect this sort of thing from Welder. There was interest in her eyes, no doubt about that. She still had the thirst for planet-hopping that Welder had supposedly given up. After hearing all the details, Oris turned to Emily and said, "I hope you know I will want to come with you."

"I'm not even sure I want to go. It's already pretty dangerous."

"You must," Oris said gently. "If you want more ships or more personnel, I can arrange it. For this, I will use a few favors I am owed."

Curious, Emily asked, "how many ships and . . . personnel?"

Oris' plumage descended an inch as she thought over it. "For certain, four ships and three hundred armed Eldrandii. I would not suggest landing with such a force. It will draw a hostile response. But we can ready them."

Emily had no way to respond. That was quite an offer, and her image of Oris was substantially altered. The disease researcher was evidently a power broker, to wield that kind of influence. What kind of favors had Oris done to justify that kind of reciprocation? If she could manage that much, something less shouldn't be a problem –

"My crew would feel a lot better about this if they were definitely getting paid for it. Could you get some credits together so that my crew'll see the whole thing as worth it?"

Brows rising, Oris' face was amused. "Mercenaries?"

"No . . . businessmen. Just your normal traders."

"This will be a long adventure, I think. My own credits are tied in other . . . business, but I can get the government to supply a quarter million every five of our days, maybe more if we can tie this journey into the murder investigation. I have received five million credit grants for research journeys before, so I can give you eighty Eldrandii days of pay, if the amount is acceptable."

Stunned, especially since the universe had somehow contrived to fulfill the only condition she could think of in no more than a day, Emily said, "that's a lot of help you're saying you'll give. Why?"

Shrugging in a uniquely Eldrandii way – by stretching her wings out a bit, and rotating them back – Oris replied, "being able to examine members of ISC species who have been in isolation for hundreds of years or longer, and all the other life that must have adapted to that world, could be very important to my research. Of course, it will also be fun. The government will be easily convinced that this is important, so it will not be difficult to get the help I have promised. Can I go with you?"

"Y-yeah. 'Course. Thanks for the credits. We can hold off on the ships and troops, I think. Maybe you can have one on standby, just in case my ship needs to get away and we need to be picked up."

Oris nodded. "That sounds right. I will arrange it immediately. If you could arrange to stay here for a day?"

That gave Emily pause. True, she didn't want to head up to the ship, just to come back down here again tomorrow – fuel was money. Oris would need some time to get things organized and just one day was very little to ask for. On the other hand, this planet was freezing, the only hotel she knew about was in the middle of a murder mystery, and the murderer might be targeting her as well.

Sensing her concern, Oris said, "the entire Vananora police force will be here soon, if they are not all here already. They are not as incompetent as they look or act. You have been cleared, and the decisions of the panel are nearly absolute. You will be safe here."

Emily looked at Welder, who nodded. It was hard to put her trust in two individuals she barely knew, but it was cold outside, warm in here, and the longer she could put off a trip through the frosty wasteland, the better. She agreed, and made arrangements with the hotel staff – still detained in the conference room – and contacted the ship. The landing pod pilot decided to use a cot in the pod instead of heading for the hotel.

In a completely unexpected turn, that night passed without incidents or memorable dreams. By morning, the hotel was running on a skeletal staff cleared by the panel. Everyone else was given quarters in the city's guard house, herded over there with great care. A few of the guests had been cleared, including the Universal Compendium council that Welder was supposed to meet with, but the rest would face the normal treatment as the police tried to discover who the hypothetical mage was. The city's guard force had limited access to mages who could help in the search, and the world was full of magical phenomena that could confuse matters. It was much easier to interrogate someone who might know about the mages involved than to actually search for them.

Emily met Oris over a breakfast prepared by one of the hotel's apprentice cooks, temporarily promoted to head cook because she was the only one left. Since she had mostly specialized in seafood so far, and had been too busy to learn anything new properly, the menu was somewhat limited and inappropriate for breakfast. Not having a clue what any of it was anyway, Emily let Oris order for them both.

Wasting no time, Oris informed the captain that the money and backup ship had been arranged, and that she was packed and ready to go. "I have just a couple of instruments and personal items. There is nothing too heavy for humans to lift, but I cannot carry much while walking, so I will need help bringing my things on board."

Emily nodded. This quick readiness was a pleasant surprise, but it also made her wonder. She shook the thoughts out of her mind, and focused on one thing she wanted to ask Oris. "I'm guessing you know a lot about the ISC species and their cultures."

"As much as I could learn, traveling to all their worlds, including yours for a year."

This was going to be a little unorthodox, but Emily had suddenly been struck this morning by how little attention she had given to Ethan, who had only gone into space because of their friendship. She wanted his time in space to be a little more interesting than it had been so far, and saw an opportunity here. "I . . . have a sort of cultural officer on my ship, a friend of mine. I was wondering if, while we're going places, If you could tell him some of the stuff you know."

Plumage tall in surprise, Oris said, "you chose a cultural officer who is incompetent?"

"No. Not incompetent. Just not as useful as he could be. He learned what he knows in a way that . . . wasn't very . . . reliable." Emily realized that trying to explain television documentaries would be too confusing. "I'm sorry. I don't know if –"

Oris waved a hand. "I will be happy to tutor your cultural officer if he will be joining us on the planet. I will not have enough time to do the subject justice otherwise. He will also need practical experience."

"Yeah, he'll be down there with us," the captain said with a taste of vicious conviction. She knew that Ethan wouldn't be eager to do hard traveling on an unknown world, but would appreciate it in the end. She could even get him to bring his guitar.

Without many more words, they finished up breakfast and picked up Oris' luggage. Emily had no trouble carrying the two bags, which were about fifty pounds combined, to the landing pod. She briefly wondered if there was a market for rolling luggage on Eldrand. They seemed to lack it, but definitely needed it. This was the sort of thing she should pay attention to, a real business opportunity that could let her make her mark.

Stepping onto the bridge as the ship remained in orbit around Eldrand, she realized that her stay on the planet had been pursuit-free. No shadows following her, and no dreams about them, either. According to signals, there wasn't an Asparian ship in sight.

She sat in her instrument-adorned chair, her mind conjured up images of Wetzler and Davison, and she cursed under her breath. If it wasn't one thing, it was another. Well, time was getting short, and before she left the ship in Kaz's hands, she would need to have at least one unpleasant conversation with the two members of the repair crew. She could take them along with her to the planet, but that would leave the ship shorthanded. No, she would have to have that talk with them.

Her head was aching, and she limited what she said to the bare minimum orders. Kaz wanted a full explanation of what happened on the surface, and who the new passenger was, but she was too tired for words. Her mind was swamped, and her face was so contorted to match her mindset that Kaz quickly gave up on his questioning glances. He did, however, turn around startled when she finally told him their destination.

"Kaz, plot a course to the coordinates I gave you for Selparis."

6
Selparis

From an orbital viewpoint, the planet could have been Earth to someone without any knowledge of geography. It was mostly seas, but had well-defined continents. Most of the surface was shrouded in a thin veil of clouds, just as Earth usually was. Revolving around a typical G-type star, Selparis was larger than Earth, but deficient in the area of moons and companion planets.

Kaz was busy monitoring the mapping computer, comparing the rendered images to the rough sketch produced by the Eldrandii investigator. Emily had explained every detail of her Eldrandii excursion to him, and he was not happy. With the captain under unusual stress, he had not discussed the subject with her, but every atom in him was against her going to the planet's surface. Seeing the worried way she spent her time staring out of the rec room windows, though, he got every sense that she would explode if he expressed his views. She knew them all too well already.

The crew had noticed her temperament, as well, but didn't know how to take it. Within a few hours, the spread of rumors meant that there was no avoiding a talk with the crew. Emily waited until after a basketball game in which she chose to participate, mainly to take her mind off things. Her speed and agility made up for a basic lack of skill in the game, so she got a generally favorable review from the crew, which had guessed why she was participating. Feeling the tiniest bit better about herself after the competition, she plunged into her discussion with the crew, explaining exactly where they were, what they were doing here, and what they would get out of it – both certain and uncertain. The crew had mixed feelings. Some were excited, seeing this as the kind of thing they had dreamt of and signed up for – the rediscovery of a lost world. The older hands were more reserved, and understood fully now why she had been looking so troubled. Despite the risk, though, there were no objections.

Emily breathed a sigh of relief. Well, of course there were no objections. The crew didn't really know all the details of what they were getting into – like what she had seen in her dreams. Tell them that they might be placed in the path of a leftover Asparian menace, and their attitudes would shift from cautious optimism to utter disbelief in a second. Some of them had caught sight of Kaz, whose face didn't hide the fact that there was more to the story than the captain was mentioning. Since the first officer made no comments, the observant crew members concluded that, whatever the secret catch, it wasn't worth mentioning. Certainly, Kaz had not held back from criticizing the captain before, so they could count on him to hold her in check if necessary.

Crossing a possible crisis off of her list, she next arranged to deal with the repair crew problem, which had been put off for as long as possible. In her ready room, waiting for the two crew members, she had no idea what to say. A part of her wanted to bring Kaz in as backup, since he was the only other person on board who knew about the issue, but she wanted to show herself that she could handle the things a captain was expected to deal with. She would just have to ad lib. Even if it turned out awkward, it would feel more authentic than something pre-planned.

As Wetzler and Davison entered, she was struck by how physically imposing they were. Maybe it was because she was still sitting while they stood at attention, but just their presence started to make her nervous. She realized too late that there was only one free chair in the room, so they would have to stay standing. On the other hand, they really didn't look like men who would plot something in secret. They had a pride and bearing about them. From their criminal records, you might have expected someone shady, but they were anything but. With all the evidence against them, only their character and demeanor challenged the idea that they were responsible for the ship's sabotage during the Ariki affair. Taken that way, their stoicism was comforting to Emily, but she was nevertheless worried about what she could do if they got seriously offended by her accusation.

After the solid silence made it obvious that they had no idea what the meeting was about, she tried her best to explain. "I called you guys in 'cause I found something out that I don't like. It might not be any trouble, but I have to talk to you about it before I leave for Selparis."

They weren't budging. Nothing on their faces hinted that they knew what she was talking about. She made a note to herself never to play them in poker, because by now they should have had at least a clue – they weren't stupid. They just didn't want to make it easy for her, the vicious bastards. Taking a deep breath, she told them about the black market charge in their record, and hinted at the connection to the Plani device that had forced the handover of Ariki. "Now, since the ISC isn't hunting you or anything, what I do about this all depends on whether you're using what you know to help us, or if you're using it in a way that might hurt the crew and my ship." That sounded all right. It could have been put worse. She waited for their reply.

For a while, they stood like pillars, not even looking at each other. When one finally broke his concrete countenance, it was Davison, and he turned to look at Wetzler. There was no way he was going to speak for the two of them, that was the chief's job, and he trusted Wetzler to say the right thing.

Wetzler kept his own gaze on the captain, whose leg was shaking under her desk. His craggy features twitched at the right cheek, as if hinting at the wince his face should have sported in light of the topic. Clearing his throat, he said, "Have you brought this up because you're still angry that we didn't go out in hyperspace?"

Emily's face scrunched up into true puzzlement. With all that had been going on, she had almost forgotten that part of it. Her mind had visualized the two of them attaching the device on the hull so many times that she had forgotten that they had resisted the attempt to remove it. With complete honesty, she said, "didn't even think about that. Listen, I just found out about this on Newport Station, and didn't want to be away from the ship for a month worrying about you two, okay?"

"You think that we put it on the ship? That's what you think?" The growl in his voice was filled with temporarily contained anger, but he could have just been putting it on to hide another emotion.

"I think that. I have a right to worry about it. I see evidence, I need to check it out. That's all I'm doing."

"Well, you can stop thinking about it, Captain. We didn't do it."

Damn, she thought, now what? She stayed silent.

Wetzler continued. "If you don't trust my word on it, then I'll just resign. I don't need this kind of . . . this kind of suspicion over me."

Nice bluff, but it didn't prove anything. Wetzler knew that she couldn't risk having him resign, since she was about to depart, and couldn't leave the repair crew shorthanded. Emily looked down at the files in front of her and decided to backtrack. "Okay. Tell me what this was all about. What were you doing to get this stuff in your file?

Considering his position for a moment, Wetzler proceeded in a professional but cautious tone. "We were hired by a Plani tech shop to tinker with some stuff. We must have worked on hundreds of things – figuring out how to remove restrictions on electronics and hardware. A lot of it was on-the-job training. They couldn't use any Plani, since for the right price, a Plani'll rat you out in a second. And they knew we would find the experience valuable enough to keep our mouths shut, coming from planets that weren't so technologically advanced. We were hired on Newport Station, and that was it. We didn't buy stuff, sell stuff, or use stuff. Sometimes, we didn't really know what the thing did. Once the shop was linked to the disaster, the one that was being investigated by the people who put that black mark in our files, we got out of there fast."

"So the thing the Inanas used on us could have been put together, or messed with, in your shop? That's possible, right?"

"Are you hell-bent on trying to connect us to it?"

She held her tongue. This wasn't getting anywhere. At least they knew that she knew. If anything happened to her ship, they would be the first to get blamed for it. Now, she had to bring the tension down so they wouldn't be driven to do something stupid.

"No. Forget I asked. Listen, we'll call this thing settled. I'll take your word for it. I just had to check, right?"

Keeping any relief carefully hidden, Wetzler nodded. "I suppose you did."

"And like I said, 'long as you use what you know to help the ship,

I'm glad to have you two on board."

Choosing to take that well, Wetzler said, "Thank you, Captain."

Emily did not say "you're dismissed" because she never did, and Wetzler and Davison knew not to expect it. The conversation was over by mutual agreement, so they turned and left, leaving her to think. She still felt uneasy about the repair crew, but she had done all she could. At least Kaz knew about it – she wasn't leaving the ship in blind hands.

Feeling claustrophobic in the ready room, she next headed for the rec room, where the massive windows facing the stars provided the opposite effect. She had recently spent many hours using the stars as a backdrop to map out her thoughts. This time, she started by appreciating how little the crew seemed to need her. Her rare trips to engineering were hampered by the fact that she had no idea how anything worked. She suspected that it was all simpler than it looked. The only questions that occurred to her to ask the engineers sounded silly – is everything working right? Anything we could do to make things run better? The answers would always be yes and no. If there was something wrong, they would tell her right away, they assured her on every visit, pushing her out as gently as possible.

The recreation room was unusually filled as the ship orbited Selparis, and the topic of discussion was what might be found on the planet. As usual, she tried to keep her distance so she didn't create awkwardness, but they still turned down the volume. Scanning the place, her eyes were drawn to two figures seated at a side table. Ethan was in a regular chair, facing Oris, who had pulled up a stool since the backed chairs would encumber her wings. With a pang of guilt, Emily realized that she had neglected her old friend. He knew he would be going with her to the planet, but they hadn't really talked about it. Well, at least Ethan had found someone to talk to in Oris. Emily had been hoping for that, and the Eldrandii was as good as her word. From the way that Oris was talking and Ethan was listening, there was no question that this was an intense cram session designed to shove vital knowledge into Ethan's remarkably receptive mind. Oris was throwing out words at a spitfire speed, and Ethan could only take notes directly in his mind since writing or typing would be too slow. That was all right – he had never needed to take notes from all those documentaries he had watched, and this was no different.

Emily decided that intruding would give the two of them a well-deserved break, but before she could actually interrupt their flow, Oris turned to her and greeted, "hello, Captain. Your cultural officer is in desperate need of lessons, but makes up for it by being a quick learner, even by Eldrandii standards. It is nice to see a human with the aptitude to learn by listening."

"Well, that's good." Actually, it delighted her. Not only was it great to hear someone compliment one of her crew members, but it was even better when the person was her good friend. Emily gave Ethan an approving look, and he threw a weak smile back. He only had weak smiles, as if he was always too tired to muster up a full-fledged confident one. "How are you feeling? You ready for this?"

Ethan shrugged. "I don't know. I guess."

Typical. She waited for him to say more knowing that he'd fill the silence with something better.

"I've just sort of gone along, right? It's not like I have something to get ready for, except for the kinds of things you can't predict, like starvation."

It was a point. Even ignoring Ethan's follower attitude, she could look at her own experiences and see the same reasoning. Had she been ready to command a starship? Was she ready, even now? Did it matter? She supposed that the real difference between Ethan and her was that she would have confidently claimed her readiness regardless of reality – as she had to her parents repeatedly. Knowing Ethan's parents, they had probably been thrilled by the news that their son was going out into space, and that he was finally putting his obvious intellect to use.

"Bring your guitar along," she advised him, practically quoting the instructions she had given him when they had set out on this space adventure. "It'll be a long trip, and we'll need some entertainment."

"But . . . it's heavy. We'll be doing a lot of walking won't we? You haven't asked me to play this whole time," he accused.

"Well, I will down on the planet, okay."

"You'd better."

She tried to look remorseful, but couldn't wipe a slight grin away. "Been a bit busy. Besides, I was afraid you'd try to sing."

"Hey, I've got a good singing voice. Everyone says so." It was the one thing he was defensive about. She knew it, and he always took the bait.

"Oris, you'll find a way to put him to use, right?"

The Eldrandii smiled, "indeed. I see hard work ahead of him."

"Aww," Ethan objected, then said in a halting cadence that was his particular method of whining. "I don't . . . suppose we could . . . take it easy?" He knew there was no point, but tried on impulse.

"You have been taking it too easy, I think. In the old days, an Eld who was lazy and refused to work up to his potential was sent to the mines across the sea, where the ships are built. Take this as the easy way."

"All right, then," he said petulantly.

It was nice to see good old Ethan being himself, apparently unchanged by space travel. Emily definitely felt changed and unsettled. She was suddenly beset by an insane urge to unpack all those boxes sitting sealed in her room, just to remind herself of who she had been. That was why she had brought all that stuff aboard, after all, but it made no sense to unpack on the day before she would be leaving. Then again, maybe it was the best time. For the rest of the day, she wanted to be her old self, the self that ignored the practicality of things, and just went out and did it. That was the person who took command in the first place, had taken her this far, and might keep her alive on Selparis.

The captain took her leave of Oris and Ethan with more energy than she had come in with. Reaching her quarters, she wasted no time getting started, putting the first three boxes on her bed so that there would be room on the floor to dump the stuff excavated from them. None of them were marked, so every opening was going to be a surprise. Since all of her essentials had been in luggage, everything else had been treated democratically.

Extracting items from all but two boxes, she found no solace. She could have covered the ship in punk or goth decorations, and put on a fashion show, but here and now it all seemed so ludicrous and inconsequential. What had she been doing, collecting all of it? What was it supposed to do for her? She couldn't remember. Compared to the adventure ahead of her, everything she had done so far looked meaningless. Exploring an unknown world . . . could some posters or music give more purpose to her life than that? There was a comforting side to that – the idea that everything behind her could not be weighed against what was ahead – but it left her ungrounded.

The second-to-last box contained absolute junk. She couldn't understand why she had kept the stuff – aged electronics, all sorts of things she had collected but not looked at twice, and even some stuffed animals. Quite a packrat, she had even managed a small stamp collection gathered when she was eight, before she learned that it was the dorkiest hobby in the world. Her collection of coins was worth a look, though. With her grandfather jumping from star system to star system, it was easy to forget how many countries her father had visited on business. The legends of space travel had overshadowed her father's more modest crisscrossing of Earth, but space had no substitute for an old-fashioned coin collection.

Both her father and grandfather had been generous with the stuff they brought back from their trips, and the last box was full of these artifacts. They were all excellent, and Emily thought they deserved to be displayed around the ship. Mostly animalistic statuettes or dark artwork from around the world and galaxy, they helped her tap into her imagination and dreamscape. A set of kabuki masks in particular occasionally popped up as characters in her nighttime wanderings because they had been hung on the wall next to her bed back at her Earth home. This last box was a treasure trove that she now had new respect for, to the point where she couldn't believe she didn't mark the box and pack the delicate objects more carefully. Luckily, nothing was broken.

Putting the masks in front of the viewscreen on her room's communications and command desk, she cleared everything else from her bed. Her room was in complete disorder, but she knew where everything was. The last box finally gave her some satisfaction to sleep on, so she curled up in bed without delay.

There was no way for her to know whether it was her first dream that night, but it started with the disembodied masks floating in front of her. They slowly morphed into distinct faces – a teenaged boy, an old wizened man, and a hooded spectre with a skeletal face. The hooded face started chasing the other two. Expressions on all three faces were tense and gritty. Now the floating faces grew bodies. The spectre disappeared and the other two were running across a landscape. The view zoomed out to the only map of Selparis she had until Kaz finished with the mapping computer – the one created by the Eldrandii investigator.

On waking, Emily remembered the dream, but not the faces of the boy or man. She was surprised by how straightforward and obvious it was. She could accept premonitions of a certain degree, as long as they were a bit vague and mysterious, with carefully hidden meaning. This was too much. This felt like a force-fed vision. Her mind threw up an image of Tylan, the Asparii mage, but she dismissed any connection to his accidental intrusion, as she did when her mind's eye turned to the other dream intruder, the Shadow Worker on Newport station. By setting up the masks and bringing out all the gifts from her father and grandfather, she had basically been asking for vivid dreams, so why should she be surprised when she got one?

She left the last minute preparations to Kaz's hands, and instead took the time to dye her hair a flaming red, and to tour the ship. Her hair color didn't draw comments, but got the usual looks. She would have worried if people totally ignored it – that would defeat the whole purpose. Her walkaround brought her some wishes of good luck, and a few more signs of respect than she was used to getting. Finally stepping onto the bridge, she felt a shade better, and fixed her eyes on the planet, which now occupied all but the very top of the forward view.

"Nice color," Brian said, turned to look at her with eyes on her hair. "Well, there's your planet. Sort of deceptively normal."

Emily opened the comm and asked Jessica Scott, "any odd contacts, signals?"

"Nothing so far. It's all clear. Never really seen a system with totally clear skies before. It's weird."

Arisin Oris stepped onto the bridge, looking completely unimpressed by the planet, and gave the captain a searching look. The eyes probed for readiness, and showed Oris' eagerness to set out. Well, if her employer was ready to go, Emily had no reason to delay. "Kaz, you're acting captain until I get back. You all right?"

"Yes."

"Everything all set?"

"Yes," Kaz said flatly, hiding all emotion.

"Alright. I'm heading for the cargo bay, then. Here," she tossed him the cell phone Commander Raiz had given her, "you can use that to call Raiz if you're around Newport Station. He said he wanted to help us, so you might want to take him up on it. Liam, tell the others to meet us down there. Time to find out whether this planet was worth the trip."

As the sun crept over the rolling hills outside of town, West gazed out longingly toward the horizon. He had to get moving. He had been here way too long.

The sprite-like figure jumped down from the tree, from where he looked out over the world every morning. He hit the hard soil, throwing up a small cloud of dust, and dashed into the house. Time to wake Jaik up.

Inside, West took it slow, stepping carefully through the mess on the floor. He was on tiptoes as he entered Jaik's room and approached the bed. Looking at his sleeping friend with amusement, he hesitated before tapping Jaik's shoulder. The sleeper didn't stir. Going to stage two, West whispered, "Jaik, wake up," close to his friend's ear.

Jaik rumbled, mumbling "why?"

In his regular voice, West said, "so I don't have to throw a bucket of water on you."

"It's too early," Jaik said, rolling over but keeping his eyes closed.

"It's your birthday."

"So why don't you let me sleep?"

West's grin filled his voice. "'Cause I thought we should celebrate here before you have to get greeted by the town. You've got a big family to celebrate with, remember?"

Jaik had no answer to this. Knowing from experience that West had not been joking about the bucket of water, he slowly levered his upper body to a sitting position. West tousled his already disarrayed dirty blond hair in a loving way he had never gotten comfortable with.

"I hate you," Jaik said, not meaning it, and despising himself for saying it so feebly.

Opening the room's curtains to let the sun shine in, West responded casually, "no, you don't. Happy birthday, by the way."

"Thanks."

"I'll wait for you in the kitchen."

As West left, Jaik considered flopping back down and cozying back in his blanket. Now that he was awake, though, he decided to get the day over with. He got out of bed and approached the tiny mirror on the wall next to the door. He still had a young face, but that would be normal for years to come. At seventeen years old, he couldn't see how he had changed much since thirteen. West had started shaving years ago while Jaik still wondered whether facial hair would ever make its appearance. But West was the odd one, wasn't he? He didn't look like anyone else – he was fairer, without the yellow tinge to his skin, and had a slimmer frame than everyone else in the Free City lands. No one in town commented about it, because there were plenty of odd creatures that came from across the sea to trade or explore, and at least West was the right shape. Still, living with him made it difficult for Jaik to maintain his own self-image.

Jaik wondered how he could possibly be expected to decide the future course of his life so soon. But he would be expected to. The townsfolk certainly knew his age. Pretty much everyone had taken a part in his upbringing, as they did for every child in town. He knew which two townspeople were technically his parents, but he had never lived with them, and they felt no special responsibility to him. Children in the Free Cities were raised by the town, which also built a house for the child if no vacated ones were available. It was a custom criticized by the farmers living on the lands surrounding the towns, but it had always worked well. Everyone accepted a responsibility for everyone else, and the tradition served to keep the town a coherent unit.

Then, three years ago, West had made his appearance. Entering town alone, and having the careless air of a wanderer, he had been shunned by the people more for his strange attitude than his looks. They quickly got over their dislike of him, though, as his inventiveness and ability to fix machines made life easier for everyone. They agreed to let him stay in the town after a trial week, but since the town only built homes for its own children, and they didn't want to start giving free land to any stranger wandering in, West had to live in an existing household. It was decided that the best option was another boy his own age, and Jaik's name was randomly selected from a list of all acceptable roommates. Jaik had just graduated from the babysitter phase, during which his house must have been host to every woman in town, and was thankful at the time to have some help on the cooking and the chores again. The transition from being babysat and being independent was always a difficult one for the town's thirteen year olds. Looking at himself in the mirror now, though, Jaik realized that his mercurial friend had become the standard by which he judged himself.

When the young inventor had entered the market square on his own seventeenth birthday, half a year ago, there had been no question what he would choose to be. An expectant mayor had asked, in front of the entire town, in what capacity West would serve the town, and West had answered that he would continue to be an inventor and repairman. The announcement had been greeted with congratulations, and from that day on, West had been treated as one of the town's own. After all, out of the seven hundred residents of the town, he was the only one with the skill. Before, when the machines broke down, the townsfolk had to hope a traveler on the road could fix them, or a trader could sell them a replacement. Most of the machines – like the millworks, heaters, ovens, and Gershin's automated looms – were too big to normally be in a salesman's merchandise. The town's excellent blacksmith could conjure up replacement parts if pressed, but was at a loss when it came to how machines actually worked. West was a godsend.

Now, if only Jaik could determine his own calling with such confidence and acclaim. After seeing some acting troupes passing through town, he developed a liking for their art and thought he might be good at it. But that wouldn't be acceptable to the town. He would have to travel with a troupe, and wouldn't be contributing to the well-being of the town. It would be showing ingratitude for all the help that they had given him. Everyone had invested in his future, and ignoring that would inspire hatred from people he had known all his life.

He pushed his hair back into some sort of order, picked his jeans up from the floor, wore them over his shorts, then smoothed the wrinkles out of his white shirt. That passed for presentable, even on a day the whole town would see him. They were working people, and not prudish about looks. Sure, some boys and girls bought dazzling outfits for their day of adulthood, but nobody would look down on him for being more modest and folksy in his attire. So, finding the cleanest pair of socks from the mess on the floor, he wore them, and promptly hid them with his new shoes, acquired by West in a trade for one of his inventions.

Jaik stepped into the kitchen, which doubled as West's workshop. They had the best oven in town, a special bread maker, an electric fan, and a heater that kept the whole house warm through the winter. Both the heater and the electricity-producing steam engine could be powered by either coal or oil, depending on which supplies traders brought. The appliances and generators were in demand throughout the town, but the real wonder was in West's little toys. The most useful one was the panel wired to control the oven, bread machine, fan, and heater using switches. The kitchen was full of machines that automatically chopped vegetables, sliced bread, spread preserves on bread, mixed their drinks, and used a tub of water to wash their dishes. For the rest of the town, some of this was taking mechanization too far. It wasn't a major challenge to chop vegetables or slice bread, after all. In Jaik's eyes, it was magic – as close to it as you could get without locking yourself in a tower and studying with a creepy man who had managed to grow a white beard four feet long, and that magic was not nearly as practical. West had come up with the dish washing machine after Jaik had gotten sick eating off of dirty dishes. West himself never used dishes, and ate by hand right off the table, but had also mixed together a cleaning chemical that kept the table spotless. The liquid was frankly dangerous, though, and Jaik avoided it. He had seen it eat through dropped food in seconds.

The most recent innovation was one West had heard about on his travels four years ago, and had wanted to try every since. Last year, he had asked one of the regular traders to find a glass blower who could manufacture to a specific design. He also needed some metals, and established long distance correspondence with an alchemist who could distill certain gases. In six months, the trader returned with the materials, and West paid him with some artwork and furniture that he himself had previously been paid with by the artisans of the city. Obviously thinking that he had taken unfair advantage of a naïve young man, the trader gave them a cartload of coal as a bonus, saying that his kinna, the pack animals, were overburdened anyway. West was thrilled by the bonus, and immediately put the coals to use.

The patiently collected materials were meticulously put together by West, and connected to their source of electricity. It glowed brightly, to the wonder of Jaik and West's delight, but was overheating too quickly, so it had to be disconnected. After a few days of testing how much power the light could sustain, West installed it permanently as a door lamp, where it could be seen by the rest of the town. They still only turned it on for special occasions. Every person in town had come by at one time or another to see it. They called it West's candle, though he kept insisting that he wasn't the one to come up with the idea.

Entering the kitchen after having thought of West's adulthood announcement, Jaik was hit by all of the young inventor's achievements, becoming even more depressed at how little he had done in the same amount of time. The house was more West's than his. Breakfast was neatly laid out on the table already. In a regular kitchen, West would be completely lost, but let him use his inventions, and he was a chef.

Normally, they didn't sit together for breakfast, since West finished eating before his friend got out of bed. Shaking his head, Jaik tried to clear his thoughts out and failed. He smiled weakly at West and sat down at the table. It was a special breakfast – not just bread with preserves and milk, but also egg and sausage. His meal was on a plate while West's own was on the bare wood. As soon as he sat down, the meal started without any prologue.

As he tore off another piece of bread, using it to rip off some egg and shovel it into his mouth, West threw a knowing glance at Jaik.

"Any ideas yet?" he asked casually.

"You mean since yesterday?" Jaik responded incredulously. "I haven't done anything but sleep."

West shrugged. "You've had vivid dreams before. I thought maybe one of them would bring you a sign if you slept on it."

"I've never gotten any signs from my dreams. They're all about weird things – things that can't exist. Anyway, you know what I want to be."

Nodding, West looked into Jaik's eyes with dead seriousness.

"Should we just light out? I want to go traveling. We could leave town without warning, but it'd be better to tell them something. I could tell them that I want to head out for a year to find the latest inventions and bring them back here, and that you're coming along to help me since it wouldn't be safe out there alone. They'd understand that. Didn't the blacksmith leave like that a few years ago? He came back, and he could do practically anything we asked him to – even all the stuff I wanted."

"But they'd know I'm avoiding it."

"Then tell them you want to be an inventor, too. And since we'll be learning all sorts of new things to try, I'll need the help."

Jaik shook his head. "I never showed a hint that I'd be interested in inventing. They'd wonder."

"Let them wonder. You haven't shown a hint of interest in anything else, either. Listen – you've been living with me for years now. They've got to figure it rubs off."

Leaning back, away from his half-empty plate, Jaik thought it over. While he did so, West added, "or you could say you're heading out to become an apprentice mage. The town'll be thrilled that they could get their first resident magician. And you always like the part of the wizard in all the plays, so you can at least act the part."

Jaik opened and closed his mouth mutely, mind cleared to digest this new idea. "Or they'd treat me like some sort of . . . degenerate who couldn't figure out some real work to do. Every lazy kid is a future mage apprentice. They already think I'm a bit lazy –"

"Then how about being another inventor. We'll head out in a few days. Then you can be an actor, and I'll come back and tell them you were kidnapped or killed or something. And that'll be that. Just make sure to hide in the wagon and get someone else to play your part if you swing back into town."

"Seems . . . wrong."

"If you can think of a better way out, go for it," West said, without implying that his idea was the only possible solution. He had a way of robbing harsh words of any menace, and putting a friendly face on them.

Finishing off his meal, Jaik didn't leave his seat. The idea was a solid one, and it should work without a hitch. The problem was, the idea wasn't his. He barely knew what he wanted. He wasn't even sure about acting. Nothing the schoolmaster taught was especially interesting to him, though some of the other youths in town were captivated by her. Farming was out of the question. Acting just came easy to him. He supposed it wasn't easy for everybody, so maybe it was his calling. That was about as far as his thinking had gotten.

Well, he didn't have much choice at this point. "All right," he said finally, "we'll go with your plan."

"Not saying that traveling'll be easy. Geography lessons don't –"

"I know, I know. Let's just get it over with. I knew I'd have to leave some day. I just don't fit in."

West shrugged, not really knowing what 'fitting in' was. Finishing up his breakfast, he cleaned up his section of the table, and decided to leave Jaik alone for a few moments. His friend was agitated, as expected, but it wasn't normally so tense between them. He hoped Jaik would smooth out once they struck out on the road. Time to get moving.

Outside, the town was fully awake. Their house was on a slight hill, perched so that it was possible to look straight down the town's road. It was a market day, so farmers were streaming in on the road. Stores were already open, and the ladies of the town were loitering around, sharing the latest rumors. Eventually, everything that happened within a day's walk of town would be discussed by the ladies. A few words murmured in the basement of an unknown farmer's house would be repeated here if it was juicy enough. The townspeople probably didn't think much about it, but West knew it was the town's way of preventing citizens from straying too far from the norm. Folk could get vicious, and Jaik feared them. It was already well-known throughout town that Jaik was having trouble choosing his calling. West didn't know how the actor thing would eventually get out, but it would. He sometimes wondered whether magic was involved.

For his part, West could not have cared less. If anyone got unfriendly, he'd just move on. They weren't really comfortable with him because they needed him more than he needed them. He could walk away from town with confidence and without a glance back at it. No one who had lived their entire lives here could say the same.

He wondered about Jaik. Looking over the town – a village,

really – he saw some of the boys he had known since his arrival. Not one of them had acted civilly toward him when he first came in, but he knew how to deal with hostility. The town had warned its kids about associating with 'his kind,' and it had taken weeks to convince people that he was safe. He had only bothered because he felt – for no reason that could be put into words – that it would be worth it. And it had been. But would Jaik be able to do the same, to bear up under the same scorn? Would he be able to fend for himself? They would definitely meet with some trouble on the road. Actors were never seen as upstanding citizens, for that matter, and were always treated like dirt when they weren't entertaining people on a stage.

It was time to head back into the house. By now, Jaik would have finished brooding, and would be wondering where West was. A few minutes after that, he would sneak back into bed to hide from the world. Before intercepting his friend, West took a last breath of town air. For the rest of the day, his mind would be focused on places far away, tasting what the wind had to say about them. He didn't have to worry about the plan, at least. Jaik was an excellent actor. When the time came, West could just stand back and watch his friend convince the town. No script or rehearsal would be necessary.

The house was still filled with the smell of breakfast. Jaik was standing up from the table and, instead of moving toward his room, he strode confidently to the front door. He seemed brighter, almost cheerful. Putting on a weak grin to match West's, he said, "guess we should go."

West hadn't expected this – things were already getting interesting. It was about time.

"Guess we should."

The sun had been up for a while now, but was still far from its noonday pinnacle. The farmers remained outnumbered by the townsfolk, but that would change by afternoon. Now was the best time to make the announcement, since farmers tended to show their displeasure at the age of decision rituals, and Jaik wanted a sympathetic crowd to support him.

After getting past his instinctive reluctance, Jaik was ultimately excited about leaving town. With a full stomach, he felt fortified and ready to move. Once out of town, no one would be telling him what to do, and he wouldn't have to prove anything to anyone. West was the most resourceful person he knew, so there was no worry in his mind about starvation or any other trouble. In the shed outside their house, there was a mechanical bow that could fire a bolt twice as fast and four times farther than the most experienced archer could manage with a regular bow. West had not put it together for show.

And there was something oppressive about being around people who knew you, and already had a clear idea about what they thought of you. In distant lands, he could be different.

The short walk down into the town square was quiet and dignified. Jaik looked every bit the part of an adolescent confidently declaring his calling. Now that they were out of doors, they kept their mouths shut. The moment they were sighted by the women in the marketplace, an intense whispering shook the cobblestones of the main road. A few of the men, especially those who had helped Jaik most through his parentless youth, were clearly standing in wait for his announcement. They had a more serious and ceremonial look on their faces than the women had. In older times, this had been an elaborate ritual with dances and manhood tests, with the women doing chants. According to legends, that was when they had just come to this land, and they used the events to foster social cohesion in the midst of the hostile land. Very little of those times now survived, but maybe a few popular songs were ultimately derived from the ancient chants.

Jaik preferred this way to a complicated celebration, since he would not have to bear scrutiny for quite as long, and he lacked confidence in his ability to prove his manhood. The downside was that everyone was staring at him as he entered the town square. West stayed beside him, so that was sort of comforting, but the others were making a shifting ring around them as they moved. The farmers got the picture and stood aside – not participating in the ring, but not breaking it either. It started with only a dozen people, but quickly swelled to include a hundred, then more. By the time Jaik stood in front of the fountain at the center of the square, he could already see around two hundred at least. It was no surprise – they had been ready for him. Some had signs and banners, even.

The stone blocks surrounding the fountain's pool were the town's soapbox for speeches. At the last moment, Jaik was reluctant to ascend them. The churning of the stomach, the wide-eyed dismay, and the audible thumping of the heart, were all manifestations of his stage-fright. He knew that, but the knowledge didn't make life any easier for him. There were children in the crowd staring at him as if he was some kind of hero, and women tearing up – both those that had helped raise him, and the ones imagining other children going through the same moment. He had done nothing more than survive for seventeen years, for heaven's sake, yet some of the men were a bit shaken, too, though most were cheering loudly. Jaik failed to match up to the physical standards of the town, but he sounded like a bright lad when talked to, so there was something to hope for. The expectations in their cheers set Jaik on edge.

"Don't worry," West whispered, "they'll be wanting the Lord Mayor to introduce you first. It'll all seem more natural after he gets through his speech."

Chief official of the town, the Lord Mayor's main function was to be the final court of appeals in disputes. His more common use was to preside over ceremonies of all sorts. He had been chosen based on simple virtues – he never offended anyone and kept his speeches short. As he hobbled into the square, the crowd cleared a path for him, and some of the younger spectators shouted comically, "the Lord Mayor approaches. Make way for the Lord Mayor!"

The aged figure had an emaciated face but a slight plumpness the rest of the way down, borne out of an easier life than he had originally been built for. He walked without a cane, but his stride was slow and unbalanced, favoring the left leg. It was painful to look at. The town doctor had warned him that if he continued to walk without a cane, he would have trouble in his right knee within the year. The mayor ignored the warning – the one thing he was adamant about was his walking. Jokes abounded about the potential need to carry the mayor into the square like some ancient princess, but the whole issue had really endeared him to the town.

So did the way he perpetually spoke in proverbs. As he moved into position, standing next to Jaik, he began to speak in words they had heard a hundred times before. "Truly, there is no sunrise like the bloom of youth. It . . . it is a gratifying thing to be woken by friends to such an auspicious occasion. And while a good sleep calms the mind, a moment in sleep is a moment wasted. So, I thank you for . . . waking me up." He carefully kept any resentment out of his voice, making the words even more humorous.

"Gentle women and forthright men, we are gathered here to witness the coming of age of one of our own. To be a man is to have a sense of duty and responsibility for the community. No man is an island, and every man requires the help and support of others. If everyone fulfilled their responsibilities, the world would be a better place for it. And so we gather here to . . . to hear what this young man feels will be his proper place in this community. What can we expect him to contribute? For without contribution, there is no community."

It was one of the mayor's best speeches – among his shortest. Clearly, having just woken up was impairing his repertoire recall. He had not given Jaik enough time to think his part through. Well, there was no choice now. Jaik remembered talking to some traveling actors a few years back, and some of the profound things they had to say about performing a horribly written part. Without exception, they advised playing it as big as possible, because if you're going to fall flat, it will at least be entertaining for the audience if you do it obnoxiously.

Jaik hopped up onto the stones of the fountain with all the false bravado he could muster. He was suddenly in his element. In his mind, he saw the picture of a brave young lad, the darling of the town, proudly proclaiming his destiny for all to hear. That destiny was a grand one – leading him on a sweeping adventure through the frontiers of the world in search for anything that could better the lives of his people. It would be a great sacrifice to give up the comforts of home and the stability of the familiar, but he had a duty to his people, a clear calling in his heart, and had no choice but to bear the burden.

Over the top he went. "Friends and fellow travelers on this journey of life, you have given me so much. For all my years, you've helped me, giving me everything I needed to survive and succeed in life. You built me a home. You fed me. You clothed me. You educated me. The folk of this town have given me more than any person could ask for or deserve."

His praise for the town continued with glowing adjectives and the most poignant examples of goodwill. West couldn't stop grinning, and applied every ounce of self-control available to stop from laughing. It was so fake, so inconceivable for Jaik to talk, or act, like this, that the town would very likely believe every word he said. They may have helped him, and in a distant way loved him, but they didn't really know him. Otherwise, they would have been offended by the inauthentic way he was speaking to them. But Jaik knew what his audience thought of him, and they were enthralled, impressed by this articulate man their town had produced. If his speech was less than ten minutes long, and he threw in some of the more popular proverbs and idioms, he could run for mayor right then and there.

He wound his way down to the core of the occasion, hinting at, but not outright saying, his decision. Midway through, he was quite pleased with himself and overflowing with confidence. Most declarations involved the person in question slinking up, stating their chosen calling in a simple sentence, then slumping away. Jaik's was a work of art, proving his acting acumen to himself, and beating even West's pronouncement, which had been delivered not only with the inventor's natural charisma and flair, but also some of his special effects devices. Jaik had the rest of his speech mapped out in his mind – the reasons for his choice, the burden he would have to endure being described in excruciating and exaggerated detail, the necessity for both West and himself to leave and support each other in the endeavor, and the rest of it. It would be fabulous.

And he pounded in the dramatics as he led up to the moment. "But now the time has come for me to bear my duty to this community, which has certainly done its duty to me. Now it's time for me to start repaying my deep debt to you –"

In his rhythm, he had not noticed that the attention of the crowd had shifted away from him, but now he stopped in his tracks because it was impossible to ignore. A heavily armored figure, face encased in a helmet, parted the crowd as if an intense flame evaporating a sea, even creating a sort of haze around him. The metal-encased man stopped to a standstill right in front of Jaik, leaving the speech caught in the young man's choking throat. Jaik desperately wanted to step down from the stones of the fountain, but was immobilized. Thankfully, the man of metal turned to face the crowd, not giving the scrawny speaker a second thought.

"Townspeople," the armored man began. "You will surrender and work for us or you will die. This is your final warning."

The declaration was delivered by a voice that, though muffled by the helmet, was absolutely stony. A stone drenched in blood. No words in combination with any other voice could have created more of a stir, even before the crowd fully registered what had been said. For some unknown reason, this man was eager to kill them all. One man was no match for them, though. No, this man must be out of his mind if he thought a bit of armor and steel would be enough to compel the town to surrender. Of course, he had said 'us.'

As if he had read their minds, and had given a hidden signal in response, dozens of grey cloaked figures appeared out of their own artificial mists ringing the crowd, designed to strike the most profound panic. These were mages. Whether from a high or low order could not be told, but they must have been rogues to be pulling something like this. Any magician was worth ten warriors, and a good mage could be worth a hundred, easily. Women and men in the crowd, already off their emotional normal because of the ceremony, were suddenly breaking down, and many were openly weeping.

These were not bandits. Isolated though they were, the citizens of the town were well-aware of the common dangers of the world. They knew of towns attacked by bandits, and had prepared for that, but these weren't bandits. This man had demanded their enslavement or their death, and had not even mentioned what they were surrendering to. No war had been declared – not that the town would have joined battle, anyway.

The Lord Mayor piped up with admirable bravery, or dimwitted stupidity. "This is a free town. We are not affiliated with any nation or other people. We have no quarrels with you."

"No quarrel. Accept our demand."

Having seen enough, West looked at Jaik, and motioned downward. Barely able to move, Jaik leaned down to hear what West had to say. West only gestured more insistently. Forcing his muscles to unlock themselves, Jaik gingerly descended from the fountain. He managed it without distracting anybody from the tense confrontation. Standing next to West, he found himself a bit less of a target, but just as tense.

Through carefully pursed lips, West whispered into Jaik's ear, "We have to go."

"What?"

"We have to get out of here. Now."

"But –"

"If we stay here, we'll be killed. We can't talk to these people. We were going to go anyway. Let's go."

The armored warrior had just heard an entreaty from the mayor, stood silent and menacing, then took a step forward. The grey figures tightened their circle. From behind his helmet, their leader growled, "surrender or die. We want this land. We do not need you."

Courageous but foolhardy souls from the crowd started to shout defiance at the warrior and the mages encircling them. To the dismay of the Lord Mayor, who clearly knew he would be cut down immediately if fighting broke out, the men of the town who weren't speechless were actually threatening the attackers.

"This is bad," West said, not needing to whisper anymore.

In a flash, three random men in the crowd were writhing on the ground. Without any other prompting, the most militant members of the crowd rushed the mages while the rest ran for their homes. West grabbed Jaik's wrist and almost pulled him to the ground with the first tug. Jaik got to his feet moving, but still had trouble keeping up with West. They made a beeline for their house, which was thankfully well away from the center of town, and didn't look back as screams filled the square.

Reaching the front door of their home, West was composed but far from calm. He shouted to Jaik, "pack," then dashed in to get his own things together.

"But . . . ," Jaik stumbled as he tried to catch his breath, "don't you think –"

"No!" came the immediate reply from deep inside the house.

Jaik couldn't focus after being thrown so far off his course. He trusted West to pack the necessities, and simply took the things he absolutely had to – about half a pack's worth. None of it would actually help then on their journey, so he kept plenty of room for everything West would need him to carry. Since most of West's load would be metallic, Jaik readied himself for a heavy burden.

He was not disappointed. In the middle of the house's entryway, West heaped his inventions haphazardly, alongside a pile of empty sacks. Wordlessly, Jaik set down his own sack and started packing all the gadgets. He was excessively careful with the more delicate-looking creations, but after taking his time despite his pounding heart and flight instincts, he began to wonder what was keeping his rushing companion. His skin crawled with apprehension. There was no sound. Reasoning that any enemy who could have attacked West would shortly be in to take care of him, anyway, he searched the house, then went outside to see whether his worst fears were justified.

Outside the front of the house, the coast was clear. There wasn't a soul in sight. In the distance, though, a column of smoke was rising from the city, and anguished cries were still carried by the wind. Jaik moved to the right corner of the house, set his back to it and peered around cautiously. Seeing nothing, he followed the wall to the next corner. Looking around this one, he saw two figures – West was talking to another boy. Exhaling, though still on edge about who this interloper was, he walked hurriedly towards them.

As he neared, he recognized the new figure as Arron, a boy about his own age who managed to be even spindlier. Jaik knew only one thing about Arron – he was guaranteed to disappoint the town when it came time for him to announce his chosen field of work. It was the prevailing gossip about him. Otherwise, he had been a quiet sort who spent most of his time in the woods to the north. Maybe it was to avoid accusing eyes. Now that the town was aflame, all that seemed so petty and pointless.

West and Arron spoke quickly and seriously. Arron had no idea what was going on, and had come down from the forest after seeing the smoke or hearing the screams. West did his best to explain everything while carrying a sack of food on his left shoulder. Spotting Jaik, he finally set the sack on the ground.

"Damn. Taking too long," he muttered by way of apology. Turning briefly to Arron, he said, "We need to get moving. You need to get moving, too, unless you want to be in the middle of the mess. If you want to come with us, we've got plenty to carry and could use another shoulder."

Arron looked dubious. "I . . . don't think I can carry much. Not for a long way, at least. I know my way around the forest and the hills, so I'll stay there for now."

"If you're sure . . . you won't have to carry much –"

"I'm sure. Where're you headed? If you're heading to another town or one of the coast cities, it could be attacked just like this one."

"We'll head your way first, then maybe the empire's lands through the hills."

Jaik perked up at the thought of seeing the empire, but his recollection of a hundred vague stories was broken by a shrill shriek. With an overwhelming sense of urgency, the two would-be travelers parted with Arron, darted to the front of the house, threw the filled sacks over their shoulders, and made for the woods with West in the lead. Arron was nowhere in sight, making a lightning getaway of his own.

The forest was only a short run away, but West led them deep inside it before halting the dash. Adrenaline rush passing, Jaik's legs collapsed under the weight of his burden. Realizing the leadership role was his, West kept his composure despite an overwhelming urge to sit down and rest. He checked to make sure he knew the way ahead, made certain that his companion was all right, and offered words of encouragement and comfort.

"I don't think the enemy will bother to follow us in here. We'll have to be careful to stay away from others trying to flee, but otherwise we'll be fine."

Regaining his breath, Jaik said, "This feels wrong."

West furrowed his brow. "What, you mean the town getting attacked? I'd say it does."

"No . . . can't explain it. Maybe it's us running away without trying to help . . . but we'd definitely have gotten killed."

"We will be trying to help. Listen, they say anyone can appeal to the emperor, right? Every trader I've ever met says that's the best thing about the empire. We'll tell the emperor what happened, and he'll stop it from happening to any other towns."

"Someone that powerful wouldn't care about us. I was thinking more of like . . . I don't know –"

"You watch. Powerful people don't like other powerful people nearby. A bunch of rogue mages should get the emperor worried enough."

"Maybe they were sent by the empire," Jaik suggested darkly, "and maybe the emperor is tired of having free towns near his lands."

West grinned at him. "They wouldn't need to kill us to take us over. They wouldn't need to hide who they are. Everyone says that if the empire wanted the free cities, it could have them. And since that's what everyone believes, I don't think they'd put up much of a fight when the empire comes knocking."

Jaik accepted the truth of this, but still felt dislocated. He wondered why it should happen today, of all days. Why had these people attacked on a day when he and West were planning to leave town anyway? Had West known something would be coming? The last question was nonsense, though. West had been eager to leave for the past year or so – he wasn't the stay-put type. He had just used Jaik's coming of age problem as an excuse.

"Come on," West said, motioning for Jaik to get back to his feet and follow. "Let's head for the hills."

The foliage below the landing pad was dense, covering the hills through which the border of the empire ran. It was an unadulterated forest – the type that only existed in protected parks on Earth. If their goal was to avoid frightening the natives on their arrival, it was the perfect place to land. But unless they could find a substantial clearing or a landing strip, surviving touchdown was not in the cards.

They were traveling further and further from where the border was supposed to be in search of a road that Kaz's mapping had found, but their naked eyes failed to spot. With the eagle eyes you would expect from a species shaped like a massive, sleek bird of prey, Arisin Oris pointed out a tiny cobblestone road winding its way through the forest. Hovering thousands of feet over the land, all Emily could see was swatches of green and brown. Maybe some grey, but nothing that she would call a road if their lives depended on it, which they did. Oris guided the pilot to the road until he could see it for himself. From then on, he was looking at it dubiously throughout the descent. Tough to tell from this height, but the road looked barely wide enough to accommodate the pod. Good thing the pod's undercarriage was wheeled, since there was no way they could leave the pod on a path like that – they would have to move it deep into the trees to conceal it from wandering travelers.

"We've got some work ahead of us," Emily moaned, looking around at her fellow passengers. The pilot was of a good build, and she had been sharp enough to bring a cargo crew member – Max Schroeder – for some muscle. Otherwise, she had Ethan, who hadn't lifted more than twenty pounds in his life, and Oris, whose weak, flighty frame promised little help. Not that Emily would have asked Oris to help anyway. "John," she said to the pilot, "could you find some place where the trees by the road are thin, so we don't have to chop down half the forest to get this thing into the woods?"

Not taking his eyes off the land below, he said, "I'll try, Captain, but I've never landed on anything this tight before. If I don't find a spot wide enough, we could clear half the forest with fire. Good news is that it looks nice and damp down there. But I haven't done this before."

Emily rolled her eyes. As if any of them had done any of this before. Well, maybe Oris, but otherwise, they were all rookies in the planet exploration business. She didn't like shakiness in her pilot, so she said, "I'm sure you'll do all right. Don't rush it, we've got time."

"Umm . . . no, no we don't. If we want to get off this rock, we need to keep fuel for it. I'm already not keeping much. We'll have to get the *Azar* down to a low orbit, and even with that, we only have a few minutes before we need to set down. But that's all right," he said, pulling them back to level flight, a few hundred feet over the road, "this spot looks good."

The pod was on the ground in a minute, and without any incident. Emily congratulated the pilot, then had him do a standard check of the outside atmosphere. It was all good, as the in-space readings had suggested, so they opened the hatch and exited. There were only four translator headsets available – the rest had to be kept on the *Azar* in case jobs needed to be done – so the pilot kept one, and Emily, Ethan, and Oris took the others. Max was left out, but didn't seem concerned about this. Emily and John also took comm units that attached to the translators, giving them the capability of communicating with the *Azar* and each other.

The stone road was typical of its type on Earth – uneven, but better than a mud trail. The spot picked by the pod pilot was perfect, right beside a gap in the trees that was clear twenty feet into the forest. If they really wanted to hide the pod, they would need to get it in deeper than that, so there was no avoiding a bit of tree-cutting, even if it was only to cover the pod in the local foliage to camouflage it.

Fresh air fragrant with a smell similar to eucalyptus, Emily was overwhelmed after breathing stale ship air, even staler Plani air, and trying to avoid the Eldrandii wind of death. It had been a long time since she had tasted smells like this. The trees were only similar to Earth variants in that their tops were green. To call their protrusions 'leaves' and 'branches' would be a misnomer. For one thing, there was irregularity in them. On an Earth tree, you'd expect a tree to have one type of leaf or fruit, but these plants were diversified in both shape and color, as if they couldn't decide which branch of evolution they wanted to take. Specialization was definitely shunned by this planet's nature. Emily could live with that, but she doubted whether trees like these could actually work efficiently. But who was she to challenge the reality of this planet?

On the other hand, this part of the planet had been colonized by Asparii, and that species carried its own peculiar reality with it. These plants could have been some mage's ancient experiment, brought from Asparis itself by the exiles. Or they could be a home-grown abomination. Suddenly, the forest looked a lot less convenient for hiding, and more menacing. If a mage decided that a metal-eating animal would be a useful beast to populate a forest with, they could be in for some serious trouble.

The pod was the size of a recreational vehicle – thirteen feet in length, and eight in width – so concealment wasn't much of a problem once they put the work in. They carefully pushed it into the trees with the pilot making sure that none of the pod's parts were damaged. A highly sophisticated machine, any scratch could make it potentially unlaunchable. Oris didn't provide any muscle, but after asking permission from the pilot, she used the pod's ducted fans – its main lower atmosphere propulsion – to give a slight boost from the cockpit. Clearly, she had flown similar pods before, even though they were unusual on Eldrand.

Anticipating trouble, Emily had brought two laser rifles to the surface. Using a continuous beam from them, they cut down some of the trees to move the pod deeper into the forest. The rifles on their own couldn't sustain a continuous beam for long, but connected to the pod's electrical system, they could take care of whatever weeding the crew required. The problem was which way the trees would fall. None of them had any experience in the timber industry – in fact, Oris did an elaborate prayer for each tree before they so much as touched it. She wasn't unreasonable about it, recognizing the necessity rationally, but she also explained that they were starting off badly by killing something on this planet so quickly after first setting foot on it. That was a point they could all understand. Ethan came up with the best solution to the falling-tree-could-smash-pod problem, suggesting they pull the trunks away from the pod using ropes. They used the cargo pallet's ropes for the job, and found that while the suggestion worked, the trees were tough to cut with the laser, and it took all the force of John the pilot and Max the cargo hauler to sway the taller ones. The ropes were also too short for John and Max to be comfortable with their own safety. Max joked that Oris should say a prayer for them, as well, just in case. She did.

An Earth hour and six trees later, Emily was satisfied. They had alternated the use of the two lasers, but both were now over-heated and needed time to cool. Again, they weren't really meant for this. The pilot covered the ducted fans with their reentry sheath to protect them from the elements, and then they draped the pod in a net created from the trees they had taken down. That done, Emily, Ethan, Oris, and Max left John to the comforts of his ship, where he had a week's food and one of the rifles, with which he could hunt for more. The four explorers each shouldered three days' food, Max carried their mini-stove, Emily bore the other rifle, Ethan his guitar, and each of them except for Oris had a sleeping bag and a change of clothes.

"Feels like a real adventure," Ethan commented, more in dismay than in any excitement. He was awkward under his load, and set it all down regularly as they made their way north on the cobblestone road. Max looked at him with something bordering on contempt, and got a warning glance from Emily in return. Emily's eyes said, with absolute clarity that, if Max had any problem with Ethan, he could just get back to the pod and stay there with the pilot. For the cargo crewman, a genuine survivalist who actually liked this sort of traveling, being sent back was a legitimate threat. Personally, Emily was already feeling uncomfortable about the whole endeavor, and guilty for putting Ethan through this. Careful not to show it, she kept a confident face on, having practiced that expression a lot the past few weeks.

Oris experimented while she walked, doing on-the-fly examinations of samples she had collected from the trees they had killed, and debris from the forest floor in general. She used an ingenious handheld multi-tool that seemed to contain a whole lab. Emily mostly left the Eldrandii to it, but asked Oris to check especially for any diseases, or anything that looked like a disease. Ethan had brought this up on the flight down, pointing out that the Asparii were genetically very similar to humans, and any virus or bacteria that had evolved in isolation on Selparis would likely be able to jump species. They would not be immune to it, since the rest of the ISC would not have added the inoculation to the standard package. Oris had heard his comments, but had not commented, as if it was obvious. Emily, on the other hand, had turned hypochondriac in an instant.

"Captain," Max suddenly said, speaking up for the first time in an hour on the road.

"Yeah, what is it?" Emily said, checking the system's sun to get a sense of time. Either it was a hot planet, or just a hot place on it. The net result was that her glance at the sun was resentful, and her voice could have used some water.

"What if we meet someone on this road. Should we be ready to . . . you know . . . do the first contact thing? Or are we going to ditch the road for the bushes when we spot someone on the road?"

Huh, good point. "Oris, I think we had you here for this. What do you think?"

Oris took her eye off her tool's display, which was currently magnifying a leaf so its cell structure was visible, and said quickly, "If they are Asparii, I will be able to see them before they see us. From the look of them, I will advise whether we should meet them or not. I think we should avoid most travelers, but if we meet one on a beast of burden that will reach the empire well ahead of us, and that one looks friendly, then we should announce ourselves that way. The rider will carry word of us, and perhaps soften the reception when we arrive."

"But you're staring at that thing," Emily pointed at the multi-tool, "the whole time."

Oris gave what must have been an exasperated look, though Emily was not well-versed in Eldrandii facial communication. It was a twitch of the protruding mouth and an upward tilt of the head which briefly threw the forehead plumage forward. "I will sense any approaching life, especially sentient life, before it is visible. Do not be concerned."

"Handy thing to know," Max grumbled after asking Ethan what Oris had said. "Is it just sentient life, or are we talking animals, too?"

In her limited English, Oris said, "animals less. For them, I see first, feel second, unless my sight is blocked."

"So, in the forest, you'd be able to detect them before they get spooked by us. We could get some easy meals like that."

Oris stared with an unmistakable expression of disdain. "Is killing all you think of? I say I can do something you cannot. You do not wonder if it is possible for you to learn how to do it as well. You do not think how it can be used for general benefit. No, your first thought is how to use my ability to kill."

It was typical Eldrandii paternalistic criticism, or in this case, maternalistic, but Max didn't take it well. "Look, we've got to have food."

Oris held up a satchel of collected leaves, berries, and fruits she had been gathering and examining. "I am checking if these are safe to eat. They are all over the forest. Some are similar to the known plants of Asparis. This, human, is food."

"Food for the animals I usually eat. I need solid meat, lady. Berries might be enough to satisfy your fairy body, but mine needs more." Emily winced at Max's rudeness, but had to agree in principle. Even right now, the rations in her pack had huge meat courses and minimal fruits and vegetables. That's how she liked her meals. Conveniently, the Plani companies who packaged the most compact space rations available also tended to the carnivorous. Max didn't have to be so coarse to Oris, though. The Eldrandii was turning out to be more useful by the minute.

"Nonsense. The plants have all the nutrition you need, and more than the meat has. I have studied human biology using the texts of your scientists. Welder brought me translated copies."

Max was about to respond, probably planning to say something about the physique of the scientists who wrote those books, but Emily interrupted. "Get in line, Max. If Oris doesn't want to use her abilities to help you hunt, it's her business," she left out the obvious corollary that, if the humans in the group wanted to eat meat, it was their business. Also unspoken was reminder that Oris was technically their employer – a fact that Emily, herself, had almost forgotten. The nod Max gave her suggested that he got the point.

Oris went back to her work and Emily let out a long breath. Strife within the party only a few hours in did not bode well for their continued cohesion over the days or weeks they expected to be on this planet. She vaguely recalled the way the original astronauts would train together and get to know each other before they went up into space. The mission organizers would make sure the astronauts worked well with each other before trusting them with expensive space vehicles. She probably wouldn't have thought about training for this mission, but being stalked by shadowy figures and mysterious ships effectively threw a wrench into the calm, rational approach anyway.

With a suddenness that almost made the other three stumble, Oris stopped short, snapped her head up, turned around to face their rear, and held out her left arm to signal them to halt. Squinting her eyes to focus them on a distant object along a mostly straight stretch of the road, the fine feathers on her head and the back of her neck stood in alarm.

"Hide in the forest, quickly."

"What?" Ethan and Emily said together, but Oris was already moving.

"Follow. Quickly."

Hesitation wasn't an option with the Eldrandii so flustered. Here was someone who had seen dozens of worlds and all the dangers they had to offer, and that kind of experience gave weight to a warning. There was a convenient row of bushes to the right of where they stood, flanked and backed by trees with low hanging branches. It was practically a natural hideout.

"Too close, though," Max commented as they sat down behind the four foot high plant wall. "With the way we're sweating, whoever it is could probably smell us."

"Not what I saw," Oris said, laying on her belly so that her wings didn't protrude over the hedge. "It was metal. Solid."

"Like armor? Or a robot?" Ethan asked.

"Armor?" No surprise there. It would have been a shock if Eldrandii had that concept. They would have recognized 'shielding,' but the idea of armor didn't fit with their mode of battle.

"On Earth, we used to fight battles encased in metal to protect us," Ethan explained. "That was before we had modern weapons."

Oris thought it over. "It could have been that. The Asparii fight like you do, and this planet does not have modern technology. I was puzzled, because I thought it was a robot, but knew that was impossible. Maybe this is a guard on patrol . . . in armor."

"Still don't want to meet it," Emily decided. "Totally in metal armor? On a day like this? That's the kind of guard I don't want to meet."

There was a slow, steady clanking coming up the road, and all four of them ducked lower. The bushes were lacking in viewing gaps, but Emily found one about an inch and a half in diameter. At its height, all she'd be able to see was the figure's foot and shin. At least this looked like a native, and not one of the shadow types. It was too noisy to be one of them. The banging of the metal was like an announcement made by someone who owned the road and sought to strike fear in anyone that didn't belong. Emily was persuaded, barely breathing as the armored figure stopped right in front of their hiding place.

Both Ethan and Max looked like they desperately wanted to say something, but held their tongues and tried to communicate through their eyes. Emily couldn't tell what they were thinking, but when she looked out of her gap, she saw the figure crouch down – amazing, considering how solid the armor was – and examine the ground. She suddenly realized that the cobblestone road might bear some indication of their tracks, unlikely though that seemed. The armor itself caught her interest. It was spotless – shining with an absolute perfection that was blatantly unnatural, as if even the weather dared not tarnish it. Maybe it was just a new set, freshly forged, but her hunch was that magic was at work. She knew next to nothing about smithing, so maybe she was underestimating the ability of armorers. Still, the likelihoods unsettled her.

After a few slow seconds, time filled with tension and sweat, the armored figure rose back up and continued North on the road. As the rattling of his metal faded, Oris took the chance to stand. The rest stayed down. Once the road was clear, she said, "it is all right," in English, and they stepped back onto the cobblestones. Max checked the stones himself and said, "there's a faint trace of us, but I only notice it because I know we passed through here. That thing's heavy prints wiped most of ours out. Don't know what it thought it would find by looking at the ground – maybe wheel tracks."

"Could be that he wanted to give us a false sense of security," Ethan said. "With the rifle, we could probably take him on. Maybe there's some sort of trap – "

Max shook his head. "I think he just takes a look at the ground every now and then, just in case."

Emily chose not to think about it, and arrived at a quick decision. "We'll have to stay in the forest. We can't risk being out in the open if something like that can spot us."

"'Could've just been a guard," Ethan said.

"Not alone," Max said, "I don't care what species – no one patrols alone. Looked like a thug to me."

"Even thugs come in packs. I don't think anyone walks down this road alone," Emily said. "There's something wrong with this picture. C'mon, let's go forest side. No more surprises."

Max was eager, but Ethan held up short. "Umm . . . wouldn't just going on the road be better? I mean, we'll go faster, and Oris can still sense stuff. There could be other things in the forest – things that don't wander out into the open."

"He's right," Oris said. Of course he's right, Emily thought, feeling stupid for not thinking of that before opening her mouth. That was a dangerous mistake for someone accustomed to giving orders, and who wanted those orders obeyed. Her grandfather had always been insistent on the think-before-you-speak idea. You never know when someone might actually be listening. Tongue heavy in her mouth, she nodded at Oris silently, and started walking up the road without ordering them further. They followed, giving her a wide berth. Her inadequacy in this role could be fatal. On the ship, there were twenty-six people, all competent at making sure the ship worked, and who could make up for her mistakes – to a limit. No such luck here. Would it would be best to rely on Oris, who had traveled to so many worlds, or would Emily's human instincts have a better read on the Asparii inhabitants? Oris couldn't tell the difference between a robot and an armored person – where else might her experience be limited?

Sighing, Emily tried to fill herself with her old spirit, potentially dangerous though that might be. She didn't want to worry until she was in danger. All this preemptive worrying was really weighing on her, and she still had no idea how to bear it.

Emily didn't notice that Oris had once again held up short, and she continued to walk for a few seconds before Max hissed, "Captain!" She snapped her attention back, and found herself embarrassed for the second time in what must have been less than an hour. Reddening as she strode back to the other three, she was the last to hear the footsteps and talking coming out of the forest. Two young voices were heading their way, chatting in a language difficult to identify at this distance. The translators weren't picking anything up yet.

"What do we do now?" Max asked in a whisper, as he, Ethan, and Oris looked at Emily for orders.

7
Into the Empire

After a difficult two days in the forest, Jaik and West were finally nearing the crest of the hills which formed the boundary between the Free Cities to the south and the empire to the north. In a day, they would be reaching the border town, and might find some authorities who would listen to their desperate news. West did everything he could to transition Jaik into their new life on the move, but it was a sharp break from their old comforts, and Jaik was taking it badly.

"It's too hot," he moaned. Actually, the forest was much cooler than the open road, and what Jaik was really complaining about was the heavy load he was sweating under. It was true that their old home had been well-cooled by electric fans, maintaining a temperature some degrees lower than any other home in town could manage, but Jaik was hardy enough to deal with a bit more heat. Which was good, because the further north they went, the more the sun would beat them into submission. The northern border of the empire was a desert of proverbial death. This was no time to start complaining about the heat – they would have enough chance for that later.

"We'll have to head for the road now, the ground's getting too rough for us to lug this stuff over it. It'll be hotter, but the going'll be smoother and the load'll feel lighter," West promised.

"The only way this is getting lighter is if we eat all the food, and melt down some of the metal to make a cart. We should've brought a cart in the first place."

"No good in the forest –"

"Yeah, but we could've taken the road from the start –"

"– and we could've met the metal guy who was checking the road, remember? We would have left tracks. Think we could have taken him two-to-one?"

Jaik was silent, sensing the beginnings of irritation in West. West used to be so rarely agitated that the sharpness in his voice was like a slap in the face. They said nothing more to each other as West guided them toward the road. Jaik had no idea whether they were headed in the right direction, and chided himself for not trusting West's judgment. After all, where would he be without it? Probably dead after staying petrified in front of the town fountain, too clueless to react quick enough to save himself.

Busy with regret, he failed to notice the puzzled look growing on West's face. If he had, he would have immediately asked what was wrong, since confusion was another emotion West didn't take stock in. Then again, maybe this was the real West, the way he was when on the move. When settled, he might as well have been sedated, for all the range of expression and emotion he showed. He had always been his mildly energetic, affable self, crafted to be likeable. Away from society, his attitudes ran the entire gambit with all conceivable nuances, and new facets cropping up hourly. This was more natural, in a way, but the vicissitudes left Jaik disconcerted, since he had been conditioned to West's consistency for so long, trusting in it as much as he would a stone bridge.

He reflexively halted when his companion did, dropping his load, assuming that this was a pause for rest. His bags hit the ground with a thud, and West whirled around to stare at him furiously, venom flashing in his eyes. By the time Jaik had registered this, taking a step back from the force of it, the flame had softened and West spoke in an even tone.

"I get the feeling there's other people around," he said softly, "I think I heard voices. I'll go check it out. Try not to make any noise while I'm gone." He set down his own load gently, then dashed off without disturbing the ground enough to make a sound.

Jaik was shaking, and held up his unsteady hand to his eyes to make sure it was just him, and not an earthquake. For the briefest moment, he had seen in West's wild eyes the piercing, merciless gaze of a bird of prey. A brutal hunter, a murderer, was in there, suited to this life not only because it was more intelligent than the beasts of the field, but because it could beat them at their own game, on their own turf. So intimidating had the look been, that Jaik wondered whether West could have tackled the armored man, sans mages, on his own. If there was a gap in that armor, Jaik's bet was on West.

He sat down on the ground gingerly, and stilled himself. He was dealing with a paradox. On the one hand, West was a technological genius at the cutting edge of what passed for civilization in the Free Cities. Suddenly, though, he was proving as primal as one of the forest's vicious denizens. Maybe Jaik was overreacting, with an imagination that combined with the circumstances to reach previously unfathomable conclusions. Part of it had to be West's frustration – as long as Jaik was tagging along with him, he would not have the full freedom he craved. It was an unexpected snag in the arrangement. The civilized, society-friendly West was Jaik's friend, and wouldn't for a second consider leaving his friend to fend for himself. West the nature sprite, though, was a lone wolf, and saw Jaik as extra baggage. That, too, could have been Jaik's imagination, but he didn't think so.

As if guessing Jaik's worries and wanting to lay them to rest, West returned with his old beaming smile and twinkling eyes, and the grin was waiting on standby. To explain his change of temperament, he said, "We've got some interesting people on the road. Very interesting."

Jaik's brow furrowed. "What do you mean?" He didn't think interesting people on the road boded well for their travels.

"I mean they're strangers, and they look totally lost. And there's a winged one with them," West said, dropping the last point casually.

"A winged one? An Eldgil?"

West shrugged. "Well, it's got wings and moves real graceful, but it's a bit thin and birdish. It's different, anyway."

"Birdish –"

"There's four of the them – the Eldgil and three that look more or less like us, but with pale skin – like me but paler. Like they don't get out in the sun much. But they've got all sorts of weird things – inventions, I think."

"Weapons?"

"I saw one thing that looked like a rifle, but that was it. Only saw a rifle once before, so I'm just guessing by the shape."

"A rifle . . . ," Jaik repeated in awe. The weapon was rare and legendary. Only the elite units in the empire's army had rifles in numbers.

"Yeah. And they were talking in a different language, but it was one I recognized. I think they're the good guys. Maybe they can help us against the people who attacked the town."

Jaik was dubious, but followed along without comment as West started off. He tried to tread quietly, then noticed that West was making no such effort.

"You're . . . making a lot of noise, aren't you?"

"We don't want to sneak up on them. This way, they won't attack us on sight."

That made sense, so Jaik switched gears to another pressing question. "So . . . you can speak . . . another language?"

West brought out his grin. "You don't know everything about me."

"Didn't think I did. What's the language?"

"You'll find out. Tough to explain right now. It'll make more sense when you meet our visitors. Maybe I'll make more sense, too, but that's something else."

"You're talking in circles. I hate when you do that. You don't end up saying anything, you just . . . waste words."

West kept his lips shut, just smiling. This was his usual tact when answering Jaik's more probing questions – to throw out some nonsense, then keep quiet with a knowing smile – so Jaik was used to it. He could only hope the mystery would be solved as soon as they started talking to the newcomers.

Announcing themselves by treading loudly and chatting, they did not surprise the group they were approaching. As they emerged from the trees, grim faces met them, attached to bodies ready to bolt rather than to fight. One of the four, a fairly young person about Jaik's own height, had the rifle pointed right at him. From the face alone, he couldn't tell whether it was a man or a woman, with its strong jaw, hard eyes, and short, wildly red hair. The rest of the body gave hints that it was female, though the clothes did their best to hide the fact. That alone didn't strike Jaik as unusual, since many farming women preferred what the town's women called "men's clothes," requiring practical clothes for heavy work. Many of them had stronger jaws and more muscle than the woman before him, too. But no one he had ever met wore clothes of such absolute black, or sported flaming red hair. Her duster could have its uses as a blanket, but the black color was altogether unreasonable for the weather in the region. The sheer inappropriateness of her clothing marked her as an outsider.

Another of the three normally-shaped ones was also badly dressed, but the last was a boy – maybe a man with a youngish face – who wore jeans and a tee-shirt, much like Jaik himself. The boy also had a black jacket of an unknown hide, but it wasn't unwieldy and, considering how thin the boy was, he could use the extra skin. Only the winged creature, the Eldgil, seemed to be dressed for the weather, with flowing light blue robes that protected her skin from the sun while letting air get in to cool her. The dresses of the townswomen were sewn along the same lines. On the surface, the Eldgil looked more like a skinny, overgrown bird than the creatures of legend whose realm was somewhere across the seas. But when you saw the bearing, the hidden strength in the expression, and the depth behind the eyes, you could see that West had not simply judged by the wings.

Jaik's mind was thinking fast in the seconds after they confronted these strangers, but he had no idea what to do, so he lapsed into quick observations. Always having trouble dealing with people, he tended to notice details about them that would help him figure out how to act. If he had to guess, the Eldgil would be expecting abject respect, and was probably the one in-charge. The two badly dressed ones were clearly the muscle, though the way they were standing made them seem unsure of themselves. And the last? He had a studious and sullen look, but Jaik noticed something sticking out from his pack. Maybe he was a specialist of some kind who would react well to interest in his field. He and the Eldgil would be easy to deal with, and the muscle would be the hard-headed types resistant to reason. They were West's area. Then again, Jaik's eyes were constantly brought back to the red-haired woman, who didn't seem quite muscular enough to qualify as the muscle, but had the appropriately dim look on her face and the rifle. She didn't look that old, either, and her grip on the rifle lacked the conviction with which West held his crossbow. Her smooth face reacted badly to the creases of worry, but without the fierce look, she had a certain beauty. Jaik was dimly aware that women in the southern cities were expected to be frail and graceful, but here in the foothills, women with a bit of grit were both necessary and preferred. Girls with too much flightiness and not enough down-to-earth sense could be as beautiful as they wanted, but weren't any good as wives.

West's aura of calm confidence allowed Jaik to muse on all this with a rifle pointed at him. Every atom in West was proclaiming mutual friendship and peaceful assurances, and different though these travelers were, they would not fail to pick up on this. All Jaik could do now was to wait and see how West handled the first step.

Talking was good. In the split second she had to decide, Emily chose to stand her ground instead of taking cover. "We'll make this our first contact," she said in a whisper, the low tone hiding the uncertainty in her voice, "but let's not take any chances. Get ready to run. I'm pointing the rifle at whatever comes out."

"That might scare them, Captain," Oris protested. "We do not want our first contact to start like this."

"Although," Ethan interjected, "if there're people running around in armor . . . maybe they don't even know what a rifle is."

"They will know by the context."

"Quiet!" Emily said, bringing the gun level with the ground and setting it to low power.

Two people emerged from the forest, one with a winning smile on his face and the other wary. The wary one was definitely Asparii – he had the yellow tan skin color that didn't occur naturally in the human skin spectrum, looking a bit jaundiced. He also had the young face paired with a fully mature body that all Asparii teenagers featured. His companion was much more human-like, with a skin color not far from Emily's own and a slim form that suited his face well. He might have been close to twenty in Earth years. Emily could have taken the serious one on easily, but the other one looked dangerous despite a lack of muscle. He looked like a surprise waiting to happen.

Emily's rifle was aimed at the first one, and she tried to shift it to the second, but couldn't. He was smiling, and not showing an ounce of hostility. The word "disarming" took on new meaning. Emily lowered her weapon and relaxed, prepared to bring the laser to bear again in an instant. They were practically human, and young ones at that, but why weren't they running? If she had just come out of a forest unarmed to find four grim people confronting her on the road, she would have been at least a bit startled. Were they confident because they worked for someone powerful, like the armored man? She could not bring herself to think so, whatever her natural inclination to paranoia.

That was when the look on the cheerful one's face struck her as familiar. The face bore little resemblance, but when the boy's build and stance were thrown into the picture, Emily was forcibly reminded of Tyler Raiz. Taking another look at the cautious boy, the one that was definitely Asparii, she realized that he was acting exactly the way she would have if Raiz had been leading her through a forest – alert, but comforted by Raiz's powerful charm which could convince most people most of the time. That recognition brought Emily's breath back, and she relaxed further. The idea of a second Tyler Raiz in the universe was a bit disconcerting, but she could deal with it.

She was lucky to have worked all this out so quickly, because the natives had another surprise in store for her that might have otherwise pushed her suspicions to the breaking point.

"Hello, my name is West," the smiling one said in halting English, "I speak English a little. Who are you?"

Before Emily could respond, West hastily mumbled something to his companion, who had not understood the English. The translator picked up the words between the two, though it seemed to take some time on a few words, which might have been part of the local dialect instead of the common language. The device was finding approximations for words it did not recognize, which could be a problem if it was already tripping over the simple phrases like "my name is –" and "I speak –"

Getting over her shock, she decided that this coincidence was a bit much, but left herself open to a reasonable explanation, which she would insist on hearing at the first opportunity. Realizing that she had limited options in this conversation for the moment, she stuck to the obvious. "My name is Captain Emily Pierce. I'm from a planet called Earth," of course, West probably already knew that, "and we're here to speak to your leaders about trade." The translator automatically rendered her words into Asparian, and West's companion was adequately surprised, to Emily's satisfaction.

West pointed to her headset and said in Asparian, "that invention she is carrying on her head can translate."

" . . . not clear . . . talks in ancient language. It is difficult to understand. It is like . . . our teacher showed us," the other one said, knowledgably. "Knew already. Was surprised because I did not think she was in charge."

West grinned at Emily. "This is Jaik," he said in English, gesturing carelessly to his friend. "I hope he does not make you angry."

Emily finally broke into her own half-smile. She looked at Oris and deduced that the Eldrandii certainly had all the marks of a leader that Emily lacked. "No anger," she replied simply, imitating the awkward mode of speech she was hearing in the hope it would translate smoothly, then got straight to the question she had in mind. "How do you know English?"

West replied in Asparian this time, probably for the benefit of his friend, but maybe because his English was too limited to say what he wanted to. "My grandfather was from Earth. He came with other Earth people to . . . here. My mother came with him, but she was too young to remember Earth. My father born here and is like Jaik. They call themselves "Free City people" and do not have a name for this world. My mother told me Earth people call people of this world "Asparii." She taught me . . . English, but . . . from disease when was six. She said might meet Earth people . . . , should learn to speak English, and she was correct."

All this came as a shock to Jaik, but Emily had been prepared for it, remembering her discussion with Raiz. The station commander had told her that some humans had joined the last group of Asparii exiles, among whom must have been West's grandfather and mother. His mother must have been in her forties when she bore him, though. "Are there any other Earth people here? How many live here?" she asked.

Shrugging, West said, "no one else known. My family is all dead. They were . . . only Earth people in Free Cities. Maybe more in Atparis Empire, but cannot say."

At the word "empire," Emily's eyes widened and she turned to the three behind her. Oris and Ethan were following along, but Max was clearly lost and remained tense. "Relax," Emily said, "it looks like we're with friends." To West, she said, "could you show us the way to the empire? We want to speak with the emperor."

"We go there," West said, bringing his pack around to show that he and Jaik were doing some hard traveling. "We can go together."

Jaik listened to all this placidly, but felt intensely uncomfortable. West had, until now, been the odd one in a world filled with Jaik's people, but that had been all right since West was good at ingratiating himself with strangers. Now, West had found others of his own kind, and Jaik was the one that would be alone in this company. Already, he did not like being around these humans with their devices that could speak in other languages. Something about the tough woman and her red hair made him more comfortable in her company than he normally was in West's. Maybe it was because she did not make him feel hopelessly inadequate. Gazing at the ever-engaging West, though, she did not seem to take notice of Jaik.

"Why are you two going to the empire, anyway?" Emily asked. A picture of the situation was forming in her mind, and she did not like how it looked. Images from her dreams were now beginning to make sense, and that steel-clad menace now up the road would no doubt haunt her the next time she slept.

West sensed awkwardness from his companion, and gestured for Jaik to deliver the explanation. Having lived with Jaik for years, it was hard not to notice the boy's insecurities, and this pass of the baton, however artificial, would make Jaik feel a bit better about himself. Prone to quiet brooding, Jaik nevertheless needed a speaking part before he could feel like he was an equal in company.

Knowing why West had stepped aside for him, Jaik reddened a bit at the thought of being so easy to decipher, but took the opportunity without complaint. "Our town attacked by . . . mages and man of metal. We are hoping . . . Empire can help."

Emily sighed. This was really too much. What were the chances? This reeked of planning, though for a mind to have come up with this, it would have to be so convoluted that her own straightforward mind couldn't fathom it. If she had been a bit more superstitious, she might have hit upon the idea that some god or another, or perhaps the fates, had meant for all this to happen. Either the Shadow Workers funneled her into this for some reason, or Raiz, or the culprit was still completely hidden from her. Could it also be Welder, with all his world-hopping and interest in Selparis? That would explain Oris' eagerness to come along and to pay the crew. She could be Welder's agent in this affair, acting in lieu of the old ambassador. Emily wouldn't have brought Welder to this planet, since he would steal the show. Oris could be Welder's way of managing things from afar without stealing the credit.

There was no avoiding it, though. Emily continued the script as planned, asking the necessary question. "The mages . . . . They were hooded, cloaked, shadowy types that hid their faces, right?"

"Y-yes."

She nodded. "I've heard of them. We also saw the armored man walking up this road. We hid from him. Sounds like that was a good idea."

Jaik nodded. "Very good idea. I hope mages are not hiding somewhere waiting for us." He looked ominously at the forest. "But I guess they would immediately attack us, if they were. We do not have any protection against them."

Thankful that the translator caught all of that, and seemed to be adjusting its database based on context, Emily said, "don't know about that," adjusting the strap of the rifle on her shoulder. "We might have a few surprises for 'em."

"No, we do not," West said, with sudden sternness, leaving it at that.

Emily understood him, and did not think to contradict. There was a brief silence, then she broke it, saying, "c'mon. Let's head for this empire of yours. Tell us about this world while you're at it. We're here to set up trade. Do you know anything about that?"

West let Jaik do the talking about land merchants, the ships that docked in the Free Cities along the coast where West was from, and how only the traders really left their homes and explored the continent. Jaik gave West curious looks throughout his talk, trying to reconcile himself with the idea that his friend was only one generation removed from people who had been born on another planet. Why had West refrained from telling him, after all this time? Maybe West thought he wouldn't believe it, but more likely it was just one of many secrets between the two of them. Actually, he still couldn't entirely believe it, even though it made a kind of sense. If it was true, then West probably had knowledge of all sorts of inventions, and it was easier for him to make the mental leap as an inventor than for someone else. The idea that aliens came to this world regularly was a bit frightening, but the four newcomers were living proof of it. No doubt, if arrivals like this had happened before, the imperial government had made an effort to keep it quiet to stifle unnecessary panic.

What if all the new technology – all the electricity, and the trains of the empire – had been introduced to his world by outsiders? What if all the changes that had been brought about were the product of outsiders like West's grandfather and mother bringing their ideas in. Jaik eyed West with newfound suspicions as he described placid town life to these aliens from Earth, and how that had all been disrupted from alien magic users that could not have had a specific grievance against his people. There was an added edge in his voice, but that could have been explained away by the recent trauma of devastating loss.

As the party made its way north, Emily became increasingly involved in her own thoughts, and it was Ethan who was conversing with Jaik, after introducing himself. He was fascinated by this new world, and had more questions ready for the asking than Emily could have come up with in months. Oris was in her own world, using her experimentation apparatus to collect data, and didn't say a word to the natives. Her silence certainly magnified her mystique, which West and Jaik were already in awe of. Unable to bring himself to trust in Oris' superior perception, Max was on the lookout, occasionally moving ahead of the group in a fruitless search for any signs of others on the road. Aside from the continuing stride of the armored man, though, there was nothing.

West had noticed Max's behavior, and saw for himself the massive tracks left by their mutual enemy. He didn't want to be worried about it, but had a nagging question that he needed to share with someone. Since Emily seemed the likeliest choice for an ear, he approached her and said without a hint of actual concern in his voice, "you said . . . that metal man was walking up this road, and that he is ahead of us. What if we get to town, and it is already destroyed?"

Emily had been thinking along the same lines from the second that Jaik had told her why the two boys were fleeing their town. Ethan looked at her in alarm, overhearing what West had said. Too involved in learning about this world, he should have arrived at that logical possibility himself.

Anticipating that West had something more to say, Emily didn't tell him her own answer to that problem – she and her crew would get off this rock and not look back. Somehow, she felt that this solution wouldn't impress West, so she kept it to herself.

"You have a spaceship," he said, seeing immediately the obvious advantage in this. "You could take us to town fast, so we could warn them before anything happens."

Not at all surprised by the idea, Emily stretched the truth a bit when she said, "it'd take us as much time to get back to our ship as it would to walk to the next town. Anyway, we're not here to save people. We're here to trade, that's all. You know traders. If there's trouble on the road, traders go around. They don't just walk right into the middle of it. If it turns out we can't make money from this world, we'll go somewhere else. Understand?"

Suddenly, his face always reflecting exactly what he thought, West broke into a full-fledged laugh. "You are not just a trader, Captain. I do not think that is what you came here to do. People do not always end up doing what they planned to do, but you do not look like a trader, Emily Pierce. None of you four looks like a trader."

Sensing eyes on her, Emily turned to see Oris giving West and her an appraising glance. The Eldrandii then smiled and turned back to her work. Irritated, all Emily could think of saying was "we'll see about that. If there's trouble, don't expect us to wait around for you. We'll be outta here in a blink." It was a stupid thing to say. They were just following these two to the empire's capital – why should Jaik and West expect Emily to care about them if some sort of disaster struck? But the fact was that she would, and in saying what she said, she had proven the opposite. Even Oris had caught on to the contradiction between Emily's words and the premise behind them, and to Emily's surprise, she turned to wink at West.

West worried her, and she was not getting the better of the conversation, so Emily turned her attention to Jaik, who seemed in every way straight-forward, and much more her type. He was still casually talking with Ethan, though both had an ear for what was going on between Emily and West. Every so often, Jaik would glimpse curiously at Emily, usually while Ethan was asking another question. Emily wondered how old he actually was, since Asparii were longer lived than humans, and looks could be deceptive. He had lived in a town on this planet all his life, so her appearance must be strange. He probably was not used to women like her, if his planet was anything like Earth two hundred years ago, and women were still oppressed. That could be why he sometimes stared at her. On the other hand, she didn't see any tinge of disapproval in Jaik, only passive interest. There had to be a hundred questions in his mind, since his universe had suddenly gotten a whole lot bigger and more complicated, so Emily decided to write it off as understandable curiosity. She was an alien from outer space, after all.

"We do not really have parents," Jaik was explaining. "I know what you mean. We know the two people we are from, but we are raised by the town. It is . . . difficult sometimes." Jaik wanted to mention the expectations surrounding his adulthood ceremony, but the shock was still fresh and, while he was tempted to discuss all the pressure with these strangers who would not judge him for it, he hesitated. He could say that mages had attacked his town, but had trouble acknowledging that the attack had come on his day, with all the town eagerly listening to his every word. Never before in his life had he been so fully in his element, and the effort was defiled in the most brutal way imaginable. Would he ever be able to stand on a stage and face an audience again without remembering the start of the slaughter? Probably not.

Any attempt by Jaik to continue was stopped short by Oris, who called out in English, "Stop! Metal one ahead of us, returning this way."

Before Emily could say a word, West shouted, "here! We could have one person behind there, three more behind those bushes, and last two there on left."

"Who do you think you . . . ," Emily started.

"No time. Maybe he cannot smell well in armor, but we are all sweating waterfalls. Some plants can hide your smell, others cannot. Move!" He wasted no time heeding his own advice, yanking Jaik to the position on the left.

Deciding it was not a time to grandstand or to make points, Emily gestured for her team to take the places West had indicated. This time, when the armored man passed, he continued moving, and seemed to be in a hurry. Emily lacked a view of him this time, but heard the clanking footfalls rush back down the road. West stood up and emerged onto the road before Oris gave the all-clear. Emily waited until the Eldrandii was convinced of the road's safety, but Ethan and Max returned to the road when West did.

That was quick, Emily thought, giving West a look of loathing.

The sprite-like youth didn't need to read her mind to know her thoughts. He had been around, coming into contact with many figures of authority before. Uniformly, they all felt threatened by him. With deliberate formality, he said to her, "Sorry, Emily Pierce. I acted out of instinct. From now on, Jaik and I will be under your command."

Not buying it for a second, Emily spat back, "it's Captain Emily Pierce, by the way. Captain – you know what that means?"

"Yes. It means you command a ship. We only use it for sea ships, but you use it for a starship. You know I am not stupid, Captain, so let us not pretend I am."

"Hmph." She was being petty, of course, but he brought it out in her. They started north on the road again.

Jaik was somewhat comforted by the official-sounding West. That was how West used to talk to the adults in town – with full formalities so that, from the day he had walked into town, they could never accuse him of being uncivil or have reason to throw him out. The townspeople took it as a sign of good behavior and upbringing, but that was not how West meant it. To him, and eventually to Jaik, it became a sign that he considered himself apart from their society, and didn't plan on becoming a part of it. The way West had spoken to the Captain was a bit sharp, but he was also not a child anymore, and didn't have to put up with being treated like one.

Their latest brush with the enemy gave them mixed hopes about the next town. In the time between the two encounters, he could not have reached the town ahead and returned, as long as magic was kept out of the picture. Magic could play merry havoc with convenient assumptions. But if not to launch his next attack, what had he been doing up the road?

Ethan was the first one to propose an answer. "Jaik said that the armored man had wanted the town whether the people were alive or not. Maybe he wanted the land as a staging area, and he's just scouting out the road ahead."

Oris added, "that would be my assessment as well," then turned back to her instruments. She gave the impression that she had already come to the conclusion long ago, but considered it unimportant to voice it. For some reason, Emily didn't buy it – as intelligent as Eldrandii no doubt were, their aura of superiority was built on how they portrayed themselves more than their actual prowess. Oris was certainly doing a job on West and Jaik – maybe she was afraid that this world had not been adequately instilled with the basic knowledge of Eldrandii supremacy that the ISC worlds took for granted, and was trying to sow that seed now. Even though Selparis' inhabitants had arrived here on spacefaring vessels, the fact that they had done so in desperation, and had not established a space traveling community here because they lacked either the resources or the expertise, meant the Eldrandii monopoly on hyperspace travel had no significance for them.

Emily smiled to herself. Could she really figure out the psychology of alien species with her own observations and reasoning, or was she just applying her own psychology to them? She was the one who was insecure, and trying to find ways to prove herself. It was a stretch to assume that Oris was apprehensive for the same reason, but the thought that the Eldrandii was unsure of herself as much as she was tickled Emily.

After a few hours of further journeying, the great furnace of the sun became hidden by the trees on their left, trying to send a few spare rays through the dense and tangled growth, succeeding only to light some corners of the road's cobblestones. Much of the sky was quickly turning dark blue verging on black, and the party needed to find a good spot in the woods to sleep. They were at the summit of the hill range, and could reach the empire's border in a few hours according to West, though Jaik was less certain. There was no point trying for it tonight, though, since the border town would likely turn away nighttime wanderers.

West was the first to suggest that they stop for the night, noting the fatigue of Ethan and Jaik when he did. The two of them might have been close to passing out, from the strained and dazed looks on their faces. None of the travelers had exerted more effort in their lives, including Oris, who had never spent so much time on her feet, so it was only a marginal commentary on the physique of those two. Actually, Ethan and Jaik had held up fairly well, though they would be painfully sore tomorrow and probably unwilling to move at the start of the day.

If he had been willing to admit physical infirmity to himself, West would also have noticed that he was eager for dinner and a good night's rest, but part of his strength came from not recognizing such things. He carved his reality out from useful and constructive things, and ignored difficulties and impossibilities offhand. Without that, he would have been one of the silly people who believed a boy his age could not be a master inventor, or a skilled survivalist able to cross the continent alone.

Settling down for the night, the party shared the chicken-like meat that came in the standard rations Emily was carrying with her, with some bread and jam from West. After the long day, they were positively craving the over-manufactured mess, and were in bliss when they got to taste the bread and preserves. Emily mused that, in other circumstances, such a craving would normally be considered a sign of insanity. Obsessing about the stale, characterless, reheated meats specifically designed to disgust consumers out of hunger was a genuine ground for concern. She made a note to establish more regular mealtimes.

West set up camp exactly as he had while traveling with Jaik, and warned the others about his traps. Max looked on, and expressed approval of West's efforts. For her part, Emily was comforted by the presence of two outdoorsmen, whatever their personalities. West had already taken some time in the twilight to gather berries and fruits he considered safe, though only he and Jaik dared eat them until Oris was done with her analysis, so the rest saved their share for breakfast. Anything that West could eat was, in theory, safe for the other humans, but this was not the place to take chances and get indigestion.

Showing off his inventions, West also gave the spacefarers a sense of the technological position of this world. Electronics were out of the question, at least in this part of the world, but all the trappings of the Industrial Revolution were already in place. Jaik talked about trains traversing the breadth of the empire, though they weren't in use in the Free Cities yet. The capital was supposedly fully lit by electricity, though West injected some skepticism on the grounds that the light probably had yet to touch the working-class neighborhoods.

She didn't want to seem like she had a one-track mind, but Emily had to ask a business question. "Does the empire have anything valuable it could trade in exchange for technology?"

West hesitated. His mind quickly ran through the implications of a flood of machines coming from Emily's planet, and was wary of what that picture did to his way of life. Nevertheless, he answered honestly, figuring that he could catch up to the changes as they came. "They have diamond mines along the desert border and the two ports are rich, bringing in all sorts of things. But I guess diamonds will do where you come from?"

"Diamonds will be fine," Emily said, clearing her throat.

With the campfire dancing in the silence of the night, all six were soon lulled to sleep. Oris found a very strong branch to perch on, flying up to the amazement of Jaik and West, but Emily's jaded scorn. West assured everyone that it wasn't necessary to set a watch, and the stillness of the forest supported his assurance. They had not seen the slightest sign of large animal life on their trip up the road, though there were bizarre squirrel-like creatures in green fur.

Once the others were asleep, West whispered to Jaik, "Still think this is all wrong?"

Jaik thought it over and said quietly, "our town got destroyed, and there're crazy mages running around, gods know where they are. Is that supposed to feel right?"

"But meeting these people. It doesn't feel like running away anymore, does it?"

"No. But I don't know what we're doing with them. They don't really need us. What we're looking for in the empire is totally different from what they want and the Captain looks at you like she hates you. I don't think she likes people showing her up, and you can't help it."

West grinned. "Yeah. But she knows better, I think. I like her."

Jaik felt a brief blow to his stomach, but got over it quickly.

West continued. "Their enemy's our enemy, Jaik. That's all I need to know."

Turning his head to look at his friend, Jaik asked earnestly, "did you know it was going to happen? Did you know we were going to meet with these people?"

"Not the way you mean," West said, eyebrows arched, "how could I have known? But I had a feeling yesterday morning, and it was as strong as I had ever felt it, but that was it."

"Hmm."

"I think we should stick with this bunch. I think interesting things are going to happen, and they're the right people to be with."

"Why, because they're your people?"

"Don't be stupid."

Jaik had to admit, on reflection, that the comment was flawed. West was West – he didn't have a people. "But why? They're going to get off this planet as soon as there's trouble. You heard the captain. Are we just going to run away again?"

"I don't believe her. Do you?"

"No . . . I guess not."

"I don't even think that scrawny one, Ethan, is a coward. The way he looked when you told him about the attack on our town. Did you see it?"

Jaik nodded, side of his head brushing the pile of leaves he had made for his pillow. "He looked like . . . it had happened to his family, and he was just hearing about it."

"He acts like the entire universe is his town. If the Captain wasn't the type of person to help us, he wouldn't be following her. You can tell a lot about leaders from the people who follow them."

"What about the Eldgil?"

West looked up, as if worried that the birdlike creature could still hear them, then said in his softest voice, "I like her less and less."

"Why?" Jaik asked, surprised.

"She's always playing at something. She's a better actor than you are, Jaik, and I only like actors when everyone knows what they're up to. I like it when she smiles, but that's it."

Jaik felt cold at the thought. He had a lot of respect for the Eldgil, and couldn't imagine doubting her authenticity. Had he been so easily fooled? He had faith in West's instincts, but it was hard to be suspicious of the Eldgil, who's presence had given him such a sense of safety the past day. For his part, he would reserve judgment, and trust West to be wary for the both of them. Somewhere in the dimness after these thoughts faded from his mind, he fell asleep.

Emily woke up a few times during the night out of discomfort on the all-too-solid ground. The first two times, she saw West sitting upright, clearly keeping watch despite what he said to the others. The third time, though, he was asleep. She smiled inwardly after that last glance, thankful for companions who were only human. Waking up for the definitive time at dawn, she remembered none of her dreams and decided, as compensation, to quietly daydream during this planet's casual sunrise. Not a naturally early riser, Emily preferred to enjoy herself in the nighttime hours, and to make up for it by sleeping until noon. Space had thrown her off of her old habits, forcing her to be practical, and maybe that shift in her personal clock provided some side benefits, including a lazy enjoyment of Alpha Mensae's rise through the trees of Selparis. Could it have also been the reason for her recent vivid dreams?

The sun itself was out of sight, but its presence was felt by everything, imbuing every particle with its radiant magic. The air was pure and fresh, cleansing her lungs of the filth she had been breathing all these years. Muscles rebelling against her after yesterday's strain, Emily forced her body to stand and stretch, using what energy the morning had to offer. Her legs and shoulders were locked tight, and would probably stay painful throughout the day. Feeling eyes on her as she exercised, she looked up at Oris, who gazed down like a hawk or vulture. Emily sensed both interest and humor there, but didn't shout up any comments, afraid of waking the others. She was half tempted to suggest that Oris should bear some of the load on this leg of the trip, just to see the look on the Eldrandii's face.

The others woke as the dawn turned into day, which turned out to be a quicker transition than Emily had expected. Everyone except West woke up with a groan of pain, while the young inventor did a series of stretches and exercises that looked like a morning routine. He knew how to absorb the morning energy far better than Emily did.

It was a surprise to see Max, sturdy as he was, complaining about how he felt. He had shouldered the heaviest load out of all of them, of course, but with his chiseled face and sergeant's jaw, he didn't look the type to voice feelings of physical pain. Ethan, on the other hand, was acting exactly as predicted.

"Couldn't we just . . . rest today," he suggested hopefully. "I mean . . . we've got plenty of food, and the next town's close by."

"The next town's close, so why don't we just get there, then we'll have beds to sleep in tonight," Emily retorted.

"I'll play my guitar for you," Ethan offered desperately. He had refused to do so the night before on the grounds that he was too tired.

"No deal."

With Ethan communicating exactly how he felt, Jaik decided it was safe to flop back to sleep. Ethan had taken the time to wear his translator, but Jaik didn't need it to understand what was being said. He heard the desperate fatigue in Ethan's voice, and that was enough.

West knew what to do to get everyone on the right footing, and started preparing breakfast. Slicing some of the fruit he had gathered yesterday, he spread the pungent aroma of food throughout the encampment. Emily took the cue and started doing the same, though her sausages and bacon had less enticing fragrances. By the time she finished her meal, Ethan, Jaik, and Oris were starting theirs. Oris had been delayed by an early morning flight to reconnoiter the area. She reported no towns in sight and estimated her visibility as eight hours of walking distance, so they would be on the road in the scorching afternoon again.

By lunchtime, they were already desperate for the shade, and settled beside the road under the benevolent protection of four trees whose branches arched over the entire width of the path. While there, they heard the approach of a trader – unmistakable because of the sound of many fully laden carts rolling over the stones. He was heading south from the empire into the Free Cities area, into danger. After they agreed to warn him, Jaik, the most normal and believable of the travelers, walked up to the trader and told him about the attack on the town. The trader thanked him, and said he would be on his guard, but didn't trust the story about a bunch of mages attacking a village. No surprise there, so Jaik continued to insist in the hope that his earnestness would sway the traveler. The words might have been to no avail, but once the trader got a good look at Jaik's companions in passing, he was stunned into promising that he would take a secondary road that went well west of the town.

"Well, he had his warning," Emily said. Jaik looked at her with disdain, as if to remind her that she was a trader herself, and that West and himself had certainly made the effort to warn her. He only wished he could do more for his own countryman.

Oris, with a curious look on her face, approached Jaik as he was sending this silent message to Emily and, for the first time ever, asked Jaik a direct question. "What animals was trader using?" She said it herself, in Asparian, to calibrate the translator, then put the headset on to hear the answer.

Speechless for a heartbeat, Jaik said, "W-what? Oh, they are . . . kinna. That is what we call them. That is what everyone uses. They do not eat much and store fat for long journeys. Their meat is no good, though, so they are not bred for food." Aware that he was about to start babbling out everything he knew about kinna, he stopped.

But Oris wanted to hear more. "What else could you tell me about them?"

Jaik thought it over. From yesterday, they had gotten used to talking around the limitations of the translators by keeping phrases simple. Describing something using basic vocabulary was tricky, though. "They can be bred fierce, for war. Those types have sharp teeth, but the ones you see do not. They do not get bigger than this," he measured out a volume with his hands that was about seven feet long, three feet wide, and five feet tall, "and their . . . legs are very strong. They can pounce on enemies in battle. Their front legs are only useful for keeping their . . . moves smooth. The ones you saw were . . . not to run. I heard from a trader that they do kinna racing in some cities. My pants are made from kinna skin," he said, pointing to them. Emily noticed that what she took to be jeans also had a slightly leathery look to them, and at a close look lacked the threading that would be evident on normal jeans. "These are . . . blue, but the only kinna I have seen are white, brown, grey, and black. In colder places, people wear clothes with the fur still on, but here that would be too hot."

"Thank you," Oris said, smiling. Jaik couldn't help smiling back, feeling both relief and satisfaction that he had fulfilled the request of this magnificent creature. Emily stared at the two and rolled her eyes, suddenly regretting that she had brought Oris along.

The Eldrandii continued. "As I suspected, these are what, on Asparis, were once called kantha. I am not surprised they were brought here, since they were almost indispensable on Asparis. I had never seen one before, of course, since Asparis had been under ISC quarantine since I was born. Kantha were meat eaters, though capable of eating plantlife, and much larger than these. This sort seems to be . . . a plant eater. Is that right, Jaik?"

"Yes."

"Must be due to adaptation to this planet over thousands of years. It was quick adaptation, and good adaptation, since they were inefficient eaters on Asparis, from what I heard."

"Asparis?" Jaik said with deep curiosity.

Oris, having maintained an economy of words until now, looked to Emily to do the explaining. It was a dicey issue – telling a person so far removed from his origins that his homeworld was now an uninhabitable wasteland.

Emily shook her head. "Hey, you mentioned it. You tell him."

She loved the scathing look Oris gave her, since it revealed that Oris, under her calm exterior, was still much more human at heart than the other members of her species. Other Eldrandii would not have flinched at telling the hard truth to someone, and certainly would not have looked to pass off the difficult responsibility to someone else.

"Captain, I believe your world was the determining factor in the fate of Asparis. Perhaps it is more your place –"

"No need," West said, stepping in. Now that Emily thought of it, West would obviously know the whole story, since his grandfather and mother had arrived alongside the latest wave of Asparii exiles. Why he hadn't told Jaik before was between the two of them. She was just thankful that he was ready to broach the subject now. Emily did not understand all the words due to the limitations of the translator, but West was speaking for Jaik, who caught every word. "Jaik, your people didn't evolve on this planet. They came from a planet called Asparis, probably thousands of years ago, since Asparis was blockaded for a long, long time until about eighty years ago. Asparian ships managed to break through eighty years ago on a mission to attack Earth, my planet, because they still claimed it from when it was called

Atlantis. Fifty years ago, Earth attacked back with the help of other worlds, and some sort of accident happened, and no one can live on Asparis anymore. Earth helped to get people off of Asparis and some were brought here, because this was labeled as a refugee planet. My grandfather came here with them. Everyone on this planet's from somewhere else, my mother said. Somewhere, there are Eldgil cities, too, I'm sure. That right, Captain Emily Pierce?"

Emily nodded. "What I understood of it sounded right." She didn't mention that she had no idea what an Eldgil was. She wanted to see how Jaik would react to the bluntly relayed story.

The young man mulled it all over. Emily appreciated his rationality and ability to digest information, since she had been forced to do the same more and more these days. The quiet, concentrated look on his face was not unlike her own. On him, it was an acute look, having both a childish innocence thanks to his fair, creaseless face, and an adult intensity that came from living a contemplative life.

"We have some legends . . . ," he said, directing his words more to Emily than West. "They say we fled some people called mancers. It is sort of a joke now, but adults used to scare little kids, telling them mancers will take away children who do not behave. Some adults still try, but it never works. The mancers were on Asparis, right? And we must have been desperate to get away, so we only brought what we had to. Inventions would have broken down after time if we did not have people who knew how to fix them. Is that right?"

He looked at her, and Emily nodded, impressed. He thought it through much farther than she could have, even given more time. Never the sharpest intellect, she was still proud of a deductive streak fostered by an early interest in television mysteries.

Attention turning to West, Jaik said, "is that why you're an inventor? Your mother, or whoever, thought it would be a good idea to teach you how to make things because we . . . we're so –"

"What do you think?" West interrupted. The words suggested anger and impatience, but instead West had his normal grin, appreciating his friend's silliness. Maybe there was also some admiration there, for how quickly Jaik had connected the dots.

Jaik knew that he had made the same mistake as he had last night, and said, "you did it . . . on your own, then. I guess people from Earth don't all know how to build generators or electric things. They just use them, just like us."

West tousled Jaik's hair in approval. Jaik usually hated it when he did that, but this time bore it, assuming it was a compliment for his perspicacity.

"Yeah, wonderful, whatever," Emily said, still having trouble liking West. "We should get going, or we'll be back in the forest tonight, too."

The hills were falling away now, and the road was steadily descending into the vast plain extending throughout the center of the continent. Seeing it magnified from space had given Emily a better idea of the landscape than West could possibly have, so the idea that they needed him as a guide was a joke. They had full color map printouts and everything. What they really needed now was someone to put a local face on their arrival in the empire, and that was Jaik.

Their pace quickened when they saw the road narrowing ahead, passing though a town wall. It was about half an hour away, and they took no longer than necessary to get to it. The wall was a mud-brick affair that looked like one slam with a battering ram would bring it down. But that was appropriate, since it was facing friendly territories from which no threat was expected. Getting closer, they saw that its tall wooden doors – easily twenty feet in height – stood open with only two guards in the entry way. No guards stood atop the wall, which probably wasn't wide enough to accommodate a walkway in any case. A sign post in the ground, about ten yards ahead of the wall, had writing in a language the humans could not read, so West read it aloud as soon as he could make the worn lettering out.

"Anduhalipar, Border Town. All travelers must submit to searches."

Emily looked at West and the rest of the party one by one. "Umm . . . we're going to have a hard time explaining some of our stuff, aren't we?"

There were frowns all around, even on Oris' face. She was clutching her device protectively, and said in explanation, "I have had all sorts of items confiscated before when traveling. We cannot let them have this, or your rifle, Captain. There are items they should not be exposed to, yet, by ISC rules."

Jaik looked furious. He had been silently aggravated by the issue for the past day, and needed to let his thoughts burst out, whatever awe he had for Oris completely eclipsed. "And just what is that supposed to mean?" he said, not caring whether their translators understood him. "You are going to carefully feed us inventions and protect us from dangerous things because we are not ready for it? We are not a planet full of children. If you can use it, we can use it. We are not stupid. And it sounds like you space people have wars, too, so you are not so much better than us. I have seen you working on that thing. I know you are some kind of herb master or alchemist or doctor. I hope you were planning to share some of what you found, because I have seen people die in horrible ways. It would be nice if someone could help us instead of keeping knowledge from us."

Emily felt a surge of pride and admiration in Jaik. Jaik, despite his normal reserve, had asserted himself with minimal reluctance. He was simply not conditioned to respect the Eldrandii the way she was. Even with her strong anti-authoritarian streak, she lacked the nerve to talk to an Eldrandii the way he had.

Oris had been hoping that the Asparii here, so far removed from their thoroughly offensive progenitors, could be brought around to respect the Eldrandii. Respect on equal terms based on achievement, of course. The old Asparii had something in them that made them oppose, unthinkingly, everything the Eldrandii stood for. The respect she had seen from this boy had given her hope, and his composure while hearing about the destruction of his homeworld at the hands of the human race even more so. But this outburst diminished her hopes. He was as irrational and prone to sudden passions as they had all been, Asparii mancer and mundane alike. Like Earthlings. Without thinking, he had attacked her spiritual purity – her ability to do the right thing for the less fortunate, and for those in pain. It was necessary to put him and any of the humans who might agree with his words in their place.

She spread her wings with indignant anger. "How dare you," her translator crackled as her voice turned into the high-pitched screech of an eagle, with words barely distinguishable. "I am no beast. I do not lack compassion. It is only because you do not know about my people that I do not kill you for your insult."

Without a doubt, no human had ever seen an Eldrandii like this. Emily quickly decided that Jaik had struck a real nerve, and every indication was that this was a religious matter, since that was the only thing that could set an Eldrandii off.

Jaik didn't back down. "If we do not know about you, it is your own fault. You had spaceships and we did not. You have been walking with us for a day and you have barely said a word. I do not even know your people's proper name, much less anything about them."

"Fool! We are Eldrandii, and there are Eldrandii on this planet. You have called us Eldgil."

Those words caught Emily completely off guard, and Oris herself looked surprised at the words escaping her lips. Except for Jaik and Oris, everyone was looking at Emily. Even West seemed to be indicating that it was her role to step in and end this. Max had caught the under-the-breath murmurs of Ethan, who repeated, "other Eldrandii . . . here," and soundlessly said "ask her" to Emily.

Having a tall order to deal with, Emily took it slowly while the two combatants fumed. Oris was in no mood to be pushed into an explanation, so the approach would have to be delicate. "Okay, first Jaik. Jaik, I don't know about Oris, but I'm here to sell some of our technology to the empire. I thought I had covered that already. I'll give your people everything you can pay for, I promise, but I can't have them getting a look at the goods for free. Do you understand that?"

Jaik realized that he had gone too far, and so hastily nodded and turned away from the glaring eyes of Oris.

"Now, Oris, umm . . . what Eldrandii? I mean, how did they get here?" That would do for starters.

At first, Oris looked like she would just answer "none of your business" or something else dismissive, but then her wings dropped and through that gesture she accepted that she owed some answers. "We . . . it is a penal colony. It is on another continent. I do not know specifics. Except for prison ships, Eldrandii ships are forbidden to or from this world, so even if exiles know space technology, they know we will destroy their ships if they try to leave. When you told me of a planet of exiles and refugees, I knew it was this world, and that is why I was eager to come. Other ISC ships, following Eldrandii lead, would stay away. I should not have even brought the penal colony up, as it is an Eldrandii internal affair."

Emily mumbled to herself, "you sure need a lot of penal colonies for a peace-loving bunch." Emily recalled that Plani had started out as the same sort of colony before the Plani evolved into a sentient species. On a planet where murder hardly ever occurred, what crimes could possibly get a person kicked off? Was immorality enough? Out loud to Oris, she asked accusingly, "why didn't you tell us about this before?"

It was tough to tell through the translator, but Oris' voice had some grit in it when she said, "it is an embarrassing topic . . . to my people I mean. We do not openly announce the flaws in our society."

Letting that go for now, Emily said, "all right, then. Listen, Jaik had a point. We're here to trade, and we want to show off what we can give them. I think we'll have a much easier time seeing the emperor if we bring impressive gifts."

"Nothing of mine," Oris said firmly. "I am not a trader."

"Fine, fine. I think we can impress people with other things. What do you think, Ethan?" This was good. She would get to put Ethan to use, now that Oris was not so ready to give answers.

"We'll have to explain things so that they don't seem threatening. I think the rifle will be the thing they'll be most interested in. Umm . . . West . . . do you have –"

"We have rifles. If you show them your small stove, they will understand that. But when you start talking, they will notice your invention which will be most difficult to explain, and will make them suspicious of magic being made to look like technology."

"Oh . . . ," Ethan said, "the translators. Yeah, that's a bit . . . tough."

"Should we go in without translators maybe?" Max suggested, having been able to manage fine without one. "Let West here do the talking. We're going to be pretending that we're from far away, right? It'd make sense for us to bring someone to translate for us."

Emily did not like the idea of putting away the trusty translators just when they were walking into a population center of this alien world. She liked even less the idea of trusting West to do their communicating for them. The proposition made sense, though. There was no denying that. She pictured the kind of traders that would be expected at the gates of this town, which stood large within shouting distance ahead of them, and having West translate would certainly be better than needing to start with a bunch of quick explanations. She had a good look at the guards from here, and they looked bored enough to make someone else's life miserable.

Jaik, regaining full control over himself, piped in before Emily could finish her train of thought. "West can do translating, but I can talk to them. Ask him." He nodded towards West.

"He is a great actor," West said without a moment's hesitation. "I did not see how good he was until a few days ago, but if anyone can talk his way through, he can." The absolute expression of confidence made Jaik's face flush with even more heat than when he had been shouting at Oris.

Emily messed her hair a bit. She decided she liked the idea. "All right. Oris, keep your thingy hidden, and let's stash the translators. If they ask us about them, we'll call them hearing aids or something. Will that be all right, West?" The inventor nodded. "Okay, and Jaik, do you think you could make that sort of thing up, if they ask you about our stuff, and you really don't know what something is?"

"If I have trouble, you can feed me explanations through West. But it should be pretty easy, after seeing everything West has come up with. I think I could pass it all off as things like his, and just say that your people can make huge numbers of them for low prices."

"Sounds good."

Translators off, but rifle in full view, they approached the gate. The guards were both stocky and around six feet tall, making them a bit below average by Asparian standards. They were the type of guards that got drudge duties because no one could picture entrusting lives to their care. The upside was the lack of expectations – they weren't really there to keep the realm safe. At best, their job was a subtle way to redistribute the wealth that accumulated in the imperial coffers, and at worst they were simply bodies filling an expected post. The downside was that the shabbiness of their official armor, which was all hide or cloth and not even slightly metallic, lacking even a rudimentary helmet, was a severe hit to their pride. The city's insignia, whatever it was, couldn't be made out at all, since the colors had faded into a patchy dark brown and sickly green. As a result, they were tempted to overcompensate for this blow to their self-esteem by nitpicking and exercising a mean streak on the basis that they should give the world as bad as they got from it. Of course, a propensity for this way of thinking played a large part in how they were brought to this low in the first place.

"Who are you?" the guard on the right, distinguishable from the other only by a thicker beard since they both had the same brown hair styled in the same diminutive manner, said with contempt. West translated, and the guards noticed. "Foreigners, are you? Look like it, you do. Talk about weak skin."

Emily noticed that his eyes were fixed on Oris, but his expression was one of casual contempt rather than surprise, curiosity, or reverence. Maybe he just didn't have the imagination for those more intricate reactions.

Jaik started the introductions, but only West and the guards understood his words. "We are from southern cities," he pointed to himself and West. "But these others are from far off lands and across seas, and they hired us to bring them here. They are traders with amazing goods that only our empire could afford in quantity. See this magnificent winged one," he gestured to Oris, "and do you doubt that such a one comes from places unknown to us? Let us pass, for these are visitors who seek an emperor's audience, and have journeyed far for that honor." It was far less impressive in West's English, but the delight West showed made clear that, in the Asparian dialect, this was a pronouncement worthy of Shakespeare.

"Not impressed," the other guard said, looking at Oris dismissively. "Big birds is all. Our emperor's seen everything from sea to sea. Besides, he is a bit busy right now, what with Great Sharing and all."

Jaik wanted to ask what Great Sharing was, but felt that he would lose initiative that way, and the act would subsequently fail. "We are not in Atparis yet," Jaik said, using the name of the imperial capital. "Good guard, for today, we will only wish to pass into this land. We will concern ourselves with seeking an audience after we take our first step in imperial lands."

"Yeah, well you are suspicious," big beard said.

"Mighty suspicious," the other one agreed, nodding gravely.

"And we don't even need to search you to tell you are up to no good. Take that rifle on this red-haired girl's shoulders, now. First of all, no woman ought to be given a weapon more dangerous than a cooking knife –"

"Never."

" – that's right. And then there's a bit about only our army having rifles, and our law that says anyone else caught with one will be hauled in no questions asked."

"Never see a rifle around town, I can tell you."

"Right. So, if this girl who wants to look like a boy will be good enough to explain what she plans to do with that, we might not arrest you on suspicion of planning an assassination plot."

The other guard's mouth hung open for a moment. Clearly, he hadn't actually worked that idea out for himself, and needed time to catch up. His eyes narrowed and he glared at Emily with a furrow-browed intensity that almost made her laugh.

"Gentlemen, gentlemen," Jaik said, needing time to recover himself after the surprise accusation. "This rifle, as you call it, is nothing this empire has ever seen, and thus cannot be something you have banned. It deserves a different name altogether. Call it instead a –" He looked to Emily for guidance.

"Energy launcher," she decided, and West relayed.

"Energy thrower," it turned out, and Jaik was thoroughly unsatisfied with the name, hoping for something more glamorous. "Please allow my friend here to demonstrate it. You may pick a target. Please pick something well away from your empire's walls – we would not wish to be accused of using this invention illegally."

Being offered a show, the guards couldn't resist. Suspicions had to give way to entertainment after a long stint standing around staring up an empty road. Besides, Jaik had spoken to them as if they were important, so their mood was softened in inverse proportion to their burgeoning ego.

"Let us see what that thing does to that tree over there," big beard said and pointed.

Emily waited for the translation, then questioned Jaik with her eyes to see whether this was all right, or whether there was some sort of trap – like something about hurting trees. He nodded, so she brought the laser to bear, and fired at full power. The burst left a clean hole in the green trunk of the tree, which sagged and fell, no longer able to support its own weight.

"Holy Katerz!" big beard said, hand on his head. "You can't bring that thing in here. That's a menace, that is."

"Please, sirs!" Jaik said, fully expecting this reaction. "Imagine if your emperor's army had weapons like these. Guards of Atparis will no doubt have security well taken care of, and we will certainly hand over this merchandise sample when we arrive. One of them is not enough to conquer a land, after all. Do not worry – it is tamper proof, so no one can discover its secrets. If it falls into other hands, it will not function." Jaik made the last bit up, but it was necessary to prevent the guards from just confiscating it, and seemed to fit anyway.

"Oh yes, and what else have you? You could show this rifle all over, and still be hiding things – smuggling them in – because no one will think to look at your other . . . objects. Weapons dealers are not trusted –"

"No, no sir. My employers are inventors, and they have all sorts of items. Take, for instance, this stove." He gestured for Max to bring it out. "And be amazed at its ease of use."

And Jaik continued to bring items out to show them, in the hope that they would eventually get tired of it all and just let them pass. He gave mundane purposes to the translator and Oris' computer, but otherwise told the correct purpose of everything, checking with Emily when he didn't know what a device was. By mixing in West's inventions, he managed to keep the interest level down so the guards would not ask to examine anything too closely. Nothing of West's was particularly new to the empire, and it gave the guards a chance to say, "oh, we have those already."

Finally, at the end of it all, big beard grunted. "Say, what are they paying you, boy? I have never seen a trader with your . . . well, you could sell anything, boy. You should be swimming in gold."

"Room, board, and a chance to travel with them," Jaik said virtuously. "I have lost my home to attack, and these good traders rescued me. And if you saw their ship, you would know that they take room and board seriously." He gave a cheery grin.

"Nice, is it?" the guard said, returning a smile, remembering distantly the dreams of his youth. "It sounds a bit like slave labor, and our empire does not tolerate that sort of thing, but you seem to be an eager young lad, and that bodes well for your employers. All right, then. You sold me."

"Me, too," the other said, still stunned by the steel riches unveiled for his pleasure.

"Here, let me give you a tag from our governor for your weapon so no one will give you trouble for it. This marks it as a southern cities trade good, protected under some treaty or other. Truth be told, a southerner could bring in a regular rifle if he wanted to, so long as we tagged it."

Jaik had to ask. "And . . . you will not get into trouble for tagging it? I mean . . . my employers would not wish to give you any trouble."

"Not at all. If you try to use that thing, it just gives something for our fellow guards inside town to do," big beard said, grinning to show that he wouldn't mind if a few of those guards fell flat on their faces. "Those . . . they just wait around, ready to practice their aim on anyone that tries anything funny. Expect that every step of your way, especially with Great Sharing and all. You just be careful to keep it on your shoulders, missy. And if you really want to avoid trouble, you might want to let the gents carry it. I know they might do things different where you come from, but some things might . . . unsettle people here, you understand."

West translated as best he could, conveniently missing the more colorful aspects of the guard's speech. Emily handed the laser over to Max as a gesture of good faith. It was an extra load she had no use for now, anyway. If the Shadow Workers chose to attack this town, the rifle would do little to turn them aside.

"Ah, good. Always nice to see people taking friendly advice. What is good for them. Okay, in you go. And if you cause trouble, do us a favor and tell them you climbed over this bloody wall and stole that tag."

Jaik and West gave twin smiles, and led the way into town.

Their eyes were filled with an idyllic medieval town scene. Before Jaik could appreciate the resolutely traditional feel of the place, Ethan turned to him and asked, "how did you do that?" before realizing that Jaik could not understand. That forced Jaik to get a translation from

West, who had his own piece to say.

"No need even to bribe them," he gloated quietly to his companions so others could not overhear. "No wonder those two were picked to guard – they were too stupid to hold out for bribes. Of course, Jaik here is really so good, he might have made them forget about trying. That was brilliant, Jaik." He said it in English, but repeated the praise for Jaik in Asparian. Jaik flushed briefly but said nothing.

"I don't know if you've noticed," Emily said to West, scanning their surroundings, "but this place looks ready for some celebration. Banners everywhere. Unless these people are all rich, they're in their best clothes." It was true – the dresses the ladies were wearing were resplendent with colors and a myriad of intricate embroidered patterns, with none of the clothes suiting any sort of work. The men were all in adorned leathers, which might have been practical if they did not mind mucking up the delicate finery. Since the designs were still in impeccable condition, it was obvious that not a single garment in the lot had been worn before. These were special occasion clothes "Must be the 'Great Sharing' thing that the guard talked about. Know anything about it?"

West shook his head. "First time I hear of Great Sharing." He asked Jaik, who gave a firm shake of the head, silently cursing himself for forgetting to ask about this vital piece of information.

Still taking a good look down the road, Emily saw all sorts of fresh tracks crisscrossing the cobblestones, clearly indicating a party-time bustle for the past few days. In a morbid moment, the worst possible realization stuck her like a hammer blow. Growing in the pit of her stomach, it was too heavy, too leaden to be voiced. But she had to get it aired, or be dragged down by it, so she made the effort to throw it out in the open. "This place is not ready for an attack. The guards . . . the people . . . everything. If the whole empire's like this town, then this Great Sharing, whatever it is, is going to be –" There was no way she could finish the thought, but she had said enough.

The words met with a cold silence from the others. West and Jaik were outright stunned by the thought, having from infancy thought of the empire as a massive, omnipotent force to the north. It had been a thankfully benevolent force, because it would otherwise have conquered the lands south of the hill range they had just crossed, and would have done so against minimal resistance. True, the empire had its troubles with the wasteland barbarians on its own northern border, but that was mostly protecting against raids. There was no hint that the desert dwellers could actually take over the empire. For the humans, the fall of empires was an almost inevitable occurrence, but the natives had different expectations. The empire was the solid bedrock of their world.

"Come on," Emily said, seeing their confused reaction all too clearly, "let's get a good look around. We should find out what this is all about before we head for the capital."

It took only a few strides into the city, though, before Oris attracted attention and curious stares. Emily would have responded to the attention by doing something humorous that would break the ice, but that was not Oris' way. The Eldrandii instead preferred to remain mysterious. The locals were in no way hostile. If anything, they, like West and Jaik, had an initial inclination to be reverential. They were also residents of a border town, and therefore used to unusual folk entering on a daily basis, and knew how to take such things in stride. If they were gaping now, it was because none of those arrivals had ever quite matched this one.

Emily suspected that if Oris decided to get opinionated, the imperials would quickly get as hotheaded as Jaik had, so maybe having Oris keep quiet was the best way to go. On the other hand, Oris could have done wonders to make herself seem less threatening by, for instance, simply chatting with Ethan using her limited English. It was true that, without the translators, the potential for conversation was restricted, but Emily was just as sure that Oris was trying to regain some of her sense of superiority after being brought down a notch by Jaik. Attributing petty reasoning to an Eldrandii was always a dicey proposition, but the image certainly fit in this case.

Ethan instantly renewed his studies in the local language from West and Jaik, more eager than ever to gain fluency since the translators would have to remain inactive. That gave the traveling party a more amiable feel to it as they entered the town proper, but between Emily, Max, and Oris, they were also projecting an unfortunately serious and menacing façade.

Emily overheard West translating some of the signs and banners stretched clear across the road, including "Gods Bless Our Emperor" and "Sharing is for All." Nothing gave a clear hint about the cause for the celebration, and the only ones who could make an attempt to ask were busy learning from each other. She looked at Jaik, wondering whether she should interrupt, just as he looked back. Somehow she knew that he had been thinking along the same lines, even as he had been interested in the study session between Ethan and West.

After sharing the moment with her, he started his work, approaching a random man and woman who had not been gaping at Oris, instead conducting some business with a street vendor who had bushels of fresh fruit on display. Within moments, it was clear that the plan had somehow gone wrong. Jaik had tried to strike up a conversation with the two, but the man immediately started shouting at Jaik, with the woman trying desperately to hold him back, attempting to prevent a scene. No luck there. So many people had already been attentive to the newcomers thanks to Oris that more than a dozen people were already listening in. Thankfully, they didn't get involved or try to instigate, though they were now throwing ominous looks at the outsiders.

West quickly stopped his discussion with Ethan and took a step toward Jaik, ready to back him up if things got uglier, then stopped. Really, there was nothing he could do that wouldn't make the situation worse. To Emily's disappointment, he also neglected to translate the shouting. Instead, he stood fixed to pounce, staring malevolently at the angry man.

As soon as the man took a breath from shouting, Jaik started calming him down. Opening his pack, Jaik pulled out and showed some of West's inventions. He gestured for Max to approach. When West tried to move forward as well, he indicated that his friend should stay back. He then moved to take the rifle off of Max's shoulders, but Max resisted, looking at Emily for guidance.

"Give it to him," Emily said as soon as she realized what Jaik was up to. It was basically a repeat of the scene played out in front of the town walls, except this time it was for the benefit of the townspeople. Clearly, the xenophobic man had accused them of something and Jaik was trying to explain what they were really here to do. Max handed the rifle over, and Jaik showed it as a salesman would, displaying the trade goods tag prominently, but careful not to touch it anywhere that might accidentally set it off. The man eased off and the tension in his face faded. He apologized grudgingly, did some explaining, then led his wife away from the scene. The crowd melted as well, curiosity about the newcomers mostly satisfied.

Jaik and Max came back to the rest of the pack, and the latter shouldered his weapon again. West wasted no time and questioned Jaik, having missed the start of the argument. He then turned to the others and finally explained.

"It is complicated," he said, calming down, but not his usual effervescent self. "Their emperor owns all land because he bought it from nobles and rich men. Great Sharing is him giving equal parts to all people in his empire. That man was angry, thinking we had come to get a part. Jaik told him no, that we are traders coming to offer people something, not to take from them. He did a good job again." And now West smiled to his friend, a bit embarrassed for doubting him.

Max frowned. "Sounds like we're not going to get much of a welcome. Everyone'll think we're just trying to get a bit of land for ourselves when we don't deserve it."

"No," West said, "that man was wrong. Everyone has put their names on lists already. We could not get land if we tried. That man thought we did not know that, and were trying anyway."

"Stupid," Max spat, but he saw the reasoning. No doubt plenty of people had flowed into the empire for land. It was a once-in-a-lifetime chance.

Emily furrowed her brows. "Weird idea. Can't imagine anything like that happening on Earth. Sort of . . . what do they call it –"

"Communist," Ethan said, "but they don't need to keep just that same land, right? I mean what would a . . . shoemaker do with a lot of land?"

West thought it was a good enough question, and asked a kindly looking old man passing by. The man was good enough to answer him with a smile, and West returned with the answer. "All pieces of land have equal value, and there is land in cities, too. A shoemaker would ask for a place here. If anyone wants, they can sell their land afterward. After Great Sharing, everything is normal."

"Not communist, then," Ethan decided, "not really."

Emily shook her head. "Still a weird idea. Let's get rooms and food. Do you think you could find us an inn or something like that, West?"

West didn't understand the word "inn" but got the general idea. "I will try, but it will be difficult. Everyone from farms is here to find out what land they received. It is like a market day, or worse. Rooms are . . . kept for people –"

"Reserved, yeah, I get the idea," Emily mumbled miserably. She was really looking forward to a bed. And a shower, if these people had gotten heavy-duty indoor plumbing worked out. Speaking of which, a toilet would make for a good change of pace after the last day of trying to find a concealed spot where some alien bug wouldn't crawl up her leg. She brought along some of her ship's emergency gold reserve to ensure a good time once they reached civilization down here, so there was no problem on that front. No doubt Jaik and West had some local currency of their own, and would make sure she didn't pay too much for things. She had been worried that people would try to gyp her, but now she wondered whether there would be much to spend the money on. All the gold in the world couldn't help you if all the rooms were booked, and nobody was willing to throw people out in the face of more money with the Great Sharing going on.

West wandered off for a while, leaving them to look around in the center of town. Emily had missed it before, but the buildings were all brick longhouses with thatch roofs. Each longhouse was divided into what she supposed were four to eight condos. Sidewalks surrounded each longhouse so that the streets were simply the gap between the building islands and were, as a result, irregular and bent rather than straight. All the doors were at sidewalk level, so there were no steps or staircases in sight. Makeshift stores occupied the fronts of half the condos selling whatever its occupants made. In some cases, these stalls were hodgepodges of goods, like garage sales, and it was clear that these were the houses of traders rather than craftsmen. There were no food stalls, though. Emily had been looking for anything that looked edible and found only dubious fruits. There was nothing like a taco cart in sight.

"Where do they keep the food?" she asked, stomach uneasy.

"Umm," Ethan said uncertainly. "I could try asking. West taught me how to say "I want to eat" and "where is their food?" already, but

I probably won't understand the answer."

"No food," Jaik said pointedly in English, his voice plaintive. "No food," he repeated. There was no sign that he had actually understood what they were saying, but it sounded like he was making the same observation that Emily had.

Ethan looked at Emily, sharing a moment of amazement with her. Jaik had obviously been paying some attention. Sure, they had been walking together and sharing meals for more than a day, and they had been speaking English more than Asparian, but that didn't mean the young native had to pick up on English. Why would he want to? Well, "no food" wasn't much, but it was something.

"That's right, Jaik. No food," Emily said, trying to show that she was complementing his attempt to speak her language. "Now, where food?" She gestured to his show that she was looking for something and not finding it. "Where food?"

Jaik smiled, getting the point. He shook his head and shrugged.

"Hmph," Max said, "lots of good that did."

Understanding the frustration of the group, Jaik added, "West. West where food."

Emily nodded. "Yeah, I guess he's out looking for it and we just have to wait."

Jaik's brow furrowed in thought for a moment, then he brought out the coin. He pointed to Emily, said "no", then held up the coin. He look worried.

She fished out one of her gold coins and held it up for Jaik's inspection. His eyes widened. She said, "okay?"

Uncertain how to respond, Jaik just nodded. It occurred to Emily that by nodding and shaking his head, he might be only imitating the human gestures he had seen. Asparii likely had different gestures, and very different ones at that, if a species like the Plani were any indication. Similar anatomy did not necessarily mean the same body language. Maybe she was over analyzing, or maybe Jaik was really that observant. Being an actor, he was probably very good at imitating behavior he saw. Trying to figure out why he would go to such lengths, Emily found herself reluctantly flattered. She didn't know why, but it was almost as if Jaik wanted to fit in with the humans.

Jaik knew exactly why he had paid attention to English words and human gestures. He barely admitted it to himself, but he wanted to impress Emily. As much as his performance in front of the gates of the city had been directed at the guards, he had also wanted to show the human woman what he could do. He had never considered the possibility of a woman like her, and every hour that he passed in her company made him more attached. In his eyes, she had some of the strength and cunning of West, but kept her feet firmly on the ground. She had his sort of grim view on life.

From what he had gathered by talking to Ethan, Jaik knew that Emily did not have a lover, and was not attached to anyone. At first, he had been worried that Ethan was with Emily, but that had turned out not to be the case. It was tough to tell what Emily would look for in a friend, much less a lover, and Jaik didn't bother trying to ask Ethan. The human customs for all this would be quite different from what he was used to, so he had to move slowly. She seemed to react well when he tried to impress, so that was a good sign. There was interest in her eyes, and that was enough to keep him going.

West returned, bearing gifts.

"West where food," Jaik repeated, still smiling. West gave him a quizzical look, then corrected, "West has food. West brings food." He held up six objects that looked like sandwiches, handing one to each of them. "West shares food."

"Thanks," Emily said, not waiting to dig in.

Oris was more cautious. She almost reached for her analysis device before stopping, contemplating the sandwich without it. Her manner was reserved. Of all of them, she drew the most attention, but had the least interest in everything around her. At first, she had taken the stares with patient dignity, being accustomed to the awe her form generated, even among the other spacefaring species. But this was different, and she caught some sniggering and what sounded like rude comments. Evidently, she did not live up to their image of the magnificent Eldgil, and they gawked at the specific areas in which she was deficient. Her species' latent hatred of the Asparii flared up in her again, and had she not been more tolerant than her brethren, her blood would have boiled.

She could not bring herself to trust the food, especially since she was not as hungry as her companions and was in any case better at holding her appetite in check. She decided to keep the food for later, when she would be able to use her instruments in private. Also, seeing the effects of the food on the others would be instructive.

The rest ate the food, and they all followed West as he led the way, trying to explain the situation. "Only one room. They will bring more beds. There is plenty of space for us to sleep, but not to move, so it is better if we do not all go in until night."

"Well, one room is better than nothing," Ethan said.

"It is a good room. We are lucky. There is nothing else in town. Tomorrow, we can go to capital," and here the excitement grew in his voice, "and, if you have money, I can get a kinna carriage for us."

He said this all again in Asparian to Jaik, who said something back. It might have been about the gold because West then turned unsurprised to Emily and said, "you have money, then."

"If gold is good enough."

"Gold is good. Gold is always good." He led them to a longhouse that was a single establishment instead of divided up into individual houses. Over the main door – a double door instead of the usual single sported by houses – a sign swung on a hinge in the gentle breeze. "It says, in your language, South Road Hotel. That is Alforanis Navera. Alfor is south, and Alforanis was the road we came on. If my mother had wanted my name to mean West in this planet's language, she would have called me Dalkat, but that is not considered a good name for a person," West explained pleasantly, leading them inside.

The interior had the feel of an Old West inn, but without the swinging doors. The place was full, everyone was drinking heavily, and it was obvious where all the food in town had gone. From what Emily could tell, the town was currently playing host to about five to ten times its normal population. This couldn't be the only inn in town, but everywhere else must have been packed as well. Nearby towns must have been shoved into this one for administrative purposes. But there was no way that this hotel could fit all the people in its first floor restaurant, so they had to have found other accommodations.

A burly, jovial, and thoroughly bearded man approached West and shouted at him through the din. Emily supposed that this was the manager, though he was on the verge of drunkenness. His cream-colored tunic had food stains all over it – though these could have been due to anything, not necessarily eating – and his pants were rough, lacking the embroidery of the clothing seen on the people walking the street outside. Among the patrons of the hotel's restaurant bar, the clothing fit right in. Some of the better dressed revelers looked awkward and more reserved. They were probably thinking of fleeing to their rooms instead of staying in the midst of this dissipated devilishness.

"Uh . . . Captain," West said, after speaking to the manager, "he says others want room. You will need to give a lot of money."

"How much?" She asked warily, unwilling to flash too much gold in this company.

"One gold coin will do, I think."

She brought it out, and handed it to the manager. He growled something to West.

"I did not know your coins were so small. One more will do it."

Emily took a good look in the manager's eyes. "Tell him that's all we've got. At least, all we've got for a room since we'll only be here one night. Tell him I've got more gold for the food and drink."

West relayed the message, and before he got done talking, the manager was barking back. "He says he does not have a place for outsiders without money."

"Tell him we're sorry to bother him. We'll go somewhere else."

"He says he will not discuss the price."

"Tell him that if he expects us to outbid other people who want the room, he'll have to take a bit of haggling. Tell him I'll give him two gold coins if he throws in food and drinks for free."

"Three coins, and he will give us a bottle of alcohol instead of what they make in . . . I do not know how to say . . . place where we wash."

"Bathtub. All right, deal," she gave over the three coins, each a half ounce of gold. It was a hefty price to pay, no matter where, but she had an additional request. "But while we're here, we don't want any trouble. Can we get him to promise our safety here?"

"That . . . we will be safe?" West clarified, puzzled. He didn't trust anyone else to keep him safe, no matter who it was or how much money the person was paid. Actually, he didn't trust anyone who wanted payment at all.

"That's right."

West translated and the manager nodded, gesturing toward two muscle-bound men standing unobtrusively, but conspicuously, near the staircase to the rooms above. Nothing else needed to be said.

"All right," Emily said. After the scene between Jaik and the man in the street, she had only wanted to ensure some privacy. "If there's no trouble while we're here, I'll give him the extra gold coin. Let's see this room."

It was no more and no less than six mattresses laid out in a row with blankets on them, and a foot of walking space around each one. There were two windows overlooking the street, but they were fogged and smudged up with unknown residue, so that there was no view to speak of. Emily went to them and tested whether they could open – six people in such a tight room could make a place real stuffy. They did, albeit with a lot of reluctant creaking and the need of extra force with every inch. The walls were a dreary gray plaster peeling away in patches to reveal the wood underneath, which was mercifully not yet rotting. At least the walls weren't bare brick, since that would have given a more stifling feel to the place. For what she had paid, though, they should have gotten all the amenities of an upscale Manhattan hotel.

West sighed and said, "it is all there was. I talked to some of those with rooms here, and they paid about one of your pieces of gold each for two or three bed rooms."

Emily shook her head. "Don't worry. It's better than sleeping in the forest. I'll manage our money – I brought more than enough to cover this sort of thing."

Eyebrows raised, West said, "you must want a lot of trade with us to spend so much on this journey."

Emily glanced at Oris when she said, "we've already been promised a lot of money for our trouble."

Smiling at the brief acknowledgement, Oris said in English, "Captain, you may remove a mattress. I do not sleep on ground. I see a tree nearby I can perch in, and that will be enough for me."

"Great," Max said with uncloaked sarcasm, "a couple of inches more wiggle room. Wonderful." The way he looked at the room and the shakiness in his voice betrayed a hint of claustrophobia.

The accommodations aboard any Eldrandii-built ship were naturally spacious and high-ceilinged, so no one could feel cramped aboard a starship. Maybe he just wanted a bit more space and privacy, but if Max really had a touch of claustrophobia, there would have been no way to tell before. He wasn't shaking or doing anything crazy, so whatever he was thinking, he had control over himself. That was enough.

For the rest of the day, the land dwellers took part in the town's revelry, while Oris decided to stretch her wings and do some flying. Emily sensed that Oris wanted to get away from town for a bit to do more research. By the time the five got their first drinks, though, people were coming up to them to ask about the Eldrandii. Jaik fielded all questions, making some of it up as he went along, and looked quite worn out by the time the sun set since every person in town wanted to hear the story for him or herself. The residents were accepting of all travelers, living in a town that derived its wealth from them, but no one like Oris had ever passed through, and while they wouldn't have had the guts to walk up to her, their curiosity drew them to Jaik like Plani to a sucker. Or maybe a Plani vampire to someone wanting to be sucked, Emily mused.

Having nothing else to do except for drinking and eating, West continued the linguistic education of Ethan, with Jaik listening in whenever he could. Emily pulled Ethan aside, just as the natural light outside of the hotel dimmed below the lamplight inside, wanting a few minutes to talk with her old friend. She brought him back to the bedroom, and they sat down on one of the mattresses. Ethan sat crosslegged, but Emily hugged her knees to her chest, her boots making it awkward to cross her legs.

"How are you feeling?" She asked, not knowing how else to start.

He thought it over. "All right, I guess. It's almost like a dream. Sometimes I think about what I've been doing, I can't really believe it."

"The whole language thing between you and West. You want to keep that going or –"

He shrugged. "It's all right. It's a good thing I can keep up with him. He is not a very patient teacher. But I always wanted to learn languages – I never really got down to it – so it's . . . fun, I guess."

Emily smiled weakly. "Great. Nice that something's working out right. I don't like anything about this planet. I don't like people in metal armor, bars with no food or drink I recognize, an entire town of people I can't talk to, this Great Sharing thing, or the chances that we will actually get to see this Emperor. I have no idea what to think about Oris and Max, except that Oris has totally forgot about teaching you now that she's getting what she wanted from here. I know what I think about West, but I'm not sure I'm being fair. And –"

"And you like Jaik," Ethan said for her, knowing what was coming.

"What? Well, yeah, but –" She was about to say that it was just because of all the help the Asparii had given them, but knew the words would ring false. "Is it that obvious?"

"No. But I've known you for years, and I've seen you with other boyfriends so . . . I could tell."

A part of her wanted to ask Ethan if he thought Jaik liked her in return, but her very essence rebelled against the childish notion. She was a couple of old boyfriends and one-night-stands beyond the point where she should be wondering whether a boy liked her, wasn't she?

"Yeah, well, he's a bit young," she said dismissively.

"Smart, though," Ethan said, proddingly. "And he's got a dark side. You like people with dark sides, right?"

There was something in Ethan's words that jolted Emily – a subtle bitterness that suggested a hundred things that might be off the mark. She didn't know which question would get him to open up, so she decided not to bother. Instead, she got down to what was really troubling her.

"Kaz has been trying to comm us, and I just got his message. The ship's got a job and was getting ready to leave orbit yesterday. Nothing from the ship since, and they aren't answering, so maybe they've left. I tried to check in with John at the landing pod, and didn't get an answer. I've checked in the few times since we left him, and he didn't say anything was wrong. Said it was good hunting, actually. But now –"

Alarmed, Ethan said, "should we go back?"

"He didn't call for help or anything, so that means either it's just a messed up comm thingy or whatever got him was so quick he didn't have time. I think we're too far along to go back anyway. We'll have to wait until the *Azar* gets back before we know anything for sure. I . . . It's tough. I don't want to tell Oris and Max yet, 'cause I'm not sure how they'll take it, and we're all under it already."

After a moment of contemplative silence, Ethan said earnestly, "t-thanks for telling me."

"I was just getting it off my chest . . . I needed to tell somebody."

"Yeah, I know. But thanks for telling me." Feeling like enough had been said, he stood up and left the room

Huh, Emily thought, he took that well. For her part, she had been on the edge of panic and confusion. For what must have been the first time, she had talked to Ethan about something serious, and his simple trust in her served to calm her down. It usually made her feel mildly guilty, since she knew perfectly well she didn't deserve that trust, but this time it bolstered her. A bit lighter on her feet, she left the room thoughtful, but a shade less worried.

That night her dreams passed unremembered and, when she woke up the next morning, she felt energized for the long day ahead.

8
Atparis Nightmares

The kinna were everything Emily had imagined from West's description – hulking, smelly, and massive. They had a buffalo's size and shape, except in the legs, which had the power of a cheetah's magnified to match the added mass. It seemed impossible that such beasts were tame, but one of them nuzzled her affectionately in the back while she was negotiating the price for a ride to the capital.

"You will be just in time for our emperor's announcement of Sharing and our capital's celebration," the carriage driver said, through West's translation. "You outlanders may even get an imperial audience. He will be in a good mood for visitors after this, I think, and you are interesting enough to get through." The carriage driver was looking at Oris in particular, who would be riding on top of the carriage despite Emily's objection that it would attract too much attention. Emily was getting tired of the Eldrandii's single-mindedness – the whole reason why she wanted to sit atop the carriage was so that she could fly around, conduct experiments, and return. It was true that the avian could easily outpace the carriage and catch up to it when her business was done, but Emily couldn't help feeling that they should keep their profile low. Why else had they landed so far from the capital? Really, without Oris, the party would have blended in with the locals fairly well.

Despite the throng of onlookers gathered around the carriage, gawking at them, they got underway with minimal hassle. The journey itself was sheer boredom, with Emily spending her time staring at the landscape, Max snoring on the seat beside her after having trouble staying asleep the night before, and the other three intermittently doing language lessons and talking about different places and worlds. Every now and then Emily would catch Jaik's eyes on her, they would look at each other for a moment, and then both turn away. She did not know what signals to send, and he didn't either. They were at an impasse, both trying to take the tactical approach while neither of them was especially good at it, used to plunging in and relying on instinct instead.

Luckily the roadside scenery was varied and eclectic, so Emily always had a plausible reason to look out the window. Right out of the city, she spotted a flight of enormous creatures, each at least twice as large as an Eldrandii. Her first thought was that they were Karisi – a sentient species with a world of their own – but saw that these avians were bearing Asparii on their backs, and the Karisi would never stand for that. Besides, the one thing everyone knew about Karisi was that they did not look like dragons. Scholars were very active in combating this mistaken first impression, brought about by a clueless diplomat with a bad habit of oversimplifying everything when placed in front of news cameras. When the ISC first provided details about all its member species to the World Council, the idiot had come up with nicknames for each of the species based on Earth fantasies – the Plani were elves due to their slender form (which might have been the grossest of the misconceptions), Karisi were dragons because of their webbed wings, Delauri Gol were giants for the obvious reason, Delauri Kai were dwarves by the same token, and so on. Of course, it was all ludicrous, but the associations made the unknown familiar, so they spread like wildfire.

But these creatures really did look like dragons, so they were definitely not Karisi.

West had seen her looking out at them, and smiled as he said, "bierka."

At the word, Jake had leaned toward the window, delighted to see one of the common but marvelous beasts. The other two humans also looked, in surprise.

"There are fewer and fewer of them these days," West said, musing to Jake, "that's what old men always say. We hardly ever saw them over town. See more airships now."

"So you have airplanes, then?" Max asked.

"Not many airplanes. My mother taught me about airplanes and airships. Airplanes have wings, that's what 'plane' means. Airships are big balloons."

"Zeppelins," Max said, "yeah, we had them, too."

And sure enough, Emily spotted one in the distance. It was difficult to tell how far away it was because the enormous size of it could not easily be gauged. If the sky didn't provide enough marvels to catch and keep the attention, monuments and buildings did the trick. Out of the city, this was once again an imperial road, but that status was more obvious now than it had been in the forest. Every few minutes, they passed by another statute. And these weren't the pale marble statues of Earth, all austere imitations of ancient leftovers – these were in full color, and gleaming bright in the sun of the plains. Some warrior statues actually had their swords out with blood painted on. Very nice. Most of the statues were of lone figures, but some depicted scenes. Emily was sure that if they stopped, and were able to read the writing on the bases of the statues, they would learn the history of the land they were passing through.

The roadside buildings were mostly inns, and by the looks of them, they were all actively competing for business. Emily was reminded of the monument imitations of Las Vegas, except these were all on a smaller scale. Not one building at the side of the road had the simple brick longhouse construction of the border town.

Every town they passed by was offset from the road, so that they didn't go through any of them. From the outside, though, they were fascinating little units of life. For one thing, they had very definite boundaries. Cities on earth tended to fade into the countryside in a smooth transition. These towns looked like neat boxes, as if they weren't allowed to grow any further. As the capital neared, the very nature of the towns morphed. Whereas the earlier towns had regular roads surrounded by buildings, these towns had roads on the roofs, and the buildings were underneath. The roofs were often uneven, so there were ramps all over the place, but there was a clear central road under which all the roofs matched in height. Only that central road could have accommodated vehicles, and the rest were obviously pedestrian affairs. Emily got the sense that the townspeople spent little time in their homes, which were so tightly packed that Max would certainly be claustrophobic in them. Their lives and their business were conducted in the outdoors, on the rooftops.

Even West and Jaik were stunned by these constructions, not having heard of them before. Somehow, this little detail had escaped the stories traders had brought to them about the empire. What would the capital look like when they finally reached it? Within an hour of arriving, the sun starting to set on their left, they started to speculate.

The city itself did not disappoint. Everything they expected was there, starting to be lit up for tonight. Emily was the first to see the massive step pyramids, but these were just gateway buildings – probably containing something administrative. They were perfect twins, and each at least eight stories tall, if each step was one story. Out of each of them, a strong wall stretched out, so that the only way to enter the city on this road was between the two pyramids. The lights made them glow golden in the dusk, and reminded the Earthlings of Egypt.

Entering the city without any hassle from the guards at the gate, who were better armored, but no less surly and disgruntled than the border guards, the carriage immediately started up a steady slope. What had previously been obscured by the pyramids was now visible. Calling it a hill would have missed the grandeur of it completely, but that was the basic shape of the terrain. The incline was gradual enough to make the obscuring effect of the pyramids work, yet also to make the central tower prominent on the summit. That tower was in the form of an obelisk, but was again not a bleak solid color but decorated in a mosaic of distinct images. Alone, though, it would still have been unremarkable. Instead, it was encircled with twin flyways spiraling around it in a double helix. From a distance, it was hard to see whether they were functional or just decoration, but they were impressive. Tearing her eyes away from the spire, Emily saw flyways all over the city. Some were clearly exterior stairways for the taller towers. Others danced above the uneven rooftops as elevated highways so that the city's roofs would not have to bear the load of the heaviest traffic. Most of the city was built like the nearby towns, but from this vantage point, massive courtyards and parks in the midst of the buildings could be seen. There were parks on top of the roofs, too, and these were often tiered like the pyramids at the gates, though only three or four tiers high. Still, they were massive.

"Like the Hanging Gardens," Ethan murmured.

One thing the city was missing was people, but that was expected. The Great Sharing celebrations were going on at the heart of the city, and anybody not required to be somewhere else would be attending. Absent its denizens, the place was eerie. The streets were well-lit, as were public places like parks and official buildings, but otherwise, entire neighborhoods were shrouded in a creeping darkness that was only kept at bay by street lamps which had an old Victorian style to them and, as far as Emily's limited experience could tell, ran on electricity. The darkness didn't bother her as much as it did Ethan, who walked haltingly and stared at every shadow in case something foul materialized. No, she was bothered by the silence. This was a legitimate city, while everything else they had seen in this empire had been a glorified village, and any true city generates noise. Even on a special day, noise meant life. That was probably why people liked fireworks, marching bands, and all the other loud trappings of celebration. Noise was essential.

Emily felt better about the city as they neared its center and mounted its pinnacle hill. A boisterous racket was first announced by rhythmic pounding, reverberating in the hollow caverns beneath the road. The drumbeats were soon joined by the cheers of an entertained crowd and the flares of fireworks. These weren't the fireworks Emily was used to – they were alive, dancing about against the background of the starry night sky. Without a doubt in her mind that magic was involved, she marveled at fiery figures forming dancing pairs, or the explosive equivalents of balloon animals. The firework kinna were obvious as were the bierka, but Emily didn't recognize some of the creatures, and frankly felt a few of them were worth avoiding at all costs. Their tooth-to-brainspace ratio was on the dangerous end of the skull scale.

The lighting of the city's central square, set in front of the emperor's citadel and tower, cast a glow for blocks around. The travelers knew they were nearing their destination, not only by the now deafening noise and babble, but also by the light that let them examine the fine features of the architecture around them. No longer were the buildings constructed from mudbrick or wood – these were opulently dressed in polished stone, in such close proximity to the powerful liege lord of this land that even they had to maintain appearances. Elevated train tracks now crossed over the street, bringing travelers from the west into a tall station barely visible on their far right down one of the side streets.

This square opened up in front of them, and was packed with uncountable bodies. After the long climb up to it, Emily was glad to see that the Empire had taken the time to flatten this section of the city out – it would have been painful to stare upward to see the stage, where musicians were currently performing a form of native music bearing some resemblance to Earth rap music. Their tiny distant forms were made visible to the crowd thanks to huge holographic projections – magic again. No doubt the amplification of the music was also handled by some magery. Deep down, Emily felt it was cheating, since these people didn't have to put the work in to get their enjoyment.

Dignitaries walked onto the stage in costumes that looked like inaccurate attempts to imitate traditional garb from times long past. Actually, the robes looked vaguely Eldrandii, except with a flat color and no accommodations for wings. On the avians, robes complemented their plumage and fit their characters. The humanoid figures onstage looked like peacocks, trying to impress others in a way totally unsuited to their stature. Or maybe trying to remind others of the status now lost to them. That was more like it – these had to have been lords of huge estates before the emperor decided to share land. In the holographic projection, their faces looked unusually solemn, and even grim.

Emily jostled her way into a position right behind a family, but didn't want to push her way through them. They made such a quaint picture. The mother and father, both dressed in drabby work clothes, were carefully keeping hold of the hands of their children – three girls and a boy, all four in overalls. One of the girls, not more than seven years old, stood right next to Emily. Having tired of the fireworks and the loud music, the girl took an interest in the outlandish woman.

The girl tried to speak to Emily, but Emily couldn't understand a word she said. Luckily, West was right behind them and said, "she wants to know where you're from."

"Well, just tell her that I'm from another country."

West did, but the girl's curiosity was not satisfied. "She wants to know if all girls dress like you do in your country."

"No, they don't. I like to be different," Emily said with a bit of cheek. "Ask her what her name is."

"Her name is Havala. She says she likes your clothes and hair. She's never seen anything like them, and she likes to be different, too, but she doesn't get a chance to show it like you do."

"Tell her that if she goes to other countries she'll get plenty of chance to be different. That's part of the fun of traveling."

The girl smiled thoughtfully, and was about to say something when a woman stepped onto the stage after all the dignitaries had ascended, and stood at the front to speak to the crowd. Deciding that the woman on the stage was more interesting than Emily, the girl returned her attention. Judging that no one would pay much attention at this point, and that the crowd was quiet enough, Emily took out her translator, turned its volume low, and motioned for the others to do the same.

"As mayor of Atparis, it is my pleasure to welcome you to this long-awaited occasion," the woman on stage began, pausing for cheers, "and in this great city, which since time's dawn has been our world's heart, we have rejoiced and will rejoice at a great gift given to us by our realm's lord. Every year, during this same week, we will rejoice again, since every year, our land will bring forth new gifts, making us all rich and all content anew. Let me not babble any further. Please show your gratitude to one who deserves it – his honor, Lord High Chancellor, Davin Tayron."

The shouting and applause was deafening as an aging, though still vigorous, man strode to the spot the mayor had just vacated. If the crowd had not already been standing, they would have gotten to their feet for this man. Emily had to turn the translator off, since all it could do was buzz in response to everything that was being said around her. It was some minutes before the Lord High Chancellor got a chance to start speaking.

"My countrymen," he said with relish, and to further cheers. "I thank you and our mayor for this wonderful reception. I have looked forward to this for a long time . . . and it was well worth the wait." Excitement rippled through him, and spread out from him as an aura of unbridled vitality. "Our world has moved steadily away from our ancestors' struggles, and we can now enjoy fruits from centuries of their labor. With so much of their old world fading away, we stand at a threshold, a new beginning, and Great Sharing is only our emperor's attempt to give his people an appropriate fresh start. As we were at time's beginning, we will once again be equals. What happens to you from here on will depend on your diligence and skill . . . and perhaps a little bit of luck. So, let me wish us all good luck."

The chancellor paused again. Close by, Emily heard some murmurings in the midst of the delirious approbation. If these people thought anything like humans did, she could guess what they were saying. However precisely the wealth of this land had been divided, there was no way a farmer, with all his skills, was equal to a High Chancellor or, the gods forbid, the emperor.

"Now, would you please give your welcome to your emperor, his magnificent and indomitable highness, Fenarian, king of Atparian lands in an unbroken line for centuries, whose grandfather conquered Rath'rainol and built our empire, who –"

Though the chancellor continued listing the emperor's legacy, his words were drowned out by a cheering crowd. He made no attempt to quiet them as he plunged ahead with his introduction, smiling warmly at the crowd's enthusiasm. With a pang , Emily wondered at the spectacle, and found it almost too perfect. Grumblings of a few discontents aside, the scene was fantastic and dreamlike. Too dream-like. She remembered vaguely a snippet of a dream in which she had seen this being played out, but couldn't remember what happened. Couldn't be anything good – her dreams were never about anything good. A chill swept through her as His Imperial Majesty appeared on the stage, flanked by bevy of bodyguards who, being unarmed, must have been mages.

The emperor did not immediately return to address the crowd, but instead gestured to his chancellor, who had taken a few respectful steps back. Chancellor Tayron hesitated, but at his lord's continued beckoning he stood alongside the emperor on the stage. The emperor then extended his hand and, in that instance, Emily saw what would soon happen. She looked around at her companions, and her eyes met West's. His face was full of anguish, so there was no question he was thinking the same thing – this place, with all the residents of the capital gathered together, would provide the perfect target for any group bent on attacking this planet. If the enemy was a real asshole with some sense for the dramatic, this would be the exact moment to start blasting.

Emily held her breath as the chancellor grasped the emperor's hand in his and shook it, once again delighting the crowd. There was no getting away now – the mass of people was pressed in on them, and just maneuvering through it to get out of the plaza would take half an hour. She started anyway, signaling to the others to follow. Little Havala marked their departure, but made no mention of it to her parents.

Emily had barely started moving when the cheers turned to screams. In a single second, the mages onstage had been blasted – some were burned in pillars of fire, while others simply exploded. The attack occurred so quickly that there was simply no defense. Left without protection, the Emperor could only stand in shock. He had only just let go of Tayron's hand, when weapon blasts defeated the anti-magic charms he wore in an amulet, tearing first through his chest, then his skull. The amulet would have protected him against magery, and his mages had been focused on shielding against mundane weapons. Only the combination of both kinds of attacks, in precisely this manner, could have worked. The enemy had come prepared.

Panic erupted immediately. Emily could no longer see what was happening on the stage because the crowd's pushing had turned her around. There was no chance for them to stick together now – she and her cohorts would either have to move with the crowd or get trampled.

A mist was building in the plaza, making it difficult to see what was going on. The crowd's shouts offered no hints, since people were as likely to cry out in fear as from death. But then the bloodcurdling screams started and there was no question that the enemy's might was being unleashed on the populace.

Forced into a stumbling run through the nighttime haze with no idea where she was going, Emily's heart was pounding painfully as if trying to rip apart her ribs to free itself. The thick air was quick to choke her lungs, which were doing more work than they had in years. As if she needed further excuse to have a heart attack, a hand suddenly gripped her wrist and pulled her forward. Whoever it was pulled her forward, weaving its way as if it could actually see in the clouded nighttime air that turned the most intense lights conjured for a ceremony into vaguely brighter regions of grey, providing no help to the blinded.

Running behind whoever was leading her for what seemed like forever, her legs were shooting bolts into her brain. When they finally escaped the fog and slowed to a cautious measured walk, coughing the thick mist out in the face of pure air, she was unsurprised to find that her companion was West. Having faced so much shock already, maybe she had become desensitized to it.

"Captain, we must find our friends and leave."

"You mean you didn't see where they went? Seemed like you could find your way through that –"

"I could not see more than an arm's length away. I took your hand so I would not lose you. It was just luck we got out of it. But we are in an open area now, and we are even more in danger."

"How did you know it was me?"

"Red hair," West said simply, scanning the field of smoke in front of them. Sometimes a mage hovered up above the mist, then plunged down again to wreak more havoc. A few of the enemies were also at the edge of the plaza, trying to kill any potential escapees. It wouldn't be long before she and West were sighted.

Emily couldn't say anything. Ethan, Jaik, Oris, and Max were all either still in there or dead. Or maybe they escaped. Certainly Oris could have escaped, unless the Asparii mages had spotted her as a member of the species that was their ancient enemy, and had attacked her soon after targeting the Emperor. God, what a mess.

"Get back!" West shouted, pulling her into one of the smaller roadways off of the plaza, shoving her back against a brick wall of the nearest building. A radiant mage, all aflame, hovered past without a look down their way. There was enough prey in the square, and a few escapees were nothing to be worried about. Emily would have instinctively brought around the laser rifle and shot the bastard if she hadn't left the weapon in Max's care. As it was, she took out her comm link, trying to contact either the pod or the *Azar*. No luck. Too bad she didn't have a link with Ethan or Max. Ethan especially – Max could take care of himself.

Not in this, she reminded herself. No, they were out of their league, as Kaz had said in the first place. Boy, she hated when he was right, but she would give anything to hear him gloat about it over the comm right now. All the danger aside, she also felt some sense of guilt, as if she had brought this doom to a peaceful planet. She had seen it all, hadn't she? She had seen it in her dreams, and back at the border towns she had even told her companions what would happen.

With a start, she suddenly realized that West was no longer standing beside her. Damn that idiot, where had he gone now? Looking around, she couldn't see anyone in sight on the narrow street, but the oppressive darkness made any search futile. She was paralyzed with indecision, unable to simply run away, nor able to return to the battle zone where the enemy mages were still indulging in the slaughter, causing the crackle of flames, roar of explosions, and the now fading sounds of suffering life.

Hopefully West had left for a reason, and with the intent to return, because at this moment, she was felt completely lost. Of course, he had no ties of loyalty to her except the recognition that they were of the same species, which had never stopped humans from abandoning each other before. If he had run off to save his friend, Jaik, then maybe the two of them would simply flee the scene, leaving the outlanders to deal with their own lot. Her mind, having nothing better to do at the moment, imagined Jaik admirably insisting that West and him should stay with Emily and whoever else had survived, because of his still undefined feelings for her.

West didn't leave her wondering long, popping out of an alley to her right with Ethan in tow, and not looking happy about it. "A mage came between us, Max, and Jaik. That idiot Max was shooting at a mage. What do they teach humans on Earth, anyway? I am going back for Jaik. No hope for Max – these mages will not let anyone who has shot at them live."

Emily bit her lip, but said nothing as West turned back down the alleyway. There was no refuting it – if Max really had fired at one of the enemy, they couldn't let him survive, and he was no match for them. She looked at Ethan, who was standing mutely beside her, trembling in every limb. He was still in shock, and when he raised his shaking hands to rub his eyes irritated by the smoke, he looked on the verge of breaking down. Emily went to him and held her old friend. He turned to face her, his eyes squinting up into hers, and she gave him the best comforting hug she could manage. She wasn't, as a rule, the mushy type, but if there was ever a time to be sensitive, it was now. Besides, she needed the reassurance almost as much as he did.

It still took a few seconds after they separated before Ethan managed to clear his throat enough to say "thanks" without his voice cracking horribly.

"West said that Max shot at one of the mages."

"Max . . . was protecting me. I couldn't help him. Had to get away."

In the midst of the carnage, Max still shielded Jaik, covering the young man's escape from the onslaught. Spells rained down on him from furious mages bent on torturing him to death, and Jaik was having trouble bringing himself to stand and run. He had no idea where to go, and even if he did, his limbs were stiff in horror as Max's form was stretched and twisted, writhing in pain from the malevolence contained in the magical words. Still, in his anguish, Max had enough presence of mind, and care for a fellow innocent, to look at Jaik with seething eyes, trying to wordlessly will the boy to run, as he knew his own time on this, or any, world would soon be over.

But Jaik couldn't budge. It was just like in his town, when the armored man had first appeared. He had needed West to pull him away that time. Now, frozen again, he had no hope. With the ability to think, he would have berated himself for his foolishness and complete lack of survival instinct, but as it was, fear occupied every cell in his mind, and took residence in his stomach as well. Meanwhile, three mages surrounded Max, providing Jaik with excruciating images that would haunt him for a lifetime. The mages now ripped limbs from the noble warrior, and then repaired them magically so they could tear him apart again. Careful not to reassemble him properly, they eventually created a creature with arms sticking out of his chest and legs out of his back. Max remained alive through it all. The true horror of it, at least in Jaik's mind, was the way the fists on the arms clenched and unclenched in such pain that the fingers ripped the flesh of the palm, causing blood to stream out.

Jaik didn't know how long he spent sitting on the ground, staring desperately at the scene, before a hand grabbed his arm and stretched it to his limit, and his heart lost all rhythm until he realized the grip belonged to West, and that he was saved.

"Too bad you didn't get the gun from Max, but I guess it wouldn't have done us much good now, anyway. Oris, though, damn her, where's she gone? It won't help the grief, but I'd sure like to send some of that money home to Max's family. This will be a total blowout if we don't get what she promised us."

Ethan's expression morphed from distress to outrage so quickly that he caught Emily by surprise. Her friend had always been slow to emotionally respond to things, but not this time. "You're thinking of money . . . now?" There was an edge to his voice that told her more than his words.

"Was trying to take my mind off of now, actually. Listen, this isn't our fight. We're here on business, and it isn't happening, so we're leaving. All we're waiting for now is Oris . . . and maybe we should be moving without her. If she's alive, she'll be able to find us from the air."

"You didn't used to think like this," Ethan grumbled.

"I didn't used to have Asparii crazies chasing after me and killing thousands of people in front of me."

"Yeah, about that. What if we're responsible? What if we led the bastards here –"

"They were here before us, remember?"

"Not by that much."

"There weren't any ships in the system when we came in. That means it must have been here a day before us at least." Then it hit her – what if there had been a spy aboard the *Azar*? Kaz would have entered the coordinates and plotted the course to Selparis while she was down on Eldrand, and once the course was in the computers, an unscrupulous hacker could easily access it. Had she misjudged the Wetzler-Davison situation? If so, she could have led the Shadow Workers here, a planet that was supposed to be somewhat of an open secret. Emily swallowed. Ethan glanced the question at her, but was interrupted by the arrival of West and Jaik, the latter looking even worse than Ethan had.

"We must get out of here," West said immediately. "Those mages are almost done. Some are already scouring for survivors."

Emily was in full agreement. "Any idea where we should go? After we got done with business here, I was planning to go straight back to the landing pod, but I bet the mages are keeping an eye on that road. I haven't been able to communicate with the pod pilot, so –"

"I had a map . . . I do not remember much of it, but I do remember big cities. North of here is Mankared, to our east is Atacren, and to our west, there is Dakatanis. They are all very far. Mankared might be a week away, but it is surrounded by desert, so no escape there. Atacren and Dakatanis are ports, so we can take a ship to Free Cities, then, if you still want to, you can get to your pod from there. Dakatanis is two weeks away, and Atacren, maybe three. Going straight back the way we came without the kinna carriage will take us a week and a half. Dakatanis is further south and closer, so it is probably better."

"Any idea how we get to Dakatanis?"

West shrugged. "Head west until we hit ocean, then head south. Unless there is a road with signs."

Emily sighed. Nothing about this sounded like a good plan, but it was better than anything she could come up with on this unfamiliar terrain. West had the best idea of where to go, and without Max, who had been carrying all their hunting and cooking gear, he was their best hope for food. Problem was, that meant the key elements of their escape were out of her hands. She desperately hoped that she would be able to get contact with Kaz and the *Azar* soon, otherwise there would be some hard traveling ahead.

The four survivors moved quickly with West in the lead. While in the city, the roads helped them orient themselves, and their guide's instinct for concealment kept them hidden in the shadows while enemies swept overhead.

"Fucking hellish things," Emily murmured, trembling slightly at the sight. "Didn't know they could fly. Makes them . . . so much creepier. I liked it better when they were the ones hiding in the shadows."

After what seemed like hours, they were halfway through the city. Taking a good look at him in the occasional lamplight, they saw that West was growing increasingly worried and anxious, frequently twitching nervously. While there were myriad reasons for him to be concerned, she guessed that there was something specific nagging him.

"What's wrong?"

West hesitated, then said dejectedly, "I have been thinking about the city wall, and I cannot figure out how we are going to get past it. All gates out will be guarded by mages. They would not want anyone escaping to warn other cities."

"That's easy," Ethan said, adjusting his translator because it had shifted down a bit and wasn't picking up his whispering voice. "We use the train tracks. Those trains must go out of the city, and I'm betting that they pass under the wall in a tunnel. This whole city is full of tunnels already, so I doubt they'd miss a chance to build one more."

"And you do not think that tunnel will be guarded?" West asked scathingly. He hadn't given the railroad a thought, and was bitter about missing such an obvious possibility.

"If I could fly around and blast things, I wouldn't be spending my time in a dark tunnel hoping some victim wanders in," Ethan explained. "It would be sort of like the guards at the gate who can't leave their posts even though everyone else is celebrating. Somehow, I don't think these mages would let themselves be treated that way."

"Know them well, do you?" West bit back.

Ethan furrowed his brow, not seeing why West was angry at him.

"Fine, tracks it is, but do not blame me if we find ourselves facing a fireball."

Jaik was giving West a puzzled look now, too. He was still jittery from seeing Max being contorted and crushed, and West's attitude was doing nothing to help his nerves. Noticing this, West cast an apologetic glance back and said, "sorry," before continuing to lead them, now heading in parallel with the elevated train way.

Fires in the city center made a false dawn breaking the dark of the night, and the smoky haze reflecting the flickering light spread at an incredible pace, threatening to overtake those trying to escape. Shouts carried by the cold night air now seemed distant and random. Judging from the flames back up the hill, the haze created by the enemy was thinning as it spread, revealing the full extent of the carnage. The center tower and its surrounding keep still stood out behind the smoke.

Was there any sense to all this? Weren't Shadow Workers supposed to manipulate things from the background and try to control realms by persuasion and threat? Maybe these mages were not Shadow Workers at all, but an altogether different group. It was an unlikely coincidence, but possible. Far more likely, they were so close to their goal that they had abandoned secrecy and were going straight for it. That goal couldn't be blasting a backward empire to kingdom come, so what was it?

Emily shook her head. Not her problem, dammit, not her problem.

The tracks were finally descending at a rate greater than the hill was diminishing. For five blocks it ran at road level, necessitating elevated crosswalks. Then the tunnel started, just as Ethan had predicted, heading directly west into a tunnel seven blocks from the city wall.

It looked exactly like a subway on earth, making Emily feel dazed and displaced for a second. Everything else on this planet was just alien enough to remind her that she was not home. They hopped the short fence, and followed the trackside walkway down into the dark depths. A few yards in, West fished through his sack and brought out one of his devices and a tankard. He poured a liquid from the tankard into the base of his invention's cylinder, then flipped the switch. It was an oil lamp, with the switch providing a spark to light it. Throwing the switch the other way would douse it. With the lamp, which was bright beyond what she would have expected, they could see details on the tunnels opposite wall and the two tracks in between. The light was a beacon, though, and would have given them away immediately if lit outside.

There was no telling how long the tunnel was, and its abyssal gloom dared them to proceed. The sounds of destruction from the city were carried to them, amplified by the reverberations off of the tunnel walls, urging them forward. Eventually, as they distanced themselves from the tunnel entrance, there was silence, and none of them spoke to break it. Emily was weary beyond belief, and the flickering light of the lamp did nothing to keep her awake. At the edge of her mind, she could see dreams creeping up on her, and she pushed them away with all the mental force she had left. Perhaps if she didn't see what was going to happen, she would not feel as responsible for the disasters around her. Of course, she could not deny sleep forever.

Her increasingly bleary eyes, staring forward without really seeing as long as the view remained monotonous, now registered an out-of-place gleam in the murky gloom. The others also saw it and slowed. It moved towards them. By the time they could think to retreat, the outline of the armored man solidified and all hope of escape had left them. West and Jaik had seen the steel monster summon mages before, so turning around and running back to the city held no hope for them. There was nothing else to do, though, so they ran.

Not a word was said, as their tired minds were slow to acknowledge the futile situation or voice the anguish they all felt. No sooner had they started their dash than something was flying in from the city, heading to meet them. They were surrounded, and the choice between the metal man and the flying mage left them without options, panting for breath, sweating in the hot night air, and terrified.

"I don't . . . suppose . . . you've got some kind of . . . weapon in there," Emily said in between breaths, pointing at West's sack.

West brought his pack around when, taking a new look at the flying figure, his eyes widened, and he smiled. He hurried with renewed vigor to get his mini-crossbow out. Unable to see why West's attitude had changed, Emily came to the logical conclusion quickly. Ethan was the first to voice it.

"That's Oris, isn't it?"

By now, though, there was no doubt. The Eldrandii was carrying a hunched man on her back, who jumped off at her bidding as she continued without slowing to fly at the armored enemy. She had the laser rifle, Max's rifle, aimed and ready, but its beam might not be enough to pierce through the metal skin – there was no telling what these attackers had come prepared for.

"West!" Emily urged, not knowing what the crossbow could do, but reasoning that any bit would help.

Oris started firing with the rifle, fully intending on flying straight at her opponent in the hope that her momentum would do some damage if the rifle did not, but that plan was dashed in short order. Laser fire went right through its target and by the time Oris had reached it, the armored enemy had disappeared. A horrendous squawking cry of fury later, the Eldrandii turned to face her companions and the squatting, hunched man she had brought with her.

Face contorted in an unmistakable smear, Oris shouted, "Where is it? Damn magicks! It could attack us from anywhere now." She was burned in patches of her skin and wings, and all the muscles in her face were tight, pained from exertion in the midst of intense action. To have managed the retrieval of that rifle, she must have done some impressive flying, and was now twitchy, ready to evade any further attacks.

"I . . . I don't think so," Ethan said, voice filled with uncertainty, "I mean, I don't think we were much of a threat to it, if it wanted to kill us."

West and Jaik looked at each other. The latter said, "that one attacked our town. We did not hear any fear in him, then. Even when he walked alone, he did not seem very weak." There was such great pain and trembling in his voice, that Emily instantly knew that he was being plagued by whatever he had seen before West had rescued him.

"Then why did he not? Why did he not kill us if this rifle was not going to kill him?" Oris spat, with a deranged look in her eyes. "He is here, I tell you. Get ready."

Emily was taken aback, never imagining that Oris could act this way. Granted, the Eldrandii had a bad reputation for handling trouble and surprises, but Oris had so far acted like a more adaptable sort who could take the unexpected in stride. Then again, Emily had never seen the Eldrandii pitted in open conflict against their mortal enemies. Could the existence of an Asparii opponent be enough to turn the aloof Oris into an avenging angel? Emily couldn't help thinking that there was more to this – something that she was missing.

Even worse, she had a strong suspicion that she knew why the six of them weren't dead, and desperately wanted to talk to Ethan about it. They were being followed to some unknown destination. She had thought it was this planet, but clearly the enemy was expecting to tail them further. Considering all she wanted to do was get off this planet as soon as possible, though, she couldn't understand where they were expecting to be brought. Unless . . . it wasn't her that they were following this time.

"Who's our friend here?" She asked with a sneaking suspicion. She recognized the robes as similar to the ones worn by the dignitaries on stage during the sharing ceremony. The dignitaries . . . and –

"Lord High Chancellor Tayron, Captain," Oris said, cooler than she had been since her arrival. "I flew to rescue him knowing that he would be the next target of the assassins. I, for once, would like to know what is happening here, and think he might be able to tell us." After speaking, she returned to her search for signs of the armored man's reappearance, not at all ready to believe he was really gone.

"The . . . omigod," Emily slapped her forehead. "Great, now we're totally involved. That knight is probably coming with backup. He could kill us on his own, but he wants to capture the chancellor to see what he knows. Or maybe they'll follow us, see where we go, and kill everyone there, too. Let's move, fast."

"Finally talking sense," Oris murmured as she led the way, her multitool far from her mind and her awareness at its height. The rest needed to run to keep up, but they didn't mind, sensing the necessity and desperate to get out into the open, free from the confines of the tunnel. High Chancellor Tayron, still out of breath, didn't speak but kept up with them. All the others were new to imperial culture, and had no idea how to treat their new fellow traveler. Emily's outburst had also made them aware of the added danger that the newcomer brought with him. It made them cold to the political leader, who himself was stricken mute by this disaster on his day of triumph.

After a few minutes, they were still alert, but Oris had slowed their progress down.

"There is a train ahead," she said. "I think it is safe to approach it. It has stopped, probably waiting for a signal from the station."

"That must have been what the armored man was doing. Remember how he was checking the road?" Ethan said. "I think he was checking the tracks for trains."

Jaik nodded, but had other thoughts he was not ready to voice. He opened his mouth to speak, but then shut it, as if realizing that what he had to say would not be taken seriously. Only Emily noticed, wondering what was going on in that enigmatic boy's mind. Truth be told, she felt guilty about her momentary willingness to flee without West and Jaik.

Oris stopped for the first time since she had entered the tunnel, and turned to look at the rest. "Perhaps it would be better if I stayed back. I can catch up with you easily, and it would be best for everyone on the train to see . . . familiar faces giving them the bad news."

Emily nodded. "West, could you take the lead and do the talking? I think they'd rather hear it from someone who speaks their language, and if it's you, they won't be so suspicious of us other humans."

Without a word, West stepped forward and brought them to the stopped train. It was on the city-bound track and looked mostly empty. No surprise there. Its headlights cast a bright ray at them, and the conductor poked his head out of the control cab window to yell, "Hey! You there! Any idea what is going on up ahead? They stopped me here, and I have had no word from them since."

West gave him the news about the massacre, causing the conductor to blubber about the impossibility of it, but evidently he believed the news wholeheartedly nonetheless, because he decided on a course of action quickly enough. "I am going to put this train in reverse and back right out of this tunnel. No good sitting here until we are blasted by mages, is it? Best to get back to Aftari station, and park it there till everything gets sorted out."

"Yeah . . . but you could just back into another train," West said, stating the obvious patiently. "Unless there's someone at the other station controlling things."

"Good point. I've been talking to them about this hold up, and they had no idea. Now I've got some word to pass along, I'll get them on wire."

They waited while he did so, wanting to know whether the way was clear, or if the mages had already moved their attack on to neighboring towns. The news was good – the last station was blissfully unaware of the capital's situation, shocked by the news, and the track was clear for a train to reverse its way back.

"Whew, that is a relief," the conductor said. "We are pretty much empty, so if you do not tell anyone, I will let you hop on free. I was kicking myself all day, not getting to see . . . Great Sharing and everything, but now it looks like some god was keeping his eye on me. Puts me in a good mood, that."

Without hesitation, they took the offer. If there was trouble on the train, they would just get off again, and anything that sped them on their flight from the capital was a blessing. According to West, Oris should have no trouble keeping up with one of these trains, so no problem there. This familiar mode of travel would be a rare comfort after so many bumpy rides and exhausting walks, not to mention after their run to get this far from the plaza.

The train's passenger cars were elegantly upholstered, but the intricacies of the interior only made its long history of gradual wear and replacement more obvious. Some of the seats were faded, while others had cloth fresh from the textile mills. Though it looked a bit more upscale, Emily saw no appreciable difference between this Selparii train, and those she had seen on Earth. As the train pushed its way backward, she made herself comfortable, settling into a nap, sprawled on a pair of seats. The others followed suit, exhausted.

Before they knew it, the station was alongside, lit by oil lamps as the long night was still going strong. Weak legs barely obeying, the group stumbled onto the platform, and saw around it a town blessedly free from mist, smoke, or screams. Looking back up the tracks, the landscape and darkness obscured the capital city, but the heights of the smoke columns were clearly visible. The conductor locked the train and walked past them toward a stern-looking woman rushing to meet him. From her rigid attire and attitude, she was probably an official. Exuding a great deal of energy for such a late hour at night, though, she was obviously to the night shift.

The conductor must have recognized she was important from her clothing, because the first thing the woman did was introduce herself, so he couldn't have known exactly who she was. "You in charge of this train? I am Captain Terivelle of the Aftari security force, and I demand you tell me what has happened in the capital city. We have had no communications for hours, and by the time the town wakes up, I want news for them. I have already got the night shifters panicking. It is usually solid buzz on the wire from the capital day and night."

"Well, ma'am, it is my train, but I didn't get to Atparis station. I got a stop and was stuck until these folks came and told me what happened. Guess someone threw the emergency cutoff for that section of track."

Captain Terivelle ignored him, stepping past him to face his passengers, and didn't bother to repeat herself. "Well?"

West handled the explanation, but the captain was a sharp observer and noticed the translator headsets picking up what he said. "Not from around here?" she asked with the requisite suspiciousness.

Looking into Terivelle's, strong, honest eyes, Emily decided to take the chance and speak. "We came to make a trade agreement with the Empire. We have technology for the Empire, and wanted an audience with the Emperor."

"An interesting coincidence. And how is it you alone of the city's people managed to escape to our city?"

Emily frowned. It was a good question. "Hopefully, we are only the first. Me and my people have experience in dangerous situations through our travels."

". . . and me and my friend here," West said, gesturing to Jaik, "we knew the danger beforehand, and told Captain Pierce. You see, our town in the south had already been attacked by these mages –"

"Enough!" came a voice from behind them. Striding forward was the lord chancellor, so far silent and unobtrusive throughout the proceedings. Now, his commanding tone rang out and his elaborate attire finally marked him as nobility, rather than a man in a costume. "I am His Majesty's chancellor, and I require conveyance from here to Dakatanis for me and my rescuers here. I want fastest travel possible. We have to outrun magic, and I do not like our chances if we are stuck on trains."

Shaken, her jaw hanging open, Terivelle took some time to answer, but Tayron was used to this sort of reaction, and waited patiently. "I . . . my lord, a flight of bierka can be arranged. Whether they can out-fly magic . . . but they will beat trains, that is why we keep them around. We . . . we could get some flying machines, if lines to Queisis are still up."

"Not necessary, a bierka will be fine. Make it one six seater."

"I will go to arrange it then," Terivelle said, snapping a salute, and marching off.

Tayron turned to Emily and said sharply, "we need to talk. Let us take a seat over there." He pointed to a bench on the lamp-lit platform, sitting lonely in the night. It occurred to Emily that she had never been in the midst of a more important person – neither Welder nor

Raiz could match the sheer power in this man's hands. And Tayron had been in complete control of his presence – unobtrusive when necessary, and stepping forward to take control of the situation when it became essential. Whatever influence technology gave to Earth politicians, none of them, at least as far as she had seen on television, could compete with the noble chancellor's stature. He was born to this role. Emily was as ardent a democrat as anyone, but even she had the modesty to recognize that she had just met the real thing – a politician so well groomed to power that he knew it was corrupting muck and felt secure sharing it when necessary.

She had expected iciness from the bench, but the summer night had kept the wood warm. It was a good thing that Chancellor Tayron had a clear idea where he was going, because she sure didn't. Actually, one question did come to mind – how did he know we were going to Dakatanis? – but she got a definite feeling that there were already more answers on the way than she wanted. To get a grip on her thoughts, she turned briefly to Ethan and tried to guess what he was thinking. The most obvious answers suddenly struck her like epiphanies. Tayron was going to Dakatanis because it was the closest port city and he needed to get somewhere, maybe somewhere with the forces he would need to strike back against the invaders. But more than that, Tayron had expected the arrival of the humans, and might even know what they were here to do. Otherwise, he would have been asking questions about their presence immediately. Turning her suspicious eyes back to the chancellor, her intensity melted when she saw the deep worry that creased his energetic face.

"I will start," he said, looking up at the stars instead of directly at her. "Generations ago, Captain, your people brought refugees from Asparis, a world we had only heard of in legends. They tried to be inconspicuous about it, but my father had a talent for paying attention to our empire, and did notice. He even noticed that some humans stayed behind, and that they had means to communicate with Earth. Through agents, we have kept good relations with our human residents, learned of other species and recent events through them, and sent some veiled messages to your leaders, even though those communications were technically directed to family and friends on earth. That you are here means that your leaders were listening in."

Well, Emily swallowed, her mind racing to keep up, that pretty much confirmed all her suspicions about Commander Raiz. "And you're not telling your people about all of this, are you?" she asked, thinking about suspicions of government UFO cover-ups over a hundred years ago. Of course, those conspiracy theories had been bogus, but here on Selparis, they seemed to have the real thing.

"It is a frightening time, Captain, and we are preparing our people as fast as we can. But everything that I have heard tells me that we will not be welcome in this Interstellar Community of yours. We were castaways, and if we start raising a fuss now, we had better be ready for a backlash. So, we started by launching unprecedented efforts to explore our world. And even though bierkas had always provided efficient flying transportation, we sponsored the development of flying machines because that could eventually lead to space technologies while bierka would not."

"Great, but that still –"

Chancellor Tayron held up his hand to silence her. "And on our explorations, we found something. A library of ancient knowledge. We could read some of it, but some technologies described were so far beyond our own that we had no chance to put what we found to use. We needed a spacefaring species' help. A species we could trust. So, we dropped some hints, and here you are. Unfortunately, other, more sinister parties, heard our news as well. Not a surprise – you cannot keep something like this a secret."

Baffled, Emily returned to some simple facts she was clear on. "I'm here to trade. That's it. I don't know anything about ancient technologies, and I don't think my crew will be much help, either."

"This is a trade, Captain, but it is between your government and mine. We need protection, and your government gets all information in that library. We have to get there before these mages, and we cannot lead them there. At least, we have to get there well ahead of them so we can contact your people and have them secure the area."

She felt horrid for saying it, but had to make the point. "I trade for money."

"Captain, you can make your own deal with your government. I can guarantee you a wealth of gold every year for every year of your life if we can save my empire, but nothing if we do not. That library though, is of incalculable value, and even a small fraction of all profits it would generate . . . even you could not have needs beyond that."

"Why, what do the books have in them?"

Tayron looked around, then spoke only for her ears, though the others must have caught some of the words. "Do not tell your winged friend about this. Am I right in saying that it is an Eldrandii, and that they are somewhat . . . dominating over other species?"

"Yeah, but I don't think they'll get jealous of any technology we might find in there. They're not that type."

"I think there is material in this library that would make even them jealous."

Emily motioned for Ethan and repeated what the chancellor had said. "What do you think? Could there be something like that?"

Her friend stroked his chin. "Asparii don't write their secrets down in books. It's a cultural thing. But if . . . Atlantian refugees ended up here . . . they would have had the technology and plenty of books about it. If there's an ancient library here that an Asparii could understand bits of, it's probably Atlantian. They say that Atlantis used to be as powerful as Eldrand, too. Plus they would have plenty of stuff about magic that the Eldrandii might consider dangerous. The refugees wouldn't have had all the machines and stuff to build what they needed to make spaceships, and they would have been more interested in food when they landed here anyway, so all the extra technology would be left in the books for us to find. It's possible . . . I think."

"Okay," Emily said, trying to grasp the enormity of this, never having believed the Atlantis story in the first place. "Okay. That would be worth something."

"Yes, in bringing your Eldrandii with us, we will be taking a risk. You will be bringing information to your people that would challenge her people's supremacy."

"She just saved your life," Ethan said, not comfortable with this machiavellian man stepping in and sowing discord against his former tutor.

"For what reason, I wonder. Why is she here in the first place?"

Emily looked at Ethan. Now that came to it, the reason sounded a bit lame. "Disease research." Wouldn't Oris have found it much easier to get the money to fund this venture if she had been telling people that some valuable secrets from one of the ancient competitors was buried here? And that Earth was now trying to recover its legacy. That was the sort of thing that would have gotten her anything she asked for – millions of credits and a fleet of escort ships. Emily shook her head. Eldrandii didn't think the way humans or Asparii did, and Tayron was just projecting his own attitudes onto Oris.

And this game could get even more interesting than she had planned. Even if Oris wasn't secretly trying to betray them, and Emily found it hard to believe that she was, that didn't mean the Eldrandii government wouldn't oppose their keeping control over the library once the secret of it was revealed. And if some Asparii mages had found out about it, assuming that this was what the Shadow Workers were after, how long would it take before the Eldrandii found out? They had to have known already. Of course, she didn't need to secure the entire library. If she could just find the right books, the most important books, then she could carry out a treasure in her arms. What if the Atlantii had planted other libraries around the galaxy as they ran from the destruction of their civilization? This could turn into a huge treasure hunt.

Could she back out of this now? Maybe, but she'd hate herself for the rest of her life. Imagine if she could bring some long-lost secret back to Earth, whether it was technological or magical. There was no better opportunity than that. There was no better way to guarantee hero status for as long as humans traveled through the stars. It was what every explorer dreamt of doing. Anyway, they wouldn't be getting to the library tomorrow, so there was be plenty of time for her to think her away through this morass.

What if Tayron was lying? One look at him told her that he wasn't. He was too spent, too absolutely drained of spirit after the loss of his capital and his emperor, to bother fooling around. At least, not about anything important.

With a tinge of worry in his voice, the chancellor asked, "are you with me, Captain?"

"Yeah, yeah, I'm with you."

9
Transoceanic

Oris rejoined them once they were in the air, as they clung for dear life to the bierka's six-person saddle. Their legs were stretched out in front of them, strapped onto the massive hide structure. Backrests almost made the saddle look comfortable, but in the air, comfort was far out of their minds, as they desperately tried to find things to grip. As the dragon-like animal beat its wings, the oscillating motion was nauseating. Emily and Ethan found it hard to keep their composure, but could not complain since West and Jaik, frightened though they looked, seemed to bear with it without a word.

Tayron alone was amused. "Flying in space ships, I would have thought this sort of travel would not concern you. Surely you are not afraid of flying?"

The Eldrandii supplied the answer for them. "You will find that gravity is not a present threat in space travel, Chancellor, and your planet has slightly greater gravity than Earth, or most other nearby habitable planets."

"It does not seem to affect you, though?"

"Flying here is difficult, but easier for me than walking. If I had to ride that animal, though, I would be . . . affected."

Tayron gave a boisterous laugh, seeming to need it desperately, with tragedy otherwise hanging over him like a death shroud. Emily was surprised when Oris cast her own demure smile. The Eldrandii had been haughty lately, and it was easy to forget that Oris was not nearly as icy as others of her kind.

In Emily's eyes, Oris was Wetzler and Davison all over again, and she could not know whether Oris was trying to sabotage this journey. She based her suspicion only on Tayron's suggestion – not even his word, just a hint casually thrown out there – and the devil was that it all made sense. Could a person believe something just because it sounded right? She usually did, but somewhere deep in her mind, she suspected that this sort of thinking had gotten people into trouble before.

Unable to appreciate the scenery passing below them as she struggled to keep herself firmly in the saddle seat, she would not have seen anything of note anyway. The carriage ride to the city had provided a much better view than the aerial trip, since the landscape was a nondescript rural pattern, with fields of various textures chopping the land up into an enormous checkerboard. Tayron seemed to grow bored easily, and struck light banter with Oris, keeping carefully away from topics of importance. The rest kept their minds on ardent prayers that the ride would soon be over.

They must have been in the air for two hours before the chancellor decided to set them down for a break, a little past halfway through the trip to Dakatanis. The location was ideal. A grove of trees surrounded, at a distance, a placid lake, producing perfect shade for summer heat and a lakeshore that had just enough landing space. Since there were farms all around, dangerous beasts were unlikely to be present.

Until she dismounted, Emily had no idea how sore her body was. It did not want to budge. When she tried to stand firmly, pain shot up her legs, only to meet her numb rear end. Her back was aching. It had never ached like this before, but thanks to that damn animal and its unwillingness to just glide, she felt like an out of shape wreck.

"Ow," Ethan said with every slow, jerky step. Shaking themselves out and stretching a bit, West and Jaik did not seem too bad for the wear. Tayron, of course, hopped down lithely like a veteran, breathing the fresh, moist air deeply. He did not make it obvious, but his eyes were fixed on the horizon where the capital, now too distant to be seen, would have been.

"How come," Ethan started to say, but then took a breath to calm himself. "How come the wind wasn't pounding on us while we were flying? There wasn't any windshield on the saddle."

"Oh, there was," Tayron said, preoccupied. "A spell. Magic," he said the word bitterly, "on that saddle. All bierka saddles have windshield spells – totally safe and reliable."

"Umm . . . couldn't they have done some sort of spell to make the flight smoother? Or keep us from getting so sore from the ride?"

Tayron shrugged. "Why do they not just enchant a box to send us anywhere we want to go instantly? I am not a magician. I have been privileged, until now, not to have to worry much about magic in my day-to-day administration of an empire. I have been thankful for what our mages could do, and I never bothered to ask them to do more."

Oris was down at the lake, floating in it much like a swan would, though the water came up to her abdomen. Her cloak streamed behind her as her feet paddled, moving her across the surface of the water with a swift grace that was somewhat cartoonish. With Eldrand as icy as it was, finding temperate water to wade in must be a rare pleasure.

West wasted no time jettisoning his extraneous clothing, and taking a dip wearing his shorts. Jaik took his lead, but the other two were more dubious. The most obvious excuse was that every muscle in their body would crap up immediately in the water after the horrendous ride. A bit of prudishness was at work as well – they had not packed swimwear, and were not willing to dip in their underwear, especially without a towel in sight.

"Could use a bath, though," Emily commented, doing a smell check of herself. "Hope that diving into a lake's not the only option in these parts." Wearing black clothing had been a case of bad planning on this hot planet, but she didn't mention that to Ethan.

Tayron walked along the shore alone, absorbed in his own thoughts. With all that was on her mind, Emily should have been doing the same, but her body objected to any attempt at refocusing attention away from its pains, and sent blades into her consciousness.

They waited only a minimal time between the swim and lunch, and only because of Ethan's pleading did they let the meal settle in their stomachs before taking flight. Emily did not like the idea of airborne vomiting, either, but Ethan did a good enough job stating the case that she was able to keep her mouth shut. Just thinking about another hour or two on the bierka made her queasy, but she hated looking weak in comparison to . . . anybody. Ethan had long accustomed himself to it.

The second flight seemed smoother than the first, though that was more a testament to human adaptability than any care the bierka was suddenly taking. Actually, it was almost completely a product of the large-scale desensitization that still pervaded throughout their bodies. Maybe that was how Tayron bore through it – he couldn't feel anything at all anymore. Shaken up for life. The thought was not enough to put a smile on Emily's face – the flight was better, but not by that much.

Dakatanis was abuzz with activity, and thankfully untouched by any sign of disaster. The trains were running, planes were flying, and from the air as they circled into a landing at the bierka field, they could see massive cargo haulers inching into and out of the harbor. Unlike the cities of the Empire's interior, its buildings were built to great heights, as if to give pilots more of an adventure on their way in and out. The skyscrapers were no more than fifteen stories, but still taller than all the buildings they had seen in the Empire with the exception of the capital city's tower. Of course, the capital's hill had made even the smaller buildings seem to loom over them while, approaching these beachside towers from the sky, the travelers were unimpressed by the features of Dakatanis.

The bierka field was a menagerie containing all size and color variants of the flying beasts of burden. It was a full-fledged airport, and a mark of the struggle the government would have replacing the old method of flight with clunky, fuel driven machines. Even if a bierka was slower than an airplane, it would not crash when it was hungry, and would automatically do its best to land safely, no matter what happened to it. No engineering talent required.

Making another wobbly dismount, Emily spotted a charming white single-seater bierka. Regardless of the discomfort of riding one, she decided that it would be extremely cool to have one as a pet, even if she made only some short flights with it. Unable to stop herself, she asked, "how much would one of those cost . . . Chancellor?"

"Oh . . . I do not know your currency . . . A gold bar about your forearm in length and another your upper arm in size. That is my best estimate. It also depends on the animal's breeding potential."

Tough to translate that into credits, but Emily guessed it was easily over a hundred thousand – maybe a million for one of the larger ones. Too much for an impulse purchase. Emily sighed and took a broader view of the field. The price of purchase did not include people to take care of the animals, and they seemed to need a lot of attention. Cleaning up the mounds of crap they produced, in particular, did not look very appealing. More trouble than they were worth.

Emily loved sour grapes logic. Despite a privileged life, she did not always get what she wanted from her parents, who had read books about how children should be raised, and regularly applied the "saying no" part. Her grandfather, of course, had always indulged her.

Leaving the bierka port, the tension of the situation returned as they struggled to keep one of the most famous political figures in the Empire from being recognized. With Oris around, this was easy. Dakatanis, being a port city, had heard all about the Eldrandii, though they did not call the avians by that name. Eldgil, the word familiar to Jaik, was the local term. Instead of gawking at a respectful distance, they readily approached Oris, and started asking her questions. This drew attention that the party did not want, but allowed Tayron to stay in the background, sometimes pretending to be an onlooker instead of a fellow traveler.

Hotel rooms were not hard to find – after the Great Sharing celebrations, people were rapidly heading out to their new possessions and business for in-town establishments was at an all-time low. Only those looking to sell their share were sticking around, except for the city's regular inhabitants, who had already made arranged exchanges with locals before the sharing had taken place. The hotel proprietors were thrilled to have customers in, and did not ask questions as long as the customers paid for the first day upfront.

Having an open field to choose from, the travelers picked a place overlooking the harbor, and asked for rooms with seaside views and access to a shower. West negotiated the price down, sensing the lack of weight from his money pouch, and not wanting to rely on Emily to pay for his and Jaik's room. The chancellor was not carrying even a small percentage of his own wealth, and though he could have instantly gotten credit by revealing himself, that could cause trouble, especially if they were trying to stay one step ahead of their pursuers.

"The Shadow Workers are just following us straight to whatever we're trying to get to," Ethan grumbled, considering it absurd to hide Tayron, and generalizing his discontent to the entire mission. "This is completely pointless."

In the privacy of one of three hotel rooms booked by the party, Tayron finally stood to his full height and spoke with authority. "If I know anything about magic, it is that a mage cannot instantly teleport to an unknown location. Since our destination is across an ocean, they can follow us as much as they would like, but not on bierka, which do not have enough range. And only a few flying machines can make it across."

"That doesn't matter. They have spaceships." Ethan looked at Emily. They were supposed to have a spaceship, too, but the dejected expression on Emily's face showed that there was still no signal from the *Azar* or the landing pod. She had dutifully pinged her comm link regularly, getting no answer.

"The Empire is not completely blind, Ethan. We have very powerful telescopes observing our skies. We saw ships – though we did not know they were enemies then – we saw them, your ship, and two others. I checked before Great Sharing, and there were no ships in space above this planet. There is no chance to check now, but my guess is that space is just as busy as we are, and enemy mages would not find it safe to return to their ship –"

Emily was enraged. "Why didn't you tell us? I've been worried about my ship for days."

Calmly amused, the chancellor said, "I thought you knew. We are backward people, after all."

"When did the ships come and go?"

"What I believe to be our enemy's ship entered orbit first. They left after making many trips with a lander, then yours came. We saw a small lander from yours making only one trip, so I know your small party came on it. I did not see it, but I was told our enemy's ship came back, your ship fled, and two new ships of same shape as yours came, making no landing, and our enemy's ship left. That is all I can say for certain."

Almost gasping halfway through the chronology, Emily just could not decide what to think. The implications were clear, but the result was being played out somewhere, maybe a hyperspace jump away. Her ship was faster than most ships in regular space, so that was an advantage there. Kaz was . . . well, a better captain than she was. It would be pushing it to call him experienced, but he was further in that direction than many. Those two other ships could go both ways – two Shadow Worker ships from Ina Cur, or two Eldrandii. The Eldrandii possibility made more sense, since otherwise there was no reason for the Shadow Worker ship to run off when the two newcomers arrived. She was missing too much in this picture to see what was going on.

Without comments about Tayron's news, they settled down in their rooms. The chancellor sent Jaik into the city to speak with a pilot friend who might be up for the cross-ocean trip, explaining to the young actor that this was a daredevil journey by all accounts, having only been completed a half dozen times, and only twice with so many passengers. In other words, there wasn't much of a choice of pilots available, and those ready to fly at a moment's notice . . . Tayron only knew of one. The burden was on Jaik to reel him in.

Emily tried to look calm as they waited for Jaik's return, but she discreetly tried the communicator, attempting to contact either the landing pod or the *Azar* every hour. Her concern visibly spread to Ethan, who could come up with even more bizarre scenarios than she could to fit Tayron's news. She decided to take the long-desired shower in the hope that it would take her mind off things. The barely adequate plumbing and horribly heated water managed to make the shower a bit of an adventure, but not enough of one to occupy her mind.

Anyway, she looked at it, she was trapped here. She had not intended to get trapped. As far as she was concerned, she had done everything in their power to prevent it, but that did not change their predicament. And Max was dead. That was really hitting her now. Her choice to pursue this unlikely and dangerous chance had led to the death of one of her crew members. Maybe two, depending on what had happened to John the pod pilot. Not wanting to think crassly, but finding herself doing so anyway, she realized that this would definitely damage her reputation as a captain. She really knew little about Max or John, so it was hard to figure out how she should feel about this loss, except in terms of her own failure.

As always, when they found themselves ensconced in rooms, Oris escaped to do some flying and perching outside. With every passing hour, Emily felt more and more hostile to the Eldrandii, and increasingly suspicious of her seemingly good intentions. But every time she thought of Oris as scheming, her mind immediately turned to Raiz, who had nudged her along so unassumingly, and who had cheerfully fed her exactly the knowledge that would draw her to Selparis. Was everybody in the universe taking pages out of the Plani book of manipulation? It was really too much.

Jaik returned with good news. The pilot, Draken Veris, was willing to carry them and would be ready tomorrow. Veris had made a big deal about the overnight effort that would be necessary to get ready, and how lucky they were that he was always ready to dare gravity and the elements. Jaik's impression of the pilot was far from glowing, and his distaste showed in the scowl on his face as he recounted the meeting. As far as Earth's popular culture was concerned, though, pilots like that were the norm, and you had to expect some hotshot behavior and grandstanding. The complaint about the overnight effort sounded a lot like the starship engineer stereotype. If this pilot was anything like that, they were in good hands.

Worries aside, Emily had hoped to get a sound sleep that night. More often than not, her Selparis sleeping had been minimalist on the ill-boding dream front. No such luck this time. Not knowing whether these were real premonitions or just fears and hopes manifesting themselves, she still accepted their demand for attention and interpretation.

The night started with a hint of looming shadows that broke with the breeze and started stalking her, blocking every path of escape. A good old-fashioned symbolic dream, but also one that left nothing to the imagination. After waking up for the first of many times that night, she recalled that the shadows seemed to waiver with agitation, and she could guess why. Without their spaceship in orbit, they were at a disadvantage on this world, and trapped as much as she was. It was somewhat comforting – not a great relief, since she still saw no way out from the midst of them – but something,

Falling back to sleep, she dropped into a rapidly sinking aircraft being knocked to the left and to the right. It was difficult to tell whether the plane's descent was controlled or not, especially since the pilot's voice was drowned out by the unruly roar of the engines, the creak of the wood frame, and the buckling bits of steel, but she guessed it was not. She had thought the bierka ride was uncomfortable, but this cramped and tempest tossed travel left her unable to imagine moving her extremities again. Her arms and legs were so numb that she had to conclude her body was masking dire pain that would shoot through her nervous system as soon as she tried to reposition them.

The dream was so powerful that on waking she was paralyzed, unable to roll around as she usually did in the middle of the night. After a pregnant moment of enforced stillness, awkward and mildly frightening, she was back to dreaming.

The last dream of the night that she could remember in the morning was simply and completely explicit – a spaceship exploded. She could not tell whether it was the *Azar* or some other ship. What she did know was that she was on board a ship that was observing the destruction. Her dream was not turning her around, so she could not see what kind of ship it was, but felt that she was not truly on board. Her eyes fixed themselves on the exploding ship.

It looked like a movie explosion. Of course, she had never seen a real ship explode, so she had no way to judge to realism of it, but it sure seemed like the elaborate special effects. When she awoke from this one, she wondered how a dream could so deliberately confine what she could understand from it. The lack of fluidity in this last vision was so different from anything else she had experienced that she suspected it was not of the future or present, but instead of the past. Or was it that her mind simply didn't want to know the whole truth, and was preventing her from seeing the full reality? She shook her head in dismay – they were just dreams, for heaven's sake. She was taking them way too seriously.

Back to sleep again, and this time for good until morning, when she was brought awake again by squawking animals she could not recognize, communicating with each other outside the window. The creatures were early risers, starting their calls right at the break of dawn. So was Tayron, and he knocked on her door before she could summon the will to sit up on her own volition.

"Captain, the pilot awaits." The chancellor had borrowed a translator, and Emily would have to thank whoever had handed theirs to him. She hoped it was Oris, since it would add another solid grievance against the Eldrandii, but it had probably been Ethan, who would be more than willing to hand his over on the asking.

There was a small mirror in the room and, hesitant but compelled by curiosity, she took a look at herself. Somewhat relieved that she could still recognize herself, she still noticed heavy bags below her eyes, the red hair coloring fading badly revealing her natural brown near her neck, and her eyes. Staring back, her gaze was haunted and haunting, even more so than she remembered from her last look in a mirror. Instead of stepping back, or turning away from her reflection, she continued staring, as if trying to find some truth in herself. She tried to remember if she had ever looked at herself this way before, but could not. If she had, it had to have been so long ago that the whole meaning of it would have been different.

She had work to do, and could no longer be reluctant to do it, even if it was not the road she had wanted to journey down. The enemy was all around, and delay was not a luxury she could afford if she wanted to leave this world on the *Azar*. Maybe she was thinking movie instead of reality, but she lacked anything else to go on.

It took hardly any time for them to get to the airfield, which whirred with activity. The news of the attack on Atparis had reached Dakatanis finally, and pilots of both aircraft and bierka needed to get a reply organized, and to send support to the besieged center of the Empire. It was a good thing Jaik had already convinced a pilot to help them, otherwise there would have been absolutely no alternatives left. Pilots were, by and large, thrill-seekers who were, with few exceptions, gung-ho in response to everything. Considering what some of them were flying, they had to be. Hiding Tayron had been an even better idea, as everyone would now turn to him for leadership, trapping him on this side of the ocean, where he would be able to do nothing to stop the Shadow Worker onslaught.

Continuing to decoy the locals away from Tayron, Oris drew more attention from the flock of pilots at the airfield than from the people of the city, and the questions from pilots and engineers alike were pointed and specific. They asked about her range, speed, glide ratio, and whether she thought a plane with flapping wings would be practical or even more efficient than a propeller driven model. The Eldrandii was indulgent within limits as the rest of her companions strode ahead, confident that she would be able to catch up. She did, but not before snapping angrily at an engineer who tried to use a tape measure to get the exact dimensions and curvature of her wings.

Vast hangars shielded most of the airplanes from the elements, so that the machines were huddled together at their sides, surrounding a taxiway down the middle. At the far end of the field, though, was a collection of smaller hangers privately owned by successful pilots who could afford the privacy and secrecy. A plethora of "No Trespassing" signs proliferated on that side of the field, and in every guise imaginable. Emily did not need to be able to read the language to get the gist – the visuals said it all. One of them depicted a sneaky-looking shadow with eyes walking into a hangar and getting impaled on a spike trap, blood spurting everywhere. This sort of twin-paned comic strip was the most popular warning format, and the text under the images was irrelevant.

In these hangars, pilots and engineers guarded Selparis' cutting-edge aviation and latest aerodynamic innovations before their unveiling. One of these hangars belonged to Draken Veris, their pilot, but Emily was justifiably wary about approaching his closed enclave – its signs showed some outright demented examples of excessive gore, including photographic detail on the intestines. Thankfully, Veris came out of the hangar to meet them.

He was a lanky fellow burdened under hide clothing that sat badly on him, clearly worn for image instead of comfort. His hair was unwashed, in utter disarray, and roughly cut at the shoulders, probably in haste and for expediency by Veris himself. On his face was an affected scowl that served to hide what he was actually feeling, but failed to suggest that he was upset about anything, once again being put on to satisfy expectations. He seemed to think that a scowl was the appropriate expression for a person like him to have. His face was clean-shaven, making his messy hair seem like another unnecessary affectation. It was easy to see why Jaik disliked the man – Veris was trying too hard to act a part, and botched the job badly.

In his eyes, though, there was a glimmer of intelligence and a sense that he was very good at one particular thing, flying, even if he was not so good at fitting into the local aviation culture. Tayron was glad to see the pilot and that was good enough for Emily – at least until Veris made his first mistake. She was not so far out of high school to have forgotten what the pressure to fit in was like, and how many people failed miserably at it. It practically made her feel sorry for Veris until he opened his mouth, at which point all sympathy was lost.

"You didn't tell me that there'd be a woman along, Tayron," Veris started, his words matching the programmed dialect of Asparian so well that even his mannerisms were rendered into English equivalents. "You know they're not up to this sort of thing – they're not built for it, you know. Nothing against this one, you understand, she's clearly an outlander and might be hardier than most, but this is a long trip, we don't need any complaining, and in my experience that's what women are best at. Makes 'em good politicians, but bad company except on the cold nights, if you know what I mean. I was worried enough about having a kid along, but young Jaik here proved himself a bright young lad, but I don't see how the girl will be helpful on any sort of journey to save the empire."

Emily socked him, right in the jaw, sparing no strength. Veris was thrown clear off his feet and onto the grimy taxiway outside the hangar. For a moment in which she realized what she had done, Emily panicked, worried that in a second's lapse of self-control, she had condemned the entire mission. Against all instinct, she prepared to apologize, but could not bring herself to debase herself, having meant from her very soul every pound of the punch. She looked at Tayron for guidance, but he was grinning. On the ground, she saw that Veris was grinning, too, as if he and the chancellor were sharing a joke. Bewildered, she waited mutely for an explanation.

"Okay, looks like I deserved that," the pilot said, getting up quickly and checking to see if any of the locals had seen the embarrassing moment. A few did from outside audible range, and the story would therefore spread to everyone on the field. Veris did not seem to mind. "You got some punch. I'll take everything I said back, 'long as you don't throw that hook at me again."

The translator was doing such a good job with Veris' speech that Emily was impressed, having never heard better from it. Picking up on the humor, she said, "fine. Next time you decide to open your mouth like that, I'll kick you where it hurts."

And that seemed to be understood as intended, because Veris broke out in laughter. The mirth was a bit forced, as if this is all a macho show. Tayron still smiled over the proceedings calmly.

“Let’s get inside,” Veris said levelly, leading the way. The side door of the hangar brought them into a tunnel, and along the way, the pilot was either deactivating traps or making a show of it. He warned them about two tripwires before the tunnel opened up into the main hangar, which was just big enough to hold two planes. The one they saw immediately was a tiny model that had been all over the place outside, and was probably the stock plane Veris used for daily flying or testing the effects of minor alterations. The other was much larger, but it didn’t look very special to Emily – though, of course, she had been conditioned to expect jets and rockets on state-of-the-art planes, and more sleekness in the fuselage. This plane was decidedly blocky. At least it wasn’t a biplane, though its very rectangular wings and wooden propellers didn’t give Emily much hope for a smooth ride.

“It’s a piece of junk,” Emily spat, quoting the movie line that had instantly jumped into her mind. Out of the corner of her eye, she saw Ethan snicker.

Almost getting the response right, Veris replied indignantly, “it’ll cross the continent in a day and get you to where you’re going, lady. She’s not the fastest bird in the sky, but she’s the only one that can guarantee a round-trip to the western continent, mark my words.”

Emily decided that continuing the scene any further would probably be pushing it, considering she had already punched the man. The pilot was also dead earnest about the plane, and it would probably hurt him deeply if she made any more sign that she rejected it.

It wasn’t a bad looking plane anyway, when she compared it to what Earth might have had so early in the era of aviation – a comparison Emily could not really make except in vague terms based on the number of wings and engines. In her mind, if the number of wings equaled or exceeded the number of engines, that was bad. This one had a single wing and two engines so, in theory, it was good. Sort of. Mostly metal, it beat out the wood-fabric constructions of the dawn of flight on that score as well. It still had a bit of wood on the window frames and anywhere a bit of lightness would not hurt, including the body’s ceiling and the skin of some surfaces. Chances were that lightweight steel was an expensive commodity on this planet, and Veris included as much as he could afford.

There was no one else in the hangar, so either Veris was his own engineer, or his help was out at the moment. Emily wondered about this, but had no chance to ask. Taking the cue from her last words, he was now showing them around the plane, pointing out the subtlest of improvements. He kept using units of measure that failed to translate, so it was hard for her to follow along, even if she could guess at the meaning of all the successfully translated aerodynamic terms. Plenty of the specialized terms also got lost in translation, but Veris seemed oblivious to the language barrier.

Her appreciation of the plane was superficial. It had both engines within the body – one as a pusher in the back and the other as a puller in the front. Mounted high above and behind the passenger compartment, its wing had a huge span that suggested good gliding but not much speed. The bits painted at all had a base coat of white, and these were usually the wood portions. The rest was bare metal and gleamed in the hangar's flickering lights. Emily did not like having the engines in the body, perhaps because most Earth passenger planes had them mounted on the wings. The high wing was also a bit distracting, for the same reason – only slow wind-tossed planes had high wings on Earth.

Still, it had to be a smoother ride then a bierka, didn't it? She recalled her dream and decided that there was every chance it could be worse.

"So, what do you think of her?" Veris asked, hungry for validation. "Good enough for you?"

"'Suppose so. Like you said, if it gets us to where we're going, there's no point complaining."

That didn't really satisfy Veris, who was looking for some expression of amazement. He obviously had not guessed, despite the presence of Oris, that the individuals he was speaking to had seen far more flight that he had, and found it entirely mundane.

"Hmph. Well, fine. Your young friend tells me you're in a hurry, and the sooner I am out of here, the better. Already arranged to have it spread around that while everyone else has been chatting about what to do, I left on a secret mission with the lord chancellor here. Won't those idiots outside be red in the face when they hear that," Veris chuckled, then turned suddenly serious and stared at Tayron. "I will get to return to enjoy my joke, won't I?"

"Veris, if you can get us across safely, then I do not see how our mission could put you in any further danger. As far as your joke goes, my family used to believe that some god in heaven smiles upon that sort of thing, so you might even have given us divine backing."

"The god Tayl," Veris sniffed, "don't take me for a fool, Tayron, I know the strange beliefs of the aristocracy and where your family got its name."

Tayron was taken aback by the sharp retort, but recovered smoothly. "My apologies. I did not think it was within your particular realm. It is an old superstition that is barely more than trivia now."

"When you tempt the fates like us pilots constantly do, you gain a better appreciation for superstitions and divine entities, let me tell you. I don't quibble about whether any of it's true or if any of them exist. As far as I go, whatever's there, I want it on my side."

"You could spend quite a long time praying and making offerings with that doctrine."

Veris' upper lip curled into something between a smirk and a sneer. "Some are better proven than others. Your god Tayl, for instance –"

"I think we can leave religious talk for later, Veris. We have a long flight ahead of us, and need to be off."

The dodge was obvious, but the urgency was also real, so none of them protested. They stowed their luggage and, as they were climbing aboard the plane through a door under the wing, Veris deactivated some traps and cranked open the hangar doors, letting the sunlight pour in.

The cabin was cramped, especially for Oris, who was given the copilot seat because she simply could not fit at all in any of the others. All indications were that she would be flying alongside for much of the flight, so letting her have a seat by a door made sense. Behind the pilot and copilot seats were six more, tightly packed between the plane's walls. The seats were removable to make way for cargo, and did not look very well integrated into the plane. The backseat was loaded with food and supplies, and Ethan squeezed in beside the bags.

Veris briefly leaped into the cockpit to release the brakes of the plane, and towed it out into the morning air. After heading into the hangar again, closing everything up, and emerging out from the side door, he finally settled into the pilot's seat, strapped in, and started the engines. Emily was pleasantly surprised that they didn't have to give the propellers a few turns to get them started. This world figured out automatic starters early.

Since the field lacked runways, all they had to do was taxi out to the pavement and scan to see if there was enough room for takeoff. Their plane was substantially heavier than the usual flight, with all the fuel needed for a round trip, and it would require a proportionally longer takeoff run to get off the ground. Knowing this, Emily and the others were looking around nervously. As it turned out, they had more to worry about than they had bargained for.

"What in the world is that?" Veris said, spotting it first as he applied the brakes at the edge of the field and revved up the engines. He didn't need to point, since in the second after he spoke, all heads followed his line of sight and saw instantly what he had. A linear mist had formed at the edge of the field the closest to the ocean, and was beginning to clear enough so that they could see the cloaked figures in the midst of it.

"Aw, hell," Emily said with absolute fervency, all doubts about the accuracy of her dreams set aside.

"Okay. I know it looks bad," Veris said, "but how bad is it?"

Tayron bit his lip before speaking, hesitant to admit that the collapse of the empire his family had helped form over the past generations was now imminent. "They attacked Atparis and won against our mages, Veris. I think that says it all."

"It definitely doesn't say it all," Veris grumbled as he hastily released the brakes and willed the plane to accelerate as if it, too, should be afraid for its life. "Should we be doing something to stop them, instead of flying to a continent where, believe me, we're not going to get any help, either? Or are you just trying to save your own skin, Lord Chancellor?"

A less controlled man would have choked Veris at that point, but Tayron kept that side of himself buried. It was there, visible in his expression, but Veris would only hear the even-toned words that Tayron spoke. "There is something that these mages are seeking," he shouted over the combined roar of the ground rolling beneath them and the engines at full might. "We must get to it first. These enemies are not looking to conquer us – they could have done so long ago if they had wished to."

That wasn't true, though, Emily reminded herself. They might not have known about the planet if it had not been for her. Her assumption of all the guilt was overstating it, of course, and considering the way she had stumbled into all this while being led to it by Ariki and Raiz, she could hardly be to blame. But she couldn't shake the feeling as she looked at the lord chancellor's increasingly dejected face, sitting slumped next to her, that the lack of caution on the way to Selparis had played a large part in the demise of his land and dreams. Maybe she could have attempted to shake off the Shadow Workers. So much had happened that she was a bit confused about the sequence of events since she had railed against the Shadow Worker on that night on Newport Station, but there had to have been more that she could have done. With so little preparation and thought going into this mission, it was a minor miracle only Max had died.

After what seemed like an eternity, they were in the air, barely leaving the ground before the mages started working their magic. Wanting to keep the planes on the ground, the enemy line started literally throwing clouds out to make an instant storm. Veris' plane was thrown by the turbulence, as the masses of condensed water vapor were hurled at great velocity. The force shot the plane into the vertical, forcing Veris to bring it back level with all his might to prevent a stall, giving them all red-outs as the blood rushed to their heads. Then another magical torrent pushed a wing up, putting the plane into a steep bank. With the clouds blocking visibility, Veris had few chances to tell if, at their low altitude, they were heading into something dangerous. He put the plane into a steady climb as often as possible with the storm winds slamming it around like a ping-pong ball and putting enough stress on its structure that a completely wooden plane would have snapped in a dozen places by now. He was wary of losing too much speed in the climb, though, since at any moment a gust could throw them up again, and the resulting stall would have this overburdened plane, filled to the brim with fuel, plunging into the ground.

Ethan threw up in the back, and Emily firmly avoided looking back at him, feeling her own breakfast high in her throat. Tayron, veteran of many bierka flights, remained stoic in his seat, almost meditative. Jaik was in the same place as Emily was, and his face was so pale he looked almost human. West . . . well, West looked like he was thoroughly enjoying the ride, though he could have been putting on a brave face.

When he saw Emily was looking at him, he tried to look as if he was concerned about their safety, but failed. By the time they were clear of the magical storm, the ocean was stretched out beneath them as far as the eye could see, and only a glance through the rear windshield revealed the city, completely covered in an isolated overcast so that not a single building could be seen through it.

"If any of you vomited, I don't blame you, but if you could clean it up using a towel I packed, I'll fly low so you can throw it out the window. The last thing we need now is a stinking plane all the way across the ocean." Emily relayed the message, which Ethan couldn't understand without translator. Ethan did as bidden, spotting a stack of towels in the middle of the supplies placed next to him and cleaning up the mess that, mercifully, had not splashed much on any of his clothes. Gaining some control over his bowels, he managed to shout over the engine whine, "why did you pack so many towels?"

"I'm serious about hygiene. They're also made of eferei, so they're edible in an emergency. After you've thrown the towel out the window, dig around for a bottle of anta scent – it's a yellowish bottle about as big as your palm. Throw some of that around to kill the smell."

The clean-up complete, Veris brought the plane up to a high cruising altitude and warned the passengers not to open any windows. It was difficult to say over the ocean, but Emily guessed that their height was less than two miles. That was still in the troposphere, where weather could foul things up, even for high-tech spacecraft. A midflight hurricane would really kill this adventure unless Veris' piloting skills were truly phenomenal. Actually, after the rough takeoff, Emily wondered whether Veris would be interested in a job as a pod pilot. Then her thoughts wandered to John, who she had tried and failed to communicate with, and she grew depressed again. She was already thinking of replacing him, giving him up for dead before being certain of it.

Rough start aside, Veris was good at reading the air, and the turbulence was minimal. After reaching the cruise altitude, he cut the rear engine to save fuel, and the cabin was quiet enough for them to speak without yelling. They didn't speak, though. Maybe it was the serenity of the ocean that put them in a contemplative mood. More likely, it was because each of them was confronted with the reality of loss more than ever before, as they dramatically left the land where those losses occurred. Emily and Ethan had lost Max and possibly John; Jaik and West had lost their home and town-family; Tayron had lost his empire and emperor; and Veris had lost the piloting community he had spent so much time cultivating a reputation in.

What about Oris? Well, she wasn't one to chat anyway, but she was certainly grimmer than she had been when they had started out on this expedition. What had she lost along the way? Perhaps she had been hoping for something, and had found these hopes dashed. Whatever she had been looking for on Selparis, this flight was clearly carrying her away from it.

Because of language difficulties, there was no way for Veris to communicate precisely how long the trip would take, except to say that they would be in flight during the night and land sometime during the next day. West had no knowledge of Earth time measurements, so there was no help from that quarter. Emily considered telling Veris to skip saving fuel for the return journey because they would have another way – a faster way – to get him and his plane back to Dakatanis. Having Veris use the second engine would get them to their destination faster, but could she really promise the return trip? Until she heard differently, she was as stuck on this planet as everyone else.

The tedium of the flight quickly washed the excitement of the takeoff away. Emily was wary of eating or drinking since the prospects of a restroom break were nonexistent. That made the boredom much worse, since having some food or drinking some water would at least break the monotony. Veris seemed busy with charts, instruments, and calculations. Every now and again, he would bank in search of more favorable winds, making their empty stomachs queasy. He had an air of confidence that made them less concerned for their safety, which was a shame, because having something concrete and immediate to worry about sure helped to pass the time.

"Can't even play any road trip games," Emily mumbled. "I could say that I see something starting with 'w', but you'd guess what it was. Well, Ethan would. I guess the rest of you would have no chance."

Clearing his throat, the chancellor said, "we have a great struggle ahead of us, Captain. Our explorers had some traveling to do on this western continent before they found what we seek, and saw many strange things. I guess that some creatures may not be as much of a surprise to you as they were to me, considering your travels. I suppose you know of vampires?"

"Vampires?" Emily said, almost jumping out of her seat.

"No? You seem to react as my people do – as if they were nightmare tales and nothing more. Or did my word mistranslate? It is hardly common to speak of vampires, and your device might not have –"

"Yes, yes, I know about vampires, but I'm not sure that yours are the same as ours."

"They drink blood."

"Right, I think I got that part."

"We do not know much about them, except that they are thin, pale, and very dangerous."

"Dangerous? Well, that's more like the stories and less like the actual vampires I know."

Tayron was thrown off by this. "Vampires . . . that are not dangerous?"

"I know, I know. I can imagine them getting violent, though. They're oppressed on their homeworld so maybe once they are let loose, they go with their instincts instead of trying to hide them. If these were exiles from Plani, they probably don't know how to synthesize blood or don't have the technology for it. The vampire I met did, so he didn't have to drink blood the . . . I guess, the hard way."

"You have . . . met a vampire?" Tayron almost paled to a Plani shade. It was obvious that vampires were a personal fear of his.

Emily grinned. "Yeah, and no one was more surprised than I was. Remind me to tell you about it sometime."

Tayron made a show of looking around for something to do, then said, "I think we have time now, Captain, if you would care to entertain?"

Emily looked at the back of Oris' head, wondering whether the Eldrandii would object to or be offended by a description of A'anfu En. Nevertheless, she plunged into the story of, as she put it, the Night of Three Weirdoes, describing her encounters with Tylan the mage – leaving out their connection to each other in the dreamscape – and proceeding through A'anfu En's rants as well as the Plani vampire. The Eldrandii sat through the account of the night without comment, making Emily slightly irritated. She wanted to see some more of the human emotion and manner that Oris had shown on their first meeting in the company of Marcus Welder. Had that been just for show? A diplomatic ploy she used to gain Welder's trust, but which was otherwise unnecessary when dealing with lesser humans?

No, that wasn't it. Oris had shown a loose and relaxed manner on board the *Azar* as well, when first instructing Ethan on interspecies relations. The change must have been brought about by something else.

Emily's thoughts were interrupted by Veris, who suddenly asked at the end of her story, "so, Tayron, she's told us a good story, hasn't she? Why don't you tell us yours? We have plenty of time now. Tell them about your family and the god Tayl. I've always wondered about it myself. I've only heard the odd rumor, the clever hint, or the off-the-wall theory. The old nobility's been washed away anyway – you're really the last of it. Give me the answer – are the gods real?"

Tayron sighed, and for the longest time remained silent. It was difficult to tell whether he was preparing to avoid the subject again by making some excuse, or getting ready to give the answer. As it turned out, it was a rich mix of both.

"I do not know as much as you think I do. This knowledge has been completely lost to most nobles, and I have no idea who gave you your hints. Of course, even in Alevan Tayron's time, he being first of my ancestors to be chancellor, those whose knowledge was greatest were those who wanted to break into ennobled ranks by earning a title. Nobles themselves spent too much time on political intricacies, which godly powers are rarely involved in, so ancient superstition did not merit much attention."

"Superstition you call it, Tayron? Does that mean you don't believe it? You'd better be careful."

"No, I was merely describing two hundred years of neglect, which has led to my ignorance today. I certainly would not want to imply that I disbelieve in any divinity's existence. Maybe divine neglect has played its part in our recent disaster."

"Now that is going too far the other way, Tayron. You won't

convince any gods like that."

Tayron smiled as a silent indication that he was less devout than he would dare to claim in words. "Tayl has been of some use to my family, or so my ancestors have said, though they do not give details that would remove doubts."

"So," Emily started, trying to understand some difficult new concepts, "your family . . . had its own god?"

"Yes, it was a major benefit allowed to nobles. Presumably, it still is a benefit. I do not think that I put my god too much use, but I assume Tayl has other business to attend to."

Veris actually turned to Tayron, looking at him eye-to-eye. The plane felt less stable for the moment as Veris said pointedly, "I don't believe you," and Tayron responded with serene simplicity, "you don't need to."

Having nothing else to say, Veris returned to the controls. Emily still felt curious, but did not know where to begin the questions. "How could you believe something like that?" would be too rude even for her, and besides that unfair. The chancellor was clearly not dogmatic about his beliefs, and Earth religions featured at least as much absurdity, if not more, being prescribed vehemently. Still, it was a weird idea – sort of like guardian angels. Whether or not Tayron believed in it, Veris seemed to think it was important and might have been hinting at something. Maybe, with his country in jeopardy, Tayron still had some tools to save the day, and this trip would help him get access to them. The empire had magic; that was certain. To convince people they had gods protecting them, the nobles might have had potent magic at their disposal. If so, Veris was hinting pretty heavily that he would like to see some of it being put to use.

West had been thinking along the same lines, but did not feel like dancing around the issue. "Lord Tayron, will anything we do actually help beat our enemy? We have all lost our homes – will it ever be safe to go back to our lands, or is this a one-way trip? Even if we stop them from getting what they want, they are not likely to leave now that they have taken over everything, are they?"

"No. But as soon as I got word from my explorers, I started planning to bring more powerful allies to our side. Spacefaring species have mostly left us to our own devices as a rule, but there was one that could legitimately interfere if involvement of Asparii refugees was proved to be causing mayhem. As it so happened, I had a means of passing information to humans, and wanted to establish formal contact immediately using our discoveries as leverage, but everything has happened much faster than I had expected. It is lucky that humans are so willing to jump on minimal information with necessary speed, otherwise I suppose you would not be here, Captain Pierce. I am not so foolish as to fight Asparis' ancient magic with our pathetic reconstruction of it. As for my god, Tayl was never one for direct confrontations unless his charge did enough planning to ensure victory."

"And have you?"

Tayron laughed mirthlessly. "I hope so, but I have never in my life found myself less certain, and dozens of different aspects can still go wrong. I am far from declaring victory. Too much is in our enemy's hands, and my first goal has already failed. Or did you think I planned for my empire to fall? I could never have guessed how ruthless and powerful those who seek ancient knowledge could be. Nor could I anticipate our seemingly solid defense's fragility. I cannot, even now, fathom what malice they had towards us, to desecrate our people's moment of glory and triumph so deliberately. It was not a coincidence that they chose to move so quickly after arriving on this world, of that I am certain."

"But it had to have been," Emily said. "How could they have known about the Great Sharing? We didn't, and we had some communication with this world. It had to have been by chance."

"Magic users have ways of divining events. All they had to see was that a large gathering or celebration would be taking place, and that would be enough. Even our mages could manage that much. Only very specific information – like coordinates – would be difficult to see into, I think."

Emily shook her head, feeling a bit dumb. She would have to remember about magic, or pay the price for forgetting. Glancing out of the window, she closed her eyes and let the intense glare of the alien sun wash over her face. Her limbs felt heavy and tired, and in the soothing sunlight she soon fell asleep.

There was only one memorable dream this time, but it had even more clarity than she had seen in her most striking dreams, and when she woke from it, the knowledge that she still had this secret and mysterious gift gave her comfort that the dream itself had not. First, there was a flash of vampire fangs sticking out of a darkened face, but the vampire was thrown back and fell into a wall of mist. Emily then walked into the mist and, once it cleared, found herself at the edge of a cliff and took a step back, unsteady. The cliff overlooked a dark landscape at least five hundred feet below. It had to be at least five hundred feet because the land was pocked with towers, some more than thirty stories tall with glittering lights in their windows. Below the cliff, an entire city stretched to the horizon, and all except the tallest towers and major roads remained unlit. Looking in the distance, Emily saw that there was no distinguishable horizon. Overhead, weak lights from the city provided enough illumination for her to see that everything was surrounded by a massive dome-shaped metal ceiling.

The mist behind her receded, revealing . . . everyone. Tylan the mage came out, as did Kaz, Raiz, Ethan, West, Jaik, Oris, Tayron, and dozens of others. They all had faces of awe, and not one looked pristine. Every face was worn, except perhaps Raiz, who was immune. Quite a few, including Ethan, West, and Jaik, had obvious injuries. Ethan had a bandage on his neck, Jaik had his arm in a sling, and West had a scar on his forehead. But as she looked all of them over, she saw that the mist still hung behind them, and from that mist came a scream.

As far as she could remember after waking, she had seen nothing else, but just the detail of the look on her companion's faces convinced her that the dream had some level of voracity. She wondered what the appearance of all those people meant, but there could be no doubt about the mist and the scream, not after their escape from the Shadow Workers in Dakatanis. All those people she recognized in the dream . . . they couldn't all die in this, could they? She couldn't imagine how Raiz, Kaz or Tylan would die on Selparis, though that seemed to be what the dream was suggesting, with all of them at the edge of the cliff with the menacing fog behind. What if a fight with the Shadow Worker ship destroyed part of Newport Station while Tylan, Kaz, and Raiz were on board? That was possible. The thought, especially that of Kaz dying, sent a chilly dagger into her heart as she finally opened her eyes.

Actually, the chill had come in from the open cabin door as Oris stepped out and took flight in the dead of night. The Eldrandii's launch knocked the plane to the left briefly, but Veris quickly corrected course and shut the door after Oris started her initial glide and adjusted to the ocean air. There were no clouds, so Emily had a perfect view of Oris flying in the night light, a shadow passing over the brilliant field of stars.

"Awake, are you?" Veris said, looking jealously at the rest of the passengers, all of whom were napping in their own way. West was restless, much more comfortable sleeping on the bare ground than in a machine, despite his love of inventions. Emily wondered what his sleep might be troubled by. Maybe meeting people from his world of origin and seeing them wield technology that he could not come close to matching was enough to disturb him. He had taken advantage of his foreknowledge of technologies and their value, but that life and world was now in his distant past, with only the unknown ahead. Of course, his nocturnal distress might have simply been due to the severe trauma of the past days, the horrors of which would have been enough to put nightmares in anyone's mind.

Jaik was certainly being troubled by it, but he did not toss and turn like West. Rather, he seemed frozen, though the strain of the visions appeared on his face. The others were sleeping more soundly. Even the chancellor seemed to have felt a need for recuperation, and was finding it without any of the tumult experienced by the younger members of the group.

"Didn't take much to get you asleep, did it?" Veris continued, needing the conversation to stay awake. "Odd sleeper, you are."

"I have a lot of catching up to do, sleep-wise," she said, then heard his final words. "What do you mean, I'm an odd sleeper?"

"Well, for a bit of it, you were sitting up, rigid-like, as if you were in a trance. Spooked me a bit, and I could tell that your weak-stomached friend in the back was a bit surprised by it as well. The rest of the time, you were slumped over like normal, though you slept more soundly than most people I've flown. Unless they take the trains often, they don't like sleeping on machines, especially not flying ones."

"I've slept on plenty of machines where I come from." Suddenly curious, she asked, "how many people have you carried to the western continent?"

"No one else until now. I normally take out the seats and carry trade goods both ways. I only use the seats for runs within the empire. Not that I'd take passengers to the west anyway, but the imperial government carefully restricts who goes there, and only three pilots can really make the trip at all. As far as I know, there have only been two groups of official explorers sent, and only one has returned."

"One group's lost over there? The chancellor didn't tell us that."

"I didn't say lost, did I? The pilot who brought them over wasn't told to bring them back. For all we know, they were sent to make a permanent base, or they're still waiting for a flight back, or maybe they just saw the place and decided to stay. It's pretty different over there, and you have to be a pretty different kind of person to want to leave a comfortable life here to explore an unknown land. I don't know."

"Were the ones that stayed the first group or the second?"

"The second. They flew out only a couple of months ago. Why? You think you know what they were up to?"

Emily looked at Tayron and it didn't take long to see the signs of preparation in this. "I think they were sent so they'd be ready to guide us to where we're going. We don't really have a guide with us, and I don't think the chancellor would know the way on his own, but he was definitely expecting someone like me, from my . . . land, so he had to be ready to get us to . . . wherever it is we're going."

Veris was amused. "Good theory, and it fits. But I'm not sure you're right about Tayron not knowing the way. I think he reads reports very carefully, and he would be the type to know the way just in case the guides had, you know, gotten killed or something. He'd probably have a third group ready, too."

Emily nodded. Veris certainly seemed to have Tayron's number. "Why were you so curious about his god and everything?"

"Because he's not being completely honest, of course, and I wanted a way to get a few more hints. He knew what I was up to, though. My family is closely related to nobility in a couple of directions, and my grandfather tried to get a title for himself in his time. Like Tayron said, it was the ones who wanted it but didn't have it that paid the most attention to it. Who a noble's god was and what that god can do used to be a closely guarded secret, especially when it came to the nobles at the top, but over time, word leaks out. Our dear Chancellor was very good about covering up the shock when I showed that I knew. My great-great-granduncle was a friend of Tayron's ancestor Alevan when both started working in the palace. He carefully passed down the information, and since his line failed, the inheritance was left with my grandfather. I think Tayron suspected the secret had been compromised, but wasn't sure until our recent conversations. Information about the nobility is always useful, and has been handy while I'm searching for funding. Doesn't even count as blackmail, I think, since the secret isn't embarrassing or anything."

"What's the big deal? I mean, even if the gods are real, how would knowing about someone else's help you?"

"They do exist, though maybe not in the way people normally think about gods. They are probably just simple magical forces. Anyway, knowing which god a person is defended by can tell you what to avoid if you challenge them, what their strength is. If a noble is protected by the god of corporate law, then you certainly don't want to pit your business against his, or bring up a lawsuit against his company."

"The god of corporate law? Really?"

"Well, the normal gods, like of love and war and fertility and that sort of thing are pretty rare, so I don't think nobles are given the protection of gods like that. Take the god of doorways or the god of kitchen tables, though. If a noble knows their stuff, they'll make important things happen in those doorways or at the kitchen table, and they'll have their way when they're there. They'll also use misdirection to keep others from guessing their god, and sometimes you can't avoid being at a disadvantage. Whoever has the god of conferences can pretty much sit and enjoy."

"But that can't be right. I mean, how does it work?"

Veris shrugged. "No clue, but it does. How does any magic work? Most mages don't even know. Anyway, that's why, when the emperor said to the nobles, let us buy your land or I'll take away your title, the nobility took the money and kept quiet about the Great Sharing. That's how much they think their gods matter, and everything I've heard tells me that Tayron was flat lying when he said they've mostly forgotten it."

"Why would he lie, though?"

"Because these days the noble cult can get the attention of the public, the newspapers can constantly run stories about it, and no secrets would be safe. So they make it seem like it doesn't matter, and that it's old superstition that ought to be forgotten. Besides, now that he knows I know, he wants to throw me off so he can stick to his plans and I won't mess it up."

Veris sniffed and continued, head cocked in Tayron's direction. "Funny, us trying to figure him out with him sitting right there. I wouldn't be surprised if he's listening to us. Are you listening to us, Chancellor? . . . No? . . . Well, I suppose it was too much to hope for that you'd spring up and answer."

Emily smiled at this causal mockery. Veris had a comfortable, effortless way about being coarse and irreverent, as if he really had been born that way. He wasn't the quiet, brooding type that she was attracted to, but very much like her old friends who, with the exception of Ethan, had been authority-hating hellraisers in search of adventure, trying to prove themselves in the world by daring each other to ludicrous feats, usually while doused with alcohol. Maybe that had been because all the real feats available on Earth had already been taken. Here on Selparis, there were real adventures to be accomplished, and nobody had to dare Veris or tell him how to prove himself. Emily figured that most of her friends would have made good hotshot pilots on this world.

The suggestion that Tayron might be listening ended the conversation, and Emily continued to watch Oris soaring outside, occasionally falling behind the plane and needing to flap to catch up. Her stomach threw a sharp pain to remind her of its priorities, and she decided it was time to take a bite. She struggled down the foot-wide center aisle, bent at both waist and knees down to four feet in height, and was careful not to jostle any of the sleepers, especially Ethan who was curled peacefully next to the supplies.

When dawn came, her companions also ate immediately, and were generally more upbeat for the rest of the flight. At Ethan's request, Jaik and West continued to teach him the local dialect of Asparian, and Emily participated eagerly as well though she was a bit behind, and far slower at picking it up than Ethan was.

With the coast of the new continent in sight after midday, Ethan asked Veris in Asparian, “do they speak same language, or different language?”

“Some speak so I can guess what they mean, but it’s never easy. Others speak in a way I completely can’t understand, no matter how slow they go. The people on the coast seem like they’re used to dealing with others who don’t know their language, but go just a short journey inland, and there’s no chance to communicate with anyone unless you bring someone with you to help.”

The coast ahead looked like any beach from a distance, with bright sands gradually merging into rolling pasture lands, and didn’t show any signs of human habitation. Veris pulled out a new map, scrutinized it carefully, and compared it to what they could see of the land. It was too much to expect that, after the long flight across the ocean, they would hit land precisely where they intended. Banking the plane to the right, to the North, Veris brought them parallel to the land, but kept them over the water so he could keep sight of undulations of the coastline. Before long, some indication of life was in sight on the left, on top of the highest of a chain of dry coastal hills. A few distinct triangular shapes could be seen, and only after a few minutes was Emily sure that they were not Eldrandii cones, but rather pyramids like those at the gates of Atparis. The pyramids themselves could not have accommodated much living space within them, but it was unlikely they would be built except to serve a substantial population.

“Huh, that’s weird,” Ethan said, “it’s sort of like being in Egypt and seeing the pyramids, then flying across the world to Mexico, and finding the ones built by the Mayans. Except, I don’t think anyone else put them on top of hills. Usually, the civilizations that built them don’t have hills around. Maybe they were compensating for that. Building pyramids on top of hills, though, that’s . . . weird.”

Four distinct pyramids, each equal in size and placed around a central square, could be clearly made out by the time they started seeing the roads. Because the hills were rocky and a grayish-yellow all around, the cobblestone roads had been hidden from a distance. Now they could see literally dozens of parallel roads with switchback connectors between them encircling each hill. Veris brought the plane closer to the hills so they could take a look. Small figures could be seen moving along the roads on the nearest hill, and every so often one would disappear into a darkened spot in the hill – tiny cave apertures that, in context, must have been entrances into homes built right into the hill. If every such spot was an entrance to a home, and there must have been a hundred just on one side of one hill, the four or five hills within view could have contained more than a thousand families.

Veris took the plane in very low – perhaps a hundred feet higher than the first hill's pinnacle, and banked left. A few of the hill-residents could be seen clearly, and they looked even more human than the Asparii did. For all Emily knew, they were human.

"I think you see another reason why I thought Earth a good place to find help in this matter," Tayron said. "I do not know how to explain it, since your world has not had space travel until recent times, yet these people are of your kind, and have been here for at least hundreds of years to have built mounds like these."

Ethan was nearly out of his seat in his eagerness to say something and immediately spoke up once the chancellor was finished. "Atlantis. They must be from Atlantis. According to the ISC records, Atlantis had spaceships of their own, and if it fell, then maybe some of them came here as refugees, too."

Emily never liked the whole Atlantis version of Earth history, and stated her main objection to it now. "Yeah, but weren't they supposed to be real advanced? A whole bunch of technology and magic? Where is all of it, and why aren't they building spaceships?"

"Maybe because they were hiding from the people who caused the fall of Atlantis. That would explain the way they live in hills. At first it was because they had to hide, and now it's become sort of a tradition."

While he said this, Veris was looking around at Emily with confused anger. "What do you mean spaceships?"

Emily quickly covered up the gaffe by saying there were legends of a people called Atlantii who had the ability to fly through space, which was true enough. She didn't want to deliver a dose of culture shock while Veris was at the controls of the plane, and their continued safety was in his hands. Her words subdued him for now, but he had proven himself intelligent, and it would have been out of character for him to trust her words blindly. Their translator devices alone suggested to him that they had technological secrets beyond his comprehension.

Spaceships, though , were something else entirely, and he was eager not to ponder their potential existence while trying to bring the plane to a landing.

"Well, then," Veris replied, "I can tell you why this bunch might be your Atlantii, but might not have the technology. There aren't any resources on this side of the ocean. It's good pasture land, but horrible for mining. Iron would be worth its weight in gold here if they had gold to give, which they don't. I normally trade for cultural artifacts, information, and books that the imperial authorities might be interested in. I'm sure the chancellor here has quite a collection, since these people have plenty of books to spare, though none of them are bound half as finely as ours. See here," he said pointing, "take a look at that."

They were on the inland side of the hills now, and Veris banked the plane right to head for the pyramid studded hill again. On their left, they saw a huge expanse of pastures pocked with feeding animals. On the horizon, far further inland, a hint of forest provided a boundary to the otherwise unbounded field.

"Nothing grows here except . . . ," the translator missed the word, but from context, Emily guessed it had to have been something like grass, "and tall trees. They say their ancestors tried planting crops, but failed. Every chance I get, I bring them seeds from our side, and they tried them. The trees grow, and they never stop thanking me for the new fruits and nuts, but none of the grains or vegetables work. I can't understand why – this place has the mildest weather I've ever seen thanks to the coast. It's a good thing they brought some –"

"Those are cows!" Ethan shouted in rabid excitement. "They look a bit different. They're smaller, I think. But they're cows."

"Not what they call them," Veris said, slightly peeved by the interruption of his tour guide repertoire and flow. "They call them vani. Close enough, I guess. There's the pyramids coming up. Strangest thing in the center, though. Take a look."

Emily's heart picked up its tempo when she saw it, and Ethan was breathless, finding no need to state the obvious for Emily's benefit. It was Stonehenge, except with polished and smooth marble stones, and a much more elaborate arrangement of four concentric circles and markings on the ground. Flaming like a beacon, the central altar's fire would, at night, cast a brilliant glow on the sides of the pyramids facing it. The pyramids themselves were polished and reflective with almost reprehensible care given the relative poverty of the citizens that maintained them. Then again, if constrained by their resources, how would these people have better spent their free time, except by improving their one source of pride – this monument to whatever they worshipped or held dear.

If there had been any doubt in Emily's mind that those below were ancient refugees from her planet's long forgotten glory days, before the magical equivalent of nuclear holocaust wiped the great Atlantian civilization out, those were now set aside in the face of this evidence. She could have reasoned that the Asparii seemed to like pyramids as well, and that the Eldrandii lived in cones not unlike the pyramids, but the entire picture was finally coming into focus, and such evasions of the likely fact did not interest her. A great circle of events was now at its close, and there was every indication that two different branches of the human species, long alienated from each other, would finally be reunited.

Veris brought the plane back to the coastal side of the hills, and told them to brace for landing. He explained that this landing should be smooth because the fuel tanks were still half full. On the return trip to the empire, the lack of extra weight made keeping the plane on the ground difficult, and bounces on landing were a serious struggle.

His normal landing patch was a clear, flat dirt field close to the hills that looked like it was meant to attract aircraft to this shore, so perfectly runway-like it was. A real old-style airport could easily have been built on the same location with no obstacles, and if this planet really did attract Earth intervention or interaction, then it would take no time to identify this place as an ideal location for a makeshift spaceport.

The landing was far better than the sudden stop Tayron's bierka made, but was nevertheless mildly gut-wrenching for everyone on board. Ironically, Tayron actually squirmed in his seat as they neared the point of touchdown this time, perhaps because he was not in control. Flat though the land was, the coastal wind gusts and thermals near the hills tried to force the plane into a stall. Compared to the takeoff, with the mages doing their level best to destroy them, it was nothing. Being badly fed and desperate to rush to the nearest toilet or outhouse as soon as their feet were on dry earth, though, their stomachs protested with every minor lurch.

At they hit it at over a hundred miles an hour, the ground felt rougher than it looked, but Veris kept the plane from hopping and brought it to taxiing speed in a minute, then turned it to a wooden fence that marked the great field's edge. On the other side of the fence, one of the locals looked on as they stepped gingerly out of the plane, trying to regain feeling in their legs and stumbling as they tried to walk in the meantime. Jaik actually sat on the dry grass as soon as he scrambled out, stretching his legs. West was spry almost immediately, and after relieving himself with his back to them, he sauntered up to the fence and looked at the local man, who was dressed in earth-tone trousers and a button up shirt, curiously. The vaguely middle-aged man was not the least bit interested in him, though, and was focused on Veris without calling out to the pilot or showing any sign of recognition. His stance was entirely passive.

Veris ignored the stare as he anchored the plane with four ropes. This allowed time for his passengers to straighten themselves out, work on the kinks in their muscles, and in Tayron's case make all sorts of elderly groans as his muscles showed less resilience, briefly reminding him of his age. Only after being sure that his plane was secure, and that his passengers were ready to stand dignified, did Veris say, "why hello there, Trinkilion, you old devil. They still got you watching this place?"

The translators picked up the response flawlessly. "To guard the ocean coast is an honor and privilege, Lord Veris." The terse reply bore no indication of malice, nor anything resembling friendship. Emily could have easily hopped the three foot fence, so the gate Trinkilion guarded was superfluous, but it did not take much intellect to guess that trying to bypass the sentry would be a big diplomatic mistake. And though the stretch between the fence and the hills looked empty except for a four-legged creature standing too far in the distance to make out clearly, the guard stood at the gate with a firm confidence that was either faith in some unseen force that would oppose them if they transgressed or the product of delusion. Or both, which might be even more dangerous.

Tayron was appropriately the first to look at Veris amused and say, "Lord? Lord Veris?"

Veris shrugged a single shoulder unabashed, as if to say that certain kinds of politics had to be played out when establishing initial contact with a new civilization. Tayron smiled knowingly and didn't argue.

Veris continued with the formalities that would get them through the gate. "These behind me are esteemed travelers and ambassadors, and their aides. Here are three similar to your kind," he said, pointing to Emily, Ethan, and West, who scowled at being lumped in with the humans, "who are explorers with technology even greater than that of my own land. They were curious about your people, on hearing that, in the physical respect, you seem to be related."

"The physical is no indication," Trinkilion replied.

"Ah . . . yes," Veris said quickly, then veered away from what was evidently touchy ground. "More important than these is Lord Chancellor Davin Tayron, who is second in power in our empire, only to the emperor himself."

That made Trinkilion's eyes widen, but he immediately dropped back into his stony calm, as if the least facial expression took more effort than was warranted for mundane events. "Is the empire in such dire peril that it sends its right hand to treat with us? Our seers have sent preliminary visions down to us, but much of it is . . . unbelieveable."

"I have long been curious about your people, and have matters settled in such a way as to free my time to allow for this journey."

"You are an important man, and therefore I do not take offense when you lie to me. Our card readers have said that your capitol has fallen, though I did not entirely trust their findings until now. The stars and the winds had confirmed the card, but still I did not find the interpretations likely. Now, I have changed my mind, because you are here. But tell me, were the signs and portents in error and has my change of heart been misguided?"

"No," Tayron admitted heavily, "no, they were not."

With utterly impassive bluntness, the guard said, "then you bring a great evil to our shores. Why should we not keep you right where you are for your enemy to find, instead of allowing you to pass into our lands, which would surely lead to our ruin?"

"Our enemy will destroy you when they arrive in any case. They are not in pursuit of us, but of something beyond your borders."

"And you are wittingly leading them to it. We have seen this as well. We have seen great changes ahead for this world, and for the peoples represented by your companions."

"Then you know more than I can tell you."

"What we do not know is whether your haste will result in your success or theirs. The consensus among the elders is that the most immediate possible steps should be taken, but there are some, like myself, who believe that if careful preparation is made while your enemy searches fruitlessly, perhaps there will be a better outcome. Haste has, so far, been your enemy."

Insulted by the guard's intransigence, Tayron snapped back in the manner befitting his high station. "Haste alone has kept us alive. Your cards, stars, and winds are quite verbose. You assume for yourself great wisdom on their account. I do not claim wisdom, but have been in company with some who are truly wise. Not one would claim to know all ends, or be as sure of matters as you pretend to be."

Trinkilion paused, gauging how far he could press this dignitary before he would face reproach from his superiors. Probably not any farther. In his mind, the duty of a good guard was to get as much information in exchange for allowing someone to enter. Travelers all had their secrets, and were also bringers of news from other lands. Knowing the secrets would keep his people safe from present threats, while the news would contribute to the understanding of the whole situation. That was why the coastal watch was so prized – news from this quarter was rare, and insight about doings across the sea hazy. Trinkilion would have hated to admit it, but all the significance of his duty rested on doubt in the signs and portents he loved to cite. If the people of the hills really placed absolute faith in their divinators, and if those seers could cast their eyes on the farthest reaches, information from the gates would be old news and uninteresting.

"You may pass, but only after the introduction of the last of your party, who will be of interest to the elders."

Oris had been so silent that the rest of the travelers had temporarily forgotten how striking she must be to Trinkilion. Unobtrusive and statuesque as usual, she preferred to keep silent and let Veris handle the introduction. Unfortunately, the pilot was at a complete loss, having lost his thread after listening carefully to the exchange between Tayron and Trinkilion, and looked around hopelessly to indicate he needed someone to rescue him.

Emily, shuffling impatiently in the hope that a private toilet was in her near future, sighed and said, "this is Arisin Oris. If your people are who we think you are, then you'll know plenty about her kind. She's a scientist." If she had wanted to be completely honest, she would have added "I think."

"Indeed," Trinkilion said, oddly refraining from some kind of contradiction or retort. Emily had almost expected that his card readers had found out some interesting secret about the Eldrandii, but no comment to that effect was forthcoming. Pointing at the translator on Emily's head instead, he said, "that is truly technology unlike any our people have seen in a long, long time. Perhaps the elders may have interest in you, though the seers said nothing in particular about you. You may look like us, but you are not us, and can only be pale imitations."

Emily felt like punching the man, and would have at least come up with something snappy to say had he not opened the gate after speaking. Trinkilion reminded her of A'anfu En, and she once again wondered whether all of his people were as self-important as he was. What right had these hill-dwellers to such obstinate pride? At least the Eldrandii had won respect through their accomplishments, the fact that they were essential to hyperspace travel, and were willing to share the precious knowledge they had, albeit at a price. Could Trinkilion possibly know how inadequate his people seemed from her point of view?

No roads led to the hills, and no signposts were placed to indicate their names, if they had any. The absence of both showed all too well the kind of welcome they could expect from the natives. If you didn't already know how to get where you were going, you could not expect any help reaching your destination. Trinkilion offered no guidance, and they could be sure that none would be given if they asked, considering how long it took him to simply open the gate.

"I'll take you to the city center, where the elders spend their time grumbling about how standards have fallen since their day," Veris said. "I know you all want to piss and get a bite to eat, but you can't do anything with these people until the elders decide whether you deserve hospitality or not. After I get you to them, I'll need to make arrangements for my plane and look after my own business. I guess you'll be all right after I get you to the elders?"

"That will be more than enough," Tayron said, "thank you for your help Veris. Your flying, especially during that magical storm, proved your reputation."

Veris smiled in satisfaction, even though the compliment was mere formality, and proceeded to speak as if, at least to Emily's ears, he was making an award acceptance speech. "Well, some credit has to go to my bird. That's a fine contraption there, and I couldn't have done it without her."

"No doubt, no doubt. Tell me about these elders."

Veris rolled his eyes. "Practically anyone in the hills above a certain age is an elder, and they all feel like they have the right to make decisions. Their word is law, always, but if one makes an important decision without consulting the others, and they decide the decision isn't the right one, that elder is exiled for a year into the forest to meditate on where he or she went wrong. There's plenty of food in the forest, and not many dangerous animals, so the elders don't usually hesitate to use their power, and you can usually get some quick decisions when you need them. It's an interesting way to run things, especially since it doesn't take much explaining. And since they're pretty traditional, the flexibility of the system doesn't lead to chaos. You don't want to make the mistake of angering one of the elders, though."

"Yes, I read in a report that these people had such a system, but it was hard to believe. Such a government, traditions aside, should have collapsed long ago. Young people inevitably stop respecting their elders' words."

"Well, in my experience, it's their parents they disobey, but they adore their grandparents. Anyway, none of the usual patterns work here. They take their ancient wisdom seriously, and their religion is . . . well, I don't really understand their religion at all, to be honest."

They reached the base of the pyramid hill, and started on the path up. Practically no one frequented the lower levels, but they could hear plenty of chatter above them. Everything about the hill felt artificial. What plants there were existed primarily to keep the soil from eroding in the blasting winds, and their color was matched to the hill so the deliberate human touch would not be obvious. No foreign powers would be encouraged by the semblance of these hills to anchor the ships and come ashore. The pyramids were the only clear sign of intelligent life here, and their magnificent obtrusiveness must have been an unbendable requirement, since they broke the evident purpose of everything else here – to hide the signs of habitation. Without traditions mandating the contradiction, it might have been expected that, with the construction of the pyramids, the people of the hill would abandon the attempt to hide from the world. Since these mutually exclusive facets of their culture were both demanded by their ancestors, probably for specific, logical reasons long forgotten, both were done dutifully despite the irrationality of it.

The first natives they met on the way up were a dark-skinned woman and her girl, both heading around to the inland side of the hill, perhaps to do some herding. Both were dressed in rough stitched undyed hides which, to Emily's complete lack of surprise, blended well with the ground and hillside. After seeing the denizens of the hills from a distance in the plane, she knew there were some who were not so conservatively dressed, and either less observant of ancient edicts or simply less paranoid than these two. The mother and child did not speak to the newcomers as they passed, but gazed warily, curious to see any signs of ill intent. Veris did not engage them or try to reassure them, and the others in the party followed suit, skirting around the two while avoiding any sudden or jerky moves, as if dealing with wild animals.

Every encounter on the way up was another case of mutual caution, making everyone but Veris and perhaps West increasingly tense. Having been known by everyone around him all his life, and generally liked by them, Tayron was especially nervous, massaging his forehead and running his fingers through his hair constantly. Steadily improving her observational skills, Emily decided that the chancellor would have been significantly calmer if he was given a chance to test the local plumbing. Between encounters, Veris explained, "don't expect any warm welcomes. Until they're told how to treat you by the elders, the natives will not react. They won't make a move until you're declared friends or enemies, just in case they ruin some delicate negotiations that the elders need to conduct."

"What about you?" Ethan asked. "They must already know about you."

"Not everyone recognizes me – it's not as if my picture is posted everywhere. Since there's usually only one bunch of outsiders around, they just pass the word around that the outsiders can be trusted, and you basically get a license for that week. Anyway, being friendly to me would be taken as an approval of your presence, which is an extra step no one is going to take. Don't worry, they're not being hostile, either. For them, this is perfectly neutral."

Before residents quieted as they passed, conversations could be overheard and snippets picked up by the translators. Back in the Empire, some of the Asparii-style slang and colloquialisms could be recognized by the device, but the casual talk here was more difficult to parse. The words that did make their way through conversion were either recognizably Asparian or clearly something else – presumably Atlantian. The latter was used by people speaking in an official or parental tone, while the former for trading and negotiations. The words used casually between friends or acquaintances in passing had more difficulty getting through.

Paying careful attention to their mannerisms, Emily noticed that they did not break off their conversations abruptly as the newcomers passed, which would presumably have been a sign of rudeness in any culture, but concluded the sentence they were on, and paused a bit as if to consider what had been said. This practiced mode of smoothly quieting as strangers passed indicated that visitors were expected and prepared for, if not frequent. Emily was reluctantly impressed. Humans, Earth humans, rarely showed so much tact, even when their elders insisted on it.

More striking were the eyes. Every single person who mutely observed their passing had intense intelligence, or the appearance of it, behind their gaze. Even the children took patient and careful measure of the visitors with practically scientific curiosity. Looking back at them, Emily felt inadequate, and though they did not mean to be insulting or hostile, being confronted by so many sharp eyes put her on the defensive. Unlike the mother and child they had first encountered, most of the rest thankfully refrained from staring, but even brief probes were so practiced and precise in their purpose, she was thrown off balance. Not that her circumstances gave her much equilibrium, being far away from her home turf with little chance of returning at the moment. Still, she had enough awareness of herself that she knew to keep her mouth shut. These people, all of them it seemed, had something that she couldn't pretend to have, and if she chose to behave as she normally did, too much of her uneasiness would be revealed, and her actions would not fail to count against her.

A peek into doorways along the path up made it clear that the hill could only have been kept from collapsing by the artificial reinforcement built by the inhabitants. Any metal found in the vicinity or acquired through trade must have gone purely for the rivets, bolts, and brackets that the tunnel structure depended on. The actual supports were wood from the nearby forest and polished stone similar to that used on the pyramids and the henge. Aside from the structure, little could be seen in the entryways to the caves, though some glimpses revealed aesthetically pleasing carpeting and tapestries providing an essential sense of home that the austere exterior of the hill did not. Evidently, none of their precious traditions bade them to deny themselves comforts within private confines. There was no avoiding a lack of natural light within the hill, though. Skylights and mirrors carried as much in as possible, but candles would have to do in most of the rooms.

Enjoying the sunlight and wind blasts all the way up to the pinnacle of the hill, they were all eager to see the stone monuments up close. While most of the plaza was paved in stone, the henge at the center stood in bare soil, without either grass or stray pebbles that might break the perfect pattern outlined by the grand monoliths. The pyramids were simply unfathomable. The effort it would have taken to get all the stone up here had to have been tremendous, and to what end? They could not have been used for the Egyptian-style burial of a great leader, since there were four equal pyramids, clearly constructed as a unified plan. With no grand staircases or anything at their tops, they could not have been Mayan-style temples, either. So what were they? Surely their ancestors had at least done them the justice of telling them why they should undertake such an enormous task. It would be a real tragedy if the pyramids were just for show.

Filled with people, the plaza grew steadily quieter as everyone wrapped up their conversations, gathering around to hear what the elders would have to say. The elders were marked as such by both the usual ways – the physical, including white hair, bald patches, and deeply crevassed faces, and the clothing, which were robes of the deepest red. The robes stood out because no one else wore dyed clothes, but they were otherwise plain and unadorned. With the stone circles in the background, there was something faintly druidish about the elders, especially since the robes were rough, and unlike the silkier, luminescent cloth Oris wore. Since the elders were concentrated in the center of the plaza, even though some were scattered on the edges and corners of the hill, the travelers proceeded onward to the henge instead of approaching the first red robed figure they encountered. No one objected to this, but in between two of the pyramids and before they reached the circles, they were intercepted by one of the elders, who hailed them from fifty feet away by raising his right arm high above his head.

He had the expected stately grace of a leading figure among the local council, though with a hint of stiffness in his step that he carefully hid as he passed a pack of his peers. Not one of them had the bent backs or other physical infirmities Emily was used to seeing in seniors on her world. The one preparing to speak to them had skin lighter in tone than Emily's, and the flecks of color left in his hair were brown, but most of his fellow citizens had darker skin, similar to that associated with Africans on Earth, but something about the facial features made them look different. So many centuries living in an isolated but heterogeneous society might have led to a moderation of some features. In any case, no one clearly matched the physical form associated with the peoples of Earth, and all looked like a healthy mixture instead. Perhaps they were more prototypical, embodying all the traits seen among humans.

Speaking to them in the official language, which the translator could handle without difficulty, the elder said, "I, Penulasen Geramintor, greet you on behalf of Seli, this refuge of our people. We understand you are dignitaries from your worlds, and will be treated as such by us."

There was palpable relaxation in the crowd, and even some random buzz breaking out in the peripheries. Emily and Ethan looked at each other, both catching the word "worlds." It made sense, if these were really Atlantii who knew something of their past, that they would realize travelers could come from other planets, though the people of the Empire did not.

"How did they know so fast . . . ," Jaik started to say after a Selian translated the official language into Asparian, caught off guard by how quickly word had gotten up the hill. It revealed his naïveté, since even this impoverished place could have easily developed a rudimentary communications system – anywhere from light signals to some sort of telegraph. Granted, a small town like the one Jaik had lived in until a week ago had no need for a network of that sort, but even West thought his friend a bit dense, shooting him a brief contemptuous look.

Tayron stepped forward and, looking to the citizen who was translating to indicate his services would be required, said, "we accept your gracious welcome, and will do everything in our power to be worthy of it. I am Lord Chancellor Tayron of Atparis, from which Veris . . . Lord Veris here . . . has frequently visited you. These others –"

"Please allow us to hear their introductions from their own lips, Lord Tayron, if they are not of your own people."

Smoothly taking this in stride and appreciating the reason for the request, Tayron bowed slightly and said, "of course. In that case, let me only mention young Jaik here, who was resident in a town outside our borders until he came to us as a refugee. West here came from that same town, but his full tale will take a longer time to tell, and if you choose to hear and he chooses to tell, you shall hear it from his lips. I will now give way to these others."

Knowing that Oris would hang back and go last, Emily took the liberty of stepping up. "I am Captain Emily Pierce from Earth," not entirely satisfied, and wanting to test the notion, she added, "once known as Atlantis." The addition had been unnecessary, as the gasping had already started at "Earth," which had been translated appropriately. Suddenly realizing that the revelation could be taken in two very different ways – nostalgia and dread – Emily fervently hoped that she had not made a terrible mistake, and that these people would not mistaken her for the descendant of some ancient enemy they had fled from. After all, who would have been left on Earth after these people left for the relative safety of Selparis?

Ethan stepped forward next, and said in Asparian, “I am Ethan Johnson, Captain Pierce’s cultural officer.” Emily could have introduced herself in Asparian, too, but since it didn’t seem to be the main language of these people, what was the point? Still, it was nice to see Ethan stepping up and looking competent in the role she had harangued him into.

West gave a brief account of his dual background, explaining that he was not happy being lumped in with either Earthlings or Selparii. Unable to upstage West’s unique introduction anyway, Jaik decided to be content with what Tayron had said about him. As usual, until bidden to speak and given a clear stage, he would be reserved and keep to himself.

Finally, it was Oris’ turn, and the crowd was all ears, silent to make out not only what she had to say, but also how she said it behind the mechanical tone of the translator. For reasons unknown to Emily, everyone in the square seemed on edge as the Eldrandii stepped forward, and the atmosphere was suddenly hot, tense, and confrontational.

“I am Arisin Oris of Eldrand, and act as an ambassador from my world,” was all Oris said, neglecting her scientific background. Her incomplete answer was enough to set Penulasen Geramintor on edge, and he decided to snap her arrogance like a twig.

“Arisin was a name given only to the family of government agents sent by the masters of Rev’Nor, or so the ancient books say. Is this not so, Arisin Oris?”

Oris’ face flushed to a midnight blue quite darker from her normal hue. Emily struggled mightily to avoid laughing.

“Those are ancient naming conventions not often followed today, and mostly forgotten.”

“Mostly forgotten, perhaps, but we have a saying: the old ones never give up the old things. The saying, we know, refers to your people. You are an old one.” Oris tried to say something, but Geramintor was just taking a breath, and he continued, “and there is another saying. The old ones never do anything except for two reasons.”

“Ancient prejudices and stereotypes are an unbecoming subject for a first encounter between peoples. I do not recall our peoples having strife with each other, so let us be civil here today. If you require two reasons, then I am both an ambassador and a scientist examining the diseases of this world."

The elder was not ready to yield, and passed casual glances to Emily and Tayron as he spoke, as if trying to suggest something to them. "It is not a question of our past, but of our future. To be sure, there are good words said about your people as well, but I have a mind for our circumstances. Your party brings danger in its wake, and we wonder whether divided motives might complicate matters further." His last words were blunt, and gave Emily's worst fears about Oris new fuel. She decided to see how Oris would react before passing judgment.

"My motives are not divided, and I am shocked by your accusation. This is not the welcome you promised." Her tone was imperious, but unconvincing, and lacked the sort of details a person with a truly scientific purpose might offer as a defense.

"Perhaps your motives are not divided, as you say," Geramintor said in a suggestive growl. "And if my welcome to you has been marred by my recent words, then I apologize. It is the considered purpose of this council to provide you with all possible aid. Our diviners are firm that the danger you bring will destroy us if we fail to do so."

A short, stout elderly woman stepped forward and, pulling at Geramintor's cloak, said, "the prophecy Penul. Do not forget the prophecy."

"I was getting to it, Marlata," he said, irritated. Emily had to smile. It was nice to see that not everyone in this place did like they were supposed to, and she felt a special kinship to Marlata.

Geramintor continued, "there is a . . . a legend of the sort you often hear. A woman and a man from our world, that which we came from, would lead us to our long lost heritage, and back to the stars. You are the first from that world to come to us – forgive us, but we do not say the name of the world here – and, by chance, the two of you who were born of that world are a man and a woman."

"Oh hell," Emily said, unintentionally aloud. A prophecy. It figured. "Sorry."

Geramintor looked confused. "I do not recall an underworld being part of the prophecy, but I suppose it is possible. Or is it that you live underground as well, and that you refer to it –"

"No, no. Nevermind." Emily's mind wandered to her dream about the underground city, and caught a hint of an idea she couldn't take hold of.

Seeing something else in what had been said, Tayron retook the stage and asked, "what aid will you be ready to provide? I must admit, our enemies are quite capable of destroying your people regardless of your actions."

"Save one. Indeed, if we stay here, we will be slaughtered. But, as you walk ahead of the storm, we will walk with you, and thereby win our safety. We are prepared to follow you part of the way, then find some safe ground down a branching path – one which your enemies will not pursue us on, lest they are delayed and lose their prize. We are herders, and our provisions are always mobile. We will send them ahead of us along the coast, which will be a shorter path to the safe ground, but will eventually be far away from your route. After that, we will stay in seclusion for a season, which should be enough time for your adventure to reach its conclusion, and we will then return to these hills."

"How long have you known we were coming?" Emily asked, barely catching on that Geramintor was speaking of the wholesale uprooting of Seli's population. "How long have you had to prepare?"

"Fifteen days. Fifteen days ago, our seers came to an accord on the signs. That was enough evidence to allow us to make a decision. By tradition, we are always prepared to leave our homes. We keep few possessions even though we have lived in these hills for eons. Our people were surprised by our edict, but ready. We have always been ready."

Fifteen days ago, she had probably been on Newport Station, far away from this planet and not at all certain that she intended to come here. It sent a chill down her spine, to think that her freedom of action was so limited that they had already known she was coming. At the same time, she fervently hoped that she wouldn't disappoint them. How would she bring these people back to the stars? Surely that was up to the Eldrandii, if anyone. Earth would not part with any of its expensively bought ships – not for anyone lacking even iron to pay for it. She couldn't be sure, but it was probably fair to say that everything in the hills combined wouldn't pay for a landing pod, much less a ship like the *Azar*, unless they could sell their plaza as a tourist attraction. As for carrying them as passengers to, for instance, Newport Station, Earth's military fleet would take one or two trips to carry all the Selians to space, packing them into the cargo bay in cots. The cost of that, again, would be way beyond their means or hers.

Prophecies would have to take care of themselves for now. Tayron exhibited no skepticism, though, when he said, "I must commend your seers, Penulasen Geramintor, for their absolute accuracy and foresight. To have seen our arrival two weeks ago, before our enemy was even on our lands, is a great achievement."

Geramintor bowed. "Thank you, Lord Chancellor. It is a skill we have cultivated, since of the ancient arts it requires the least by way of material, though more in thought and insight. We have not been bound to this planet by want of intelligence, but rather because of the material poverty of the land."

"That is fortunate, that your people are so skilled. In so short a time since our arrival, we have already benefited from their knowledge." This was Tayron's way of saying, to everyone, that he believed the conclusions of the local seers to be true, and would act accordingly. His words won him a harsh glance from Oris, who was no longer the graceful paragon of patience, but fury incarnate, contained only by her sense of decorum and propriety. The lack of a middle-ground in her behavior was more than a bit disconcerting to Emily, who didn't need cards or stars to foresee a struggle against the Eldrandii in the near future. Of course, Oris only showed her dark side when facing accusations of duplicity or dishonesty, as any of her species would, given their strict moral codes. The problem here was that Tayron had basically declared his permanent distrust of her, and as long as he maintained that posture, her attitude was bound to be hostile to him, and anyone she perceived to be on his side.

Emily felt compelled to step in to avoid strife. They were facing potent enough enemies already, and didn't need to create new ones from within their own ranks. That Oris was her employer and Tayron alone knew the way to their goal meant that neither was dispensable, however much Emily might dislike them. Both of them had to be scheming in their own particular way, but that had to be tolerated for now, until Emily could extricate herself from needing them. The one absolute in her mind was that she had to beat the Shadow Workers to their goal, and to lay claim to the secret they wanted so badly before they could. That alone could, in the weakest possible way, justify Max's death. As long as they succeeded, Max had died in the line of duty, fighting against a dangerous foe, and trying to complete a legitimate job.

"I don't know what this is all about," Emily said in all honesty, "but I don't like it when strangers I don't know cause trouble with the people I travel with. We have important things to deal with, and I don't want to waste time with . . . well, dealing with anything that doesn't destroy cities is probably a waste of time."

The elder was obviously distressed by this rebuke and hastened to say, "no offense was meant, Captain. I only sought to report findings and no more. As you say, we have more important concerns to attend to. If you consent to wait until sun-up tomorrow, we will join you on your way. The guides the lord chancellor sent are here living in the hill to the north, and have been sent for. We have treated them well, as you would expect of us, and they are, as all of us, ready to leave. The only reason for delay is to wait for the herds to get a substantial distance ahead of us, so that they do not slow our progress. We have charted pasture lands to cover the entire journey for our animals, while we will beat the harder path through the forest. Some of our livestock will have to travel with us, of course, and we will be with you as long as our beasts can sustain us. Afterwards, we will have to make directly for the planned holding ground."

West looked troubled. "Your herds will slow us down and attract attention," he said, carefully dodging what he really meant to say – that the hundreds or thousands of Selians themselves would slow the progress of the travelers, and leave an unmistakable trail. "I cannot see why we should not travel separately – you to your safe place, and us to our goal."

"Our numbers will protect you from an unforeseen danger. At least, that is what we have read in our divinations."

"With all this seeing, could you just tell us what this unforeseen danger is?"

Geramintor shook his head. "No details were evident, and the danger continues to be identified as unknown, though it is associated with distant forest lands. I apologize, as this is frustrating for us as well. We . . . due to some of our views on magic, we have not produced a lucid seer in many ages, and only such an individual would be able to focus the mind on details to answer specific questions. We can only gain a general understanding of large events."

Emily's ears prickled, but as much as she would have liked to have such a rare gift, she couldn't really believe that she was a "lucid seer," whatever that was. Her dreams were anything but lucid, and she certainly didn't do any magic. Still, it was interesting that the Selians had talked about seeing the future in cards, in stars, and in winds, but not once had they talked about dreaming.

West was less impressed with what Geramintor had to say. "Sounds like a neat excuse –"

The elder scowled. "Captain Pierce has said correctly that we should not waste time insulting each other. Divination is our greatest art, and our strongest tradition. Do you insult it by suggesting we manipulate findings to suit our whim?"

"No," West said softly, realizing too late his mistake and lack of diplomatic etiquette. "Sorry. I apologize."

Turning away from West with some disgust, Geramintor went on. "You will all have accommodations for the night in the spare quarters of this hill, which I will personally guide you to, and your guides will meet you there. I will make myself available, and any questions you have about our people will be answered by me. Nothing will be held back from you, because to do so may be to deny you the help you need, which will result in our own demise. However, you should know that your guides have told us only the beginning of your way, and not the entire journey's path. Our divinations do not produce maps, and show little about your goal. If you ask us what lies ahead, you should know that we are limited by the information you give us. Interpretation requires both the ability to ask the question and a basis for understanding the answer."

Tayron nodded. "We will tell you all we can, but must keep much secret. We thank you for your hospitality, and a night of rest will be something to be thankful for."

Emily felt that she should have been the one to thank the elder for his hospitality since, last time she checked, she was the leader of the party despite the fact that he had taken the initiative for the past few days. Seeing now that his purpose was likely quite different from hers, she was dubious about how much rope to give Tayron. Without question, he wanted to bring Earth in to save his people, and while she thought it a good idea, and would certainly advocate the intervention, all she wanted right now was to get off this planet and onto the *Azar* as fast as possible, preferably with something amazing to sell to the highest bidder. And, she reminded herself, if that bidder happened to be the Eldrandii government, what was wrong with that?

It would concern Tayron, though. He wanted to exchange the treasure his explorers had found for whatever military and technological aid it could buy. The Eldrandii would be far less sympathetic to his cause – a fight between Asparii mages and an Asparian empire – than Earth would be. Emily felt a certain sense of guilt for leading the Shadow Workers here, and an indirect responsibility for hastening the collapse of Tayron's empire, so she was supportive of his cause and rooting for his success.

For now, though, she stayed silent and followed the elder as he led them to the spare rooms in the hill. To enter the interior, they used a pulley elevator on the side of the plaza, where two heavily-built operators stood ready to take passengers where they needed to go. Dropping steadily through the higher floors, they saw that the corridors surrounding the shaft were lit badly by candles, with a morbid atmosphere filled with the oppressive sense of being buried alive. It was no surprise that, in this bright hour of the day, everyone was outside and the hill's interior was empty of residents.

The actual rooms, quite apart from the corridors, were reasonably decorated and comfortable looking. Still not comfortable feeling, though, with tons of rock overhead. After they took turns using the facilities, which turned out to be simple basins attached to pipes, lacking any sophisticated plumbing and reeking violently with lingering odors, they all gathered in an anteroom. This room served as a combined kitchen, meeting room, and reading room for the cluster of five bedrooms immediately around it. They waited in it for the guides to arrive. Fortunately, this did not take long. Four hardy men dressed in the local manner strode in and saluted Chancellor Tayron, who gave them a nod back, then stood at semi-attention in a row. If they had seen fit, any one of them could have beaten Emily to a pulp, but their expressions identified them as the thoughtful, silent types incapable of using their strength on a whim. All four were, at the moment, affable and eager to please the lord chancellor, who had given them the opportunity and the funding to become only the second group of explorers in the new world. There was a shade of fear and doubt in their eyes as well, as they were concerned about the state of the empire and why the chancellor should travel across an ocean to a badly charted land.

"Lord Tayron," a guide with black hair and a chiseled face began, "it is truly an honor to have you here."

"Forgive me, Daeltin, but we should skip pleasantries, I think. It was not desire to bring you honor that brought me here. A dire situation has developed in our homeland, and efforts here may be our only way to bring aid."

Daeltin looked ominously at his companions, whose eagerness to hear what the chancellor had to say faded away into concern. "We have heard from local seers . . . many things. We are not sure what to believe."

"From what I have heard of their abilities already, probably all of it," Tayron said bluntly. His imposing and commanding attitude while dealing with these subordinates was distasteful to Emily, who found this line particularly coarse and insensitive.

"Indeed, Lord. If it is your wish, we can show you our route and give you details that will astound you. It is difficult for us to decipher what we found, but our expedition was well worth your funding, and may bring technology of great value to Atparis. It is a shame that one or two of us were not trained as technologists or linguists instead of just being survivalists, since we would have done more to examine our find."

"Your efforts, such as they have been, are much appreciated and will more than suffice. Now, I am impatient to know exactly what you found."

"Umm, my lord?" Daeltin nodded meaningfully at Geramintor. Having kept the secret from the Selians for so long, he was understandably dubious about suddenly telling all.

"I think it is time we let our hosts, who have shown their good intent to us repeatedly, know what we plan to do. They are being forced to make sacrifices because of a danger we have brought to them. Sharing our secret will be our way of recognizing this."

Her recent dream in mind, Emily interrupted, "Let me guess. There's a huge underground city with massive towers surrounded by a metal dome. Parts of it are still lit by electricity and . . . well, that's all I remember."

Jaw hanging unceremoniously, Daeltin whispered coarsely, "how did you know that? We kept it secret, my Lord, an absolute secret, I swear. Not a word to anyone. How did she know? Even you did not know about that metal dome, my lord."

"Calm down, Daeltin. I'm sure you are not to blame."

Thoroughly pleased with herself, Emily tried now to shrug the surprise off, saying, "I saw it in a dream, that's all."

The simple truth seemed to work wonders, and Daeltin's shock cleared, making way for a pleasant smile. It was amazing how quickly the man changed temperament – perhaps it was a survival technique. "Ah, well then, our friend Elder Geramintor here might be willing to take you in as an honorary resident. A natural seer."

In fact, Geramintor was definitely looking at her with interest, but said nothing. He did manage to indicate wordlessly that he would be interested in a private word with her later.

Daeltin proceeded to tell them about the city in vague terms. For most of their journey through it, the explorers were in a state of wide-eyed wonder and completely incapable of making an incisive examination of their surroundings. Knowing, thanks to the previous expedition, that there was something to find, they had mostly concerned themselves with surviving their way through to the site, and returning to Seli in preparation to guide a more substantial team to the underground city. They headed straight for the main building of interest identified by the first party – a massive library with books that were merely screens, with buttons to scroll through the contents. Unable to read many of the words, they nevertheless recognized some of the names of the major sections of the library, including the magic section, which easily held thousands of books on the arcane arts, and the technology section, which occupied ten times as much space. At the very center of the library's fourth floor, from the top down, was a book on a pedestal sealed in a glass case. The lettering on the cover was completely alien to them, so they could not guess what the book was. It must have been profoundly important, though, because no other book in the place had been given a more prominent display.

Also scattered throughout the underground city were vehicles of all sorts. In a massive area on one side of the city, huge winged craft were placed in neat rows, though there was no field or runway to take off on, nor any way to get past the dome surrounding the entire city. The only logical conclusion was that the area was more of a museum of technology than a functional part of the city. Emily could see a potential solution – if the vehicles could take off vertically and there was actually a retractable window through the dome. Or maybe the runway and opening were actually under the surface of the city, and elevators carried the aircraft and spacecraft down to the launch bay. Such monumental mechanisms had not occurred to the imperial explorers because they had nothing even remotely like them in their experience. Her scope was a bit wider.

To close, Daeltin said, "locals, who live in a city that looks like it was built to protect it, call the underground city Raljar Canti, which just means Forbidden City. They absolutely refuse to go down there, because there is a spirit that lives there that bid them not to. We saw the spirit, and it let us pass, but gave us stern warnings about what we could and could not do."

"We have something like this city in our legends," said Geramintor, searching for a book from one of the bookcases huddled in a corner of the room. He flipped to a page he had long held in memory for reference and read verbatim, "the people of . . . ," he cleared his throat and looked curiously at Emily, "the people of Atlantis built great cities in space as sanctuaries during times of magical civil war. After the fall, these were filled with those fleeing the destruction, and they left the devastated planet, landing on habitable planets throughout the galaxy. The space cities had been built, from the beginning, with adequate fuel for a one-way exodus." The elder placed the book on the table and said, "that is the essential part of our foundation legend, and what I understand from you is you have found the space city that brought us here. Is that correct?"

"Space . . . city," Daeltin said, trying to catch up. "I suppose . . . yes. Maybe."

Geramintor was remarkably downcast for someone whose cherished beliefs might have been confirmed, and he immediately revealed why. "How is it that you, in our land for less than a year, found this treasure, while all this time we have not?" The question was directed at Lord Tayron, but the chancellor did not have an answer. Daeltin had already considered the issue, and gave his opinion.

"Your people rarely travel more than a ten days' journey from here, Elder, and never beyond what you call the boundary forest. Land from here north forms a slim curve, like a massive peninsula, and it is easily a month's travel long. Since it is ten times longer than it is wide, that makes exploration . . . straightforward. As I said, locals around this Raljar Canti stay out of it, though they let us through because Raljar Canti's spirit could decide if we deserved entry or not."

"They stay out of it," Geramintor mumbled to himself. "They live so close to the remains of our ancestors, and could learn such secrets that we could only imagine, and they are content to live at its doorstep without entering." He became angry, and his voice sharpened to a point. "We have copied over and over again our ancient books to preserve them. We have kept alive knowledge we could rarely understand and never use, in the hope that, someday, we would return to our old glory. Who are these people who have so broken with our ancestors that they fear to approach a mountain because of . . . of a spirit. I doubt such a spirit. It is a mechanism of some sort, if anything. Where is the thirst for knowledge? Are these people of some other mold that they are so faint-hearted and lack all imagination? If we had only known –" And it was that last point that most grated on Geramintor's sensibility. It would have been so easy for his people to have explored just a bit further, and to dare the dangers of the boundary forest, if only they had known the source of their heritage was so nearby.

Made nervous by Geramintor's sudden caustic comments, Daeltin spattered, "I cannot answer your questions, Elder. They . . . they look like your kind, and certainly are not ours. As for the rest, I can only report what I saw.'

Geramintor nodded and softened his tone. "Yes. I will have to suggest to the elder council that we send some people with you to investigate these neighbors to the north. Clearly, we have been lax in our scouting, and too complacent. This departure from our hills will do us some good."

The gathering broke apart in some haste and discomfort, as Tayron wanted to go over the state of the empire and the specifics of the journey ahead with his men. Aware that it was vital for her to know this information as well, but not wanting to poke her nose in too obviously, Emily tasked Ethan to hang around and to get a clear sense of the path to the underground city, as well as he could. If anyone could remember details after hearing them once, he could. Exiting the anteroom, she noticed that Oris was waiting against the wall outside. But why would the Eldrandii want to know the way to the underground city for herself, unless some of the accusations leveled against her might be true? Emily had to give her some credit, though – she could simply distrust Tayron.

The rest of the group departed to their rooms after grabbing some leftovers from the kitchen. Geramintor followed Emily out, and when she reached her room, she stepped aside for him, letting him through first, to show that she knew they had something to talk about. Eager to talk about it with someone who might understand, she jumped right into the middle of the topic.

"I have dreams that show me what's going to happen. I didn't used to get them very often, but now they happen every few days. Any ideas?"

"Yes, Captain. I had a clear picture as soon as you mentioned your dream. You are a natural seer –"

"But I don't really understand them, and I don't feel like they help me at all. And I don't remember having any dreams like this when I was a kid."

"Please, let me finish. You were born with this gift, but it required a certain store of magic to activate it. When you were young, your environment must have had very little magic, and I assume you were never taught any incantation to gather magic. Recently, I suppose your travels have brought you in contact with more, and so you are able to use your talent."

That rang true to Emily. "Are there a lot of . . . people like me?"

"Not at all. While there are many mages, few have abilities that automatically activate in the presence of magic. Most need spells to harness their power. Someone born with the complex ability to see into the future . . . we have very little magic here, but we have records going back over a thousand years to make up for it, and a natural seer has never existed in these hills. You may be the only one on this world. But you have seen more than I have, Captain. Surely you are in a better place to judge?"

Emily shrugged, and he continued, "we could do much to help you to hone your skill, especially in the area of interpretation. We can also show you how to prepare before sleeping so your visions are on the subject you wish to have revealed to you."

"Listen, I haven't had a single vision about something I haven't been involved in. I don't think my dreams are all that useful, and especially not to anyone but me."

Geramintor paused for a moment to ponder the information, then said, "however, you have never tried to focus your mind deliberately, have you? You have only dreamt about your own affairs, because those are the only ones you were thinking of before you slept. Captain, I believe your skills could become abundantly useful, even while you are awake. Consider what must be happening when your mind shows you glimpses of the future. It is choosing the correct path in a multitude of possibilities. We can all see various possibilities ahead of us – your mind simply sees farther down the road, and selects the true road. Whether you see down your road or someone else's simply depends on where your mind starts walking."

Emily was getting confused. She knew the elder was making sense, but couldn't appreciate conclusions that were so far beyond her experience. She was a practical person, so the only solution was to try the theory out.

"Okay, so how do I start on a different road, then?"

"There are a number of ways that could be tried, but my first suggestion is that you focus on the person or place you wish to study for at least an hour prior to sleeping. I cannot say that this simple method will definitely work for you, but it is worth the attempt."

"All right. I'll tell you what, Elder, I'm going to try it tonight. I've got something I want to know, and we'll see what happens."

"Thank you for having an open mind about this, Captain. Among our own people, magical abilities are stifled by superstition and mistrust of those arts, which according to legend brought down Atlantis. Otherwise, we would have many powerful mages in our midst, and I think we would be better for it. I would not be surprised if the galaxy was full of people with amazing abilities who never put them to use for one reason or another. Believe, Captain, and all else will follow."

And that was that. Emily laughed a bit to herself after Geramintor's departure. Yes, she was exactly the type of person who could have amazing powers. He had made her sound like some sort of superhero, and maybe in a town where predicting the future was the biggest business going, she was. Anyway, she had said she would give it a try, and she meant every word she said. Focusing on the *Azar*, she would gladly accept some news of what was happening there now, and set her thoughts on the tiniest fraction of time in the future, a single tick of a clock.

It was still a few hours before sunset, but she spent the afternoon lazing on the bed. It wasn't a very comfortable bed – the blanket was rough, even though it looked brand new, and the pillow stoutly resisted her head's weight as if a solid rock. Having spent the previous day and night in an airplane with minimal leg room, ever-intensifying pains were flaming up in all parts of her body from the neck down, and getting off her feet had become a necessity, so she was prepared to enjoy whatever bed she could get.

Her thoughts were on the *Azar*, and it did not take much effort to keep them there, with all the possible perils that might have befallen her ship. Normally, she would have tried without avail to dispel the thoughts of worry as a waste of effort, but this time there was a purpose behind them. She had to endure the pessimistic conjurations of her mind, punctuated by the occasional brighter options that broke the monotony of dread, hoping that Geramintor's hunch was right, and that her dreaming would reveal the definitive truth, whatever that might be.

At some point, she fell asleep and started the dreaming. By the time her eyes opened again in the candle-lit room, she had a new perspective on herself, and everything. It had worked, and she dashed to Ethan's room to tell her only shipmate within communications range how their crew was faring. If it had been bad news, she would have been more hesitant.

Ethan was still sleeping, but she didn't think twice about shaking him awake, knowing he wouldn't be angry with her. In fact, he would be thrilled to be the first to know, after he got over his fatigue.

"Yeah, what?" he said blearily, rubbing his eyes before reaching for his glasses from the bedside table, "we aren't being attacked, are we?" He yawned. "I heard the way to the underground city, if that's what you're wondering."

"I had a dream about the *Azar*, but I made it happen this time. The elder suggested it, and it works. I can see into the future . . . well, at least a short way into the future."

Ethan was immediately excited, having taken no time at all to fathom the implications, and said, "that's great! What did you see?"

"They're all right. I saw them docked at Newport Station and Commander Raiz was on board. They were talking about some sort of fight – I couldn't tell whether it had already happened or if they were planning for it. There was something about Eldrandii around Selparis. The way I figure it, the Eldrandii ships are keeping the Asparian ships from helping the Shadow Workers already here, but might not be strong enough to actually destroy them. So Earth will send help to finish them off, and then it'll be safe for the *Azar* to come into the system again."

Ethan's enthusiasm was not powerful enough to overwhelm the innate morbid pessimism that fueled his music. If the news had been bad, he would have been instinctively more likely to believe it. "You sure this dream wasn't just . . . wishful thinking?"

"Totally sure. It was that kind of dream."

"All right . . . so, I guess all we do now is hold out. I guess . . . you'll want to see this whole underground city thing through, right?"

"Yeah. I mean, it's what we came for. From what the guides said, there's probably a boat load of money in it."

"This sort of thing never turns out good in the movies, you know."

"Well, the good guys win, don't they?"

"Sometimes. But how do we know we're the good guys?"

"We don't go around randomly killing people and blowing up

cities," Emily said sharply.

"Good point. Still . . . I don't think we should go with movie logic on this one."

Emily sensed some rebellion in her old friend, whose docility she had so far taken for granted. She would have been amused at some other time, and would have found it cute, but she did not have the patience for it now. "Ethan, are you telling me we should just give up and go home?"

"Well, no, not if you put it that way –"

"Then just go along with it and get back to sleep. I promise we'll try our best to keep you from dying."

"Thanks." To Emily's surprise, he did tuck himself in again, though petulantly, without further comment. Taking this as a sign that most of the night remained ahead, having no other way to check, she went back to bed. This time she set her head down without a specific purpose to her sleep, and had no dreams.

10
The Slow Road

The Selians, perhaps two or three thousand in total, flooded out into the broad plain on the inland side of their habitation. They were a dour crowd, but did not complain or seem disgruntled about this uprooting. Rather, they were resigned to fate. Here was a tribe that could truly predict the general layout of the future, and yet were always prepared to leave home if some unexpected event should befall them. If that didn't speak to their chronic pessimism, nothing could.

Of course, this move was not unexpected, but rather preemptive based on foreseen dangers. Even with time to prepare, though, this was a huge population to move, and Emily hoped that the elders had considered carefully what they were doing. After her own experiences, she would be the last to discount their divinations, but she prayed deep in her heart that they relied more on planning and less on the stars for their welfare. She didn't want to be responsible for any more tragedies, no matter how tangentially.

The great plain had held at least a thousand head of cattle the day before, but was nearly empty of them now, except for the dozens that would sustain them on their journey. In the place of the ruminating animal was a new flock of humanoids, crossing the expanse in a day, reaching the first trees of the sparse nearby forest by evening. The Selian scouts went ahead, but what had become known as Lord Tayron's Party followed closely behind them for this first day, and walked well ahead of the great mass of the people.

Veris had returned to his plane yesterday, and was already on his way back across the ocean, to one of his emergency fueling fields far outside the limits of any town or city. Ethan had asked whether he would be willing to fly them to the site of the underground city, but as far as the pilot was concerned, that option was out of the question. Flying was his livelihood, and as long as there was no fuel on this continent, he had no intention to get stranded here.

"I don't understand why ships don't cross the ocean . . . ," said Ethan, suddenly realizing that he wanted to know, and had failed to ask. "I mean, if they did, you could just bring your plane back on one of them."

"You're a bright lad," Veris replied, indicating by his tone the complete opposite, "but maybe you need to save your brilliant mind for later. They don't cross it because the winds and currents make it impossible, not to mention the cost of maintaining the crew doesn't make it worth it, since there's so little to trade for here. Listen, I'm not debating this. I'll be fine once I get to the fuel I stashed away, and my patriotism takes second place to my flying. That's the end of it."

Tayron nodded stiffly to the pilot. "We thank you for taking us safely this far," he said, and that was the last they saw of Veris.

Tied to the ground, Emily couldn't help but feel vulnerable. While the hardy folk of the hills traveled faster than she could have guessed, Shadow Workers would soon be hot on their tails, moving much quicker with less effort. It was too much to hope for that the mages, after ripping the airfield apart, wouldn't find a way across the ocean. Unable to imagine them taking a plane across, huddled together in a tiny cabin, Emily appreciated more than ever that magic was an unpredictable tool, and extremely malleable to the clever mind. She had seen nothing that suggested her enemies were clever, but her only hope was nevertheless to be far away from the coast before they got their collective brain cells together.

Once in the trees, they had some cover, but spending a night in the forest, tame as this one might be, could never be entirely comfortable to someone used to all the amenities of modern life. The alien flora and mysterious nocturnal creatures of this world added to Emily and Ethan's unease. Fortunately, the ground was at least dry and firm, having not seen rain in many summer weeks, so there was no worry in her mind about a random monsoon or hurricane wiping them out. That would have been just their sort of luck.

The bizarre company offered by the Selians made her even more anxious, and she relied increasingly on Ethan's presence for a sense of stability. She was also beginning to think of Jaik as part of her team, even though West seemed, to her, to be totally unreliable, and even volatile. Other than these three, though, she was surrounded by people cut from a very different mold than she was. Tayron's leadership also served to rob her of her natural confidence, since everyone looked to him as the leader of the adventure, and she could only stay silent in her resentment of this usurpation. She had certainly never been a follower, never giving way even when it would have been better to do so because someone else had more talent or experience. In this case, though, she had not been given any choice. It had been hard enough gaining the trust of her crew of thirty, assuming she had really finished that job. Getting a hundred or so elders to look at her as a leader when they were already familiar with Tayron's position of authority was impossible. So, she was forced to just tag along.

Only Oris was more irritated by Tayron's leadership than Emily. The Eldrandii was still a member of her species, and entrusting an Asparii with power was anathema to her. Since this particular Asparii had directly challenged her honesty, and was supported by others who had done so as well, she was intensely tempted to insist that Emily and Ethan, who were technically in her employ, should abandon their association with the hill people and Tayron. She knew the way to the underground city, but she knew better than to make her move. The Selian diviners had been mostly accurate so far, which meant that these people would likely provide some essential help along the way. There were many dangers that five or six people could not cope with, but that hundreds or thousands could easily handle. So, she did not make demands, and was, like Emily, forced into temporary irrelevancy.

Unlike practically everyone else, Jaik and West were thrilled. Desperately escaping from danger in Dakatanis, they had now found themselves on a real adventure – one that every young man would dream of being part of. West saw in the underground city a wealth of possibilities. If he could only come to learn some of the technological secrets unknown to Earth, he could become a universally relevant inventor, rather than one considered competent only by this backward world's standards. Jaik was of a similar mind, and was suddenly flushed with ideas he had long ago considered absurd. If the ancient city held marvelous secrets as promised, and some of those secrets were magical in nature, why not become a mage? They certainly could have used one on this journey. Why not become an inventor or an engineer, for that matter? All it would take would be some way of translating those ancient books, and he could have abilities that no one had seen in thousands of years. Ethan was proving that he had a way with languages, and would undoubtedly be quick to learn the ancient language, so maybe they could work together to decipher the secrets, and to put them to use.

Jaik especially wanted some way of impressing Emily, since he had no other idea how to woo her. She had so far been the model of strength, with a private fragility and lack of self-confidence that made her so easy for him to understand, despite the language and cultural differences. Though they put on very different faces when dealing with others – she had her blunt act of bravado, and he had his silence punctuated by moments of passion and inspiration – their quiet demeanor behind closed doors was the same. He often imagined that he could read her thoughts, especially in her most introspective moments. He had no way of knowing that she had spent an entire childhood void of inner dialogue, and was still uncomfortable with the necessity of it, but otherwise, Jaik had the measure of Emily. What made it hard was the seemingly certain knowledge that he would never meet anyone like her again, and that this was his only chance.

There was a time when Emily would have paid attention to Jaik's feelings, taking delight in playing around with him a bit while getting to know him before, in all probability, letting him down gently. She would have exchanged hints with him, giving him an opening through her rough façade. But now, with all that was happening, she had stored those instincts in the back of her mind, deep in her subconscious, so that she might still have been giving off some signals, but not intentionally.

Feeling weak and dazed after the long walk, she gladly took a seat on a rock when the elders called for the halt in the late afternoon, being worn out themselves, and more than ready to encamp. She was surprised by her sudden sense of fragility, which had actually been there since morning, increasingly weighing on her through the day.

Was she getting ill from some peculiar local bug? It was certainly lucky that they had not encountered any fatal sickness here, and she was long overdue for something like this, having exerted herself so much lately. There was no way her fatigue was anything normal, since it was accompanied by an inability to put thoughts together or focus on any object in sight. Maybe it was something about the air of this continent, or spending the night in the stuffy hills. If it was something simple like that, Ethan should also be feeling down, but there was nothing unusual about him as far as she could see.

Geramintor had noticed her heavy descent onto the rock, and walked over to her stiffly, as if he was desperately in need of a lie-down himself, but to do so this early in the evening might damage the esteem others had for him. He had a reputation for being solid and stalwart, which had won him the right to be the first to speak with the newcomers. Unfortunately, his sort of person didn't rest until the sun had fully set, and certainly didn't groan about the aches in his back and knees. It was a great sacrifice on his part, but worth the trouble.

"You seem to be tired, Captain," he opened.

"So do you," she replied sharply, not in the mood for a conversation and lacking the patience for niceties.

"Yes, but your weariness, if I may guess, is not physical. I am surprised you did not come to see me this morning. You have depleted your magical store in the attempt you made last night, which must have required more magic than any accidental attempts to delve into the future would have. Your body has become tolerant to a threshold level of magic, and –"

"You're saying that I've got some sort of magical withdrawal. I'm hooked on the stuff and I need my fix."

"I do not understand, but if you are referring to addiction, this is not an addiction. There is simply a minimal level of magic that magic users are used to having at their disposal for the regular rigors of life. That threshold, once established when young, does not increase. They say even regular people require a small amount of magic to function. All magic users will occasionally use more than they should, and need to recharge. We do not use magic often among our people, so we only know weak recharging methods – simple recharging spells and the like. It is yet another resource we lack."

Interested, Emily asked, "but it's not like you need iron for it, and from what Lord Tayron's explorers said, the underground city is full of magical books. You must have some that tell you more. I mean, the Atlantii and Asparii and everybody's full of magic. Practically everyone except us humans and the Plani, I think. I always wondered why we were left out."

"The same reason we lack it – the fall was blamed on arrogance and corruption bred by the power magic provides. It is a surprise to me that there would be so many magical texts in the ancient city. Our ancestors certainly made clear what they thought about magic. Beyond divination, they considered it dangerous, and a temptation that the greedy could never moderate. I suspect that the same sentiment reigned on your world, where the last magic, according to legend, was spent to clean up the last remnants of the old, failed civilization." His voice was filled with deep emotion, though his account lacked it. He spoke of the end of hope, the human species' greatest failure, the expulsion from Eden, and the fall of man.

At least he wasn't blaming it on a girl eating an apple, Emily thought in a brief moment of clarity in the haze. Satisfied by the explanation, and desperate to get back to normal, she said, "all right. Could you teach me a recharging spell, 'cause it's hitting me hard right now."

"I do not know any spell myself, since I have never used magic, but I will find someone who does. The magic users among our people know I am a sympathetic ear for their ideas and troubles. Wait here."

It didn't take long, and Geramintor brought the same elderly woman who had interrupted his initial greeting on the hilltop by mentioning the prophecy. She skipped any prologue or introduction, looked around to see if anyone was listening to what they were doing, for fear of being punished or ostracized for breaking the taboo, then told Emily to repeat after her.

The translator device did not convert the words at all, or even try. That made sense, because all words associated with magic itself, which used languages all its own, had been deliberately kept out of the device's database. Emily heard the nonsense words, and repeated them. She missed the tone and inflections the first few times, but after correcting the mistakes, she felt a sensation similar to an adrenaline rush. It helped immensely, almost like a good strong cup of coffee, and she was up and walking in a flash. She repeated the phrase to the old lady over and over again, getting a minor rush on the second successful recitation, but nothing after, as she was presumably up to her magical limit. Once certain her student was hitting it every time, the teacher nodded, and left with some satisfaction in her quiet smile.

As the woman left, Emily saw a faint purple glow around her, which diminished in intensity the further way they were from each other. The glow was barely perceptible, but unmistakable. Looking around, Emily saw others with the tiny glow, and when she neared them the effect grew more distinct. The conclusion was obvious – she could now see other mages. Looking at her own arm, she didn't see any such glow, but knew it had to be there when others looked at her. Thrilled with the realization that she was now a genuine magic user, however feeble her abilities were, she could not wait to try her only ability out again that night. Dinner passed, and before she knew it, guards had been set around the massive encampment, and she was free to sleep.

Right after dinner, she had started to focus on something even further removed from her own context – the current state and future of Marcus Welder. Again, she focused on a tick of a clock to indicate that what she was looking for was as close to the present as possible. She had no doubt that she would eventually be able to see further in the future, but so far her sight had, at most, shown her events within weeks of the present, and the further away it was, the less clarity she had. Looking years into the future would probably produce nothing more than the barest symbol, and in the process exhaust her meager magic. Choosing a more specific focus would also make a bigger demand on her energy. She knew, with instinctive certainty, that to push too far in either time or specificity would result in dire consequences, including the loss of the essential spark of magic that all sentient beings required.

Sleep plunged her without prologue into the vision, of which she would only remember flashes. Welder, speaking to a bunch of highly-perched Eldrandii similar to the interrogators at the hotel, looked far more distraught than he had been before. Quite noticeably, his wife was not with him. The name "Raiz" came up, but that was the only word she heard. The next scene was of Welder alone in a reasonably furnished room, pacing furiously with glances at Eldrandii guards at the door who turned relative comfort into a prison. The last flash was of the map – the one they had gotten from the crime scene investigator – in the hands of an Eldrandii questioning Welder.

She woke up in the middle of the night, right after the dreaming was done, which allowed her to remember what she had seen. It didn't look good from any angle. Clearly, the Eldrandii trust in the troubleshooter had run out, and for some reason they suspected him of something. From the appearance of the map, she guessed this still had to do with the original murder, but there had to be something else behind it, since Welder was so obviously clear of guilt that even the most paranoid Eldrandii would have to be brain-dead as well to be concerned about him. Maybe it was something about her own mission that had gotten Welder into hot water.

Why had she decided to look in on Welder in the first place? It had been a whim, but behind it must have been a realization that what was happening on Eldrand was important. She wanted to know more in connection to Geramintor's suspicions of Oris, and had hit upon Welder, which was the kind of misfire a person could get when unaware of their own purpose. She had not tried looking into the past before, but it might have been worth a try to see where Oris had been before their meeting on Eldrand, and the night between that meeting and their departure. The past should be a clearer picture than the future, since her mind didn't have to figure out which of the many possibilities was the correct one.

She said the spell to refill her magic, but didn't intend to do more dreaming. Instead, she wanted the adrenaline rush effect to get her a bit more awake, in the hope that she could think through everything with greater care in the peace of night. In a few seconds, she realized how obvious it was. Thinking first about what she could possibly find at the end of this road that could interest Earth's government in the form of Raiz, the Eldrandii in the form of Oris, and the Asparii in the form of both Tayron and a swarm of evil mages, the options were fairly narrow. Add to the equation that it had to be something that could be recovered form Atlantii remnants, and that Atlantis had been a force to rival Eldrand in its heyday, and the picture became far more focused than any dream could be. To her knowledge, which was admittedly thin assurance, Atlantis and Eldrand had never been enemies, so the secret had to be information that Eldrand had not been concerned about at the time, but now valued a great deal.

Emily's eyes widened with the ultimate thought. The status of Eldrand was upheld primarily by one thing: their exclusive production of hyperspace craft. They had not always been the sole possessors of that secret – the Asparii had lost the knowledge generations ago, and irreversibly after the fall of their world, but had maintained some of their own fleets throughout that time so that a few, such as those in the hands of the Shadow Workers, had survived into the modern day. Those that didn't survive simply died, suddenly unable to make the jump into hyperspace. Atlantis had been able to make ships as well, according to ISC records, but after over ten thousand years, there were no lasting examples of their work.

Physical weariness catching up with her, she left it at that, satisfied that there was a great likelihood that the secret of hyperspace technology was in her future. She did not remember any of her subsequent dreams in the morning, though she felt there might have been some significance mixed in with the usual nonsense. At the first sign of dawn, she woke fresh and went straight to where Ethan was sleeping, telling him all about her night as soon as he was aware of his surroundings. Annoyed about being woken early for the second night in a row, he pretended to be bored when she explained what she saw, but couldn't help being impressed when she explained what she thought their goal in this actually was, and why the Eldrandii government had deployed Oris to sponsor the expedition. Far from being surprised by the theory, he was impressed that she had managed to come up with it, and in his irritation said so.

"No offense, but you usually have trouble putting two and two together, much less anything like this."

"I know it. I was surprised myself. I think magic had a lot to do with . . . you know . . . inspiration. Getting all charged up with it . . . I hadn't really thought much about magic until now, now that I can use it."

"Crazy," he said in admiration. "I've got a friend you uses magic."

"Sort of makes the whole trip worth it, huh?"

"Well, no. But Emily," he whispered with deliberate strain to indicate she should lower her excited voice back down as well, "we should keep this from . . . well, pretty much everyone just to be safe. I'm sure Tayron and Oris know the elder spoke to you about your dreams. If they think you're good at it, they might get worried that you'll see into their plans."

"I get why Oris might be worried, but what do you think Tayron might be up to?"

"I don't know, but I don't think anyone as powerful as he is doesn't have plenty of plans up is sleeve. Bringing us here was one of them, and so far that's worked out for him. If you just take all the stuff out of the underground city, how can he be sure that Earth will help his empire? All Earth needs to do is secure the city, and the chancellor wouldn't get anything out of it. He has to have a way to get what he wants before we get what we want. I think whatever that plan is, it probably involves his explorers."

"Good point."

"I really don't like this. I mean, it's just the two of us, isn't it? I mean, maybe Jaik and West, too, but they have no clue. And they're really big on the empire and Tayron, really patriotic about them, so we can't really be sure they won't take up his side." Ethan hesitated, finding it distasteful to doubt their companions, especially since he had gotten on so well with them. "I don't think they're more loyal to us than to the empire, Emily, I really don't. I mean, have you seen West's face when he's lumped in with us, with humans? He likes it here. This is his home."

It was a grim assessment, and Emily couldn't help but notice that Ethan was ignoring Jaik's feelings towards her, which she often ignored herself, but could easily use to sway him, On the whole, Ethan's words were accurate. West and Jaik had journeyed north to the empire for the sole purpose of seeing the emperor, in the confidence that he would act against the enemy and prevent the destruction of any more towns. That was a wealth of symbolic trust, and Emily had done nothing to win as much from West or Jaik.

Her mind was making her aware of the way Jaik had been looking at her, and she cursed herself for not taking more note of it before. The way she had treated him so far bordered on neglect, and if he ended up favoring Tayron's position, it would be because of her failure to appreciate and address his feelings. He wasn't a bad sort at all, and a lot like the quiet, brooding boys she had always gone out with, and seemed to find floating around without any effort. He was a bit younger than her, but she didn't know by exactly how much, nor what counted as normal where he came from. Asparii also looked younger than they were, having proportionally longer lives, so it was difficult to tell. Way back on Newport Station, she had been so desperate for companionship . . . how had she gotten by without thinking about it until now? Hopefully, her suddenly resurging impulses, suppressed because of the pace of the recent action, didn't lead her to do something stupid – something that would hurt Jaik.

She shook her head. No point treading old ground, and that train of thought could only lead to reminiscences that were best forgotten. She was different now. The magic alone was good enough reason for a revolution in her life, and everything else that had recently happened only compounded the sense that she needed to make some changes in her way of thinking. There was no point resisting it – part of the point of an adventure was that the journey changed you. Those who come out winners make sure they are changed for the better. Her new, more serious and probing, way of looking at life was definitely due to the distance she had put between herself and the suburban environment of her youth, and the flippant and fickle attitudes it had fostered. She was adapting and suiting herself to the situation, which was as dire and perilous as her old life was carefree and thoughtless.

Well, nice to have that settled, she thought as others in the camp began to wake up. What had she been doing? Ethan was still waiting for a reply on whether she thought Jaik and West were trustworthy. It must have seemed as if she had given it a lot of thought when she finally said, "yeah, we can trust them. But I won't tell them anything yet," and Ethan didn't offer a word of counterargument. He also had to be slightly relieved, since he had become good friends with them, benefited from their company, and didn't want to treat them as suspicious or keep them at a distance. As for keeping a secret or two, that was just in the normal course of things.

If the past days had tested her ability to adapt, the next few were replete with boredom that made her regret not bringing along some portable entertainment. It was fortunate that the Selian cows were more athletic than their cousins on Earth, though it meant tougher meat and more limited milk output, or the progress would have been tortuous. Emily had time, while they traveled through alternate patches of plains and savannah forestland, to muse that the tough meat might explain the stern Selian manner. The hill folk were quick to tell the newcomers which fruits were to be eaten and what creatures were hunted. In both cases, the numbers were plentiful, and the food easy to find even without the accompanying cattle. Any offensive creatures were taken care of by either scouts or guards long before they threatened the bulk of the population, and Emily only caught glimpses of the battles and their aftermath. She did get a chance to taste the meat of some of those dangerous animals, and had to admit that these people could cook enticing dishes out of anything. Even better, she didn't have a clue what the beasts were when they were named, saving her from any preconceived distaste.

She decided not to try any more focused dreaming until there was a concrete reason to, even though some revelations would have broken the monotony of travel, on the logic that she couldn't do anything about whatever she might see. She really didn't want to know about Tayron, Oris, or Raiz, whatever they might be playing at. Only the Shadow Workers interested her, and she knew what they were doing, and how little she could do about it. Even though she had not intended on it, she spent some time on the fifth night of the journey thinking about how the enemy mages might get across the ocean without a plane, and the truth came to her in a dream-vision, in what she now considered the "normal" way instead of the "magical" way. She did not need to recharge after receiving her answer, but also lost some clarity.

The Shadow Workers were ready to cross the ocean but, in her vision, had not made the journey yet. It was impossible to tell whether the scene was of the past, present, or future, but it must have been fairly close to the present, since it would have otherwise taken more magic out of her. The method being planned by the mages was intriguing. Only able to transport themselves magically if they had a clear idea of their destination, they had deployed the horrendous knight she had seen on her first day on Selparis to scout forward areas and psychically send the necessary information back. They were evidently unable to create a projection that could cope with the ocean – a bird, for instance – so they couldn't use the same method to cross to the western continent. However, because the ocean was more or less open and free from obstruction, they could risk an arbitrary teleport a certain distance away. So, they were going to take it in stages, build platforms of a predetermined design in the water along the way, and eventually the lead group would hit land, and likely be buried alive by it. Emily couldn't see what the forward team of mages would do when they finally came to this end, but supposed that one of them would have to send a message back that random teleportation was no longer safe. Perhaps from that distance, a bird projection could be sent as a scout without depleting the magic of the mage that created it.

With the details obviously sharper, and the results better, than on any previous night, Emily concluded that the dreams were coming more freely now, as if some mental block had been removed. Testing the magic and building confidence in it had probably been the key. Part of her mind had rejected the possibility until it was provided with absolute proof.

The sixth night out brought something new. Dense forest surrounded them, and the portion of livestock the Selians had brought with them for food had to be diverted by a different route, since the going was simply too difficult for the cattle. Trying to get the dozens of cows through even sparse woodlands had been a chore, though the animals were clearly of a different ilk than their pathetic brethren on Earth. Getting them through a true forest was out of the question.

Everyone was hunting and gathering as they went, fanning out to be as efficient as possible. Moving in the forest was, itself, an energy-intensive and exhausting exercise, as the terrain grew increasingly erratic, eschewing any attempt to be flat. The younger folk mostly rose to the challenge, climbing eagerly up the terrain they could not walk across, but many had to be carried. Even ardent hikers found it a tough walk as the seemingly dry and solid earth lacked cohesion, and the brittle soil gave way to dust unexpectedly. Only West seemed unperturbed by it, leaping lithely even with heavy packs on his back, and he was increasingly impatient with the others, often joining the scouts who moved far ahead. Jaik stumbled regularly and, more than ever before, Ethan openly complained, saying he would have rather traveled with the cows. He even considered abandoning his guitar, though he had actually been putting it to use during the evenings to entertain the folk, drawing crowds of dozens impressed with his skill and interested to hear the new music.

According to the elders in their public discussions, this land had last been explored long ago, but had now grown foreign to their experience of it. The trees of this forest, crowded together despite the dry and dusty ground, were known to the elders as "andrenits," and they said the roots of the trees ran deep through the soil layers into an underground water source. From Emily's point of view, they had to be the most normal looking trees she had seen on this planet so far – brown trunks, green foliage, and a slightly creepy gnarly visage.

By the next day, rumors were spreading like wildfire among the normally stolid people, and the word "vampire" was being tossed about. Tayron was furious, because he suspected that one of his explorers had been the first to mention the vampires which had dogged them, though had not attacked them, through their first journey in these woods. The elders assured him that the Selians were more than capable of applying their legends to interpret signs without any external help. Nevertheless, the chancellor found it an unlikely coincidence that the main danger his explorers had cited was the one that now struck at everyone's morale. Emily saw a certain irony, though – Tayron's own minor break in composure when confronting his men about the rumors did as much to panic people, confirming the truth of the word being bandied around, than anything which had been said before. He had gathered around himself so much authority that his brief lack of control, perhaps due to his own fear of vampires, sent ripples throughout the population.

"He is not as perfect as he likes us to think," West commented wryly, on one of the rare occasions he decided to speak directly to Emily. He rarely spent much time with Jaik and Ethan these days, either, exploring this new landscape at a fast pace, away from everyone else. His normal wild streak was tempered by the presence of so many strangers, so he preferred to distance himself from them, getting as much true freedom as he could manage without abandoning them. His activities had not blinded him to the facts of the situation, though, and he took the liberty to ask her pointedly now, “when are you going to tell us what is going on?”

Emily was unsure of what to say, trying to gauge what he had meant. Could he have already guessed something, or was he just throwing a net out in the hope that some secrets would get caught in it? If it had been Jaik asking, she would not have hesitated to pull him aside and tell him, especially because she had started breaking the ground between them, and he was acting progressively more at ease around her. West was a different animal, and she had not gotten an inch closer to figuring him out. He was so fickle that, at times, he didn’t even seem to have any particular loyalty to Jaik, who was pretty much his only friend in the world at the moment. Too confident in his ability to win over whoever he wanted, whenever he wanted, he showed no interest in doing anything he did not already want to do. He lacked all of the illusions that held societies together, and Emily could detect in him no sense of responsibility toward others. What reason he had for being here with them, she could not imagine, and whether she could trust him was beyond her to determine.

She prided herself on loyalty to her friends, and they had often reciprocated by following her blindly. Ethan was still following her. Lacking the trappings of a competent space captain, she had not won the same devotion from her crew, much to her frustration, but she cared about her people, and desperately wanted to prove herself to them. She did not automatically expect loyalty, like Tayron and Oris might, but earned it by having an open ear, by caring, and by being accessible. West simply did not fit into her existing way of dealing with people, because there was no way to create a stable association with him, nor did he deliberately try to position himself as a leader over others. He had natural charisma and talent, and put it to work effortlessly, making his way dissonantly because it suited him, but not so the music of the world was in any sense ruined.

West would be useful on any journey, and was proficient in vital ways that she and Ethan were not. Her rifle was great, but she wasn’t much of a hunter, and had originally intended to rely on Max for the survival element. Left alone in the woods, the two of them might be able to learn a few essentials quickly, but the steep learning curve would eventually catch up to them, and they woud die. For this plain reason, West had already earned his right to hear the facts by virtue of being necessary, just by being who he was. Maybe Jaik could do as much, but Emily doubted it. Jaik had been a townie, and while he had already put some of his skills to use to their advantage, and had a sharp enough mind, he could not stand in for West.

Having given the matter due consideration, and forcing the impatient West to wait through her sticky mental flow, she ultimately decided. "All right. Get Jaik over. He should hear this, too."

West hopped away to find his friend, who was straggling behind with Ethan. Ethan had temporarily recovered his translator from Oris, but was needing it less and less, acquiring the Asparian language with a phenomenal rapidity that fully justified his desire to be a linguist. Jaik was more than happy to pass the time with Ethan, who was so soft-spoken and non-threatening that even a squirrel wouldn't feel it necessary to run away from him. Ethan's curiosity and ability to ask questions also made it very easy to have a conversation with him. Jaik also enjoyed watching Ethan's guitar performances, and might have asked to learn how to play the instrument if there had not been so many people watching.

West brought the two of them to Emily, and they were all aware that a small conspiracy was now in its infancy. Ethan knew what was coming, was thankful for it, was interested to hear how she phrased what she had to say, and to see how the others would react to it. Emily looked around to check if they were being overheard, paying special attention to every angle of sky around them. The extent of Oris' senses was an open question, but it was safe to assume that if the Eldrandii was in sight, anything confidential they wanted to say to each other was at risk, and there were no guarantees even without her in sight. Still, they had no choice but to take the chance.

Speaking as laconically as possible while ensuring that West and Jaik would understand, Emily told them of her dreaming ability, what she had so far seen, and what she suspected everyone, from the Shadow Workers, to Oris, to Tayron, to her own people, was after. They kept walking as she talked, and she was careful to steer them a good distance away from everyone else in sight. It was too much to be truly aware of her surroundings while delving into her mind, so West helped by keeping a sharp eye out. Whenever others neared, his eyes darted in their direction, and she no longer had to look around, since occasionally looking at him sufficed.

When describing her dream ability, Emily noticed that Jaik's face suddenly turned downcast, as her newfound magic had placed a great gulf between them, so she tried to minimize the significance of the dreams in complete contradiction to her growing confidence in them. Jaik had a fragile aspect that, like cotton candy, melted away at the merest flick of the tongue. At the same time, she was also attentive to Selparii sensibilities, conveniently neglecting the dreams about Newport Station and Marcus Welder, while being blunt about Tayron.

"He's going to try something to make sure me and Ethan don't get whatever secrets are in the underground city, at least not without helping his people first. I'm perfectly fine with helping the empire, you understand, but I don't like the idea of being trapped somehow while the chancellor negotiates with Earth. Those explorers outnumber us, so I don't think they'll have trouble keeping us as prisoners if they like."

"I do not think so," West said with spirit, tapping his handheld crossbow and the newly fashioned bolts slung at his side.

Jaik's thoughts went on an entirely different track. "So . . . we do not trust Chancellor Tayron?"

"I never did," West said. "He is just a politician. It is not as if he is emperor."

Emily was struck by how human West's reaction to politicians was, compared to the devotion some species, including the Asparii, showed to their most detestable leaders. Maybe the sentiment was just an American one, since there were places on Earth where blindness to a leader's flaws was the norm. It cheered her to see that he exhibited some reasonable tendencies.

"Okay, but what are we doing here? Chancellor Tayron is trying to help his empire, and that was why we went to Atparis, to make sure those mages were defeated. Why not trust him to do what needs to be done to defeat them?"

West cast an apologetic grimace at Emily, as if to ask forgiveness for the political naïveté that confused Jaik's otherwise bright mind, then explained his view of what had happened. "We left town because we had no choice. Going to Atparis was our only idea. There was nowhere else to go. We are here because we had to leave Atparis in a hurry, and we have been in Tayron's company since then because there has not been any other company to be in. If Tayron went one way, and Captain Pierce and Ethan went another, I would go with them and not with him, since they have helped us more. You would, too, right Jaik?"

Cornered, Jaik said, "yes, of course. But we want to help Lord Tayron's empire, too, right?"

"Sure, but Captain Pierce will bring help from Earth if she can get this ship engine invention to her people, right Captain?"

It was a promise that was far beyond her ability to fulfill, but there was only one correct answer. "Yeah. Absolutely."

There was a chance, albeit a slim one, that the prize at the end of this road was everything she could hope it was, and that she would be able to name her price in exchange for it. Raiz would probably still find a way to get it out of her clutches at a discount. The priority now was to get to the underground city before anyone else did, or any promises she made were moot in any case.

Jaik nodded. "I guess Lord Tayron will need Earth's help anyway, so instead of helping him, we should help people who will really beat our enemies back," said Jaik, acutely aware that he could not have said "no" to Emily. Besides, if what had been said was true, and the people who had built the underground city had been from Earth, then Emily's people and the Selians had much more right to it than the Atparian Empire.

"But why did Geramintor not warn us about Lord Tayron when we first met?" he asked suddenly. "Why did he only warn us against Oris?"

It was a good question. Geramintor would not have fabricated the findings of the seers, since it would be a stain on him in the community. What about omission? The elder was not required to state every fact gleaned from the oracles. That Tayron was not planning anything was hard to believe, but perhaps the Selians had not seen into his dealings, or thought that his goal – to destroy the Shadow Workers – were in line with Emily's own, and so did not warrant warnings.

"I don't know," said Emily, "but I really don't understand these people. I don't think the elders mean us any harm, but it's hard to tell what they're about."

The others nodded, all feeling the exact same way about the bizarre Selians, prone as they were to extreme traditions and superstitions.

That night, the superstitions won out. The four of them had separated after their conversation, so that each one heard a different version of the night's events. The first rumors that reached Jaik claimed that one of the encampment's guards had been drained of all his blood while his partner in the shift had been standing only fifty yards away. The culprit had vanished into thin air without a sound. West heard that the vampires were abroad en masse, and that they were readying to attack the camp outright by testing its defenses, leaving animals drained of blood to frighten the guards. Ethan listened in as two of the natives discussed the time of year and the position of some of the stars, which made it likely that the Harindes, an ethereal tribe of semi-opaque creatures, were the real danger. These same monsters had last appeared centuries ago under similar circumstances, and were also known to drink blood in an attempt to become corporeal.

What Emily heard turned out to be the truth, but that would only become evident in the fullness of morning. A guard, hearing a noise in the distance, had strayed away from his watch partner. Investigating, he saw that the decayed body of an elderly female Selian was lying there, bloodless. Morning brought clarification. The woman had not been a current member of the elder council, but an exiled elder forced to leave the hills two months ago. Clearly, she had set herself on exploration during her year away, and had overreached herself.

That news, on top of sleep deprivation from all the increasingly explicit buzz spread through the night, brought the steady progress they had been making through the forest to a halt. Few of the Selians believed the revised story, suspicious that it was a cover-up meant to keep them calm, and there was still plenty of talk about vampires testing defenses and Harindes sightings. As one, they began searching for herbs to place in amulets. Magic users huddled into packs to avoid those who would condemn them employing their art in the open, and poured their little magic into whatever charms they thought would protect them. Emily was more concerned about this change in attitudes among the stalwart folk than about any potential dangers looming in the dark. She knew that vampires really existed in the universe, that

Plani vampires had likely sought refuge here from persecution on their own world, and that from Tayron's account, they were legitimately hostile. Still, she feared blood drinking Plani a lot less than she did Shadow Worker mages. She could take on even the strongest Plani with no problem.

As Ethan reminded her when she expressed her frustration at the lack of movement, she was not taking into account the possibility that the vampires could seriously outnumber them. The Selians made a big difference in the equation, and if there really were vampires lurking, then it would be unwise for the four of them to strike out on their own now, lacking what advantage more than a thousand extra bodies could give them. This was a hard argument to swallow when those thousand bodies had been driven insane.

"Besides," Emily pointed out, "what about Tayron's explorers? Most of them got through all right."

"Most of them."

Emily decided that the best action was to find out as much as they could about vampires, and that meant speaking to Tayron and his explorers. If what they had to report did not seem too bad, then maybe it was time to suggest a parting of ways with the hill people, but possibly not from Tayron and Oris. She was not eager to test the navigation skills of anyone in her miniature conspiracy yet. Tayron's response to their inquiring would tell them a lot about his intentions. For the past week, there had been little contact between her and the chancellor, so even the barest conversation would give her valuable insight into where he stood.

It was growing difficult to speak with Lord Tayron. He was himself again, or at least trying to be, and made an imposing presence. With strong followers at his side, he was in his glory. As usual, he was active and interested in the affairs around him, but he dealt with those affairs in a more organized and less direct fashion. He was the embodiment of authority, and if he was approached by anyone, it was with recognition of his powers and responsibilities, and not through any sense that he was a fellow being in the midst of the same struggle. The vampires could take all the rest of them, but the gods would protect Lord Tayron.

Emily had never thought of anyone in those terms, and did not intend to start. Breaking the invisible barrier required her to build up some gall, though. She sauntered up to him after gathering all her arrogance into an easily accessible pile, and said, “Lord Tayron, I want to know what your people know about these vampires. You said they were out there, and I need the details.”

“Captain,” Tayron said, pausing to emphasize the difference in their ranks, as a slight jab in response to her coarseness. “I have not spoken to you in a while, have I? I think that discussing vampires where we might be overheard would be unwise. We understand certain issues differently than our fellow travelers do.”

He pulled them into the forest far to the east of the Selian masses. Half of his explorers were up ahead, attempting to organize the scouts and guards who remained after many had temporarily abandoned their duties. The rest were still with him, a devoted retinue to their leader. Since there were only three of them, though, they gave more the sense of toady footstools than a formal court.

Emily did not like the surroundings. The trees were a sickly gray, not getting their fair share of water, and reminded her of the similarly colored Plani. The forest as a whole managed to foster the worst of forebodings with its dank smell, claustrophobic density, and in this patch especially, its decay.

“Well, Captain, you want to know all, do you?”

Acting after a nudge and a comment by Jaik, Ethan quickly stepped in to forestall any more impolitic missteps from Emily and said, “we want to know everything you can tell us, sir.” Not sire, Emily was thankful to hear, appreciating what Ethan was up to. If he wanted to play the good cop, that was fine by her, as long as she did not have to subjugate herself to Tayron. Delicacy was not her hallmark. As long as they were here to get information, her desire to spurn Tayron’s pretensions to power could be an obstacle to their cause. Also, her unwarranted rudeness could tip the chancellor off that they suspected him of malfeasance as much as they did Oris.

Tayron found Ethan’s interruption curious, but not unprecedented. “Does he speak for you, Captain?”

“Yeah. Of course”

Tayron nodded to one of the explorers, who started by saying, “we do not know much, but they are dangerous. A vampire killed one of our men. We did not notice until morning because not one sound was made to wake us. He was dry of blood, yet bone and muscle were left untouched. Before that, they had toyed with us. They would follow us, letting us see glimpses of them. We would find animals dry of blood along our path, and they got larger and larger as we went on. We understood that they did not like us going through their territory, and we went through as fast as we could. We were only a day from this forest's edge when . . . when we were attacked. I guess . . . I guess they could not let us go without paying a price."

"But they didn't try to take all of you? They went just for one person?" Ethan regretted the cold way he phrased the question as soon as it was past his lips, but the explorer did not react to the wording or the tone.

"Yes, but that only shows their intelligence. A bloodsucking beast would go on a killing rampage. They deliberately struck fear in us, putting their killings in an order that only a sentient being would bother with, and we knew what was coming. It was their way of showing us what price we would pay for passage, and of showing that they were vampires. I do not think we were meant to be food for them."

"And now, we're really invading their territory," Ethan pointed out.

"Hell," said Emily, "bringing all these people with us made things worse, not better."

The explorer shook his head. "I do not think so. Perhaps if it was just us explorers, Lord Tayron, and yourselves, then we would be killed by vampires without a second thought. They would recognize us as repeat offenders. Our numbers now might be too much for them, even if they attack quietly. During our first journey, we did not see any sign that there were even dozens of them."

"Have you seen any sign of them this time, like you did then?" Ethan asked.

"Except for a dead person, no," he replied, making sure the sarcasm translated. "I do not think they will play games this time. Not that they need to. These people are frightened enough already."

"None of the glimpses of them, then?"

Thinking it over, the explorer said, "no. Not this time. But, honestly, that only frightens me more. They are serious this time. I do not think that woman's body being left there was an accident."

"Real cheery thought," Emily murmured. "That's all I wanted – a bunch of vampires serious about killing us." She looked at the other three, and the message was clear. Any plan to leave the Selians behind was not happening. Ethan made an attempt to poke holes in the threatening story, but the picture of vampires planting drained animals to taunt and scare travelers was too chilling. Though she hated trusting anyone out of fear, she was not ready to bet that the explorer was lying.

They thanked Tayron for allowing the explorer to give them some details, but were not so foolish to believe every detail had been vouchsafed to them. Oris flew in to meet them as soon as they were out of sight of the Tayron party. Her expression was as wild as it had been in the tunnel during the attack on Atparis. She tried her best to be subtle about her intentions, but the juxtaposition between their discussion with Tayron and her immediate intervention now made her purpose all too clear. Surrounded by distrust from the hill people, and underlying hostility from Tayron, Oris had never faced such antagonism to her will before. Since it was all under the surface and rarely explicit, she was unable to respond to it with appropriate indignation, leaving her progressively more infuriated. To avoid the hundreds of meaningful glances cast her way, she stayed in the air, perching on the highest branches that could carry her. No Eldrandii had ever experienced such a reception outside of wartime, and Oris was utterly unprepared for it.

Emily almost felt sorry for her, but was cautious not to let her sympathy get in the way of the cold calculations she had to do. As Captain, she could not allow sentiments to get in her way, as they had when she took the wrong tact with Tayron. Thanks to her lack of care, she had gleaned little or no information about the chancellor's plans. This time, she wanted to handle the exchange without Ethan's help.

Unlike Tayron, Oris had nobody behind her, was acutely aware of it, and a touch paranoid because she lacked backup. Emily decided that a show of friendship and some casual interaction was called for, and might bring some accidental revelations.

The Eldrandii started speaking immediately in a calm tone, but her eyes darted around, irritated by the sight of every Selian nearby.

"Captain, these people slow our journey. They claim to be helping us, but force us to stop when our enemies come ever nearer," she said in English, as if to remind Emily that she could. "You spoke with Tayron. What did he say?"

Emily noticed the exclusion of the chancellor's title, and the clear implication that the Eldrandii had spotted the meeting without being seen herself. By her question, Oris indicated that she had not heard the conversation, but it could easily be simple deception to hide her abilities. For Emily, the truth was harmless, so she answered, "not much. We asked him about the vampires, and one of his explorers told us about what had happened when they went through the forest."

"And the . . . explorer said the vampires were dangerous?"

"Well, yeah."

"And you believed him?"

Here, Emily decided to play naïve, and shrugged. "Why not? He had some pretty good reasons." She knew the answer, but wanted to hear what Oris had to say.

"Because Tayron wants to keep you from going without his friends. If you think vampires are dangerous, then you will not travel to Raljar Canti without these . . . people."

The argument seemed scripted and ready for delivery, which suggested that Oris had heard the dialogue with Tayron's man. Emily ignored this for the moment. "But we can't take the chance. Anyway, it's certain that there's something out there that drained that woman's blood, and I've met a Plani vampire before –"

"So you know they are usually harmless. I know the disease that causes . . . need for blood in Plani. Tayron's explorers told you vampires were here, but what if they set up the body and the legend months ago, when they made their first journey to Raljar Canti?"

Emily had to admit, it was an intriguing scenario. If she had not known Eldrandii to be phenomenally suspicious, she would have guessed Oris had spent time watching Earth television, perhaps purely for research like Ethan did. Smiling despite herself, she said, "I didn't think of that Oris. Why, have you seen something?" She tried to get her face into an expression of concern for the question, but failed miserably.

Oris either did not notice, or mistook the smile for a wince. "What do you mean?"

"Well, I was just wondering if you saw something suspicious while flying. You could see much more territory than even the scouts manage to when they do their sweeps."

"I am not scouting, Captain," Oris shouted with wings spread in anger, her hair-trigger temper unleashed. "When I fly, I am busy conducting the experiments I came for." She stuck her unique computer out and shook it in front of them, as proof of her work. "Flora here is a rich mix of species from different worlds. Such a perfect mix, in fact, that one would think each plant was placed here deliberately. This land may be poor in metals, but it is rich in medicinal plants."

"Right. And you didn't see anything by chance? I mean, we all know your eyesight's very good, and on our first day on Selparis, you spotted that armored man form a mile off. I just thought –"

"I have not seen anything," Oris said defensively, dropping her menacing posture. "If I had, I would tell everyone."

Emily doubted that. The lie was simply too blatant, and the evasion too obvious, to miss. She was sure, now, that Oris had seen vampires in the forest, and might even have conveniently ignored their passing in the hope that they would attack, and force Emily and her companions to flee. By lying, Oris proved that her sense of morality was divergent from the norms of her people, but she was likely innocent of Emily's worst charges, though guilty of lesser ones. Oris had seen vampires, but genuinely believed they were harmless.

To resolve her lingering questions, Emily was almost tempted to use her dreams, and to see into her future one or two days from now, but did not dare. She could not know whether the future was alterable, and if it was not, there was no point to knowing it beforehand. For the sake of her sanity, she had to maintain an illusion of free will, and if it turned out that she could not change an undesirable end, the circumstance would be a heavy blow to her worldview.

Returning from her thoughts, she read the concern on Ethan's face and realized she had once again drifted off. The others did not seem to make as much of it. West and Jaik were speaking quietly to each other, and Oris' people were prone to far more extensive thoughtful pauses. The Eldrandii was herself thinking of what else she should say, and chose to speak next.

Almost back to her old demure self of Eldrandii wisdom combined with human flexibility, she said, "I apologize, Captain, truly. I do not know what has . . . why I am acting like this. I am not . . . comfortable with . . . how these people think of me. I have lived a long time with respect and dignity, and I know not getting respect . . . changes me."

Emily was at a loss to stifle her deep sympathy, since the admission of a failing was no doubt awkward and difficult for Oris. Begrudging the Eldrandii a few points for it was unavoidable. Oris had shown similar rage when Jaik challenged her at the gateway of the imperial border town, but had never apologized for that confrontation, though neither had Jaik, so fury was not entirely surprising behavior from her. Requesting forgiveness for it was. Given the choices, Emily decided to offer the warmest possible reply.

"We understand totally, Oris. These people are giving you a hard time, and it's really not fair. And I'll be honest, I'm not too thrilled about them, either, especially now that they're holding us up. I need to plan out what to do. I don't believe all the superstitions, but I don't think the woods are safe, either."

Oris nodded dejectedly and said, "as you wish, Captain," and flew away. They kept a close eye on where she went and, once it was beyond all chance that she could hear them, Ethan whispered to her, "you shouldn't have been able to bluff her."

"What do you mean?"

"I remember people used to think you were lying even when you were telling the truth. You were never a good liar."

" . . . thanks –"

"But just then, you lied to her and she didn't realize it."

"I didn't really lie."

"Close enough. You never used to get away with stuff like that, and Oris is as clever as anyone gets. And Eldrandii have great natural lie-detecting skills, so she should have been able to see you weren't acting honestly. She must have been too preoccupied with her own feelings to notice how you were behaving, and I don't think it was just the anger."

With warranted smugness, Emily said, "I was able to tell she was lying though, about not having seen anything."

"I've got a theory. I think she doesn't trust her lie-detecting instincts any more because she knows she's had to lie to us all this time and hates herself for covering up whatever she's hiding. She doesn't trust herself anymore."

Emily was in awe. "That's brilliant. Very psychological. You make it sound like a conspiracy with the covering up bit, though."

"Well, it is, isn't it? There's no way Oris would go against her honor unless her government asked her to do it for the good of her people. A government conspiracy."

"And we know what they're after," Emily said, excited and convinced that she had the whole picture now. "Ethan, we know what's going on. After all this time, we've got it, and we could really get one step ahead of everyone."

Ethan grinned. "Yeah, but what are we going to do about it?"

West and Jaik listened intently without commenting, unable to add anything substantial in the rapid exchange. The lull in the brainstorm allowed Jaik to say, "I do not know about all of this. Captain . . . Emily . . . why can't you all share this space engine secret? Why do you have to fight over it? If everyone has it, there is no problem. No one would kill for it out of greed. If you get it, would you share it?"

Emily was unprepared for the suggestion. She wanted money and fame, and theoretically she could get more of both if she sold the secret of the hyperspace drive to every ISC species.

"We could, you know," Ethan said. "We could make a deal, even if it's a bit tricky."

She liked the idea at first glance because it would effectively piss off everyone that had tried to play her like a pawn. Of course, for precisely that reason, every person with power would prevent her from doing it, making it an improbable if not impossible plan. The trick was explaining this to Jaik, who did not have her competitive spirit.

"We can't deal with the Eldrandii," she ultimately said. "If we were ticking off everyone equally that'll work, but the Eldrandii lose everything from the deal, and'll get nothing out of it. There's no way they're going to let us off this planet with this technology unless there's a force going against them that will keep it a stalemate. Whatever that force is, we're pretty much at their mercy, and will have to hand the technology to them. If we're lucky, that will be Earth."

"You don't have to leave," Jaik protested. "The different species can come to us if you send a message."

"That only works if you have a chance to turn them away, Jaik. If we had weapons to stop them from getting to the city, or wherever the technology is, then we could bargain with them. As long as they can come in with guns blazing, though, we've got no choice. If we don't get off this planet, all we can do is hand everything over to the world that gets down here first, then they fight it out, and the ones with the biggest guns win."

"She's right," Ethan admitted to Jaik. "As long as the Eldrandii want to keep it for themselves, we don't have much choice."

Jaik knew they would reject his next suggestion, but wanted to see how the humans would react. "Why not just let Eldgil Oris have it? They have it anyway. If they get it, nothing will change, right?"

Emily wanted to shout out "you're missing the whole point – it's not fair that the Eldrandii have the hyperspace drive and we don't, and this is a one in a thousand year chance," but did not. That would just take the whole argument in a circle. Instead, she conceded, "that's possible. We have two ways out – give it up to the Eldrandii or give it to whoever can stalemate the Eldrandii. We can't let the Shadow Workers get it, no matter what, so that's our first goal, and only Eldrand, Earth, and Plani really have a chance to fight them off."

Jaik nodded. That was good enough for him. He was expecting Emily's impulse response about the Eldrandii monopoly not being fair, and was happy to see she gave the question more consideration.

West, passive throughout because he agreed with Emily but did not want to take sides against his friend, detected an end to the topic, and switched to his own plans. "I am going to scout around myself, and check whether there is real danger from these vampires. I will go today and come back tomorrow."

None of the others liked the sound of West's intended course, but he was adamant about it. He did not like having uncertainty about his surroundings, and fear could not leash him. West's bane was to stand around talking when positive action was needed.

"And as long as these people refuse to move without their charms and enchantments, I can be out and back before you move, and find out how much farther we need to travel before we are out of the forest. I climbed some trees as we traveled, and even though there is plenty of forest in front of us, east and west of us, we can get to its edge in two days. If there is real trouble, that is what we should do. While we are waiting, though, I want to track down these vampires. They do not get to have this forest all to themselves while I am here."

The firm and confident grin on his face brooked no objection, but Jaik did anyway.

"You are not telling us everything. What is it? You have seen something. I know it."

"Yes, I have, but I am not going to talk about it until I am sure, Jaik."

There was no chaining him, but not one of the other three felt his departure, however brief, was a good idea.

When West failed to return the next day, his companions were not the only ones worried. The elders had noted his participation on scouting and hunting missions, and he had made numerous reports to them. His confidence and competence had instilled in them the respect he gained from everyone eventually. They cast divinations to discover his situation, but reached no definitive result, except that he was still alive. The readings would not be so muddled if he was dead.

For Emily, Jaik, and Ethan, the forest now filled them with fear, and they gave more credit to the Selian superstitions. Only a formidable force could prevent West from returning when he said he would. Emily hoped that the force might be his curiosity, if his investigations had led him to some enticing discovery that continued to hold his attention and made him forget the time. There was also a chance that he had wandered too far, perhaps frustrated by the lack of signs, and the extra distance traveled would delay his return. However, for each rosy scenario they could think of, ten others put West in dire peril.

Oris spent some of her time that day consoling them and reassuring them that West knew his way around better than anyone. She phrased her words carefully and, when combined with a soft manner, they made the desired impression. Oris was back to her angelic self, and wanted to spread some of her grace in this time of need.

Lord Tayron was less helpful, though still sympathetic. Instead of being clear-cut about his reactions, though, he mixed in further warnings about the vampires, and how unwise West had been to wander off. Jaik listened with clenched fists as the chancellor used West's disappearance to personal advantage, but kept his indignation to himself. He had the measure of Tayron now.

"Does it seem to you," Ethan commented once Tayron left them, "that whenever Tayron's more reasonable, Oris is less, and whenever Oris acts like our best friend, Tayron's an ass."

Emily snorted with laughter. If felt good, but she couldn't keep it up. To quell any remnants of mirth, her mind conjured up a vicious thought. "What if Oris kidnapped West? What if she planned to –"

Ethan shook his head. "Thought of that already. First of all, we're more frightened of the vampires because we don't know what's happened to West, so that goes against Oris' point. I also don't think Oris is strong enough to deal with West."

Emily nodded. She did not bother suggesting that Tayron was behind West's absence, seeing the flaws in that theory immediately.

Soon after their meeting with Tayron, the Selians were ready to move again, this time defended by wards, amulets, and an entire day of prayer to various deities. When Jaik heard that they were preparing to move, he went on his own to the elders to object on the grounds that West would return here to find them, if he was free to, and that they should organize a search for him instead of just reading his fortune.

Geramintor, who was now permanent liaison to the outlanders, responded to Jaik's plea evenly. "If West is free to return here, then he will also have no trouble following the tracks we will be leaving, and will catch up with us easily. If he is trapped, then we can only hope it is on the road ahead, for otherwise we have neither the time nor the will to conduct a search. We need to be out of this cursed forest as soon as possible."

Jaik continued to make his case for search parties, but to no avail. Broken and weary from worry, he returned to Ethan and Emily. Never expecting that he would one day need to rescue West, he was now adamant about finding a way to repay his friend for saving his life twice. West might be prone to wander, but he also did not say anything he did not mean. Knowing that, Jaik was more certain than anyone that West was in danger. Assuming West was alive as the seers said, he was no doubt wondering if Jaik would manage to mobilize an attempt to retrieve him. But how?

All it took was for Jaik to think about Emily, which only concern for West had kept him from doing for a few hours, and he had the answer. He got her attention with a beckoning look, and she gazed back with solemn eyes and walked towards him. Out of inexplicable neglect, he had never paid due attention to her eyes before. There was so much behind them, so much that she never showed anyone else, even as she wore her emotions in plain sight. As she drew closer, he tried not to stare.

"Emily. I wondered . . . you could dream about West. Could you see what happened to him?"

She paused, caught by the worry and strain in him, then said, "yeah. I was planning to tonight. No guarantees, but I'll try."

"Thank you."

That night, she did as she promised, and focused on West. There was nothing vague or choppy about the dream this time. He was a prisoner in some kind of hut, and twelve foot chains tied his outstretched arms to the walls of it, his body lit by light from a single torch. His eyes were closed, but he was breathing heavily, so he was alive though exhausted. No one was in the hut with him. There was something odd going on, since a rabid vampire had no reason to keep him captive, at least not in this way. West was almost on display, as if bait to draw a larger catch. More flushed than drained, his face was too red with the blood, some seeping through a cut on his forehead, to mark him as the victim of a blood drinking Plani.

No matter how much she wondered about his captor's motives while dreaming, Emily saw nothing to answer the question. Making sure she had her priorities straight, she redirected her mind and forced it to show her the route to him. In her first successful attempt to focus her vision in the midst of it, she saw the paths in a flash, and the exertion woke her up immediately. Feeling horribly empty, she started frantically repeating the refueling charm, and regained some sense of herself.

Slowing her breathing down after the shock of her dream's rapid end, she remembered some of the way to West, and definitely where to start. It was enough, and she went straight to Jaik and Ethan, woke them up, and told them what she had seen. Night was the perfect time for them to get away from Tayron, Oris, and the rest, but the worst time to travel safely. Nevertheless, a mad rush by the Selians to the hut would probably lead West's assailants to simply kill him and run. On top of that, neither Tayron nor Oris was free from suspicion, and telling them would reveal the full extent of her talent.

Contrary to expectations, Jaik and Ethan made no fuss about being woken, guessing why she interrupted their sleep, and were keen to hear her account. Seeing the two scrawny young men, neither one having the slightest chance against her in a fight, Emily wondered how she ever got to the point where her backup was so thin and uninspiring, but sheer urgency overtook her thoughts. She was able to conjure a solution to their sleepiness, at least, with an energy drink in concentrate she had packed for just such an occasion, but they had to get a safe distance away from the camp before mixing it up, otherwise the smell of it would likely wake others.

Drinks down and eyes wide open in the eerie darkness of the forbidding woods, they followed Emily as she tried to remember fleeting landmarks. Just when she thought they were lost, another distinctive tree would come into view. Getting past the camp guards proved not to be a problem – they were so focused on detecting enemies trying to come in that they did not give anything going out a second look, assuming it to be one of the many harmless creatures resident in the forest. Jaik made deep marks in the dirt to indicate the path they had taken, should they have to retrace their steps. Failing to get back to the camp was not a major worry, though, with the potential of nocturnally-gifted vampires in every shadow. Emily recalled that the one vampire she had actually met had chosen to feed in the hyperspace night time, when most of the *Azar*'s crew had been asleep. None of the stories told about the vampires so far had broken that pattern.

So here they were – walking vampire juice with minimal protection at their disposal. On the bright side, West was not the captive of vampires, so they were not up against the bloodsuckers directly. The problem with seeing that optimistically was the inevitable corollary that there was something else in this forest that had taken him, and whatever that was, they did not want to meet it in the dark. Whatever had forced him into those chains had left him alone in the hut, and could now be on the prowl for them. Going out on a quest to rescue West sounded great on the surface, and fit right into the adventure they were supposed to be having, but at the moment they felt pathetically exposed. Making the ground as they walked was all Jaik could think of doing to provide some sense of security. At least, if they lived, they would not have trouble remembering how to get back.

"We could go back and tell everyone what we know," Ethan suggested, the drink opening his awareness to the almost insurmountable danger he was walking into. "We could say we went out at night and saw him – that way, nobody will ask how we found out."

Emily whispered back, "even if they believe that, it's too dangerous to bring them all along. The enemy, whoever they are, would know we were coming to rescue West, and you know what happens then. Anyway, they must have known when they took West that he had a thousand friends in the forest with him. They must be ready to deal with the hill people."

"We could ask the elders to get people into a small rescue party. You know, people who might actually be good at the whole rescue thing. Maybe people good at sneaking, or fighting, or anything but playing the guitar."

She gave him a devastating look that said with perfect clarity that he could head back to the camp if he didn't have anything helpful to say. This was personal for her, and she realized that all her other rationalizations for going it alone boiled down to a single fact. Somewhere along the way, she had subconsciously added Jaik and West to her crew list – the list she had maintained since her earliest days in school to identify who she was willing to defend. She did not wait for others to step in when someone on that list was in trouble. It was an instinct in need of reexamination, now that she was so far away from the school grounds of its inception, but now was not the time.

Ethan turned away from her to show he understood, but did not feel any better about their chances. Jaik was firmly behind Emily, and was glad to see the way she had shot Ethan's suggestion down. Keeping a grim, determined visage, he hoped his own resolve would steel Ethan's nerves. As it happened, it only served to make Ethan feel more out of place, with the attitudes of his friends so at variance with his own. His only weapon was his guitar, and while he was sure Emily would buy him a great replacement if he knocked a bad guy out with it, he was not at all sure he could do much damage. Thinking practically, he also did not like the idea of being stuck on this planet without being able to use his only valuable skill to make money.

The hours of travel to the hut was excruciatingly tense, but no sudden attacks harried them. Emily immediately saw why, as she crept ahead and peered out from behind a tree. The fact that there were half a dozen huts and not just one did not bother her. Horrendous monstrosities gathered together in between the huts, and she was sweating bullets at the sight of them.

"What the hell are they?" Emily whispered under her breath to no one. Ethan and Jaik were nearly next to her, but still too far to hear. They also could not see what she did, and she motioned for them to stay back, since this threat was far beyond what any of them could be able to contend with, and there was no reason for them to risk being seen. The creatures resembled nothing more than immense worms eight feet tall. They had tiny arms that might have suggested a lizard-like nature, but their constant movements and their hideous heads betrayed them. A dozen of them slithered on the ground, sinuously curling around each other, only propping themselves upright to emit a deep noise similar to a howl. The sound had the same chilling effect, and a clear viciousness to it, but it hardly carried out of the clearing.

Their heads left Emily stone cold. She could see nothing more than a tooth-ringed hole – a massive mouth easily wider than her body – without any of the features such large animals should have, like eyes. Any one of the worms could have swallowed her whole, making the likely assumption that the rest of their body was stomach.

The horror of the sight aside, there was more to worry about. As they moved constantly, the creatures did not make much of a sound except for the occasional howls. Their skin also camouflaged them into their surroundings like chameleons. While she had her eyes on them, they were easy to see, but they would be the epitome of stealth when still, ready to pounce and consume their prey.

Extrapolating from both their form, just large enough to gobble up a standard sentient being, and their ideal concealment, Emily suspected that the worms were not a naturally evolved species, but rather built to purpose. The presence of the huts, which the worms could not have built, and the capture of West, which they could not have thought to do, were both evidence of a higher intelligence at work. Emily shuddered to think what kind of person would think to create and train the monsters, but the list of possibilities was thin. Either this was the work of the most deranged breeder in the galaxy, or magic was behind it, and a crazed mage was much, much worse than a pack of vampires.

When the worms suddenly dispersed, heading in a pack the opposite direction from Emily, she had no idea whether to think of it as fortunate or as the prelude to an attack from behind. She was not stupid enough to believe that the clearing and the huts were truly deserted except for West, but with the worms gone, this was the time to act. Motioning the other two to join her, she started moving forward, acutely aware that her heavy footfalls were making more noise than the worms did when they moved. Jaik and Ethan were both lighter on their feet, but that was a small favor. She did not tell them about what she saw. There was no reason to, and any unnecessary talk could tip off whatever forces might still be around.

Emily knew which hut West must be in, based on her vision, which had shown her his location at an angle that had hid the other huts. From their direction of approach, only one hut could be seen separately from the rest. They went around the perimeter to it, and saw it was windowless, and there was no way to check inside before entering. Rudimentary at best, the hut was little more than branches tied together and supported by wood beams. The construction was so flimsy, that Emily was certain, especially after seeing the worms, that some enchantment was required to keep it up. If her own magic had given her an appreciation of what such powers could do, she was all the more apprehensive about crossing a threshold built by them, but there was no choice. Creeping around to the front side so that she was briefly standing in the center of the clearing, Emily wasted no time there. As soon as the doorway was in sight, she went in, ready for a fight.

Except for a bruised and bloodied West, standing chained, there was no one else. He was paler than when she had envisioned him, just a few hours ago, but was still breathing. She let out her own breath in relief, the fear of getting here too late to save him set aside.

"We don't have anything to break the chains with," Ethan said in anguish, desperate to leave quickly and get back to the safety of the encampment. Emily was way ahead of him, and had spotted West's pack in the corner.

"No," Jaik said when she went for it. He brought his own pack to the ground and rummaged through it for a metal cutter that looked like a wrench, but with a machine-sharpened inside edge and a fully adjustable width, allowing it to cut through both wire and piping. West insisted on carrying so many such tools with him that Jaik had to bear a few, and it was nice to see one of them finally coming in handy. Emily took it from Jaik and attacked the link closest to West's right wrist. The wrist cuff itself would have to stay, since in the weak light, Emily saw no seam in it, or any way to get it off easily.

After a minute of trying to break the one link without so much as scratching it, and testing the cutter on her belt buckle and finding it sharp enough to cut straight through, Emily concluded that all her fears about magic were justified. She refused to give up, though, until West himself opened his eyes, looked at her, and said in a parched voice, "magic." Looking into his pained yet fiery eyes, she could have fallen in love with his wild willpower if her desperation was not so acute and her disappointment so painful. Spots of dirt and blood on his face and shirt only hinted at the strain she saw inside him, revealed only through his traumatized eyes. What had they done to him? She was aware, for the moment, that he was human and only human, and was hurt in a more than physical way.

"Run," he said through clenched teeth. "Nothing you can do."

"No way," she said, dazed from the surreality. Even if she brought hundreds of people from the encampment to rescue West, she doubted all of them combined could do so much as break these chains, much less defeat the one who had forged them. The Selians might have some magic, but she did too, and tried with all her might to pour it into the cutter while struggling with the chain to no avail. What of the others? Oris was a scientist, void of any sign of magic or the ability to counter it. Tayron would be the type to have emergency spells memorized, but Emily knew, just from looking at him, that neither he nor any of his men had any magical talent.

West was right to say there was nothing she could do, but she refused to leave him.

"Well, well," Emily's translator buzzed, and her heart stopped.

The voice form the hut's entryway was devoid of humanity in every sense, and when she turned to look at the speaker, utterly grey and soulless eyes stared back at her. "The boy has friends after all. How convenient. I hope those thousands of juicy mortals you entered this forest with will be willing to come rescue you. You will, of course, not be leaving."

He was an Asparii male by his facial features and style of clothing – rugged pants and a loose unbuttoned shirt revealing a skeletal body underneath tattooed with sigils. Instead of the flushed yellow skin of an Asparii, he had a chalk white pigment. His white hair fringed an otherwise bald skull, which was again uncharacteristic of his species, since Asparii rarely experienced thinning hair at all, much less full-fledged baldness. This one had lost hair for some other reason. Emily knew he was the mage she was dreading, because of the bright violet aura of leaking magic surrounding him.

"Mmm," he said, walking straight up to Emily without any concern for his safety. "You look . . . quite tasty. Quite vital with that touch of power." Turning to Jaik and Ethan, he added, "these two others have very little in them. Golakor food if I have ever seen it."

"Big mistake," Emily said, throwing a punch directly at the apparition's face, certain the force would demolish his flimsy form. It didn't land. Some sort of field, an inch around the mage's body absorbed the blow, and her knuckles felt as if they had just hit a wall.

No real surprise there, Emily decided, and in an attempt to keep her rising terror down, she said, "just checking."

"Indeed. You have spirit. That is good. That is very good. I could teach you so much." He touched her – first stroking her hair, then steadily moving his hand down. She was paralyzed, and saw that Jaik and Ethan were struggling to get to her, to draw her away from him, but had no control over their bodies, either. The devilish spectre gloated over her, delighting in her anguish as he showed his dominance over them. "I would never teach you everything, but there's so much. You would never feel so powerless again."

The mage's outpouring of magic, at this close range, made her tingle, and she felt the different frequencies of the waves flowing from him, almost able to distinguish the different spells she was being exposed to. The waves of paralysis were most noticeable, but mixed in with them was a weak magic that charmed her and enticed her. Able to make her bend to his will completely, the mage was exulting in the sheer revulsion she felt as he flexed his power. The enticement waves were not sent out intentionally – they were his spare magic leaking out, so much more potently than her own. From the feel of it, magic attracted magic.

"On second thought," said the mage, "your intelligence is clearly not adequate, and bringing up an apprentice would take up so much of my valuable time. I think I will just . . . amuse myself with you."

He kissed her, but it was far from an ordinary touch of the lips. As he pulled away, a thread of deep purple beads left her mouth, entering his. He swallowed each one in turn, and by the time he had gulped down the sixth one, she felt the same weariness as when she was empty of magic, and was desperate to recite the only incantation she knew. Beyond the sixth, every bead that left made her feel as if her very soul was being ripped apart, and she knew immediately that West had faced this same deep torture. She was losing the ability to hold onto a thought, even one encapsulating the trauma.

Jaik and Ethan watched on, fully realizing what was happening but just as powerless to stop it. By the eleventh bead, they saw Emily's legs waver as if she was going to faint. Blood rushed to her head, and her face was flushed. When their shouts of fury grew too loud for the mage's tastes, he lashed out with his right arm, extending his magic like a sword between the two of them, cutting Jaik's left shoulder, and Ethan's neck. Both started to bleed freely, prevented from moving to wrap cloth around their wounds.

Before Emily lost consciousness, new arrivals stormed into the clearing, and could be heard breaking into each hut. They only existed at the edge of her awareness, though, as a huge impenetrable haze filled the center of it. The mage himself was unperturbed by the invaders, but broke off his feeding. After licking her cheek with a sickly green tongue, he said, "I'll come up with something more creative to do with you and your friends in a moment." A half dozen of the newcomers rushed into the hut behind the mage, who turned with a show of mock shock on his face.

"You," the mage said, still with a hollow voice lacking any connection to nature. "Very brazen of you to invade my domain. I have tolerated your kind, and your presence in my forest, for as long as I have because your bloody, degenerate activities amused me. You are, in your own way, a pale imitation of me, and I am mildly flattered by your existence. It is a shame you will have to die."

Emily regained a measure of focus and saw the six new figures clearly for the first time. There was no question about it – these were Plani vampires, each one sporting blood-stained lips. In spite of the fear spread about vampires, she was glad to see them, though she doubted they would be able to defeat the dark mage. They were as incompetent at magic as the average human. As far as she could see, they were as defenseless as she was.

One of them answered the mage in a rasping, clotted voice. "Try your magic on us, then. We dare you."

Never doubting himself, even when challenged in so suspicious a fashion, the mage acted to paralyze them before taking another breath. Emily saw the power of the spell, but like her punch, the waves were deflected by some sort of force field around the vampires. She was able to see the wall of the field this time, but only as the spell struck and the magic was turned aside, marking the interference point. Otherwise, the field was invisible until encountered, even to the foul mage.

"How?" he said, finally with some audible frustration in his voice. "You have no magic, nor any item of magic. How have you done this?"

Instead of chatting, the vampires attacked the mage with fangs bared, but were halted by his own field. That brought a mirthless laugh from him. "Prone to idiocy as usual, I see. If I cannot strike you, you can be sure that not even a particle of your stench can reach me. It seems, though, we are at an impasse. If that were the case, you could justify a claim of victory, having drawn against a superior being. Appearances, however, are deceiving. I have friends."

And, as if on cue, bloodcurdling scream came from outside, followed by the concentrated howl of one of the great worms. The beasts had returned to the clearing quietly, and were now beginning to feast on the vampires who had remained outside the hut. The six who had come in swiftly sprinted out to aid their comrades and, in a blink, the mage was alone again with his captives.

"This is getting too interesting," he commented. "And that means my personal touch will be required, or that rabble might do some harm to my lovely Golakors." He conjured three new pairs of chains and bound Emily, Jaik, and Ethan in tight parallel to West, so that each of them was yanked into position and had three chains taut against their backs. Once he was out of the hut, the paralysis effect was released, but that was of little use to them. Ethan, unable to see how badly he was bleeding at the neck, had enough fortitude to say "it could have been worse" in a vain hope to console the barely awake Emily.

She was bereft of the energy to react, but she wanted to apologize profusely for bringing them into this nightmare without better preparation. Not that any preparation would have helped, of course, but maybe hundreds of hill people would have distracted the mage while . . . while they still failed to free West.

"What a rescue," West said, coughing a bit, but gaining some of himself back. "You should have made it easier for him and brought your own chains."

"Hey, we did our best!" Jaik shouted feebly, his shoulder shooting more pain into his nerves than he had experienced in his entire life up to this point. He let the chain bear the weight of his arm, which he tried his best not to move. "Why did you go out on your own, anyway? Was it worth it?"

West made an effort, and got a bitter grin on his face. "I guess not. I thought I had seen –"

"What?"

West sighed. "Something from the sky, that is all. I saw something fall from the sky, but it might have been anything."

Ethan looked around with darting eyes, thinking quickly through what had just happened as if actually seeing the replay in front of him. "You know what? I think we might get out of this just fine."

"What?" West said sharply.

"Why did those vampires decide to attack here right at that time? I mean, it's pretty convenient, isn't it?"

West yanked at his chains, at the same time brushing them across everyone's backs. "I do not call this convenient."

"I mean someone must have sent them."

"Quite correct," came a new voice from the door – one that Emily recognized from somewhere, but only from a brief occasion. When he stepped forward, though, her synapses blazed and threw up a whole array of associations. Unfortunately, her mouth was still too heavy to deliver an appropriate response, so she just said, "you," and tried to imply as much as she could in the single word.

"My name is Raznar Eldael, Captain. You brought me from Plani to Newport Station. I am sure you remember, since you had never encountered a vampire before. Commander Raiz had a conference with me aboard the station, and found I knew about a vampiric population here on Selparis, which was a legendary haven for us centuries ago. He enlisted me to make contact with them on behalf of Earth. A very open-minded man, the commander is, and much like yourself, Captain."

"Can you get us down?" Jaik asked, what strength he had slipping away.

"No. My vampire friends know this mage, and told me the chains were magical. He is a known terror to them and some of their number have been captured, tortured, and released by him before. The vampires have a name for those which translates to 'lost souls.' But do not worry, we have someone nearby who will be able to get you down. He will have to choose his own time to appear, though. This is a delicate situation."

Three local vampires had snuck in with Raznar, but none looked enthusiastic about his company, or entirely friendly toward him. The rasping voice of one now broke through Raznar's explanation. "I do not think we will let these four go with you, Raznar."

"What?" Raznar said, shocked. He was naïve beyond belief, attributing the best of intentions to his fellow exiles.

"You offered a way for us to strike our ancient enemy, the dark lord of these woods, and we thank you, but our pack will lose many warriors today, and fresh blood can be the only compensation. Worm blood is tainted, and none of us would be so foolish to drink the blood of the dark mage. These four will do nicely. They were in the company of men warned previously, in the manner required by our laws, not to enter this forest again, so they and their companions are now fair game."

As the three moved to Ethan, licking their canines, West noticed that the young man was curiously unafraid. Perhaps Ethan's mind was lacking blood, and he no longer appreciated the situation, but West saw the corner of a smile on his face indicating confidence that some unseen force would intervene. Whoever Raznar was, he would be the last person to rely on for a rescue, but he had mentioned someone else who was prepared to step in. That person must be known to Ethan, and must have substantial power to prevent these vampires from having their fill of the blood leaking from his neck.

To West's surprise, Raznar shouted "no!" and showed unexpected bravery by positioning himself between the three and Ethan. "We had an agreement. You were not to touch these. The only reason you have the chance to defeat the dark mage now is that great powers want these four to remain alive and protected."

"False blood may do for you, outlander, but here we live the way we were meant to, the way we were created to be."

New shouts from outside broke the confrontation, as hundreds of new voices thundered and roared nearby. The Selians, noticing the absence of Emily, Ethan, and Jaik, perhaps because of the night sentries realizing what they had seen, mobilized in mass and followed the trail left by Jaik. Now, armed with all the trinkets they made to protect them, the hill folk charged at the objects of their worst fears, vampires and worms alike. Raznar stayed in the hut, but the others were forced to respond to cries from their embattled comrades, who were fighting on two fronts.

"Looks like the people of the hills really did end up saving us," Ethan commented before closing his eyes, drained of energy. Raznar would have tried to keep everyone talking, but the sudden betrayal of those he trusted left him disillusioned, causing him to take a seat on the ground to lament his folly.

With a sudden cock of the head, Emily perked up and, pointing with her nose at a cloudy purplish glow, she said, "he's here." She kept her face in the direction of the magical emissions, but with her eyes closed, as if basking in bright sunlight.

Sure enough, a mage materialized, though this one was garbed in traditional flowing robes more fitting for someone of his occupation.

Emily opened her eyes and said "you" again to indicate she recognized him, but was too weak to remember what his name was, though she would recall it if she tried to. This was beyond bizarre now, and she lost interest in keeping up with all the shifts in fortune. She would sort it all out later. It was enough to know that they were now safe.

With a flick of the wrist, Tylan made their restraints vanish, and all but West fell to the ground. The mage quickly looked over the visible wounds of Ethan and Jaik, and shook his head. "I cannot heal these wounds magically. They will have to heal themselves." He stopped the bleeding for both and conjured a large bandage for Ethan, and a sling and compress for Jaik, explaining that it was the best he could do. From within his robes, he brought out a vial and poured a golden liquid into the mouths of everyone, including Raznar and himself. Jaik and Ethan were brought fully aware by the liquid, as its magic temporarily allowed them to operate normally despite their blood loss, but the other two were beyond its effects.

"We must leave immediately," said Tylan as he used a charm to float Emily's limp body.

"Where are we going?" Ethan asked, realizing that he was, by proximity to Emily, the speaker for the group.

"To Commander Raiz, of course. Thanks to some negotiations we managed to get a single ship through the Eldrandii blockade around this planet. Thankfully, Captain Pierce's communications link was still trying to ping the *Azar*'s system, so we were able to locate you. We saw you moving towards this area, which Raznar said was held by a malevolent mage, and we organized this effort to retrieve you. Come now. Raznar, you will have to help the captain."

"Can't we, you know . . . teleport like you just did?" Ethan asked hopefully.

"No. I am afraid maintaining some protection for the Atlantii is draining me. We will have some shielding ourselves, but as long as I try my best to help those you traveled with, we will have to travel on foot."

With all the carnage raging nearby, they left the confines of the hut barely noticed. The Selians had realized their more potent foe was not the vampires, but the dark mage and his Golakors, and were, for the moment, unified with the vampires in the fight. Blood and guts were spilt whenever the worms broke through, with their master's help, the magical protection projected by Tylan. The beasts ripped vampires and Selians apart ruthlessly with their massive mouths, spitting out the pieces to make way for more prey. Thanks to their betrayal of Raznar, the vampires found themselves at the center of the slaughter without any magic on their side. Their deaths would be now be incidental to the larger contest between the two other forces.

Tylan's magical shield kept the escapees safe from a worm that departed from the main fight and tried to crush them, throwing its massive tubular body around to no effect. Stray arrows fell short and no sword landed on their unarmored flesh. The dark mage detected their departure, and tried to attack them with a thrust of his right arm, his magic sharpened to pierce through to them, but with a look and a complex gesture, Tylan threw the fearsome enemy off his feet and the purple bolt disappeared. The hill folk suffered, though, as the protection on them briefly weakened, and three fell to the worms before Tylan restored balance to his attention.

"Come," he urged, and they were on their way. Neither West nor Emily were at all aware of what was happening. Jaik walked on West's left to support his friend using his good right arm. Otherwise, West walked as if in his sleep. After half an hour of travel like this, Ethan asked, "can't you do some more magic to help them? I mean, what did he do to them?"

"He fed on their . . . spirit, the underlying energy that makes them who they are. It is the energy that allows some of us to do magic, and all of us to think. I cannot help them. If I did, it may do their psyche more damage. Transfer of . . . spirit from one being to another is an intimate process, and I will not intrude on them the way their assailant already has, not unless it is a matter of life and death. They will be able to regenerate their own essence over time."

"How long will it take?"

"A day before they will be able to act normally, but many days or weeks before the last effects disappear. Your captain will recover sooner, I think. She has started to use magic and to channel the energy. The other, I cannot say. Humans are normally inefficient with spirit, and I see no reason to believe he will be different."

"Is –" Jaik spoke up in a wafer thin voice that would have shamed him if either Emily or West had been conscious enough to hear it. "Is there anything we can do for them? Not magic, I mean."

"There are herbs and teas that will aid the process, but I do not know the plant-life of this world, so we will have to wait until we reach Commander Raiz's ship. I have some ingredients there that may be of use. As for yourself, you are doing enough to simply bear some of your friend's weight, and by the time we are done with this journey, you will be bearing him holding him up with every step, and will have asked others to carry the burden for you at least twice."

It turned out to be four times, during which Ethan took West's other arm and Tylan put a slight flotation spell on West as he had on Emily, before they reached the eastern edge of the forest. Tylan left the escapees halfway through the journey to see what he could do in the continuing battle behind them, and their travel slowed in his absence. The walk took them past the dawn, and into the better part of the morning, but the end still came surprisingly quick.

"I thought that there'd be more to this forest," Ethan said, thirsty for more of the mage's golden liquor, but thankful to finally depart the confines of the trees. "It didn't feel like we were ever going to get out of it."

"There is more in the direction you were headed in with the Atlantii, to the north," Raznar explained, "but we have made a detour to the east coast of the continent, which provided Commander Raiz with the closest possible landing point to your position."

They were still well away from the coast, though, with no apparent need to get any closer – Raiz's ship had landed right at the forest edge, where the underground water fed upon by the trees evidently ran out. The dry earth was scorched by the landing at a distance from the ship, but as all Eldrandii ships were equipped to do, sanitized waste water had poured out near the landing spot to prevent the possibility of fire, and to dissipate the heat. As a result, the ground near the ship was unnaturally muddy and dank smelling. Work parties had been sent out immediately after the landing to restore the ship's water supply.

The ship so much like the *Azar* from the outside, with the same twin body design and center mounted engine, that Ethan was briefly dazed into thinking he was finally back to his relatively comfortable home away from Earth. Even Emily woke at the sight of it, and scowled, at first thinking that it was some sort of illusion, then recognizing that it was not her ship. She hated the idea that her ship was just one in a mass produced lot, and her hate turned to loathing at the appearance of the first person to emerge from this ship – a bright-eyed and practically gloating Jack Wilson.

"Hello, Captain Pierce," Kaz's former captain said with his fake charming smile plastered on his face, hiding the contempt he wished to show her. "Nice to see you again. Are you all right?"

Feeling a surge of energy, powered by her desire to show confidence in front of the opposing captain, Emily said, "oh, hell no." She was prepared to tell Wilson exactly what she thought of him, with every last ounce of effort she could muster, and ask him in no kind terms what he was doing on her planet, when Raznar interrupted.

"Captain Wilson, where is Commander Raiz? I expect he chose to stray from the ship on a bright day like this."

"You expect right," Wilson said, souring a bit at the combination of three people who failed to fit into his worldview – Pierce, this simpering vampire who walked around in daylight, and the commander of Newport Station who seemed to treat his important position flippantly. "He's with the water acquisition crew on the coast."

Emily grinned insanely. "You mean he's at the beach," she said, and started walking down to the coast with the rest of her team in tow. They took around half an hour to get from the ship to the shore, where Raiz was waiting for them. He wore an outfit similar to the one Emily had first seen him in when they had met weeks ago on Newport Station, except this time the tank top and swim trunks suited the surroundings. Everything else about the commander was the same as well, right down to his bouncy personality and his need to be in close proximity to computers. Even here, he had brought along a laptop and was working to the rhythm of the waves until they were in sight. Once they arrived, though, he dropped everything to meet them, earnestly joyful to see them intact.

Just at the sight of him, their worries seemed to melt away, and they felt as if the ultimate prize, still buried in the underground city of Raljar Canti, was already theirs.

11
Relics

The cheerfulness Raiz showed at first sight of them gave way to earnest concern when he saw the state they were in. The hike to the beach had been long, and having missed last night's sleep and literally running on raw fear, everyone was ready to collapse. With Raiz exuding such an absolute lack of care, they couldn't hold back the need for relief any longer, and fell into the sand and dirt. Ethan and Jaik took a seat, but the other two were less graceful. Only Raznar remained upright.

Raiz was unsurprised, but he felt a bit of concern was warranted. "Looks like we got to you a bit late Emily. Are you all right?"

"No," she said bitterly, curling to sleep.

Raznar stepped in and tried to explain. "That mage I told you about. He did something to these two. Tylan explained it to us, but we were all so tired, I think he'll have to repeat it all. I cannot recall a word of it. The others are a bit better off, but completely worn out."

"No, that's not it," Emily mumbled, struggling to get her point out. "What's he doing here?"

"I tried to explain that to you," Raznar started.

"No, not you, him."

Raiz knew what was on her mind. "Captain Wilson's ship was the only one ready in dock for departure. Earth Force ships were either in dock for repairs after the engagement with the Shadow Worker ships, or already here around Selparis. By the time we got here on Wilson's ship, the Eldrandii blockade made it impossible to transfer using a shuttle pod – especially when the Asparii jumped in and a full space battle broke out. So, there was no choice at all but to land the entire ship, which could at least defend itself on the way down and maneuver away from danger. According to communications from Earth Force ships, the battle ended a few hours ago with the Shadow Worker ships destroyed, but that only means the Eldrandii have restored their blockade."

"Everybody's here," she said, getting up on her elbows, looking up at him with a squint. "Everybody from that dream I had that I thought was symbolic is here. Everyone from that stupid trip I made to Newport station . . . except A'anfu En. Where's she?"

"In space negotiating with the Eldrandii fleet. Right now she's the only thing keeping them from blowing Wilson's ship up. It's a bit exposed on the ground here."

"And what about the guy I slept with that night on Newport, did you bring him along, too?" She shook her head. "Never mind. What about the *Azar*? What about my crew? What about John, the pod pilot?"

Raiz cleared his throat to indicate not-so-subtly that there was bad news on the way, but he intended to save it for last. "The ship is in dock at Newport, and should be fine after some repairs, which the World Council is paying for. Your crew is intact and, except for Kaz, is still on the station. I believe Marquez, your cargo chief, is in charge of the crew while the repairs conducted. He is also trying to find you repair crew candidates, since I detained Ben Wetzler and Jason Davison on suspicion of sabotage."

That brought Emily to her feet. "What?"

"There's evidence against them, not including the recent incident on your ship you are already aware of. It came to light after you left the station."

"Oh".

"As for your pod pilot, I'm sorry to say that your ship lost all contact with him. It is possible that there was simply a communications problem with the pilot's link –"

"But there's no way to tell, I get it. Okay, now the tough one – did you plan all this?"

Raiz grinned. "Captain, the answer would take far too long, at least while you're in this condition. We've set camp up along the beach. The weather's pleasant and we'll be staying here until nightfall. That should give you six or seven hours worth of sleep in the tents."

"I want to –"

"And after that, I'll tell you everything you want to know, and have some questions for you, too. I'm interested to know whether this ambitious gambit was worth it, Captain, but you don't look ready to give me the answers I need. I also want to hear the story of the young human native here, who's either descended from the party that accompanied the Asparii refugees decades ago, or has an even more interesting story to tell. But now is not the time. Get some rest, all four of you." The last words came out as an order, and Raznar escorted them to the tents Raiz pointed out.

They were awake again in a blink, but when they opened their eyes, the world was dark. Coastal winds had picked up and, as Emily emerged from the tent, she marveled that Raiz was still clad in his shorts. There had always been something alien about him, but he certainly seemed at home here, whatever the weather. A lot like West, she thought as the Selparii human emerged from the tent behind her.

The water team had constructed a fire close to the tent, and it crackled away, occasionally drowned out by the howling wind. Raiz was on his feet, pacing nearby, and three others sat around the fire. Two were part of the water crew, enjoying some time out of the confines of the ship's hull. The last was a man Emily had not seen in what seemed the ages, and had half thought, during her most devastated moments, she would never see again.

"Kaz!" she shouted as he stood up in his lanky way to greet her. The rush of enthusiasm she felt at seeing him, and the sense that a heavy burden was off her shoulders, led her to run up and give him a bear hug. To her surprise, he didn't complain or pull away in shock, but gave her a pat on the back in response.

"Captain. It's . . . I'm glad to see you're all right. The crew's been worried. Things have been crazy since you landed here, and as bad as it was up there, we knew it had to be worse down here."

"Yeah. Yeah, it was."

"You look pale. What happened to you? I've heard the craziest things from Raznar."

"You mean something about a mage sucking out my soul?"

"Something like that, yes."

"Well, that's pretty much what happened," she said, looking carefully at him and getting the desired look of distress. She took a seat about ten feet away from the fire, facing where Raiz was walking, and Kaz sat beside her. Sleep had by no means wiped away the empty feeling inside her and, though it had been worse before the sleep, there was every indication that life would be difficult to bear the next few days. Emotionally and mentally, she was as fragile as a baby.

"So . . . has the crew really been worried?"

He shrugged. "After we escaped from those Asparian ships and docked safely at Newport, that was pretty much all we had to think about. Some of them wanted to rescue you, even with the ship in bad condition and the repair crew short, but Commander Raiz told us Earth Fleet was mounting it's own mission. We have good people in the crew, and since Raiz told us we were still being paid, there are no bad feelings against you for . . . you know, putting us in danger and everything. The commander did a good job explaining things to the crew."

Emily smiled. "But they blamed me for whatever those crazy mages were doing?"

"Well, I did warn you about all this, Captain," Kaz said pointedly. "And you knew the crew was already . . . skeptical of the chances of success."

"Don't start with me, Kaz, I'm not in the mood. There's definitely something big going on, and we need to get a few things straight with the commander over there. Do me a favor, and get him over here. I don't think I'll be able to stand up again without blacking out until I get something to eat."

Kaz decided not to argue, and went to call Raiz over. The commander followed him back, replacing the pensive look on his face with a cheerful vigor. Despite the instantaneous gear shift, which would normally suggest affectation, Raiz was always completely authentic. It was part of what made him a master media manipulator. But here, it made him the ultimate rallying point – a walking morale booster.

"Well, Captain, shall we talk over dinner? Your young friend seems to be a bit circumspect," he said, nodding to West, "but perhaps we can persuade him to join us?"

West sauntered up from the shadows. He was in his forest animal mode, and everything was fight or flight. Whatever the mage had done to Emily, he had tormented West far further, maybe to the brink of his existence. He still had his essential fire, but right now it was bare, without the complex façade of humanity or his well-developed intelligence to cloak it. Those two higher functions required energy that he did not have, and might have to do without for some time.

As they gathered together, the two crew members obliged them by bringing over rations then departing into another tent. Jaik and Ethan had woken up, but reserved the energy required to get out of their sleeping sacks. The meeting would involve only Raiz, Emily, Kaz, and West.

"I know what you would like to ask me, Captain," Raiz started, "but, if you'll indulge me, I have a few questions that will show you what I don't know, so you will have that in mind when I tell you what I do."

"Whatever. One question first, though. I've been through hell over here, and I want to make sure of one thing. Will that asshole –"

"Captain Wilson will not receive any of your much deserved credit, assuming the prize is what I think it is. As I have already told your crew, your work may well go down in history as one of the most consequential expeditions in human history, and I already have press release prepared. Now, tell me Captain, what are you doing on this continent? What is it you are trying to find?"

Emily hesitated for a moment. The thirst in Raiz's voice was a touch more manic than she would have liked. "An underground city that's supposed to have ancient texts."

Raiz pumped his fist excitedly. "Yes. Question number two. Who were the people following you into the forest? Raznar says they looked human, but that there were hundreds of them."

Clearly, Raiz already guessed the truth, but needed it confirmed. For the first time, Emily was keenly aware that she, along with her ship and crew, were at his mercy. His benevolence in negotiating money from the World Council was all that was keeping this thing profitable. If the commander chose not to give her any credit, could she really mount some sort of opposition to him? All she could do at the moment was answer his questions and hope that his good heartedness would trump anything that could go against her.

"They live in hills they call Seli, along the coast. They're Atlantii, or at least they say they are. They say their ancestors escaped from Atlantis and landed here."

Raiz clapped. "Excellent. Have you guessed what this might mean, Captain? I will answer your question. I knew only that a major artifact had been found here and that a group of Asparii mages were after it. Oh, and one other thing: in the ISC archives we discovered the Atlantis evacuation plan, in place since the end of the first Atlantian Civil War, long before the fall. That plan showed that this world was the closest point that would serve as a destination for evacuees, with other safe locations hundreds of light years further. Putting those three bits of information together, I developed a hypothesis, and I bet you can tell me what it was, can't you, Captain?"

Emily nodded. "Somewhere in that underground city, there's a book that explains how the hyperspace drive works. How to build one, I mean." Even now, the enormity of such a prize sent chills up and down her spine. It was the sort of thing that could give the most jaded politician goose bumps.

Kaz was stunned. Raiz had clearly forgotten to mention what this was all about to him. Emily could imagine his sharp mind getting crushed by the sheer extent of the implications. "But that's impossible. That's the biggest secret in the galaxy," he said flatly.

"Not impossible. Two fallen civilizations – Atlantis and Asparis – both had the technology. No surprise there, since the two were related to each other and collapsed in sort of the same way. Anyway, you have to figure that someone buried the secret somewhere, and there's every reason to believe that the Atlantii buried it here, on Selparis."

"But, that's still –"

Having a rhythm going, Raiz was not about to be interrupted. "The Eldrandii seem to think the secret's here, too, don't they? They wouldn't have the place blockaded otherwise. Dear Marcus was unusually dense when he sent Arisin Oris with you. I can't tell you how worried that made me, but I suppose it was necessary since I hadn't offered you any money. And you've done all right, haven't you? What a daring way to escape from Oris' gaze – to walk straight into the clutches of a demented mage and magically super-sized Lumbricidae.

Very creative."

"We could have died," Emily mumbled, trying to come to grips with how stupid she had been to lead them into that situation.

"I don't think so. Your Atlantii friends were very eager to rescue you. Their abundance of magical charms caused some trouble for that mage. Tylan mentioned that with his protection, they practically didn't get touched except during the few moments he was distracted. According to him, they would have been able to rescue you on their own. It would have been bloodier, of course."

Emily shook her head. "I'm surprised Oris hasn't already found us."

"Oh, she has. She passed overhead a couple of times. But it's a flat out race now, and she didn't bother to get you. Each side is trying to get to the underground city as fast as possible, and the Eldrandii would have a head start if A'anfu En wasn't talking their heads off."

"What can she do to stop them?" Emily asked.

"Ah, you didn't know, of course. The Dunorii sect of Eldrand has secrets of their own – one of the components of the hyperspace drive is manufactured by them and it's their primary export. I took the liberty of negotiating a little deal with A'anfu En, who is the Dunorii speaker and the matriarch of its largest clan. The Dunorii are odd, even for Eldrandii, and they're obsessed with the greater good. I convinced them that Earth getting its hands on hyperspace technology would satisfy their goals, as well. In exchange for her helping us, the World Council has agreed not to manufacture that one component the Dunorii specializing in for at least ten years. Actually, the World Council signed the deal without realizing that what we're after is the whole secret to the drive, but that's another story. Right now, A'anfu En is threatening to sell the component to Earth only, if the Revnorii Eldrandii ships try to stop us from reaching the underground city. That would mean Earth would share in the monopoly and be able to mark up the price until the Eldrandii were forced to turn over the secret anyway. At least, that's what A'anfu is telling them."

"Okay. So, now what?"

"Now, I have one more question. Do you know the way to the city?"

Emily nodded. "I've got a general idea, but Ethan looked at the maps and overheard the explorers talking in detail, and I bet he has every word memorized. The other two, Jaik and West, might also know."

"Do you trust them?" Raiz asked with a rare serious look on his face, looking at West curiously. The young man remained absolutely motionless.

"Yeah. Totally. Wouldn't think to try without them."

"And what about me, Captain?" A voice, instantly recognizable, came out of the darkness. Emily had only understood it because she had reflexively put her headset on. The other two had not, and so stood up, puzzled.

"Look like someone important, and an Asparii at that," Raiz commented. "Who is he, Captain?"

Emily was briefly on the verge of laughter. Raiz and Tayron had, through their unofficial communications with each other, been the architects of her mission here, and they couldn't even recognize each other. But there was something that puzzled her. Since her translator had been detecting only English for a while now, it had long since stopped rendering her words into Asparian. If it hadn't, she would have needed to turn it off. So, how did Chancellor Tayron know what she had said?

"I can understand English, Captain," he said, still in Asparian, "and can write in it, though I cannot speak it, except for basics." Sensing that he needed to introduce himself to the others, he added in English, "I am Lord Davin Tayron, Chancellor to Emperor of Atparis. Who are you?" He had clearly prepared this introduction before hand, anticipating a potential need to speak to Earthlings without benefit of a translator.

Kaz went first. "I'm Kazuhiro Kamiki, Captain Pierce's first officer on the *Azar*."

Tayron was too tired to disguise the contempt he had for underlings. It wasn't a revolting snobbishness and certainly the least Kaz expected from a man of Tayron's position, but Emily had come to think well of the chancellor, even during his recent lordliness in the midst of the hill people and his competition with Oris. This brusqueness struck her as beneath him, or at least beneath what she thought of him. She would have to readjust her expectations.

Amused by the whole situation, Raiz held some of his mirth back, since it would very likely set off the tense and touchy Tayron. "I'm Tyler Raiz, Commander of Newport Station."

Emily realized that this conversation was now heavily tilted in Raiz's favor. Tayron had no idea what to make of Raiz's title, but the commander now knew exactly who Tayron was, and guessed what part he had to play in bringing Earth into this mess. The interesting thing about Raiz was that, if you didn't already knew any better, you would think he was some sort of buffoon, or otherwise inconsequential, though that opinion would quickly be complicated by his immense charisma. He had his charm carefully switched off , so all Tayron could base reactions on was Raiz's title, which still made him the highest ranked human in attendance.

"My English is not very good," Tayron said, repeating another memorized line. "Do you have translators?"

Raiz didn't waste a breath, and dashed into the water team's tent, emerging with four headsets, handing one each to Ethan, Kaz, and West, the last looking gratified by the consideration. Once the devices were active, the chancellor continued. "I brought you here. I had a message about our discoveries delivered through channels to your people, guessing your government would listen in. Now, I want assurances that you will come to aid my people."

Emily wondered what bargaining chip Tayron had left to make this deal. He no longer had exclusive knowledge of the location of the site, so what could he be using for leverage?

Raiz was miles ahead, though. If Tayron was expecting to be asked about what he could possibly offer in return, and eager to reveal his secret, he was destined for disappointment. "Sure, no problem. One thing, though. This planet is surrounded by the ships of a species called the Eldrandii. If I'm right, you've already met one named Oris. The problem is, we can't get our people onto this planet right now to help us much less you. I don't even know if it's safe for us to leave, 'cause last I checked, the Eldrandii are madder than they've been in quite a while. But, if you could find a way to clear them out, we'll be happy to help."

The commander said it all with a perfectly straight face, and Emily marveled at his freewheeling self-control. He left Tayron with no possibilities, using no statement that could be shown as untrue. Tayron was certainly in no position to insist on anything. All he could do was make the threat that he had already planned on."

"Well, sir, I am not interested in your problems. I know details about the security system of the underground city which will be essential, if you wish to pass through unharmed. Either you will render aid to my people or you will not reach your prize. These Eldrandii ships are your problem."

"But Lord Tayron," Raiz said calmly, as if the chancellor's remarks didn't surprise him in the least, "if we don't get to that library before our enemies – the same ones that attacked your empire – I don't think you will be able to negotiate with them to save your people. Our mutual enemies will get what they came for and will use their newfound knowledge to enslave every nation they encounter, including yours. You don't want that, do you, Lord Tayron?"

That left the chancellor mute. Everything he could say, Raiz could parry with reasoning, and finally the realization struck him. "You received my messages. You planned all this. This is your game, is it not?"

"You're not yourself, Lord Tayron. I think you must be a bit tired. Why don't you rest a bit in the tent? We'll be here until morning, so there's no rush."

Tayron took a seat on the ground near the fire, so thoroughly outplayed that he barely knew himself. Holding his throbbing head in his hands, he murmured, "I am a disgrace to my ancestors."

"Now, now, we all have our off-days, Lord Tayron," Raiz consoled earnestly. "The key is to make sure they don't get to you. Best policy is to sleep them off, and clear your head for the next day."

With the light of the campfire casting itself on Tayron's form, they could see how wretched he actually was. His clothes were ripped at the edges and muddy in places. His face, once filled with youthful exuberance back at the capital before the Shadow Worker attack was now worn and slightly scarred, showing his true age. No longer was he reminiscent of the forever young Raiz, and the contrast was stark. Emily would have pitied Tayron if she thought he deserved it. Over the past few weeks she had slowly learned that pity was a completely useless sentiment when directed at the powerful. The more ruthless of them manipulated it to get what they wanted. Pity was useless for the truly unfortunate, too, now that she thought on it. If a person is starving, they don't need pity, they need food. If a person has lost a loved one, they need comfort. Pity is what people choose to show when unwilling to give others what is really needed.

Tayron needed nothing from her, but tried to inspire pity in the hope that it would melt the memory of his previous posture of superiority. Realizing that his plan had fallen to pieces, he wanted to get his way by tapping into convenient emotions.

She wondered whether her recent experiences had somehow hardened her heart. Would she have fallen for his act before? Would she have been so gullible? Her thoughts drifted back to Ariki. The Inana had played very similar games with her, and she had bought every minute of it. And there was Oris, who had seemed so gracious, at first, and ultimately turned out to be an agent of her government. Powerful people got where they were by toying with others, and the most powerful were exceedingly good at it. Looking back, she realized that she was now far more cynical.

Raiz was no exception to the rule, but despite the objections of her developing cynicism, she felt that there was something different about him. He had never actually lied or put on a false face; he simply omitted certain information. Everything he did focused on his self-declared duty, to help bring Earth into the stars, and he adhered to that limitation faithfully. This entire adventure revolved around getting access to hyperspace secrets which would give Earth an equal footing with the Eldrandii. Not once had he misrepresented his intentions. Nor had he ever forced anyone to do anything. She had known the dangers as well as he had, and had decided to come to Selparis for her own reasons. Nothing at all about Raiz's hidden purposes invalidated the fame and money she expected to get from this journey.

The confrontation between Tayron and Raiz was telling. There was no hint of a lie when Raiz told Tayron he would be glad to help the empire, and Emily certainly believed that he had every intention of fulfilling his promise to send aid as soon as possible. Tayron felt it necessary to threaten to get his way, though it was a pathetic threat by any account. Ariki had used self-sacrifice. Oris had used outright deceit, which the Selians had rightly called her on. Raiz just asked, mixing just the right amount of information into the request. He knew that knowledge was power, and was careful about making sure any expenditure of information had its payback. He could bombard a person with revelations while retaining the key piece that would decode it all.

They had been silent around the fire for a few minutes when Emily turned to Raiz and said, "I think I get you, now."

Raiz smiled winningly, "I'm a very simple person, Captain Pierce. The only reason people get confused is because they're expecting something complicated. I've still got some surprises in me though, I think. Still some surprises."

As he repeated the last words, Jaik approached them with a dour look. He had heard some of the exchange between Tayron and Raiz. The argument about the Eldrandii ships sounded to him like a way to dodge a real promise to send help. He did not doubt Raiz was an important man, and that meant he was entirely qualified to sign an agreement with Lord Tayron. That was what should have happened, and exactly what he intended to have done.

"Will you help us?" he asked Raiz point-blank, in English.

"My word, you have a serious face," Raiz said, legitimately shocked by the stern stare he was given. The translator was still rendering in Asparian, so he continued, careful not to sound patronizing or disingenuous. "Yes, I will help you in any way I can. I think an empire on this planet capable of defending itself will be in Earth's best interest. Certainly, seeing you fall to these rogue mages will do us no good. There's only the practical problem of being able to bring our forces in."

"But if you agreed with . . . these other people that you would share what you found here, they would let you bring help in."

Raiz shook his head. "Not the Eldrandii. They already have it, you see. And, as it turns out, they've had their eye on this place far longer than we have, and they have a bad habit of sterilizing anything that doesn't suit them. I know you won't want to accept it, but the politics of the situation are far more complicated. I wish they weren't, but it's not in my power to change people's minds."

"But you will help us?"

Raiz shrugged. "Sure. Absolutely."

"Then you will not mind signing an agreement with Lord Tayron saying that."

That finally got Tayron's attention. "If this person had that kind of authority, he would not be here. Agreements only function if they are made between equals, and Earth overmatches . . . whatever is left of our empire."

Raiz scratched his head. "I don't know about that. Throw in the underground city and this planet has some hidden strengths. As for my own authority, Lord Tayron, I think I have enough force under my influence, if not my command, to have destroyed your empire without ever landing an army on this planet's surface," he said cheerfully. "And, in fact, if anyone here lacks legitimacy to sign an agreement, it is you. But I think an agreement is an excellent idea, which is why I already had one drawn up, just in case."

He fished into the pocket of his shorts and brought out two triple folded sheets of plastic paper, and a pen. English and Asparian writing appeared on alternate lines on both sheets. Raiz handed one to Tayron, who read it over incredulously.

"You planned . . . even for this?"

"Well, I'm only really here as a representative from Earth, so the only way any sort of intervention here on my part will be seen as appropriate on my planet is if we are invited in. So, I would definitely appreciate it if you sign, otherwise I'll catch three kinds of hell for all this, not that it hasn't happened before. And I'll still probably catch one kind of hell, but there's no avoiding that. I think you'll find the terms reasonable."

The chancellor slumped even further where he sat, shaking his head. "Unbelievable, very well, guaranteed access to underground city, as far as Atparian Empire – you even had our empire's name correct, even though I had not mentioned it – can ensure. In exchange, my people have Earth's guarantee that our empire will be defended from attack and rebuilt to pre-attack levels with Earth's best support. An elegant agreement, since neither side can fully fulfill these terms, you added necessary qualifiers. And your people have already agreed to this?"

"Amazingly enough, yes. I can be very persuasive sometimes," Raiz smiled radiantly.

Tayron said no more, taking the pen from Raiz and signing both his copy and Raiz's. The commander followed in suit, leaving Jaik completely speechless. Raiz decided to be indulgent to the young man, saying, "You had the right idea, nothing wrong with that. You might say that your logic was so forceful, I got the message ahead of time."

"How did you know?"

"Ah, well," Raiz mused, "you're very used to thinking like you do. Let's just say, I'm used to thinking the way other people do, and they rarely expect it."

Emily grinned, dazed. "You mean you don't predict the future in your dreams?"

In full puzzlement, Raiz said, "No. What an interesting idea, though. Is that from your own experience, Captain? Can you predict the future through dreams?"

It was amazing. She had wanted to throw him off, and he turned the tables in no time at all. From the way she said it, he guessed that she had personal experience with dream divination. Even more impressive, he was immediately willing to believe it with perfect open-mindedness.

She needed to dodge the topic – at least as long as Tayron was still in listening range. "Yeah, right, If I could predict the future, do you think I'd be in this mess?"

Raiz opened his mouth to reply, but stopped, looking straight into Emily's eyes. He didn't pry too deeply, and got the hint almost immediately. "Then, Captain, if you can't see the future, I can't see why you'd think I'd be capable of it. I only know what is possible and which path will be most beneficial. I try to increase the probability that the beneficial route takes place. Having a treaty handy is a minimal step that would inevitably be convenient."

Skeptical, and seeing Raiz as a dubious conjurer rather than the genius he was known to be on Earth, Tayron said, "What else do you have in your pockets? Anything else useful?"

"Not at the moment, but if you have any requests, I could arrange it."

Defeated, the chancellor said, mumbling again, "We believe in . . . gods here you know. My family god . . . I get a strange feeling that he would prefer you to me, you are so far beyond me."

Raiz didn't say anything, but gazed levelly at Tayron until the latter finally said, "I think I'll go to sleep."

"You do that. I'll wake you up when it's time to leave."

Their new traveling party was substantially larger than the original group Emily had landed with but a sharp reduction from the thousand that they had entered the forest with. On the way from the beach to Wilson's ship, Raiz was firmly at the head of the venture, though he frequently deferred to Emily for no particular reason, careful to also give her some time alone because she was still recharging. West, Jaik, and Ethan formed their usual trio, leaving Tayron to brood on his own. Tylan was interested in the magic of Selparis, but the chancellor was short with him, and the mage was wise enough not to press for answers. Raznar had stayed behind, trying to work with his fellow vampire Plani in the hope that they could be, in his own words, civilized.

Aside from these primaries, there was also a full support staff that would accompany them to Raljar Canti, including four members of the Newport station security detail, two linguistic experts, two space engineering experts, two physicists, and three other multidisciplinary specialists. It was a good thing Raiz made a point of giving her a command role, otherwise Emily would have literally had nothing to contribute. Until she got a chance to dream, at least.

The new additions were saved from slogging it on this planet the hard way, though. Captain Wilson, seeing really no choice, gave them full use of his ship's four landing pods to cover the distance to Raljar Canti, so they would be covering the hundreds of miles remaining in a day. Wilson discretely secured a promise from Raiz that any damage to the pods would be covered, but not so quietly that Emily failed to hear. She also noticed the condemnation in his eyes whenever he caught sight of her. There was no mistaking it – Wilson knew the credit for this was going to her despite the fact that, in his eyes, she was far less competent or deserving than he was. His discontent gave her a warm, fuzzy feeling inside. From her now obviously superior position, she was almost prepared to forgive his snobbishness. Almost.

As they stood waiting for the pods to be prepared, Emily approached Raiz and commented, "I still can't believe you managed to get . . .

well, almost everyone . . . from my visit to the station together."

As if admitting that he had taken a cookie when his mother had told him to save them for after dinner, Raiz said sheepishly, "Well, that whole thing wasn't exactly a coincidence. I deliberately got everyone on board for that time so I could coordinate the whole thing directly. It's so hard making sure things work out right when you can't talk face-to-face with people. I even had our experts there, though I'm sure you didn't get to mingle with them. I invited A'anfu En, Tylan, and Raznar to the station. I had actually planned to use Wilson for your mission – don't tell him – but then Ariki picked you, and these Asparii mages showed up and started chasing you. So, I gave you an opportunity to involve yourself. If you had chosen to stay out of the equation, it would have been Wilson. Again, please don't tell him."

"So, you had nothing to do with Ariki and the Inana thing?"

Raiz shook his head firmly. "No. I've looked into it, and they must have intercepted the messages between Selparis and Earth, or might have heard about my interest in that planet. Ina Cur must be genuinely under the influence of these Asparii mages. Ariki leaked information about Selparis to them, probably under torture, and hoped that we would be forced to engage them here. It was a brilliant move, I must admit. It was Ariki who brought you into this Captain, though I'm now glad that you were the one. You're much more interesting."

"Well . . . thanks."

Before they were all packed into the pods, Emily also managed a private word with her first officer. Her memory of the previous night was hazy, and she now had some concrete things to say to him.

"Listen, I wanted . . . I want to thank you for taking care of the ship."

Kaz was almost offended. "Don't you think I deserved your trust. I mean, did you think I –"

"I'm just saying thank you. Good job," she said wretchedly. She looked at him and from his stern, confident brow to his weak, academic chin, his face gave her the right words. "There's nobody I would have trusted more than you. If we get what I think we will from this, your name will be right next to mine."

That was enough to make him flush. She couldn't have come up with better words if given direct access to his mind. Liking the result, she went on. "Actually, we could have used your help down here, too. I'm not always the best at thinking things though, and this isn't really Ethan's thing."

"I don't think so, Captain –"

"Call me Emily. I bet Captain Wilson let you call him Jack, right?'

He paused. "Well, yes, in private. Anyway, I don't think you could have done better with me around. You got here safely, and Commander Raiz seems excited. I can't tell you how excited he was when he saw your signal wasn't coming from the continent –"

"Yeah, whatever, I mean I . . . got two crew members killed."

"One killed and one missing."

"Right. Doesn't make me feel any better, by the way."

"But, Captain, I don't think I could have done anything to save them, either. We saw the smoke from the fires in Atparis from space. You were in the middle of all that, and you managed to survive. It's . . . it's more than I expected after we saw –"

"You mean you didn't trust me."

"It wasn't a matter of trust –"

"But admit it. You didn't think any good would come out of us landing here."

Challenged, Kaz reacted in the normal way and threw out his strongest defense. "Well, nothing good has come out of it. Not yet, anyway, and I think Commander Raiz –" He might have gone on, but he accidentally bit his lip and massaged it gingerly.

She couldn't believe what she was hearing. All she had wanted was a little recognition from him that she wasn't as incompetent as she had always thought she was, and he had completely missed the boat. It was so much worse, because she desperately wanted that acknowledgement from him specifically. It would have meant so much. Abjectly disappointed, she turned and walked away from him, and it took him a few heartbeats to understand why. Too long, really.

"Wait, I didn't mean . . . Dammit, Emily, you're still so –" It was no use. He had meant what he had said, of course, and he simply had not developed the esteem for her that he showed to Wilson. But Wilson had earned it over a period of years. Emily had stumbled onto this planet and her every step had been attended to by more luck than skill.

Yet, given a choice between her ship and Wilson's, regardless of the possibility for advancement, Kaz would have picked the *Azar*. Having a choice between captains, he would pick Emily. Why, though? He wished he could explain it to Emily, but he had trouble explaining it to himself. He liked her. All his criticisms of her actual command ability aside, he admired her eagerness to improve, and was gratified by the way she always took him seriously. There was more to it, though. Not all of it was logical.

They were both careful to pick different pods when it came down to packing in for the flight. Each pod could carry five passengers in the tightest of arrangements, not including the pod pilot. Emily insisted on having her old comrades Ethan, West, and Jaik along over Raiz's objection that there should be one person who knew the way in each pod. Raiz relented, but forced a delay while Ethan, Tayron, Emily, and himself poured over an aerial photograph of the region, going over the route. Tylan filled the final spot in Emily's pod, and his reaction to this assignment was so mixed that Emily had no idea what to make of it. He seemed to want to speak to her and avoid her at the same time, and she thought she knew the topic that was on his mind, if not the actual words he would choose to say.

She had not paid much attention to it last night, completely out of focus as she had been, but Tylan was glowing with an aura of magic similar to the one the dark mage had sported. Drawing the obvious conclusion, she must also have the tiniest of glows of her own, visible to other magic users, and Tylan would have noticed. As someone who had come to Earth in order to set up a school of magic there, he would no doubt see her as a potential student. But why was he hesitant?

Perhaps it was just the presence of the others, but she guessed it was more than that, because at any point during the preparation for departure, he could have asked to speak to her privately. The answer was obvious once she put her mind to it. Her dreams had only become vivid after that night with Tylan aboard the *Azar*, so maybe he thought he was responsible for her magical abilities. There was a good chance he was. Maybe he thought she blamed him for doing it deliberately. Even if he had, she was more likely to thank him, sneaky though it might have been. Of course, the reason he would fear her accusation was because he was definitely not the type to do something so underhanded. Just the image of him coming to the rescue in the dark mage's hut was enough to convince her of that.

Eventually, he finally took up the subject after the pod's ducted fans got them safely off the ground.

"Captain Pierce, I am not sure that it is good to take up this subject at this time...."

"Anything you can say to me, you can say to them," Emily said. The pod pilot and West were sitting up front, unable to hear any of the conversation between the four facing each other in the back. West had immediately opted for the forward position, eager to discuss and examine this example of off-world mechanics first hand.

"I had hoped that you had broached the subject with your companions already."

"If it's about my magic, I have."

"Indeed," Tylan said uncomfortably. "And, since you undoubtedly know of your own ability, might I ask what nature it has taken?"

"Seeing the future in my dreams," she answered promptly.

"Ah", he said, his worst reasons for anxiety realized. "I hope you understand, Captain, I –"

"Don't worry, I don't think it was you – not mostly, anyway. It was mostly thanks to my meeting a Selian elder on this continent just a few days ago. I didn't really have control over it until I talked to him, and I definitely couldn't see magic. Actually, I couldn't see it well until I was in the tent with the dark mage." She was rather pleased with herself. For her to be outthinking a mage was definitely special. Outthinking anyone was rather rare for her. Sure, he was helping her by trying to guess what she was thinking, which meant he was taking his thought level down a few notches. That didn't negate the sense of achievement.

"You are not yet as sensitive to it, so you can only see magic when it is in large enough quantities. You would probably not even see it in yourself."

"So . . . you can actually see yourself glowing?"

"After a while, a mage becomes desensitized to his own emissions much like a person may be unaware of his or her own smells, though a greater than normal emission will be sensible."

Emily yawned without wanting to and said, "Sorry, still trying to catch up on sleep. That's really interesting, though. So, the glow is actually magic leaking out or –"

"Yes. And your more vivid dreams while I was aboard your ship might have been due to my presence. You absorbed my residual magic, and it reached a sufficient quantity to trigger the dreaming in which we conversed. When I first saw you, your magic was within the normal human range, though at the high end of it. Now you're slightly above that." There was every indication in his voice that he was impressed, though because he was faithful to the stereotypical persona of the magical teacher, he was carefully subtle.

Emily felt an ounce of pride surge through her. "Yeah, I've learned a sort of spell to recharge and used it whenever I felt a bit low. If I wasn't full up, though, I suppose sitting next to you would get some more magic in me, right?"

"Yes, though not nearly as much as any spell would add. It is fortunate, too, that you have not attempted any feat too far out of your abilities."

"The visions just get fuzzier and shorter when I try to see further."

Tylan nodded gravely. "There is that safety valve, but if you tried to see to the end of the universe, even an infinitesimal success would be too much for you, and if you press magic hard enough, it will rarely achieve absolutely nothing."

"So what would happen?"

"Typically some sort of magical vacuum would form. I have seen a mage's body torn apart as the binding magic in his atoms was released to supply the spell. That is very unusual since the force to break apart a body is also quite great, so the magic already being exerted by the mage in question was already more than great enough to accomplish that feat. You would not be able to do that, and chances are that you would simply lose consciousness and become comatose. Consciousness requires a certain minimum amount of magic."

"How powerful can a mage get?"

"Millions of times more powerful than you, Captain. And that excludes legends and figures whose power is only estimated. We have actually developed ways of measuring magic."

"And the mancers?"

Tylan sighed. "Should not have existed. That is complicated. They did not follow the rules of magic as we know them. It is a little known fact that Asparis existed within a rift between realities, and that the power of the mancers diminished a great deal when they left – or were eventually removed – from our planet. That is why Asparii mundanes felt confident that, if they managed to escape as refugees, the mancers would not follow. That is why Earth survived the attack from Lord Heinly, and why Earth's attack on Asparis was so legendary."

"Between . . . realities," Emily repeated, deciding this was too much, even for her peculiarly open mind.

"It is . . . complicated. Reality theory is far from adequately explored, for obvious reasons. Even a master of magic cannot easily poke a hole between realities, much less make a thorough examination of the process."

"Right . . . well, we won't go there, then."

"As you say."

"Anything else you'd like to tell me?"

Tylan thought it over. "There is much I could say, but perhaps this is not the time for it. Would you be interested in pursuing your gift, or are you satisfied with your abilities as they are?"

Emily had decided the former when Geramintor had given her a similar choice, but what Tylan seemed to be asking was whether she wanted to become a mage, and on that point the answer was definitely no. Before saying anything, though, she wanted to examine her options further. "Can I . . . pursue it? I mean, what could I do?"

"That is entirely up to the individual, Captain, but I would say that you have great promise. I would be delighted to have you as a student."

Emily laughed, and saw Ethan grinning as well since he knew her well enough to get the joke. "You don't know me very well, Tylan. I'm not much of a student."

"This would not be like academic learning, Captain. It is more practical and, in a way, athletic. Magic requires practice and precise control like a sport. The theory is only for those interested in that sort of thing, like myself."

It was in an intriguing idea, she had to admit. Emily the mage.

Emily the witch, in fact. Magic would definitely give her an advantage in the business side of things, assuming the other end was clueless about it. Then again, a fair portion of her psyche still insisted that magic was cheating. She had retained some latent sensibilities and biases that were assumed as common sense on Earth, and therefore not questioned. It had been so easy to question all those things that rebels were supposed to doubt, that no one ever bothered with all the other daily assumptions everyone made. The unnaturalness of magic had definitely never crossed her mind as something to challenge.

As she was thinking it over, the pilot was receiving a communication from Captain Wilson's ship. Once it was over, she shouted back to them, "Captain Wilson reports seeing an armored figure heading our way, Tylan, and wondered if you knew anything about what it might be. He says it was flying low over the ground along the coast a bit slower than us, but not by much, so it's pretty obviously magical."

"That thing can fly?" Ethan burst out loud.

"You have seen it before?"

"Yeah, it sort of scouts out places before the bad guys materialize. We guessed they need to see a place through it before they try to pop in."

"Very good, that is logical. A projection of some sort, then. It would be extremely dangerous to have it fly, however, and must be taking unusual effort. If so much as a pebble was thrown at it, I would wager it would be dispelled, and the mage who formed it would not have the energy to recreate it immediately. Inform Captain Wilson that he should attack it if possible. That will set our enemies back a pace."

There was a wait as the response was sent, and a new message was received. "He says it's already gone too far ahead. Since they don't have any pods available, they can't catch up to it. The Captain's ship doesn't have a clear shot."

"Ah, well. We can only hope that a gust of wind hurls something at it or it fails to navigate properly around a boulder. Trying to control it from such a distance at that speed must be horrendous."

Emily's mind was doused in temporary relief that they were still firmly ahead of the enemy, but there was no question that the Shadow Workers were now on this side of the ocean. She said as much to

Tylan.

"Yes. They were surprisingly dense, were they not? Taking so long to cross an ocean. These mages are no doubt very powerful, but they lack sense and basic intelligence. All bang and no brains, as a human once put it. That is a very common problem with magic – it does not encourage the development of wisdom or virtue. In that way, magic is again similar to athletics and technology."

Emily didn't feel at all comforted by the apparent stupidity of her foes. "Yeah, but they sure don't mind showing their power. They ripped apart the capital of the empire."

"Yes, and that was an absurdly stupid move. If they wanted to follow you to the underground city, it was counter productive to engage in such destructive acts, which made it apparent to you they were after you. I assume they realized that an official of the empire had knowledge of the Atlantian city, and could have captured him, but they allowed their bloodlust get the better of them."

"But Ariki thought they were manipulating governments on Ina Cur. They can't be that stupid if they were doing that."

"On the contrary. If they had been intelligent about it, he should not have known. They were likely making blatant threats rather than employing more subtle means."

"You mean wizards aren't subtle and quick to anger?" Ethan asked, amused.

Tylan cracked a smile. "Commander Raiz told me of that Earth phrase. It may not be as poetic, but a more accurate saying would be 'meddle not in the affairs of wizards, for they are subtle and/or quick to anger.' I think of myself as the subtle sort, while our enemies are obviously quick to anger."

Emily had just one question left. "Could you take them on? I mean, given you're smarter and all."

"No," Tylan said firmly. "If they were kind enough to attack one at a time, then yes, but they will not, and no matter, how clever I am, I will fail against a half dozen of them. I could survive in the midst of them, but would not be able to protect you."

"No surprise there."

Jaik had wanted to say something, and in the silence that followed found the opportunity to do so. He had never considered it seriously, but in the company of a mage, while interested in a woman who could do some magic, and heading to a place with a treasure of lost magical texts, how could he be blamed for asking?

"Could you teach me to be a mage?"

Tylan looked him over carefully and said, "Yes, I think so. Mind you, most Asparii find it easier than Earthlings in any case, and I have a bad habit of claiming everyone is capable of learning magic even though, strictly speaking, it is not true. But yes, I think I can teach you if you want to learn."

That satisfied Jaik for the moment, and he looked briefly at Emily before casting his gaze back down to the bare metal floor.

Emily found his innocence unbelievably cute. The question about his age was long overdue, but she had some trouble figuring out how to put into words so that he wouldn't think she was disparaging him, or suggesting he was a child. Deciding that only the straightforward wording would work, she tried to say it in an even, purely curious, tone.

"Jaik, how old are you?"

"I just had my seventeenth birthday," he said without thinking, then guessed why she had asked and added, "which is when boys in my town become men, and announce their calling in life." Considering how his pronouncement had turned out, he tried not to inject any false pride in his voice.

"Ethan, how old is that in Earth years? Do you know?"

Ethan did a quick calculation in his head. "That's almost twenty-one." He, too, had guessed where this was going, and as much as Jaik was his friend he couldn't find it in himself to be happy about it. Nevertheless, he answered the question honestly.

"Close enough. Jaik, how would you like to join my crew after all this is over?"

That made West turn, reminding Emily that his hearing was sharper than the average human's. She decided to add, "and West, too, of course. We'll probably go straight to Earth after this, and go back and forth a few times assuming Raiz manages to win this against the Eldrandii."

Jaik knew what his answer to her would normally be, but he was nothing if not a loyal friend, so he turned his eyes to West, wordlessly asking if the plan was alright with him. West gave no sign, though, indicating that it was Jaik's choice, and he was just listening in to hear what the future portended. Neither staying to help with the rebuilding of the empire nor leaving to discover new worlds, perhaps at the same time pushing Commander Raiz to send the help that he promised to Selparis, seemed like necessarily bad ideas. Emily was a compelling factor to Jaik, but he also knew that her offer was no guarantee that she was really interested in him. She liked his company as a friend, and was interested to get to know him better, preferably in her native habitat.

Well, why not? "Yes, I would like to go, but maybe we should wait until after all this ends to decide things for sure."

"It's always good to have something to look forward to," she said, satisfied. He smiled back. Between them, a continent of ice was breaking, and it made her sigh to think that she was hoodwinking him into a world – a universe – unlike anything he could imagine. The culture shock would be tough. Everything was going to be tough. West would help him adjust, she supposed, though Jaik gave his friend too much deference from her point-of-view. They were friends, but that didn't mean Jaik had to look to him before making a decision like this. She supposed that, given all they had been through together, some mutual attachment was to be expected, but she wondered if West would have glanced at Jaik the same way. Would West wonder what his friend thought before making a decision? She didn't think so.

On principle, she had always given her boyfriends room with their friends, not believing that the start of a relationship should mean the end or diminishment of friendships. Most of her friendships were emotionally fulfilling, with her love interests being physical affairs until now. Now, she was looking for something different, though she couldn't decide by how much. Jaik was probably too different.

While it was nice to have Jaik a bit more relaxed around her, she wondered whether she had given him too much hope. He was bright, and knew her tendencies well enough – not that she held much back. But, as far as she knew, he had never had a girlfriend. He certainly acted like he had little experience on that side of life, and she usually preferred a slightly more mature brooding type – the type that brooded to attract girls like her. Jaik was more legitimate and authentic, and that scared her because she was used to putting on a show and leading a double life, like most humans did. Jaik drew a firm line between acting and real life, but she had been conditioned to a culture that expected a certain amount of fakery. Did Jaik know that? Was it the same with his people? It was hard to tell. He had in him the rural naiveté – the honesty of the countryside – and an actor's calculated guile. Did he understand that people could spend their entire lifetime playing different parts when with others?

It was funny, because until now, her show had been her life. Only now, when she had more going for her, did she realize how shallow her young self had been. She still hated introspection – it was like running around in circles – but some careful self-reflection had helped her develop some reality to her life, and gave grounding and increasing maturity to her actions. She had never needed that before, always being around people who were quietly more solid than she was. Ethan was a good example. Having him around to rein her in, she had been free to do all sorts of crazy things. Kaz was the same way. Jaik had the makings of that sort of anchor, but he also had a bit of the unpredictable and immature in him, and he could catch some of her craziness.

Her mind wandered to Kaz. He was easily the most firm, most real thing in her life right now. Seeing him brought it all down to Earth. When she first started as captain, she hated him for precisely that, because she was trying to escape Earth literally, and reality metaphorically. But he took none of her nonsense, and kept her away from the road of self-indulgence and failure. Compared to Kaz, Jaik was more like one of her old friends – someone she really wanted to hang out with. In the quiet charm department, Kaz was –

She stopped, shocked at what she had been thinking. Well, it wasn't that crazy, was it? He was cute in his way, as practically every male on the *Azar* within ten years of her age was, and right from the start they had bickered like newlyweds. And what about the wave of comfort she had felt when she hugged him on the beach? During her conversation with Raiz, she had looked at him every other second, and his placid yet haunted and weary face brought back some of the strength sapped from her by the dark mage. There had been something there, and it was more than her imagination.

Just as her lips silently moved to murmur 'aw, hell' in response to her last thought, turbulence threw the pod to one side in a manner all too reminiscent of the attack by the mages on Veris' plane. They were only fifteen minutes from their destination.

"What the hell?" the pilot shouted in frustration, as the pod was no longer responding to his determined pulls on the controls. After a few seconds, the turbulence ended, but had not left the pod unscathed.

"We've lost two of the fans and I don't have enough altitude to troubleshoot them. Either we try to land, or we light the rocket," the pilot yelled over the comm to the other pods, waiting for the decision from Raiz. The answer came, though only West and the pilot could hear it, so none of the others knew whether to hang on for the rocket jolt. Using the rocket on this planet was a dangerous proposition, since controlling and landing the pod afterwards would be problematic on a planet without long landing strips. Within a second, it was clear they were landing.

The pilot kept the craft reasonably stable through the descent, but brought it down in a spiral instead of a regular vertical landing. They landed on the shore of a tiny lake, surrounded sparsely by trees. It was so similar to the site Tayron had landed the bierka in on the other side of the ocean that Emily felt a brief bout of déjà vu. The other three pods followed suit, and soon the entire party was flowing out, wobbly from the hours in the tight compartments. All four craft had sustained some damage, and the engineers went to work immediately, speculating.

Raiz's team was greeted by a local in rough jerkins and a complexion to match. There was a cabin on the opposite shore of the lake, and this man looked every bit its owner. Instead of looking surprised by them, or angered that they had trespassed on his land, he was wholly entertained. His worn leathery face, so similar to his clothes, also matched the smooth yet rugged texture of his voice. "It figures you would be off-worlders. Everyone around here knows not to try and fly over this place, if anyone around here could fly. And nobody from somewhere else on this world would want to come here, because the people here are poor and can offer nothing. So you had to be off-worlders, because no one else would be stupid enough to come here in a flying machine."

Raiz confronted the man amiably, translator in place, but Emily noticed West wary and ready to pounce, instinctively aware that something was untrustworthy about this man. Neither of them could see what she saw – the corona of magic around him – but Tylan could. She looked for the Asparii mage's reaction, but found none. He was scrupulously passive, waiting for the magical man to make the first sign of intent, one way or the other. Emily imitated Tylan's posture, realizing that as one of the two magic users in the lot, she would also be one of the first targets if things got hot. Tylan and the leathery man looked more or less evenly matched in magic, as far as Emily could tell.

"I am Commander Raiz from Earth," Raiz said brightly, "and if I can be any judge, you look to be an Atlantii descendant yourself, an Atlantii mage." That caught Emily off-guard, but not the mage, whose amusement had not flickered in the slightest. Raiz didn't seem to be magical, though since she wouldn't be able to see the magic in herself, maybe he just had very little power. More likely, he used the way Tylan and Emily had been looking at the man to make a chance deduction.

"You are more intelligent than you look, Commander," the mage said, certain that Raiz lacked magic. "You may call me Makis, or perhaps Mark would be more common in your language. It has become more of a title than a name, mind you, but to the degree that anyone calls me anything at all, that is what they call me."

"And there's no point in me asking how you know that 'Mark' is a name in my language, even though you mentioned it so I would ask, because you have no intention of telling me."

That did give Makis pause. It gave everyone a bit of a start. Even if Raiz wasn't a wizard, he had found ways to compensate. It was uncanny.

"Remarkable," Makis said. "For an obviously inferior being such as yourself to presume to read my mind is remarkable. And can you guess the secret hidden in the grove not too far away? It is the same one that brought you down here, and which also keeps me here. If you can guess it correctly, I will guide you to the forbidden city, which I know all too well brought you to this planet. It is the only thing of value in this wretched place as far as off-worlders are concerned."

"But you know about it, and are not interested?" Raiz probed.

"Interested? Perhaps."

"But this secret of yours manages to keep you here. So it is something more compelling to you than the magical secrets of Atlantis."

"Magical secrets of Atlantis, indeed," Makis scoffed, rolling his eyes.

"Ah, so what you have here is an even greater magical secret. It creates such a large magical field around itself, much larger than any mage has, that it disrupted the electronics of the landing pods. I've heard about magical artifacts like this. They once had many on Asparis, and still have a few on Eldrand. Let's see . . . it can't be something that simply recharges your magic, since there are other ways you could do that, even living here on your own as you do. You knew of our world's language, but spoke about it vaguely. Your name is a title, which means it has been handed down from person to person," Raiz said, piecing everything together vocally for the benefit of the others. He had already zipped through all the steps in his mind, coming to the obvious conclusion.

"Go ahead and say it. You're not going to get any points from me for hinting at it," Makis said, with a great deal of grumpiness now in his voice, and his demeanor falling perceptibly. He had accidentally given away his best riddle, and was now at the mercy of a clever man. With Tylan standing behind Raiz, breaking his word was not an option.

"Your secret, Makis, is a gateway between worlds, though not one that can be controlled by just anyone. You were taught how to use it as an apprentice to the last Makis, who learned it from the one before that. You stay here, because from here, you can go anywhere. And I suppose it was an Atlantian product."

Emily shook her head. It must be such a trip to have a mind like that. She remembered the old detective shows she loved as a child. Never, even at that age, did she think someone with Sherlock Holmes' mind could actually exist. And yet, here he was.

"That's . . . impossible," Tylan said, referring to the gateway rather than Raiz's derivation of its existence.

Tylan's expression of shocked disbelief put Makis back on familiar ground. "There are more things between heaven and earth, friend, than are dreamt of in your philosophy."

Raiz laughed. "You've waited all this time to use that line, haven't you? I can't imagine there are many people around here who recognize Hamlet when they hear it."

Makis scowled. He was developing an intense dislike for Raiz. "Given the low quality of the degenerate branch of Atlantis left on Earth after the fall, I doubt there are many Earthlings who would recognize it, either. Enough talk. I made a promise, and I intend to keep it."

"You're going to take us through the gateway?" Raiz asked eagerly.

"No, no! With so many people at once it would be unstable. Besides, shutting it after it is open is a tricky business. No, we are close enough to go on foot."

"We're in a bit of a hurry."

"I know, but how long will it take for you to repair your aircraft, hum? And if you repair two, I don't suppose you would care to leave half of your people behind here, would you?"

The engineers and pilots had already gathered around the non-functioning engines of the worst hit pod, and they were standing grim.

Surveying the situation, Emily's eyes fell on West, who was still on alert. Maintaining a hostile stance ever since the night in the forest, except possibly while sleeping and talking to the pod pilot, he was the only one who seemed ready for action. In everyone else's eyes, Raiz had everything under control. While Raiz talked the repairs over with the engineers, Emily sidled up to West and asked, "Why are you so . . . you know . . . looking so serious? Doesn't look like the mage is going to be a problem." Jaik was looking at his friend with concern as well, and gave Emily a thankful glance for her intervention.

"I don't trust him."

"Well, none of us do, but I think Raiz has it covered. You know, you reminded me of him when we first met. The way you walked right up to us, all smiles and confidence was exactly the way he talked to that mage."

"He is not like me," West said, adamantly fierce and practically shouting. "I was confident because I knew you wouldn't try to kill me. I could talk to you, because you would be interested to know why there are humans here. Otherwise, I would have avoided you. He . . . he acts like nothing in the world can touch him. It is wrong. I don't trust him."

"You . . . don't trust Raiz," Emily said, forcing herself not to laugh. Bizarre as it was, she knew exactly what this was about – it was the old testosterone problem. Well, a form of it, at least. It was pure jealousy – an emotion she would never have guessed could come out of West.

At the same time, West was right, in a way. Raiz was profoundly unsettling. Was he ever jealous, or afraid, or anything? Was this a façade he showed all of them, or was it all really him? She had honestly pictured West as the exact image of the young Raiz, sprite-like and excited about life, acting in the exact same ways. Right now, in a side-by-side comparison, the differences were more striking.

Raiz strode from the engineers to the mage a minute later, and announced, "I don't think there is any reason to trouble Makis any further, except perhaps to leave some of our people here in his cave. We don't have parts for two of the pods, but the other two can fly in an hour, so we'll have to leave behind ten people, not including the two pilots. I will need the two linguists, at least one physicist, and one engineer. That means –"

"What? But . . . wait a moment!" Makis said, confused.

"We already know the way to the underground city, Makis, otherwise we would not have come this far already. Answering your question was an interesting diversion, but we won't be requiring you to fulfill your promise."

"But I –"

"Unless, of course, you needed to go with us for some reason, and you were simply trying to make it seem like a favor."

If he had been as human as he looked, the mage would have bit his lip. They all waited for his explanation, staring intently for signs of deception.

"The . . . the gateway is not working as it is supposed to," he admitted, air of superiority evaporated. "I was hoping to find a book in the Atlantii library that would give a hint about the problem. Unfortunately, the locals have certain superstitions, and there's an entire city of them in the shadow of the mountain under which the library lies.

They think that a magic user's only reason to seek the underground city is to increase his own power, but they have no appreciation for my gateway and the power it has. As long as it remains unstable, they are all in danger. They have magicians of their own, though none with meaningful power individually, and they take great pleasure in banding together to prevent me from passing through to the mountain. They control all its entrances. Perhaps if I am helping you, they will not be as suspicious. You will have to convince them to let your own mage pass anyway, so one more should not be a problem. And it is for a good cause."

"You haven't done anything to anger these people or make them suspicious of you?"

"No more suspicious than they would be of your own mage. Superstitions and jealousy are a bad combination."

"But perhaps convincing them to let one through will be easier than convincing them about two."

"Commander," Tylan stepped in, with severe concern printed on every inch of his face, "a gateway between worlds . . . it violates physics to such an extent . . . the magic needed could rip a hole in the universe if not channeled properly. If it is not . . . working correctly –"

Once again put back into his normal spirit by Tylan's reaction, Makis said, "Actually, it is a hole in the universe that is being channeled. And yes, if problems with it continue, there is no telling what would happen. A galactic-sized black hole, for instance. Or maybe the end of time itself. I hate to be over dramatic, but there you are."

A tunnel between worlds. Emily had trouble believing what an uncanny coincidence this was. Could a gate like that negate the need for a hyperspace drive entirely? It depended on how big the gate was and how accurate. As usual, it was a case of magic cheating, and there was no telling whether it was reliable or not. She preferred the hyperspace drive, and would gladly leave this hazardous artifact that damaged one of their pods to Makis.

As far as Raiz was concerned, though, it was too good an opportunity to pass up. "Makis, do you have an apprentice? You said the secrets of the gate were passed down from master to apprentice, right?"

"Yes, they are, and no, I do not. But if you think I will take one of you scruffy Earthers –"

"Now, now, Makis, think of your position. You need our help. We would like something in return. It's not unreasonable, surely. If this is an Atlantii gate, then our people have as much claim to it as you do. Besides, if the local people are as restrictive about magic as you claim, I would guess that it must be difficult to find a young person willing to follow in your footsteps."

"There's always one . . . but you're right. Very well, if you help me, I will consider an Earthling for my apprentice. Consider, mind you. You will have a better chance if you give me a choice of candidates. I refuse to take on some politician's son, or anyone otherwise unworthy."

"Done," Raiz said, satisfied. "Let's get on with it, then."

If she tried to, Emily could feel the tendrils of magic from each of the two mages clashing against one another. Each one was sending out magic with their own particular . . . smell attached. Smell was the only sense that really worked for the analogy, but it was still far from accurate. She could tell which magic was coming from Tylan, and which was coming from Makis. She didn't try for long, though, feeling awkward about it, as if she was really trying to smell out a distinction between body odors. A part of her was fascinated by it, though, so she opened her mind up to it whenever she became bored.

There was also the substantially different clash going on between Raiz and West. Unlike the one between the mages, this one was overt and completely one-sided. It was all about West's distrust of Raiz. Emily was just beginning to appreciate the fact that the former was a creature of instinct, while the latter was one of pure logic. They might both end up in the same place, but only one of them had calculated his way there. She didn't like the cold calculating types, either, so she appreciated West's apprehension. But Raiz was a warm calculator, and his nature somewhat confused the issue. He actually cared about what he was doing, and the people he worked for, so there was no sense that he had a mechanistic view of the universe. He also projected an image of spontaneity, even though he had proved himself fond of meticulous planning.

Emily found the prospect of West insisting on a conflict with Raiz disquieting. She had no way to imagine what West was like when irrationally angry, but guessed that he was vicious. Not knowing what exactly might set him off made it even worse. She set the worry aside for now, but kept an eye on the human native, just in case.

It was ironic that they had crashed so close to their destination, but it did save them from thinking twice about leaving the functional pods behind and striking out on foot. If there had been more than a three-day walk ahead, going with two pods and leaving part of their group behind would have been unavoidable. Having an extra mage along also somewhat balanced the threat implied by the speedy travel of the armored man.

"Do not worry about that," Tylan said to Emily when she mentioned it. "I had a good look at this land while we were in the air, over our pilot's shoulder, and though I missed the magic of Makis' gateway, I did see the coast rise from beaches to cliff, and large barriers in our enemy's way. I am sure that, whatever magic our enemy has, they either had to slow their avatar to a normal walk, or they lost control over it because they were unable to maneuver it quickly enough."

"Are you sure?" Emily asked, doubting their luck.

"I am certain."

And that was enough really. Tylan wasn't the type to be confident without good reason. Lacking a swift means of travel made her acutely aware of the advantage they had while using their technology, and she wanted every reassurance she could get. Otherwise, to abandon that advantage just so they could have some so-called specialists along didn't seem worth it.

She looked at the scientists and scholars with a skeptical eye. They tended to huddle together in a mini mobile ivory tower. On the way to the town around Raljar Canti, the specialists also tended to slow their progress down, getting tired easily and utterly failing to absorb the urgency of the situation. West's reaction to them was interesting to watch. If they complained of weariness in earnest, he was sympathetic to them, as he would be to Jaik. He seemed to recognize that they were useful and interesting people, and often led Jaik and Ethan close to the academics to overhear their theories about this world. He understood few of the words, but that was all right, because Ethan was interested as well, and could explain some of the jargon used.

Fond as West was of hearing the ideas, and respectful as he was of the scholars, he had a marked distaste of the ones who complained about the exertion and tried less than their best on the hike through relatively flat fields and occasional groves of trees. Whatever rough terrain Tylan had seen on the way, the pods had carried them well past it, and this was the smoothest walking they had come across on this planet for a while. On top of that, the specialists only carried what they needed to conduct their exploration of the city's contents – dictionaries for the linguists, basic meters and tests for the mechanics, and so on. All of that seemed light enough, just looking at it. The four guards lugged the rest, compensating for the frailty of their companions.

The worst grumbling came at night, when the ivory tower was treated to general rations, and rough bedrolls brought for them by the guards. Aside from Raiz, who seemed to sleep like a baby, and woke up before dawn the next day, no one got much sleep. Those not used to sleeping outdoors tossed and turned, and woke sore. Emily, Ethan, Jaik and West were all excited by the prospect of finally being so close to their goal, and their minds raced through the night. Tylan, Tayron, and Makis were all thinking about what powerful people like them thought about. With the two mages so obviously still awake, Emily had additional trouble closing her eyes, wondering if she, too, should be more careful about letting her guard down. There was also no telling how her dreams might act up with all the magic around.

For the first time in her life, she found herself outright afraid of knowing what lay ahead. Her concern bordered on panic, and she was resolute in avoiding a vision of the adventure's end. She already knew that the dream where they had all been standing, looking down at the city, could really happen and was not merely symbolic. That being true, it was all too likely that, from the screams she had dreamt, they would also be attacked by the Shadow Workers right at that moment. Should she tell Raiz? She was sure he would believe her, but would that really change events? So far, all of her dreams had been right, which suggested that there was nothing she could do to change the predestined course.

There was a slight kink in that dream, though – it had not included Makis. Now that she knew them, she recognized that the specialists and guards were the additional, so far unrecognized figures, in the vision. But Makis had definitely not been there. Possibly, the mage would be stopped by the locals from passing through to the mountain, and that was the reason, but what if he really did change the equation? This was about magic, after all, and wizardry had a way of altering reality in unpredictable ways. It was one of the reasons why she had not objected to having the perennially suspicious and untrustworthy Makis along, and maybe why Raiz had been so quick to accept him, as well. Tylan had said that Makis' gateway did not follow the rules of magic. Maybe something that went against the fabric of the universe was enough to change fate.

Maybe, but Emily didn't want to check by dreaming. As long as there was hope of a way out, the slightest possibility that her vision was no longer accurate because a variable had been added, she could keep going forward. This need to maintain momentum was familiar to her, and a throw back to her old vital spirit. She could not allow herself to be paralyzed by fear or uncertainty. One more time, she would show the determination that had convinced her grandfather that she would be able to take on the challenge of commanding a starship

Her stubbornness could get her killed, but if it had been just her, she would have gone on without a second thought. Whatever hesitation she had was due to her desire to keep the others safe. She knew that there was no way to convince Jaik and West to stay behind. They had nowhere to go back to, and were short the extra years it took before a person started worrying about danger or mortality. Like her, they would plunge in with conviction. Like so many young soldiers, she thought, her mind betraying her resolve.

Ethan, on the other hand, could probably be convinced to stay behind. Not because he was a coward – he was, but that wouldn't matter with her going ahead. If she asked him not to follow, and made a logical argument, he would probably listen to her. Without that kind of discussion between them, though, his attachment to her would induce him to follow along. He had so far, through countless trials and inconveniences. Unfailingly, even when he had known her idea was stupid, he had done what she asked him to. Not that she asked much. She had never asked why he listened to her. In the middle of the night, with her thoughts keeping her from sleeping, she decided it was about time she did.

Ethan was immediately to her right and, though technically asleep, he was tossing around so much in his bedroll that it was not possible to believe he was getting much rest out of it. Emily knew she would have woken him up even if he had been deep into sleep, but was glad the issue had not come up.

"Ethan," she whispered, nudging him, with an eye on the mages and Tayron, who were awake to hear this conversation. She didn't think they would be interested, so there was no need to be secretive. If West and Jaik had been awake, Ethan would be too reluctant to speak his mind.

He moaned and rolled over.

"Come on. I need to talk to you."

He turned to face her with squinting eyes barely open. "What?" he croaked, a bit too loud.

"Quiet down. Listen, why do you follow me? I mean everywhere. I totally like having you around and everything and you're like a solid rock I can depend on, but I don't get it. I guess it's 'cause I'd never follow anyone around the way you do."

Ethan propped himself up on his elbows, still bleary eyed but not eager to clear his vision, hoping that Emily would just let him fall back into his choppy slumber. "You ask me this now?"

"Well. When should I have asked you?"

"Maybe before we came down here."

"But . . . but it was all right, right? Bringing you down here, I mean."

"Yeah. Wouldn't have missed it. People dying everywhere. Max dying right in front of me. Having to lug heavy bags around all over the place. Do you know how many times I've thought about leaving my guitar behind?"

"You've gotten stronger, though," she said, realizing that she was totally derailed now, "and you've learned a new language. I mean, it's only been like a few weeks. That's incredible."

"But I'm totally useless here."

"No, you're not."

"Yes, I am," Ethan insisted, and sat up fully now, finally rubbing the fog out of his eyes and opening them fully to absorb the grays of the night. "Sorry, I guess . . . I'm just a bit cranky about being woken up."

"No. I think . . . I wouldn't have been able to do anything here without you. Back at the capital . . . when I thought I might have lost you . . . I was totally lost."

"Don't say stuff like that."

"But it's true."

"But the way you're saying it. What you mean isn't what I'm hearing."

"What do you mean?"

Ethan shook his head. "You wouldn't understand. If you could, you would have figured it out by now. I don't care, though. I don't need you to understand me."

"What if I want to?"

"You don't. And that's all right, because just being around you I've done more that I ever would have on my own. I would have ended up behind a desk somewhere, playing gigs with a crappy band on the weekends or something. Your world was always more exciting, and the only way I could have felt comfortable in it was because you were there."

"But the way you said it, about being here, made it sound like you're not comfortable."

"I am . . . I am as long as you're here, too."

"Well, that's how I feel about you."

"No, it isn't," Ethan said, frustrated. "You'd be all right just on your own, or with Kaz, Jaik, West, or anybody. Even Arisin Oris. As long as the person you're with isn't crazier than you are."

Emily had to smile at that. It was true. Ethan was, in a coarse way, a little piece of home for her, but if he suddenly decided to go for the quiet life, she would continue just fine without him. "Can't be crazier than me, huh? Not West, then."

Ethan cracked the slimmest of smiles. "Anyway, it's different for me, okay?"

Pausing for a second, Emily finally got to grips with what Ethan was saying. "You . . . you like me, don't you? You've had a crush on me all this time and you never told me?"

"Listen, we're just friends, all right? It's . . . it's all right if we're just friends."

"You idiot, why didn't you say something? Or do something?

You've had girlfriends before. I know you're not shy about that."

"Well, maybe. It was a long time ago, when I met you. I didn't know what I wanted, and I didn't want to risk it. You...you never really stick with your boyfriends very long, do you?"

She had to give him that. If someone really wanted to hang with her for a decent stretch of time, being her boyfriend was not the way. "But I don't want you to keep –"

"I'm fine, all right? After a while, I found other reasons to stick by you. Like I said, I would never have done all these things otherwise. That's made it worth it."

"Listen, I don't think this is going to turn out well. I think maybe the enemy mages are going to surprise us in the underground city. If you're just coming because of me –"

"I'm not just coming because of you. I want to know what's down there. Let's just stop talking about it, all right?" Ethan's face was a subtle mixture of anguish and relief, as if he was devastated by the need to admit his feelings for her and afraid of how she would look at him now that she knew, but relieved to finally have it out in the open. Without waiting for her to respond, he tucked back in and turned away from her.

Emily wasn't really stunned by the admission. She had detected some hints of interest from Ethan, and read into his near-constant presence in her life, but the continuing intensity of his feelings after so long was a bit of a shock, especially since he had seemed to have solid relationships with at least two girls while he had known her. Maybe it was because of the stress, being on this planet. She was his only existing link to his past and the only consistent part of his life, so that perhaps magnified his attachment to her while they were here.

At least she had given him an opening – an option to stay behind as they went into danger. She had never done it before, always expecting him to take the harder road with her. This time was different.

The next morning, even Raiz was eager to bring the journey to a close, losing patience with his specialists for holding them up. When one of the linguists asked if it would be possible to stop and rest only an hour's walk from the start, the commander looked at the man dryly and, though he had a smile on his face, something in his eyes made the man abandon his plea and trudge on.

They made good time thanks to the pure flat terrain touched neither by seismic forces nor by creative erosion. Emily guessed that they covered something like thirty miles, judging only by the pace they kept up and the time they spent traveling. Another way to measure the distance covered was to count how often Makis tried to start a conversation with Tylan, only to have his opener squashed by a brick-wall answer. It happened every four miles. Tylan, for reasons of his own, staunchly opposed interaction with the other mage, seeing him as the caretaker of a mistake, and as much a violator of the universal fabric as the mancers were. Makis just wanted to impress Tylan, and to elicit the dumbfounded awe that he thrived upon. Tylan was starving him.

"I have seen the future, you know," Makis said at one point. "The gateway can open into other times as well. It is unfortunate that it is malfunctioning or we could have walked right into the Atlantian city at any time you chose. We could even have seen it in its heyday."

"Which is all completely unacceptable according to the laws of magic," Tylan insisted. "And I would prefer not to hear more about it. As it so happens, we already have someone in this party who can see into the future, so your gateway is superfluous."

For a moment, Emily's breath caught in her throat, fearing that Tylan had just outed her, but Makis didn't even turn around to look at her. Hearing Tylan's statement, everyone who wasn't already aware of her abilities looked at him in surprise. They thought he was speaking about himself, so she was still safe for now. For all she knew, he was referring to himself. If the hill people could have been so good at divination without having much magic, he could be even better. She doubted it, though. Somehow, she felt she would be able to tell.

If anything, Tylan's misdirecting comments hinted that he was curious about her ability, and what she saw in their future. She had no intention of telling him. Having done some more thinking, her reasoning was now marginally clearer. If she decided to tell them, and they chose not to continue, and they were saved by that decision, then that meant her visions were not inevitable. Therefore, other factors could change the result as well. It was a paradox . . . or was it a catch-22? Anyway, the ultimate conclusion was that telling them was completely useless.

Was Tylan suggesting something different? It was easy to read too much into his words and expressions, her guilty conscience gave her an additional dose of anxiety that complicated her interpretations. Why did she feel guilty, though? She knew. Not knowing, there was no way for her to feel guilty about it. Ultimately, the key was the realization that the others had a right to think through the decision for themselves. By denying them the information which could help them better make their choices, she was limiting their freedom, and in her mind, that was the worst thing one person could do against another.

So, that night, the last before they would reach the foot of the mountain and, if the locals permitted, begin their descent into its depths, she told the others what she knew. It wasn't much, and took all of two or three minutes, hesitations included. The tensest point was right at the beginning, when she had to describe her ability. Keeping their opinions to themselves until hearing everything she had to say, their reactions were predictably mixed. When Tayron demanded to know why she had kept it from them, suspecting that this was how his plans had been circumvented, she was forced to admit to her distrust of him and Oris. She then proceeded to explain her thoughts leading up to the conclusion that they should be told about her dreams. Her reasoning, now that she had to explain it, sounded poor, but Tayron's attack was blunted by her straightforward account. At least it showed that she had thought it over. As she had hoped, Tylan came to her defense, saying something vague about the burdens of such an ability, especially since no one can be sure whether changing the expected future is possible.

Of all the people around the fire, Emily was most nervous about revealing her ability to Makis, who was still an unknown quantity. He enjoyed manipulating people primarily for his own amusement, especially intelligent men like Tylan, and became dangerously petulant when his attempts did not have the desired effect, as with Raiz. The smile on his face when she shared her secret sent shivers down her spine. She was now a target of interest.

No one asked her to look into the future that night, to see if things had changed. They all recognized the futility of it, since the gamble had already been made, and trying to leave without the prize would, overnight, turn a group of genocidal mages into the second greatest force in the galaxy, next to the Eldrandii. Even if the Shadow Workers didn't build hyperspace ships, they could easily amass a fortune and an army by offering the secret to every species in communication range, mining all they could out of it. The Eldrandii would not be able to stop them, since no weapon on board their ships had a chance of destroying an underground city. That had been the entire point of the Atlantian refuge ships in the first place – to protect their inhabitants from any and all threats. On top of that, Eldrandii ground troops were so rarely used that they would be massacred in front of the Atlantian stronghold. Eldrandii mages had no destructive magic to speak of, so no luck there either. Thinking about it that way, the Shadow Workers could easily become, outright, the greatest force in the galaxy.

Airing all the angles out, they knew better than to ask her to dream again. No one slept soundly that night. Not seeing any point in prolonging a fruitless night, they set out hours before dawn. They made slower progress than they would have with a full and solid night's sleep, but none of them complained.

Luckily, it seemed as if Raiz had prepared his team of specialists for the worst in terms of peril, because they made no complaints about the danger. To a person, they might be too old or too lazy for hard traveling, but they were essentially brave. Considering that they entered this with full awareness, Emily considered them a notch more courageous than she was, since she had practically stumbled into it and at no time felt brave. It was a hard thing to admit to herself, but in terms of the thin line between courage and stupidity, she had never been on the virtuous side. Looking back on her high school years, everything she dared to do was so . . . stupid. She had thought so highly of her antics then, because they won her approval from her peers, but not one thing could really qualify as courageous. Only someone intelligently walking into a horrible situation to achieve something concrete was commendable.

That view gave her a different read on Raiz, who was unquestionably a sharp thinker, yet stepped into this personally, taking control of the situation here in Selparis. Aside from preventing potential strife between her and Wilson, he must have had other reasons for assuming direct command. Was it some sort of plan he had in mind – perhaps one that would require the kind of timing that only he, in person, could provide? So distant from his regular command, he never wasted a second during their rests in between the long marches. She had no idea what he was working on, but he was persistent at it, pulling out his laptop and accessing its data with percussive ferocity while simultaneously holding up his end of any conversation. It was enough to put anyone in awe, though West, who spent much of his time looking over Raiz's shoulder, preferred to be suspicious. She suspected West had never, until now, been truly humbled by anything or anyone in his life.

Raiz also brought hope to their cause. Indeed, it was hard to imagine losing all optimism in the unflappable commander's presence. When their pods had crash-landed and their one advantage was eliminated, they retained confidence that they would reach their destination. Could she have instilled the same confidence in their place? Confronted by a mysterious mage of unknown power, Raiz bested him with words – a feat Emily knew with certainty that she could not match. In fact, only when Emily herself told the others about her vision did a real chill set in, leaving Raiz unable to bounce them back to an upbeat orientation. He tried to point out alternative interpretations of the final scream in her vision, but knew that to emphasize it too much would only make matters worse. Despite the failed effort, he continued to be his normal self, and as buoyant as ever, with no reason to be otherwise. He could succeed against many obstacles, but not the future itself.

His attitude did give Emily something new to think about – the nature of heroism. She had never taken heroics seriously, nor identified anyone as her hero, but only because the people normally identified as suitable targets of hero worship were never her type. Military heroes were right out. Until now, she had never been able to articulate why, except that she didn't like anyone willing to take orders. Political leaders were either sleazes or otherwise so self-righteous or identified with a particular cause that she found them unpalatable. Athletes never impressed her. As far as musicians and artists were concerned, she appreciated their work, but could not hope to emulate them, since she was not particularly creative, never sensing the need to put her thoughts into words, pictures, or music.

She supposed Raiz was a politician, but one of them would never do what he was doing. He was something else. Instead of Raiz's actual ability, which she could not match, she aspired to his refreshing way of walking through life, which not only exhibited confidence, but spread it to others as well. In her best moments, she could be like that as well. Raiz got things done right with minimal obvious effort and enjoyed himself in the process. Maybe she lacked his charm, charisma, or intelligence, but she saw that those were only the fancy architecture on a building with firmer foundations in planning, hard work, and information gathering – foundations anyone could duplicate.

For the remainder of the journey, she appreciated his unique brand of understated heroism, which only someone who had rejected the other sorts could recognize.

12
Under the Lonely Mountain

Before long, they were within sight of the city and the mountain concealing its predecessor. It was immediately apparent why it would be necessary to get the permission of the citizenry before they could pass through to the mountain. A thirty-foot high wall ringed the lonely peak, and the city was arrayed around that wall, on its outside, as if built specifically to bar their way.

"My, my," Raiz said as he surveyed the scene from a low hill, shielding his eyes from the sun, "Our Atlantii ancestors were certainly focused, weren't they? A very utilitarian people, judging from this. I guess there's no doubt these people know there's something important in that mountain. Lucky for us that they haven't been eager to pry into it or share it with others, or it would have been taken by one of the space powers before we had even reached the moon."

Ethan was taken aback, coming to a further conclusion. "But then . . . Lord Tayron, how did your explorers know to come all this way, anyway? From the looks of it, only the people who already knew what they would find would be allowed in past the city."

Tayron smiled. "There, we were in luck. Our expedition's leader was a clever and dangerous man. He learned quickly from everyone he met, read their histories, took them seriously, and found out what he needed to know. I do not know how he judged where to look, but it was from details in sources he had studied from. When he saw what you are now seeing, he knew he had found what he was looking for. He deduced that there was something hidden in that mountain and, based on that, it was not hard to convince people he knew what it was already, having read Selian histories. After they checked him for magic, he was through."

"I can't imagine how –"

"Discovering long buried secrets by interpreting local stories was his specialty. If he had not been amazing at it, he would not have been given such a vital position. It is a shame he is also a restless man, and immediately joined another exploration team after returning to Atparis, otherwise it would have been valuable to have him here with us."

Ethan nodded, appreciating the kind of mind that the expedition leader must have had. On the journey down to the city, he also reluctantly brought up the point that they might encounter some trouble due to the magical members of their team, and the possibility that the rest would have to leave the magic users behind in order to pass through. The physical nature of the city itself, and the almost certain fact that the only entrances into Raljar Canti were located there, gave them little hope of circumventing whatever rules the people of the city had in place. Ethan's hesitation was mainly due to Emily's inclusion on the list, unless her magic was so weak that no one would notice. He knew that she would resist anyone keeping her, after traveling all this way, from doing what she had come here to do. At the same time, he felt it his responsibility, as the one closest to her, to prepare her for that potential disappointment.

Raiz had the same sense, and artfully dodged Emily's status when he said, "I'm afraid Tylan and Makis will have to remain in the city if the people insist –"

Makis flushed with indignation. "The whole reason why I came with you –"

"If, despite our reasoning, the people still object to magic users passing through, I can't see how we have any other choice. Surely you must have realized that, Makis. Whatever books you need, if you tell us what to look for, we'll try to find them for you."

"I do not know what they might be called," Makis whined. "That is why I must go with you. For all I know, the study of technology behind such a gateway could have its own name and terms, long lost to time. I and my predecessors have come up with our own words to deal with phenomena, but I do not even know if the ancients called it a gateway, or a word your translators would not recognize."

"If you show me an option, Makis, I'll be glad to hear it," Raiz said, with a slight edge in his voice to indicate that he really had thought it over at length, and despite the effort, found no viable alternative.

Makis got the hint, as did Emily. She had, of course, wondered about whether she would be able to get through, but had concluded that either her magic was so minimal that she could easily make the case, or Raiz would talk his way around the issue. She had hoped a third option would be unnecessary, but now that Raiz was signaling he wanted one, her mind was aflame with doubts. He was clearly most concerned about her status, since leaving Makis and Tylan behind, though a diminishment of their ability to understand some of what they might find underground, would be a surmountable obstacle in terms of discovering the secret of hyperspace. So would failing to take her in, but Raiz was keenly aware that he owed her a great deal for taking an immense risk and getting them this far. He wanted to repay her by, at minimum, guaranteeing her most of the fame that would come with the discovery, but that would be difficult if not impossible if she never managed to see Raljar Canti for herself.

West's sighting of a blue flying creature at the edge of his visual range shattered her thoughts. Even though Selparis' skies were full of birds and wild bierka, some of which were easily the size of an Eldrandii and even larger, he insisted that it was Oris making a beeline for the city. None of the others could see it, but doubting West's senses was out of the question. Since Oris would beat them to the city, and could take possession of the secret if it existed in only one volume, they faced an added dimension of difficulty beyond their already copious concerns.

"What are the chances that Oris knows the Atlantian language well enough to figure out which book has the secret?" Emily asked, nervously staring at the sky between the city and the spot West had pointed to.

"If she was sent for this purpose by her government, it is almost certain that she will know translations for essential terms in a dozen languages," said Tayron, knowing he would have provided his explorers the same preparation, had he been able.

"Agreed," Raiz confirmed, no happier at the thought of Oris beating them to the destination than Tayron was, "our linguists used records that the Eldrandii gave us to learn the Atlantian language. I'd even go so far as to think Oris, being a specialist in Asparian, Eldrandii, and Earth medicine, probably knows the most important languages from all three worlds."

"She didn't seem to know Asparian very well," Ethan pointed out.

"Just because she chose to use a translator doesn't mean she didn't know the language," said Kaz, knowing similar tricks were played frequently on Newport Station. "But I have a question – if there are books on the hyperspace drive in the Atlantian Library, shouldn't there be more than one? Any library on Earth would have dozens, maybe hundreds, of books on rockets and engines, so I can't see why we're thinking there's only one book about the hyperspace drive. And if there're entire shelves of books about it, then Oris can't carry them all out on her own."

Raiz sighed. "I think you have missed the point. To answer your question, though, I'm hoping there are plenty of books, but of course, we can't be sure. It's such a closely guarded secret now, there's no reason to believe it wasn't thousands of years ago, so maybe they only allowed one copy, and kept it behind a secure glass case. But times could also have been very different then. In such a long time, any information once commonly known could become obscure, especially if one group or another had a reason to make it that way. My biggest worry is that Oris will get it into her head to destroy the books rather than to steal them. It would not take much to burn them or melt them."

Kaz looked grim, hopes dashed.

"Don't worry, though," said Raiz, face now lit in his usual upbeat optimism, "I suspect that she will meet some resistance in the city. These are traditionalists, and Oris will either be something new to them, or something they know all too well. Either way, I think she will have to be patient while they decide whether to let her in, and that will give us time to catch up to her." The commander seemed so definite about this, that none of them thought to say anything further about Oris.

The city itself was, in form, much like what the human travelers were familiar with, barring the fact that it encircled the mountain so precisely. There was no continuous roof, as they had frequently seen in Tayron's empire, nor was it an anthill town like those of the Selian coast. Rather, the city surrounding Raljar Canti had regular buildings separated by streets of narrow width, though how they had known to build it that way, Emily had no idea. Nothing on this planet had been so straightforwardly Earthlike, and the sudden revelation of such a standard city was a bit jarring to her.

Tight streets were only wide enough for four or five people to walk abreast, and certainly not enough for vehicles to travel through. Since the builders of the city would have expected few outside visitors, Emily had anticipated the lack of vehicular accommodations, until Jaik reminded her that a city of this size had to expect regular visitors – farmers on market days. As long as people in the city wanted to eat, it was odd that they had made passage through the city so difficult.

Dismayed by how obsessed these Atlantii must have been, Kaz came up with the obvious answer immediately. "It's all for defense. The narrow streets would destroy any ground army that wanted to attack here. You couldn't even get a tank into the city. If there had been other hills around Raljar Canti, I bet they would have turned them into massive bomb shelters."

"Why didn't they build some sort of outer wall, then?" Ethan asked.

"They're not defending the city itself. They're defending the mountain, so the wall is around that."

"But if the only entrances into the mountain are in the city . . . ," started Ethan, but knew no one had an answer to his question, so concluded the thought by saying, "weird."

Once in view, they saw that the citizens themselves looked exactly like the Selians, and just as human. Their clothing, however, wasn't made to blend in with a hillside or, indeed, anything. A distinctly bohemian style marked their garb, which was somewhat patchwork, and heavily dyed. The layers of cloths used were profuse yet gauzy. If their mode of dress reminded Emily of hippies, their demeanor certainly shocked her out of it. She had never seen such despairing faces in her life, and the awe with which they stared at her gave the strong impression that their clothes were patchy by necessity, not out of choice. Not at all happy with their own quality of life, the locals expressed muted enthusiasm at the sight of obviously wealthy visitors. Whatever their ancestors might have believed, or built this city for, the current residents were down to earth and eager to find some way to escape their deprivation. There was no contempt or jealousy in them at all, but a meticulously fostered hope hidden beneath the pain of their tortured reality lest it was destroyed when exposed to the open air. Maybe these were the slum dwellers, and this first impression of the city was inaccurate, but even if the heart of the city contained people living comfortable and normal lives, the desperate denizens living on its fringes already scarred her image of it.

Emily was aware that pointing out how horrible life in the city seemed, based on the complex expressions of the locals, could affect the reception they would get from the city leaders if she was overheard. She kept her mouth shut tight, though she was eager to voice her consternation. Being aware that the impression she made was vital to success, and adjusting accordingly, was new for Emily, but she felt the adding of basic social caution to her range of action was long overdue. It would be better if, like Raiz, her natural behavior was already suited to charming people on first encounters however, since she had a jagged personality, settling for a less authentic approach was the best she could do. She tried to smile the way Raiz was doing as they walked beside each other, but felt her face contort into something mangled between anxiety and sneering disdain, and chose a passive expression instead.

For obvious reasons, the city lacked a true center, but the path they entered the urban area on curved into one of the city's many plazas – a simple circular market and fountain affair that recalled into Jaik's mind his old town. Perhaps it was purely by chance that some of the city's mages met them there, but if Kaz's theory that everything about the city focused on defense was correct, then this was a case of forethought. All paths in the city lead to a plaza, and each plaza was properly defended.

"I'm willing to bet that the entrance to the Underground City is somewhere near this plaza," Kaz whispered to Emily as three mages approached them menacingly while three others held back a safe distance away.

"So?"

"And the wall around the mountain is just a rouse to make people think that there's a way into the underground city on the mountain itself. Maybe they built it before they buried the entrances and built tunnels to them."

"Oh." The thought tickled Emily. If Oris tried to circumvent the city by passing directly over the wall, she would search in vain for the way in. Raiz must have realized this when he expressed confidence that Oris would find a roadblock, and Emily wondered whether there was anything Raiz had not already figured out, right up to their return to Newport Station. Rather than see it as an example of Raiz's genius, she considered the inability to examine different contingencies before acting to be her primary failing. When asleep, she could see the future, but when awake, she was running blind.

Before she managed another thought, the mage at the center of the three confronting them spoke. "You cannot pass any further. You have magic about you," he said in a deep, rumbling voice that could have come from the earth itself. Emily mused that he must practice at it, or at least had to have subsisted on a steady diet of dirt as some sort of penance. His language was close enough to pure Atlantian for the translator to deliver the English rendition smoothly, and with minimal delay for grammar.

As usual, the mages were dressed in a way that contrasted themselves from others in the city, except that this time it was by wearing solid black trousers and shirts. Theirs was a style after her own heart, but it was apparent that it simultaneously marked them as wealthy enough to afford new clothes, but also shunned from regular society because of the role magic played in the fall of Atlantis. If it had not been for the clothing, only magic users would have recognized them for what they were, so they were made to wear their particular clothing as a stigmatizing mark anyone could identify, but paid well in compensation for their voluntary subjugation to this rule.

Before Raiz could speak, Tayron stepped forward and, translator borrowed from one of the specialists in place, said, "I am Chancellor Tayron from Atparis, representative of that land's emperor. You have received my explorers. Please understand that these mages are only here for my protection."

"You lie! This one is known to us," the mage pointed at Makis. "We can taste the energy of the Gateway from him. He is a Makis, and not wanted among us. As for the other, it has been our tradition since time immemorial that users of magic must not be allowed to pass into the Forbidden City. If to enter the city is your goal, as we are sure it is, then your mage must be left behind. The Makis must leave our city entirely." Emily noticed that her magic had not triggered comment and let out a breath of relief, but also felt a tinge of resentment at the casual dismissal.

"Now, come on," Makis said with a bad attempt at a winning personality, after having mumbled audibly "I could have been in the Forbidden City in a blink if the Gate was stable," while the mage had been speaking. He scrupulously avoided eye contact with his companions, who uniformly felt that he should have mentioned something to them about how hated he was. "You don't think I would come all this way for nothing. The Gateway is acting erratically, and I require the knowledge of the ancients to restore it to equilibrium. Surely you can see how that would be to your benefit as much as mine."

"No, indeed, we do not. We see that the deliberate intent of our tradition was to eventually bring about the collapse of your gate."

"But it could rip a hole in the universe that could destroy us all," said Makis, not without a bit of pride in being the sole protector of an object capable of such ultimate carnage.

"Or the magic that sustains it will fade and the gate will disappear from our world. The wound in the fabric will heal, and all will be right again."

"And you would take the chance that your picture is more correct than mine, though I have knowledge about the Gateway that you do not?"

"Admit it, Makis, you are interested in keeping the gate open, regardless of the cost. If it came down to a choice between the definite safety of this world and the final closure of your toy, can you honestly say that you would not risk our lives, unable to bring about its end? None of your kind has been able to promise us this before, at least not in honesty."

Makis thought it over, but with an awareness that he had to give the answers to get him through, regardless of how distasteful the promise was. "Yes, I will seal the gate if there is any question of safety. I give you my word."

"And, of course, we require more than that. We will come with you to the Gateway and ensure you speak the truth about it, and your actions."

Not at all surprised, and having prepared for the intervention of the local mages a long time ago, Makis took the caveat in stride and said, "I am shocked that you do not want to go down into the Forbidden City to make certain I do not take some extra books."

That brought a spontaneous raucous hissing from the six mages, and some of the regular residents gathered in the plaza. The taboo against entering the Forbidden City was so strong that the locals reacted with instinctive revulsion to the idea that they would ever break it, but there was something else there – a gap in their armor. Ever since Tayron's men had gone in and come out unscathed, a steady undercurrent of desire and curiosity had grown among the people. It was one thing to maintain the tradition in the belief that it would be fatal to break it, and quite another to persist when others had seen the wonders of the underground city without so much as a scar. Makis had wanted to needle the locals a bit, but in doing so revealed the complexity of their feelings about their core belief.

The deep bass of the mage's voice reinforced the sentiments of the crowd. "We have not decided whether to allow you through yet, Makis, so do not overreach. This decision must be made in the presence of the full council, and the non-magical authorities. We do not sweep aside generations of unwritten law on a whim. Our discussion so far has merely established the parameters within which the further negotiation will take place."

At these words, Raiz finally chose to step in, having made the best possible use of Tayron's willingness to take the lead. "With all due respect, we are pressed for time. We have been pursued by a group of perhaps a hundred mages who leave only destruction in their wake and seek the knowledge hidden here. Our goal is to reach the essential secret before they do and, perhaps by bringing it to where it can be defended, we can divert any ruin they intend to bring to you." Emily was surprised, because this qualified as an obnoxious distortion for the normally straight-shooting Raiz. Regardless of whether every single reference to the hyperspace drive in the underground city was brought to Newport Station, the residents of the surface city would likely face utter ruin at the hands of the Shadow Workers, simply out of spite.

Unfazed, the mage said in his profound and unshakable tone, "the secrets are protected."

"I think that this group of mages may be beyond your capabilities, and they would not hesitate from destroying your people whether you give way to them or not."

"The secrets are protected," was the immediate reply. The statement was patently a matter of religious faith among these people.

Raiz grew impatient with the mindlessness of the reply, and said sharply, "in any case, we would rather not be here when the terror rains down on you, your city is leveled to the ground, and thousands die."

The piercing words struck home, reminding everyone that while long buried secrets might be safe, the city leaders still had to take care for the exposed population, which would face the wrath of a frustrated foe. With the potential pain and suffering of the people imminent, this was the wrong time to trumpet traditions, good and reasonable though they might be. Even the austere mages were shamefaced, caught emphasizing obscure taboos and customs over the good of their fellow citizens. Emily appreciated their willingness to listen to logic; there were many leaders on Earth who would stick to their peculiar ideas, and insist others do so as well, regardless of whether those ideas would do more harm than good. Fortunately, these people had their priorities straight, though there was evidence that their ancestors and elders had been less flexible.

"And you are certain of this threat?" The deep, resonant tones of the mage were now less firm, though still heavy with gravity.

"Very," Tayron offered convincingly, trying to regain some face after the revealing of his initial deception.

Wanting to drive home his understanding and interpretation, Raiz continued, "If the ancients wanted you to keep magic users out of the underground city, then I believe they had our enemies, our mutual enemies, in mind. You should be on your guard against people who would use magic for evil purposes or the acquisition of further power, those who would take by force what they have no claim to by right. Did you build your walls and stand ready to defend against us, who ask for passage humbly, wanting to preserve peace in the face of horrific odds?"

Forced to ground by Raiz's explanation, the mage finally asked the basic questions which, until now, his official concerns preempted. "You are not of this world?"

"Lord Tayron here, your Makis, and the two young men there are . . . of this world. The rest of us are from Earth, which was the world that was once called –"

"Atlantis. You are from Atlantis."

"Yes," said Raiz, throwing a brief grin back to Emily, amused by the idea that they were now the Atlantii, "I'm glad we're finally getting to this. And we know what we seek in the Forbidden City. There is knowledge that has been lost to us that we must now secure before our enemies get their hands on it."

"Your enemies . . . are not from Atlantis."

"No. They are from Asparis. Maybe you've heard of that world, too? We're all sort of related."

The mage nodded gravely. "The world of magic that the people of Atlantis originally evolved on."

"Well . . . ," Raiz said evasively, "some people on my world might take issue with that idea."

"Then you are here to fulfill the prophecy."

That forced Raiz to pause from his otherwise relentless flow. Assuming this was the same one, Emily had heard of the prophecy from the Selians, but had missed mentioning it to Raiz. She was interested to see how he dealt with a twist he was clearly unprepared for.

A millimeter of upturn in his lip revealed his distaste for the idea as he said, "what prophecy?" in a noncommittal monotone, aware that simply asking the question might undermine his chances to get through to Raljar Canti with minimal hassle. He had a good idea of what the prophecy might be, and certainly what he would want it to be, but guessing incorrectly might be even more detrimental than simply asking for clarification.

The mage cleared his throat and intoned his words gravely and reverentially enough to make gods blush. "That someday, those who survived the . . . unexistence of Atlantis . . . would rebuild and lead their brethren back to the stars."

"Oh, that prophecy," said Raiz, relieved that it was, in fact, the one he had hoped for. "I don't know much about rebuilding – I don't think we've got Earth up to Atlantian standards yet, not if they could build entire cities underground – but as far as getting you back into space is concerned, that is definitely in the cards. The information we look for in the underground city will help us."

"You know how the ancient technology works?"

"What we know brought us here, and I'm sure that's enough to satisfy you. What we don't know, we'll be able to figure out in the ancient library. We are a bridge to your past, friend, and can not only help explain it all, but also give you the resources to make use of the knowledge. Earth, Atlantis, is a rich world in a wealthy star system, and we would be eager to help our long lost brothers. I know that Captain Pierce here would be thrilled to trade with you, and that just a few of your books – not the ones underground, mind you, but the ones that contain the story of experience on this world – will be considered valuable enough on Earth to compensate her for her trouble. So, not only will we be able to give you what you need, but we will be equal trading partners."

The mages and everyone else gathered in the place were elated at his words, as if at the coming of a savior. Certainly, Raiz had a great deal of natural charm and charisma, but the effect of his words went far beyond the power his talents could have imbued them with. All question of barring the way of the visitors forgotten, there was a rush to get them before the city administrators so that a final judgment could be rendered. The mages led the visitors in a tight procession down the narrow lanes, across two plazas and finally stopping near another, in every important aspect identical to the first, except people packed this one. The crowd spilled into the connecting streets, even though from that distance people were unable to hear the proceedings, and relied on word from others closer to the events transpiring.

To get through, the mages escorting them had no choice but to use their magic, though they looked intensely unhappy about the necessity, and they built a ramp and walkway over the heads of the crowd. Emily was awed by this demonstration of magic, which she had actually experienced fairly little of in her life, and thankful that the walkway included side railings, because walking twelve feet above ground on a structure created in such a dubious way was unbalancing. Even though she had eagerly jumped down from greater heights than this, landing unfailingly on her feet, this magical construct with no tangible support unnerved her. Not understanding why she was afraid, she nevertheless gripped the handrails as if they somehow gave more support to the illusion.

As they descended into the center of the gathering, they saw that Oris was already there, pleading with the local authorities to let her into Raljar Canti, having discovered no other way in. The dozen leaders were easily recognizable, crowned in simple circlets studded with uniform stones of a specific color, though, except the two chief mages who were in black, they wore the bohemian stitched cloths like the other residents.

Oris was in full fury, with wings spread and her back to the newcomers. "Erem Kantor, I see no reason why you should bar my way."

"And I can see no reason why we should let you pass," a bear of a man replied, easily a head taller than all except Oris herself.

"You have allowed explorers sent by Lord Tayron to enter."

"They approached us in the correct manner, and their mission was sensible to us. Your manner is imperious, and you give no adequate reasons why you should pass. The explorers proved themselves to us and were, after they returned from out of the Forbidden City, gracious enough to share with us what they saw, of which our only accounts are many hundreds of years old."

Oris flapped her wings once, creating a stiff wind that forced some to take a step back, and others to clutch their headdresses, which threatened to fly off in the gust. "I have told you, there are others coming to seek the secrets you protect, and they will steal the most valuable of them from you for their own greedy purposes. My people already know these secrets, and want to help you safeguard them."

"That is not acceptable," Erem Kantor growled. "The secrets are protected. Your help is unnecessary, though we thank you for your concern."

"But –"

"Your people, known by many names to us, including that of Eldgil, have a mixed reputation among us. In any case, the ancients were clear concerning our place, and who would . . . safeguard the secrets. It is not you."

"That's right!" Tayron said, stepping forward. Oris froze for a blink, and then turned murderously toward him. The two of them had, by degrees, become each other's nemesis, and the loathing they had for each other was beyond estimate. "This Eldgil spoke truly when she said her people already know all knowledge your ancients had, but . . . misrepresented her purpose. She wishes to deny that same knowledge to other peoples, so hers can maintain a monopoly on it." Emily marveled both at how willing Tayron was to stick his nose into things, and how patient Raiz was, to let him have his say instead of demanding the translator back to effectively deny the chancellor a voice. Of course, nothing Tayron had said so far ended up damaging their efforts, so there was no reason to stifle him, but Raiz could have chosen to exercise logical caution instead of giving the Asparii lord a free rein.

Kantor roared, "Who are you? How is it that with magic users as companions you have been brought here rather than immediately expelled from this city?"

"I am Chancellor Tayron of Atparis, imperial advisor. I sent explorers to your land, those same explorers you have just spoken of."

Kantor remained standing in an aggressive stance, waiting for the answer to his second question. Tayron had hoped to gain ground by relying on the footholds established by his men, but was now forced to credit the influence of his human companions. Given that, he decided the best tact was to make his next words as grand as possible. He had, after all, been responsible for bringing the humans here in the first place, so he said, "I bring representatives from Atlantis, who stand prepared to fulfill your prophecy."

If he had expected excitement, it was because of a gross overestimation of the populace's optimism. Compared to this crowd, the people who overlooked in their arrival in the first plaza had been boundless Pollyannas. Centuries of poverty, of knowing that a treasure existed nearby but having no raw materials or machinery to put it to use except by cannibalizing the Forbidden City itself, had given them a healthy bit of cynicism, but a nearly lethal dose of pessimism. There was a matter of practicality involved as well – they would have been far more enthusiastic if Tayron had declared that he had come to donate enough free food to the city to feed them for a year, or enough coal to heat their homes through the winter. At least that would have been believable and useful. Stating outright that their greatest hope for salvation was about to be fulfilled elicited some suspicions and confusion, but mostly failed to register at all.

Fortunately, the six mages escorting them had been convinced by observation and by Raiz, and believed their eyes and reasoning. Their reputations were on the line, as well, since they had allowed the outsiders to remain in the city for this long, and had even judged them worthy of an audience with the magistrates.

"Honorable Kantor," the mage with the weighty voice attempted to explain, gesturing to Raiz, "this is the one who says he is from the planet Atlantis used to be. They use devices on their heads to translate their language into ours, and have technology beyond our own, just as this Eldgil seems to have. They are being pursued by a group of mages that they believe the ancient edicts meant to protect the Forbidden City against. They have employed these two mages for protection."

"And you believed them, did you, Bentrell? You were always a credulous fool. They have the Makis with them, and he could have told them all they needed to know to concoct a clever tale. But we shall see. Have the offworlders step forward. This Tayron had the pomposity of a man once important, but now defeated. I do not need to hear more from him."

That brought a vicious grin to Oris' face, but the Eldrandii said nothing, surprised to see Raiz here in person, and curious about what he had to say. She knew about Raiz almost as well as she knew Welder, and recognized that any attempt to take the offensive against him would backfire. It was far better to hear what the commander had to say, to play defense, and aim to have the final word.

Raiz took the stage with Emily and Kaz close behind him, and said everything almost exactly as he had done before, so that there was practically no discrepancy between the two tellings.

"What nonsense," Oris scoffed as soon as he finished. "These people are simply trying to frighten you into giving into their will. Have them give proof of their origins. Have them show evidence of this force of mages they claim will destroy you. It is all too convenient for them to create such a story to get their way. You note that I have not used fear as a tool to convince you."

Kantor turned to Raiz. "Well?"

Raiz brought out his laptop and, with legendary keyboard dexterity, loaded a video to the screen in a second. After handing the computer over to Kantor, he pointed to a tiny thumb-sized cylinder attached to his translator headset above his left ear. Emily neglected to notice it before, but realized what it was before Raiz explained, "This records everything I see. When we passed over Lord Tayron's land in our starship, we saw the aftermath of out enemy's passing – a corridor of devastation across that country. I think this proves that we have the technology we claim, and goes some way to proving we have the foes."

Without even glancing at the image on the laptop, Oris said, "it could have been fabricated."

"And you would say the same about any evidence he brought before us," Kantor pointed out. "Do you have anything else . . . Earthian?"

Raiz took back the computer and called up another video, this one of Newport Station around Earth. It had interactive hotspots imbedded in it, and Raiz instructed Kantor on what to click to access the information concerning Selparis. He had already configured the console to display in the ancient Atlantian language, which was intelligible to Kantor, and readable as long as the words used were common rather than specialized. A quick learner and even more efficient reader, Kantor took little time to declare himself satisfied by Raiz's offering.

"This is acceptable. I believe what you have said." Those words burst the pessimistic bubble of the crowd, and such a commotion broke out that the other city leaders had to motion for everyone to be quiet so the proceedings could continue. Oris, though now silent, was slowly losing her grip.

"However," Kantor continued, "I do not approve of your magical companions. Even if prophecy was fulfilled today, I do not see why it should be at the expense of our unwritten law and the simple commandments of our ancestors. No magic users may enter the Forbidden City."

Raiz stroked his chin, on which some definite stubble had emerged after a few days without time to shave. "I think that the approach of the enemy threatens all of you, and our arrival . . . heralds an opportunity for a drastic change in your way of life. There really is no choice, of course – you will either have to take advantage of whatever protection the Underground City might offer, or die out here."

"What are you suggesting?" Kantor asked, knowing the answer very well, but realizing from the absence of gasps that much of the crowd did not.

"Bring everyone in the city into the mountain. It's time for you to change your ways and embrace your past firsthand."

Emily could feel the disbelieving stares form the crowd tickling the back of her neck, and the wall of silence behind her was frightening. She didn't dare turn around.

Kantor cleared his throat. He had risen to leadership primary due to his unwillingness to blindly obey, and his promise to improve the lives of his people even if doing so might go against common sensibilities, but even he had trouble digesting the idea of this much deviation. "Even if we considered that . . . option . . . and I in no way suggest we will, there are obstacles. We have heard of peoples who live their lives underground, and the ancients were not averse to that lifestyle, but we are more accustomed to life in the sun. That aside, food is the major consideration." He detected that his words, falling far short of a condemnation of the blasphemous suggestions, were unsettling to the crowd.

"Oh, I'm not saying we'll be down there for long. You see, once the mages are here, I can call Earth's forces in," he patted his laptop, "and then the first question is whether the Eldrandii will step aside to let them through. Our special forces have dealt with Asparii mancers before, so I don't think these mages will be that much trouble. I've got three thousand men and women ready to land on my signal, and my ships can get up to twenty thousand more where that came from. If getting the troops through works, then our only problem is having to seal up the underground city so that our enemy will be forced to lay siege to it. As long as we can hold out for a few days after their onslaught starts, Earth Forces should be able to clear the way for us to emerge. Your people keep saying that the ancient secrets are protected, so I was hoping that it was more than the wall we have all seen."

"It is. In fact, it is the ideal place to wait out an attack. We will need to discuss this matter." Kantor moved to confer with his peers in a huddle.

"Do not bother," Oris said smugly. "Commander Raiz neglects to inform you that my people would never allow him to land his forces on this planet, so if you trap yourselves in the Forbidden City, you will starve there, or be killed by these mages if they happen to break in. If you fear this phantom foe, then it would be better for you to flee your city on land. I can tell you that others have been driven to do the same by the stories these humans have spread, so at least you can be comforted that you are not the first."

"Earthian?" Kantor turned questioning eyes to Raiz.

"Oh, I thought of that, of course. The only reason that the Eldrandii oppose us is because of the hyperspace drive secret. Once we get to the library and find the key information, I'll scan a copy and send it to Earth using my computer, through the hyperspace relay on Captain Wilson's ship. After that, Oris' people will have to decide whether they really want a group of rogue Asparii mages, their ancient enemy, to get hold of the secret as well. I think they'll conclude it's best to allow Earth Forces to take care of this extra threat."

"And you are sure you can find the information that you seek?" asked Kantor.

"I managed to put together a team that should be able to spot it in record time. That's not a concern."

"Very well. We will take that into consideration."

Back in their huddle, the city leaders tried to make the decision quickly and publicly. To deliberate behind closed doors would have been more natural, but they wanted to convey a sense of urgency in light of the warnings, and also to reveal their recognition of the misgivings everyone in the crowd had. The discussion was anything but calm, and frequently loud outbursts and moving sermons punctuated the key ideas for everyone to hear. At the same time, the city council was giving its people the opportunity to get used to the idea that this was, in fact, the prophecy's fulfillment, and that being the case, the laws they had lived under for so long would no longer hold. Whatever might be said about the lack of curiosity among the people around Raljar Canti, they had the same sharp minds as the Selians, and the same propensity for hampering themselves with traditions obeyed as absolute doctrine.

Giving due time to the issue, the city leaders turned to face outward, to the public, after their decision was established by a vote. Kantor announced the result for the benefit of the rest of the crowd.

"It is our belief that changes intended by our ancestors are at hand, and that this will require of us some . . . flexibility. However, we will not enter the Forbidden City until we have no choice. If these mages you speak of come . . . there is no choice but that we should enter the city to join you. If that which protects the city deems our reasons worthy, it will let us pass, so the decision to break the unwritten law will not be ours. We have seen that you do not lie about your origins and your intentions, though we are not so naïve as to think you have spoken the whole truth. We are, of course, most interested in assurance that you will fulfill your promise to us, and bring us the benefits of your technology to free us from our bondage to this world."

"As far as I'm concerned, you are my people, and fellow humans," Raiz said sweepingly. "Captain Pierce here is a starship captain. Emily, could you please tell Erem Kantor how I describe my duty?"

Emily smiled, having found his self-developed job description goofy from the very start. "Commander Raiz believes that he needs to do whatever it takes to help Earth and the human race compete with the other space species."

"And, Captain, to the best of your knowledge, have I ever done anything to contradict that purpose?"

She genuinely thought back to the little she knew about Raiz, even to what she remembered hearing about him in the news during her Earthbound youth, and answered, "Nope," making certain to keep any hint of doubt out.

"Oris," Raiz continued. "I think you are as biased against me as anyone here, but that you won't lie in this case. I have a reputation in the Interstellar Community. Is there any doubt that my focus has always been bringing Earth to an improved standing among the ISC species?"

Oris hissed. Emily had never seen an Eldrandii hiss – it was too snakelike, and not appropriate to the avian nature of the species. "Oh, you will do anything for your people, that is certain. Even stab these people in the back, I think."

"Well, Erem Kantor, there you have it. Now, the question is whether you think I see you as one of my people. If you do, then even my enemy is willing to admit I will do all I can to bring you to the stars."

As if he had finally developed a migraine from all the new information, Kantor shook his head in the hope that a different angle would relieve the strain. He said, "You do not speak our language."

"But we do share the same history and legacy," Raiz rejoined effortlessly.

"You do not know our ways."

"There are hundreds if not thousands of cultures on Earth as different from one another as my ways are from yours."

"Thousands of cultures . . . how many people are there on . . . on Earth?"

"Nine billion. So, you see, the differences you see are not so striking to me."

"Nine billions . . . Atlantis itself, according to legend, never had a hundredth as much. If you see yourself as . . . beholden to so many, I suppose our thousands would not be many more. You said you had three thousand soldiers ready to land from your world. With those same ships, it would not take more than four journeys to take every man, woman, and child from this world to any other. Not that we would wish to leave that way, but it gives your promise credence. Tell me, is it necessary for you to bring mages into the Forbidden City? What you look for is technology. I cannot see what use they will be. There is nothing under the mountain that you would need magical protection from, unless you do not deserve to be under the mountain in the first place."

Raiz looked at Tylan and Makis, as if considering whether to abandon them here, then said diffidently, "I chose them as companions because there was a chance I would need their expertise. Now . . . I'm still not sure I won't need them . . . and we only have one chance at this. I'm sorry, this business is risky enough as it is, and I don't want to roll any more dice. Both my calculations and my instincts tell me that these two will still be useful to me."

"But how? Give us at least a reason, and we stand ready to make way."

"I can think of two. First, the specific secret we need access to might be protected somehow by magic, since that would explain why your ancestors were so keen to keep a mage out. The other possibility, which gets more and more likely every time I think about it, is that the information itself involves magic and requires an understanding that our engineers and scientists so not have. I'm sorry, they're not very good reasons."

A smile twitched Kantor's lips briefly. "You have dealt honestly with us, so let me make a confession. Our desire to learn of our legacy has overtaken, especially in the younger generation, our humility in the face of our ancestor's will. The arrival of the Asparii lord's explorers ended the final justification used by the elder generations to dissuade the younger – the one warning that anyone attempting to enter the Forbidden City would surely die. Since then, we have all gone through the normal motions, with the more pious of us intoning the ancient commandments and maxims more vehemently than ever, but we knew the time would come when, if we did not make good use of that which was left to us, others would. Now you come and . . . I think it is time. We will not bar the way against any of you, including the Makis, though we have long hated the peculiar impiety of his kind. If what you say is true, then you will enter the city, and we will soon be forced to join you."

At this admission, the crowd's restraint broke. A few were outraged, damned Kantor, and presaged doom for the city and its citizenry, but the rest accepted the good news as a fulfillment of prophecy, and were now eager to explore their birthright. Now that the dam was officially broken, speculation filled the air and drowned out the increasingly crazed ranting of the dissenters. Kantor made no attempt to quiet the city down, and instead led Raiz and his team away from the throng and into a building at the side of the plaza.

Judging from the interior, it could have been a home, if someone had chosen to furnish it. Certainly, the room spaces and corridors had been built with family life in mind, but every inch of it was bare.

The brick of the walls and wood of the floor were in good repair, but without the punctuations brought by furniture and decorations, they existed in an eerie vacuum, serving no clear purpose. In a room down the corridor, at the back of the house from the door, there was an iron grate in the floor, not unlike a sewer cover, except that it was engraved with delicate symbols.

"This is not the most common sort of gate," said Kantor, "and certainly not the only one into the Forbidden City, but it is the closest, and we did our best to mark its significance. This is as much iron as we can find or trade for in half a year. I suppose you cannot imagine such a lack."

"No. Especially not with wealth buried in a mountain so close by," Raiz said suggestively.

To Kantor's credit, he avoided Raiz's bait, and addressed it calmly. "Even if using the materials in the Forbidden City would not constitute sacrilege, I doubt we would be able to build adequate flames to make malleable even the weakest metals the ancients used."

"I guess not. Not to change the subject or anything, but before we go down . . . could we discuss what to do about her?" Raiz pointed at Oris, who had very quietly followed them here.

Kantor looked uncomfortable. "The Eldgil has guessed rightly that if you are allowed to enter, she is allowed as well. We cannot take sides in your competition, weak as we are in comparison to both your peoples. Perhaps when you have fulfilled your promise to us, we will be able to support you, our brethren, with confidence. For now, we cannot risk antagonizing anyone. Certainly you can see that."

Raiz sighed with resignation, not ready to press Kantor for anything further. "I can see it, but it will be . . . inconvenient. We can't race her to the finish, since she has wings and we only have legs. At this stage, I don't see that we will have any choice but to kill her –"

"What!"

Oris was seething. 'How dare you! You take any action against me and you will have an interstellar incident with the Eldrandii on your hands, and I assure you that it will mean war."

Raiz waved her off. "We already have an incident with the Eldrandii on our hands, starting with the hiring of an Earth ship for deceptive purposes to maintain a monopoly by stealing from the people of Earth their birthright. But don't worry, Oris, I would not kill you, unless there was no other choice. The deal is simple: you can come with us if you don't take flight. As long as you're on the ground, you have nothing to fear from us. Start flying, though, and my guards have the standing order to fire at will. I think that's reasonable, under the circumstances."

"You dare –"

"Yes," Raiz said firmly. "Many, many people have died to get the knowledge your species has kept from the rest of us. Many innocent lives have been lost, especially in Lord Tayron's empire, because you wish to keep your hegemonic domination over the other spacefaring species."

"We have not been irresponsible stewards. We have always used the power for the good of all. How would it have been if Earth alone had the secret? Domination and conquest. I know your history, and you cannot deceive me with high-minded talk. None of the other species has been given the secret because none deserves it. None would have used it as we have, for the mutual benefit."

"For the mutual benefit? Seems to me that you get paid a hefty price for those ships –"

"Not as much as we could ask for them."

"Yes, but enough so that the ship construction and maintenance sector drives your entire economy. Don't try to fool me, either. I don't pretend that humans are perfect, but we have learned from experience that the road to perfection is built on choice. If you refuse to let people choose their own path and reap the consequences of their choice, you're preventing them from improving. That's what you've done. You've cleverly built a stasis in which no species except yours has a chance to excel, and then you make yourselves out to be the most perfect. Very convenient. But I know some of your history, too, and in the early days of your space exploration, you weren't so peace-loving as your make yourselves out to be now, were you?"

Raiz articulated the words without the slightest flaw in his rhythm, as if he had rehearsed them to himself a hundred times, just waiting for a chance to explain the human point of view to an Eldrandii. The others breathlessly anticipated Oris' next attack, but she was forced into an intense silence, the reminder of Eldrand's history cutting deep and throwing up in her mind revolting images shown to Eldrandii children as a reminder of their flaws, while kept hidden from other species to avoid embarrassment and any potential blow to the Eldrandii reputation. While giving her something to think about, Raiz had also been careful to deny her anything to sink her claws into.

With a voice that trembled with the collision of immense emotions, she managed to say, "Your people had their chance, and made their choice. Atlantis has fallen, and it failed in its time, with all its power and promise, to show the enlightened attitudes that we have," but before she had finished speaking, she knew what Raiz would say next.

"Atlantis has not failed yet. Not while we can pick up from where our ancestors left off and do better."

Oris was left with nothing else to do but scoff, and to give in. "I will not fly while I am with you, but this is not over, Earthling."

Raiz smiled brightly. "Well, that's settled. Shall we get on, then?"

Kantor insisted on lifting the grate himself, and did so reverently. The bear-like man was now looking at Raiz in absolute awe, convinced by the exchange that the commander was, in fact, the savior meant to bring his people to the stars. His heart throbbed with excitement, that he should live to see a day his people had waited for in anticipation for eons. The majesty of the moment was marred by the smell hitting them once the underground tunnel was open, and the putrescence of decay was like a wall set against them, forcing them to turn their noses away in revulsion. The stench was far more successful a barrier than any amount of iron could have been.

"Why does it smell like that?" Ethan asked first, though everyone had the same question.

Shamefaced, Kantor said, "over time, our sewer system has . . . everything under the city has been in such disrepair . . . and we never go into the tunnels to the Forbidden City to clean everything out and make basic repairs. There is a door of some kind at the other end of the tunnel, or so the Asparii explorers told us, so the Forbidden City itself remains . . . uncontaminated."

Kaz said, with his nose pinched shut, "funny, it's such a good defense, I would've thought it was deliberate."

"I commend your explorers for their bravery, Tayron, if they went through that without protection," said Raiz wryly.

"They would have used their high-altitude air tanks," Tayron said, breathing through his mouth and making faces at the taste of it. "Standard equipment."

"Well, we have better, I think." With a nod, Raiz signaled Tylan to start his work. The mage formed bubbles in the air, each one expanding from a tiny point into a size just large enough to encapsulate any of their head with four inches of spare room in every direction. He directed bubbles over each of their heads, and the clear spheres eliminated the rank stink. The bubble's surface added a shimmering tint to Emily's view of the world, but was otherwise clear. When she breathed in, pristine air flowed into her lungs as the bubble filtered out the air's more extreme impurities. Tylan told them that as long as there was air in the passage, they would be fine.

"There is air," Kantor guaranteed. "That is part of the problem. We think the air system used in the tunnel allowed our waste, which flows out of the city in a system built closer to the surface, to seep through. It is complex, and I do not know the workings of such systems, but there will be air."

"Of course there will be. I would like to point out, Kantor, that we are not even in the Forbidden City yet, and I have found a use for my mages. Please inform your people about this. I don't want them to think we were eager to break their traditions without a reason."

"I will. And you, Commander, please leave all the entrances you pass through open. This is not the only way in, but it may be that my people will have to follow you soon, and will need to do so in a hurry. With thousands of people to move, every barrier removed from our way could save a life."

Raiz nodded. "If there is any way we can help, we will."

"Good luck be with you, then."

Rather than have them climb down one by one, Tylan levitated them down gently, making sure to send guards before and after Oris, and to take special care of her wings, which the aperture was barely wide enough to accommodate. Thankfully, he managed to get her through without clipping any feathers.

Once in the dark tunnel, Makis created an illuminating flame in his hand, despite the fact that they had half a dozen flashlights between them. Upstaged by Tylan's air bubbles, he wanted to beat the other mage to the next magical solution to even the tally. This amused Emily, and she remembered what Tylan had said about Makis being quick to anger rather than subtle. The gateway mage was so predictable, even to her, that he was almost childlike in his simplicity.

Muck leaking into the tunnel had gathered at the very center of the floor in the curving corridor, so they walked in double file along the sides to avoid it. They avoided contact with the walls, as well, suspicious of the dark, uneven surface revealed by Makis' light, though the irregular bumps were probably harmless. At least, they were motionless. Emily remembered a number of movie scenes where a similarly shadowed wall would be covered in creepy poly-legged insects swarming over each other. The silence of the tunnel, and the fact that nothing in it except for the bipeds seemed to be shifting, gave her some reassurance that this planet's equivalent of a centipede was not crawling up her leg. Every few steps, though, she still shook one limb or another violently, just in case. Ethan had stuffed his hands resolutely in his pockets, but stared nervously at every shimmer, reflection, or bend of the light. To Emily's surprise, Kaz walked with almost as much confidence as West the survivalist and Raiz the indefatigable in this eerie environment. At first, she thought that his lack of imagination had saved him from picturing foul entities here, but then she caught him glancing at her. The nervous look in his eyes was all too familiar to her, and she could have laughed. He was more concerned with what she thought of him than anything disgusting this passageway could produce. It was the same way with Jaik, but he was less obvious about it, carefully evading eye contact with her.

After plodding down the path for fifteen long minutes, they reached a steel door at the side of the tunnel with a ten-inch wheel at its side. One of the guards stepped forward to make an attempt at turning the wheel and, after a few bursts of effort, the grime finally gave way. A telltale hiss accompanied the wheel's rotation, and as the door slid open, Ethan remarked that the mechanism might use a transfer of air, which would save the need to keep it powered over thousands of years. He was impressed, but Emily considered it needlessly complicated. She had never seen any problem with a simple hinged door and a trusty doorknob, even though everywhere she went except her home on Earth had automated sliding doors.

Seeing that Ethan was still looking at the door in interest, Raiz said, "Time to move on, I think. If you stop and stare at every little thing, it'll take a year to get to the library."

Nodding, Ethan followed the rest through the door and into a corridor, this one in excellent condition and dimly lit by a glow contained in tubes running alongside at waist height. They were now officially in the midst of creations produced more than ten thousand years ago by the people of Atlantis, and the surprising thing was that it all still worked. Makis scoffed at the light provided by the iridescent tubes, carrying his conjured flame higher as if to show he could do better using his magic.

The door at the end of the passage was identical to the first, except that it opened onto a tight stairwell, with steps winding their way twenty flights down. Tylan noted as they descended the stairs that the air was growing thinner, and only his bubbles prevented them from noticing, since the magic compressed the air to normal pressure.

"Of course," Makis said, "this spell is just depleting what remaining air there is in here. Very inefficient under these circumstances, if you ask me."

Scratching his chin, Tylan said, "I will take care of that when we reach the city, which should have enough air trapped in it to refill the tunnels, as long as we leave all the doors open as Kantor asked."

Wide-eyed in mock surprise, Makis said, "My word, is there anything you can't do?"

Not detecting the sarcasm, Tylan shook his head, "I specialized in air magic when I was an apprentice. When I was young, my goal was to be able to fly."

"And can you?"

"Certainly. Can't you?"

That left Makis silent, and Emily grinned behind him as they reached the bottom of the stairs. Exiting through another door, they met a sight that gave her a start. They were overlooking the Underground City, high on a cliff. She had partly expected to see this scene, having developed some faith in her dreamings, but to have such an exact, and enormously spacious, replica appear immediately after the confines of the tunnel was unnerving to her. She looked at the others, and sure enough, everyone who had been in her dream was there. Jaik, Ethan, and West all had the injuries, sustained at the hand of the dark mage in the forest, which she had seen on them. There was no mist, but not once in the past week and a half had she felt the peril posed by the Shadow Workers so strongly, and she spent more time looking behind her in the fear that they would appear than at the amazing panorama transfixing the rest of the team. Her dream had been deliberately vague about whether the enemy would actually enter Raljar Canti and assault them, but the suggestion was now enough to put her on guard.

"How do we get down?" Jaik asked as they assembled precarious feet from the edge, hoping that the rock outcropping was safe.

"I think this is an elevator," Kaz said, standing by a massive carbon composite cylinder with doors on it. Its base extended right through the rock and, for all they knew, right down to the ground level of the city. There was no way for them to see whether this was the case, nor whether the elevator tube had any break in it. When Kaz stood directly in front of it, its door opened automatically, leaving no doubt about its purpose.

"Emily," Raiz said suddenly, his casual tone throwing her off, "I guess this is the spot you saw in your dream? The part where it suggested we would be attacked once we got here."

"Y-yes."

"Well, it maybe a bit premature, but I'd say we've determined that the future is not set in stone, which should be of some interest to theological circles."

"It could be that I misunderstood what it was trying to say."

"True, but the way you described it to us made your interpretation very convincing. We'll have to set up a better experiment some other time. I don't think we should press the issue by lingering around here. Everyone into the elevator, please."

They stuffed into the cylinder, which Emily estimated to be about twelve to fourteen feet in diameter, and managed to all get in so there would only be one trip. To put all their eggs into one basket, Raiz pointed out, was a risk, but since Tayron's explorers must have been brought down this way as well, it was not an ill-advised one. Everything else about the ancient city so far indicated phenomenally durable workmanship, so the chance that the elevator would not have lasted the millennia convinced no one to hold back. Even Oris, who could presumably have flown to the surface, refrained from arguing about being bound to her feet.

As soon as the last person – one of the physicists – was in, the doors shut, the sensors confirmed that no one else was outside, and in a heartbeat later, the elevator started descending smoothly in its tube. Once they passed through the rock of the cliff, the opacity of the tube and the elevator wall faded out, providing them with a clear and stunning view of the city as they approached the ground. While hoping, now that they were at its mercy, that the machine's braking was still functional after all these years, and that the end of this ride would not involve them smashing into the floor, they nevertheless took the time to examine the city.

Dozens of supports extended from the base of the city's cavern to the roof, each dwarfing in height the actual buildings. Some, especially those closer to the center of the city, also lent support to skyways – grand overhead roads spiraling around what would have been the most congested part of town. The design of it made clear that this had been a genuine lived-in city. The precise lattice of the surface streets looked a bit pre-planned, but they were also functional, and of a size that could manage reasonably large vehicles. Why anyone would need to drive around in a city you could walk across in an hour, Emily had trouble understanding. She had the suspicion that this space city had not always been enclosed in its dome, or isolated, and her imagination pictured many such cities around Earth, each connected to the others with space corridors. Having trouble fathoming the implications of such an enormous idea, she brought the city back down to a level she could understand. Unlike Newport Station, Raljar Canti was about more than towers and commercial buildings, though these were necessarily common given the tight space within the dome. Emily could spot neighborhoods with more or less regular-looking condos and somewhat San Francisco-style housing. The residential areas would be familiar in form to the citizens of the city outside, except one that Emily saw, populated with the cone-shaped homes of the Eldrandii, marking the fact that the avian species had maintained a small presence here. Perhaps they had even gone local, adopting Atlantian citizenship.

It was difficult to remember, here underground, that this city had been a space station, much as Emily tried to remind herself of the fact. After a devastating civil war, Atlantii built it to ensure the survival of their culture, and after the final magical conflict that remade Earth in a new image, cities like this were boosted out of orbit to destinations far away from the troubled planet. Raljar Canti had preserved the essence of Atlantis here, all this time, in the hope that the civilization would revive on Earth with the knowledge contained here, and her own arrival here was part of its fulfillment. What Kantor had called a prophecy was actually the purpose of the place his people had protected for so long.

The elevator chamber descended into a building, but the walls of it remained clear, so that the contents of each floor flashed in front of them, empty of life but filled with computers. It was a center for city services, not just a station for the elevator. Emily imagined the building filled with workers ready to solve the problems of the residents, which must have been many considering the space that was required to deal with them.

Exiting the elevator at the ground floor, everyone stepped out in relief, thanking silently the genius of the ancients for enduring work that put the safety requirements of virtually every other species to shame. A circle of panels, three times the diameter of the elevator, stood arrayed around them, with gaps to the left and to the right. The panels were about four feet high and two feet deep, so they were a grossly inadequate barrier. Once they were all out and the doors of the elevator closed behind them, a large projection screen dropped from the ceiling in front of them, and they all fixed their eyes on it, confident that there would be some sort of welcome message and curious what it would say. Emily had other ideas, and approached the left gap curiously, disconcerted about the arrangement of the panels. As soon as she was a step away from it, twin bars from the ceiling came careening down into slots in the floor and, in seconds, bars came down all around them and behind the screen, no more than a foot apart, effectively caging them in. Oddly, Emily felt satisfied, finding that the Atlantii were sensible people, after all.

Unsurprised, though everyone else except Emily was in a state of shock and West was almost growling in frustration at this turn of events, Raiz said, "Well, now we know what they were on about when they said this place is protected. I wondered why it seemed so easy to get in here, aside from the stink of the tunnel. Speaking of which, Tylan, I think you can get rid of these air bubbles now. I imagine we're about to be addressed, and we want to look as innocent as possible."

Tylan did as bidden, and no sooner had he completed his task than the projection screen filled up with the life-sized image of a middle-aged female Atlantian with a hostile disposition. Black hair capped her head, and matched her clothing, which Emily guessed was some sort of advanced body armor – supple to the touch, but harder than steel against penetration – made of synthetic fibers. If allowed to pick the wardrobe of the woman in a video like this, she would have chosen the most menacing armor possible, and sure enough, the distant ancestors of the human race had thought the same way. She wondered whether the city had any spare armor of that sort lying around, maybe in the home of a guard, because she was determined to get her hands on a set. It had the perfect combination of menace, coolness, and protection. So far, her clothes had done nothing for her but stink from sweat, and with any luck, the Atlantii had developed clothing that was self-cleaning. Everything else they had built was capable of working perfectly well without anyone around.

It was an odd time to admire clothing, but since the armor was the only element of this situation she liked and knew how to react to, she stuck to it. For the rest, she would have to take pointers from Raiz. This little confrontation could be the principal diplomatic test of his career, and the fact that the negotiation was with some a computer program that looked utterly human was ironic, but in no way diminished the difficulty or significance of the meeting.

The woman in the projection spoke. "This city is forbidden. Who are you, attempting to enter?"

Once again, having achieved reasonable result every time, Tayron took the lead before Raiz could respond. In this case, however, his answer was easier to formulate than any his human counterpart could offer. This barrier had not prevented the entry of his explorers, presumably meaning that he, too, could pass without hassle.

"I am Chancellor Tayron from Atparis, and my explorers have already entered this city twice. I simply wish to assess their findings . . .

hoping that something here will help, and perhaps save, my people."

Without warning, blue beams swept across them from the front, left, right, and top. The light show was a mundane demonstration of Atlantian technology to most of them, but shook Jaik and West. Tayron had heard of something similar in the report from his explorers, and knew nothing hostile was meant by it.

The projection continued. "You and your Asparii companions may enter on the same warning we have given your explorers. The gifts of this city are not for your people, and if you attempt to remove any item from its proper building, you will die here. You others, do not try to follow them."

The right bars rose and Tayron went past without hesitation. Jaik, realizing that he was cleared as one of Tayron's companions, was slower to move, looking first at West, then longer at Emily, with neither giving him any indication about what he should do. His instinct was to stay with the two of them, but if he acted in a way not anticipated by this security system, they could all be in danger.

"Come on, boy," Tylan, the other Asparii in the team, said urgently. "This is out of our hands."

Jaik, seeing the truth in his words, followed him out, and the bars returned to their slots in the ground. At first, Tylan and Jaik remained directly outside the circle, with Tayron leaving them and heading out of the building into the city proper. Raiz, however, motioned for them to follow the chancellor, and they quickly obeyed.

The projection took a moment to switch to the rest of them, and the awkward transition gave Emily time to glance at Kaz, who had nothing but doubts on his face, then return her eyes to Raiz. She wondered how smart this security system really was. Would Raiz's plan to scan books in this city's library and send those scans to Earth count as removing the book from its proper building? The city's computer should be able to detect the message going out, and if it chose to, interpret it as a violation. If so, then Raiz would have to convince this automated response system that the city's gifts were meant for him and his people, and that would be a trickier task than convincing the confused people living on the surface. The program speaking to them lacked any dreams or hopes for Raiz to play on, and vague prophecies were, for it, concrete specifications.

To her surprise, the system threw them a curveball. “There is an Eldrandii among you. Please step forward and address your purpose here.”

Oris was uncertain in her step, at the mercy of a computer whose reactions she was at a loss to predict, with no ready justification for her presence that could possibly satisfy it. The truth was that she was only here to prevent the others from getting through, but that would tie her fate to them, and the computer’s judgment of her on Raiz’s ability to convince it of his purpose. Since that tactic had already failed her once today, she had to try a different approach this time, and had only one hint available to direct her.

“My people were here, living alongside yours, in an amicable arrangement. I am here with respect to that tradition of mutual cooperation and benefit.”

“The members of your species who lived here were not your people, but ours.”

“Yes, but their history and legacy is still important to us. Surely we have a right to . . . research their lives, and to study their part in your . . . civilization.”

“And you swear on your honor that this is, indeed, your purpose here?”

The question caught Oris off guard, but she did her best not to give a hint of it. “Yes, of course.”

The computer seemed to think it over, then said, “very well, but on your honor, and with the same warning. These were not your people, and you have no right to the gifts of this city. If you attempt to remove any item from its proper building, you will die here. You others, do not try to follow the Eldrandii.”

“Oris,” Raiz said, practically choking the name out, “I –”

“We will see each other again soon enough, I think, Commander Raiz. If you do not mind, I will fly now, but I will try to fly slowly.” Smug and haughty in her success, Oris walked smoothly through to the other side, and took flight as soon as she exited the building. It was aggravating to watch her go, and Raiz in particular had a brief, pained look on his face, but at least she could not remove the books from the library. On the other hand, she could easily hide them, delaying them from sending the scans to Earth. To what end, though? After all, that would only mean that the Shadow Workers would pen them in successfully, with no hope of relief. Maybe that would be enough, since the mages would presumably be unable to break through into the city. Odd that Tylan was able to just walk in, but he alone might not have been powerful enough to trigger alarms.

The computer was less casual in its treatment of Makis. "There is a mage among you Atlantii. Let him declare himself and his purpose."

Makis cleared his throat then spoke. "I am Makis, protector of the gateway between worlds. I seek the knowledge to stabilize it. It has been fickle recently."

"The gateway . . . between worlds. Searching database. Do you refer to a reality rift?"

Makis shrugged. "I suppose so. I have not heard it called that, but I have only ever heard one person, my master, speak of it intelligently."

"Then you may pass, but no mage has a right to the gifts of this city. If you attempt to remove any item from its proper building, you will die here. You others, do not try to follow him."

This was the second time Emily had been considered unable to use magic, and she was peeved at this dismissal of her abilities . . . or ability. Sure, she couldn't throw flames around, create breathing bubbles, or build a walkway over a crowd, but looking into the future wasn't exactly child's play, was it?

"Those of you who remain are recognized as Atlantii. Let the leader of you step forward and declare whether this is the case."

Having been remarkably patient so far, Raiz said eagerly, "yes. Or more precisely, we are from Earth, the world once called Atlantis."

"So you were not born of the world of our refuge?"

"One of our number was," Raiz said, indicating West, "but not the rest."

"Is this place still protected by our descendants?"

"Yes, they live in a city outside, but they consider the place forbidden, and don't come in."

"And until now, that was the case. Step forward a single stride."

Raiz did so, and from the floor two feet in front of him rose a tiny platform, about a square foot in size, on a cylindrical piston. It reached waist-height before stopping.

"Place your palm upon the reader."

Doing so, Raiz felt a slight ticking sensation that almost made him draw back his hand reflexively.

"You are indeed a genetic descendant from family lines known to have been on Atlantis at the time of our departure. Some of those families were our friends, and others were our foes. On our initial scan we read the contents of your computer, which support your claim."

"And you read Oris', the Eldrandii's, computer, too, didn't you?"

The projection did not answer, but instead continued, "whether we allow you to pass will hinge on the following question. What do you seek in this city?"

"The secret of hyperspace entry. We are currently dependant on the Eldrandii for this technology."

There was some processing time after this response, and then the projection said, "very well. You may take a single book from the city library, though you can copy any information from any book you require. We limit you to one book only to ensure others seeking the knowledge will be able to access it. As you exit this place, a . . . robotic bird will be released. Simply follow the bird, and you will be led to the section of the library you seek. You may look through everything else in the city behind unlocked doors, but may not take anything but the book of your choosing. State your name."

"Tyler Raiz."

"Then, from here on, your people should come here in your name, and we will identify them accordingly. If there are today factions of Atlantii, then your faction will be known here by you. Know that if you had lied, you would have been killed. The Eldrandii has already met her fate, and our systems are examining the actions of the Asparii closely. We will examine your actions similarly. You may pass."

Finally, the computer lifted the cage, and they left the building of their confinement in haste. Outside, the street was lit, revealing a pristine and almost sterile world. There was, within sight, no sign of wear, or anything out of place. It was not unlike the empty home from which they had descended into the dank tunnel – bare and unused. In this case, it felt wrong, since people had lived here, and there should have been signs of it. Emily had just enough time to grow apprehensive again, suspicious of the plastic landscape, when the bird promised to them fluttered out. It was a metallic robin-like model programmed to emit a birdsong.

Following the bird down the street, West was the first one to voice what they were all thinking.

"How does it all still work? It must be thousands of years old, and with no one to take care of it. How does it still work? Is this possible on . . . on Earth?"

"No," Raiz said with absolute certainty, "at least, not anymore, and not yet, but I know what the next team I send down here will be looking for." Already, behind his glowing eyes, intricate designs were being calculated.

West was dismayed rather than impressed, and mumbled to Ethan, "I do not like it. It is too . . . clean. Technology should have some grease and oil in it. I understand why they left now – this would drive me crazy." He was exaggerating the point a bit. In the weak streetlight, there could easily be grime in some shadowed corner unnoticed by them, though Jaik chose to have faith in the idea instead of checking whether it was true. Emily, on the other hand, was actively looking for imperfections on every surface as they walked, examining the finely curved edges of the buildings, and the paving of the sidewalk. At the sight of some grit on the ground, enough to produce a crackling noise as her boots strode through it, she pronounced delightedly, "Not as clean as we thought."

"Actually," Raiz said, and then cleared his throat tentatively. "Actually, I believe those were the remains of Arisin Oris. I'm sure this city's automated systems will clean it up . . . promptly."

"You're kidding," Emily said, knowing that Raiz had a decent, not a crass, sense of humor. Turning around to look at the ashes she had walked through with such glee, she saw that a little robot, nothing more than a trash pail on wheels with a broom extending from an arm on its right side, appeared from nowhere, swept up the remains, and zoomed away. It was as if the city's system had wanted them to see the reality of its threats.

"Creepy," was all she could think to say, and she was much more sympathetic now to West's scowling distaste for the city.

West spoke up again, biting back at Raiz and unnerving them all. "How do you know it was not Jaik? Why would this place kill people like that? How does a place get to kill a person, anyway? It did not even give her a warning . . . how could it tell she was lying, anyway? She could have explained –"

"Since Tayron told the truth as far as it mattered, I think our Asparii friends are safe," Raiz reasoned. "As far as the city's computer is concerned, it is a bit lacking in hospitality, but . . . we are relying on it to keep us safe from our enemies, so I can't say I blame it for being . . . protective. I want it to be protective." He was as troubled as they were, and put fixing the antagonistic Atlantian system on his to do list. If anyone could negotiate with a computer, he could, so this would most likely require his personal touch.

The buildings they passed were typically unremarkable, though the linguists took great pleasure in reading every sign on every building, happy to see that specializing in a supposedly dead language was paying off. The lack of vehicles in the streets left the physicists unsatisfied, and when one voiced a hope that one of the clean-up robots might come close enough to be corralled and examined, so that they could see what sort of motor it ran on, Raiz warned against it.

"Let's not do anything that might give the city a reason to blast us into trillions of pieces," he said, visibly pained by the childish suggestion. "Now look, that's something interesting." He pointed down the street at their bird-guide looping around twin stone statues, one on either side of the road. The statues had a classic Roman look to them – both were male, clean-shaved with short-cropped hair, and carved in austere standing poses. Unlike the Roman statues Ethan was familiar with from documentaries, though, their toga-like robes were ornamented with colored fringes, and the marble used was darker than the usual chalk white, and far from uniform. Between the whites and the grays, the statues tended to be green.

"Connemara marble, or something like it," Raiz said, amused. "I'll have to tell my Irish friends. They'll have kittens over this. Those two men don't look very Irish, though, do they? Facial structure looks . . . what would you say they looked like Ethan? Just from the faces, I mean."

Surprised that, with the scholars in attendance, Raiz was consulting him about anything, Ethan nevertheless offered an immediate response. "I guess . . . Ethiopians? I don't know much about countries in Africa and how different peoples there look."

"So why did you pick Ethiopians, then?"

"Isn't that where, like, all humans were supposed to have come from? I mean, before we started learning the ISC history and things got a lot more complicated and confusing."

"Maybe it's not as confusing as we think it is, and we were just missing some puzzle pieces. Maybe we weren't so far off the mark after all."

They passed by the statues without further comment and entered a monumental neighborhood of the city. The buildings were suddenly supersized and domed, with columns proliferating in the oddest places, including right in the middle of the street. Each column was heavily inscribed, often with a combination of words and portraits, and as they proceeded up the street, the pillars in the center of the street grew steadily taller. Up the street, they saw that a tall building, glinting in gold and perhaps a hundred feet tall, sat directly inline with these growing spires, in their way. On closer examination, Ethan remarked that it had the form of a pagoda.

"Actually, it looks more like the Taipei 101," one of the linguists said. "The roofs of each tier aren't as curved as the traditional pagodas I've seen. Do you suppose that's real gold?"

Raiz smiled broadly. "I don't think they'd go to all the trouble, putting it in the middle of the road, and then fake it."

The road curved around the pagoda in two great semicircles, and they followed the bird along the left side. There, their bird-guide slowed in front of a colonnade thirty feet tall and a dozen columns wide, each carved with sinuous vines and moss patches as if the off-white stone was a living tree trunk. The carvings had the appropriate, almost convincing, paint, and their hue had not faded over time.

"Look at that!" another of Raiz's specialists said, pointing to what looked like a green ladybug on one of the vines. "It's a little bot. I think it must keep up the paint. Imagine that – a little robot bug specializing in maintaining the green pigment on the architecture. That's –"

"A waste," West said disgustedly. "And somewhere, there must be a factory that still makes green paint, and a power plant burning some kind of amazing fuel to keep the lights going."

Raiz gave West a wink, approving of the young man's staunchly contrarian stance, but then pointed out, "unless that little bug eats the decayed paint and excretes fresh pain. I don't know how it could do that, but I don't make robotic bugs."

"And it's all so complex," a physicist added, "that the builders' descendants, all those poor souls living on the surface, had no chance to imitate it. They wouldn't know where to start. I bet that after generations living in this place, having everything work automatically for them without needing to figure out how it works it was completely baffling to them by the time they had to leave. Now, after struggling for centuries to survive in the outside world, I bet they would have the drive needed to figure this place out, like we have."

Their guide was now immediately in front of the open gateway of the column-fronted building. Doorless, it featured a simple open arch set atop a flight of stairs, inviting them in. At the top and on both sides of the arch, boldly etched lettering was clearly visible, and the linguists wasted no time deciphering it for them.

"Over it, the word just says 'library.' No special name for it or anything. On the left side, it says 'know yourself,' and on the right it says 'too much of nothing.'"

"I think," Raiz said, with increasing humor and inexplicable giddiness in his voice, "the words would be better rendered as 'know thyself' and 'nothing in excess.' At least, that would be more . . . traditional."

"I don't see a difference," the linguist said.

Raiz shrugged, still beaming at the two inscriptions, "just a suggestion. It's all Greek to me, anyway. I prefer the pagoda myself." He let a few of the others go into the library after the bird before striding in himself, and Emily wondered what he saw in the two phrases that had him rooted to the spot. For a moment, she thought she saw a shade of doubt cross over his face before he finally moved. The library's atrium was vast, and filled with museum-like displays – twenty cases Emily could have slept in, each filled with artifacts.

"But these are just normal things," West said. "Pots, plates . . . and why animal bones? Why put them on display?"

"These things . . . were ancient to the ancients," the historian said in awe, dismayed by West's lack of appreciation. "The Atlantii preserved these things because they were keys to their past. Even a small dinosaur by the looks of this one. Fascinating."

A straight hall without side passages, the museum atrium led directly to a grand staircase covered in a red synthetic plush – the first deviation from the cold, smooth surfaces of the rest of the city. The lush red fuzziness even encased the handrails, confirming that, whatever else might be said about them, the Atlantii were uniquely single-minded about the use of materials. Up the flight of stairs was a crosswalk connecting an arch on the left to an identical one on the right. The back wall in which the arches were set was a plain gray holding no tapestries or ornamentation, so that the bold color of the staircase stood out, as if it some significant symbolism was involved.

Before they reached the steps, Jaik rushed down to them from behind the left arch and, once he was in sight, West dashed forward, delighted that his friend had avoided the fate of Oris. They hugged briefly in profound relief, and West's overall demeanor eased and brightened, though he retained his overall misgivings about the city, and his discomfort in the midst of it. Jaik also hugged Emily, though she greeted him in kind with more hesitation. Emily had a view of Kaz's face while she was hugging her Asparii friend, and the confused look from her first officer was priceless. On the one hand, Kaz saw nothing about Emily that would deserve such an embrace from Jaik, who had known her for less than a month. Then again, Kaz himself had known her for only a little longer and, for reasons he assiduously failed to acknowledge with diminishing success, he felt a pang of jealousy at the sight. Kaz had already turned away, examining the last exhibit on the right a bit closer, when Jaik let her go. For his part, Jaik gave Emily an apprehensive stare as he distanced himself from her, as if sensing that her attention had been elsewhere.

Ethan stood behind Emily, gathering in the whole scene with a bemused nonchalance. By speaking to her about his feelings for her, he had smoothed the edge on their peculiar relationship, and no longer felt as nonsensically attached to Emily. She had, from his new dispassionate point of view, a few concrete features in her favor. Even when she dressed in clothes that obscured it, she had a plain neutral beauty that was readily apparent. Thoughtful and clever, she never assumed she was intelligent, even though she was. She was daring and irrepressible – willing to take on challenges that few would ever think to undertake on their own. Being around her was exciting because she was always left unsatisfied, steeling herself for the next challenge. All that said, he was certain that her magic played a part in attracting people to her. There had always been something different about her, and now he knew what it was.

In a way, Ethan pitied Jaik, because ever since they started bickering like a couple, Kaz and Emily had been liveliest when in each other's company. Emily paid such close attention to what Kaz thought of her, it was hard to avoid concluding that she had feelings for him, even if she failed to show it in a normal way. Parted for a little over two weeks, the pair had become more civil to each other, and Kaz was beginning to see all there was to like about his captain.

Jaik shifted gears quickly enough, and told Raiz that Tayron was unable to find anything in the library, not having any way to read Atlantian, but Makis was already among the stacks, trying to find what he needed to know. Tylan was with Makis, curious about what he might find. Wasting no time, the team was up the plush steps and through the left archway, and found the chancellor waiting for them. He received none of their attention, though, because the view past the blank gray wall was breathtaking enough to draw their eyes immediately. Ethan literally choked on a sharp intake of air, and started coughing. They were standing on a platform with a clear floor, overlooking a cavernous pit, dozens of floors above its base. Each level down was staggered slightly inward so that the central aperture gradually shrank in size, making visible the first rows of bookcases on each floor. Taking the likely breadth of the huge building into account, the number of texts contained had to be in the millions. Mirrors placed in strategic locations purely to reflect it made the library's bright lighting even more intense.

"The funny thing is, the whole lot of it could have been put into a single disc, or maybe a case of them at most," Raiz commented. "But I'm glad they didn't build a library of discs, since that would be a tad difficult to scan."

"They are not normal books, Raiz," Tylan said. "We had a look at some of them a floor down, and the books are electric. I think even your discs might have trouble storing what one bookcase contains. This library may contain everything your ancestors ever knew. They were trying to preserve their civilization here, after all. This method is inefficient, however. They would have served their purpose better by creating some sort of compilation of key information."

"An encyclopedia, we call it," Raiz said, "and I would agree with you, but the damnedest thing about encyclopedias is that they always happen to leave out what you need to know. I prefer the kitchen sink method myself. Now, let's have this metal bird take us to the book we are looking for."

The bird obliged, first leading them to twin platform elevators at the center of the walkway, both thankfully with opaque floors. The team had to divide itself between the two, and the bird performed a tap dance on the control console of both, instructing them down to the proper floor, seven down from the entry level. Everyone except a historian and a linguist exited the elevators and started tailing the bird once they reached the correct floor. When Raiz turned to inquire why the two of them were holding back, the historian explained that they were both interested in finding a history of Atlantis, and the platform controls were straightforward enough that the search for the ideal text should take less than an hour. Raiz let them do so, with a reminder not to remove any books from the premises. To all of them, it seemed that Raiz, despite his cheerful demeanor, was nervous about unnecessary incinerations, and wasted no opportunity to remind them against doing anything monumentally stupid.

Making a straight line to their goal in the bird's wake, the key books turned out to be unobtrusively nestled among other books on physics and theoretical engineering in a bookcase, not standing apart proudly in a display case. There were, in fact, three shelves of similar books identified by the remaining linguist as being on the topic, and the specialists had the lot of them off the shelves in seconds, much to the dismay of the only one who could manage the translation. They sat down on the floor immediately out of the tight aisle, fascinated by the digital books that, once opened, displayed a contents menu on a touch screen. None of the books was more than an inch thick, and what little heft they had was mainly due to the need to protect their sensitive electronic components. Buttons were set into the base of each book, allowing the readers to turn the pages and, on most pages, control the viewing of embedded video. Thanks to the detailed visuals, the physicists could get started trying to understand the material, and identify the specific passages that most urgently required translation.

Looking back at the empty spaces on the shelves, Emily saw electric contact points coursing along both the bottom and top of each slot, which kept the books charged. It was her turn to shake her head in dismay. "This city must have used a huge amount of energy without anyone living here . . . and we're talking centuries."

"Maybe . . . ," Kaz said, "maybe it's a closed system, and the energy's recycled somehow. The dome could catch some of the energy and, if they figured out a way to put the heat . . . I don't know. It can't be perfect, but if it's very, very good, it could work. There has to be some technology making it more efficient than it looks."

"Or there's some magic behind it," Ethan said, looking at Emily.

Kaz sighed. "The great game-changer again. I swear, the less we have to do with magic, the better." Then, catching the implication of his words and darting a panicked glance at Emily, he added, "I mean –" in an attempt to backtrack, but stopped. She was paying no attention to him, instead moving to look over the shoulders of the specialists, who were in a tight circle with the books arrayed around them.

The linguist was in the middle of saying something sheepishly. "It might not be wise to judge just from the diagrams in each book and their captions, but it doesn't look like this secret is an engineering one at all. There're plenty of lines that look like equations, and you say it looks like physics, but –"

"Dammit, that can't be how it works. Maybe . . . maybe that's just how the Atlantii did it. Maybe the Eldrandii do it a different way."

"Still, if it works, it works. Really, though, we shouldn't judge at first sight. There're lots of books to go through."

"No, let's get this straight right from the start. We can't accept that sort of solution. We're looking for the physics in these books, nothing else."

"Why? Because the rest of it makes you irrelevant?"

"It makes all knowledge irrelevant. What's the point of linguists if magicians come up with a spell that translates anything, huh? At least we know the translators don't rely on magic, but imagine how you would feel if they did. I'll tell you – if this is the way we develop our own hyperspace drive, there'll be a flood of people into magic and out of physics and engineering. Can you imagine them teaching magic at the universities? It would be a catastrophe, especially since there's every chance that a real, scientific solution for hyperspace could be found. If people go around changing reality to suit their needs, they won't have any curiosity about the way things are supposed to be."

"It doesn't have to be scientific to be real, to be the way it's supposed to be."

"In my mind, it does. I'm sorry if I'm clinging to old ways of thinking, but the new model is destructive, not constructive. Listen, maybe one of these books has a purely physical explanation in it. We really shouldn't be judging based on one book."

That animated conversation having given her more than enough to think about, Emily wandered off, blankly exploring this floor of the library as she considered what to make of the new revelation. She had been interested, of course, in what the great secret was, prepared that the explanation would be far beyond her ability to understand. Now, it turned out that maybe the answer was all too easy to understand. She was sensible enough to realize that there was every chance they were completely wrong about the contents of the books, spending only a few minutes so far examining them, and she sincerely hoped they were. Despite her newfound aptitude for the esoteric art, she was also more comfortable in a world governed by scientific law, and in ships that functioned in what might have been a mysterious way to her, but one that was nevertheless explicable by physics. In terms of what they knew, physicists might as well have been wizards to her, and the reason for her preference of one worldview over another was impossible for her to put a finger on. While trying to find some way to articulate it in her mind, she saw Makis, who had found information on his gateway on the same floor the hyperspace technology was located. He stood reading a volume, looking up in frustration as she approached.

"It cannot work this way," he said, as if trying to convince the book to change its contents. "This blasted things says that I have to pour magic into the gateway at its . . . its default power level . . . to recalibrate it. It says magical interference is causing it to fluctuate, and that only sending magic into it steadily at the exact rate will . . . but that is not the problem. The problem is that there are symbols I do not understand in here, placed in equations, that are supposed to tell me how much to use. Even if I do find out the correct amount by . . . by decoding this, the gate must need an incredible amount. It will take me years of practice before I can direct this much magic at a specific frequency at a constant rate."

Emily grinned. "What did you think it would be? A reset button?"

"This is not funny. Until I do this, anything can happen. If the gateway accidentally aligns with the . . . the wrong type of worlds, and the wrong type of creatures notice and walk through . . . and it all depends on me. It is not fair."

"Well, you're not the only one saying that right now. Our bigshots aren't happy with the way the hyperspace drive works, either."

"What does that have to do with . . . wait a minute," he stared at her wide-eyed, and she remembered too late that Makis was quicker on the uptake than anyone she had met except for Raiz, "the way you said that . . . it is magic, right? They think it has something to do with magic. That makes so much sense. Hyperspace is just another . . . just another world, and your ships match the frequency of that world to break into it. Your ships are like simple gateways."

"I don't think my people would like to hear you talking like that, and it doesn't make any sense anyway. I mean, you're leaking magic right now, and I don't see different worlds opening up."

Makis rolled his eyes. "It's not enough energy, and it is being emitted at my personal frequency. It is me. If I brought all my magic to bear, I am still not powerful enough, which is why I need the gateway. With luck, the amount I need to send in to stabilize it will be a threshold, and not actually enough to go from one world to another, because otherwise it will be too much for me."

Emily sighed. "Still don't get it."

Makis shook his head. "Me neither, to be honest. The theory is far beyond me. I am more into the practice," he said with a toothy smile. "Perhaps Tylan will know better. He wandered off some time ago, and I would like to speak with him. He might recognize the symbols in these equations."

Emily was rapidly losing interest in the technical side, though, and instead of seeking out Tylan, she looked for Raiz, who was more likely to have the kinds of answers she was looking for. The commander was walking with Jaik, West, and Ethan in his wake, analyzing the contents of scattered display cases, which were in the dozens on this floor alone, and voicing his thoughts about the library and the ancients as if a tour guide making up the details en route. Amused by the scene, Emily trotted up to them, but before she reached, a newcomer had run up to Raiz in panicked urgency. The woman, one of the locals from the city above, was glistening in sweat and taking in breath rapidly. She desperately tried to get words out, but the syllables were too choppy for the translators to recognize.

Raiz helped her out. "The enemy mages have arrived, then?"

The athletic though winded woman nodded, partly in thanks for Raiz's understanding.

"Will the people of the city be able to get down here in time? The elevator was rather cramped and slow."

"We have . . . other ways. Ways that . . . can be used . . . once."

"Really?" Raiz was genuinely surprised. "Our ancestors gave this more forethought than I imagined. They guessed you would need to use the underground city for sanctuary?"

"They . . . they knew . . . they knew we would have to."

"Right. My mistake. And I bet they thought to make the tunnel a ramp straight down to the street level of the city. So, will you be able to get everyone in here?"

"Most of us. Some . . . our mages are fighting while the rest escape. The council told me to tell you that they have sealed the Forbidden City according to the secret instructions. Until the threat is no longer present, this place is to remain sealed."

Emily's instincts threw up a warning sign and she interjected, "how will you know if the threat's gone? Is there a way, in here, to see what's going on outside? There must be, right?"

"The council, in sealing the city, specified the threat. The city will tell us when the threat is gone. The council believes it can detect the magical field outside, and will notify us when it has dropped. We are . . . nervous about the system, but have no choice but to trust it."

Raiz said, "I think we might be able to provide an alternative." He patted his laptop bag, always a fixture on his shoulder.

"We will be congregating in the circle outside this building. If you wish to speak with us, simply send a runner up . . . or maybe a walker will do," the messenger said with a wry grin. "Did you have any message to the council?"

"Simply that we regret what has befallen your fine folk so soon after our arrival, and that we mourn your losses alongside you. If there is some formal ceremony of remembrance, we would like to attend."

"There will be, once the toll is counted. I will go to the council with your words." She bowed, and left as quickly as she came. Her departure made way for the return of the linguist and historian who had wandered off to find out about their Atlantii forebears. They, too, were excited with their news, and had trouble getting what they wanted to say out, but in their case it was more giddiness than exertion.

"We found this!" the historian declared, presenting a nondescript digital book to Raiz. The elderly man was glowing with pride at his accomplishment.

Raiz cleared his throat. He had been speaking to others a lot more than usual recently, since he usually managed things through Newport stations systems. "Good. Great. What is it?"

"A history of this city. Even better," he said as he turned it on for Raiz and quickly flipped the pages to one of particular interest, "it's a children's book, complete with pictures on every page and oversimplified to the bare essentials. It's not the source I would normally choose, but things being what they are, I'll take it. It's an absolute revelation."

"And what exactly is the revelation?"

The historian turned to the linguist, indicating that the translator should proceed with the details. Raiz smirked, figuring that the two of them had already decided to share credit for their discovery, and had probably outlined a co-written book that would cite tantalizing snippets from a children's book.

"This planet was lifeless and barren before the Atlantii arrived. It was chosen as a place of refuge because it was a suitable distance from its sun, had water, but didn't have existing life."

"So no nasty native diseases or hostile creatures. Good choice. I assume that the Atlantii were somehow able to terraform this planet, but from everything we've heard so far, the people that landed on this planet wouldn't have known a screwdriver from a wrench."

"It was all automated. This city was preprogrammed thousands of years before they had to take it out of Earth's orbit, that's how the book starts. The people that lived in here didn't even realize that, when they landed, the terraforming process would immediately bury the city, and they had to spend some time digging their way to the surface. By the time they reached the surface of their new home, the process was already complete and the first plants were starting to grow."

"You know what," Raiz said thoughtfully, "I think that really explains everything. They must have used nanobots, to be able to terraform a planet so quickly and successfully. This place keeps giving us reasons to come back, doesn't it?"

West, unimpressed as usual, said to Jaik, "and they forgot how to do everything. These Atlantii forgot every useful thing their ancestors knew, and replaced it all with superstitions."

"Yeah," Jaik said, "but it wouldn't have been very useful for them to know all that stuff, since they were just trying to hide and survive. They needed to know how to farm and build homes."

"But that would be a whole lot easier with machines, if they had known how to build them."

"If they had the metal to build them."

"They had plenty of machines here, and plenty of energy to put them to work. There wasn't any excuse," he said, more to make the case than in actual disappointment at the sorry state of fellow members of his species. He had exhausted his disappointment an hour ago.

"Well," Ethan said, paying as much attention to them as he was to the continuing conversation between Raiz and his scholars, "if this city works like a closed system, like Kaz said, then . . . they couldn't take the machines out of the city or use the city's energy outside, because anything lost to the city would reduce how long it would stay working."

"And that . . . computer would keep anyone from taking anything out anyway."

West had to accept their logic. Adopting an entirely different attitude, switching gear as he was prone to do, he wanted to hunt for inventions in the city, and to show the curiosity that he berated others for lacking. He planned to stick around Raiz as long as doing so remained interesting, then begin exploring on his own, hopefully with Jaik and Ethan along as well.

Raiz had taken everything in, and told the two eager discoverers, "go ahead and work on that. Give me an abstract with some details and I'll transmit it to Earth before we leave here. Don't forget that you'll need to get all your notes in the next few days while we're stuck in here, and that the book stays. If you could credit Captain Pierce for bringing you here, I'm sure she'll be thankful for the mention."

"But you –"

"I made a deal with the Captain here that she would get credit for the discovery, and you should reflect that in your paper."

Realizing that Raiz was asking them to place their names alongside a relative unknown instead of someone who could overshadow them, the linguist and the historian made no further objections. Meanwhile, the noise of the thousands of surface dwellers, gazing for the first time at the fabled wonders they had protected for so long, was carried into the library through its open arch, and echoed around its hollow core. In this moment of change, the local Atlantii abandoned the restraint they showed on the surface, and delighted in everything they saw. Emily resolved to avoid stepping outside if possible, because she invariably felt embarrassed when people, usually her parents, acted like tourists and pointed out the most mundane things in amazement. It was a mark of how human she found them, that she saw no difference between her reactions to them and to her own family. Raiz had said nothing more believable than his inclusion of them, with enthusiasm, as humans to whom he had a duty to aid. She felt the same way, and lamented the fact that she had brought such danger to them, even if they ended up benefiting from contact with Earth.

"All right," Raiz said, "time for a little checkup on the main event. Let's hope the intellectuals haven't gotten too carried away."

"I was listening in on them before," Emily admitted. "Sounds like the secret might not be what we expected."

"What, magic? Maybe not what you or they expected, but I didn't drag Tylan all the way here for nothing."

Emily shook her head firmly. "No way. You couldn't have known it'd be magic. I don't care how smart you are. Why did you bring engineers and physicists, then, huh?"

"Well, just because there's a mage at the center of it doesn't mean it doesn't have moving parts."

"Come on."

He grinned. "Yes, yes, there was a chance it could be purely physical, and there was also a chance for it to be magical, and I prepared for both possibilities."

"'Course you did," Emily said, exasperated.

Tylan was now with the specialists, giving what input he could against some stiff opposition and resentment. He played his hand carefully, soothing the challenge he posed to their scholarship by occasionally saying that he would need more time to parse something out even if it was as plain as day, so that he only emphasized what they urgently needed to know. Raiz spoke briefly with all of them, but Emily ignored most of what they said – a mixture of gripes and attempts to translate the details involved, especially those that might contradict their first impressions. Jaik's face, visible in the corner of her eye, was distracting her. The young man was looking back and forth between her and someone else behind her, and she knew without turning to look that it was Kaz. She sighed. This was not good. Kaz must have been staring at her, contemplating whether hitting on his captain was appropriate, leaving Jaik to experience a mixture of emotions that Emily wanted to avoid dealing with at all costs. It was her fault, she knew, for not distancing herself from Jaik in the first place, but why did the awkward part have to happen now?

"That's fine," Raiz finally said, looking through the book identified by the linguist as most complete in its details, and inclusive of all the topics mentioned in the major headings of the other books. Fortunately, Atlantian books showed advanced formatting development, complete with contents and index, though both were placed at the front of the book, as well as margin notes and internal cross-references accessible at a touch. What Raiz liked about the book, though, were the videos and the list of essential equations after the index. "This will do. I think we will be able to convince the Eldrandii with this." He held up the book to show an image of a female mage, magical aura encircling her in bright purple and extending well past the bounds of the picture, standing in a chamber permeable to her influence, with feeding and life support tubes connected to her. Her eyes were closed, and her body was limp despite the massive outflow of magic.

The sight of it revolted Emily, and she was horrified at the realization that there must be a mage at the center of her ship, confined in much the same way as the figure in the picture. It made her sick to the stomach. More than anything else, she had so far identified her ship with freedom, so the need to keep another being captive in order to keep it running defied her sensibilities. Why did the mage have to be confined and connected to life support? She chose to ask the question aloud.

Tylan, finding the question firmly in his territory, explained, "the mage has to focus on releasing the correct amount of magic, surrounding the ship with it, then adjusting its frequency to that of hyperspace. After that, the mage must recharge as quickly as possible to allow for the exit from hyperspace, which will require another exertion. To output that much power in a burst might cause fluctuations in bodily functions, and the brain especially. The life support systems protect the mage from shock, since that would probably collapse the hyperspace bridge and tear the ship apart, or leave the ship stranded in hyperspace. We all know that it is impossible to make hyperspace jumps of less than three light years, or approximately three hours of hyperspace travel. Now we know why."

"But . . . but maybe the mage could just connect up to the life support system and everything when it's time."

Tylan held his left hand up. "While that is possible, if the mage is allowed to engage in daily life, there is every chance that some emotional situation or trauma might be distracting at the key moment. If this is truly how the hyperspace drive functions, then the mage is the most valuable part of the ship, and anything that happens to the mage could leave the ship adrift in space, or worse. Taking such a position is . . . not something I would choose to do, but I can well imagine a community of mages in which being selected to be part of a ship is an honor, and may confer some benefits to one's family. I cannot pretend that I understand it. It must be voluntary, since I cannot imagine a mage of such power being forced to do anything."

"What . . . what do you suppose happens when we press the hyperspace jump button?"

Kaz cleared his throat from behind her before saying, almost unwillingly, "I know you don't take many trips down to engineering, Captain, but there's no button. Actually, until now, we really didn't know what the instruments measuring the stability of the hyperspace drive actually meant – we only knew what to do to compensate when the needles went into the red. Now we know it was the mage's vital signs. Anyway, once the course is programmed into the ship's computer, the hyperspace jump happens automatically at the plotted point."

"Then what in hell is Brian doing tapping . . . oh, right," she slapped her forehead, "maneuvering the ship so we hit the point exactly. That part's not automatic. It's been a while since I've been on board the ship, sorry."

The apology shocked Kaz, but he made no indication of it.

"So, all right," she continued, "we reach the jump point and . . . what happens? The mage gets an electric shock that starts her up?"

The suggestion appalled Tylan, but he responded to it coolly. "I doubt that should be necessary. The location and timing of a jump point would not cause any significant distraction. It is usual for a mage to focus on a specific . . . stimulus while in a meditative state. The course plot itself would be the perfect thing, or perhaps a simple light that changes color when the jump point is reached. Whatever it is, it must be simple, since complex stimulus would force the mage into full consciousness."

The idea of spending the rest of her life staring at a line on a map or a blinking light revolted Emily as much as her electric comment had troubled Tylan. In fact, the life Tylan was suggesting would make the occasional shock therapy an act of mercy, at least in her admittedly inexperienced opinion.

At the start of the talk, Raiz had taken out his laptop and by the time Emily and Tylan finished, he had scanned every page of the book that he considered essential and convincing. Now, he was sending the first batch of scans, and everyone looked on, eager to hear the news that this phase of the mission, which would end the logic behind the Eldrandii blockade and bring help from Earth, was successful. Raiz's face was enthusiastic at first, but after a few minutes of waiting, the color drained from his face and a distorting shadow crept onto his normally calm, unlined face.

"I can't connect to Newport Station through Wilson's ship. I can't even connect to Wilson's ship, or any ship in orbit. The residents of this city must have been able to get a message out while it was in orbit around Earth . . . and I know the metal shield alone can't block the signal from this laptop, and the dirt of the mountain definitely can't."

He tried to send the signal repeatedly with no good result. To his credit, he did not, as others might, get angry with the computer or treat it indelicately the third and fourth time around. Rather, he was clearly disappointed in himself for not anticipating, or inaccurately judging the probability of, the inability to establish a connection to the outside world from Raljar Canti. Emily found it impossible not to be panicked, but was convinced that there had to be a way around the problem. Unfortunately, there was only one entity in this city that could give them the answers they needed, and it had a programmed malevolence that made it unlikely to lend them any aid.

"Computer!" Raiz hollered in vain hop, looking up at the ceiling, addressing the city's system, not his laptop. "Forbidden City computer, or whatever you're called, I need to talk to you! Where's that bird of yours?"

To their collective relief, the bird appeared above them and, after flying in circles then landing at the top of the nearest bookcase, it said, "what do you require?" in a chirpy high-pitched tone reminiscent of a cartoon canary.

"I want to transmit a message to ships in space outside this planet. Now, unless the dome is made with dozens of feet of lead, and there isn't a single gap left in it, there's no way it alone is blocking my transmission. Supposedly, you can detect the presence of enemies outside. Is there some way you can send my message?"

"This city is surrounded by a superdense compound unlikely to have been rediscovered by you, and it would block most signals. On the sealing of the city, there are no gaps in the shield. An interference field is also established on the sealing of the city, and if you believe the shield is not blocking your signal, then the field certainly is. As you are almost certain to ask, the field will not be brought down for your benefit before the external threat ends. Some mages are trained to use waves to manipulate or destroy electronic equipment, and that risk cannot be taken. Our detection devices are precisely that – they are integrated into the surface of the hemisphere to receive information and cannot be reconfigured to transmit. All communications arrays were placed within the shield so that, in times of danger, absolute radio silence could be enforced. Otherwise, a traitor within would be able to use the transmission of a message to point out for an enemy that weakness in our defenses."

"Better than a turtle in its shell," Raiz grumbled. "Those must have been some bad times you guys lived in, to be so ready to seal yourself, and in the dead of space at that. But with all that forethought, you must have some way to get around the restrictions in case something went wrong, like if something malfunctioned and the seals couldn't be lifted."

The bird sounded defiant when it said, "we do not malfunction."

"Everything malfunctions," Raiz said, with absolute certainty. "There must be at the core of this place either one of two things. Either there is a mage holding it all together, or a power plant combined with a superbly intricate computer. My guess is that even the greatest mage couldn't survive forever, and this city was created to be as perpetual a system as possible. So this place is purely technological. Is that right?"

Seeing no reason to deny it, the bird said, "that is correct."

"How long has it been since you have had human input into the mainframe? You know, actually programming the artificial intelligence that runs things."

That brought a pause, but the bird conceded, "fifty-six thousand four hundred fifty-three point six two seven Atlantian years."

"And how, exactly, do you know you are not malfunctioning? Circumstances change, and the input of real people is required to adjust your parameters accordingly."

"Do not try to confuse us. Our makers saw through this potential ruse. We are self-adapting, by necessity."

"Good. That's what I wanted to know. Now, would an appeal to reason be able to persuade you to give me what I need, being that you are, as you say, intelligent?"

"There is no probable line of reasoning that would result in the lifting of the interference field."

"I was speaking in theory, in the abstract. Could I convince you of a notion?"

Another pregnant pause, then, "proceed."

Raiz was pacing up and down, establishing a rhythm with his body to facilitate the flow of his thinking. "First, the premise, that there is an enemy outside this city that your creators would not have wished to relinquish their secrets to."

"Agreed."

"And your creators would have wished to protect their descendants."

"Definitely."

"And protection of their descendants includes securing the best possible lives for them.'

"Yes."

"And this city was built out of necessity, not out of preference for a confined life."

"The history of the city's construction supports that claim."

"And therefore the best possible life for the descendants of your creators implies a life outside of this city, and not merely one confined within it, despite how comfortable life within its wall might be."

"Absolutely. Our systems were programmed to urge residents of the city to leave as soon as the world of refuge was reached, and to declare this place forbidden for that exact reason."

"I maintain, then, that the enemy outside can effectively lay siege to this city, and survive outside indefinitely. They will choose to do so because they believe, probably rightly, that the materials contained here would give them immense power. If my forces from Earth are allowed to land, they will be able to dispel these mages and not only would the descendants of your creators have the preferable life, being free to leave here, but will also be brought into contact with Earth, which is filled with other Atlantii descendants who will be able to work with them to restore the glory of Atlantis."

Raiz cleared his throat and caught his breath. "So, we need to send a message that will convince the ships blocking our ships from landing that the blockade is unnecessary. If you accept my reasoning, let me get my message through, because it is obviously the best option for all concerned, and in accord with the purpose of your creators."

The bird took off from its perch and flew around a few times in a smooth circle, indicating that the system was processing the proposition. Its flight was similar in purpose to the hourglass on older computers with slow loading times.

"We have heard you express interest in the technology of this city, other than the hyperspace technology you stated you sought. If you succeed, how do we know you will not plunder the secrets of this place, taking what you lacked the intelligence to create on your own?"

It was a strange change of topic, but it put Raiz closer to his home turf. His raw impulse and peculiar logic was quite clear on the matter: everything of use to Earth should be brought to his planet at the minimal possible cost. However, he knew that the computer had a different view, and had shown its willingness to punish those who it deemed to be in the wrong. At face value, any answer satisfactory to the computer would be a misrepresentation of Raiz's intentions. He did want to plunder the place. He would carry the library to Earth with him if he could, but admitting that bluntly, while honest, would be impolitic. Speaking for the World Council instead of himself would be cleverly evasive, but the bird would likely reject the answer.

Raiz had no choice but to deliver the truth. "Of course we would like to have all the technology you have here, but if you don't think we're ready for it, I'm sure you can deny it to us. But could you blame us for wanting to learn all the knowledge you have here, even if we're not ready for it? We're a curious people, like you must have been. We, on Earth, haven't been bred into complacent comfort generation after generation, but always face new struggles and improve ourselves by overcoming them. Even if we can duplicate the glory of Atlantis, I'm sure every human will know that there's always room for improvement, and always another step to climb." It was true enough for Raiz, but Emily doubted everyone on Earth was as wedded to the idea of progress.

The computer assessed his answer in a few flutters. In those tense moments, their fates hinged on whether the artificial intelligence had a temper, and could take offense at the hidden accusation Raiz had delivered. To justify himself, the commander had pointed out that the efforts of the ancients had turned their descendants into incapable individuals unfit to carry on the legacy of their forebears. They were sponges, soaking up leftovers and squirting them back out into the system, adding nothing by way of order, complexity, or development. Atlantian civilization had left humans on Earth with far less, but they had done more with it. Raiz's gambit was that the ancients would have appreciated those who were enterprising.

"Your reasoning is acceptable," the bird decided, back on its perch. "But we will not lower the interference field. Above a single opening at the very top of the dome there is a shaft to the surface emerging at the pinnacle of the exterior mountain. The surface point is one person wide and kept hidden by the city's . . . nanobots. We heard you guess their existence, Tyler Raiz, and there is no point hiding the truth of it. That exit point was the one concession made to the possible need for external communication. Since the city's original construction in Earth's orbit, this exit has never been used."

Raiz shook his head, and when he spoke, it was with an air of desperation. "That's too obvious. We'll need something better. The mages would definitely see anyone on the most visible point for miles around, and they're probably swarming on the hill trying to find some way in. If they have a way of detecting concentrations of nanobots, they'll probably find the way in before we even get there, and I suppose you'll seal it up as soon as they do."

"We have prepared for a great deal more than you can think of, newcomer that you are. The . . . nanobots are evenly distributed on the surface of the mountain, and are all that remain of our original terraforming force. Should we choose to, they can be used to defend any entrance as well, so no mages or group of them will be able to force entry. Their abilities will not extend to protect any member of your party that you choose to send to the surface, however."

Unhappy with the circumstances, Raiz said, "Anyone who tries to use the exit will probably be attacked as soon as they hit fresh air. The choice you give us is . . . unacceptable. And you won't order the nanobots to give us protection."

"That's not their purpose."

"Beside the point. You call yourself an artificial intelligence; are you able to transcend your programming and to recognize the necessities of the situation, or are you rigid and unable to deviate from the programming?"

"Again, you try to appeal to our nature in your favor, but the choice you provide is a false one. We were created with an explicit purpose in mind, while you were not. To us, free will is not an issue, and we take pride in fulfilling our reason for existence. We will neither help nor hinder you beyond revealing the secrets we have already conceded to you."

Raiz turned his back to the bird and murmured, "You should have put it somewhere less obvious. Right at the top. It's insane."

Raiz's attitude clearly insulted the bird, and it said, "this place was not designed with your . . . peculiarities in mind."

Catching the implication when no one else did, Raiz returned his eyes to it with a sour grin, bordering on a sneer. "My peculiarities, is it? Have a sense of humor, do you? My desire not to get killed by a fireball, or at all, is peculiar?"

"If doing this mattered to you, you would take the risk without hesitation."

"Oh, a test, is it? I'm afraid I don't work that way. I'm not much for the mindless heroism thing, and I don't buy into tests of faith."

"That is not our concern. This city obeys its own rules and will hold firm to them regardless of you."

"Just what I need, a fundamentalist computer," said Raiz in a huff, sitting cross-legged on the ground with his right forearm supporting his chin over his knee in a traditional thinking posture. No one could blame Raiz for being frustrated and incensed, since the city's computer failed to value life in the way . . . in the way those who were actually living did. Tayron, however, materialized out of nowhere, and did his best to take a dig at the formerly invulnerable Raiz.

"Now, now, Commander, do not get sour when your plans fail to work out. It happens to me constantly."

"I suppose you're happy that a measure of justice has been done to balance out your own failure, or is there something about this that's actually useful to your cause?"

"Just gloating over the measure for measure."

"Well, I'm still trying to think of a way out of this, and I haven't given up yet. You might have forgotten, but if we don't get the signal out, it will be your failure as well as ours. No one will come to Selparis to help your people."

Tayron smirked. "I am not worried." He looked at Jaik, West, and Emily. "I think if you are less than willing, we have plenty of people here who are ready to prove themselves. Your problem, Raiz, is you do not know how to delegate."

Catching the drift of the chancellor's words, one of the guards stood up and said, "sir, if you'd like, I could send the signal."

Raiz rolled his eyes. This was just the sort of ill-considered heroism he hated. "No I wouldn't like. Quite apart from anything else, it's not just a matter of pushing a button. If you only had to send the message to one location, I could make it that simple, but these scans need to be sent to both Newport Station and the ships in orbit – to both the Eldrandii ships and our own. If I had anticipated this situation, I would have given Captain Wilson the access codes to Newport Station computer, so we would just send the message to him, and he'd be able to send it on to everywhere else. I can settle for sending it to Newport and to just one of the Eldrandii ships in orbit, but we need to do both, and this laptop can't have both connections open simultaneously. I have a laptop that can, but –"

Ethan helped him out, knowing the feeling, "but you didn't think you would need it."

Raiz nodded. "This one was more efficient on the battery use. And it gets worse. I actually had one of these guards carry a backup laptop all the way here for me, but instead of bringing a different type, I chose the same model." He sighed. "Anyway, the point is, I can put my password in and get this ready to send the message to Newport, but then the person who sends the message will need to reconfigure the program to access Eldrandii ship comm systems."

"We have come this far," West said with a savage contortion to his face, "and here you are, too afraid to finish it. Do you know what we have been through? If I could do it, I would."

"My being here was as much of a concession to danger as I was willing to make. I think presenting myself as a sitting duck for a pack of mages, standing around in plain sight, would be sheer idiocy. If you think differently, it is more likely that you're out of your mind than I am. Unless . . . Tylan, could you protect us? If we went up there, could you fend off the enemy for, say, five minutes?"

Tylan was downcast, and the answer was clear even before he spoke. "I did not study defensive magic. My air magic can be of some use, but not against more than two mages of Shadow Worker caliber. Most of the magic I have used for the past few years was for investigative work. There is . . . I have heard some theory about automatic magical defenses, something a mage does not need to study, but which is inherent in the magic itself. It is unreliable, though, and would . . . would almost certainly result in my death. I am sorry. These Shadow Workers are clearly more powerful than I had previously estimated, judging from that armored projection they used to scout areas and catch up to us."

"No apology needed. I expected as much. And I don't think Makis is a defensive mage, either."

"His knowledge revolves almost solely around his gate."

Raiz was back to his own ruminations, and dissuaded other comments by saying, "if you would all be quiet for a moment, I might be able to think a way around this. I can't believe these people would seal themselves in without a way to communicate out that didn't involve suicide."

Shifting uneasily, putting his weight on one leg, then the other, and back again, Kaz worked himself up to state the obvious after a minute of silence had passed. He stepped forward so that he was standing next to Emily before saying, "Except . . . except for you Commander Raiz, I think I'm the only one that could send the message to the ship comm systems."

"You can't –"

"I know that I'll have to use the backdoor method – I guess you already have all the frequencies for that – because they're probably maintaining first level radio silence. I'm fully qualified."

"I know you are. That's not what I was about to say," said Raiz, a tinge irritated, but also amused by Kaz's visceral need to state his credentials. "As I was saying, you can't be serious. You strike me as a levelheaded sort. Why would you be willing to sacrifice yourself like that? Don't you have any family, or someone who'll miss you?"

"Not . . . not anyone that I talk to anymore." Emily's heart filled with pity at the sound of Kaz's broken voice, though it quickly made room for pride in her first officer.

"Sorry to hear that. I thought that would be a sure-fire way to change your mind. Listen, this city almost certainly has plenty of food for us in some sort of hydroponics gardens – enough to feed thousands of people perpetually. We shouldn't be hurried to find a solution to this."

"I thought of that. But how long do you think the World Council will keep Earth Forces ready to . . . to intervene here? You're not there to convince them to keep it up. How long before one of your political enemies convinces the council that the confrontation with Eldrand isn't worth whatever might be found here on Selparis?"

Raiz barked out a laugh. "Good point, good point. I'd give it a week more at most. All right, so we don't have that much time."

The admission gave Kaz a bit more steel, and he continued. "Do you really think you'll find another way to send the message?"

"It's . . . improbable. If this place wasn't shut up tight, we'd be fried by mages by now. But there's still a chance."

"Then . . . then if you're not going, I will," Kaz turned to look at Emily, to see if he was making the right move. Her amused and slightly awed stare back at him was enough to confirm that she was supportive of his decision. Of course, she was hardly the vanguard of good choices, but she was an excellent marker for the line between courage and stupidity. She had walked that line and survived.

"There's a good chance that you'll die. Even Tylan thinks he would die, and he's a bit more talented in the magic department than you are."

Kaz stayed silent. Now that he had stated his decision, he could only keep his mouth shut and look more resolute than he was while Raiz tried to talk him out of it. If Kaz responded to the attempts to dissuade him, it would be a sign that he wanted his mind changed for him, and Raiz would absolutely refuse to let him go. He had to resist the temptation to take the easier road.

"Well, I'm going with him," Emily said promptly, delighted that Kaz was more her type than she once guessed. Actually, she wondered whether getting a night's sleep before deciding might be a better way to go, but there was no way she could sit back when he was ready to go. To do so would be an embarrassment to her for years to come. Besides, if they delayed, Kaz might lose his will, and no one could blame him if he did. It was a minor irony that, in this case, he was the one being impulsive, while she wanted time to consider their course carefully, but her preference was due to her unique gift, not from the sudden blossoming of cautious decision-making. She was itchy to delve into her lucid dreams as soon as possible, now that they were firmly in Raljar Canti, and the Shadow Workers were safely outside. Since the traumatic night in the forest, her fear of what she might see, and be unable to change, kept her from actively seeking the nocturnal knowledge. Those fears had since melted away, perhaps because of the combined company of Tylan and Makis, and the magic she had recently seen in use. She had to set all that aside, though. Kaz had stuck his neck out, and she loathed responding in any way that might turn them away from positive action. Everything said between Raiz and Kaz convinced her that this was the only way.

She also acknowledged the fact that she was growing fond of Kaz. She admired the way he carried himself outside of the ship and the environment he was more accustomed to, and was consistently comforted by his presence. Ever since she had named him her first officer, much of the old sniping between them had diminished. Some tension and frustration had remained, especially when she told him that she wanted to pursue the mission to Selparis, but their talks had become markedly more amiable. Now, whatever friction there was between them, it was purely due to their . . . she couldn't quite pin down where they were at right now. Her previous relationships had evolved in a carefree atmosphere and without the employer-employee complication. In contrast to those easier times, Kaz and her were embroiled in a high-stakes conflict that, to say the least, complicated their ability to express their feelings toward each other, whatever those might be.

Ever perceptive about the subtle realities around him, Jaik said, "Why?" in English, with such anguish in his voice that Emily knew he was aware of the subtext behind her offer to join Kaz. He had caught the exchange of looks between the two of them, and even cultural barriers were inadequate to prevent him from understanding what had pushed Kaz to his courageousness. If Emily had known enough to use Raiz's laptop, and decided to go on the mission to transmit the secrets, Jaik would have been the first to volunteer to join her, with absolute disregard for the dangers, and no one would have to wonder why. Now, with competition in the picture and taking the lead, his impulse was to tear her away from the other. "You can't," he continued to say in English, but then articulated himself better in his own language. "You cannot fight mages, and you cannot use Raiz's machine, so why risk your life for no reason?"

Emily could find nothing to say that would satisfy Jaik, since he would dismiss any claim that she was simply standing by her first officer.

Seeing that Emily had no explanation, West said, "she's going because he's her friend, Jaik, you know that." The reason caught Emily by surprise, since it was obvious, but had not for a moment crossed her mind.

Jaik turned to West and knew that his friend, who had learned over years to understand him, fully comprehended his jealousy, and the blow this was to his low self-image. There was also a hint that West wanted to do something proactive, and to join Emily and Kaz to the surface.

The disappointment and confusion was too much for Jaik, and the condescending pity from West was the last straw. Unable to keep his composure in their midst, he bolted off through the nearest aisle at a fast walk, maintaining enough dignity to prevent his legs from breaking into a run, and turning out of sight before anyone could say anything. West followed him, though allegiance to his friend only marginally trumped his desire to join Kaz's vital mission. He tailed Jaik at a distance to allow time for the distraught young man to cool down, and before he disappeared among the stacks, he threw a half-apologetic, half-accusatory look back at the rest.

Looking back and forth between the retreating figure of West and Kaz's pale countenance, Ethan quickly decided, "I'd better talk to Jaik," and left them, jogging to catch up to West.

"I . . . ," Kaz said, trying to broach Jaik's bizarre reaction, having some idea of his own part in them. Realizing that Emily had played a more significant role, he said, "You . . . ," but lacked any way to complete the thought.

"Damn, I mean geez, out of all the –" Emily shook her head, her fists clenched in fury at her own misguided treatment of Jaik, a tear or two of frustration in her eye. "He's such a –"

"He's a kid, Emily," Kaz said pointedly, certain of this fact, at least.

"But he's past twenty in . . . in Earth years. I didn't think –"

"Don't worry about it," he said, judging that she was more than appropriately remorseful for her actions, and eager to get them refocused on the task. "He'll get over it."

"And it's not like there was anything between me and him anyway. I've had boyfriends, real boyfriends, and some of them got emotional when I dumped them, but that was because there had been something there. I didn't feel too sorry about dumping them, though, so why do I feel like crap right now?"

"Because he's a kid."

"No, he isn't. He hasn't acted like one once this whole time."

Kaz looked directly into her eyes and she almost took a step back. "Maybe in other things he acts like an adult, but in the part that mattered, the . . . his crush on you, I guess, he was –"

"I know, I know," she said, desperately wanting to change the subject with so many people listening to the conversation. That was odd, too. How many times had she gloated, at the top of her voice at a club with only one or two friends and a host of other people overhearing, about all her exploits, however embarrassing or disgusting, and every tawdry detail about her relationships. Since when had she become so self-conscious? It only took a look at Kaz to know the answer.

She had to change the subject. To move the only other logical topic forward, she said, "well, anyone else coming with us?"

As if obligated to do so, the guards immediately stood at attention as a sign that they were ready to serve. Even though he had initiated the mission, Kaz was now prepared, and even eager, to accept Emily's leadership, and let her decide whether to recruit the guards or not.

"Uh . . . how about we take two of you along?" She peered at Raiz for confirmation, but he just shrugged to indicate that this was her show now, and he had no interest to take part in it. He had even reached for one of the guard's sacks to bring out his backup laptop, showing that he had already given up his other one for lost. That was just one of his games, though. If he had a better plan, or even the inkling of one, he would put it forward firmly so that no one could even consider an alternative. He simply wanted to establish that he was not responsible for their actions and that, insofar as he had identified her as an equal partner in this adventure, Emily bore the responsibility for this surface expedition. The arrangement was suddenly very convenient for him. Emily was also ready to bet that Raiz had allowed Kaz to tag along, instead of insisting that the first officer should stay on Newport Station, precisely because Kaz knew enough about computers and ships to manage certain things in the commander's own absence. Things that no one else in the party would be able to take care of. It would just have been a matter of covering all the bases.

Doubts about her place in Raiz's scheme set aside, she readied herself to lead three other people on a ludicrously perilous undertaking. She was hoping that, if things got hot, they could save themselves simply by leaping back down into the hilltop aperture. As long as they hustled back down at the first sign of trouble, the city's computer had expressed confidence that the nanobots could seal the city behind them. They would have to avoid wasting time, though, or risk getting sealed outside. She forced herself to find every possible way to survive, trying to exude a minimal sense of self-confidence for the sake of the others.

Already, Kaz was less sure of himself. He carried Raiz's laptop as if it was a newborn child. Of course, there was a good reason to treat it gingerly, since all their hopes rested in it, and with it already set to send the first message at the push of a button, he had to avoid any mishandling. Nothing would break his ability to move forward more than an error forcing him to head back to Raiz in disgrace, to ask the commander to fix his computer. Kaz even opened it periodically to check that it was still on the correct screen, half of the time hoping that there was some sort of error that would save him from the pickle he had put himself in.

The city's computer assigned them a new guide-bird – this one ominously crow-formed, complete with jet-black plumage. It had an impatient character, cawing at them unnervingly when they were lagging, and preferring to perch on the highest point in visible range while waiting, instead of circling overhead as its predecessor had. Hard as it was to believe that the crow symbolism has the same meaning to the ancient Atlantii as it did to Emily, she was nevertheless convinced that this was another sign of the city's malevolence towards them.

Immediately after they exited the library, Erem Kantor confronted them, eager for news but hesitant to enter the hallowed ground of any ancient building. They quickly updated him, continuing to follow the crow as they spoke. Kantor sensed in them a strong sense of urgency, and accepted their unwillingness to stand and speak, not knowing that only their diminishing courage pressed them for time. Telling him all they could before leaving him, they hustled down an unfamiliar road to the center of the city.

Skyscrapers worthy of any Earth city grew around them, making the most efficient use of the in-dome space. At the heart of the downtown cluster, they saw four great and equal towers that, from a distance, looked like a single building, being so close to each other. The elevator shaft rising to the ceiling from the midst of the four was so clear and non-reflective that they only made it out when already under the towers' shadows. Closer, they saw that the buildings had a curved exterior, so that each one was a quadrant of an ellipse. Considering everything else in this place had proven to be more complex than was strictly necessary, Emily was sure the familiar look of the metal and glass constructions belied the same excesses that offended West.

Passing between the looming, intimidating heights of the two towers, they entered a garden filled with robotically maintained plants, and a relatively tiny control center at the base of the elevator. The small, overshadowed building was an exact duplicate of the one they had arrived in on their descent. Because of their harrowing confinement on that first occasion, the structure engendered apprehension in all of them. While the entire city was under the domination of its artificially intelligent systems, and subject to a moral code punishable by death, these nodes were, in their minds, the computer's home. What if it decided Raiz's argument was unconvincing after all, and chose to detain and interrogate them again instead of letting them pass? One wrong answer in its eyes, and –

Of course, it could get rid of them much more efficiently by letting them pass, Emily's pessimistic and sarcastic core reminded her. It was sort of silly to worry about what a demented computer would do to them when they had volunteered to face people definitely ready to blow them to bits with a magical blast. Her mind reminded her that even if Raiz was a coward, she was anything but a soldier, and could appreciate why he was so reluctant to take on this task himself. She had done tremendously stupid things, usually on dares, but she had never been up for sacrificing her life, whether the cause was worthy or not. Then again, the survival rate might preclude anyone from doing something this idiotic more than once. From her perspective and sensibilities, no cause was worthy unless it was possible for her to enjoy it after the struggle was over, so she wondered what exactly had brought her this far. Taking a good, long look at Kaz, her subtlest thought processes pointed out his substandard appearance – she could do better – and expressed a vain hope that she had other motives, except for him, for making the choice to be here.

Her pessimism was abruptly swept aside by the realization that, even now, she did not believe that she would die. For some strange reason, she was able to visualize success very clearly, and the loss of one or both of the guards, but despite trying to do so, she failed to conjure a convincing image involving either her death, or Kaz's. It could be wishful thinking, but the tone of her recent thoughts made that conclusion dubious – nothing about her recent thoughts was rosy. So, maybe it was safe to draw comfort from her failure to see her demise, or Kaz's, but her corresponding ability to see clear scenarios in which the two guards met their end made her feel too guilty to do so. Any attempt to justify her visualizations, to see them as outcroppings from her dreams leaking through into the waking world in which her mind was trying to select from possible futures, made her uneasy for the same reason. However, that idea, breaking down the wall between the waking and dreaming worlds, making it permeable in both directions instead of just one, was appealing to her. It suggested a subconscious method to her decisions, so that instead of the manipulations of powerful people bringing her to Selparis, she might have chosen this course somewhere deep in her mind, where hints of the future gathered and waited to be rendered into dreams.

She filed that thought away for later consideration, and refocused on their progress through the control center. They entered the ring of panels surrounding the elevator without any resistance, and faced with nothing of note except the departure of their crow. It went off to some unknown hold, to wait out the eons before someone would need it again.

The two guards were growing increasingly anxious, realizing too late that they were walking into danger without anything constructive to do. Unlike Kaz and Emily, they had no justification for leaving the sanctuary of the city, since they lacked any way to do their job – to protect the others from harm. They needed the special battle armor Earth Forces battled mancers and mages in, and the anti-magical tactics training those elite troops received. A mage would swat away the energy of their weapons with ease or, even worse, redirect it back at them. Increasingly aware that they were nothing more than cannon fodder, they found their limbs stiffening against their movement forward.

The elevator gave no hint of menace, opening invitingly and sliding its doors closed behind them without an ominous slam. Although the transporter had lacked the benefit of human inspection for thousand of years, Emily knew now that the city computer continued to manage the necessary repairs, so there was little need to worry about safety this time. She had to admit that the city had run itself quite well despite the absence of humans. As it shot up, leaving the semi-lit city behind, the elevator's ascent was so smooth only their mordant ruminations kept them from drifting to sleep. They had no way of knowing whether it was night or day in the outside world, but the underground city's sky was perpetually dark, and there had already been enough activity in the day to warrant the need for some rest. As they had so far, they would have to rely on the momentum of events to carry them through to the end of their mission, anticipating no further lulls in the tension.

High above the city, at its very pinnacle, they exited onto a platform forty feet wide supported from above by webs of metallic ropes extending to the dome. On each of its corners, spiraling staircases led down hundreds of feet to the roofs of the four towers, though these dizzying heights made the use of those stairs unlikely except in emergencies. Opposite the elevator entrance, there was a door, again identical to the hydraulic one they first saw when passing into the city. Because the entire structure was suspended from above, the exterior of the tunnel behind the door was visible. It rose steadily, up into the ceiling-dome of the city.

Emily led the way through the door and into the neon-lit corridor that, once within the dome, started making corkscrew turns to the left. After three complete turns, they reached a cube-shaped cabin about twelve feet in each dimension. Huge glass panes filled most of its wall space, and it no doubt once served as an observation deck atop the dome when the city had been in space. Now, those panes revealed nothing but dirt surrounding them, since the terraforming of the planet had covered even this high point. The pressure on the cabin from the earth around it was, of course, nothing the high-tech composites used to build it, and the nanobots used to maintain it, could not handle.

"Do you suppose it'd work in here?" asked Emily. "I mean, we're pretty close to the surface, and we're outside the dome, so maybe the signal isn't blocked anymore."

Kaz let himself absorb some of that hope, but logic prevented him from accepting the idea outright. "If you were as paranoid as the people who built this were, wouldn't you shield this place, too? If they are worried about traitors trying to get people in, wouldn't this be an obvious place to protect?"

"You know what, I really don't get the whole thing," she said, throwing her hands up. "Okay, I see the ladder up to the . . . what do you call . . . the wheel-locked hatch in the ceiling, and I know that's the way outside. If there was going to be a traitor, what's the big difference between being in here, and being up there?"

"That's an airlock, Captain," Kaz said, with a hint of his usual exasperation.

"What?"

"This place was in space, so that isn't just a hatch. It leads to an airlock and pressurization chamber. That means there's a big difference between being in here and being out there if the city's in space. As long as they didn't let people in spacesuits up the elevator, traitors wouldn't have been able to send the signal, as long as this place is also shielded."

"As long as this place is also shielded," Emily repeated dejectedly.

Kaz sighed. "Right. Nice thought, though." Then, because he wanted to make up for discouraging her, he smiled at her. By reflex, though it was the last thing she felt like doing right now, she smiled back. They were both in the same place, with the same fears and hopes. Turning to the guards in unison, they also both had a very concrete idea about not being the first up the airlock.

"I suppose . . . we should go first," the one on Emily's right said.

"Oh, come on," said the left guard, who was seriously rethinking his chosen vocation, "what do you want us to do when we get up there?

We can't do anything. And this was not our idea, by the way."

Kaz and Emily just stood on, looking at them silently. Emily felt a bit guilty about it, especially after visualizing the two of them dead, but why had the two of them come in the first place, if not to be guards? Moreover, in every depiction she could think of, guards stepped through first. It was practically in the job description. These fellows weren't the Secret Service, nor did Kaz and Emily expect the presidential treatment. Reluctance on the part of the guard was no surprise, yet there was an expectation that the type of person who chose to be a personal guard would have sentiments like honor and duty that would ultimately sway them to be self-sacrificing in a way Emily and Kaz were not.

The guard on the right – Emily was acutely conscious that she had failed to ask his name – definitely had the requisite tendencies in spades. "Well," he said, faithfully, "I'll go first." Without another word, he started up the ladder, turned the handle on the airlock door, and climbed in. In space, the vacuum on the other side of the eight-foot tall airlock would require someone in the cabin to seal the astronaut in. The depressurization controls were inside the chamber itself, to prevent its use as a tool for murder or capital punishment. In this case, the guard just climbed through, leaving the first hatch open as he completed his ascent to the top. Without the base of the airlock to stand on, however, he had trouble balancing himself while trying to force the lid open. Emily was afraid that he would soon ask them to shut him in so he could get more leverage against the outer hatch. Now that she had egged him to take the lead, she felt nervous about losing sight of the brave guard, lest something happen to him.

Before the brave guard, as she now called him, made the dreaded suggestion, though, the more sensible one snapped, "get down and let me try."

The hesitant guard had more bulk on him, and stood with such firmness that gravity despaired of ever bringing him down against his will, so the brave one gave way to him. Sure enough, he was able to push it up and open on his first try, knocking aside the tight layer of earth covering and jamming it. Genuine sunlight poured into the chamber for the first time in millennia.

"I loosened it for you," the brave one mumbled, attempting to save face in the traditional way.

The fresh air battled with the machined air of the city as it poured in, while they ascended the ladder eagerly, once it was clear mages weren't hovering directly above it. Emerging into the open, Emily realized that there was little difference between the hill towns of the Selians and this underground city of the ancients in terms of feeling buried alive. How humans, or any species like them, could get used to living like this was beyond her. The top of the artificial hill was a brilliant release from the oppressive environment, as long as she looked up. Down the slope, only the outer circuit of the ravaged surface city was visible due to the bulge of the mountain, but it was enough. Covered in flames and a thick layer of smoke, the smell of which was starting to saturate the air even at this altitude, the city's buildings were no longer visible, and for all they knew, the enemy had reduced every square foot to rubble.

Tiny specks were visible, floating above the choking smoke, and they occasionally dove below the haze as if fishing. The Shadow Workers, having found no way in on the mountain itself, persisted in their search for the inevitable secret entrance. The one used by the residents of the city was already blocked off and impenetrable. Emily saw no sign of the local mages who had stayed outside Raljar Canti, forestalling the advance of the enemy, so either they were fighting closer to the mountain and therefore out of sight, or their opponents had overwhelmed them.

Since some of the Shadow Workers had combed the peak firsthand, many of them, if not all, were now able to teleport to the summit in a flash. There was no time to waste. Before Emily could indicate for him to proceed, Kaz had already sent the message to Newport Station using the hyperspace relay via Captain Wilson's ship, and was waiting for confirmation before reconfiguring the laptop's wireless communications port.

"We're good on that one," Kaz said finally, with some relief. The Newport Station connection was the one he could not handle on his own. Now, it was only a matter of how much time their enemies would afford them. Kaz tapped out a constant rhythm, using the ISC emergency channels to link to every nearby ship, then sent the secure signal to make sure he had everyone's attention. Because most ships in the ISC were of Eldrandii make, and had the same comm system installed, establishing uniform ISC procedures was straightforward. The emergency line would be uninterrupted for the next minute – enough time to get the files through, judging from the quick transfer to the hyperspace relay. It was unlikely that any ship in the vicinity would interrupt the message, even after secure time expired, since the header indicated its striking contents, and the fact that the same message was on its way to Earth. The Eldrandii would want to know the extent to which their most essential wisdom had been unveiled. Kaz crossed his fingers in the hope that no Shadow Worker ship was listening in on the channel, and therefore poised to get the secret without a fight. Presumably, the host of Eldrandii and Earth ships would destroy such a ship immediately, so there shouldn't be one in orbit, but what if Earth and Eldrand were already embroiled in their own fight?

The transfer initiated, Kaz was visited by a centuries-old plague – the progress bar inching its way across the screen. With every notch, his heartbeat accelerated and its pounding intensified. Past the halfway mark, he could have sworn his skull was about to burst from the throbbing. He tried to relieve the pressure by turning away from the screen, but his eyes unfailingly drifted to the sight of the city below, and the mages at their foul work.

The other three waited with their attention fixed on him, a soft wind cooling their faces, standing on a yellowish-brown patchwork of nanobots-tended grasses and soil. Emily became increasingly alert, and when Kaz took his focus away from the laptop screen, she snapped her head in panic, concerned that by staring intently at his work, she had missed the enemy's approach. Seeing nothing new made her no calmer. Though the intuition that she was going to survive this was still strong, the competing claim that danger was fast approaching also filled her. More than a concern or foreboding, it felt now like a firm certainty.

In Emily's mind, one thought began to occupy every spare space – that she could not let anyone die. The notion went beyond her normal protectiveness of crewmembers or friends, taking on a life of its own, and branched into reinforcing ideas. She was just starting to like Kaz. After dragging the guards along, it would be her fault if they died. The deaths of those she was responsible for started to elicit a visceral horror in her, as if promising a hell of eternal nightmares for her failure to protect them. She was not a general capable of putting thousands of troops in harm's way to secure a victory, and the contrast was poignant to her. Already, she knew the name Max would haunt her for the rest of her life, and every time she heard it, she would imagine his tortured death. John, the pod pilot whose fate she couldn't even be sure of, would probably occupy the same place in her mind, unless a miracle had transpired and he had escaped danger.

Microseconds after her mind became saturated with this concrete set of thoughts, a faint glow – the glow of magic – appeared around them in four cloudy spheres. Under her breath and in an eerie trance, Emily said, "they're coming."

"What?" Kaz said, unable to control the pitch of his voice. "It's at ninety percent."

"Why the hell's it going so slow?" the burly one asked, his weapon already prepared to fire. "Just tell me where to shoot. Dammit, why couldn't we have brought our own mage?"

"Won't work," Emily said airily, standing tall, eyes glazed over. The guards looked at her puzzled, wondering whether she was referring to their guns or the potential help Tylan would have provided.

The four mages appeared a full second before Kaz shouted, "Almost . . . done!" They launched their blasts before he closed the laptop in triumph. To their credit, the guards stood ready to protect Kaz and Emily, resisting the temptation to scramble down the stairwell. As a result, they witnessed a minor miracle. The blue-hot plasma launched by the mages dissipated in midair feet away from the targets. The deflected energy outlined a large sphere centered on Emily, leaving no mystery about the cause of the attack's failure. She was rooted to the spot, and showed no sign of awareness.

Kaz worked out what had happened before the guards, and shouted at them, "get back down."

"You fir–"

"I said get back down!" The two guards were closer to the hatch in any case, so they didn't object further, dropping down the ladder and clearing the way for the other two.

The mages let loose another salvo, and this time Emily's protective shield was smaller – about twelve feet in diameter. Kaz was at the lip of the airlock when he panicked, seeing Emily was still standing in the same place, not moving to escape. Whatever she was doing prevented her from initiating any other action. Desperate, he charged at her, grabbed her right hand, and tugged. The pull forced her to take a step back, but she was still entranced and unresponsive. He took her arm with both of his hands and, on his next effort, brought her stumbling backward to the ground.

Once again, either lacking enough imagination to attack the two prone figures physically by simply tackling them, or being too orthodox in the use of magic to resort to such base measures, the mages launched the same spells again, trusting that this time they would break through. They didn't. At the stairwell and placing Emily's feet in the aperture, Kaz shouted for the guards below to catch her. The third volley flashed an inch away from his face, the intense heat leaking through. A look back showed that Emily was still fully protected, but that was the last gasp for her shield. Wasting no time, he anchored himself and launched her into the stairwell, with the bodyguard inside it catching her, and keeping her from knocking her head on anything.

Kaz jumped in after her, shouting incoherent words as he got as much of his body down as he could fit with the guard and Emily still partly in the way. The mages were closing in, and he could not reach for the external seal to cover up their escape route – not if he wanted to keep his head. Looking down and seeing the way clear, he released his grip on the rungs and fell through instead of climbing down, which at this point was the only option to avoid the fireballs that would be sent down mere seconds later. He desperately hoped that someone was ready to catch him, but was unable to shout for them to do so in the second he made his decision to risk it. The brave guard did, though not before the mages were standing right above them, looking down into this entrance into the underground city with wild and hungry stares.

It was all up to the city computer now and, before the mages could bake the occupants of the observation deck, a new seal to the airlock emerged from its edge. The unseen nanobots created a new, more permanent closure. One mage attempted to get into the chamber before the nanobots completed their work, and the ruthless metal sliced him in half. No one had time to get sickened by the gory legs still perched on the ladder down, because the city computer was continuing its efforts.

As soon as outside light no longer leaked into the underground, liquid metal started dripping downward along the sides of the stairwell. They hurriedly closed the lower hatch, understanding that the computer was securing the place in a final, anti-magic manner, but the hatch itself burst and the metal continued to pour through. They had to get out of the observation deck, as the entire place was under demolition. With the burly guard carrying Emily, who was now asleep and breathing slowly, they rushed down the spiral through the great dome of Raljar Canti with the city's tiny agents following close in their tracks.

The pursuit stopped when the liquid metal reached the end of the spiral, not continuing with them onto the platform. The four of them were in the elevator before the nanobots rebuilt the corridor's entrance into a solid wall.

Almost out of breath, more from the entire experience than just the exertion of carrying Emily down, the burly guard said, "this computer thing is pretty serious isn't it? When it says the mages aren't getting through, it means it."

Kaz nodded, hyperventilating and struggling through choking coughs to get a chance to say what was on his mind. By the time they were halfway down the elevator shaft, he managed to say, "How is she?"

"Fine, I guess. Looks like she's sleeping, but I can't tell what's going on . . . you know," he tapped her head gently, "in there. Did you know she could do that?"

Kaz shook his head, his heavy breathing under better control, but still making it hard for him to get words out. As his brain was also numb with confusion, he decided not to speak at all until there was a real opportunity to get some answers.

"Didn't think so," the burly guard continued. "Better question – did she know she could do that?"

Kaz's brows furrowed. He doubted that Emily was the sort to hide a useful ability, especially when they were all eager to find some source of hope. Since she willingly disclosed the magic associated with her dreaming, there was no reason to hold this aspect of her abilities back. What if she had done it before, initially misunderstood what had really happened, but now guessed the truth? By not telling them, she would avoid giving them an untested reason to risk themselves. That was a bit like her, but Kaz found it difficult to credit her with that much consideration and secrecy. Emily was anything but tight-lipped, and in that respect was the opposite of Kaz, who already knew a host of secrets he would keep through his death.

While he preferred to think of her in this analytical way, he increasingly felt a dumbfounded awe and wonder whenever he looked at her, and not only for the obvious reason. Were there other humans, perhaps millions, who, if brought in close proximity to the magic abundant on most worlds, could do the same as Emily had? The one thing he was sure of was that he was not of that number, having shown no inkling of unexpected abilities despite spending ample time in space and many ISC planets. Would Emily begin looking at others like him differently, if placed among many humans like herself? Was this an unbridgeable gap between them?

Unable to calm himself down, he faced a persistent turmoil that prevented the filtering of his thoughts. In a normal frame of mind, he would explain his concern in purely professional terms, but not now. He would find adequate excuses to blunt his overt affection to Emily when she woke up acting normally, or when he was in the company of Jaik. For now, he only had energy for raw and unrefined reactions.

Their journey back to the library was somber, but relieved. After all, the mission, which Raiz had considered unacceptably risky, was a success. They were alive. Kaz first grasped the debt he owed to Emily – which they all owed to her – when the library was within view. The word "hero" crossed his mind for the first time, and he found to his surprise that he deserved the title as much as or more than the others did. As long as Emily woke intact, his choice to volunteer had proved a solid one – a decision to be proud of – and his rescuing of her was . . . not something he would find easy to recount. Had he actually chosen to save her, or had it been instinct? It was all a bit hazy, and he remembered the struggle as if he had only watched it happen. Unless the action was deliberate, he doubted that he could take credit for it.

Emily was still asleep when they reached the library steps through the parted crowd. The local people wanted to ask how the venture had fared, but they kept silent in deference, seeing the sight of Emily and fearing the worst. Jaik, West, Ethan, and Tylan met them in the library's entryway, each one showing worry and impatience in his own way.

Jaik was seated, back to one of the doorposts, quietly cursing himself and murmuring that he should have gone with the surface expedition instead of getting emotional for no reason. West paced vigorously, and if there had been a tree to climb that he was comfortable with – one not tended to by robots – he would have taken to the better vantage point in a heartbeat. Finding a good use for his guitar, carried by him all this way mainly at Emily's bidding, Ethan alternated his playing between aimless improvisations and furious tunes, reflecting the cycles in his interior monologue.

Tylan turned out to be the one most beside himself. Seated just inside the doorway, he was in the middle of the most agitated meditation he had experienced in decades, since his world was ruined in the attempt to save the galaxy from the mancers. Sensing the return of the four, he leapt to his feet and rushed down the steps to them.

"I knew it! I should have gone with you!" he shouted, confessing his guilt in an embarrassingly loud proclamation. "Now, look at her! Poor soul."

Taken aback by the emotion displayed by the elderly Tylan, whose normal stoicism would have delighted Roman philosophers, Kaz desperately tried to reassure the mage. "She's not dead. She's all right. She's just . . . sleeping, I think."

"I know, I know, and it is not sleep, you fool. Magic reacts to the processes of the mind and, when her mental activity indicated life-threatening danger, her magic initiated a self-defense mechanism. This was what I was speaking of when I told Raiz of the inefficacy of my own magic. A magic user schooled in defensive magic would know how to control it so it did not go this far, but this poor girl."

"Why? What happened to her?"

"She's drained herself of almost every particle of magic, and is now below the levels every normal human would naturally maintain."

Kaz paled and, stuttering, said, "s-so . . . w-what does that mean?"

Jaik, West, and Ethan listened intently, and looked drained of vitality. Each one turned a pair of pleading eyes to Tylan.

"It . . . it means she is in a sort of coma, and one that some people recover from, and others do not. I will do my best for her, and the next week will be critical. After that, if she does not absorb magic, those higher functions that require some magic may never return to her."

"You mean . . . her magical abilities?"

Tylan shook his head impatiently. "I mean her mind. Her ability to think as sentient beings do. Her personality. After two weeks, we would be lucky if she recovered to even non-sentient functionality. Now, please, I need to start helping her. Bring her into the atrium and lay her down there. If some of you search for a bed or somewhere comfortable for her, that would be better."

West volunteered himself, Jaik, and Ethan for the task, sensing that they would otherwise remain moping at Emily's side. He was more than ready to do some exploring, already stifled from action once due to Jaik's antics. Having a goal that would bring the other two along would help them to get a grip. He was in no mood to be patient with them or to coax them along back to the land of the interesting. West's longtime failure to wander off depended partly on Jaik being an intriguing out-of-the-box thinker who, though admittedly lazy and quiet, never accepted anything fed to him at face value. If his old friend chose to spend his time being a soppy mess, there was no reason to hang around and watch the melodrama unfold.

Kaz would have eagerly gone with the three to find a bed for Emily, but having Raiz's laptop in hand, he decided that he should return it to the commander before engaging in any other task. Guessing what he was about to do, Tylan quickly pointed out, "Raiz is not in the library. There is a spaceport nearby, or maybe a space museum according to what Tayron said. Everyone is there."

Thanking Tylan and casting a last, furtive glance at Emily, Kaz descended back down the library steps and cut through the crowd quickly, trying to show that he was still not ready to answer questions. He was peeved that Raiz had rushed off instead of waiting for their return, but reasoned that this at least showed the commander was working on something constructive in their absence. Finding the spaceport without some guidance in this city would be a trick, especially since he understood none of the street signs. Kaz risked looking foolish, and shouted, "Computer, I need a guide to wherever Commander Raiz is."

Sure enough, a swift appeared within seconds, circled his head once, and then started flying a zigzag down the road. Kaz considered chasing down Ethan to suggest the use of a computerized bird to help in the search for a bed, but decided against it. For one thing, the swift was overeager and almost out of sight, forcing him to jog in its wake to keep up. He also understood quite clearly that the longer the search, the better it would be for them, just as a long excursion away from Emily would benefit his troubled mind.

The space museum turned out to be so large that though its borders were not far away from the library at all – five blocks at most – the trek to where Raiz stood examining one of the ships was easily twice as long. The swift left once Raiz was in sight. "Like it has something better to do," Kaz mumbled, finding he had much to say about how the workings of this city could be improved.

Raiz was looking around distractedly as the scientists talked to him about their findings in one of the massive ships, which were totally unlike the prevalent Eldrandii designs. Once he caught sight of Kaz, he ran up to the first officer with both delight and a sense of foreboding. A planner who believed in balance, and that no situation was entirely good or completely bad, he was prepared to hear what must have gone wrong, because something surely had. Just the sight of Kaz's sour face confirmed it.

Kaz was bewildered about what to say and how to say it. Tylan had, after all, done the most difficult part for him, knowing even better than he did about what happened. Raiz was clever, but could he guess, without seeing Emily, how they were all saved at the cost of her comatose condition?

What did Raiz know? It was never possible to overestimate the extent of his knowledge, so could he have foreseen Emily's use of her magical defense? The question resolved Kaz's confusion and transformed it into something approaching anger. He worked himself up to it, realizing that even if he was being paranoid, the best way to get answers from Raiz might be to put the commander on the defensive. Had it been Raiz's plan from the start to see the extent of Emily's powers, knowing that the magic would protect her as much as it could? It was ludicrous, of course, but plausible enough to spark Kaz's anger and get his energy pumping.

Without any prompting, he shouted, "did you plan this?"

"Did I plan what?" said Raiz innocently, reaching for his laptop, the backup still at his side. Kaz wanted to trust that guiltless look, but recalled that it had effortlessly led them into this in the first place.

"Did you plan for Emily to use her powers to protect us?"

Raiz scratched his head, "I seem to remember you two volunteering –"

"Don't give me that. You could have gone yourself with Tylan's protection. You came all the way here yourself even though you could have delegated the responsibility, so you can't be as much of a coward as you make yourself out to be. And what's with carrying two laptops when neither of them can do the job right, anyway?"

Raiz cleared his throat. "I'm not a coward, but I don't take unwise risks. And, for the record, Tylan is a coward, and you can tell him I said that. We've had a few talks since you left, and he eventually confessed that there was a good chance he could have protected you for the few minutes you needed, even if a dozen mages saw his magic at the top of the hill. More than a dozen, and maybe not, but it would still have been better than what we sent you with. The problem with him is that he's never been in the thick of it. He's more of a behind-the-desk sort, and I don't think he's seriously had to shield himself against anything, ever."

"And that was your plan," Kaz realized, "you had wanted him to go with us."

"I considered it a good possibility, but I don't know as much about magic as I should, and when Tylan expressed doubt that he could do much good, I had to take him at his word. When you stepped up . . . I didn't know what to think. It's not my job to keep people from making choices or mistakes, but I was pretty close to insisting in your case. When Emily backed you up, though, I thought she had a trick up her sleeve. Maybe she had seen something in a dream. Why? Didn't she have something? Didn't it work?"

"If you mean did we get the messages through, then yes. And we're all alive. But Emily . . . I don't think she knew what she was doing. She used her magic to defend us, but it wasn't . . . deliberate. It was automatic, like Tylan had talked about before we left, and it drained her magic. She's in a coma. Tylan says . . . he doesn't know if he can help her."

Raiz swallowed. "I'm sorry. I definitely didn't mean that to happen."

"I don't think she had any tricks. She was just following her instincts. She . . . does that sometimes. I think she likes to live that way. It would drive me crazy. It does drive me crazy, because I can't tell –"

Sighing, Raiz said, "for some people, that's knowing. That was why I preferred her to Wilson. I can take care of the calculations. What I need is someone who's less predictable, and who can deal with unpredictable situations."

Kaz shook his head, but didn't say anything. In the silence, a thought struck Raiz. "You know, she's very good at dreaming. She was able to see the inside of this place from hundreds of miles away. Granted, it wasn't sealed up like it is now, but somehow her mind was able to penetrate the future here. When you think about how hard it is to get in here physically, and how touchy this city is about magic, it must be that her dreams can break through barriers that normal magic would not be able to get through."

"What are you saying? That we should have sent the scans through her dreams?"

"No. Apart from the problems of getting the information back out again, she can't store adequate copies of anything like that in her mind. Not to send it with any fidelity. No, but I remember Tylan telling me that their minds met in her dreaming one night on your ship. I'm willing to bet that, if we have any chance of getting her out of that coma, we should try to replicate the conditions when their minds met that day."

A rush of adrenaline pouring through him, Kaz nearly shouted, "Should I go tell Tylan to do that?"

Cheerful in the hope brought by his plan, Raiz smiled slightly as he said, "yes, I think so."

13
Revival

No one was as frustrated and anxious as Tylan for the next few days. At first, his efforts to pour magic into Emily resulted in her shield reappearing. He explained that the remnant of the spell was still working itself out, and should fade. On the third day, the shield spell completed and stopped consuming magic, and Emily went into a dream state. Since she still failed to retain the magic, and lacked consciousness, they knew that her dreams were of the prophetic sort, though her mind was in no condition to make sense of them.

Raiz's idea was, so far, a dead end. Emily's dreams were impenetrable, no matter what tact Tylan used. He tried a nearly exact replica of the conditions on board the *Azar* on the first try, and made gradually more direct attempts after that failed. After the fifth session, he told them, "I do not know how it happened in the first place. I am sorry. Since I do not know why the connection between us happened, I cannot duplicate the phenomenon or find an alternative to cause the same effect. I am sorry."

Makis offered no help, either, and hardly seemed interested. The only reason he paid any attention to Emily's plight at all was because it prevented him from getting Tylan's help on the gateway problem. He pestered his fellow mage, but Tylan rebuffed his attempts harshly, taking the opportunity to vent his anger and tension. Returning in irritation to the Atlantian books, he found more complexity than he was prepared to deal with. Of all things he had expected to find in books of magic, equations were not among them, and yet the magical section of the library was filled with mathematical tomes. He mumbled to anyone that cared to listen that he suspected someone had mislabeled the rows, but knew better. Left with no alternative, he joined the vigil for Emily's recovery.

The specialists were actually learning more about magic than Makis was, though the explanations of their findings were no help to him. They had a love of equations, and spent most of their time matching the Atlantian formulas with those they already knew. As Tylan had suggested, magic had constraints and was subject to definite and understandable laws. Appreciating that this discovery did not undermine physics in favor of magic, but rather did the opposite, the physicists were having a much better time, confident of many awards and great fame in the future.

Raiz commented solemnly that the conclusions drawn from the ships in the spaceport would have pleased Emily. They had found the actual living space of the hyperspace mage and, at least in these Atlantian ships, he or she was not shut away as a secret, and spent time aboard the ship in relative comfort. The life support equipment was still in place, as shown in the books, but from the look of the room surrounding it, the mage was able to spend most of the time outside of it, as Emily had envisioned. The people of Raljar Canti, at least, seemed to be of the same mind as West and Jaik – that the hyperspace drive should be a matter of common knowledge rather than a secret – so the ships parked at the spaceport were completely open for study.

Though Makis and the specialists seemed to be in their own little worlds, they were nevertheless rattled by the shaking ground. A battle was raging outside the underground city, presumably between the Shadow Workers and Earth Forces, though it was impossible to be sure. Though the sound of the fighting did not reach the mountain's interior, the minor earthquakes caused by explosions did.

"What if it is not Earth to the rescue?" West asked. "What if it is the mages trying to punch their way in?"

"I recognize the weapons being used," replied Raiz, not apparently happy about having that sort of knowledge. "Don't worry, it's our people."

"I wasn't worried," West spat. He hated not having the option of leaving, and not seeing the sun in the mornings, and grew more agitated by the day. His behavior was now so wild that Jaik and Ethan spent as much time worrying about him as they did Emily. At times, he ranted loudly that he was used to the idea of destructive magic, but wondered what stupidity led humans to push technology to the same depths. West knew he was acting irrationally, but was past caring. His self-identity had never demanded sensibility, but for as long as he could remember, he had always greeted the morning sun, and that ritual was as essential to him as his name. So was freedom.

Much of West's irritation was due to Jaik, who in an unexpected turn of events had become Makis' unofficial apprentice. The young Asparii was studying magic so ardently, and practicing the Atlantian language with such focus, that it was obvious that he was running away from thoughts about Emily, and from associated thoughts about his own inadequacy. Having nothing better to do, Makis had agreed to be his tutor, and disconcertingly acknowledged that the boy had talent. The gateway mages had preserved techniques capable of increasing a person's magical potential to a certain degree, as long as there was already some surplus to work with. In a few days of applying these teachings, which he infuriatingly kept to himself, Jaik could see a slight glow around Makis and Tylan, though the difference in his magic was barely perceptible to them. Makis decided that this learning curve meant Jaik had a chance to develop decent capabilities, though nothing so dramatic as Tylan or himself were able to do.

As if the underground city was lacking in commotion, the thousands of locals seeking refuge in it created some of their own. They had discovered food, as Raiz had predicted, in hydroponics gardens scattered throughout the city, but many locals feared to eat it, as if every fruit was a pomegranate from Hades. After three days of this, the situation was growing dire. Raiz gave up pleading with those who adopted this self-imposed fast, mainly because he conceded they had a point.

"If our theory that this city is a closed system is right, then unless we all choose to live here for the rest of our lives, eating anything grown here will be a blow to its continuity. Now, it might not be a big blow, and any system worth its salt should be able to recover from it, but they have a point."

For the Earthlings, though, the gardens were a delight, and they spent time there to unwind whenever possible. Only some of the foods grown were familiar to them, but not having to think twice before pulling fruit off a tree and eating it was a rare treat. The least familiar plants, those most alien to Earth, grew in abundance on Selparis. Raiz quickly concluded that the seeds were chosen by the terraformers for utility and due to their adaptability to the warm climate of this world. His mind continued to work at full speed to learn more about the thinking of the ancient people, and the reasons for their choices.

Altogether, the calmest mind in the underground city during the days they remained trapped, waiting to be freed by Earth Forces, was Emily's. On the first two days after the start of her coma, her only brain activity involved her vital functions. After the shield spell wore off and the dreaming began, her mind automatically stored into her long-term memory all images that elicited strong associations. Without being bidden, the magic took her along innumerable "what ifs," and attempted to resolve every regret Emily had by showing the results of all alternative paths. In some cases, her life turned out better along one of the untrodden roads, but in most cases, the options not chosen would have been worse. She also saw the immediate range of choices in her future, and the consequences of each, so that though she understood none of it, every possible use of her dreaming insight was exhausted as Tylan poured his magic into her.

Tylan informed the others that the most common hurdle in this sort of recovery was clearly not a barrier in Emily's case. Her consciousness could have rejected his magical energy, since it had a signature based on his personality. Instead, she was absorbing and using his energy as fast as he could produce it and recharge. The use she was putting it, too, though, perplexed him.

"I have only attempted something similar twice before, when people who did not know they were mages expended their magic accidentally, but this is the first time I have seen this kind of . . . receptivity."

After the fifth day since the messages were sent, the plight both inside and outside Raljar Canti changed dramatically. The tremors ceased overnight, but no indications of the progress or result of the battle could be gleaned from under the dome. Raiz expressed absolute confidence that Earth was victorious, and that the troops were sweeping up the remaining mages.

Closer to home, the starving locals finally broke their fast and dispensed with their superstition about eating the underground city's food. Seeing that no god – or computer – had struck the outlanders dead, they judged that no supernatural or technological force would oppose them satisfying their appetite. Their stomachs were disgruntled by the long abstention, so they enjoyed the vast stores with caution, in case sudden bingeing caused vomiting or indigestion.

Emily's situation was similar. She was no longer accepting the full blast of energy Tylan had provided for the past days, but as long as he constrained himself to a level of magic just above his normal radiation, she was starting to take the trickle in and store it. Any more than the slight flow, though, and she threw the lot out in a burst, emptying herself completely again. So, all Tylan could do was stay at her side and wait.

As her magical store built up, her mind started churning in earnest. With an animal level of consciousness, her mind tried to make sense of the images stored during her long dreaming, aware in the vaguest possible way that the information was important, in the same way that data on predators was to a monkey. Already, the bulk of it was lost, and only finding an explanation for the images would help her retain the rest. The failure to grasp all of her visions led to a deep, primal despair that would haunt her nights for years to come.

Eventually, the magic restored her sense of self, and she sought out the mind of someone she desperately wanted to speak to, recalling the most immediately pertinent details from her comatose wanderings. She wanted to speak, with visceral urgency, to the closest sleeping Shadow Worker, and tried to stretch outward to find an open mind. Tylan felt his magical field, normally stretching evenly on all sides, was pointing squarely at Emily, as if she was a black hole drawing in all light. Comprehending that she was going through a new phase, he added more magic into the mix in the hope that, this time, it would not overwhelm her system. She kept absorbing, and because her field was not growing despite the greater input, he deduced that her semi-conscious mind was creating some new spell. In a bout of resentment stemming from sheer weariness, Tylan thought it unfair that Emily would use his magic to work spells she would otherwise be unable to do, instead of making her own recovery a first priority. Regardless, he continued to provide what she needed.

Tylan was, from the outside, beginning to appreciate that Emily was not at all a normal sort of mage. He had spent his time manipulating the physical world in various ways – from the elements to the search for evidence in the cases he had helped authorities on. Like Eldrandii investigators, he could see the recent history of a place or a piece of evidence, given a close proximity to it. Many sages could see local futures, as well as happenings tied to current circumstances. When Emily had connected with his mind, he had been truly surprised. She had the most minimal of magic – so little that, at the time, he had noticed nothing in her more than he would expect to see in a normal Earthling. What could she have dreamt of during the many days, with him producing a river of magic between them? Without an understanding of her peculiar abilities, he had no way of guessing, but knew that he would be amazed.

With Tylan's boost, Emily mentally passed the supposedly magic-proof dome of the underground city, and saw a cognitive landscape in the habitations around it, with each tower the mind of a sentient being, and each color and design their personality. She had never purposefully sought out another psyche before, though she had accidentally linked her mind to two – those of Tylan and the Shadow Worker on Newport Station. The difference was like that between accidentally dreaming the future, and deliberately tuning into it. As long as she focused on what she wanted, she could find the mind she wanted, though it took far more than the usual amount of energy to achieve the feat.

While her benefactor was brooding over her and wondering about her powers, Emily was using his to deal with one last question. In the blank white space formed by the meeting of their minds, she saw someone who could answer it. Before she could get a look at the other's face, the Shadow Worker materialized a mask for herself. She was already wearing a black cloak around a skintight grey shirt and black pants. The hood of the cloak was down, so Emily could at least see her enemy's short copper hair.

Before Emily could gather herself, the Shadow Worker started speaking in a deep, almost tenor voice, the smooth connection between them handling the translation better than any device would have been able to. "You! How dare you! You petty upstarts do not understand what you have kept from us. Perhaps your ancestors would have known what to do with it, but your lazy incurious people have no idea. By keeping this from us, you have secured Eldrandii hegemony for eons to come. We warned you Earthers to stay out of this. We warned Raiz, we warned you, and now you have brought about our collective ruin."

This was too much for Emily's still recuperating mind to deal with, and she replied feebly, "so . . . you know who I am?"

"Since that bastard Ariki chose to tell you about this world, our eye has been fixed on you, Captain Pierce. Until he broke under our interrogation, we had no way of knowing which of hundreds of specially designated systems this world was in, much less what continent to direct our forces on, except to follow you. Ariki broke after your adventure on Eldrand. You are lucky Eldrand's government is slow and bizarre in its thought processes, or you would not have left that world safely."

Again catching perhaps a quarter of what her opponent was saying, though thankful that the Shadow Worker was so willing to converse, Emily chose to continue on her own tangents. "So, our forces beat you, didn't they?"

"By outnumbering us fifty to one," the Shadow Worker said with an unmistakable sneer in her voice. "Your degenerate people . . . what do you hope to accomplish in this? It has been long known to us that hyperspace travel was made possible by magic – a secret passed down to us generation after generation. Once, perhaps thousands of years ago, it was our order that supplied Asparian ships with hyperspace mages. We simply wanted to know what spells, energy levels, and theories were necessary to put our powers to work, and to bring about a new Asparis – one with its long neglected shipbuilding intact."

"Why didn't you just open up your own ships and look inside, if you knew there was a mage in there?"

"Because all ships have a self-destruct failsafe to prevent that sort of prying." The Shadow Worker paused, then had glee in her voice when she said, "you are not entirely yourself, are you, Captain? You are weak from that exertion at the top of the mountain – yes, I heard about that – and you are not even fully conscious, are you? It was unwise of you to engage with me in such a vulnerable state. I know little of this white world you have pulled me into, but I would wager that what is done here can have true physical manifestations."

"So, what're you going to do? Kill me?" Emily asked with a droll slur.

Less cheerful after Emily revealed a complete absence of fear, the Shadow Worker said, "I suppose you would simply run away before I get the chance. If I could rely on you to fight honorably, I would engage without another word, but Earth people are such cowards –"

"You're not going to trick me into fighting you, so don't bother. I know you've got more power than me so, yeah, I will run."

"Yet you wanted to contact one of us. For what? To know our reasons?"

"Yeah, that was it. You know, you could have talked it over with me in the first place instead of threatening me. I wasn't exactly thrilled with the idea of fighting a bunch of mages, so I might have backed off if you had asked nicely."

"Asked . . . nicely? Talked it over with you, a lesser mongrel species?"

Emily snorted. "I guess not."

"Tell me, how many Earth people do you suppose there are with magical ability enough to begin a hyperspace jump?"

Emily didn't have to guess. "There might be people like me that don't know they're magical, but right now? None."

"And if there were, would descendants of stubborn Atlantii, individualists to a fault, be so willing to wire themselves to a ship in service to others for a lifetime?"

"A few," said Emily, having heard of such people, but not personally believing in them.

"So there are no people on Earth capable of using this knowledge, should they come to possess it, and if they had magical ability, most if not all would still cringe at having to sacrifice their lives to, for instance, satisfy the whims of an immature and irresponsible captain who makes money on petty trading missions. Or, what about being confined to ships sold to other species, whose purpose in buying a ship cannot even be guessed? Your obstructionism, as I have said, will only bring delight to Eldrandii, who are so far too slow and dimwitted to understand this. It is our demise that your people continually fail to appreciate your limited place in this galaxy and your utter inability to compete with species greater than your own."

"And you're the great species that has a right to it, is that it? I don't care if we beat you fifty to one, because we still beat you."

"Our right to knowledge rests in our ability to use it."

"And what about the people you killed?" Emily asked, her faculties sharpening. "All those people in the empire – they were Asparii like you."

"The true Asparii were created on Asparis' anvil battered by hammers of mancer domination. Surviving as a mage among our mancer overlords, a hundred times more powerful in their way than we ever could be, was a test of our strength and our people's worthiness. Those who came to this planet were runaways, unfit to compete, wavering under fire, and failing a test that we, through patience and ability, passed."

"I remember us pathetic Earthlings having something to do with freeing you from the mancers."

"But you destroyed our world!" the masked woman shouted in anguish, pointing accusingly and taking a step forward. Emily took a corresponding step back, indicating an unwillingness to engage in anything but talk. "You destroyed our world. I am sure simpletons, peons, and all those without a single redeeming quality except ability to produce raw labor, doted over you when you took them to your world and gave them a more comfortable life. It is easy to win over such people. I am sure they told you how grateful they were and how wonderful you are for freeing them. But to destroy mancers you destroyed our world, and you left nothing for us to support ourselves with. We Shadow Workers could have emerged from our shadows to lead our people, to create a world they had earned through their toil. Now, what are they? A scattered people without a world of their own relying on benevolence from others who, in a time not so long ago, they could have decimated. No, I do not thank you for freeing us, and I believe that, given time, we would have surely freed ourselves."

The argument was impassioned and, seeing through the woman's distasteful sense of species superiority, Emily felt the pain behind the words. It was revisionist history, of course, to say that the Shadow Workers could ever have overthrown the mancers on their own. Earth was given the right to retaliate against the mancer lords of Asparis, so the war had not been one of aggression on the part of the human race. Emily's understanding of the events was clear, though unspecific, and while she had sympathy, she did not believe the woman's argument.

"You're full of shit, you know that?" she said without any edge on her tone, as if simply stating a fact. "Look, I get that you could have used the secret better than we can, but use it for what? You killed thousands of people to get to it, and if you got it, you would have killed millions to create your new Asparis. I'm sure Earth would be on your hit list, too, so from my point of view, this was just survival. I don't know if we can compete with the Eldrandii, but I do know that we're better than you, even if surviving under pressure is your way of measuring whose better. I'm glad the secret's in our hands instead of yours."

The Shadow Worker shook her head ruefully. Emily marveled at how quickly the woman could shift gears, and control her emotions. When she spoke, it was now in a pitying voice. "You do not understand. You will have to compete with Eldrandii, and with everyone else, because otherwise your world will be shut out. You will see, Captain. Spread magic among your people quickly, and find those noble souls among you willing to give up their lives for a cause greater than themselves, even if manifestations of that cause are . . . unimpressive. If you want to prove your worth by surviving, then know that your battle has not even begun."

Having spoken to a Shadow Worker before, Emily knew that they were not all so coherent or charismatic. Curious, she asked, "Who were you? In the Shadow Workers, I mean. How . . . how powerful were you?"

Instead of standing straighter in pride, the woman surprisingly diminished slightly in stature. "I am . . . I was . . . wife of our leader. You . . . you see in me signs of leadership, do you? Our society is not like yours. While lesser people can bear under inappropriate leaders, it takes strength to lead great men."

"You mean they didn't let you be their leader because you're a woman, don't you?" Having penetrated the woman's mind already, it required no effort to decode her words. "And it ate you up inside, didn't it?"

Seething with rage, the woman bit back, "my husband was a

towering force, and deserved everything in this world or in any other. He could have been a lord of Asparis. If only he were here . . . if only – Get out! This part of me is not for your amusement. Get out of my mind!"

The woman's words were reminiscent of Emily's own attack against Tylan when he had stumbled into her most private sanctum, and were just as potent. Emily had no choice but to withdraw her consciousness, returning to herself. Doing so, her eyelids instantly snapped open and she was awake. Tylan broke off his outpouring of energy and looked over at her with concern.

"Captain Pierce, are you all right?"

It took her a few heartbeats, but she finally managed, "yeah, fine. I'm really hungry, though," she said, with a parched voice that said the rest.

"We tried feeding you, and you did take in some food, but not much. And that little, I had to use magic to feed you. Without regular hospital equipment . . . I am not trained –"

"Oh, god, you didn't have to clean me up, did you?"

"Thankfully, there is a rather convenient spell for that, one which condenses the waste material, and any waste in the room, into a small, dense pellet. It is actually an unusual application of elemental air control that I am quite proud of. Both that pellet and your urine have been magically conveyed out of you and into a waste bin."

"What does it look like when you do that?"

Tylan was not comfortable discussing it, seeing it as a flaw in his treasured spell, but answered anyway. "At various times in the day, someone in the room would have seen an arc of waste materializing out of the blanket and into the bin. I warned everyone beforehand, and no one got in the way of its . . . transit. No one was soiled, in other words, as I am sure you are glad to know."

"So you didn't need to take my clothes off or anything, right?"

Tylan sighed. "No. Though that was hardly the issue that most weighed on my mind at the time. We would have gotten one of the local women to do it, if it became necessary. Really, Captain, your priorities border on prudery. You are lucky to be alive. What . . . what was it like?"

Unsurprised by Tylan's interest, she said, "too complicated for me to explain right now. I've forgotten most of it, like I'd forget a regular dream. My mind was sort on autopilot, doing everything it could, stretching in all sorts of directions. It was almost like my life flashing in front of my eyes, but I knew I wasn't going to die, so I wanted to understand all of it, because I knew that getting a clear picture would help me. I couldn't, though. It was too much." Her unspecific language was deliberate, and she was keen to avoid the entire episode with the wife of the Shadow Worker leader. Except perhaps to Ethan, she planned never to mention that confrontation.

She didn't bother trying to get up from the bed, with her limbs numb with weakness, and patiently waited for food to arrive. While conducting an internal inventory, checking to see if her physical and mental selves were intact, she had to bear through one visitor after another asking her how she was feeling, if she was all right, and telling her every detail of the nothing that had happened during her incapacitation. Raiz was the one to bring the meal in, positively bouncing with delight beside Kaz, who had been prepared to do the honors. Though the final act was far from over, Raiz was brimming with anticipation. Emily, of course, knew perfectly well that his optimism was justified, but she reminded herself to keep the knowledge close. Telling Raiz would do nothing to change the situation, but would give away some detail of her recent mental excursions. She was no longer prepared to tip her hand to the master plotter himself.

With the substantial energy provided by her first solid meal in nearly a week, Emily finally got her muscles moving, and was soon on her feet, much to the surprise of everyone except Tylan, Jaik, and Makis. With Emily officially healthy, it was now deemed acceptable by Ethan, Kaz, Tylan, and Jaik to absorb Raiz's enthusiasm, and they were all eager to explore the city with her. Even West's mood lightened. The way Tylan still attended to her was annoying, but Makis soon waylaid him, demanding his help. Emily was careful to look at and treat Jaik as a friend and nothing more, while clinging to Kaz in a way that would have left her disgusted before, but now seemed natural. After an hour in their presence, Jaik peeled off to join Tylan and Makis, citing his magical studies. West stayed with them, enjoying Ethan's company more than Jaik's at the moment. Besides, they were at the airfield, which was far more inspiring to him than a stuffy library.

"So," Emily said soon after Jaik's departure, "what happened after I did the whole magical shield thing?" She was testing Kaz, and pitched the question at him like a baseball.

Practiced at explaining the event, and knowing exactly what to skip over, Kaz answered smoothly, "Well, you saved us, and we brought you back down into that lookout house, and the computer used its nanobots to seal everything up with liquid metal. More metal than the rest of this continent has in it, from what Ethan told me."

"Nothing else?" Emily asked. Among her most memorable unconscious visions was the truth of what had happened, complete with his rescue of her.

"No."

She grasped him in a bear hug and kissed him passionately, leaving him gasping in shock. Releasing him, she grinned and said, "Sorry, you're just so cute when you're being modest. It's so unusual for you. Almost as good as seeing you embarrassed. You saved me, numbnuts."

Trying desperately to get the blush out of his cheeks, Kaz said, "you saved us first. I would have been fried, so the least I could do was help you –"

"There it is again," she said, forcing herself on him a second time. "You're really not doing yourself any favors. Look at you, you're red as an apple. You need to go back to being horrible, arrogant, and sarcastic."

"But it was . . . ," and a second after stopping himself, he realized he didn't want to stop. "It was nothing, really."

And this time, he was prepared for it, wrapping his arms around her and returning her affection. He couldn't gauge what was going on in his own mind, but as he had occasionally done in previous relationships, he decided not to care. Believing in nothing trite, he would never ask himself whether he was in love. All he knew was that he cared about her, worried about what she thought of him, and gained comfort from her presence. For now, with her reciprocating the same sentiments, that was enough.

Emily could taste some confusion on Kaz's lips, but more confirmation and relief. She had broken through to him without overtly trying, and the give and take between them, which even while they argued drove them to improve, was bonding them as equals. While she at times acted as if she was a step ahead of him, and taking the lead, it was only because she was more accustomed to acting on impulse. All she needed to know was that he was right for her today, and she was entitled to some comfort in his company. Otherwise, she was just as bewildered as he was.

Annoyed by the scene suddenly excluding them, West and Ethan left Emily and Kaz without a word, continuing their walk around the aircraft and spaceships sitting in tight rows. They soon stumbled on the specialists, who were devoting their time to a single massive ship at least three hundred feet long. The linguists stayed in the library to work on translations, and sent notes to the other specialists at the airfield via some enthusiastic local boys and girls. The children were actively ignoring their parent's admonitions to stay out of the library, and pestered the outlanders for opportunities to help. The ship provided no practical reason for them to stay in it, after they had reached their conclusions about the state of the mage once living within it, but it provided the second best place for sheer inspiration, next to the library. The linguists had taken a drastic step four days ago, barring all the others from the library because everyone was too impatient for snippets of information. The constant requests for more information prevented the linguists from focusing on their work. Bringing their complaint directly to Raiz, the commander gave them his support for the ban.

West and Ethan were both eager to hear the latest details from the engineers and physicists, who were far more pleasant after being humbled by the translators, and after determining that the expertise of mages would not be necessary for an understanding of hyperspace travel.

"Oh, a mage will be essential to any construction of a hyperspace drive," one of the physicists explained, "but the phenomena associated with magic itself might have, according to these equations, a perfectly simple physical basis."

"All we need is the linguists to gather all the equations together and to list the interpretation of the symbols used, but they're having trouble because the language is so specialized. If they'd only let us in there, we could help, but . . . well, luckily, Makis already discussed most of the magical terms with them, but everything will come much more slowly now that he's not bored out of his wits waiting for Tylan."

This was the usual sort of summary from the scientists, but West and Ethan wanted the full explanation. Doing some study of their own, both of them had discovered a love for steep learning curves and difficult concepts, so they were ready for the worst, even if it would require months to decode. They wanted the Raiz treatment, and said so. In response came a flurry of babble about tachyons with imaginary mass, weakly interacting massive particles, and an entirely new branch of the standard model of particle physics that might negate the need for supersymmetry, which had been sought after for over a century but never proved. Magic could also be supersymmetry itself. There was no consensus about which of these actually described magic.

"The point is, everything in the Atlantian texts is related to things we know and, once we fit it into out existing models, we will be able to predict the behavior of it. I'm still not convinced that tachyons play any part in this hyperspace drive. That might be a misinterpretation, or maybe the Atlantii were using it as a mathematical convenience."

"You just want it out of the picture because it's messy."

"More than messy, I think. There was a time, about a week ago, when the existence of a tachyon was a theory-breaker."

"There was a time when magic was a theory-breaker, and also one when the luminescent ether was a standard. What's your point?"

This seemed to be the continuation of an ongoing debate, and since he was quickly getting lost, West asked, "what is a . . . tachyon?"

"A particle that travels faster than light," Ethan answered automatically. "They're not supposed to exist because they would allow people to travel back in time."

The anti-tachyon physicist sighed, not at all impressed by Ethan's knowledge, and lamenting his misconception. "No, that's not entirely the case. According to special relativity, a tachyon would actually travel in imaginary time, and would not violate causation because regular matter cannot interact with tachyons to pass information on. There are complex mathematical issues with tachyons that make them trouble. There is a problem with them that might be easier to understand. If they can't interact with normal matter, how could they possibly be useful to magic, which does?"

"Unless the tachyon can violate causation," said Ethan, picking up the scientific lingo with ease.

"That would be bad."

"But it would be magic," Ethan pointed out.

Firmly opposed to the idea, as if no self-respecting universe could structure itself in a way he did not find elegant, the physicist shook his head. "If the Atlantii were going to write equations to explain their hyperspace drive, they had to believe that those equations would be reliable. That means causes must lead to predictable effects, and all effects must have causes preceding them in time. Take that away, and equations just don't work, and there's no point writing them. Yes, that's what we thought magic was, but it looks like we were wrong. These equations show . . . or at least hint very, very convincingly, that it is possible to explain magic in scientific terms."

Ethan rubbed his chin thoughtfully. "Isn't there, like, a chance that there are . . . other realities in science?"

Another sigh. "Yes, yes. The Many Worlds Interpretation of quantum mechanics, and the initial creation of space-times or branes in string theory both have what you're talking about. And I know you're going to suggest that all this can be solved with something clever about the other realities. The problem is that we can't test anything like that because we can't go to the other realities, so there's no point talking about it."

Only after they were well away from the specialists, striking out to explore the rest of the city, did the thought strike Ethan. "Hey, do you think . . . the gate Makis has . . . he said it was a rip in the universe or something like that. What if it's actually a gate between realities? Then we could go through and find out if there's some way to explain everything."

"He did not talk about the gate like that."

"Yeah, but didn't it always seem like he was hiding something about it? You must have noticed."

West nodded. Of course, he had. "But don't tell the scientists about it. I think that one guy would blow his top."

Before Ethan could respond, one of the city's birds flew by shouting in its shrill voice, "the exterior threat has been removed. The city is now open."

14
Newport Again

Newport Station was built without any large halls capable of accommodating a truly ostentatious ceremony, so only the officers in charge of the units sent to Selparis could attend the celebration in space. There would be a more inclusive ceremony in New York by the end of the week, giving everyone an opportunity to show appreciation to those who had eliminated the Shadow Worker threat, and those who had lost their lives in the course of the fight. For now, though, Raiz needed to frame his use of Earth Forces as justified and successful before his political opponents could find some way to use the events to attack him. Selparis was a touchy interstellar situation, and the information stored there even more so. Those antagonistic to Raiz's policies pointed out that he had placed Earth in a precarious position, with species once counted as friends furious at his actions.

Emily found loathed self-congratulating ceremonies, and would have skipped this one, except that she was billed as the guest of honor. Raiz apologized to her, anticipating her reaction, yet noted that if she wanted fame from the discovery of Selparis, she would have to sacrifice some of her objections. It was nice to hear Raiz understanding her point of view, because he gloried in the pageantry she loathed. With all the officers in their dress uniforms, Raiz would don the Newport Station Commander's uniform, possibly for the first time since he took the office. Emily was adamant about resisting formal wear, and so showed up in her standard black jeans and red tee-shirt, adding a black tie to emphasize her lack of conformity. She was aware of her childishness, but felt she had earned a right to attend in a manner comfortable to her.

Dragging Kaz, Ethan, West, and Jaik with her to the ceremony, she let them dress as they preferred as well, not forcing them to adopt her own bias. Kaz already had a uniform with the appropriate rank insignia for a starship first officer, purchased on their first trip back to the station, immediately after his promotion. Newport Station had its own specialized tailors, producing consistent uniforms for all Earth officers, should they choose to wear them. Jaik surprised Emily the day before by asking her for some sort of title on her ship, so that he could get a uniform, too. The amazing journey from Selparis to Earth on Captain Wilson's ship had left him in awe, and wide-eyed at virtually everything he saw. She couldn't blame him, and after a shrug, declared him the liaison to Selparis, thinking nothing more of it.

The conversation with Jaik led her to think back across the past few days in her mind. The trip back to Newport itself had been a final shock to all of them, with a last Shadow Worker ship attempting to destroy them in Earth space. Before Earth's own forces scrambled to intercept, the turrets on Wilson's ship made short work of the brash enemy, but the intercept served as a reminder to them that this was far from over. Shadow Workers retained a firm hold on Ina Cur, and until the ISC mustered an intervention, they would continue to use that world as a base of operations.

Her first day on Newport had been no less harrowing than the journey. For some reason she could not fathom, her crew had gathered to greet her on arrival, and applauded her. She still didn't understand why. It was a pleasant surprise, of course, and their willingness to show approval for her certain put her captainship on more solid ground, but looking on all her actions, she was at a loss to find something worthy of it. Yes, she had gone to Selparis to win some fame for herself, and some serious cash by establishing a trade deal with an isolated people, and ended up bringing an amazing discovery to Earth, but all she had really done was a lot of traveling, and basic survival. Otherwise, Raiz was the one responsible for the actual success, and the one paying her crew for the risk taken. Her crew had actually engaged in as great a feat as she had, surviving pursuit by Shadow Worker ships with only a single fixed weapon on the *Azar*, sustaining significant damage but no casualties. She had actually done worse on that score.

Raiz had ordered the Earth Force ships to check out the site on Selparis where her landing pod, and the pod pilot John, had been hidden. They found John's dead body, and the pod disabled. Evidently, the pilot was attacked and, realizing that his assailants could use the pod to their advantage if he didn't, he disabled the vehicle. In doing so, he had probably saved her, Ethan, Jaik, West, Tylan, and the entire endeavor. Assuming Shadow Workers were the attackers, they could have returned to the pod in a blink after the destruction of the Dakatanis airfield, and whether they chose to use its ducted fans or its rockets, they would have beaten Veris' plane to the Selian hills. Finding all this out right after the enthusiastic reception from her crew doused any attempt her mind made to justify their approbation. She hoped they were simply expressing relief that the ordeal was finally over.

The one beneficial aspect of the celebration arranged by Raiz was the chance it gave her to think about more trivial matters than the deaths of two of her crew, and the appraisal of her actions. The sight of Jaik dressed up in his improvised attire as they entered assembled outside the hall managed to make her grin with amusement. She had to admit he looked positively cute in it. While she detested uniforms on principle, he wore it more like a costume, and it fit him because it allowed him to act a part. At the same time, it reminded her how young he was at heart, regardless of his years. This would save him from the embarrassment of not fitting in with the hundreds of people in attendance, when he was one of only a few Selparii, including the chancellor and his cadre.

West, given the opportunity to shop for new clothes on board, had been torn between loose olive trousers and a white tee-shirt, matching his normal apparel, or leather pants and a button-down black shirt, which the quirky young woman at the shop insisted looked stunning on him. Leaving him dumbfounded and speechless, she told him the dark colors complemented his wild hair and eyes, and swore they would make him stand out from the crowd. On that last note, her thoughts were in harmony with his. Since being back among his own people, West was desperate not to be seen as normal in any way. He ultimately bought both outfits, and wore the one the lady suggested, but was uncomfortable in it for the rest of the night.

Ethan followed Emily's lead and dressed causally, but looked less disposed to it than she was when surrounded by the politicians and military men. Emily was usually good about bringing him into experiences that, looking back, he was glad to be led into. In the safety of Newport Station, with its abundant toilets, beds, and air conditioning, he was able to assess favorably the excursion on Selparis. He had certainly benefited from his time there, so he forgave her for the terror, trauma, and general inconvenience he had felt in the midst of their adventure. The commendation ceremony, though, was so clearly pointless, and a waste of precious hours of his life, that he was irritated with her for bullying him into going. He regretted the added awkwardness of dressing casually at a formal occasion, and throughout the night looked jealously at Kaz and Jaik, who thoroughly enjoyed the party.

Much to her surprise, though the gathered dignitaries and officers gave her another ovation at her introduction, Raiz had not forced her to give a speech. She should have expected that he had more planned. He took the liberty of waiting until the party was over, when she was longing for a bed after the long night, before telling her that he was arranging a press conference in a few days, and she needed to prepare something to tell the public. Something to tell the billions of people who would be watching them. No thought, by simply crossing her mind, had ever made her as frightened. Raiz was giving her the perfect opportunity to make a fool of herself in front of her entire species, in as extreme an ordeal as she could contemplate. She had no clue how people like Raiz and Welder managed it. Not fond of being on the spot, especially in front of an audience, she enlisted the help of the person who had been her guide the last time she had tried. Kaz backed her up when she had felt the need to speak to her crew in Dael, and with any luck, he would help her through this unavoidable trial.

She would deliver her speech after Raiz's opening and A'anfu En's defense of Earth's actions on Selparis. The commander would then take questions from the press. Matched with compelling and charismatic speakers, Emily had no choice but to make her words quick and simple, and no desire to do otherwise. Her one concrete goal in the speech was to express her condolences to the families of Max and John, and to all those who died on Selparis. From her vantage point, she now saw how little the treasure everyone had fought for might be worth compared to the lives lost.

The bottom line was that, in her way, the wife of the Shadow Worker leader had been right – Earth had no chance to put hyperdrive technology to work immediately, or even in a few years. Whether the physicists found a way to explain the theory in terms of science was interesting, but unless they could create a device capable of duplicating magic, Earth was vulnerable to sanctions from the ISC worlds. Of course, once Earth could sell ships, all species except the Eldrandii would quickly forget their animosity toward the upstart world, but in the meantime, life would be tough.

Emily was also dubious about the discovery because, as a weak magic user herself, she could not imagine being strapped into a machine for the rest of her life, or being tied to it at all, however comfortable the room provided to her. To get exceptional people eager to subjugate themselves, you had to live in a society that fostered values like conformity and . . . fascism, to be blunt about it. You needed a society in which otherwise intelligent people like Oris would do whatever their government asked of them in the faith that their leaders were right and just. No experience on Earth could justify such faith, and the best human governments were built on distrust of powerful people.

She wanted to know what Raiz and A'anfu had to say, to see whether they would address this problem or dodge it. Set to be their most critical audience, she planned to leverage her hero status to hold them accountable if they failed to give an adequate answer. The practical method by which she would execute that plan currently eluded her, but she was certain that, if they gave the public platitudes instead of truth, her dissatisfaction would give her the inspiration to develop the tactics. Kaz was fully in favor of her point of view, though he was nervous at the prospect of challenging the powers that they had only recently depended on. He helped her write a speech that ignored the enterprise Raiz and A'anfu En would defend, but highlighted the more humble intent of the *Azar*'s crew and captain, and lamented the losses.

This time, standing alone in front of the world, she could not bring herself to appear sloppy. Reasoning that her purpose was to honor the dead, she dressed up for their sake, and for their families. The message she had to deliver simply would not be received in the right light otherwise. She chose a crisp black suit with loose pants, but kept her light blue shirt untucked, and the collar unbuttoned without a tie. After getting a haircut from the only hairdresser on board the station, trimming it back down to the short style she preferred, she dyed her hair black to match her suit. Altogether, she could have been a partner in a fresh, hip, startup company, which was not too far from the truth. If she had chosen a black shirt instead of a blue one, she could have been in mourning – also an accurate perception. Standing in front of the mirror, she noted her eyes briefly, but turned away before her mind could come to any conclusions.

Kaz was stunned and speechless when he saw her step out, and that effect alone was worth her trouble. His stare said plainly that this was how he saw her in his best dreams.

"This is as far as I go," she said with mock firmness. "You're not going to get me in a uniform. You got that?"

Regaining his tongue, Kaz shot back, "Fine, fine. I'm just glad I didn't have to ask you to look decent. I was afraid you'd make a fuss, and go with a red Mohawk or something."

"Oh, yeah? Well, that little comment's going to cost you."

Kaz furrowed his brow, immediately conjuring up a dozen ways she could make his life miserable. This was already the most complicated relationship he had managed to get himself into, but it was her magic that put him on edge. Thankfully, in all their discussions since leaving Selparis, she had avoided the topic. He simply had trouble with the implications of a girlfriend who could see the future, or potentially any of his actions she might want to look into. There was also Jaik, whose attitude towards the two of them had softened. Emily still nursed a fondness for the young man, and wanted to remain his friend, but had so far kept a safe distance from him. Kaz could easily imagine her trying to irritate him by spending more time with Jaik.

Emily had said the words without actually having an idea what to back them up with. Seeing Kaz's troubled expression, she was in a silent flurry to find an appropriate penalty. Just in the first seconds, her mind had developed such horrendous possibilities that, no matter how worried he was, Kaz could have no idea how much anguish she could cause him. Analyzing the look on his face after she mentioned some of them would be most instructive. Instead, she found a better, and more honest, option.

"I was going to ask you out after the press conference, but now I'll wait for you to get your act together and to ask me. And you're paying, of course. I won't take anything less than the most expensive place on board."

"Oh," Kaz said, relieved. "Well, I'll wait and see how you do in the press conference. If you mess up, I'll have to think twice about whether to be seen in public with you."

Nice one, Emily thought. Somewhere along the way, probably during dinner in the recreation room aboard Wilson's ship, their jabs at each other had turned from annoyances and challenges into an enjoyable game. She didn't have a real comeback this time, so she ended it by saying, "Do I look like I'm going to mess up?"

Kaz looked her over indulgently, and answered in earnest, "No. No you don't."

Tickled by the response, she gave him a peck as a reward, and then led him to the briefing room. On stage next to the other two speakers, she understood too late that, as tough as delivering the speech would be, waiting for the other two to finish, and reacting correctly and minimally to what they said, was just as trying. At least a half dozen times, she had to restrain herself from affirming something they said, or questioning them caustically, and she struggled to keep her mouth shut. Fortunately, the key segments of both speeches – the parts the press would repeatedly air and mine for soundbites – elicited no internal struggles within her.

The heart of Raiz's speech was a defense of his decisions, though he generalized by using the plural pronoun. When he said "we", he could have been referring to the three people on stage, Earth Forces, the World Council, or all of humanity. It was sometimes hard to tell which reading he meant, which was probably by design. Emily felt that the commander's speech was far stiffer than suited his character, but he knew best how to impress his audience, and she supposed this was what they expected from him.

"We took up this gauntlet, not because we were greedy for the reward, but because a dangerous enemy, who would become even more terrifying with it in their possession, sought after it. In fact, we lack the means to use the hyperspace drive information we acquired.

Our main reason for retrieving it was to ensure Eldrand's blockade of Selparis would end, allowing Earth's military to land on Selparis, to rid the galaxy of the menace. Let us make clear that we bear no ill-will to freelance mages, whether Asparii or of any other species. The Shadow Workers were not merely an association of mages, but a group as vile as the mancers before them, and as eager to dominate others. Since their defeat on Selparis, they have emerged from the shadows on Ina Cur, making their once secret rule over the Empire of the Fair overt. They invaded the strongest Inana nation without any awareness from the Interstellar Community, and against the most futile resistance. If this is not the mark of an enemy that must be actively engaged and fought, then we should all be prepared to hand over our sovereignty to a foreign power. It is practically the definition of a case for war.

"Nor did we lack a specific threat to our own people. After the fall of Asparis, some refugees from that world petitioned our World Council for relocation to Selparis, where a friendly government was known to be open to receive them. Along with them went a group of humans, albeit small, who settled on the planet and over time integrated themselves into the local society. Those humans also maintained contact with Earth for decades, and we paid close attention to their continuing welfare. In the course of our actions on Selparis, we actually encountered a local human – one not in communication with us – by accident. So, if the threshold for sanctioning intervention is simply to have members of your species in harm's way, clearly we were justified to help the people of Selparis. If we bore any responsibility for the refugees we brought to that planet, which has been the opinion of the World Council, then we were doubly justified.

"As any member of the Atparian Empire on Selparis will readily testify, the Shadow Worker force, which admittedly docked at Newport Station without incident a few weeks ago, was ruthless in its devastation on their capital. Without warning or pretext, these mages crushed the blossoming soul of a culture, purely in an attempt to kidnap and interrogate its first minister, who had discovered the Atlantian remains on his planet and knew their location. They would have, being unable to capture him, been no doubt satisfied if they had killed him, because they, in that way, could prevent the information from passing to anyone else. Thankfully, the Eldrandii government agent traveling with Captain Pierce's exploration team realized the first minister would be a target for capture, and rescued him from the clutches of the Shadow Workers.

"This leads us to another pressing issue. The government of Eldrand is holding an Earth citizen, Marcus Welder, under false pretenses, ostensibly for questioning in a murder case. As Ambassador Welder's reputation is beyond reproach, and his arrival on Eldrand occurred after the time of the murder, the justification for suspecting his involvement is extremely thin. So, what reason does Eldrand give for his detention? That he vouched for a suspected accomplice to the murder, Arisin Oris, and allowed her to escape prosecution. This accusation is patently absurd, and we demand the immediate release of Marcus Welder on the following grounds: the government of Eldrand has admitted that Arisin Oris was a government agent, but denies that it ordered her to take part in the murder. How can Eldrand argue that Marcus Welder should be held suspect for trusting Oris when that government itself trusted her?

"The denial that the murder was ordered by her superiors is also dubious. She was identified as the lead assailant by two Eldrandii mages already apprehended for the crime. Other than the desire to protect a state secret, what could have been their motive for murdering a man who was about to pass on a map of Selparis to a Shadow Worker representative? Eldrandii are quick to point out that they are not prone to murder, so Oris and her accomplices must have had compelling reasons to commit the act. She must have firmly believed, at the time, that she was doing the right thing, though Captain Pierce's account shows that Oris was eventually haunted by the act.

"We recommend that Eldrand examine its own internal workings, its own culture of blind obedience to authority, before it detains an innocent man of our world."

Raiz continued, but the salvo against Eldrand overshadowed everything that followed. The news of Welder, and of Oris' guilt in the murder on Eldrand, peaked Emily's interest in his speech, and she barely paid attention after he turned to less heated matters. She had boundless wrath at the mention of Oris' name, now that she had the perspective to see the enormity of her betrayal. That Oris had been responsible for the murder created two conflicting thoughts in Emily's mind. On face value, this piled infamy upon infamy on Oris' name, yet it nagged at Emily that Oris must have been tasked to kill her, as well, if she got too close to the hyperspace secrets. Why had Oris let her live, while being so willing to kill a member of her own people? Emily realized that Raiz must be right – Oris had a pang of conscience. And if anything had initiated it, her instruction of Ethan aboard the *Azar* must have been key. The thought of Ethan frequently brought out feelings of guilt in Emily, so she could relate. Because he was such a careful listener, and so observant, there was always an underlying impression that he heard and saw more than anyone had intended for him to. Putting that into the equation, much about Oris' behavior made sense. From her desire to distance herself from Ethan once they landed on Selparis, to keeping aloof while using her little multitool device, to her increasing irrationality as time went on, it was all clear. Oris had been torn between performing a duty for her government and a growing doubt in her mind about the morality of what she intended to do. Maybe she had even developed a genuine liking for Ethan. Had it been love? That would be something, but Emily concluded that was far close to a soap opera plot to be plausible.

For the first time in her life, Emily had to promise herself not to reveal some of her thoughts to Ethan, who was usually privy to everything she had on her mind. These ideas, though, would bother him to no end. They certainly bothered her, since she could not decide what to make of Oris. She instinctively preferred to label people "good" or "bad", and the fact that Oris might have spared her life after having many chances to kill her, whether due to guilt or not, was the only thing keeping the Eldrandii out of the "bad" column. But why had Oris saved Tayron? Her motive for keeping him out of the Shadow Worker's control was obvious, but why not simply kill the chancellor on the spot? It must have been her orders. The Eldrandii government had sanctioned the death of Emily, but had not mentioned Tayron in the orders, giving Oris no dispensation to murder him. Murder was, after all, not something she would have done on a whim. The irony was somehow beautiful. Tayron was the one person on Selparis that Oris would have wanted to kill, but she was held back by her limited orders.

Deep into her own thoughts, only the applause of the press brought her attention to the fact that Raiz was done, and A'anfu En was up. A'anfu was not a member of the majority on Eldrand, but a leader of the Dunorii sect, which was often treated as a bizarre fringe element by the ISC. The Dunorii did not share the beliefs or culture of most Eldrandii, and refused to be bound by the central government in Revnor. They were far from the only such minority, but they were the largest and most outspoken. If Emily bore any animosity against the Eldrandii government, A'anfu En would strengthen rather than complicate her views.

Haughty as she ever was, the Dunorii speaker stepped forward and somehow got the translators to ooze with her sense of absolute superiority. Again, Emily felt that if A'anfu had been human, Earth as a whole would be quick to send her as a representative elsewhere. Even knowing of the murder she committed, Emily preferred Arisin Oris' personality. Moderating her opinion a bit, she acknowledged that A'anfu could, at least, never be coaxed into doing anything she did not want to do.

"Commander Raiz and, through him, the rest of Earth, now knows what hyperspace travel requires. I speak for all Dunorii, and we are sole providers of that requirement to the Eldrandii shipbuilders. We have long felt marginalized on our world, which depends so heavily on our talents, and sought to find a new . . . buyer for our unique services. However, we could not bear to betray our fellow species, wayward though their beliefs may be, by revealing the secret of hyperspace technology, and the government at Revnor was aware of this. We Dunorii therefore waited patiently, hoping that some worthy species would find the secret, but be unable to use it, lacking the ability to . . . manufacture the key component."

"I was sent to Earth to make a general appraisal of Earthii . . . Earthlings . . . for my people. I wanted to see what use you have put our technology to, and make recommendations about how to treat our work. Earthlings fail to keep the interior of their ships natural and properly habitable, though they are not as bad as other species in this regard. After the battle between Earth's ships and the Asparian ships, I was called to see Commander Raiz. This was fortunate, because I would have demanded to see him in any case, seeking to know what had transpired. Commander Raiz told me that Captain Pierce's ship had been chased by a single Asparian ship, had sought refuge here, and other Asparian ships had joined the battle. He also told me the most wondrous news – that Earth was close to discovering the great secret, and only needed Dunorii intervention to allow a single ship to land on a certain planet, which was being blockaded by Revnorii Eldrandii ships. In asking this of us, the commander showed great wisdom and understanding about our culture and internal politics, so I was disposed to help him.

"Nevertheless, this decision was a great struggle for me because of what it entailed. I would have to use the only threat a Dunorii could use against Revnor – the denial of our work to the shipbuilders – and that would be a great risk. It could be interpreted as the same betrayal we had avoided all these centuries while we waited. I resisted the commander's request until he gave me a more complete picture of the situation. He was already above suspicion, and his additional explanation has been found truthful in the resolution of the events. I thank him for his candor.

"The revelation provided by Commander Raiz that convinced the Dunorii to act was two-fold, and these two facts would have compelled any Eldrandii to see the merit in Earth's purpose on Selparis. First, the source of the secret was not some random cache of knowledge, but rather Atlantian remains guarded still by descendants of the Atlantii. In other words, the knowledge belonged to Earth, and to Earthlings, insofar as they are the heirs of the Atlantii. Second, the same force of Asparii that sparked the battle outside this station already had dozens and possibly hundreds of their people on Selparis, seeking out the same secret. We know the Asparii once had hyperspace technology, so they would be able to put the knowledge to use quickly, and would certainly not ask for Dunorii help. To have a brutal, warlike group gain such an advantage was intolerable. The choice was clear.

"Momentous as the choice was, I contacted my people with the information and asked for a vote, receiving the confirmation that over three-quarters preferred to intervene. From what I have heard, Commander Raiz was able to land his ship only a day before Captain Pierce and her party . . . needed assistance."

Emily scowled at her need for rescue being mentioned to the

world, even if A'anfu had selected kind words, but continued listening respectfully. The speech was closing gaps in her view of events, such as when exactly Raiz became certain the hyperspace secret was on Selparis.

A'anfu went on. "As the struggle around the Atlantian ruins showed, the Asparii enemy was, indeed, ruthless and dangerous. So, to have stepped in for the good of all, and to help a people reclaim their rightful heritage, we Dunorii are proud, and stand ready to defend the choice, and the actions of Earth before the Interstellar Community.

"We Dunorii have waited long for this, and are prepared to give Earth, at the appropriate price, the same components we provide to the shipyards on Eldrand."

The press gaggle was ablaze with talk at this announcement, each speaking rapidly into the cameras on their laptops while simultaneously typing away to be the first to get instant analysis out to the public. A few had anticipated this move, and simply clicked the button to post their articles and pre-recorded video commentaries. A'anfu En had no option but to pause during this flurry, and to save her the awkwardness of standing silent in front of them, the cameras were good enough to pan to the audience.

Emily paid no attention to the rest of the speech, excited by A'anfu's offer. Too caught up in the worry that her adventure had been pointless, she had failed to appreciate that Raiz would have that angle covered. He had played a diplomatic gambit that now meant Earth could immediately start production of ships. That worry wiped away, Emily suddenly had the powerful urge to ask A'anfu about the mage in the *Azar*. She wanted to know why the Dunorii agreed to such a life, and whether it was all right to keep them in isolation now that Earth knew the secret. Emily supposed that they would have to – it was still a secret to the other species until Earth or Eldrand saw fit to sell the information. Even her crew should technically be kept from knowing, in case they could be bought out by another species.

Before Emily knew it, Raiz was introducing her at the podium A'anfu had just vacated. Her delivery would inevitably be a tad stiff, since she was reading it off of the teleprompter, but having written the speech together with Kaz, she hoped her intimate acquaintance with it would keep her words flowing instead of being chopped up by "uhs" and "ums". They had written the speech in her normal speaking pattern, so at least nothing would come off as unnatural.

The Newport Station press applauded her as they had the other two, but with more fervency, and for significantly longer time. She felt a blush rising to her cheeks, and tried to stifle it. What the hell had Raiz told them about her? Vaguely remembering a time when she had wanted credit for a great discovery, she was having second thoughts now that she was on the receiving end, grasping that her activities would get measurably more scrutiny now that she was known. Never prone to watching the news before, she supposed she should start, now that she was on it. Emily's main worry was that the photo of her used in newscasts might be less than flattering. She had produced a wealth of obnoxious photographs in her time, and until now, none that she would want representing her.

This time, though, the ovation did give her some sense of accomplishment. Unfortunately, it also got her a bit choked up, so that when she tried to calm the audience down by saying "thank you" a few times, her voice came out a croak. Once they quieted, she cleared her throat and started. "You've heard a lot of reasons for Earth's involvement on Selparis today, but me and my crew weren't thinking about any of those when we went there. I hope you don't mind if I take some time to tell you how it looked from where we stood."

She concisely recounted the meeting with Ariki's people, promising profit on Selparis, and the meeting with Raiz, in which he revealed the presence of humans on the mysterious world and the continuing communications from there. She left out her experience with the Shadow Worker on the station, since it would be quite a departure from everyone's typical conception of reality, even though the effect that encounter had on her was profound.

"But I was not ready to commit my crew to an expedition when we knew so little about what to expect. What really convinced me, so that I brought the issue to my crew, was the offer from Arisin Oris. Oris offered to pay us if we would bring her to Selparis. She said she was interested in helping us out, and wanted to do some disease research there, but now that we know she was an Eldrandii agent, it's obvious why she decided to fund our adventure. The Eldrandii government knew that the race was on for Selparis, and that both the Asparii and

Earth were rushing to grab its secrets, and wanted to have one of its people in with the lead party. They figured that Commander Raiz would eventually send some ship from Earth, anyway, so there was no harm giving me a reason to go. I can't say anything else about what she did or wanted to do, but for me and my crew at the time, we felt comfortable going to Selparis because of the support she promised.

"We didn't know what everyone was really after. We knew that some Asparii mages were trying to get to the planet, and would probably cause trouble for us, but we thought they wanted to take over, like they had on Ina Cur. That, and Oris' support, gave us a reason not to worry about the ISC non-intervention rule. We were, of course, in it for the profit, not for the desire to defend a planet against a horrible enemy. That was the type of decision the World Council had to make, not us."

That was a touchy point. The profit argument was just a cover that she had used with her crew. She went to Selparis because she had wanted to – she was drawn to it – but that was, again, not something she cared to explain. To grease the wheels of life, people needed certain illusions that, while not fully accurate, would keep the gears from sticking. Regardless of how true that was, she considered herself hypocritical for demanding truth from Raiz and A'anfu, while glossing over it in her own speech. Her only justification was that the truth would give the impression that she was somewhat insane.

She continued smoothly despite her misgivings. "The rest of our trip played out in a way we could not have controlled, and we made choices based on what would best help us survive. Along the way, we found out the story of Selparis, and what everyone was after, but we were completely powerless in the middle of the storm. I don't think that, if we had known what the cost would be, and how little we were really going to be able to do, that we would have chosen to go.

"Four days ago, I got word that a search party sent by Commander Raiz had found the body of the pod pilot who had brought us down to the planet, John Katzenberg. I had lost contact with him soon after we landed, and hoped he was all right, but for most of the time I was on Selparis, I feared the worst. I've already expressed my condolences and regret to his family, but want to recognize him today, so the world will remember him in the list of heroes and victims who died at the hands of the Shadow Workers on Selparis. He was the first person from Earth to die in the struggle that followed, and ended with the battle around the underground city. And he didn't start the fight, and didn't provoke them in any way. During the fight, he disabled the landing pod, which prevented the enemy from using it to catch up to us, and saved us. I . . . I'm sorry I can't say more about him.

"Max Schroeder was the other member of my crew who died on Selparis, and he fought the mages when they attacked the capital city of Atparis in order to save two members of our party. Without him, they would both be dead. He died a true hero, and I hope that he gets the honor he deserves. He was a vital part of our team, did more than his fair share of work, and nothing will erase the pain I feel when I remember his loss." The trembling in her voice did more than her words to convey her emotion.

"I'm sure what we did, what we found, will be valuable to the human race, and I'm glad for that, because it will make the sacrifice made by John and Max more meaningful. I want people who hear about what we did to understand that we weren't trying to do something glorious, and if any member of my crew did something amazing or . . . praiseworthy, it was way beyond what I had asked of them.

"My ship, the *Azar*, also came under fire while my away team and I were on Selparis. I'd like to thank my first officer, Kazuhiro Kamiki, for commanding my ship better than I could have in the same situation." This bit was her own insertion, unknown to Kaz, and it helped her recover from the heavier part of her speech. "He's put up with a lot of stuff from me, and never let it throw him off from doing what was right for the ship and crew. I'd also like to acknowledge my crew, who, right from the start, has gone through more than they signed up for.

"I don't mean to be a downer about the whole thing. Now that I see it all from this end, I know that Commander Raiz had a clear idea about what he was doing, and had a plan to minimize the risk to . . . to pretty much everyone in the galaxy. I'd like to thank him for looking so far ahead, and for paying such careful attention to details. I especially want to thank him for intervening when he did, because I and everyone traveling on Selparis with me would have definitely died that night if he hadn't stepped in. Now that I know what A'anfu En did, I'd like to thank her, too." Emily thought it fitting to thank both her co-speakers in one go.

"There were also plenty of local people who helped us along the way, and I hope that if what we found is as important as everyone says it is, that the people of Selparis also get something out of it. Even though we eventually had a . . . falling out with him, we would never have gotten to Dakatanis before the Shadow Workers if it wasn't for Chancellor Davin Tayron of Atparis. There was also Draken Veris, the people of the Seli hills, and the people living around the ruins. The point is, at no time was this just an Earth mission. For us, this all started with a brave Inana who suspected that Asparii mages were using his planet as a staging ground, and wanted to keep another world from falling into their hands. Only at the very end did Earth come to the rescue.

"I . . . I think that, since so many people played a part, the benefits of whatever we found should be shared. At least, the ISC needs to look into the situation on Ina Cur, and the petition of Ariki's followers should be taken seriously. We should give aid to Lord Tayron's people, and help them rebuild their country. The Selians and the people around the underground city have dreamt of traveling through the stars like their ancestors did, and we can help them do that." She wanted to add something, and prayed it would come out right. "And . . . and since A'anfu En's people are going to be so . . . generous to us, we should listen to what the Dunorii have to say about how our ships should be treated. They know a lot more about space flight and hyperspace travel than we do. I know what I think probably won't make much of a difference, but since they were giving me a chance to say something, I thought I should use the opportunity.

"Anyway, thank you for the kind reception. I hope that Earth, and the entire ISC, gets the very best it can out of what has happened. We can't change what happened, but we can do a lot to make sure the future's brighter because of it. Thank you."

They gave her another round of clapping, though this time it was due to what she had said. Kaz had been right – the press, at least, was well-disposed to her proposals. Raiz smiled right through her speech, and shook her hand when she finished, congratulating her on a job well-done. During the question and answer session that followed, her comments provided fodder for the reporters, who probed to see what Raiz would commit to. He hinted that some of Emily's recommendations had merit, but emphasized that the World Council would have to deliberate over every issue. He joked that he was already on the chopping block for advocating troop deployment to Selparis, and while he pleaded for his political life, it would be unwise to voice to his executioners a desire to involve Earth in further interstellar affairs. One firm pledge he was prepared to make, while making dozens of other qualified responses, was in regards to the reconstruction of Atparis. His support was firmly behind extensive aid to Tayron's empire.

Emily paid close attention to the questions and answers, but learned nothing new. The commander was anything but evasive, and he answered the questions honestly, but stayed strictly to what he knew and had definite control over. He avoided speculation, or any attempt at projecting his future actions. Some of it was new to the reporters, of course, but Raiz had already discussed his concrete plans with her. The Atparis reconstruction efforts, for instance, were already in motion, with Earth Force troops now participating in the final phases of a search and rescue effort, and turning to firefighting and the clearing of debris. Jaik and West would be returning to help as soon as the next ship to Selparis left Newport.

The tedium of the closing phase aside, Emily was satisfied with the conference, both with her own performance and what she had learned. She left the room with a load lifted off of her.

Kaz met her as she exited with a glowing smile on his face. He drifted straight up to her and hugged her. The embrace was unexpected and warming, but Emily quickly determined that her performance merited a kiss while he was at it. She said caustically, "So, you'll be buying dinner, then, right?"

"Yeah, yeah, of course. You did great. I could do better, of course, but for you, that was great."

"What, you thought I'd bomb or something?" She was miffed. It was apparent his reaction had been one of great relief, meaning that he had been doubtful that she could pull it off. Familiar with the irrational side of life, she could have made a mountain out of it. Instead, she chose to rein in her defensiveness. She was fatigued after the conference, though, and in the mood for a party, not any serious talk. Unfortunately, they would be heading to the crew funeral for Max and John in an hour, with the Schroeder and Katzenberg families in attendance, so it would be a while before she was allowed to unwind. The prospects left her prone to prickliness.

Kaz noticed that there was real displeasure in her voice, and wanted to change the subject. "No, no, but I think we were both nervous about this. Listen, I was just thinking about the way we got into all of this . . . we were tricked into it, weren't we?"

Emily's face turned sour, and he knew he was still on dangerous ground. "Yeah, so?"

"We need to get more informed. I think you know that already and . . . and in a way, you're more capable of it than pretty much anyone else." That was somewhat of a compliment, but one that could be taken a number of ways.

Hearing Kaz call her capable was always soothing to her ears, but this time he was referring to her magic, and he never did so without hesitation. The misgivings tied to his words served to annoy her further. "I don't need you to tell me to use my . . . my ability, all right?"

Frustrated, Kaz said what he could to salvage the conversation. "Look, I haven't thought everything out, and I'm sorry it's coming out wrong. Let me put it this way: we need to find a way to beat Raiz. You didn't see him smiling during your speech. It was like he knew everything you were going to say."

Emily snorted, not in the mood to give Kaz any room. "That's easy. I had to give the speech to the teleprompter people. He could have taken a look at it so he was ready for what I had to say. Anyway, he's a bit over our heads, Kaz."

"Right now, but do you want to be led around like this again? We need to at least try. We need to make that part of what we do."

"I don't like that sort of game." The truth was that she had already considered getting into the game.

"Who does –"

"That's not how I do things." Throwing the white lie out helped her to calm down.

"I know, but –"

Then, like lighting a sudden beacon in the midnight mist, Emily gave Kaz a sense of intense relief with a smirk. As rapidly as she had descended into the critical exchange, she emerged from it, brightening up in amusement at Kaz's distress. Her smile calmed him, though he was irritated that such a small gesture from her could have such an effect on him.

"You know," Emily said, voice bubbling with laughter, "I like you better when you're on the defensive. Now that we've got some balance in the mix, I think this could work out."

Staring at her with sharp eyes, he replied, "Don't play around with me, Captain."

"Oh, come on." She wrapped her arms around him consolingly.

"You're too predictable. Whenever I'm embarrassed or anxious, you say you like me more because of it."

"I'm trying to boost your morale," she said. "Besides, I thought you'd like me predictable."

He twisted within her arms to face her directly, and said with gravity in his voice, "No more predictable, Emily. I don't think we can get away with it anymore. Definitely not now that everybody knows about you and your crew."

She got the drift and nodded solemnly to show she understood. "Okay. Now, can you just relax. I thought I was tense enough for both of us, but you topped me again. I need a bite to eat before the funeral, so do you mind going back to being really, really happy that I gave that speech without goofing up so I get some time to catch my breath?"

Kaz relaxed in her arms. "Sure. Sorry."

A peck on the cheek from her later, they were floating down the corridor in search of the exit to the street outside. Through the automatic door, the vast field of stars met them, and Emily stopped by grasping one of the sidewalk railings, marveling for a moment at them. Clinging to the only notion that, under the breathtaking void and its infinite possibilities, seemed both certain and comforting, she reminded him, "Don't forget, you're going to be buying me the most expensive dinner this place has."

www.ingramcontent.com/pod-product-compliance
Lightning Source LLC
Chambersburg PA
CBHW060604310726
48982CB00008B/1228/J

* 9 7 8 1 9 3 1 8 3 3 5 2 3 *